RECLAIMER

– ARISE –

BOOK 3

JEZ CAJIAO

TABLE ⊙F CONTENTS

THANKS

Hi everyone! Well, we're here again?! How the hell did that happen? I swear I took a nap, and another book was damn near ready for release…

I'm joking obviously, but time does seem to blur a little atm, between the kids, the family, and travelling for things like DragonCon, not to mention that bloody Covid? Yeah. the last 6 months have been a definite scramble to keep up.

Normally I'd thank as many people as I can here, but honestly today we're doing something different. Today I'm dedicating this book to one person, or many, depending on your point of view.

This book is dedicated to *you*.

You're awesome, and that's from the heart. Have a great day, a great week, and remember, *don't be a dick*. It's a good rule to live by.

Love to you all.

-Jez
12/09/23

ARISE ALPHA SYNOPSIS

Steve, a one-time thief and enforcer, is hiding on the Greek party island of Crete. He was involved in a botched bank robbery, and rather than the hundred plus thousand pounds each of the team were promised, there was a hundred in total.

Seeing this, and having already decided that he would run as soon as he had "his" money, Steve chose to skip the splitting of the cash, and moved straight to hiding out. With all the money.

He flew via Toronto, taking multiple flights, until he finally wound up in Crete, paying a corrupt Greek policeman for a recently deceased tourist's ID.

The next few months passed as a dream: drinking, partying, and working the bars of Crete; a new friend moved into Steve's apartment and life was good.

Right up until he decided to throw it all away, risking his life to save a pair of drowning women he'd met earlier in the day. He rode his bike off the cliffs, diving out over the treacherous rocks below, and swam down, rescuing first Marie, and then Amanda.

Other tourists nearby had captured the whole thing on camera, and the footage went viral, helped in part when word spread that not only was he a "hero" for saving them, but that he'd been fired in turn because he was late for work.

The footage was shared, and quickly made its way to an enforcer named Kevin Sinclair, one of the organizers of the original robbery. He, in turn, hired a local ex-army, Russian enforcer named Mikhail to punish Steve, and his friends when they got in the way.

Steve, however, had already vanished.

His bike, abandoned in the sea, had begun to leak gas, and in turn the local police took his ID—including the fake—as well as his money, forcing Steve to recover his bike before he could flee the island.

In the process of attempting to raise the bike, Steve was pinned beneath it, underwater, when a hidden section of an old ship collapsed. His bike took him with it into the depths, and as he blacked out from asphyxiation, his last sight was a tentacled metallic-looking monstrosity attaching itself to his face.

Steve woke sometime later, alone, wet, and shaking with the cold. Once Steve realized where he probably was—buried deep in the bowels of an ancient shipwreck—he started to try to escape, putting the tentacled monstrosity down to asphyxia and a passing sea creature.

The superstructure was old, he realized, later finding it to be millennia more ancient than he'd first guessed. Over the course of the next several hours, Steve would find out just how old the ship—an actual long-abandoned spacecraft—would be.

The human race, he discovered, were biological weapons, ones long since discarded by our uncaring creators. In the process of escaping the ship, Steve was wounded, dying from blood loss and hypothermia; he begged for help, and his plea passed a level that a damaged, failing medical AI deemed appropriate to enable it to respond.

He was given a choice, and with no time to examine the options, agreed to a "Support package." Unfortunately for him, the ship's supplies of anesthetic were long depleted, and the first stage of the Support package integration involved a full skeletal "strip," with everything from muscles to eyes being replaced.

When he reawakened, over a day later, he was massively changed, rebuilt as a prime Biological Weapon Variant, and ready for war, with, in addition to a nanite harvesting tool integrated into his right forearm, his own nanites—something that all humans, or BWVs as the system designates them, have—now unlocked.

Through the wonders of the nanotech, he was able to defeat the incoming basic security systems designed to terminate the trespasser, as the security AI attempted to kill him.

By the time Steve had escaped what he had thought was a sunken and forgotten container ship—and he now knew to be Facility 6B—he had managed to unlock both his War and Hack trees, investing points to make himself more versatile and dangerous.

Steve went back to the shore, finding the bike he'd borrowed to return to the beach was still there, and used it to return—naked—to his apartment.

On arrival, Steve climbed up onto the rear balcony and looked inside the apartment, finding his friend and houseguest, Dave, being beaten for information by the local enforcer. Torn between stepping in and saving his friend, and maintaining secrecy, he hesitated, only for Marie, the girl he'd first saved, to knock on the front door and be captured by Mikhail.

Steve decided that he couldn't leave them to Mikhail's tender mercies and attacks, being soundly beaten, as the ex-soldier demonstrated that the training afforded to Russian special forces was significantly higher than Steve's own ex-army training was.

In a last-ditch attempt to escape and defeat Mikhail, he triggered the Assault specialization tree under War. Instantly, the tables were turned, as the inbuilt system guided him to a vicious and resounding victory. Steve ordered Marie and Dave out, and warned Sinclair, the enforcer back in England, to stay away or he'd suffer the same fate; then he killed Mikhail.

Using the Harvest function of the system embedded in his forearm, Steve stripped Mikhail of his own nanites, gaining a number of attuned and usable nanites, as well as a larger number of corrupted ones, that his own systems began the process of purifying.

Dave helped Steve to burn down the apartment, concealing the damage done to the body of Mikhail, and his identity, and the two friends escaped with Marie.

Marie left them in a bar, before returning shortly with her friend Amanda, and as Steve told a much abridged and sanitized story of his adventure—keeping the nanites and ship out of it entirely—they are joined by the rest of Amanda and Marie's group.

Jonas, who led the team, recruited Steve and Dave on the promise of high wages and adventure, including the opportunity to kill criminals and murderers. Steve took the position, planning to use it as a cover to harvest more nanites and upgrade himself, while Dave took it on the grounds of a lot of money.

As a trial, Jonas sent Steve to recover his ID from the police station, and to insert a device into their network, opening it to the team, while Dave was sent to seduce a reporter who had been investigating a spate of recent murders.

Steve left the group, upgraded his Hack abilities, investing nanites recovered from Mikhail and gained access to the police systems, before he bluffed his way in, recovering the ID and money, and planting the data spike, and escaping.

Jonas and the team were surprised, but pleased at his success, and they went to observe Dave's trial. They arrived, just as Dave and the reporter were kidnapped, the group she had been tracking deciding to remove the threat.

Jonas, Steve, and Amanda followed the group into the old catacombs outside of Heraklion, splitting up when the tracks led in different directions.

Steve rushed ahead, finding a father and daughter being systematically slaughtered in a pit by *werewolves*. Steve's system identified them as an alternate "viable line" of Biological Weapon Variants.

Steve attacked the werewolves, harvesting them as he fought, and using the corrupted nanites to form tentacles of weaponized nanites, slaughtered the werewolves, as Amanda—not knowing Steve's true capabilities—ran to get backup.

By the time Jonas and Amanda returned—having rescued Dave and killed several other werewolves—Steve claimed to have killed the werewolves with the silver-edged knife Jonas had given him on arrival.

The father agreed, backing Steve, and the daughter had already lost consciousness, leaving Jonas and Amanda suspicious of Steve, but without any evidence.

Jonas suspected that Steve was a fresh "Arisen," and took him deeper into the catacombs, testing him and his abilities, and in the process, disturbed several ghouls; then he frantically escaped, his suspicions met.

Once they had joined the group outside, Jonas arranged for them to be retrieved by their shadowy employers, before having an argument with Steve and abandoning him by the side of the road, warning him that the vampires and their servants have his scent and that anywhere he ran to would only ensure more locals died.

Jonas left him, believing that it would force Steve to either admit to what he was, and they would have discovered a newly rising immortal—gaining much in their employer's eyes—or that he was a "plant" from an enemy faction.

Steve invested in his stealth abilities, hiding as the vampire and its master, Hans, arrived by the side of the road, and Hans ordered the vampire ahead. Hans then spoke to Steve, unable to locate him, but able to sense his presence.

Hans offered to teach Steve, to induct him into his new world and to answer any questions, before ostensibly leaving. Steve killed the ghouls still there, before finding Hans hadn't really left; he'd simply moved off to observe.

Again, Hans made the offer, before leaving Steve to go and rescue his former teammates and Dave.

When Steve reached the others at the retrieval site, he found one of their number—Dan, their tech specialist—dead, and the others captured, wounded, and at the vampire's mercy.

Steve killed the remaining ghouls and the vampire, before being captured as Jonas's master—Shamal, a member of the Blessed faction—arrived.

Taking advantage of a distraction, Steve escaped, Dave helping him, and the friends parted ways, with Dave being forced to help the Blessed faction as part of Jonas's team in truth, and Steve hiding in a nearby gully overnight.

The next morning, Steve recovered the team's abandoned drone, hijacking it, and used it to guide himself around people until he reached an old friend and borrowed a motorbike, setting off for the meeting with Hans, needing more information.

Hans was as good as his word, filling Steve in on the ostensible history of the two groups. The Blessed were essentially believers in "guiding" mankind to their future, while keeping them firmly underfoot as the cattle they are.

The Awakened and Accursed, on the other hand, the faction that Hans belonged to—or paid lip service to, at least—believed that they had been cursed with immortality. Some, like Hans, simply viewed it as their right to party and enjoy life; most believed that they had been cheated of their meeting with the gods, and they will do anything to "fix" that, up to and including starting a nuclear war and killing all life.

Steve chose not to join Hans, but agreed to reach out when he had more questions. Hans, in turn, was glad to have an unaffiliated and apparently skilled new Arisen to talk to, having been pushed to the outside of his own faction by his unwillingness to aid in the genocides planned.

Hans left Steve to his own devices, while maintaining an unobtrusive watch over the younger man, and Steve returned to the nearby area of Malia, moving into a cheap apartment while he planned his next step. Before he settled, a local fight broke out, and he intervened to help two new holiday workers from being blackmailed, before leaving them to stammer their thanks.

Over the next day or so, he crafted prototype armor, designing it despite being too low in nanites to actually deploy it, then returned to the catacombs, hunting more werewolves and other creatures, before encountering two huge figures on ornate thrones guarding an entrance to a further section.

He was warned by the system that they were "Beta Level Threats" and were far beyond him, and escaped, looting several ancient artifacts as he went.

On his return to the apartment, he hid again until the sunrise, when he strolled out onto the roof terrace, half asleep to relax in the sunlight.

Realizing he's not alone, Steve silently berated himself for the stupidity, as the workers he rescued previously had been joined by several others, including an old acquaintance of his and Dave's. He also met two girls who were with the group; one realized he's the eponymous hero who saved people only days ago and vanished, and attempted to film him.

Steve remotely hacked and erased her phone, before making his excuses and leaving them to it. Once inside his room, he moved quickly, gathering up all evidence of himself, before sneaking out, believing that the group had moved on.

Unfortunately, outside he bumped into the second woman, Ingrid, a Danish archeologist. She recognized the dragon staff he carried—looted from the catacombs—and forced herself on him, demanding answers to where it was looted from.

Rather than cause a fuss where others might see, he allowed her to come with him, then gifted her the staff, asking her to leave him be. She kissed him, and for a brief moment he let himself just be a man with a beautiful woman on a sun-drenched island, rather than an immature immortal, hunted on all sides.

When Ingrid insisted on coming with him, wanting more details on the artifacts and unwilling to accept his refusal, he gave in, knowing it was a mistake but desperate to hold onto the last vestiges of his humanity.

He took her farther across the island, helping her to arrange shipping for the dragon staff to her own museum, before taking her to dinner and arranging a room for the pair, one with twin beds.

The pair danced around each other as he attempted to use her to translate the writing on the artifacts, searching for clues as to the truth of history and "his kind." She, in turn, tried to force him to take her to the original site he'd looted the artifacts from, unaware of the infestation of lycanthropes and other creatures that still survived there.

Ingrid called in a friend, Lars, a well-respected archaeologist, to help her, and he set off, flying in.

The pair eventually gave in to mutual attraction and slept together, moving to a larger room, and made friends with the hotelier, Val. Val directs them to a second "palace" on the south side of the island that he believed Ingrid would find interesting and where Steve would be able to find more evidence of what he was seeking.

Although the ruins were interesting, and Steve deployed his newly upgraded drone to show them the site from the air, the taverna that Steve expected to get information from—a "rescue" center for dogs injured in dog-fighting rings—instead turned out to be a cover for another group of werewolves, connected to the first.

When they attacked, and Steve revealed himself to Ingrid, she left, heartbroken and confused. Steve, hurt, decided to finish the fight, harvesting the dead and then hunting the pack leader who fled into a nearby cave.

The cave turned out to be a much larger catacomb, with a trapped creature that the ancient people of Thera and the Minoans had captured. The Reta Variant was eventually defeated, but Steve was gravely injured in the process, collapsing as soon as it was constrained again.

Ingrid, who had control of the drone, and had unknowingly taken Steve's phone in her bag, had seen the fight and the injuries he suffered. She returned, and after apologizing to him, recovered several of the bodies from the taverna. Steve, in turn, used an unlocked ability called System Replenishment—essentially an advanced and technological version of cannibalism—to strip the dead of their genetics and biological matter to repair himself.

Over the next few hours, Ingrid explored the site; then the pair got replacement clothing—Ingrid's was ruined by the bodies she recovered and dragged to Steve—and new phones, tablets, etc.

Eventually, the pair hired a car and went to meet Lars at the airport. Ingrid, who now had a friend to help her, eventually convinced Steve to come fully clean about who and what he was, back at the hotel.

The trio returned to the site, finding the owners had returned, searching for unpaid rent, and bodies had been found. Lars started the process to buy the site and its surrounding lands, to "find" the archaeological site later and have a viable way of bringing the artifacts to the light again.

Upon return to the hotel that night, Lars and Ingrid spent the entire night arguing over translations and more, deciding that Atlantis was most likely real, and all the issues that would cause for archeologists.

Steve left the pair to sleep, and on the way to visit a local potential hidden site, came across a family who had fallen victim to people smugglers. Steve rescued the mother—who'd been taken due to her looks, when the father and two children were discarded—and he killed the majority of the smugglers.

Although the rest of the smugglers were killed, the "boss" escaped, and Steve returned the mother to her family, paying for them to stay in the hotel that he, Ingrid, and Lars were staying in.

Leaving them to recover and feeling he'd finally done something worthwhile, he went to the site he planned to visit first, and found a hidden cave system. Inside it was a woman, eons old, encased in crystal that was slowly growing and converting what was left of her body into itself.

He also discovered that the crystal was actively lethal to nanites, and that the long-dead Minoans and Therians were harvesting it, using it in creating weapons that were in turn used to fight the monsters of the ancient world.

Upon his return to the hotel, though, Steve found Hans and other Arisen waiting for him. Hans convinced him to go peacefully, as the alternative was the utter destruction of the area by another Arisen, the sadistic Athena.

Steve explained the truth of the situation, and the discovery he made, to Ingrid, Lars, and Val, injecting a laptop he recovered earlier from the people smugglers with nanites and upgrading it to help them.

Then he left, and was taken to an Arisen sub, hidden offshore. Steve was examined by the Arisen scientists and doctors, and although he managed to hide the majority of what he was—they had no clue about the ship or their technological beginnings—they did know that he was special, and they set out to find out all they can.

They chose to do so by spending the next three years torturing him over and over to death, reasoning that they were expanding their species' knowledge, and that as he can't really die, there's no long-term loss.

By the end, they found out all they could through destructive methods, and had moved to drug-induced programming as methods of control, attempting to learn ways that Steve was able to sense—albeit in a limited fashion—certain metals.

The end goal of this research was ostensibly to enable them to find and recover long-lost Arisen who were bound in metal coffins and hidden at sea. The Arisen were not above cruelty for cruelty's sake, however, and were amusing themselves with the torture.

Hans, while this was going on, had been protecting Ingrid, Val, and Lars, as well as forcing their council to intervene on Steve's behalf.

The end result was that Ingrid was permitted access to Steve, while Steve, drugged and compelled, had no clue who she was, as his "wife"—an Arisen by the name of Vitoria—amused herself by making him beg her for sex and more in front of Ingrid.

The drugs used to keep Steve pliable and confused were by necessity extremely powerful, and when a kink in the feedline stopped the drug, his mind began to clear.

Confused and faking sleep, Steve managed to force the line free, and quickly regained his wits, finding, to his dismay, that the reason he's incessantly vomiting—the only constant in his life currently—was because the Arisen had been testing the effect of force-feeding liquified humans to him.

They were unaware that it was the nanites that were responsible for his, and their, abilities, but one of the strongest of their oldest members was a cannibal, and they sought to find any connection between Steve's meteoric rise in power and that ancient.

The end result was that for months they'd been essentially feeding him on a diet of nanites, one that his own systems were frantically attempting to hold onto and assimilate.

When Vitoria and her companion brought Ingrid in to clean the room, and Steve saw her, all his memories rushed back. Knowing who she was, and who she was to him, triggered a chain reaction that unlocked his nanites.

Seeing the way that the Arisen beat Ingrid and had clearly been doing so for a while, Steve went nuclear and killed Vitoria, before being trapped in his room. The hardened walls held him for a short while, but with the nanites in his system now purified and in vast quantities, he purged his body of all contamination, before activating his armor and creating a gravitational cannon.

Steve escaped his prison, slaughtering the guards on the way out and all who stood between him and Ingrid, rescuing her, and declaring "open season" on all the Arisen who stand against him, before deploying wings and destroying the roof of Athena's medical wing, escaping with Ingrid in his arms.

ARISE DARK CRUSADER SYNOPSIS

Steve and Ingrid landed on the abandoned island of Skantzoura, Ingrid suffering from the cold of flight, as Steve began to learn to control his new armor. The distributed neurons of the armor's management system prevented him from removing it for several hours, and the pair explored, catching each other up on the last few years from their point of view.

Ingrid explained how she came to be at Athena's island as a servant and that Hans had been fighting to free Steve for three years, while Steve explained his new abilities, and they made a plan.

In the short-term, they needed money, clothing, and safety, and the decision was made to plunder a moored yacht for clothes and to enable them to clean up, before hitting a cash machine and finding a cheap hotel.

The first yacht was badly damaged by Steve's inexperience in flight, and they were forced to land on a second one. Ingrid made the most of the shower, before Steve unlocked the ability to "repair" others, as the system designates healing.

Upon using the skill on Ingrid, returning her—despite horrific pain—to perfect health, Steve was issued a quest, unlocking a new "tree" dedicated to the Support classes. Before the pair could fully explore the new situation, they were forced to escape as the owners' children came to check on the yacht.

Steve and Ingrid flew to a quiet nearby town on the mainland and used an old train—after raiding an ATM—to travel to Athens. Steve unlocked more of his Support tree and researched the new quest—to heal multiple people—before scaring Ingrid witless as the data download rendered him unconscious.

On arrival, Steve talked Ingrid into staying at a luxury boutique hotel, under the false identity of the "Athertons," hacking the system and ensuring that they were classed as returning guests.

The pair bluffed their way in, and were accepted, meeting James, the suite's butler, the next morning. After they spun a tale of being the victims of a robbery to him, James set about to "replace" everything they needed, from clothing to toiletries and more, including electronics and underwear.

Steve and Ingrid set off the next night to begin their new plan to raise funds and get themselves out of reach of the majority of the Arisen, as Ingrid explained her plans, ones she'd spent the last three years working on.

The couple decided to convert a trawler, if they could find one, into a luxury vessel to provide both stability and safety, as well as plenty of room. They agreed that they'd need to hire and develop staff, recruiting engineers, soldiers, researchers, and more, eventually using the team to bring some of the more desperately needed alien tech to the world.

Steve realized that in order to gain access to more "points" to spend in his upgrade trees, he needed to complete quests, and the first of those was the multiple-tier healing one recently granted to him.

That night, while Ingrid slept, Steve traveled to a local hospital, raiding several morgues on the way and stealing any viable nanites. Once there, he encountered a doctor, just before he would have stepped off the roof to his death. Steve saved him and forced the doctor to explain, discovering that a child lies dying beneath them, due to a mixture of honest mistakes and happenchance, with her best prospect of a replacement heart now lost.

Steve realized the opportunity that the situation granted, and to prevent questions, deployed his armor, now switched to a more impressive and imposing model with glowing eyes, as he declares that he "will heal the child."

The night passed in a blur as he healed as many as he could, before returning to Ingrid, exhausted but ecstatic. The pair agreed that this situation gave them an opportunity to unlock trees and abilities that would be beneficial and help to make sure that they'd be safe in the future.

The first phase, however, was to get money, and both the local criminal and gambling elements would provide that easily, if not willingly.

On the way to the casino—having decided that as most casinos were rigged to ensure the "house" wins, then hacking them and flipping the tables so that they won instead was fair play—they found that the limo had additional hidden cameras, and Steve hacked them, shutting them down.

On arrival, Ingrid played the machines, ostensibly losing money, while Steve worked on the Hack tree, moving from device to device, completing minor quests and gaining more experience with his abilities, as well as earning extra points, before the pair started to cheat.

The casino quickly banned the pair as they revel in their "luck," winning over four hundred thousand euros, and in the limo on the way back, Steve found the cameras had been reset.

Steve explained the situation to Ingrid, hacking them and shutting them down again, but in the process, found a much more paranoid security setup on the attached storage device, failing to hack it and instead wiping the data.

On return to the hotel, they were soon visited, at the open-air restaurant, by Yanni, a representative of one of the local mobs, a Serbian gangster who threatened Steve and Ingrid and demanded restitution…"or else."

Steve, being the gracious and subtle man that he was, hacked his phone and pointed out that Yanni's family were just as accessible to him, as he and Ingrid were to the mobster.

Yanni left, furious, and the hotel apologized for the situation, with James arranging guards for Ingrid while Steve returned to the children's wing of the hospital and resumed his healing.

Several hours later, he was interrupted by a panicked call from Ingrid. Yanni and several of his men had broken in, killing both the guards and James the butler, and kidnapped her.

He tore his way through the wall, launching himself into the air, and returned to the hotel, but too late. In a rage, he threw himself into the problem of the nanites, and found a way both to unlock the basic "healing" process of the nanites in

James, and then forced his own to "fix" him, restarting the older man's heart and bringing him back to life.

Taking the pattern he had seen for the encryption on the storage device the limo had been using, he quickly identified another of the gang's vehicles, tearing the roof off and questioning the driver.

When he gets limited cooperation, he instead used the driver's body to smash the skylight on the second location he identified the encryption being used, before raiding it and slaughtering all but one of the people he found there.

The last one hid in an emergency secure vault, and Steve flipped the situation, having found the location Ingrid was being held, and locked the vault from the outside, then sent the location, as well as the unlocking codes, to Interpol.

Ingrid was taken to the gang's headquarters, where she met Yanni's mother, the gang kingpin, and she distracted them all, until Steve could arrive, shielding her with his wings as they fired on the pair.

Then she asked Steve, very nicely, to "hurt these people, please."

The pair escaped a few minutes later, this time with the gang's hard drives and the boss's laptop, including her bank access to over a hundred and forty million euros.

Ingrid and Steve decided that they couldn't risk returning to the hotel, not now, and instead went to a cheap "no-tell motel" and spent the night, breaking into a store on the way to dress Ingrid.

The next morning, the pair made their way to a local marina and purchased a yacht of their own, getting the seller blind drunk and getting a few lessons on how to sail as they went.

Steve bought some new clothes, realizing he's far too distinctive in the tailored suit he'd been wearing from the casino, and abandoned the suit in the bin at a marina shop.

The following morning, Steve and Ingrid make their way to another local shop, buying all the basics they think they'll need, introducing themselves to the couple who own the next yacht over, before being invited over for dinner later, along with their "uncle," who waited inside their yacht for them to return.

On entering, the pair were overjoyed to find it was James, the butler, who had tracked them down, then calmly requested an explanation, before joining them as the first member of the team.

James joined the team both for a flat fee of two million dollars a year, and, far more important to him, the healing of his son, Michael, who had a replication issue related to his nanites, mis-diagnosed as an autoimmune disorder.

James then assisted the pair in recruiting Zac and Casey, a married couple for the crew. Zac was a world-class engineer, with a somewhat murky background, and Casey, his wife, was a highly experienced and skilled steward and qualified marine geologist.

Next recruited was Jay Beraz, a highly qualified American chef, and finally Jack Cameron, recruited to the position of deckhand and general dogsbody, as well as tech support.

While James and Ingrid attempted to make contact with the doctor, aware that he was now being watched by the Arisen, Steve acted as a decoy, reaching out to Hans to make contact, and carried a large boulder into the air, unbeknownst to Athena and her people, who were in a yacht below him.

When Athena interrupted the call and threatened Steve, he attacked, using the boulder as an almost orbital attack weapon, devastating her yacht and killing over half the crew aboard as it impacted.

Steve followed the boulder into the yacht, dispatching the majority of the security contingent, before fighting—and killing—Athena in single combat.

Steve stripped her of her nanites, as Hans killed the last of her security contingent, with the surviving Oracan and staff swearing allegiance to Steve.

Hans took over, agreeing to loot and raise the yacht, with it being repaired and given to Steve as a conquest, and Hans covering the costs, in exchange for half of the loot.

Steve escaped, and Hans claimed to the rest of the Arisen that he was playing along with Steve to keep him close and maintain contact, while Hans instead had thrown his lot in with Steve, joining his fledgling faction.

Steve looted a safe from the sunken yacht on the way out, and returned to his own yacht, stripping the safe with the help of Ingrid and James, looting papers—both normal documents and rolled-up ones encased in wax, jewelry, bags of coins and gemstones, as well as…a desiccated body, hermetically sealed in glass.

The body was discovered to be that of Scylla, the second of Athena's daughters, kept imprisoned for centuries, according to Hans, for crossing her mother.

Steve appealed to Hans to help him set up a détente with the Arisen, basically offering to leave them alone, provided they leave him alone. Hans advised against it, pointing out that as the only one who can comprehensively and permanently kill the other Arisen, Steve was a massive threat, one that may be "resolved" with the use of nuclear weapons.

Some of the other Arisen might not want to use them, but if need be? The loss of a city to a "terrorist attack" that resulted in Steve's death would be an acceptable cost for many.

Steve agreed to keep hidden for now, and Hans filled Steve, Ingrid, and James in on more of the Arisen's ancient history, before recommending the group go off and essentially train, keeping a low profile.

Over the next few days, the remaining crew arrive, and Steve upgraded his abilities to include creation of separate artifacts, allowing him to upgrade the engines, as well as convert random matter into "null blocks," blocks of compressed high-density matter that can be used as the building blocks for almost anything.

With that done, Steve and the crew set sail for the Ambracian Gulf, a location Ingrid had identified as a potential monster nest. En route, Steve and Ingrid called her parents, having arranged a secure communication line. Steve was grilled on their relationship and condition by Ingrid's family, and over the next few days, they made several calls, getting to know one another.

By the time the yacht landed at the Ambracian Gulf, the crew knew that there was more going on than they'd been told, but trusting James, they agreed to wait until the end of the trip for answers. Jack was left aboard ship, and the others accompanied Steve and Ingrid to the suspected infestation, finding that the local rangers were very welcoming.

At first, Steve and the others put this down to the donation they made, but as the mission went on, it became clear this was not the case.

The fens were the home to two species—beyond humanity and the "known" species—the fen nymphs were more or less friendly, although they did attack the party, both for trespassing and due to being forced to capture others for their masters, the mavka.

The second species—the mavka—were far more aggressive, a snake-like naga species with a short-range hydro-warp capability. The mavka attacked Steve, and when that went badly for them, they attempted to escape using this ability, and accidentally dragged Steve along with them to the main nest.

Steve fought and slaughtered the rest of the nest, including the queen, a massive BWV. Upon killing the remaining mavka, Steve completed his most recent quest to protect the Support class, gaining three points in the War and one in the Espionage trees. The three War points were spent, unfortunately, in surviving the injuries the mavka queen had inflicted due to her terrible acidic bite and jaws.

The three points were spent on the Armor sub-tree specifically with Biological Weapons—to understand the acidic compound better—then Atmospheric Integration and Biological Cleansing, to both provide oxygen regardless of the location, and to remove the harmful buildups of toxins.

While Steve fought and recovered, Ingrid spent time with the fen nymphs, convincing them of her potential as an ally, and when Steve returned, depositing the head—almost as big as he was—of their most feared predator, the mavka queen, the nymphs swore fealty.

One of their number, Par'a'nuit, joined the crew, bonding to three trees planted in the hot tub, and began to evolve after escorting the crew down into the underground ruins.

The locals, no longer being drugged and forced unknowingly into accepting the mavka's orders, slowly awakened and were distressed over the years of events they'd been living through. Steve and the others left, filling Jack in on the realities of life, and scaring him half to death in the process.

Upon contacting Hans, they found he was under watch by the other factions, and he recommended Steve go to Russia, specifically to the wild forested lands where other monster species still lived, hidden. Then he destroyed the phone and cut off communication for their safety.

Steve agreed, and although the others weren't happy about it, they eventually accepted that with Steve headed north and leaving enough traces along the way, that freed them up to take action to the south.

The group planned to buy an abandoned recycling plant in the Sudanese desert, one filled with radioactive and biological waste, using the converters to reduce the waste to usable null blocks, which simultaneously gave them a legal and easily verified income.

Eventually Ingrid agreed to the plan, but on the condition that Steve met her parents, properly.

James arranged for Ingrid's father, Anders, to "win" a prize: an exclusive dining experience at the most expensive and prestigious restaurant in Denmark for the entire family. Although Anders knew the truth, the rest of the family didn't, and were surprised when Steve and Ingrid arrived.

Steve admitted more to Anders than he should have, and the older man, due to his navy background and current "titan of industry" experience, signed on with them as a general manager and front man for the company.

Steve and Anders agreed that the criminal element that were prevalent in the city had no need of the wealth they'd been making, and Anders sent Steve after some of the local criminals, notably an Albanian gang focused on both people and drug smuggling.

Steve's approach, and his subsequent loss of control, both horrified and impressed Anders and the crew, as Steve slaughtered his way through the lower echelons to the top of the chain. In the process, he captured the leadership, stealing their bank accounts and draining them into the one the group was using.

Unfortunately, an innocent was killed during the mission, and Steve lost control, his rage let loose as he slaughtered the remaining gang members, before being caught on camera by a news channel's helicopter.

Steve, in a fit of rage, nearly attacked the helicopter, being stopped by Ingrid calling him and demanding he back down. Steve realized the situation he'd created, and the only available solution.

He escaped, delivering the money and laptops taken from the gang, then left, heading to Russia ahead of schedule. Ingrid was furious, and her father, who had gone to the yacht, intervened, learning the truth of Steve and his situation.

Steve allowed himself to be tracked leaving the city, and Ingrid and the others left quickly, heading back to the Med, and toward Sudan.

The next several weeks flew by, as Steve vanished into the wilds of Russia, reaching and passing Tunguska, before he encountered a wild tribe of Oracan, led by Eto, spending time with them after fighting one of their number to earn a place.

He learned the language, more or less, and traveled with a small group, thinking they were guiding him, when in reality they were taking him—as ordered—to the Erlking.

The Erlking was revealed to be one of the ancients that artificially uplifted the human race, and, when annoyed by Steve, slaughtered him in several horrific ways, after the Oracan left, returning to their tribe.

The Erlking agreed to give Steve limited help and advice, on the condition that he both heal the world, and, to prevent him taking the opportunity to gain power, he must leave it.

When Steve agreed, the location of two more of the buried facilities were shared with him: one buried on Yuzhny Island and the other sunken in Lake Tengiz, with suspected ones off the coast of Jakarta and another near Algeria south of Monaco and west of Sardinia. An additional potential site was due west of the Pillars of Hercules in the Atlantic. Lastly, he was given a quest to help the Oracan, both saving them and power-leveling Steve.

While leaving the details open-ended, the Erlking was also horrifically powerful enough, and unwilling enough, to allow a new faction to rise and control the planet. Steve agreed, regardless, knowing that at the least he would be able to save Ingrid and the others and leave them in a position of strength before he had to depart.

He was joined by Maribellya—or Belle, as she was more colloquially known—an elder dryad, and one of only four left in the world with her sisters: Barishka, hidden in a valley far to the south; in the middle of Africa, Annai lives hidden on an island paradise; and Jamya, the youngest, buried long ages ago in a landslide.

Steve agreed to help Belle, due to her potential to rewild the Sahara and other places, her natural growth abilities being powerful additional tools, and took her with him to search for the Oracan.

On arrival, he found that many of the clan's warriors had been killed, and fought off the werewolves, before allowing Eto and some of the other warriors to join him, tracking the werewolves back to their village.

En route, they encountered a unicorn, one of the last of its species, and Steve, attempting to tame it, was killed.

When he recovered, they continued to track the lycans, and Steve, traumatized by the ongoing deaths, had a minor breakdown. Belle helped him through it, and the lycans attacked, giving him the opportunity to take out his issues on them. After the battle, Steve admitted that although he had great advantages in battle, he was untrained in edged weapons and more, and needed help.

He traded his portion of the loot from the lycan village they destroyed for training by the Oracan, and found that, as the trainee, he was now the lowest of the low, forced to carry the litter that Belle, who had overreached in the fight, rested on.

The next of the lycan villages was more of a trial, with a much larger population, led by an alpha, with ghouls and a vampire, as well as a pair of Minotaurs. The Minotaur, Oxus, and his calf Xous, agreed to join Steve when Belle made him aware that Oxus was being forced to fight, under threat of Xous being eaten by the vamp.

By the end of the fight, Steve had gained the rights to the lycan camp, a formerly Oracan major village, and Eto and the rest of the clan left him, to reclaim the village.

Ronai, one of the warriors of the tribe, as well as Leo, Agnin, and Tenit, joined Steve in payment of the debt of honor owed, as well as the next morning being joined by seven more Oracan: the new ex-chief of the tribe—Kim—and his immediate family, including a daughter named Oba, and two nieces.

Steve's gift of the village to Eto had been taken to mean directly to Eto, and he had claimed the chief's role, before understanding that as chief, he'd have far more work to do.

The old chief was overjoyed, and followed Steve along instead, refusing as Eto tried to recruit him or change his mind about the chief's position.

Over the next few days, trapped in a cave by an unseasonably heavy storm, Belle spent time using her abilities to help more of the group learn English in preparation for their inevitable return to civilization.

The final village of the three was in the midst of an internal "debate" when the group found it, with the losers being noticeably dead already, and the group waited until the fight was almost over, before wading in and dealing with the survivors of the little civil war.

When the group finally reached the nearby human village—with Steve fortunately finding some pants at the last lycan village—he introduced himself and tried to make friendly contact, immediately coming under fire, as one of the small number of villagers recognized his pants as belonging to a recently vanished family member.

Once things were calmed down, the villagers turned out to not only be English, but a back-to-nature commune group of hippies and Gaia worshippers, led to the wilds and summarily abandoned by a shady figure named Oberon and his brother.

The pair had stayed long enough to avail themselves of the ladies of the group, basing their community on a "free love" model, and then moving on when they grew bored, taking all the villagers' wealth with them as they ostensibly went to "get supplies" to save the failing village.

Steve explained the realities of life to the group, including that the damage to their boat, that had necessitated the pair returning to society, was done from the inside of the boat. It also looked to have been done with a survival knife, not, as Oberon had claimed, by razor-sharp rocks in the water.

The group, now realizing the facts of their situation, agreed to help Steve, and he used the remaining points he'd gained in the Support trees to improve his construction abilities. As part of unlocking so much data, however, the download damaged Steve's brain, and he went into shock.

Over a period of several hours, Steve lost control, thrashing around and breaking much of the quarters he'd been given, before burning himself on a log kicked loose from the fire.

Steve automatically pulled up his armor to defend himself, and in doing so, activated the distributed network of neurons stored in the suit to help him deal with complex tasks. In a moment of lucidity, he upgraded the communications device at the base of his brain to store future downloads, limiting the damage done by massive amounts of data being dumped into his brain unprepared.

That helped him survive the experience, although he was left unbalanced and confused for several days as he recovered. Belle helped him to deal with the situation, reducing his emotions to manageable levels to enable him to concentrate on the boat he needed to build to equip them to travel to a distant airport.

Once the situation had time to settle in, rather than, as Steve had hoped, the Oracan and Minotaurs settling with the hippies and staying there, the hippies joined Steve's group.

He led them all, while being considerably frustrated by their lack of common sense, to the airport, before sinking the boat to prevent questions, and hacking the local airport systems.

They found an appropriate plane being refueled, ready to be flown to Nepal and sold, and stole aboard, hiding while the pilot, a Greek named Dimi, flew them out of Russia.

Once they were clear, Steve introduced himself and eventually convinced Dimi to help them all, partly by converting some of the farm machinery in the transport section into gold bars and bribing him.

The plane was registered as having issues and the original buyers were in turn bought out by Steve, with Dimi flying them all to the Sudanese airport closest to the recycling plant, stopping several times to refuel.

Over the course of the flight, it was discovered that Dimi, a smuggler, had lost his license to fly in Europe and America due to a joke played on a stewardess when he was a commercial pilot. Steve recruited him, granting him permission to use the plane as he wants—provided Dimi pays for the fuel and stays within a certain radius—and sorted out his license with Interpol, reinstating him.

Dimi flew off to pick up his girlfriend from Germany, and Steve and the rest of the group were collected by Jay and Jack from the airport on a coach and were driven out to the now partially operational recycling plant.

Ingrid, her father Anders, and her mother Freja had taken more and more of a lead in things with the plant, and had it minimally operational. People who could be trusted had been hired, including a large number of Anders's ex-navy contacts, as well as a small cadre of engineers from Zac's past.

The German pair of tourists who Steve had rescued from the lycan fighting pit so long ago had also been recruited, Isolde and Lukas, and were traveling to join the group, as they were both under watch as a possible threat to the Arisen and themselves, and as they were gifted machinists.

Locals had been hired to do low-skilled, but massively important repair and uncovering work. Once the groups were reunited, the discovery was made that the plant, home as it was to a huge amount of biological and nuclear contaminated waste, was being monitored by a great many people.

Defunct spying devices were discovered scattered across the site, detected when Steve demonstrated who and what he truly was to a small number of the more trusted individuals.

Steve and Ingrid were reassured that the monitoring devices were "dead" but they continued to track them down, with Steve using them to level his abilities.

It was determined that Scylla's prison was cracked, and Steve, when checking for any potential issues, found new, and highly sophisticated, monitoring devices hidden in his and Ingrid's room. A trap was laid, and while waiting for the spy to retrieve their device, Scylla was allowed to regenerate, after much discussion.

She was provided food, water, and null blocks to assist, and left to regenerate, as the spy finally appears...and it was Anders.

An Anders, in addition to the one by Steve's side as they watched over the recovering Scylla. Belle confirmed that this was the real Anders with Steve, and Steve set off to chase the imposter, watching them through several cameras as they shifted, becoming Ingrid and fleeing, naked, from the building.

The creature masquerading as Ingrid ran to the local tribesmen, begging for protection as Steve launched himself from the nearby main structure, and the locals, having never seen Steve before like this, but knowing Ingrid, attacked him.

He forced his way through them, saving one of their number when she was injured by the changeling, and eventually fought and defeated it. He was then attacked by two more, this time wearing the forms of Oxus, one wielding his hammer, and they used a high explosive combined with a sensory overload device to stun Steve, before fleeing.

Steve and the others discovered that the trio had arrived recently, pretending to be washerwomen, and when Annabeth, the leader of the hippies, annoyed Ingrid, Ingrid asked for her help, for a "really important job."

Annabeth agreed, and was given the job of chief washerwoman, much to Steve's amusement. The site was searched and when it was declared as "clean," Steve decided that they could no longer wait.

The creatures admitted to working for Shamal and the Blessed faction, and Steve was forced to accept that the risk was too large to continue as they were. He remembered that the most effective weapon against the Arisen was the crystal spears and blades, weapons that he'd ordered the Oracan who swore to him, and were now under Hans's protection, to gather and keep safe.

Ingrid explained the truth to the entire group, locals included, and then Steve called Dimi, ordering him to Athens, as it was faster than Dimi flying to the site's airstrip that was still being repaired and then continuing on from there.

Steve set off in search of the escaped changelings, checking the area as best he could, before he turned and headed to Athens, desperate to reach the Oracan and bring them and their weapons back to defend the recycling plant.

On arrival at Athens, Steve stole a bike to get to the yachts, not wanting to expose himself too much, and spotted Dave, his old friend, observing them. Realizing Dave was being watched, presumably by his old companions, Steve left a few gifts for him in Dave's toilet, one of the few places not covered by cameras and observation devices, then left.

Steve stole into the water and crept along the bottom to the yachts, finding a network of spy devices had been deployed. Rather than attacking, he instead invested all three of his available Hack points, upgrading his capabilities through synergistic alignment until he unlocked a new ability: Contagion.

The Contagion ability was a mixture of a Plague upgrade, spreading out across connected systems, and a Control one, giving Steve ultimate control over the technological systems he accessed. It was limited in the most basic form to a single "jump" once the indicated system was infected, "jumping" to another connected system and spreading the infection there, before settling into quiescence.

Steve attacked the detection net, taking control, before attempting to slip aboard the now refloated and undergoing repairs superyacht, one that had once belonged to Athena, and had now become Steve's by right of conquest.

The sensor net in the water, however, wasn't the only one, and as he breached the surface, an additional one, separate from the first and floating, detected him, setting off alarms that were connected to a second group of observers.

On entry into the superyacht, Steve met and freed Athelas, the Oracan "First Warrior" and their local group leader, who admitted that they'd been captured by Shamal and Cristobel, a second Arisen who had arrived to claim the yacht.

They had managed to hide several of the crystal weapons, but the majority were stolen by the new interlopers. Steve recruited the group again, then fought and killed the guards on the pier nearby, before facing Cristobel.

In the ensuing conversation and threats, Dave managed to make contact with Steve, drawing his attention to two more yachts incoming, both in an extended firefight with each other.

Dave pointed out that the more damaged of the two yachts was the one Jonas and the others were aboard, and begged Steve for help.

Steve attacked Cristobel, and in the course of the fight, she managed to stab him with a crystal-tipped dagger, damaging the harvest tool.

Steve was forced to use his time compression and distortion device to give himself time to react, and the vorpal blade to carve his own right arm off at the elbow, before killing Cristobel.

The infection caused by the crystal destroyed the harvest tool, and due to the nature of the lockouts the ancients set into humanity, once Steve lost it entirely—he'd been forced to strip his own nanites from the surrounding area, essentially relinquishing control over the harvest device accidentally—it could no longer be recreated.

Steve realized that to regain the harvest tool and his primary means of securing nanites, he needed to return to the facility under the ocean and recover a second one. But for the short-term, he rebuilt his lower right arm and included a nanite creation tool instead.

Steve rescued Jonas, Marie, and Amanda, and Dave rejoined him, as Steve healed Jonas, eradicating his long-term cancer and healing him in the process, and the old team—Jonas, Amanda, Marie, Dave, Paul and his wife Courtney—joined Steve.

Steve was helped by Laia, the leader of the yacht team, to contact the local mayor and warned him to draw his people back, both the navy and local forces. The mayor agreed.

Steve was contacted by Dimi, who admitted that there was a problem with the plane—an engine had failed—and Steve in turn contacted Freja, who arranged to purchase a replacement VTOL that had been embroiled in a local legal battle.

Steve ordered Dimi to change planes as fast as possible and get to the rendezvous.

The much larger group, now including the Oracan and survivors from the yachts who had sworn to follow Steve, headed for the foot of the pier, before realizing that the incoming vehicles were not, as expected, transports. Instead, they were troop transports and tanks, sent, it turned out, by Beowulf, another Arisen.

Beowulf stabbed Steve, using an advanced stealth ability to sneak up, and declared himself, making a call to Shamal and ordering his ally to lead the attack on the recycling plant.

It was Beowulf and Shamal's plan to be "forced" to come out of hiding by the situation, before swearing to the Old Ones that they'd be guided by them, keeping the other Arisen hidden, while the pair took control of the world publicly.

Beowulf admitted to Steve that he had several artifacts of his own, and in the ensuing fight, Steve killed him, contacting Dimi and rerouting him to the foot of the pier, then gathering up the team as Dimi landed nearby with their new VTOL airplane.

Steve got hold of Ingrid, explained what had happened, and found that the three changelings who had escaped him were now outside the facility, trapping the others inside and waiting for Shamal.

Steve and the others set off for the recycling facility, six hours' travel away, and en route, Steve used the nanite-filled bodies of Beowulf and Cristobel as building materials, beginning repairs and upgrades on the old VTOL, enabling them to massively decrease the time required to reach Ingrid.

Shortly after they took off, the Hellenic Air Force surrounded them, and Steve reached out to their squad leader, Flight Lieutenant Papadopoulos, taking control of his plane and giving him a demonstration of how easily he could divert or remove them, then promised to be in touch with their leaders soon, to discuss how he could help.

Between the carrot and the stick, implying that he could just as easily take over missile silos on the ground and retarget them, the Hellenic Air Force and any others nearby backed off, leaving Steve to upgrade his new plane, installing replacement engines—one at a time so that they could continue to fly while the upgrade was done—a new stealth reflective coating and a power core, as well as a rail gun.

Dimi was unsure whether he could bring himself to fire it, but his fiancée happily took it over, after they were fired upon, discovering that she actually loved heavy weaponry, and she'd just never known until then.

Steve stormed the upper floors of the recycling plant, crashing through a damaged section and killing several soldiers, as well as one of Shamal's pet Arisen, before taking their weapons and attacking the soldiers.

In the ensuing fight, Steve was seriously injured, and had his armor integrity reduced to a bare handful of percentage points, forcing him to recover additional null blocks and repair his armor into a far less secure version, essentially coating himself in solid metal.

In the assault on the next floor, fighting his way toward Scylla's cell, having realized that was where everyone had retreated to, he managed to kill two more of Shamal's Arisen. The last of them, Festus, killed Steve with his hammer as he completed the emergency wipe of the nanites in the dead bodies.

Steve was brought to the cell, stripped and nailed to the wall, being used as a threat to force Ingrid to open the door and let Shamal in.

Shamal tore Steve's jaw free, torturing him, before turning back to threaten Ingrid, while Steve reached out, gathering the attuned and ready nanites farther down the corridor that he'd left when he was killed, and routed them through air ducts to reach Scylla, before getting Shamal's attention and making noises.

Shamal replaced Steve's jaw, curious to find out what Steve was trying to say, only to be told: "the enemy of my enemy is my friend."

Shamal dismissed it as bravado, only to hear it spoken again, as Scylla stepped through the previously sealed door, fully armored, and standing as Steve's ally.

Steve and Scylla fought together, Steve controlling the nanites as a weapon for Scylla, and her centuries of fighting experience along with the unpredictable nature of the nanites enabled them to win. Steve then converted Shamal into more blank nanites, using them to heal and rebuild himself over the next few days, splitting the cost between null blocks and the nanites themselves.

Several local leaders, including representatives from Europe, the UK, and North America reached out, coming to meet Steve, ostensibly to investigate the dark crusader, and at least in part to make sure that the facilities they were shipping their most hazardous waste to was actually doing something with it, or was pretending enough that they didn't have to care about it themselves.

As Steve met them, half in and half out of his armor, seven foot tall, winged and glistening black bones on show as bubbling nanites rebuilt him before their eyes, the questions were fairly simple to field.

Mainly being around was he, and his organization, a threat, and what could they get from him.

Apart from a brave, and foolhardy few, the majority were fine with any explanation Steve gave them, used to being ordered around by the Arisen already, and most definitely not wanting to be the one who would be used as an example to others.

Lastly, Dave had proposed in the midst of the battle to Amanda, fully expecting that he'd die in the fight, and wanting to go out on a high.

Unfortunately for him, he survived, and she was holding him to it.

PROLOGUE

"Impossible!" Zeus snarled, his massive form sprawled in his chair. Once, he'd been heavily muscled, but now rolls of fat bulged at the seams of his stylized "armor." His jowls shook as he spoke, and an odor of rank sweat filled the air, even as rare stones glimmered on stubby, greasy fingers. He glared across the table at the most junior of the gathering, who snorted in response, rising to the bait, as always.

"Oh, for...It's far from it, and you know that, you old fool!" Gustavus snapped, shifting in his own, throne-like chair. All four of the little cabal sat in similar seats around an ancient table. "We've discovered enough methods of entirely killing our enemies over the years. This upstart has simply found a new one, most likely a long-hidden relic from one of the lesser halls."

The pair, as always, glared and sniped at each other, unable to agree on anything. The other two looked on in silent dismay, seething over the fact that after all the centuries of their little alliance of convenience, the pair had to go through this dance over and over again.

"Does it matter how he's done it?" Arminius shook his head and sat forward, attempting to move the conversation onward. "Yes, we all agree that it is most likely a relic or artifact of the Old Ones, something he stole or found, or—" He glared at the last member of the group. "Or something he was *given*. None of that is *important*. What matters is that he is barely three years into his rise, and already he is guilty of the murder of several of his betters."

"Athena and Cristobel were hardly his betters. They were dogs, foul Accursed that defiled the world by simply existing in it," Zeus thundered—his opinion, as always, delivered as if a proclamation from on high.

"Yes, yes." Arminius tiredly waved a hand, accepting the eldest of their group's declaration rather than arguing, before resting his elbows on the table, steepling his fingers as he looked around the room. "They were terrible people, foul and so on, but they were *Arisen*. They spent untold centuries accumulating power and learning, improving. They were both excellent warriors..."

"Foul temptresses, more like it. Skilled more in deception and underhanded tricks," Gustavus muttered.

"Well, *however* he accomplished it, in addition to those two, he also managed to kill Shamal and Beowulf, not to mention Shamal's lesser pets. Not only did he entirely eliminate them, but their corpses, I have on good authority, were destroyed. They were rendered down into some kind of building blocks that he used to grow his own strength." Arminius finished with a sigh.

"Cannibalism?" Zeus thundered, shaking his head. His ridiculous curls bounced as he flapped his lips. "A waste of time, not to mention disgusting! We tried that—centuries ago. It doesn't *work*!"

"It doesn't matter." Gustavus ignored the comment. "None of this matters. The only truly important thing here is power! He managed to *kill* all seven. Must I remind you that a true killing of another of the Arisen, instead of merely locking them away, is a feat rarely accomplished by any of us. If he did it in three years or three thousand, the fact is that he has accomplished this, and that he possesses a relic, one that enables him to steal the life of his betters. Presumably he uses the relic to gain their powers somehow…or else how would he have defeated the others?

"Athena was known to have a supply of tears of amethyst, and occasionally imbibed them. Most likely he used trickery to overcome her when she was in her cups. Stealing her strength and then using other underhanded tricks, he killed the rest. Now he has gained strength that stands him in good stead against the rest of us. With this in mind, I vote we use one of our tactical options, and remind the so-called 'leaders' of this world who truly rules here." He jabbed his finger against the table before him as he straightened, smoothing the front of his immaculate military-style tunic.

"A vote will be held," Arminius agreed with a sigh of irritation. "But first? If it is a relic, then we must recover it, and the location where he captured it, or 'found' it." He glanced to the side again, fixing the fourth, and so far, silent member of the small group with another glare.

"You can all stop looking at me." Drusilla sighed. "Honestly, if I was going to give one of my artifacts to anyone, it'd not be a newly Arisen. And let's face it, if he was my pet? I'd have sent him after lesser Arisen first, growing his strength…or I'd have done it myself, using it on any of the lesser pets. No need to make a competitor stronger, after all, so why the hell would I give it up?"

"You've been known to spin murky webs," Zeus grumbled, staring at her.

Drusilla smiled and tossed her hair back. "Dear Zeus, you're not *still* sulking over that, are you? It's been two thousand years!"

"Some things are never forgotten," he growled, refusing to meet her eyes.

"You drank an entire barrel of tears of amethyst and passed out drunk after despoiling a dozen of my workers. What in the nine hells did you expect me to do?"

"Not seduce me, then cut off my damn staff!" Zeus snarled. "You know how sensitive that stuff makes us!"

Arminius groaned. "Do we really have to go through this *again*? Three hundred years since we last held council and still, the first thing you bring up is that ancient history? How many times have you fought side by side since then? How many hunts have we enjoyed?

"Once again, we look to the future, deciding if we should employ one of the greatest and most devastating weapons of the age, and you two have to derail the conversation to hash this out again?" He shook his head disgustedly. "I vote we keep the option to use a tactical weapon, *but*…" he held up one hand, gesturing for patience, "we hold off for a short while."

"What? Why?" Gustavus asked, surprised as he looked up from smoothing the creases in his pants.

26

"He's serving us, whether he knows it or not," Drusilla said with a smug smile. "Whatever he's doing to destroy the poisons that run rampant across the world, we let him continue, then strike when we've had the chance to capture the technology."

"Exactly. Why should we bother to waste our efforts to fix the world, when he will do it for us? We've been arguing over how to do it for decades. Now we have a nice, easy solution: we let *him* do it. He's declared he'll rewild the desert...good for him. It's theoretically possible, according to my servants, and hugely difficult and expensive. He wants to do it? More fool him. Add in that currently, even with the various factions doing their best to wipe him from the media, he's still reappearing daily. I say we should stop wasting our time."

"What?" Zeus snarled, sitting up with a jerk, crushing his goblet and cursing as the wine spilled over the rim, soaking his silken pants. "Blood and ashes!" He swore, shaking a hand free and splattering wine everywhere, much to his companions' disgust.

Gustavus shoved his chair back and frantically dabbed at the few splatters of wine that had made it to him. He looked ready to tear his dagger free and plunge it into the side of the old monster.

"We stop," Arminius said quickly, moving to distract the others before the building fight could derail everything. "But only for a short time!" He gestured animatedly as he spoke.

"Perhaps we should let the media get the idea that maybe he is what he claims, some sort of dark angel. In fact? We should *encourage* that belief. Let them see him as an angel sent from the gods. If the Old Ones step in to clean things up, as they always threaten they will? Then we gain out of all of this. First, we will know if the Old Ones are truly still involved in the world and as powerful as they pretend, without any real risk to ourselves." He lifted a hand, ticking the points off as he went on.

"Secondly, we send spies to recover both the artifact and any information we need. The humans are always drawn to these false messiahs, and we're well past due for another one to rise again. We might as well make use of the situation. This way, when the cattle swamp him in their mindless masses, it'll be easier for us to slip in some of our people."

"Go on," Zeus muttered, still regarding the stains sinking into his clothing.

Arminius paused, glancing from one to the next, making sure they were all truly listening. "Thirdly? Should he be a true threat? Well, we use a tactical option, one of the ones the humans don't know about. But we make it a messy one, something suitably devastating. An orbital device perhaps. Then we flood the media channels with stories about how he'd been a false angel, and that the gods and the true angels were forced to return, to smite him."

"We capture his relics and use them to make ourselves armor like his, but more—" Drusilla gestured, clearly looking for the right words.

"More *appropriate*," Zeus finished, cutting Drusilla off. "We make armor that reminds the mortals of what we are."

"Exactly!" Arminius grinned, sitting forward and jabbing a finger into the table for emphasis. "If the Old Ones deal with him? We've not wasted our effort, and we've captured valuable relics and information. And if they don't? If, in fact, they're proved to be a paper tiger? Then we use the opportunity to come out of the shadows. After all, we'll have to step in ourselves, if they don't."

"So there's no real risk to us," Gustavus murmured, scratching his chin and staring off into the distance. "All this costs us is time, and that's the one thing we all have. Let him make an impression on the mortals, let him convince them of his divine origins, amass more wealth and fix the planet. Then, if the Old Ones haven't dealt with him, we can truly come out of the shadows. No more hiding what we are. We can always lure him to somewhere we don't care about, somewhere that it doesn't matter if it's destroyed."

"Tell him it's a peace overture or whatever," Drusilla agreed, getting more and more into the idea. "We lure him somewhere…maybe we arrange to have the Accursed think we'll be there and unarmed. You know they'll try to lay a trap. Then we hit it with an orbital…and kill them all!"

"Then we come out of the shadows," Zeus repeated, clearly enamored with the idea of no longer having to deprive and limit his "fun" as he was forced to, long ago. "We use his relic to make ourselves new armor and we make it clear that he was one of ours—a weaker member, though—who went rogue."

"And we dealt with him," Gustavus agreed, grinning as a servant refilled his goblet. "If we move quickly, we could set up several strikes, minor ones, but possibly gamma based. Eliminate as many of the others as we can, leaving the four of us to take control, and split the world again."

"As once it was, so shall it be again," Drusilla murmured. "They drove us into hiding millennia ago. We always said it was temporary, and that we would return when we were ready. Now, I don't know about you, but I'm feeling ready." She smiled, a predatory gleam in her eye.

"Very much so," Gustavus agreed as the four looked from one to another, making sure they were all on the same page. "So, need we vote, or do we simply move to a toast?"

"To Steve the Usurper." Arminius smiled. "Enjoy what time you have left!"

"To Steve!" the others thundered, broad smiles on all sides as they lifted gem- and gold-encrusted goblets, several made from the skulls of long-dead enemies, before drinking deeply.

CHAPTER ONE

I blinked, then yawned, stretching slowly, luxuriating in the warmth of the bed as I straightened my legs, flexed my toes and tensed, then relaxed, staring up at the ceiling as I yawned again.

I must have fallen back to sleep, I realized muzzily. I'd been ready to get up not too long ago, waking with Ingrid curled next to me, her hair tickling my chin, and had decided to have five minutes more.

Now, the sun gleamed around the edges of the curtains, the room was warm, but not yet too warm thanks to the air conditioning, and the soft sounds of Danish singing came from the bathroom, along with running water.

I debated getting up and surprising Ingrid. It was a view I never tired of, after all. As much as she protested about being "pestered" in the shower, she also loved it. But after a few seconds, I decided against it.

Instead, I laid there, enjoying the calm before the madness of the day ahead could reach out and claim me.

There was so much to do, as always. Hell, there was an *insane* number of things really, and never enough time to address it all.

The last few weeks had been good ones, I reflected as I scratched my side and yawned again. After the assault on the recycling facility, the disparate groups that made up our people came together as one group, bonding in the hell of gunfire and blood in ways that a year of normal working together could never have done. There was something about sitting around and drinking with the guy who just shot someone who had been just about to shoot, maim, or maul you, that gave you the warm and fuzzies.

The sure knowledge that the other Arisen knew where we were had consumed us for the first few days. All of us worked around the clock, shoring up the damaged sections of the tower, and generally getting ready for another, much bigger assault.

Gathering the bodies and converting them to building materials as much as possible had helped with that, as weird as it was. Using the creation tool in my right forearm, I'd been able to reduce Shamal and his people to their component nanites, and then used the Emergency Wipe to render those nanites available to use.

It galled me that I was having to do it this way. Once they were blank, I could absorb them. My system was wiping them, after all, so they were reset and ready for my use, but that it cost fifty percent of them all?

This was literally millions of nanites, and aside from the small number I'd been able to use to rebuild myself as I had? Almost all the rest had been used elsewhere. It was more than a little fucking annoying.

Once again, I silently cursed Cristobel.

The bitch had stabbed me with a crystal blade, and yeah, I'd now found a counteragent to the crystal plague, but at the time, I'd not had access to it, and it'd cost me the harvest tool, and my arm.

Where before I could have drained all the corpses, including the hundreds of lycans and humans, the vamps and more, and I could have power-leveled myself into godhood?

Now more than half of the lycans had run, led by a pair of vamps who had in turn fled when they apparently "felt" Shamal's death in some way I didn't understand.

Those that had been killed by the crystal weapons had been a total loss as well. And then a load of the nanites that I'd managed to get a hold of had been needed to convert into a counteragent to purify the areas that were contaminated.

All in all, I'd come out with less than a quarter of the nanites that I could have—hell, maybe as little as ten percent, considering the dead humans and the bodies that I could have drained. But still.

I'd gained enough that I could make some basic repairs to myself, regrowing my limbs and side. And the impression it'd made on our visitors was significant, as I liquified the bodies with my creation tool, before using them to repair the buildings. The outside of the tower was currently being converted, inch by inch, into a diamond-hardened frame. It was powered by the dead assholes' nanites. And when it was done? If one of the Arisen tried smashing inside like they had last time? They'd be in for a hell of a surprise.

Bowel-loosening terror was one of the main reactions we got from our visitors, and only a few of them had accepted our invitation to stay on-site for dinner.

One, predictably, was the USA's visitor, an ex-marine who was deliberately vague about his credentials, but was easily enough verified for me.

Commandant Reynolds alternated between telling us where we went wrong in setting up our defenses, and praising the bravery of the defenders. He made it clear that he had no clue who and what I was, all the while, deferring when I spoke as if it'd come from the lips of Chesty Puller himself.

That, I was assured by those with experience of the marines, was not normal. Even if he had been ordered to be as respectful as possible, the immediate acceptance of what I said as gospel was a bit beyond.

I'd spent hours talking with James, Anders, Jonas, and Ingrid last night, as we went in circles, trying to decide whether his response had been down to the mystical crap we were selling them—that I was a dark angel sent to fix their shit—or whether he was simply conditioned to respond to any Arisen in this way.

Either was as likely as the other, unfortunately, and we'd kept a close eye on him overnight.

The other visitor who'd happily stayed was Hans. He'd arrived late last night, striding through the howling miniature sandstorm his helicopter had created on landing and takeoff as if he owned the place.

He'd refused to discuss the Old Ones until we were secure and sober, which, considering it'd been him who was wasted on another bottle of the tears of amethyst he'd looted, was a bit annoying.

That was one of the first things to address this morning: the Old Ones and their response to the situation.

Second was definitely the local area, and making more of a plan for the future.

A distant last came the damn Arisen, considering that no matter what we did, we couldn't be sure what the hell they'd do. For now? They seemed to be leaving us to it, and I was damn well hoping it was down to the Old Ones intervening.

We still needed to go over the Athena situation—yes, she was dead, and yes, I'd killed her, but we'd also resurrected her daughter—so it was sort of fifty-fifty what we did regarding her insane wealth and properties right now.

We needed to make a real decision about Scylla. For the time being, she'd been content to mooch around the base, sometimes helping, sometimes acting as if we were all beneath her and that we deserved to die for things we didn't understand.

We'd agreed for the short-term that Scylla would only move around the base with either me, or Ingrid and Belle with her. Beyond that, she stayed away from people, either sequestered in her room, or training out in the desert.

She wasn't a prisoner, we made that very clear, but she was also frankly fucking terrifying. One man, a member of the local government, freshly arrived and being escorted to a meeting room, had seen her, and decided that the shorts and small top she was wearing from the training area to return to her room were indecent.

He'd declared her a whore and that he was mortally offended by her presence, apparently trying to manufacture some kind of situation that he could turn to his advantage when we apologized and tried to show him respect.

It'd ended badly for him when rather than being all "oh no, how can we apologize," she instead took two steps, ripped his arm off, and beat him to death with it for his impertinence.

Considering we'd made it very clear to all our guests that they were permitted only in certain areas, and they'd all been warned about not offending the members of my "tribe"?

Well. It'd been no great loss to us, and only a slight inconvenience to the negotiations with the Sudanese government.

We were right at the foot of a small mountain range in the farthest north-by-northwest corner of the Sudan, literally only a matter of an hour's travel from the borders of Chad, Libya, and Egypt, and I'd already demonstrated insanely superhuman capabilities.

When I declared that the land all around us for a hundred miles in all directions was ours, and that trespassing was punishable by death, they weren't happy.

They also didn't argue that strenuously, however, as they were massively taxing the nuclear and worst wastes that arrived in their ports before they were sent onto us, and we were in the middle of a stretch of the desert viewed as uninhabitable and essentially worthless to them.

I'd played the offended dark angel role, threatened to level a small city if they continued to annoy me, then let myself be "calmed down" by Ingrid and the others. I'd informed them that my human "servants," led by Ingrid and Anders, would be dealing with them, as I'd be converting the desert to a garden of Eden, and removing all "poisons from this world." Then I'd used my armor's Conceal abilities, and I'd vanished.

Anders went on to assure the new negotiator—who stood there, splattered with the blood of his old boss, his mouth open in horror—that we would continue to pay all the relevant taxes, and that we wouldn't be stopping the conversion of the desert at the hundred-mile limit. Once we were outside of that, their boundaries would be respected, but should they continue to annoy me, or not want us to convert further deserts into viable croplands and forests, then that was fine.

Considering how little of the Sudan was actually usable, he'd taken the hint and had quickly drawn up a rough area that they would accept being converted into usable land in exchange for the government "gifting" this land to us to do with as we pleased—for so long as "the dark one" reigned here—and that it would revert to Sudanese land if it was no longer being "used."

Basically, the phrasing that was in the contracts translated into "As long as you're here, it's your land because you scare us shitless, and provided you make us some usable land in return, but you can't then sell it to our neighbors. Also, if you fuck off again, we're claiming it right back."

Anders made it clear that I was both immortal and would be leaving the earth "again" soon, but that I would periodically return. This land was to remain mine, or I'd be annoyed.

The impression that was given about me being "annoyed" translated as sinking a significant portion of Africa beneath the ocean and rendering the rest uninhabitable. So yeah, they took the hint.

Libya and Chad were similarly easily dealt with, with both countries overjoyed with the idea of gaining more arable land, not to mention a new lake or sea.

I'd explained to their representatives that I'd be creating a new freshwater lake here, one that would be several miles across, and that although that would be inside my claimed lands, I would permit water caravans access. I also intended to convert several hundred miles of the desert on their sides into arable land.

They smiled and nodded a lot, clearly thinking I was bullshitting. But considering I was telling them this while standing on gleaming black bones that were steadily being grown over by new flesh? After a few seconds, they accepted it at face value.

I hacked their phones and more as soon as they came in range, of course, listening in to find out their real plans as soon as they left.

Most of them were totally fine with the new boundaries, surprisingly, viewing that land as utterly worthless, and having the option to tax the nations of the world as they transported various crap to us being worth it alone.

Although each of them laid out plans to both infiltrate spies into our lands and take them back if we showed any weakness, for now they were willing to accept most of my demands at face value.

Provided we kept up our side of the deal, that was.

Each of the nations wanted technology, specifically weapons and armor, and shit they could sell.

They were all disabused of that notion, and were instead offered a generous counter package. Namely, I'd not slaughter them all and piss on their ashes. Also, we'd build a hospital on our lands that could be accessed by anyone.

There'd be a hundred places available to each of the four nations, and the rulers of those nations could choose to send their own people if they needed to. The lure of being able to have family members cured of cancer and so on, over a weekend, was a powerful bonus.

Egypt was the only "real" issue of the four, and that was mainly because Ingrid and I had made it clear that we would leave half of any treasure to them, but that we needed to be able to remove certain artifacts from all their lands.

The others accepted that, figuring half of anything that we found was better than nothing, and planning to beat us to anything that they could, while still believing that there was nothing left there that'd not been found already.

The Egyptians, though, were used to running the vast majority of their economy on the back of the tourist trade, and the influx of archaeologists each "season."

When Ingrid explained that some artifacts of "Steve's and Scylla's past" might be buried in Egypt, and that although anything that was of value to the Egyptians and not us would be given over, the fact that we couldn't give them specifics made the negotiations break down sharply.

I'd created a sword of nanites and I'd used it to cut through a block of solid stone before the representatives, making the level of technology clear to them. Then I'd explained—read "lied through my fucking teeth"—that should a human attempt to touch such a weapon, their soul would be ripped from their body and destroyed.

They were mostly sure it was a lie, but I knew they had contact with other Arisen as well, and that made all negotiation fucking harder than it needed to be.

The upshot was that Egypt banned us from their lands, while explaining that if we had knowledge they could use, then we were required to share it. If we didn't? We were responsible for whatever happened. And that if we entered their lands uninvited, it would be an act of war.

Then they offered to permit us to convert the local land into a forest or whatever, but that it would remain the property of Egypt, and they would be stationing forces at the border.

After getting me close to the point of stabbing them, the minister then made it clear he'd be willing to reconsider all of this, for the right price.

At this point, I introduced Scylla.

She'd already killed a member of the Sudanese delegation, and when I explained that yes, she was immortal, and yes, she was the basis of the legends of Scylla, the negotiations changed slightly.

Explaining that no, she was never a sea monster, but that she had in fact been a *pirate*, that she'd been so successful that any ships that sailed even vaguely near to her island were never heard from again? That made an impression.

Add on that she knew of several thousand years of genuine history, and that if the Egyptians were our *friends*, then *perhaps* she and Ingrid would be willing to direct them to certain locations, ones that, although not of interest to "my kind," were still treasure troves of ancient history. Lost cities and more.

OR...

Scylla might decide to simply visit Egypt and recover the artifacts that she left there in the past herself.

Anyone who got in her way would be slaughtered and their deaths would be on the heads of the Egyptian "thieves" trying to lay claim to her property.

Negotiations were ongoing, and I was thoroughly fucking sick of it.

All in all, it was a pain in the arse, and I avoided it wherever I could, spending a few hours a day training with Scylla, another hour a day working on my own abilities, integrating things like my tentacles into my fighting style, and the rest of it working on the base with the others.

Scylla and the non-humans, mainly Oxus and the Oracan, helped me work on the bigger repairs, carrying massive blocks of stone and more, holding them in place to fix the overall structure as the nanites slowly inched up and over them.

We finished digging out the runway, repaired it, and got it up to a reasonable standard, then got to work on the rest of the site.

We were low on consumables, and seriously low on luxuries. Although we had food, and lots of it, anything that we needed was being brought in by coach from Sudan, literally ten hours of driving either way, or by plane.

Dimi was more than happy to essentially fly around the world, showing off his new plane and enjoying the systems that we were integrating each time he landed.

We'd gone from the outer shell, power core, and engines being advanced beyond anything in the skies by a massive margin, and the insides of the plane being basically from the sixties and seventies, to a hybrid.

Every time he flew anywhere, we added in a shopping list of tech, food, and basics, and shit we needed, as well as minor upgrades to the plane itself. Everything from seats to air conditioning, autopilot to fucking toilets needed to be redone…transponders, radios, everything.

It meant that the space that was available for things like nice towels? There just wasn't much at all. And really? We could live without it for ourselves.

Dimi was happy to fly to and fro for us, but he was also supposed to be on holiday and celebrating getting engaged, so we'd struck a deal where he took a day at the other end of each long-haul flight for now with his fiancée. The plane wouldn't open or respond to anyone else, so it wasn't like it was going to be stolen. Just in case, we sent one of the Oracan on each flight with him, heavily armed with both an assault rifle and crystal spear, ready for anyone to try to fuck with the plane.

We'd agreed, knowing that although we could have pulled in other pilots, it was better for now to not have more planes in our skies than we needed, and certainly not anything flying in toward us to land.

Ingrid and I had been talking about hiring a large plane and doing a massive shop, extending the runway and dealing with everything in one go, when Anders had pointed out just how easily the Arisen could use it to deliver a nuke or something similar to us instead.

At that point, we'd fallen back on Dimi doing supply runs and bringing in representatives of the nations, keeping them here for a few hours, then flying off again.

Dimi was apparently loving it, especially as the plane had a top speed that was closer to an experimental jet fighter than a commercial aircraft, at just over three thousand miles an hour now that the latest upgrades had been completed.

Admittedly, he didn't fly at that speed normally. Hell, that was near to the distance from London to New York in an hour, I'd been informed, but he could. And once little things like inertial dampeners were figured out? He'd be surpassing that.

Currently he was loving life—passing commercial flights at around two thousand miles an hour for shits and giggles, with a load of the latest solar cells in the hold.

Around the base, the hundreds of older solar panels were finally fully dug out. The fucked ones were in the process of being stripped out and stacked, ready for processing into null blocks. After a few days of painstaking searching, I eventually found enough of the hidden goddamn cameras to complete the next level of the quest I'd been given when we found the damn changelings and their cameras.

Quest Complete!

Evolving Quest completed: Who Watches the Watcher? Level 4

The local area was infiltrated by advanced BWV, as well as being monitored by others. For identifying and eliminating these interlopers, as well as rendering their devices harmless, you receive the following rewards:

- **+1 Hack point**
- **+Access to Level 5 of the Evolving Quest**

I saved the Hack point with the others for now and dismissed the next level of the quest. It was simple enough, after all, following the usual advancement of these things. It'd been five of these more complex hacks to get the first level, then ten for the second, then twenty-five; now it was fifty. So far, no great change, despite the complexity of it.

It was a little annoying, because I found that "normal" hacks weren't moving the dial anymore, and all the lower-level hack quests were wiped. I was left with either harder and harder quests, requiring more effort each time, or the option to basically stop and just accept that I was best specializing, rather than doing as I was and going for a general "build."

I stared up at the ceiling, musing as I traced old cracks and recently plastered sections, my mind whirling with the possibilities.

As soon as the site was more or less sorted, I needed to return to Crete. The ship was where all of this had begun, and I damn well needed to sort it out.

The last few days before the fight with Shamal and his lot had been horrifically busy. Hell, if I'd not been involved in a fight at any given second, then instead I'd been flying. Considering that I now suspected that something had gone wrong with the brain upgrade I'd done? I didn't dare spend more points than I desperately needed to.

I'd rebuilt the remote access suite at the base of my brain into a mass storage device, something that the system had accepted me doing. I'd thought—in my confused state when my brain was basically being eaten by faulty data—that if the system let me do it, it must be a viable option.

It wasn't. The downloads I'd done since then had almost broken me. Sometimes they were minor; other times they rendered me almost brain-dead. That wasn't a feasible option, not when we could be attacked at any point.

There was also the increasingly obvious "minor" detail that either I was broken, or the system was. After all, having an army that occasionally collapsed unconscious as soon as they completed an objective?

That was a stupid goddamn design.

No, I needed to go back to the ship, get the systems up and running, and have a proper look at it all, and as soon as possible.

As I was now, I should be able to tear through the lower-level firewalls and more. And the more complex shit should certainly generate some decent quest rewards.

I also knew that I'd be able to take on the low-level sentinels easily enough now. They were pretty basic and they...

And they were armed with gamma lasers, I suddenly remembered.

"Fuck," I whispered, realizing that although they'd been basic creations at the time, and the low-level, "cheap" systems, they were specifically designed to deal with Arisen!

They had to be! That they were armed with gamma lasers couldn't be a coincidence, not at all. Shit...I'd been thinking I could breeze through the security systems. That with the access details the Erlking had given me, once I reached the control centers, I'd be able to just take over and start the rebuild. But fuck!

I needed to upgrade my armor somehow. *Make it gamma resistant?*

Or a shield maybe? Hell, I knew thick-enough lead was supposed to stop the damn stuff, but would that work with alien gamma lasers? Would my normal armor work? It was weaponized nanites, after all.

I just knew far too little. Realistically, the only way I'd know was if I damn well went and checked it out. Maybe do a raid and then back off—figure shit out and then attack properly.

Scylla might want to come, as would Ingrid and the others. And yeah, I had no right to stop them, not really. Scylla seemed to be accepting me as an ally, and although she wasn't happy with my rules at the minute, she accepted that we'd freed her and were helping her acclimatize to the new world.

Hans had helped with that last night, telling her history in a way that only someone like he could, filling her in on the last few thousand years in about fifteen minutes.

She'd refused to discuss what led to her imprisonment, and Hans respected that, refusing to tell us any rumors as he admitted they'd probably come from Athena second or even third hand, so they were unlikely to be accurate.

He was also shit-scared of her, and sat as far from her as possible.

Scylla would be able to look after herself on the ship, and Ingrid and the others wouldn't.

I gritted my teeth and sat up in bed as the shower turned off, and I banished the thoughts to the back of my mind, rolling out of bed and padding across the poured concrete of the floor toward the bathroom, reaching for the door just as Ingrid pulled it open, startling her.

"Steve!" She gasped, clearly having been expecting me to be asleep still, then smiled, stepping forward and standing on tiptoes to kiss me. "Good morning, my love," she whispered, as I took her in my arms.

"It certainly is now," I agreed, kissing her again, holding her close and feeling the roughness of the towel that was all she was wearing.

We were reduced to basically the entire lot of us using cheap "no-tell motel" levels of amenities, and the scratchy towels were a reminder of that. Carpets, rugs, nice pictures, good towels, and all that kind of shit? They were for the future.

All of that streamed through my mind at the feel of the rough towel pressed against me, and then was dismissed in favor of the lush figure that the towel concealed.

A few kisses became more, and I stooped, picking Ingrid up in a princess carry, moving back to the bed, as she wrapped her arms around my neck, before moving to straddle me as I sat back down on the bed with her in my arms.

"You know…" she whispered into my ear, knowing exactly what I wanted as she moved around, gripping me and slipping me into position, "I just got all clean."

"Is that a complaint?" I nuzzled at her neck.

"Oh, gods no," she said, a hitch in her voice. "But we're supposed to be having breakfast soon…"

"Good. I already know what I want to eat…" I trailed kisses down her neck and across her chest as she leaned back, my hands and mind full of her, as hers were of me.

CHAPTER TWO⊙

By the time we made it down to breakfast around two hours later, most of the team had already been in and were now out working on various jobs. I loaded my plate from the buffet style-breakfast bar while James filled us in on the latest developments.

"And the representative from Egypt has made it clear they're willing to agree to the sharing of artifacts, on an 'if and when' basis, at a seventy-five to twenty-five percent share, in their favor. Essentially, they're promising to share them and to let us have our pick, but insisting that they will provide security for the sites. We're not to go anywhere inside their borders without an armed escort 'for our protection.' They're blatantly intending on trying to steal anything that we recover that they want, while adding in phrasing in the contract that says that everything is theirs and we accept that."

"The armed guards, are they there to protect the sites or us?" I sighed, absently reaching out to what they believed was a totally secure email server.

I scanned the last few messages, then a few more, and shook my head.

"Did they mention 'access hours'?" I pointed out to James, and he nodded in disgust.

"A maximum of four hours a day, despite them never enforcing these conditions on any other dig teams, to the best of my knowledge. He tried to sell it as a common and hardly worth mentioning detail. We'll be removed at the end of each day and taken to a nearby hotel 'at their expense' to allow us to 'rest in comfort' while they tidy the site and make it ready for the next day."

"And tidy away any artifacts, no doubt." Ingrid sighed. "Honestly, Steve, as much as I was giddy with the prospect of exploring unknown sites in Egypt, I think we should steer clear."

"I agree, frankly." James sighed. "Lars is ready to join us as soon as we can fit a pickup in, let him fly in himself, or even sail to the port and drive himself. I think we need to stick to the current method. We should send Dimi for him, and let him deal with them…"

"And Mor," Ingrid said firmly, using the Danish term for "mum." "She's adamant that she can do more here rather than from home, and it's been two weeks since she last went back to Denmark to sort a few details out. She's ready to come back."

"Just her?" I asked, getting a slightly guilty wince. "Okay, how many?" I laughed, and she shrugged, stifling a smile when she saw that I wasn't really annoyed.

"Okay, maybe my sister as well…" She grinned. "And maybe…"

"The clan is coming." I laughed, nodding and squeezing her hand in mine. "Well, it's on you to find them somewhere to stay."

"They're bringing tents." She shrugged.

"Tents?" I asked disbelievingly. "We're in the fuckin' desert, right? That's not gonna be fun."

"They're very expensive tents," James explained, with a patient smile. "Tents that are specifically designed for use in the desert, with viewing panels in the roof, and that are rated for sandstorms. They'll be bringing ten tents, each designed for five people, to help with our current issues with quarters. Also, the first five supply trailers should be delivered to Port Sudan in three days. They'll be cross shipped to Shaddah, reaching there, I've been assured, by the beginning of next week. Jay will, at that point, start towing them back here. The sooner we can get an actual road in place for this kind of thing, or finish the railway links, the better. But, realistically, this is the best we can do for now."

"Well, if they're happy to sleep in the tents and so on, go for it." I sighed, shrugging. "Seriously, though, how the hell did they build this place without railway links?" I shook my head. "I mean, the blocks, the high-tech equipment...hell, the majority of the waste! How did it get here? It wasn't *driven* in, surely?"

"Most was carried by heavy-lift helicopters." Anders slid into a seat next to us and nodded his head in greeting after he kissed his daughter's cheek. "The railway links were intended to be cheaper for bringing in the waste and materials, but the reality is that this far out in the desert, there's only so many options.

"The railway link needs to cover over four hundred miles. The three years that the site was up and running were sufficient to have made that. Hell, with a professional team working around the clock, it could have been done easily. They didn't invest heavily in that, though, making it clear that the cost of getting the waste to the site was borne by the nation shipping it. That gave them the opportunity to line their pockets twice, by operating a transport company from the port to here."

"What happened to it?" Ingrid sipped her coffee and sighed. "Thank you. Honestly, I don't know how you do this, Casey," she admitted, smiling at the steward as Casey moved around the table, refilling cups before taking a seat nearby.

"It's damn sorcery is what it is," I agreed, sipping what was usually a bitter brew and instead finding it complex, multi-layered, and damn, it was good. "But that's a good point. What happened to the helos? I mean, if we could get a few of those..."

"They're horrifically expensive to maintain and run, unfortunately." James sighed. "I considered it, awhile back actually, but between the fact we'd need a skilled and dedicated pilot—Dimi is great, admittedly, but he flies fixed-wing airplanes, not helicopters—and the actual cost of buying such a craft, then getting it here, plus you upgrading it, then maintenance..." He shook his head. "They're horrifically inefficient machines, in all honesty."

"Best to leave it then." I sighed, nodding and moving on as I took another sip of my coffee, settling back in the chair. It creaked under my weight. "Fair enough. So, for the time being, we're happy that the site is as secure as we can make it?" I looked from one person to another.

"We've got the airstrip for when we want to fly in and out. We've got basic radar up and running. It's not going to give us much warning for an incoming missile, admittedly, but that's not something we can really deal with, either."

"You could," Ingrid said determinedly. "If they fired something at us, you could probably stop it."

"I might be able to," I agreed. "If I knew it was coming, if I knew where it was, and more. But as it is? Unlikely."

I left it unsaid that I'd also spent several days infiltrating a link into the American command and control network. They had the most advanced sensors that I'd been able to find and they were locked on us here, so why would I need to install totally new systems? Our little leadership team knew, of course, but there was no need to make it public knowledge.

Instead, I'd hacked them, slipping in watch programs, designed to let us know if anything tried to fly or fire anything nearby.

Then we'd gotten our own much more basic radar that had been included in the tower's original design, and we had that as our backup and public system, just in case of spies.

"So, what's the plan for today then, while we wait for Hans to drag his sorry arse out of bed?" I asked the others, getting a variety of grunts and responses, until Belle, who'd just entered the cafeteria area, admitted that she and Ingrid were again doing the rounds with people today, essentially continuing the "hearts and minds" work she was amazing at.

They had a constant guard with them in the form of Oxus, the massive Minotaur. But of far more concern for me was that they also occasionally had a much more violent and dangerous companion in the curious Scylla.

Scylla had expressed an interest in meeting more of the "little people" and although Ingrid hated that Scylla saw them like that…for her, it was true.

She was a little over two thousand years old, and had been locked away in the eighth century, over thirteen hundred years ago. She had been one of the premier warriors of the age, and a terrible foe, but there was also something very, very wrong there.

Scylla would alternate between talking and seeming sad, and staring, unblinking at us, clearly inches away from violence.

I'd tried to talk Ingrid and Belle out of taking Scylla with them, despite Belle's calming abilities, but the pair were determined, and I'd agreed, smiling through gritted teeth.

I *hated* this. It felt as if we had a live tiger with us at all times, and I was seriously considering taking her to the damn St. Eustace's asylum that Hans had told us about.

A normal madman was dangerous. Scylla? I wasn't entirely sure I *could* contain her, or even defeat her, if I needed to. That she was wandering around with Ingrid, and might at any time decide to kill her for some imagined slight? It fucking *terrified* me. But I forced myself to smile and nod, and moved on.

James continued to manage things directly for Ingrid and me, currently focusing on people issues and arranging shipments, stock and more with Freja.

Anders worked on the overall site plan, acting as a mixture of construction foreman, chief operating officer, and factory manager, chasing people up and making damn sure the jobs were done right, that the abandoned waste below us was fed into the converter and that the business side of things was maintained.

It was ridiculous how much of what I thought of as "hand-holding" was required in the job. Essentially, my opinion was that we paid people, and we fed and kept them safe, etc.; in return, we all pulled together and worked. Nice and simple.

Instead, every five minutes, someone was running to him or James with another issue, one that I was gloomily convinced the buggers could have fixed themselves with ease if they just stopped to think for thirty seconds.

As soon as we'd all finished our coffees and breakfast, we set off in different directions, spreading out as the next shift came in, dozens of workers who had been working on the maintenance rotation in the solar cell fields.

I nodded to several of them who I knew. The majority stepped aside to let me through as I headed to the first sub-level, and what I'd decided was the best use of my time while we waited on Hans getting up, the lazy fuck.

"Steve!" Zac grinned as I walked into his workshop a few minutes later, Corey and Joseph both in there as well. "You ready for a fun day?"

I squinted at him suspiciously. "I hate it when you're happy," I said after a few seconds.

"You see!" Corey gestured at Joseph, sitting up and nodding to me. "Thank you, boss. Great to see that someone understands."

"What?" Zac asked, confused.

"When you're happy, it means you either broke something, or you're about to, and that means loads more work for everyone else!" Corey pointed out. "So, I'm with him—I hate it when you're happy."

"Yeah, well, fuck you very much." Zac laughed. "Right, you ready to sort this shit then, boss man?"

I nodded, looking at where the various components were laid out, ready for me.

When I'd upgraded my systems to enable me to make more structures like the converter, I'd gained access to several basic plans, and then, as time went on, further investment had unlocked more and more technology, including the ambiguously named "General Technology" download.

That one had goddamn stung, that was for sure.

Today was all about making the most of this and figuring out the best way to upgrade the site, and then eventually, all of us.

We'd already established that individual constructions could be made easily enough. Taking an existing system like the solar cell panels and upgrading it, for example? Simple. Provided I had a plan.

Currently, we were flying them in when we could, just because we needed so many, but this morning was about finding a way to make our own, cheaply and efficiently.

As another example, creating a gantry system and then feeding the null blocks into it—using nanites to construct a frame and then a boat—was again, simple, more or less. There was truly little "high tech" in the actual construction, and I'd already done this once, when I needed the boat made.

Sure, the engines and control surfaces had been awkward, but the rest? Over ninety percent of the structure was literally just me using nanites to convert null blocks into something sturdier, and far thinner. Then it was like programming a 3D printer, or more accurately, like plugging the file in, and having the operating system do it.

Making a machine that could change the design as needed on the fly, though? Nope.

I had a creation tool—that hadn't been cheap but I had it—installed in my arm in place of the missing harvest tool. The issue was that it'd make only what I told it to, and that it needed nanites to do it.

I couldn't, for example, set a second one up linked to a computer and let Zac churn out different things, converting null blocks into other things.

I could use them, but I needed to use nanites as well, and that was a pain in the ass. Especially as without the harvest tool, the nanites were limited as fuck now. Also, it was in my goddamn arm, and I was kinda attached to that…which meant he couldn't just play and experiment with it when he wanted.

So, this morning was all about exploring options.

I made myself comfortable, then glanced at the others, who looked at me expectantly.

"So…?" I said after a minute. "How do we do this?"

"Uh…I was kinda hoping you knew. Come on, boss man!" Zac said, and I glared at him.

"Are you fucking stupid?" I groaned. "What would I need you for if I knew what I was doing?"

"Well…" He winced. "Okay, fair point. But you're the one with the tech and the experience of using it."

"Zac, I'm a glorified thug. Yeah, all right, I'm immortal…" I banished the memory of the Erlking telling me I definitely wasn't and I moved on. "But my main skills? I kill shit. I break things that people say can't be broken, and I don't stop. That's it. Tech?" I shook my head. "Not so much, mate. I'm making it up as I go along."

"Shit."

"Nicely put," I congratulated him, as we all sat thinking.

"So…" Corey started after a few seconds. "Your tool…"

"Heh." Zac grunted.

"The one in your hand," Corey said more carefully, glaring at Zac, who sniggered again. "Fuck's sake!" He groaned, covering his eyes. "The one that he uses to make shit, Zac, not his fucking dick!"

"What about it?" I ignored the sniggering Aussie.

"How does it work?"

"It's a molecular assembler," I said after a few seconds of examination. "Where it can, it makes things out of the matter it can access. So if I aim it at a pile of null blocks, it'll try to convert that. If it can't, if it's something that needs to be assembled from the nanites themselves, like a power core? Then it'll use some of them, even if I order it to use the null blocks. It's got some kind of safety limiters built in."

"Okay, okay, that works. So, could it, for example, make more of itself?" Corey asked excitedly.

"It could," I admitted after a few seconds, frowning at him. We'd covered this in conversations the other night…when he'd been drunk. Dammit. Not being able to get drunk was seriously annoying when it meant you had to have the same conversations again and again. "But without the actual programs that are stored in the nanites, they'd be blank, and the nanites need to be linked to something to actually work. Like, a laptop won't work for this…I think it needs to be alive for some reason."

"Okay, so could you make them for us?" He gestured to the three of them.

"No…" I admitted after a few seconds of examining the system. "Without unlocking your nanites, the tool wouldn't respond to you. In fact, it might try to absorb your nanites, and that'd kill you."

"What about a simple device then?" he tried again. "Look, take away the complicated shit…you made the matter converters, right?"

"They're *insanely* complicated," Zac pointed out.

"What they do is, sure, but the actual operating system isn't," he corrected. "You feed in the waste; it converts it. Have we been looking at this wrong? Maybe think of it as a factory production line, and take it down to the most basic level, right? Could you make a machine that would convert null blocks into…" He cast about, then found a nearby panel for the solar cells.

"Could you make it make these, not as a machine that we can change the output, but targeted and locked, like the converters are, to make just this?" he asked.

I reached out, taking it from him and examining the cell, turning it over in my hands.

It was about six inches on a side, hexagonal, and coated on the back with a reflective layer. A thick glass-like substance overlaid the actual solar cell to protect it, and to concentrate the sun. I used the system to examine it, checking over the silicon wafer that made up most of the solar cell, the various metals and more, before the wires that collected them to the other panels in relay.

"It's too complicated," I said after a few seconds of playing with the system; the others slumped, thinking it was a bust. "But…I like the thought."

"You think it could work?" Zac asked.

"I do, if we take it back a few steps." I focused and pooled a small number of nanites in my hand, then took a null block, before adding another and setting them together on the top of a nearby table, concentrating on exactly what I wanted.

The designs were there; I knew they were. I could feel that data, but they were telling me that they should be part of a much larger system, something that I couldn't unlock, not yet.

A large-scale factory plant was what I needed, and what the system wanted me to invest in unlocking, despite the numerous steps required to get to that stage, as well as the fact I didn't have any goddamn Support points to play with. I had mainly War points left. Although, I did have one General specialization one…No. I'd try to do this without using it.

Instead, I broke the problem down to tiny stages.

We needed three things, as I saw it…no, dammit, *four*. We needed the glass, to cover the front and protect the solar cells. The cells themselves, and the reflective backing; then we needed the cabling to connect them to each other and to pass the charge across.

That'd do for most of the cells, although we'd still need to make frames, and something to pass the power off the cell and into the grid. For now, though, as a proof of concept, this was the way to go.

The frame they could damn well do themselves.

I created a single factory unit on the table, perhaps eight inches long, and as thick as a ruler, maybe two inches deep and the same height. It had a slot on the top to hold the null block, and was essentially a printer inside, one with rollers that would extrude the sheet to the right once it was done.

It looked like such a small, innocuous piece of nothing, but when I triggered it?

Thirty seconds later, the first sheet of solar voltaic cells finished sliding free, slipping to the table to utter silence from us all, before Zac picked it up, swearing at how thin it was.

"What's wrong?" I frowned, thinking I'd fucked it up somehow.

"Nothing, mate," he whispered, flexing it as if it were paper and shaking his head in wonder. "Nothing at all."

"So...?"

"It's perfect." He grinned, passing it around as he gestured to me to start it up again.

I nodded, sending a message to the system that governed the printer to continue until the block was used up, then to restart as soon as the "hopper" was full again.

It was fast, sure, but it still took nearly an hour before the block was gone. And by then, three more similar machines sat side by side on the table next to the first.

One created the backing sheets, another a thin sheet of artificial sapphire, and the last churned out a thin mesh to be laid across the underside, transporting the electrical charge to the next panel in line.

Each of the panels simply needed to be pressed together, an interlocking system sealing each layer against the next, until it was done.

Each panel, from print to sealed and ready, took a little over a minute, and as Zac played with them, he made it slightly faster each time.

"This is a game changer, mate!" Zac whispered, grinning. "The solar cells aren't cheap, all right? Hell, they're not *expensive* normally, sure, but by the time they're shipped out here? You're looking at about ten thousand a panel. Then add in assembly, installation, and then replacement? Nah, they're not a realistic method of doing anything long-term. But these?" He tried to bend the now fully assembled panel, and when he failed, instead tried to do it with the "glass" composite.

"What the hell is this?" He smacked it off the end of the table, leaving only a scratch...on the *table.*

"Artificial sapphire," I said. "Stronger than titanium, thinner than glass, and cheap to make."

"How many did we get?" he asked.

All of us started to count.

For the four blocks, we'd gotten two hundred mesh backs for the electricals, sixty sapphire "glass," a hundred reflective backs, and a hundred and twenty photo-voltaic solar cells.

"So...we can replace a full panel, a big fucking one, every thirty minutes, and we're getting two an hour, for four blocks," he muttered. "Each block is converted from either a ton of fucked-up sand at the shitty end of the scale, or we get, maybe one a barrel of nuclear ooze? Maybe a few out of each fuel rod..." He made a dozen markings on a sheet, working things out in his head, before turning to me and smiling wolfishly. "We're gonna need to hire some more people."

"Why?" I asked, not liking the look in his eyes.

"Because we're building a factory!"

"Right?" I agreed, frowning, not seeing the point.

Corey clipped more and more sections together, before gathering armfuls of the completed panels. "We need to test them first!" he grunted. "Come on, you!" He elbowed Joseph, who, true to form, simply nodded and did, rather than speaking.

Ten minutes later, the four of us stood around a bodged-together panel that had been laid out on the sand, as Zac finished plugging the connectors in.

He was almost done when he screamed, jerking his hand back and shaking it, swearing. "Fuckingcocksuckingbuttholefingering…" He snarled, shaking the hand over and over, apparently trying to get the feeling back in from the electric shock he'd just received, touching the now "live" connections. "Steve…?" He half begged, sucking on the injured fingers and nodding in the direction of the panel.

"I'll plug it in." I grinned, before connecting the last few cables, using nanite tentacles.

As soon as it was all connected, though? The overall power generated by the solar field leapt upward by just over two percent.

That didn't sound like much, and I'd said that, when Joseph finally spoke, his voice ecstatic as he told us the numbers.

Then he pointed out that, first of all, the panel was laid flat, not angled to face the sun properly. And secondly? There were a hundred and eleven panels in use currently.

The half-sized panel we'd bodged together, that was laid on the sand, partially covered by the drifting, windblown crap, was carrying two percent of the load.

It was doing the equivalent of at least three full-sized panels, and had been built entirely from scrap, which was basically free to us. If we could get a hundred of these fuckers up and running? We'd have no power issues whatsoever.

I stepped back, thinking as the crazy bastard engineers all started to argue over the designs and uses for the machines.

I smiled. These panels were great, sure, but after losing the harvest tool, I'd been panicking, and seriously so.

Sure, the panels weren't going to help me massively, not really—it wasn't like I needed to sell them to make money or whatever. But it was what they *represented*.

I could still make crazy shit without the nanites, or at least without using huge numbers of them. I could set up factory production lines. Hell, I could probably make a machine that would combine the goddamn production lines…normal machines that ran conveyor belts, maybe? Feed them all into a separate machine that produced them? I could set up a line of panels…or, better yet? A mining machine.

We knew that there was water deep down. We knew that we needed a pump of some kind, and a damn drill. I smiled slowly, turning and staring out across the desert, squinting in the bright sunlight as I envisaged the land around us, before nodding at the nearby exposed large hills.

They rose from the sea of sand dunes like a pod of breaching whales, massive and slow, pausing as if ready to slide back beneath the sand, and frozen.

I'd always loved the mountains, recognizing the bones of the world where they shone through. But right now?

I was seeing a lot more than that. I nodded to myself, visualizing exactly what we'd decided we needed.

A basin to start with, one that was sealed to make sure the water didn't seep back down after it was pumped up. Maybe we could dig a few hundred meters down, then form a seal around the base of the basin with stone?

Now that I was really looking at the area, I could see a dozen different designs I could incorporate to bodge together what I needed, and the system had access to most of them already. Starting with basic mining machines that could chew up the sand and dead earth, laying the stone behind them…with a little adjustment, anyway.

It'd take a handful of Support class upgrades to pay for them, I guessed, distantly feeling the potential for certain lines at the end of sections I'd yet to unlock. I wavered between focusing on quests to gain access to them, or focusing on the ship.

I sighed, thanking the group, then left them to play with the new machines, and set off back to the main building.

An hour later, I sat in the control room of the tower, feet up on one desk, eyes closed as I worked. I'd accessed the tablet on the table next to me, and through it, a popular real-time Earth mapping software.

I was keeping my access as hidden as possible, knowing that there would be a fuckload of the various ABC agencies watching any and all data requests coming from here. So I hid mine inside a massive burst of searches that were being randomly generated.

It'd taken Jack all of five minutes to come up with a program that did what I needed, essentially randomly searching locations, websites, and images, over and over again.

It was apparently a reverse DDoS, or distributed denial of service attack. Instead of overwhelming a single target with a thousand requests a second, it made several thousand requests a second to random locations across the internet.

It wasn't foolproof—they could still trace the access, after all—but I'd had him doing this for about a week now, at random times, making it as hard as possible to find anything.

I examined the sea around the location I'd found Facility 6B originally. There was a valley that led straight through the nearby mountains directly to this point, but there had been nothing to suggest that it was anything more than a normal valley.

Looking at it again? I'd still have sworn that was all it was. Maybe it was a little longer and steeper than the surrounding ones, but that was it, if not for the knowledge I'd gained.

The Erlking had said something about it being lost to a volcano…certainly seemed like something the old bastard had said. I scratched my chin, thinking as I spun and adjusted the images in my mind.

Ingrid had said that a volcano had wiped Thera out, but that had been literally thousands of years later.

Unless…unless the explosion at Thera had just been the latest one, and not necessarily the one that had fucked the ship up? I mean, sure, there wasn't much left of the original volcano, but they didn't tend to explode just once, did they? They were one of those things that happened again and again?

If that was the case, then drawing a line mentally from Crete, back along the valley, and lining up on…*Yup. Thera.*

I grinned. If the facility had been near Thera and had been hit by its explosion? I could definitely see a line of potential damage across the island of Crete, leading right to the resting place the ship now occupied.

Add to that, the literally hundreds of thousands of years that had passed since then? I could definitely understand why nobody had found the fucker.

From what I remembered, it was on its side and badly fucked up. But at least some of it had been operational, which gave me a bit of an idea how damn well built these places were.

For a minute, I wondered how the ship had come to be hit by the volcanic eruption…then I shrugged. I'd probably never know. But the Erlking had admitted that there were three of them here, still, and that they'd been banished.

It'd admitted that they were immortal, and in a way that I wasn't. They'd also said that they wouldn't permit another race to rise to full immortality. It was pretty clear that they were expecting to live forever, sure.

One of their conditions for granting the access keys and more for the ships, though? To give me rights to unlock the systems and to enable me to essentially evolve my friends and to rebuild and take over the ships?

It was that as soon as I'd managed to "fix" the world, getting rid of the poisons, rewilding the Sahara and generally picking up the litter, cutting the grass, painting the benches, and leaving the place immaculate, was that I then fucked off.

I was to "return to the stars" and search for humanity and others of his kind. I was to hunt down any remnants of humanity left out there from the first generation they created, and I was to kill them.

I needed to see whether any of the Erlking's kind were still out there, which was a little weird and counterintuitive. If they were as powerful as he implied— and he'd easily fucked me up, I had to admit that…even if only to myself—then they should be even more powerful, right?

Thinking about it now, I was fairly sure I was being set up. If I go out there and humanity has survived all this time? Battling fuck knew what in deep space? They'd take one look at me in my piddly little reconditioned ship and squash me.

Hell, they'd think I was one of their old masters in these ships, and probably slaughter me out of hand. That, or if they weren't about, and the rest of the Erlking's kind were?

I was a human, a survivor of a genetic experiment that cost them billions of their immortal lives and fuck knew how many others. I'd be turning up in one of their fucked-up old ships, after the Erlking admitted they were all banished to Earth, along with the final generation of their experiments.

Any of their kind I met out there would probably be able to kill me, and they would, as fast as possible, and most likely as painfully as possible.

The very best situation I could hope for was that something else had killed them all and fucked off, and that was fairly unlikely as well.

Admittedly, they did make us as soldiers to fight *something*, but I couldn't really see whatever they'd been fighting killing them all and then fucking off home to leave the rest of the galaxy alone.

That was the kicker, though. If I stayed here, ignored the Erlking and just said "fuck it"? It'd come for me, and I knew firsthand that I was absolutely no match for it, not as things stood now. Maybe once I'd spent some time in deep space working on it, though? Maybe I could find some of their tech and use it.

Rebuild myself, upgrade all the way, then come back and fuck it up.

I didn't know, but considering that staying here was definitely a death sentence—and not just for me, but for those I loved—while out there, there was at least some hope? It wasn't a hard choice.

No, as soon as I was finished fixing the world, I'd be leaving, and I'd be pretty damn unlikely to be coming back. I needed a plan. I needed to get the ships claimed, repaired, and working on one of my own as soon as possible. Lastly, I needed to be as powerful as I damn well could be before I left.

The only way I could manage all those things?

I needed to get to fucking work.

CHAPTER THREE

"What do you mean, they want him to submit to them?" Ingrid asked Hans as we all gathered around the table in our quarters, the lazy bastard having only gotten up halfway through the day.

Ingrid and I were joined by James, Anders, Hans, Jonas, and Zac, with Casey both serving and joining us. We'd managed to hide what the meeting was and to send Belle off with Oxus—after explaining she was not to avail herself of any Minotaur milking opportunities until she was back in private at the end of the day—and Scylla.

Ingrid had cunningly suggested that the Oracan and Oxus were impressive warriors, and as she'd expected, Scylla had laughed, long and hard, over just how weak they were.

Ingrid had basically begged and bet Scylla in equal measures until she'd agreed that she would take over their training as a group, turning them into the base's security forces and a starter cell for an army.

It was a brilliant use of her time, giving her the opportunity to regain her strength in an environment she understood, and Belle was there to make sure that if there was a misunderstanding, it was less likely to be terminal for anyone involved. And it kept Scylla away from this meeting, just in case.

James and Anders were there as they were essentially running the business and building for us; Ingrid because she was a lot brighter than me, and would see and understand a lot I probably wouldn't.

Then Hans, because he was the whole reason for the meeting, Jonas because he could bring a lot of information to the table, as well as what the Blessed were more likely to do, and Zac because we needed to discuss the viability of rebuilding the ships.

Casey was there more or less because we needed someone skilled and trustworthy to handle the food and drinks, and it would be a bit of a shitty thing to have her serve us, and her *husband*, and then sod off while we all ate without her.

"Literally as I said," Hans replied to Ingrid, fussing with the chair as he shifted uncomfortably in its plastic constraints. "Honestly, do they make these things to be deliberately as uncomfortable as possible?"

"Hans, focus, mate." I forced a smile as I tried to get the erratic Immortal to get on with the story, rather than what was quite possibly one of the only times he'd sat his immortal arse in such a cheap seat. "You met the Old Ones?"

"Yes, well, okay, let's start at the beginning, I suppose," he grumbled, looking at the "mere humans" around him, then at me, and sighing before settling back and taking a drink of the rum I'd poured for him. "So, I made it to the Great Refuge without too much difficulty…they *do* want us to return, after all. It's a beastly place to get to, honestly, but once you're there?" He shook his head, shifting again and staring off into the distance.

"I'd forgotten just how beautiful it is. The mountains and the valley? Wonderous. They chose it for a reason: far enough from the spreading tribes of humanity that they could control all the passes that lead to it, an area where no great armies could possibly be amassed, and with places where our strengths would always outmatch that of the humans.

"The valleys and passes that lead up to it were carved over the millennia to make sure that a single figure could hold them, while massive armies, should they ever find a way to that point, would have to approach in numbers of no more than a handful abreast.

"That the Old Ones have held the valley for so long is obvious as soon as you enter it. It is truly wonderful. The human tribes who live there? They maintain it to perfection. The lycan and other trans-human populations? They're housed mainly inside the surrounding mountains, laid ready."

"Where is it, did you say?" Ingrid asked casually, and Hans snorted.

"Ingrid, I'd happily take you if I could, believe me." He sighed. "In truth, those who advise the Old Ones would love you. They'd sense a kindred spirit. And the things they could teach you? You'd love it. The artifacts they have there, stored? Not the relics and so on of *our* past, but the human artifacts? They hold samples from every epoch, from when your kind were barely able to speak above a grunt, to the great wonders of the past. They have artworks from every age, and the—" He broke off, seeing the look on her face, and those on the faces of those around the room.

"Well, anyway. The only issue, Ingrid? Is that you'd never be permitted to leave. No human who enters those lands is. Not that they want to, of course…they've mainly been bred for their roles for thousands of years. They're literally the perfect servants, and even the thought of leaving is abhorrent to them. Only the second or third generation are ever sent out on missions, and even then, it's with one of their masters." He shook his head.

"I've tried over the years, tried to encourage some of the few who deal with the outside world to jump ship as it were, to come and serve me instead. They simply cut off communication if you even try to hint at it. But I digress. You'd be conditioned to your place if you were to enter the valley of the Great Refuge, or you'd be killed. And either way, that'd be a terrible waste of one so pretty."

"You…uh…said you can only go once, usually?" I asked, changing the subject to try to move us past the awkward silence that comment had left.

"Yes!" Hans said quickly, smiling again. "They allow all new Arisen to visit once, to see the wonders of the valley, to discover the truth of the past, or as much of it as they'll share at least, and then you're given the choice. You may stay—you'll be apprenticed to one of the elder Arisen, and you'll serve until they judge you ready. Once they're sure of you? Well, I guess they give you a place there. Not sure, really. Most of those who accept the choice aren't really seen much after that.

"Not that they vanish, you understand," he clarified hastily. "They just move onto the deeper, more private areas of the valley. And when and if we do encounter them again? They've had centuries of indoctrination. They tend to view the factions with contempt, and they're generally among the strongest of us, so when a representative shows up, they come to give a specific order, or to recover something, and then they're gone again."

"And the others just accept that?" I asked. "I mean, one of them turns up and tells Athena to hand over something, I don't see her doing it very happily…"

"Oh, she wouldn't have," he agreed. "She'd have fought, most likely, regardless of what they asked or demanded be handed over. That's Athena, though. She was powerful enough and skilled enough that they'd only have asked if there was a good reason."

"So they'd have fought her if they wanted something?" I asked again, wanting clarification.

"No." He shook his head. "They'd have gone to the council and demanded it of them. The council would have most likely bargained for it from Athena, granting her something that she wanted, and the council would get something in return. It was all a balancing act, you see. No one of the factions grew too strong, and they all respected tradition.

"If the Old Ones reached out and demanded something? They'd get it, but that covers in part why most of the Arisen don't share that they have anything, artifacts of our deep past, for example. If they did? Then the Old Ones come, and they want them. They know they can't take them all, that it'd come to a war between the factions, so there's a sort of unspoken rule about keeping it quiet if you or another of your faction has something.

"Give a drunken monkey—never mind one of *us*—long enough and it'd find whatever was hidden, and whenever one of the factions is killed or locked? That generally sparks a frantic search for their personal refuge. It's one of the reasons we all like ships. We can sail around the world and relax, take our little creature comforts with us, and it means we can hide where we keep our things from the others for as long as possible."

"Okay, before we move on—sorry, Hans—but Steve, you said that you had a location for artifacts looted from Athena's ship, right?" Ingrid made notes on the tablet on the table before her.

"Laia did," I corrected. "She's pretty fucked up still. Her limbs are regrowing, but damn slowly, and it's painful for a human. She said that she saw where the artifacts were shipped to. It might be a trans-shipping place—hell, it almost certainly was—but that just means there'll be records somewhere."

"Then we need to trace them, and those crystal weapons before they get stolen by anyone else," Ingrid said. "Can you sort that, Steve? Get with Laia and find out the address?"

"I can," James said, reddening. "We're supposed to be discussing things later tonight, so I can get the details then?"

"Brilliant. Thank you, James." Her eyes sparkled over James's obvious discomfort, as well as that his discussion with her was blatantly going to be over dinner. Then she looked back to Hans and nodded to him, smiling again. "Sorry for interrupting, Hans. You were telling us where the Old Ones were?"

"No, I wasn't," he corrected, frowning. "But good try."

Ingrid smiled an apology and gestured for him to go on, as he tried to get more comfortable.

He sat for long seconds, clearly unsure about the conversation, until Ingrid apologized again.

"So...I made contact with their representatives at the borders, made my identity clear, and that while I wasn't there to join, I had information on *you*. Then I gave them the message Ingrid had given me, about 'Old Gods,' and your mission from them."

"How did they take it?" I asked, curiously, shifting in the chair and playing with my coffee cup idly.

"Well, put it this way...it usually takes around a day or two to gain permission to enter the Great Refuge, and you're allowed to go wherever, provided you stay away from the Great Refuge and you don't try to get away from the one assigned to 'guide you.' Basically, they leave a guard on you at all times. Alternatively, you're told that you had your chance and to leave, pointedly." He grumbled. "This time? Nine days."

"They left you for nine days?" I asked, surprised.

"They did. Apparently, the request was making its way up the chain of command, until finally it reached the Speaker himself. He sent for me, personally, and I was brought to the Great Refuge." He sat forward, gripping his hands together as he fixed me with a stare. "Steve, I was brought before the Old Ones themselves. Not one of the lesser Arisen, not a council member who makes the minor decisions for them, like which nations are permitted nuclear weapons to play with, or who can have a war—or peace—with whom. I was brought before the eldest of our race.

"Nine thousand years old, Steve," he said, his eyes almost feverish as he stared into the memory. "The eldest of them is nine *thousand* years old. The aura of power around her? Not even including the others? I could barely breathe in her presence! She stared at me. She saw *me!*"

"Did she speak to you?" Ingrid asked quickly. "Her accent, the language she used..."

"No," Hans said flatly, shaking his head and looking around at the others again. "I...I'm still not convinced this is something that should be discussed before you. I'm sorry...Ingrid, James, all of you. Steve has Arisen, and that the Old Ones wish to meet him, for him to be brought before the Council of Elders itself? This is an honor the likes of which you cannot understand. All your human history, all that you know and believe, she was there throughout. She guided entire civilizations that you will never learn the names of, to rise and fall. That you even ask questions about her? It is offensive beyond a level you can imagine!"

That last bit was delivered with a definite bite, and I sat up straighter, rolling my shoulders as I spoke.

"Hans, the world is changing, my friend. You need to accept this," I said categorically. "She's nothing but old, that's all."

"She's ancient and powerful beyond anything you can imagine," he snapped, before taking a deep breath, and going on, forcing a smile. "But fine, I only agreed to discuss this with you all today because you told me that you'd tell them the details after the conversation if I didn't permit them to be here. Fine, I accept that, but I will not have blasphemy! Do you understand? The Old Ones—" He broke off, clearly trying to maintain his patience.

Ingrid spoke again, her voice softer. "Hans, I'm sorry," she said. "I know this is hard for you, and I apologize for not showing you the respect she deserves."

He glared at her, and then around the table, making sure that everyone was silent, before he finally started to speak again.

"I was presented to them all, the nine of the Council of Elders—I will not speak their names—but I was introduced, and my lineage explained. My situation, as a spy for both factions, was raised and discarded as unimportant." He shook his head in disbelief.

"They knew—do you see? They *knew*, and they knew what neither faction did! They knew and they didn't care*, and they didn't care about letting me know!* That means, at the very least, that they're still as involved in the world as both factions fear. It also means that they already knew about you!

"They had me give them your message, that you'd met one of the 'Old Gods,' and that they'd given you a mission to heal the earth. It was such a stupid message…I nearly changed it a dozen times, thinking it was such a stupid and obviously made-up thing to say. Then I say it, and there I am. I could barely get the words out as the Speaker, himself over five thousand years old, asked me questions about you, pausing and looking to the other Elders from time to time, as if they were talking, yet saying nothing that I could hear."

"Could you feel anything?" I asked curiously.

"Feel?" He paused, pondering that, then waggled his head from side to side as if unsure. "Perhaps. There was a feeling of pressure, from time to time, as if the air were changing, like when a plane rises or descends suddenly. Nothing beyond that though."

"Okay, thanks." I squeezed Ingrid's knee under the table as she showed me the tablet she was making a note on.

Psychic?

She'd written that, and I connected to the tablet, printing my response below her words.

Probably something like that, I agreed. *Possibly a neural link, if they have access to any tech.*

"So," Hans said after a few seconds, clearly catching the exchange, even if he didn't know what we were saying. "After they questioned me about you, everything from our first meeting to the way you could control your drone, to the damn armor you make and the way you can fly? They said that they'd send out an order to leave you be, that you had asked for a month's grace period from them, and they agreed. You have a month to tie up your affairs, then you have to present yourself, at the Great Refuge. You're to submit to them. And until then? You're to hide who and what you are as much as possible."

"Define submit," I said slowly. "I offered to go to them, sure…I need to meet them and ask some questions. But if they think I'm going to *serve* them…"

"That's for them to decide, my friend. I'm sorry, but you don't know what you're facing here. The Old Ones are disregarded by the factions, beyond the obvious need to keep quiet about things we have, but it's because they play that they're not interested. They don't take a hand in the governance of the world; they retreated from it, or so we thought. Meeting them? Finding out just how much they knew about me, for example? And you…I was telling them things they knew!

I was shown pictures of you, in your armor, laid on the deck of your little yacht. Hell, they even had some of you serving drinks behind a bar!"

"That must have been a while ago," I muttered. Then I cursed. If they were really digging into my past, they'd be able to narrow things down fairly quickly, I was betting. I needed cash and more a few years ago, so I was obviously human then. Hell.

I'd broken my right arm eight months before I robbed the damn bank; I'd fallen down the stairs drunk and landed badly. That'd be on my old hospital records. If they checked that and decided that it was real, and not a fake—which I could have done, and I should have thought to do, or to just erase myself from all records entirely before now—then they'd have a good ballpark area to start searching for how and why I arose.

"A month," Hans reiterated. "They extended an offer to you as well, and it's a good one."

"Oh?" I asked.

"Submit," he repeated. "Go to them as you offered, but *inside* the month. They'll hold off the factions—they're making it clear to them all that you're to be left alone while you wrap up your affairs. Go to them, and they'll make sure that the others here are left alone. When I explained that you were trying to clean up the nuclear waste and more? They agreed that it needed to be done. That you'd been given a mission from an old god? Steve, I don't know what you think you're doing, but unless you found some exile from the Old Ones..."

"No," I said, then I grinned. "Well, not exactly. I did find an exile, though..." I took a deep breath. "Hans, did they tell you anything else?"

"They'll give you all the respect you're due, Steve. You'll be permitted to go to them in the Great Refuge, and you'll speak to them directly. Go to them within the month—hell, as soon as possible—and they'll teach you. They'll accept you, no matter what you've done, and they'll deal with the consequences, including the factions."

He sat forward, eyes almost feverish as he spoke. "You realize what that means? They don't care. They want you to keep quiet about what you are, and who, but all that you've done, claiming to be an angel or a demon or whatever? They don't care! They'll even declare this little project of yours under their protection! It means that Ingrid and the others are safe, truly so! They'll send a representative to rule here in your stead, to maintain everything and to make sure that the project isn't stopped while you're with them!"

"To rule in my place..." I shook my head in annoyance. "Fair enough. Thank you, Hans. Anything else?"

He shook his head, and I sighed, looking around, before settling back and making myself more comfortable. "Well, I suppose it's time I shared the truth with you, my friend. These others here all know, and it might be that you feel a little different about the 'Old Ones' by the end of my story. You might even have more that makes sense for you, *so*..."

Two hours later, I leaned against the glass of the control tower, watching Hans as he slowly climbed the distant sand dune, his head slumped and clothes snapping in the wind as he went.

I'd told him that essentially he wasn't blessed by the gods, that he wasn't chosen and had a right to rule, but that he was basically a genetic freak, a weapon made by others so long ago that time had almost no meaning, and then discarded. Unimportant.

I'd told him that contrary to his fervent, if newfound, belief that the Old Ones were somehow ancient wonderous gods, or at least only a short step below that? They were instead just old fucks, playing games while hiding everything they could, and doing a whole mystical mumbo jumbo show to maintain control.

He'd denied it at first, and more than half of the time we'd spoken had been me showing him things, like the nanites, explaining them, then reaching out and cutting his palm, dragging nanites free of his blood, showing them to him.

I'd explained it, both in simple terms, and then in more detail, showing him the creation tool again, and explaining it. I'd explained the ships, and the history as I knew it, of the local galaxy at least.

Then Ingrid and the others had gone over some of the details of our race, how we worked, the coincidences that had kept scientists awake at night for centuries, and the sections of our past that broke the rules he knew.

He'd always known some of it—or, at least, he'd suspected, I was sure. Over the long centuries before technology reached this point? So many of the things that the Arisen did were undoubtably and provably "magic." That some of them could move things through the power of their will alone? That they could recover from almost any injury?

That they were immortal, or near enough?

They'd truly seen themselves as a different species, as gods among the lesser peoples of the world, and it'd been believable.

But his face, when I'd explained some of the details, all the while wondering if I should be doing this? He was both terrified and relieved in equal measure.

One of the last things he'd said before muttering that he needed some time alone to think, was that if it was true, then it was a good thing, because at least now he knew that if there were truly gods out there? Then maybe the things he'd seen done, and that he himself had done, weren't approved by them after all.

"One of the 'tests' that some of the factions' elders did?" he whispered, standing shoulder to shoulder with me, in the doorway as he looked out at the miles of empty sand. "They wondered if the gods existed, and if they did? Well, what would it take to bring them out of hiding?"

"What did they do?" I asked, seeing the way he refused to meet my eyes.

"We, not just them," he admitted. "It wasn't just *them*. We were all ordered to participate, to see what it would take, to bring the gods out, to see if they would come to humanity's aid, to punish us...or to praise us, if they truly were dark gods."

"And?" I prompted after a few minutes.

"And when nobody came to stop us? We knew there were no gods, not anymore. That's when the Accursed faction truly splintered. There was no god to judge us, no demons to punish us for our actions, and so...we moved on. Most lost heart, diving into debauchery and worse. Others just...they just left." He gestured vaguely out at the dunes.

"They vanished overnight. Some abandoned their possessions. Others collected everything up and moved on, cutting off communication with the rest of us. Some returned to the Old Ones. But the faction as it was? It lost its moderates, and became truly lost. The council are the least insane of the group, really, but they know they have almost no power. If the Blessed knew how weak the Accursed are? They'd attack and wipe us all out.

"There are a handful like me, more or less, helping to different degrees to keep the group appearing strong from the outside, but the truth is that there aren't that many of us anymore. Learning this? I...I can understand the call to do that now, in a way that I never would have believed."

He'd shaken his head and marched out into the desert then. He'd basically scared the crap out of me, as I didn't know whether he was going for an hour, a week, or a thousand fucking years.

I watched Hans slog up the side of a distant dune, head bowed more from the sad truth than the stinging wind and driven grains of sand or the heat of the desert.

"What the hell do we do now?" I mused aloud.

"We do the right thing." Ingrid stepped up and took my hand. "I know he's your friend, and mine, but we had to tell him. It wasn't right to keep him in the dark, not any longer."

"I know," I admitted. "It just scares the shit out of me, thinking of what he might do, and who he might tell."

"He risked everything to help us, to help me," Ingrid pointed out. "He's been alone forever, just trying to get through life, did you know that? He tries to do the right thing, as he sees it, and tries to get through day by day. Honestly, I think when he comes out of this—or I hope, anyway—he'll be happier."

"I thought he had someone, a friend?"

"He's got a 'sponsor,' but his sponsor spends all of his time combing the oceans looking for some long-lost friend of his who was locked away and abandoned in a coffin out there. He's like a treasure hunter, driven mad searching for old wrecks."

"Fuck. Well, I don't know if I should wish him luck or hope that he fails. The last thing we need is more Arisen loose, especially if they're mad."

"I know, but that brings me to the next point..." Ingrid said softly, pausing as I winced.

"Scylla."

CHAPTER FOUR

"I...see," Scylla said slowly, sitting beside Ingrid, Belle, and me in our little makeshift training arena.

We were watching two of the Oracan—the ex-chief Kim and his daughter Oba—as they sparred.

The scarred and massive old bugger shouted insults at her as she tried to topple him, smacking her with a narrow switch of wood every time she failed in a grapple or strike.

I winced as she lunged forward, diving for his waist, only to meet his knee coming the other way, breaking her nose and sending her reeling. A crack rang out, as the switch whipped across either shoulder, and she staggered back, blinded.

"Damn, he needs to let her catch her breath..." I muttered unthinkingly.

"No," Scylla disagreed. "She knows the moves. She is trained and experienced with the basics, but until they are...*words*...memory?" she said, clearly trying to remember the correct word.

"Muscle memory," I grunted. "You mean until she can do it without thinking, this is the best way to learn?"

"Better a switch than a blade." Scylla looked at her own shoulder unconsciously, and I winced.

"Was that how you learned?"

She nodded, once; a hand came up and she ran her fingers over the pale, still tanning, skin.

She was dressed in a simple top and shorts, seeming unconcerned about her body, much as Belle was. Not for sexual reasons, but according to her, a lot of the training she'd undergone, and the arena fights when she was younger, long centuries ago, were done naked. It was so as not to damage perfectly good equipment, as her skin would recover regardless of the damage done.

I could understand it—hell, it made sense—but that teams of men and women had fought and wrestled with each other, literally bare-ass naked? It was wrong to my modern mind on all sorts of levels, not even looking at the "minor" detail of what might slap you in the face in a wrestling match.

No wonder the training sessions were traditionally popular for visitors.

"So...did that make sense?" I asked again, knowing that even with Belle on the other side of Scylla, and Ingrid on the seat next to us, occasionally repeating a word or explaining the meaning of a phrase, Scylla was still only learning the language, and that the concepts we were discussing had no analog in her past.

Arise: Reclaimer

A month ago, we'd literally unsealed her casket and revived her. When she'd been captured and locked away, the height of technology? Well, clocks had been considered pretty "high tech."

She refused to speak about some of the things that had happened, and we'd left it, for now. But when everything around us was basically magic to her? It caused a few difficult questions. Fortunately, she was like a sponge, soaking up the world around her.

"So...the gods existed, and they are possibly still out there in the great oceans between the worlds, sailing endlessly," she summarized coldly. "Three of the gods experimented on our kind, taking us from the monkey beast you showed me, and made us, *us*. They straightened our limbs, and took the hair, made us beautiful, and trained us. Then we betrayed them.

"They made us to protect worlds out in the oceans beyond, and we betrayed them. The first of our kind were mostly executed, and we, those in training, were abandoned. We were turned out of the gardens and punished. The other gods punished the three who did this, for the crimes our ancestors committed, and they live out there now."

"The Erlking does." I winced as I saw the way she was viewing it, and that it was us who were in the wrong, not the Erlking and its fellows. "The other two it thinks are still about: one under the sea, and one deep in the ground."

"Spending eternity in hell," she murmured, nodding. "Then you found their magic machines. They untied the magic that binds you to being a mortal and granted you immortality, as well as gifts beyond that of the other Arisen. You have control, and strength, but you are too young to truly face the old monsters of our kind. You can grow stronger by killing and eating the magic of the others, both the beasts, which you say are our failed brothers and sisters, and the others of our kind."

"Yeah." I grimaced. "Look, that's not entirely right..."

"But it is close," Ingrid said quickly. "Scylla, I know this is difficult for you. Most of the world you remember is gone, and now?" She shrugged. "We have devices, machines, like the catapults you remember, but advanced enough that we can...shoot our ships up to sail the seas between the stars," she ended awkwardly, trying to make it simpler for Scylla.

"For now, while you recover and learn, I think you understand enough." Ingrid smiled, reaching out and resting a hand on Scylla's.

The ancient warrior tensed, then relaxed. Ingrid's unthinking attempt to reassure her instead raised her hackles at the uninvited touch of another.

"If you want to know more, if you have questions? Ask." Ingrid removed her hand gently and bowed her head in apology.

"My lady Scylla," Belle said formally, drawing her attention. "I, too, while younger than many of your kind, have much to learn. I watched the sparkle of the stars and wondered what they were, before the Erlking taught me of the worlds that exist out there. Perhaps we could learn together?"

"You know of these worlds?" Scylla asked.

"Not much," Belle said. "The Erlking wouldn't discuss them, but sometimes it ranted, raving over the injustices done to it, and it spoke of the old days. As for the machines and the time of man as it continued beyond our valleys? I know

58

little. But each secret I learn, it helps me to make sense of it all. I could help you, if you'd permit it?"

Scylla nodded at her once, sharp and brusque, before standing and walking away. She took three quick steps to the side then jumped from there into the pit, to land near Kim and Oba.

"I will take over." She shucked her top and tossed it to the side, before sliding out of her shorts.

"Oh dear," Ingrid whispered, closing her eyes, before reaching over and putting her hand half-jokingly across my eyes. "Behave, dear." The edges of a smile twitched at the corners of her lips.

"Oh, I am." I forced myself to turn away, shaking my head and looking around at the few other people who were watching.

Most were Oracan, who just accepted that humans were weird, and that if she wanted to fight naked? Her choice. And that she was picking up sharp spears instead of training ones and tossing them to both Kim and Oba?

Again...humans were weird.

The only pair who were there that weren't either Oracan, and therefore pretty uninterested in her nakedness, Ingrid, Belle, or myself, were two of the idiots from the failed boy band who had come from the village I'd found up in Russia.

The pair of them and the other two who were currently elsewhere had joined that village on the promise of "free love" more than anything, from what I'd gotten from them. And now?

They stared at the naked immortal warrior goddess, with a look that, at best, was inappropriate.

"I think it's time for a little chat with those two," Ingrid said firmly, standing up and striding toward them. "Belle, with me. Steve?"

"Yeah?" I asked, still wondering where the hell I should be looking, considering training in the arena was done publicly so people could watch and learn. That meant that as far as Scylla was concerned, I was *supposed* to be looking at her. Hell, it would offend her if I didn't!

"Go somewhere else, please. I'll have a chat with Scylla again later about modesty."

"Yes, dear." I got to my feet and about-faced, weaving between the staggered seats, and left the arena, honest enough with myself to admit that I had enjoyed the view, and mature enough to know it was wrong.

As I set off jogging, moving around the cleared section of solar cells, the arena having been set up there, I waved to the other two members of the little boy band as I found them heading in, and pointed in the other direction.

"Lads, you need to find something to do elsewhere," I told them. "Scylla is training, and your friends were ogling her. Ingrid's dealing with it, but if you go there now and do the same? Ingrid will be pissed, and Scylla might stab you before I get the chance to stop her. A wise man doesn't piss the ladies off."

"But we were—" one of them started, until the sight of the other two sprinting around the corner of the piled sand caught their attention.

I winced, hoping I wasn't about to see Scylla chasing them with a spear. Fortunately, I didn't.

"I'll rephrase it, lads. I've just decided we need this sand dune built up higher, to block off the wind or something. Either you fuck off somewhere else right now, or I'll give you the job, along with a teaspoon each to do it. Understand?"

They winced, then nodded, setting off after their friends, while I snorted and headed for the entrance to the tower.

The overall layout here was massively different from the way it'd been when we first arrived. The protective wall that ran around the circular base had been more or less entirely uncovered now. The sections of it that were finished—it'd been a work in progress that was abandoned when the site was, apparently—were now entirely cleared and repaired.

The wall itself was only a few meters high, designed to try to keep the sand out of the main "working area" more than anything else, but here and there, it'd been improved, going from two and a half meters high on average, and twelve inches thick, to six meters thick with rooms inside.

In those sections, a simple corridor ran along one side; a dozen rooms led off it, each small and more like cells than anything we'd consider a home. But the local tribes had been perfectly happy to uncover, repair, and live in them, considering that the sandstorms at this time of the year were fairly ferocious.

Add in that we weren't charging them rent, that we were providing pretty much unlimited free food, good wages, and training, and as well as planning to not rape their land, but instead bring back the waters and the trees, essentially giving them a paradise to live in?

Yeah, we were pretty popular with them, even considering the whole "attacks by monsters that can steal your skin, turn into giant wolves or drain your blood," variously.

They currently worked on making a small wall to ring the airstrip that ran west from the main tower, as well as repairing and extending the inhabitable areas of the outer ring wall.

Inside the wall, most of the land right up until the base of the tower and the small parking areas that were set aside were mainly taken up by solar power cells that rotated, thanks to motors.

They tracked the sun, and fed the site its primary power source, as well as filling massive batteries to store the electricity overnight.

That *had* been the layout, anyway.

Some sections of the solar cells had been entirely destroyed in the attack, and that section, to the due east of the tower, had been cleared for the arena.

We'd taken some of the stone that was freely available in the nearby rocky hills, and the Oracan and locals working together had made a fairly flat circular space for training, along with a layered section similar to an amphitheater for observers.

Finally, behind that, was a sand dune, one that, in conjunction with the ring wall, kept the little training area more or less clear of sand.

That was for now, anyway.

The last sandstorm had virtually buried the damn place. But when it came to the constant breeze and windblown sand? That had stopped, at least.

As it was, the local area was a pain for sand or dust storms, on average having one a week. And after each one, we needed to dig the entire area out.

The walls helped cut that down, and when I had more nanites that were "spare"? I'd be making a much bigger, and open-topped converter, then leaving the fucker outside.

Sandstorms would be a lot more welcome then; hell, I'd probably make a sheet of artificial sapphire to catch and guide the sand down.

We had plans to make a better area for most things here, sort the arena, the landing strips, the…Well, I also had plans to raise an ancient spaceship sunk in the depths of time, so, you know, it was on my to-do list.

Admittedly, so was finding out how to make some sort of sci-fi dome shield and not have to fuck about with sand inside the walls. As was designing and launching our own satellites, growing our own crops, and, fuck it, probably turn back time and make 80s music cool again rather than the boy-band shite that seemed to be everywhere these days.

Beyond that? Most of the site was still derelict.

The tower itself was the main building, and aside from the covered garages that were now being uncovered and repaired, the only other intact building.

It was five stories, with the control center at the top. The luxury level, for "management and investors" originally, was on the next floor down, then normal apartments for staff. That was followed by the canteen, storage areas and kitchens, washing areas, gyms and more on the next few levels. Although it was small, it was designed to be a self-contained facility, and fortunately, things like the gym hadn't been stripped when the original owners had fucked off.

Presumably nobody had wanted to loot dumbbells.

Finally, there were three levels underground, each progressively larger, built in a ring design.

Sub-One was for minor contamination and storage of less shitty materials, mainly biologicals and general crap…refrigeration units and old batteries, that kind of thing. It was all set up to incinerate materials in a massive furnace that was powered by the plentiful electricity provided by the solar panels.

The next ring was more harmful biologicals, including, unofficially, acids, highly dangerous chemicals, plague samples, pesticides, and more.

The final ring was marked as minor and low-level nuclear storage and so on.

In reality, it was the highest-end shit, including bioweapons and the kind of nuclear waste that should be fired into the heart of the sun, never mind anything else.

When we'd found out just what kind of shit the various nations wanted to send us, and that they were marking it very carefully, and requiring it be "no return, nondisclosure" and so on?

Yeah, that explained why they were so happy to nod and smile at us and just keep paying.

At the end of the day, that they were happy to deal with me, even "knowing" I was an Immortal who was publicly claiming to be a dark angel there to fix the world—and therefore probably batshit insane—was very telling.

I got the feeling that as soon as all their nuclear and "totally safe, honest" waste was gone, they'd probably be a lot cagier with us. At this point, though, they just wanted to get rid of it before any snooping journalists found out about it.

If I'd claimed to be a magic donkey sent by the All-Father to bring everyone to the true worship of cheese sandwiches, they'd have probably nodded and smiled, and still sent their waste over.

In truth, all the waste was gradually being disposed of—fed into the converters and broken down into null blocks that we could, in turn, convert into whatever we needed.

I entered the tower, letting out a breath as I closed the doors behind me, the cooler, air-conditioned air making for a much more relaxing place, compared to the hot hell that was the Sahara outside.

"Steve," Anders called across to me. Ingrid's father strode up onto the floor from the level below, as I headed for the stairs to the next one.

I paused, waiting for him to catch up, and nodded a greeting.

"How did it go?" he asked, well aware of where we were going and what we were to discuss.

"She accepted it." I shrugged. "She doesn't really understand it, not yet, but she accepted it. Ingrid's working on it with her, as well as the whole 'naked' thing."

"She's naked again? Well, anyway, how powerful is she?" he asked me bluntly as we headed up the stairs together. Both of us were believers in using the stairs where possible, helping our fitness in little ways.

"Compared to?" I scratched the back of my neck and idly wondered how the hell sand got *everywhere*. "Honestly, Anders, I don't know. She's skillful enough that, even recovering, half dead from centuries in stasis, she killed Shamal. That her mind is even intact after all that she's been through? Frankly, that's terrifying."

"How powerful is she compared to you?"

I hesitated. "Less, for now." I lowered my voice. It was stupid—she'd not hear me—but still. I also checked the area, making sure nobody was close enough to overhear and no listening devices were around.

"As it is, yeah, I could probably take her, *but* it'd be down to tricks, like the tentacles and more," I clarified. "If we were equal, and facing off against each other? She'd probably take me."

"She's centuries older than you, boy, and most of those years were spent in a time of war. I'd be more worried if you thought you could take her as equals." He grunted. "But make no mistake, she is dangerous. Until we're sure that she's one of us, or at least not an active risk, how do we maintain control?"

"I don't know that we can. If we keep her with me all the time, we make it obvious that she's a prisoner. As it is, we're trying to make her an ally, not an enemy. If she chooses to fuck off, we're screwed, because that'll prove her condition one way or the other pretty quick."

"We need to make sure she's not a threat then." He sighed. "And soon."

"Soon?" I asked absently, and he nodded.

"You're still planning on returning to the ship, aren't you?"

"I am."

"Then we need to know where she stands before then. We can't risk her gaining access to unlocking her nanites without knowing where she stands."

"I know."

"I know you do, Steve…" He paused. "Look, son, you have abilities that are frankly terrifying to an old sea dog like me. That you know what you could do, and that you chose to live like this, to be who you are? That's a wonderful thing, and it's given me a lot of hope, as well as some sleepless nights, considering the others out there.

"Knowing that there could be more like you, only vastly more powerful? It's…well…I don't like it, put it that way. What would be the difference between you and her, if she unlocked her nanites as you have?" He glanced at me, as I winced. "That bad?"

"Honestly? Yes," I admitted. "Look, my armor? It cost me a few million nanites, all told, that's all. As to my abilities? I've invested in nearly half a dozen skill trees, spreading my points so that I can do everything. I'm a jack-of-all-trades, okay?"

"All right."

"Well, if I'd put all my points into the Assassin tree, for example?" I shrugged. "I'd be able to be invisible at will—not concealed for a short time, as I can now, but *true* invisibility. I'd be able to walk through this place without anyone having a clue that I was here. Then add in that I could form much more powerful and terrible weapons? I'd be able to slaughter all opponents with ease. That's what scares me.

"What if Scylla decides to focus all in on the War tree? I mean, fuck's sake, you know assassin is only a recent word, right?" I asked.

He frowned, then nodded. "It was the name of a religious group of professional killers, from the time of the Crusades, I believe. I'd actually forgotten that, but I'm impressed you know your history so well."

"Learned it from a game," I admitted a little sheepishly, shrugging. "Anyway, think about it this way. The ship is tens of thousands of years old, right?"

"Yes?"

"Well, what the hell is a word from the Crusades doing being used as a readily identifiable skill tree from the dawn of goddamn time? Surely it should be a word from the creators' language? Right? Or hell, why is anything in English at all?"

"A fair point…" Anders murmured as we stopped on the canteen level. He nodded to the food area, and I smiled.

"Might as well." I followed him in and nodded to Jay as he waved us over, sliding masses of meat into the various trays, ready for the hungry masses.

"So, you were saying?" Anders prompted as we filled plates of meat and vegetables, adding sauces from the end and collecting cutlery, before making our way to the far end of the room, keeping away from anyone who might be listening.

"Well, as near as I can tell, the system is adaptive, right?" I waved with a fork as I explained. "It's using details that I give it and adjusts to suit me, to make sure that it's all it can be."

"Seems impressive, but then, so is the system itself."

"It is," I agreed. "Okay, so let's take this to the next level. The system is adaptive: it changes due to the user; it enhances and rebuilds itself, depending on what the user needs. Like the Support class. It gave me access to the converter, specifically that tech, right?"

"Okay."

"Not to converters that just changed bronze to gold or whatever, but to one that could take anything fed into it and make a block that could be anything. That's not low-end tech, for fuck's sake. It didn't have me learn all the lower-level shit first, but there were a couple of trees that *had* to be taken before that, like Support. It didn't come up with a mecha that I could just pilot and take over the world.

"I've got experience with guns, and I'm happy to use them, but instead, the main things the system offers me are close-in combat armor designs, adjustments to my fighting style, and adjustments to my armor so that I can hide better. Things that make it so that I can fight, up close and personal. I mean, fuck's sake, it gave me a level of tech that can create gravity fields, and I made it into a rail gun, so that I could fight more. It could have just as easily shown me how to make a fucking robot army or something, but it didn't. It knows *me*. It knows I need to get my hands dirty, not controlling a drone or whatever.

"If the system is that advanced, what the hell could it make? You've got to remember that some of Athena's, and Hans's faction, tried to destroy the fucking planet. They wanted to kill us all, because they thought that would get them the meeting they wanted with God. What's to stop the other Arisen from turning this into an insane arms race?" I shook my head, trying to put the things I was so worried about into words. "There's nothing these systems can't make."

"You," Anders said firmly, pointing his knife at me, before going back to calmly cutting his lamb cutlet. "You, my boy, are what will stop the Arisen from kicking off an arms race."

"You've got a lot of faith in me," I muttered.

"I do, and so far, it's been well earned. Also, you're dating my daughter, Steven, so remember...if you ever want to ask for her hand, you'd damn well better not disappoint me."

"I..." I froze. My mind stuttered over the thought of the commitment that implied. It terrified me on an entirely different level. I banished it and forced a smile. I loved Ingrid, and one day? Yeah, I'd probably like that—a lot, if I was honest with myself. Just...maybe not today?

"Don't worry." Anders stifled a smile. "I won't tell Inga about the look on your face just now. So, you think the system adapts to you, providing what you need? Why not simply allow you access to all the abilities?"

"Because we're designed to evolve." I tapped my fork on the plate for emphasis. "If you give one of those kids over there"—I nodded over to where Jack followed Annabeth around like a pole-axed cow—"the same systems I have? They'd get chewed up and spit out by the first Arisen they come across. They've not got the instincts, the background, nor the will to use it. Add to that, the reason I think the system downloads hurt so much? They're literally downloading years, possibly decades or centuries and more of technological advances directly into my brain."

"So the reason you can do these things is in part because they're providing the data?" he asked, and I nodded. "Can you access it consciously? Like the details for the converters...can you bring up schematics, the actual science behind how it works?"

"I...I'm not sure." I paused to think about it. After a second of seeming resistance, it seemed that a data store in my brain unlocked. I found information there, masses of it, bubbling into my brain: covalent shear calculations, energy requirements to convert the basic atoms into their next higher or lower form, and the masses of energy given off in the process.

I watched as a standard molecule appeared in my mind's eye—one I easily identified as water, H_2O, without thought, despite the fact I'd never been able to tell one from another before.

Some of the molecules were "burned," used as energy and a catalyst, to break and shift others. Molecules were separated out by an advanced form of manipulation that was almost magnetism, to connect set molecules to one another, and alter layouts. New forms condensed into being as the atomic bonds were broken and reformed.

I watched this play out a dozen times, then a hundred as my point of view slid backward, then a thousand and millions of times, as the water continued to break down.

More methods were demonstrated as being viable, while others were locked out. I understood that the reason I could create null blocks so easily was because they were unreactive. Other things? Helium-3 for example?

It was identified as a viable fuel source, and it was banned from the system I could create. *Banned.*

I frowned, staring into the distance, ignoring the noise around me, and I unthinkingly summoned my armor, pulling it up to flood my body, the distributed neural network picking up the slack and helping me as I started to identify thousands of materials and molecules that I couldn't make.

Helium-3 was marked as too explosive to create like this; it needed to be *refined.* I quickly realized that it wasn't necessarily banned from me in a way that said "you can't have access to this." No, it was more of a "you need to make it safely" situation. I could develop the method to produce it, but I'd need other things first, including options that I dimly sensed as something like "exotic fuels" and advanced storage.

That, in turn, brought an alternative to mind about helium-3. It was available all around me, but in tiny, *tiny* quantities.

I suddenly knew that it could be separated from seawater, given the proper facilities, and I had a sneaking suspicion that the intake valves, and seawater processors had caused the riptide that had almost killed Marie and Amanda?

I had to consider that was there to do that, or something similar, refining something from the water to keep the facility going. A memory of data from the ship tugged at me. *Maybe that had been hinted at before?*

That sent my mind off on a tangent of ship design and more, until a sudden flash of light got my attention.

I retracted my armor, feeling the loss of the additional processing power my armor gave me, as I literally became markedly dumber, even as I blinked and frowned at Ingrid.

"Ingrid?" I murmured, confused, before looking around, seeing the empty room, the canteen clearly evacuated, with only a handful of people inside now.

I could see the backs of Paul and Courtney through the glass, standing on the other side of the doors, keeping anyone who got curious well away. On the inside of the room, Dave and Amanda sat at a table to my left, Marie with them. Zac and Jonas stood nearby. Anders and James watched me, as did Scylla, standing with Belle.

Ingrid, though? She looked *pissed*.

"What's up?" I asked, confused.

"What's up?" she repeated, shaking her head. "Steve, what time is it?"

"Uh, no clue?" I admitted, even more confused now. "It's not that late, is it? I mean, we had a chat with Hans, and then we went to talk to Scylla and..."

"You left the training ground five hours ago," Scylla said unconcernedly.

"Five...hours?" I asked, disbelieving. "No, that's not right. I was just...uh?"

"As I said, Inga, this was my fault." Anders rested his hand on her shoulder, getting a glare from his daughter. "I asked him if he had access to some of the data he unlocked to be able to do the things he does."

"And he went catatonic for five hours?" she growled. "What were you making him look at, Far?"

"Covalent bonding," I said softly, my mind still adrift with so many different details that I felt half drunk. "I was looking at why the converters work the way they do, and I noticed that the energy debt was higher than I thought. It's the covalent shearing factor—" I heard the words coming out of my mouth, and I broke off, shaking my head.

"Fuuuuuck," I muttered, rubbing my face and grinding the heels of my hands into my eyes. "Shit, I don't even know what a covalent shear factor is...but now I do? What the fuck is going on?"

I blinked as I glanced around the room. The looks I was getting ranged from worried and a little guilty, respectively from Ingrid and Anders, to outright hunger on Zac's face.

"No," Ingrid snapped as Zac hurried forward, mouth opening to ask a question.

"What? But Inga..." He smiled at her and gestured at me helplessly. "He knows shit, but he doesn't know what he knows!"

"It's nothing that *you* can't get from a basic science textbook," she said. "Anything else he has access to is a data download from alien machinery. We don't know what it is, or why it's doing what it does, so for now, no! Leave him to rest, and we'll see if he forgets everything again first!"

"I hope I do," I muttered, my head half full of energy equations.

"Right, everyone! We're holding up the evening meal here, so, in a minute we're going to open the doors and let people in. When we do, there's to be no more discussion about this, or Steve's abilities, his condition...nothing," Ingrid said. "Far? I think from now on, there needs to be a separate dining room for those who know important things, and those who don't. We don't need a spy learning anything new if it's accidentally mentioned in conversation."

"I'll deal with it," James said, and she smiled.

"Thank you, James. Okay, everyone, evening meal. Then you can come or go, that's up to you, but I think today has been stressful enough, and left all of us with things to reflect on. Tomorrow, Dimi is going to get Mor. I mean—" She realized that she'd fallen back on using the Danish shortened form of Mor and Far for mother and father, as Anders nodded to her.

"I think they all know by now who we are, Inga," he murmured, stifling a smile.

"I know." She sighed, shaking her head as she rubbed at the bridge of her nose with a finger and thumb, closing her eyes. "But it's not very professional for me to go around saying 'Mum and Dad.'"

"We're all family here." Dave grinned over at her, before getting a clip across the back of his head from Amanda.

"And you think that's going to make her feel better? Telling her she's stuck with the likes of you?" Amanda asked him.

"Well, you are?" He shrugged. "And I don't remember you complaining last night. Oh wait, that'll be because your mouth...yowch!"

"I'm just going to kill him—is that okay with everyone?" Amanda asked the room conversationally, smiling around as she clung onto his thumb, which was currently bent back at a hell of an angle.

"Steve, buddy..." he gasped out. "Little help here?"

"Oh, I don't think she needs any help from me. You made your bed, mate. Time for you to lie in it."

"That's a yes, from all of us, Amanda." Ingrid rolled her eyes. "I think you're going to have your hands full—"

"That's what she s— Ahhhhh!" Dave interrupted.

"With this one and a child coming soon. Best to get him housebroken while you can," Ingrid finished, ignoring Dave.

"Good luck with that," Dave muttered as Amanda released him, and he glared around at everyone, before playing the "poor me'" card as he pretended to be unable to use his knife on the steak before him.

I snorted, realizing that although everyone else had been worried over me—and I was sure Dave had, too; don't get me wrong—he'd also taken the time to grab a decent steak and had been working his way through a veritable mountain of fries while watching.

Dave never changed.

I forced a smile. "I'm sorry I scared you all." I looked around. "Thanks for the concern, but honestly, I was just deep in thought, that's all."

"You were virtually catatonic, son," Anders said gruffly. "Unresponsive until Ingrid had the idea of shining the light into your eyes."

"Thank fuck my suit didn't blank it out." I sighed. "Seriously, people, eat your dinner. Do whatever you need to do, and relax. I'm okay."

"Are you sure?" Ingrid asked in a low voice, moving in close and taking my hand in hers as the others moved to give us some room.

"I am." I kissed the top of her head, shaking clear the temptation to sink back into the numbers and data again.

That it was there, and so easily pulled up? That concerned me, and for the rest of the night, I worried about it. I kept going back again and again, checking different data downloads. I moved from detail to detail, finding that until I focused on them, it was like I had a vague understanding, but that was it.

Once I focused, though? Down the rabbit hole I went.

For the next few hours, Ingrid and the others did their best to keep me distracted, James and Ingrid clearly seeing I needed it. Then, when we retired for the night, Ingrid *really* distracted me, and for a while, all was forgotten.

Laying there later, though—the room still warm, the air conditioning working overtime to suck the heat we'd generated back out; Ingrid half laid across me, half on her pillow, her hair tickling my cheek—a final terrible thought came to me.

I'd lost complete track of time when I'd looked at that data. Hell, I'd forgotten the world around me. I'd already lost the harvest tool, which was more than fucking annoying. But that wasn't a terrible thing. What was? The more I looked at myself, at the systems I did have?

I started to worry that maybe I was actually broken. Broken in ways that had nothing to do with me being me, with my past and so on. I was a warrior, a Biological Weapon Variant, sure. I'd made my peace with that: I was what I was; it was still me who decided what I did, if I killed people or spent the rest of time on a mountain fucking meditating.

No, the problem was, now that I looked at it, that I was starting to find issues between my various forms of tech. I'd deliberately not done more upgrades on my brain than I had to. My skull had been crushed, literally demolished even.

Hell, I'd been reconstituted from bone meal. How the fuck I was still "me" I didn't know, but I didn't want to replace any more of my meat-based brain and run the risk of losing what made me, *me*.

I'd downloaded an insane amount of data, direct into my brain, and earlier today I'd been rendered catatonic as that information unlocked. A single thought had done that, and now I was terrified that I might accidentally do it again.

And when I said terrified? I meant it.

My heart rate sped up, the fear building in me…and, more than that, the need to fight. I'd felt this before, when I was up in the wilds of Russia, and hell, when I'd been roaming through Copenhagen.

The rage, the fear, the desperate need to do…*something*—it rose, and I suppressed it as best I could. I'd find Belle in the morning and have her help me.

Almost as soon as I thought that, though, I realized the trap I'd be falling into. I trusted her—I did. But she was also beholden to the Erlking. If that fucker told her to dumb me down to an unfeeling automaton, she might do it, even if she didn't like it.

I couldn't allow myself to use her like that, not long-term. That raised a point, though. The fuckers who designed us couldn't have intended us to be this unstable, surely?

Unless that was one of the reasons we'd gone rogue?

I mean, we'd have been sodding useless as weapons otherwise…And if this was what went wrong with the first "batch," they'd have fixed that, right?

Hell, I'd usually be cold and emotionless, or so I'd been told most of my damn life. Little fear, lots of anger, little emotional connection to others—so what the hell went wrong? Surely "fixing" me didn't include making me as unstable as possible? That made for a shitty weapon, after all.

After another two hours of my brain running like a hamster on amphetamines in a wheel, I eventually admitted that I knew what I had to do, as much as I didn't want to.

I needed to take the ship. I needed to go there, repair the kit that had started all of this, and make the fucker check me over. I knew that it'd barely worked at the time, and I had to think, as broken as it was? Maybe that was why I was as well. Add in as much as we had to do here? The risks we were all running every day? I just couldn't put it off any longer.

I forced myself to stare right in the face of it, and admit that this was why I'd stopped using my points beyond when I absolutely needed to. I was growing untrusting and scared of my own goddamn mind and system, and that couldn't be allowed to continue.

CHAPTER FIVE

"Okay everyone, I need a word." I started the conversation in the private dining room the next morning, predictably being interrupted by Dave. "Ah shit, I thought you'd called us all here for a gang bang," he muttered, before hissing as both Amanda and Jonas, on either side of him, did something under the table to my old friend.

"That's the evening's entertainment," I replied, not missing a beat. "Daytime is work time, not fun time."

Dave opened his mouth to speak, then spluttered and forced a smile out, shutting up as the pair did something to him again.

"So, before I was interrupted, I was saying that I needed a word." I looked around, seeing my little group waiting more or less patiently, and I counted them over, making sure everyone we needed was there.

Ingrid, of course, waited quietly, along with Scylla, who played with the coffee machine; Belle stood next to her. The Oracan and Oxus, as well as his son, or calf or whatever, Xous, were out training already, but Jonas, Amanda, Marie, and Dave were there, with Courtney and Paul guarding the door.

I'd not left them outside again for any particular reason; it was simply a case that Jonas as the leader and Amanda as his second might have valuable input, as might Marie, as the lead researcher for their team. When Jonas had ordered the pair to guard the door? Fair enough. His call to make.

Dave? Well, he was like a fart in an elevator. Nobody knew where he came from, nor how long he'd hang about. He just appeared, and you generally tried to ignore him until he left again.

We had Zac, as our chief engineer; Casey as his partner, marine biologist, and our steward for this little meeting, sorting out drinks and so on; James and Anders as the heads of our organization, and essentially Ingrid's and my own right and left hands, and that was it.

We also had Freja on the line. She was watching through her tablet, which by now was so heavily encrypted that if one of the alphabet agencies managed to get access to it? I'd have arranged a seat for them at the next meeting with free top-ups for their coffee for life, and they'd have deserved it.

"How can we help?" James asked, and I shot him a smile.

"Well, we might have fucked up," I admitted, having come to that horrible conclusion in the silent, small hours. "So, Scylla, you now know that we were all made in a facility. Jonas, you and your team don't know where it is, but beyond that, you're all pretty much on the same page."

"Oh, I've got my suspicions…" the American team leader drawled, and I nodded.

"I bet you do. Well, let's deal with that. Hans knows enough that he could probably figure it out. And when he didn't come back last night? Well, as I said, I'm starting to think we might have a problem." I moved to the screen I'd put on one wall. I linked to it with my Hack abilities and brought up the map of the world, then zoomed in on Crete, leaving that in the middle.

"So, hopefully, Hans will wander in at any minute and that's it, no stress— he's just had a busy night inspecting his belly button or whatever, and he's on our side still. Great. If not? If he's decided that after meeting the Old Ones, and hearing the truth from me? If he's decided he'd rather pretend it's all bullshit and throw in with them?"

I shook my head, stepping to the side and picking up my coffee. I took a sip and smiled at Scylla, pretending it was good, rather than the bitter mess that it really was, and I went on.

"So, we've got Hans possibly spreading the word about the ship. We've got the factions that will be looking into my past regardless, especially if the Old Ones really have ordered them all to give me a month of peace. As far as I know, the Old Ones usually stay out of this shit, so them telling the others to leave us alone? They might as well have painted a giant bull's-eye on my head." I shrugged and tossed the coffee back, seeing the look that Casey gave me as she silently returned to the coffee machine, subtly adjusting it and rebrewing a fresh cup for me.

"So..." I coughed, then forced a smile as I set the empty mug down, trying to hide the face-twisting bitterness and flavor of burnt coffee beans. "We've got possibly the factions, the Old Ones, and whoever Hans tells, all trying to find the ship. We've got the Erlking, who showed no interest in the ship, but equally, he thought it was destroyed, so he might have been playing games...who knows. Lastly, there's the fact that if *I* found it, then it's only a matter of time before someone else does."

"I was under the impression it was hidden?" James said as I looked around for any questions.

"It is. The ship was buried, then centuries of sand and general crap coated it. When I rode off the cliff, my bike hit an outer section that was gradually rotting away..."

"I knew it!" Dave and Jonas crowed at the same time, and I waved them to silence as they glared at each other.

"So, when I tried to recover the bike, I got trapped under it. I'd have drowned, if not for a custodian class automated...thingy." I shrugged. "It looked like an octopus made out of metal. It grabbed me and dragged me inside, then abandoned me when I was unconscious. I've got no clue why it saved me, why it then abandoned me, or why the security system freaked out, but that leads to the next reason that we need to get there. The ship is there, it's within reach, and it can possibly create, well, others like me. We need to do something about that.

"Personally, as well, I need to recover my harvest tool. And I'd also like to find out why the hell I can't just replace it with my nanites. That's a minor issue, but honestly, the main one? I got this installed by a system that was breaking down. Yesterday, I started looking into some of the tech that I have the blueprints for, and I got a degree-level education in covalent shear equations.

71

"I lost all track of the world around me from thinking about the wrong thing. I was useless for hours, lost in the data, and after a fuckload of thought, I think I know why." I looked around the room, accepting the fresh coffee from Casey, sipping at it and letting out a relieved sigh as it was, once again, goddamn amazing.

"I fucked up," I said simply. "Or more accurately, the system did. I'm broken."

"You're mad, that's for sure," Dave muttered, before grabbing both Jonas and Amanda's hands and laughing as he apparently defended himself successfully...until they stomped on his feet in unison. "Fuck's sake!" He groaned, leaning forward and banging his forehead slowly on that table. "That fucking hurts, you know?"

"That's why we did it," Amanda said. "So shut it, Dave. This is important."

"I'm broken, because when I went to the ship, I was badly injured," I explained. "I made it to an emergency medical wing, and I asked for help. The system agreed, and gave me three choices..." I paused, trying to remember exactly what they'd been, but only really managing two out of the three clearly.

"I was offered a nanite reboot, then I was offered something about access to a weapons system, or last of all a Support package. The first two weren't likely to succeed, the system said, so I took the one it recommended, the Support package."

I paused, reaching up and scratching at the back of my neck, feeling the ridge where the remote data access systems had been installed.

"The problem?" I looked around. "It's that I'm a War class."

"And?" Zac asked into the silence.

"And I don't think I'm supposed to have access to the Support package. I had systems like this"—the screen next to me shifted, showing a stylized image of the back of my neck, and a block that was highlighted under the skin—"installed to permit me remote access to data devices."

"That what you used for the police station job?" Jonas asked, and I nodded.

"I linked it all up and accessed their network, hacking my way through it until I found the cameras. Made a plan once I knew where everything was. That's the point, though. I managed to access the War tree easily. I could use it as soon as I earned my first points. On the other side? I managed to Hack the first of the sentinels as soon as I touched it. The harvest tool integrated with me, allowing me to access them as soon as I was physically touching things, but only when the tool was there and physically attached to them."

"Right?" Jonas said after a second as I paused, rubbing at the bridge of my nose.

"Fuck, I'm not explaining this very well. Okay, let's try this. You all know that I had the kit in my right arm, yeah?" I held my arm up for emphasis. "The blade or whatever you saw?" I ignored the confused look on Scylla's face.

"We do," Ingrid confirmed.

"Right, well, that was part of the Support package. I managed to hack the sentinel because the tool in my arm could extrude nano-filaments to plug me in. Once I unlocked the Hack tree? I could see where the issues were, and I connected up linkages that let me access this." I tapped the image of the block on the back of my neck, shown on the screen. "The Hack tree seems like it's close to the War one. Maybe it was intended that some of us would have access, maybe not, but when I started using the Support tree? That's when it went badly wrong.

"The Support package, the Hack, and Espionage ones? They need extra things…like for me to remote hack, the system at the base of my brain, or to build things, the creation tool."

"Right?" Jonas agreed, nodding that he sort of understood.

"When it comes to fighting?" I said. "I didn't need any of that. My body needed an update to my mind to integrate the Assault systems. But it was already there, a part of me that just needed to be unlocked. Each time I had to learn something complicated, like the converters? Serious pain. I had to force linkages to the Hack systems, for example, because they weren't automatically ready to be unlocked. Now, the system learns as I use it, and it adjusts to the user, becoming more and more advanced and self-directing. For the hacking? I don't generally get a billion lines of code. That'd be meaningless for me. I got a puzzle cube. Believe me, it's hard, and the complexity scales with what I need to do, but it's something my brain can work with."

"So what are you saying, Steve?" Ingrid asked slowly.

"I'm saying…fuck. What I'm *trying* to say is that I think the system that was installed in me is broken, that in choosing the Support package, when I'm not Support class? I created problems for myself. That's why I get so much pain when I try to use them the first time. I think I've basically multiskilled myself, without realizing what the hell I was doing. And the data? It's leaking."

"What?" Ingrid sounded worried.

"I did a massive data download when I was in Russia. I was all over the place afterward, seriously fucked in the head. I needed Belle to sort me out. You want to tell them what you did?" I asked her, and she nodded, then spoke in a calm voice.

"I was forced to suppress his emotions. His hormonal balance was badly thrown out, and he was ranging from rapidly building uncontrollable rage, to complete emotional collapse. Steve was on the verge of both a mental breakdown and a complete psychotic break, due to the alterations that had been forced on him. I have seen little outward signs of instability beyond that."

She hesitated, and I nodded for her to go on.

"Steve became almost unresponsive, emotionally incapable to cope, skirting the very edge of a complete mental breakdown, unable to maintain equilibrium. The only time he was able to fully self-regulate was in battle, when the more basic urges and needs were in primacy. Over the course of a week, he came close to a complete psychotic break on four occasions, and I believe he would have broken, had I not been there to regulate him. I explained part of the issue to him, when he was having difficulty controlling his temper with the 'hippies,' as he called them, and I convinced him to permit me to regulate his emotional state, keeping him in an emotionless condition for several days until his body and mind could stabilize again."

"Basically…" I paused, looking from one to another. "I think I fucked my 'build.' I unlocked different specialty trees, and I ended up a jack-of-all-trades. Sure, that's served us well so far, but the problem is leakage. If I'm going to continue to grow, I need to make sure my brain isn't getting fucked as well. When that download kicked in? It fried my brain. I ended up rolling around and trashing the little hut they gave me, until I unintentionally burned myself.

"If I hadn't accidentally rolled onto a lit log?" I shrugged. "I felt the pain as it burned me, and I instinctively pulled up my armor. Part of the design I built into the armor was a distributed neural network—not intentionally, to be clear…it was part of the design to enable me to maintain and control the power cells and shit. But once the additional neural capacity was available as well? I had a few seconds to think, and I accepted an upgrade to my brain— Don't say it." I pointed at Dave. "Just…don't, mate."

"I wasn't going to," he lied, wincing and already in pain from whatever Jonas and Amanda were doing to him under the table.

"Good." I couldn't help but grin at the pained rictus on his face, before going on. "Anyway, I upgraded my brain, forcing the download to go via this…" I tapped the kit at the back of my neck. "And then to upload into my brain over time, rather than hitting me all in one go. I'd hoped it would be the answer, and it did make it less painful."

"But?"

"But it's still painful," I admitted. "And last night, when I realized it, and started looking at myself, looking at the fight around the port at Athens? That was *after* the changes, so it might be that there's nothing I can do. Fuck it, I might just be a lunatic, and that's a bit of a bad one for all of you…But honestly? I feel a lot worse these days. It's like my brain is a jumble of shit, and the only two options I can see, moving forward? Either I abandon all the other paths, and focus on the War tree, doing my best to build on there, and hope that the rest of the data, as long as I don't try to access it, just gradually fades away, or…"

"Or?" Zac asked, unable to help himself. "Come on, boss man, there needs to be another option. Fuck, if I could transplant that data, maybe plug a download cable into you? Hey, maybe you could create a link to the laptop or something, or…"

"Zac." Casey slid into the seat next to him.

"Case, you don't understand. This is—"

"This is our boss, our friend, who might be losing his mind thanks to that information. Wouldn't you rather have him?" She raised her eyebrows as she tried to lead him into saying the right thing.

"Rather than maybe centuries of tech advancements? Fuck, no." He shook his head. "Boss man, you know I like you, and yeah, I'm sorry, this sounds shitty as fuck, and I know what I'm saying is going to make people hate me, but that information? You want to fix the planet and so on? That's how we do it. You can't make an omelet without breaking some eggs. If this was me? The choice between losing my fucking brain, but advancing the species hundreds of years? Plug me the fuck in." He sat back, ignoring the glares he was getting, and I nodded my understanding, letting him know I wasn't taking it personally.

"It's fine…Hey! I said it's fine!" I repeated, louder the second time. "He's an engineer, and I get it. This is literally the pursuit of his life's work, and more. I have shit in here…" I tapped the side of my head. "That I have no real clue about. If I could download it all? There'd be a tech revolution overnight, not to mention that there'd be practically no issues with scarcity. You need gold? Fuck it, here's a ton of unrecyclable plastic, feed it into the converter, and there's your gold. Solved the supply problem and the recycling one in a single action."

"Exactly." Zac sighed. "Seriously, boss, I'm sorry. I *am* your friend, and I'd rather have you around than not, I would, but that information…?"

"And that's the second choice." I looked around as I took Ingrid's hand in mine. "I go to the ship, I get to the medical facility, and I repair it. I take a fuckload of null blocks and I fix up that part of the ship, secure the rest. Then…"

"If you say that at that point, you'll send for us? There's going to be a problem," Ingrid warned.

"Of course not," I lied smoothly. "I'll need to secure an access point though, all right? Somewhere offshore, somewhere the Greek government can't try to claim the ship, a few miles out from their coast…"

"Six miles for Crete," James interrupted, seemingly aware of the details at will. "The Greek government is in talks currently to extend its territorial waters to the legal maximum of twelve miles, but it's causing ongoing issues with Turkey. Give it a few months and it'll probably be passed, though, even with all the issues that'll cause with their neighbors."

"If they realize the ship is there? You can expect a war to start over that," Anders said grimly. "How big is it?"

"Several miles long," I said. "I don't know exactly, but I remember an impression of long miles of machinery. I think it had something to do with providing or storing the supplies for the other facilities."

"So it might go out to the legal limit, and then others could make a claim on it." Anders winced. "Well, regardless of the legal position of Greece, if a buried spaceship that's miles long is discovered off the coast, expect Greek warships and more in a matter of hours. They'd be fools not to secure it and use it for their own needs."

"And there's the problem with us all going." I looked around. "Once they realize what it is? They'll go mad for it."

"Then we sail across that area in the yacht, anchor for the night; do the same the next night a few miles farther on…make it look like we're relaxing. Maybe we board at night and hide who we are. Have Amanda and Marie on deck, Jonas's team pretending to be partying? Any spies follow them. But as it passes over, we all dive over the side?" Ingrid suggested.

"How about we all take a little time to think about what we've been told, and have some food," James suggested, smiling. "Then we can take this up in, say, an hour? With fresh perspectives."

I frowned, about to say no, that we'd deal with it now, until Anders caught my eye, and he winked. I hesitated, then nodded. "That's a good idea," I agreed. "An hour, then we make a plan."

The majority took the hint, breaking up, as James and Anders moved off together and started to speak quickly, clearly drawing up plans of their own.

"Are you all right?" Ingrid asked me bluntly. "Steve, I don't like you keeping things from me. Why didn't you—"

"Tell you?" I finished for her, enfolding her in a hug and kissing the top of her head. "Because I didn't know. It was last night, after I'd lost myself to the information overload, that I started thinking about it, and I realized that I was frantically trying to pretend I was stable. Fuck, I've been hiding it from *myself*, not from you and the others. It wasn't until I started working on the problem, figuring my way around it, that I realized. Then, thinking about Hans and the others? Don't get me wrong, I don't think Hans will do anything, I don't, but shit…

"What if he does, Ingrid? What if he sees a chance for unlimited power, and like in the old movies, it drives him mad? If he unlocks all his nanites at once? He'll either be driven mad with the pain, or he'll become, fuck…I don't know. A god, maybe?

"The point is, if someone else gets there first? We're fucked. Hell, we've spent three weeks here getting things turned around and sorted out. Sure, we needed to do it. This place was badly fucked up after the fight, and there's been all the government dickheads who wanted to come, but shit. They'll have been searching for the ship, for anything that could have been involved, and they'll have been doing it all this time. If they found it already? We're really *fucked*."

"We'll sort it, trust me." Anders moved over. "Inga? I think Scylla needs you. And then your mother would like a word, if you could call her?" He jerked his head in the direction of a tablet, deliberately left on the far side of the room.

She paused, looking from him to me, and then at the tablet, understanding the play. She reached out, resting one hand on my arm and squeezing once in reassurance, before giving us room to talk.

"It'll be fine," Anders assured me as soon as she was gone.

I stared across the room, watching Ingrid scoop up the tablet, then move over to talk to Scylla, quickly explaining the coffee machine, again at her frustrated demand.

For all that Scylla was adjusting to things at an almost insane rate, certain things were massively beyond her, and the coffee machine was one of those, thank fuck.

Admittedly, the one we had on the yacht was miles beyond me as well. It looked as though it could be used to power a steampunk creation of world domination *and* land the space shuttle at the same goddamn time.

This one was a lot less insanely complex, but still.

Scylla was determined to master it, refusing to accept that things took time, and so Ingrid had intervened, barely making it over to Scylla's side before the crazed woman from the dawn of recorded time could tear the coffee machine apart.

Now that they were talking, Belle's calming influence and abilities were very obvious in the way that Scylla was suddenly smiling again.

"I don't know…" I murmured, shaking my head. "Seriously, Anders, this is not a good idea. You don't know what the hell I faced on that ship, and it wasn't ready for me. I killed its creations and escaped. The security AI won't have taken that well."

"It's a security system," he pointed out. "Its aim is to keep people out. Once you were out, it probably stopped caring about you."

"Or maybe it decided that if one fleabag human can get in, then another can, and it went mad, creating a billion psychotic tiny robots. Each with fucking gamma lasers…you know, one of the few things that can actually kill me."

"Steve, Ingrid and a small team will be going with you. You know that—you agreed to it. So as you've already lost that battle, you need to work on the next one. Can we at least agree on that?" James asked me calmly, and I glared at him.

"Excellent." He went on, unperturbed. "So, now that we've agreed that we're all going, all that remains to be decided is when."

"I told you, if Hans decides to spread the word, or the Old Ones put two and two together and—" I started, only to have James smile and hold up a hand to implore patience.

"No, Steve, we agree that *you* need to go, and as soon as possible. Your point about the likelihood of the other side getting access to the ship first was a good one. My point, on the other hand, is aimed at the rest of us."

"Go on." I looked at him, as he smiled and waved at Casey, the steward doing the rounds and handing out Scylla's latest attempt at coffee to a few people. She nodded and diverted, making sure that Scylla's attempts were disposed of, and went back to make some for us, herself.

Thank fuck.

"All I'm suggesting, is that if, as you say, you need to find a safe access point for the rest of the team, then perhaps you should fly there yourself, today," James proposed, with Anders nodding.

I finally realized they were running interference for me, keeping the others away.

"You go today, you get in there as fast as you can, and you clear a section and get it ready for the rest of the team...take out the security systems or whatever," Anders said. "Then, when the yacht sails over, let's say by the time we all fly across to Khartoum, then sail the yacht up to the coast, load whatever equipment we need from Egypt aboard the yacht, then set off? It'll be the early hours of the day after tomorrow at the very earliest before we could reach Crete. Possibly likely the day after. That gives you the rest of today, tomorrow, and all of the next day to establish a safe zone. Can you do it in that time?"

"I thought—" I broke off. "Anders, I thought you were demanding that I let Ingrid run the same risks as I was?" I growled, thoroughly confused.

"Don't be so bloody ridiculous. She's my daughter." He snorted. "I love her, and I agree—she's her own person; she'll go where she wants to. But you don't win a fight with a hurricane, boy. You step aside, and when it's passed, you fix things." He fixed me with a glare, as if to say I was being bloody stupid, then went on.

"This is a similar situation. You don't confront the person you love and say you won't permit them to be put at any risk. That's demanding control over them and treating them as a possession, not creating a partnership. When you love someone, you respect them and you let her pick the risks she'll face."

"You just try to minimize them where you can," James finished. "You need to accept that Ingrid and others will be there, and at risk. That's non negotiable. But what is, provided it makes sense? There's no reason for you to wait for the rest of the group, not when you could be there in a matter of hours."

"It's about manageable risk," Anders finished. "And you'll let us explain that to her and the rest of the group."

"Yes, sir." I sighed, relief washing over me.

"Oh, and we'll be sending Dimi for Freja and the family, as well as Lars," he said, and I nodded, accepting that as fine.

"Actually, that could work out well for me too..." I said after a few seconds, smiling as a thought occurred to me.

CHAPTER SIX

"You're fucking mad, mate, you know that, right?" Dave said as the pair of us looked out of the windows at the wine-dark sea. The dim lights of the last settlement on the coast winked out behind us, leaving only the rolling waves crashing below.

"Only one of us here is going to be a parent soon."

He grimaced. "That's low," he grumbled. "Besides, for all you know…"

"Don't start that shit," I growled at him. "Seriously."

"You wrapping it before you pack it? I mean, if not, then there's a chance the old spam javelin—or let's face it, mutton dagger in your case—well…" He grinned at me, knowing he could be scaring me shitless.

"Nah, mate." I shrugged and lied. "I'm a jaffa."

"A…jaffa?"

"You know, like the oranges."

"Uh…"

"I'm seedless!" I laughed, winking, then walked toward the door. "Might want to get ready!" I called, tapping the door open button.

"Fucker!" Dave snarled, grabbing his stuff as the howl of our passage tore around inside the cabin. "You bastard!"

I shot him the finger from both hands, then threw myself backward and out of the door.

The last thing I heard him shout was a question, or part of one anyway. "Really…a jaffa?"

I couldn't help but grin. I had no clue whether I was firing blanks. It wasn't something that had ever crossed my mind, but it won me the argument with Dave, and for now that was all that mattered.

I twisted, my armor already sealed over me, as I lined up. Dimi changed direction to head for Copenhagen, even as I unfurled my wings and aligned on Crete.

Between the two of us? There wasn't much chance of any fucker actually following us, not to make sense of what we were doing, considering the advanced stealth composite that made up the plane's outer hull.

They'd have seen it taking off, and it was still visible to the naked eye. But to radar? Not a chance.

When I'd jumped out? Sure, there was probably a blip then, nothing I could do about that, but that was also why Dimi had changed direction at that point. And thanks to the VTOL capabilities? He was going to be landing in the garden at the back of Anders and Freja's home, as apparently it was massive.

As for me?

Well, I was literally coated in a stealth field, and tiny in comparison to any conventional radar's systems. They weren't tracking me, but just in case, I activated the Conceal field and blurred into limited invisibility.

Forty minutes later, I dipped down, a handful of meters above the rolling waves as I shifted onto the new course, lining up for the cliffs ahead, and at their foot, right where I'd entered the ship, so long ago.

I flared my wings; the gravity field flared as well. Water splashed up as if a boulder had been dropped as I killed my momentum, then retracted the wings and tombstoned into the depths.

I plunged down. My eyes adjusted to pick out the sea bottom in grays and greens, fish and various denizens of the watery places appearing and flashing away.

An octopus, or maybe a squid—the fuckers were all the same to me—twisted around, erupting from hiding to dart away. Fish raced in all directions, driven away by the sudden impact and the strange invader to their world…before drifting back in. I stared after the multi-tentacled thing, making sure it was a real one and not a sentinel, then banished the thought as I sank deeper. It was too small, and certainly looked organic, so fuck it.

I hit the sandy bottom. My feet kicked up a cloud of disturbed particles and general crap as the fish drifted in closer, dull curiosity in their eyes.

I waved them aside, their darting movements all the more alien in this world of dim lights and foreboding. I stomped across the bottom of the sea, squinting at the various sections of rocky outcroppings and trying to make sense of it all from faint memories.

Looking upward, I saw the crustacean-encrusted and coral overgrown pillars of the water exchange system, and I adjusted, searching for my goddamn bike.

Ten minutes later, I was cursing, having stomped back and forth a dozen times across the same area, sure it was here, when I finally noticed something that stood out as unusual.

A regular stretch of sand.

I'd walked across it at least three or four times now, seeing nothing out of the ordinary, until I considered that there was nowhere else nearby like it.

There were hundreds of rocks, piled up with random growths of coral and sponge; there were dips, peaks, and troughs, all where the sand coated the supposedly rocky and natural seabed.

Here, though? There was a level, bare surface that appeared perfectly flat, with clean sand spread across it, and only the occasional section that looked to be colonized by the local sea life.

I moved straight for it, crouching down, and started to dig, grinning when, after only a few inches, I found gray metal. I scoured a section clear, moving steadily to uncover as much as possible, before cursing. In doing so, I left a trail a blind man could follow, if anyone came looking, considering I was only a few dozen meters from shore.

That set me off for twenty minutes, working to cover the section up again, before drawing an imaginary line across the seabed from the valley the ship had carved while crashing, and then out to sea.

I set off, reforming my wings, making them better for swimming, and headed deeper. There was a noticeable drop-off a few hundred meters out, and I vaguely remembered Ingrid explaining that most of the area was like that—that when the last ice age was around, the sea level was much lower, and for long enough that there were beaches now, rather than just rocky outcroppings. The sea did the same back then, grinding the land to sand.

It was clear straightaway that I was in the right place, though. To the left and right, there were the significant and expected drops. But right ahead? It went on into the darkness, smooth and straight.

Knowing I'd found the ship, I continued on, using the grainy radar-like sense that I could generate from my tentacles to map it out.

With my eyes closed, it was easier. I swam onward, floating above the huge mass, passing areas where it sank suddenly, then rose again.

I recognized these, and the way they were filled with detritus of the sea, as long-forgotten rooms, sections of the ship that had collapsed inward and had been abandoned to the ocean's encroachment.

Here and there, I passed sections that looked as though they had been more maintained than others, even though they were clearly long dead. Occasionally, now that I knew what I was looking at, I saw areas that I could almost guess at, spotting overhangs that led into caves.

I passed several of these in a row, speculating that they were some kind of intake sections, double-checking before I tried them that there weren't any signs of recent activity, as that was all I'd need, before picking the next in line as my entry point.

I was about two miles out from the shore now, and although the best situation would be to access it at the full twelve plus miles out? I seriously doubted the ship was that long.

A mile or two, maybe three or four, sure...but thirteen plus miles?

I just couldn't imagine why you'd do that, especially when it was only a few hundred meters wide at this point.

It'd be like a finger in deep space...a massive, easily broken thing. But hey. It wasn't me who designed it, so I'd not judge what kind of a screwup had created it.

My wings folded in around me, and my tentacles elongated, reaching out as I floated downward, to land on the bottom in a cloud of random matter.

There was nothing else about, not really anyway. I sensed some bigger fish a little way off in the distance, and a shark had swum past a few minutes back, angling in to look me over. Apparently, I wasn't that tasty-looking though, as he fucked off after only a short distance.

I clomped along the bottom. Clouds of crap floated up, stirred by my feet, and I looked up into the darkness, scanning for anything alive.

Nothing.

I winced, realizing that I might have been swimming for miles alongside totally submerged sections. There might be nothing inside that I could use, no access to the greater ship, and nothing that Ingrid and the others could survive in for long.

Fuck.

I jumped, tentacles extending and grabbing onto the underneath of a section, dragging me upward as I reached out. My systems clearly interacted with something, as I kept getting little flashes of...something.

It was like when I focused on a target and the system provided me with data, identifying it as a lycan or whatever. Except this time? All I was getting was a partial activation, and seemingly an order to fuck off.

The screens kept trying to populate, and then vanished.

As I clambered upward, the intake changed shape, becoming more circular; ridges formed in regular repeating patterns. The intake turned, angling to the right and then down, narrowing until I started to get seriously claustrophobic. Then, I cursed myself for being a fucking idiot.

It wasn't as if anyone was going to be sitting on the other side of the damn wall and would be complaining about the damage! I slid the vorpal blade out and made a small cut in the wall, finding it a hell of a lot harder to cut my way through than any mere steel.

I pressed harder, bracing my back against the ridged metal behind me, then pulled it back, hesitating. When no air escaped, I was satisfied that the other side was already filled with water, and I went at the wall with a will.

Thirty seconds later, I retracted the blade, bracing myself and booting the middle of the cut-out section.

It twisted then sank backward, sagging inward. I grinned as I dragged myself free of the tube, staring around, damn thankful that I'd upgraded my armor to provide air so many weeks ago.

The room on the far side had been underwater for a long time. There were piles of growths, things that looked like stalactites and stalagmites—I could never remember which were which—but considering that we were in the rotting remains of a goddamn spaceship, I had no clue why they were here.

The first few sections I swam through had slurries of settled ground, like someone had grabbed buckets of almost hardened concrete and poured it into the room.

The floor-to-ceiling ratio was tiny on one side, and much bigger on the other, making me wonder just how much of the ship was buried under this crap. I spotted a door on the far side and headed for that.

The crap of centuries—hell, *millennia*—had half buried what must have once been an open, or damaged, door. Wedging it in a half-open configuration, sections of overlapping metal might have once stood before me as I swam through the gap.

Now it was a weird sagging mess of dead, coated muck, with the occasional darting fish here and there. I swam out of the smaller room, and out into what had clearly been a storage area: high and wide, with sections of the wall to my side— the floor, I assumed it once would have been—ridged and with more twisted muck grown across torn sections of metalwork.

To my "down"—what would have been the side of the ship once—there were huge masses forming ridges, slumped hills and valleys, here and there. Thanks to the wonder of my helmet and my enhanced vision, I saw scuttling sea creatures, crabs, and lobsters...I hoped. But fuck knew, really.

Patterns of bioluminescence lit the darkness, and occasionally, entire colonies of creatures—and coral—grew around them.

Huge sections that I swam silently over were dead, the bottom literally covered in sand and slurry. But then, at the next bit? There were weeds and more: great explosions of fish that darted out of sight as I neared, eels that appeared and vanished again just as quickly, crabs scuttling away, and...

I jerked around, then sagged, before setting off again.

I'd been so entranced by the undersea world that when I'd caught a glimpse of another octopus, I'd panicked, thinking it was a sentinel! It was a telling point, though, and I forced myself back on track.

I needed to find an air lock; there had to be a sealed one somewhere. The damn sentinels and custodians or whatever they were needed to get in and out, and they'd taken me inside, so there had to be a way to get in without flooding the entire damn ship.

The thought of having to cut my way in, and permanently flooding a massive section of the ship, wasn't a good one. I swam on, passing piled remnants of what I guessed would have been machinery, and possibly long-lost stores. A ship this big would have to be used for something, after all, and I was again thinking that it had to be some sort of a supply vessel, judging from the sheer scale of it.

A few minutes later, I spotted the next wall in the distance and closed on it. I found two doors before the floor—or wall, as it had been—was buried.

The first was open, the second sealed, and I hesitated between the two, before swimming through the open one, and into the next section.

The sealed area might have been just a closed door—hell, it might have been a recessed pattern; it wasn't exactly clear from this side what it was. The damn thing was covered in crap.

But a little logic said that if I was going to find an air lock, it was most likely in the outer sections, and I needed one of those, like the one I'd escaped through, to find my way back inside.

Of course, as more than one ex—and a few friends—had pointed out, my logic wasn't exactly logical at the best of times, so I might have missed an obvious entrance to the "good" areas.

I set off, picking up speed, conscious that I had two full days to make the place safe for the others, before I was going to start getting into dangerous waters, literally.

The next few rooms were smaller, mere minutes to pass through, but the section after that was sealed. All the doors in the wall or floor or whatever were closed, and when I approached them, landing and sweeping as much of the crap off as I could, I quickly found a pad.

I remembered these from the other, working sections: like a tablet screen, but soft, like pliable plastic or rubber. I hesitated, unsure, before reaching out and pressing my hand to it, remembering that the doors I'd tried before needed you to press and turn to activate, or they closed again.

When I laid my hand on the pad, though, it was clearly long dead. There was so much crap on it that it barely shifted when I pressed my fingers into it. And when I tried to turn it? No chance.

I growled, searching for another door, and then another. They were all dead, or at least locked to prevent the ocean rushing in, and I did what I'd been worrying I was going to need to do.

I headed back, passing through a few sections, then up and out into the open sea again, cursing as I searched for another way in. There *had* to be one. Hell, *somewhere*, not too far away, was the way I'd escaped, but I was fucked if I could see it.

I shifted here and there; an hour became two as I dragged myself up and around boulders, down and into collapsed sections of the outer hull, and then back out again, searching dozens of flooded rooms, before finally finding areas that looked more recently abandoned.

The section I found myself in now was buckled inward, as if something had crushed it, and relatively recently. The outer section I'd been swimming through was clearly old, full of the crap of centuries. But as I peered through some gaps into the next section? It was clearly only a few years old.

The damage was—at least, considering the bioluminescent mass that covered one wall—much more recent. There were also sections of the walls that looked to have been recently repaired, and that made me smile.

The small amount of crap that coated the surfaces near the walls had been disturbed, with multiple tracks in it, but none near the door. That made sense: the fuckers would need to repair the outer sections first, then open the door and repressurize.

I set off, moving slowly, tracking the occasional mark here and there, before getting annoyed as fuck when I realized that for several minutes, I'd been tracking a small crab.

I did the underwater version of the "for fuck's sake, why does the universe hate me" dance, before punting the crab and moving on, returning to where the little bastard's tracks crossed over the much fainter ones that I assumed belonged to the custodian.

Ten minutes later, I was close to simply tearing a hole in the wall and repairing it with my creation tool while the sea flooded the facility, when I finally found what looked to be the entrance and exit it'd been using.

It was about twelve inches across, a small porthole that was clearly well maintained, and far, far too small for me to use. I snarled in fury, before grabbing the sides of the overhanging rock I'd found it under and dragging myself up.

The morning sunlight filtered through the sea now, granting a little illumination, even at this depth. I made the most of it, swimming faster. I decided I'd give it two more hours…then I'd be cutting my way in, and to hell with the consequences.

I mapped the ship out roughly in my mind, unfurled my wings and set them to flowing fast, propelling me over the buried structure repeatedly.

I stopped "looking" with my eyes, and went back to using my tentacles and the grainy radar-like vision I could manifest. I washed it over and over the surface below.

The first pass was pretty crap—more peaks and occasional dips than anything else. But I stuck with it, passing back and forth, picking up more and more details each time. For an hour, that's all I did, swimming back and forth. And then, my mental alarm went off.

I broke off the last pass and landed on the superstructure, finding a clear-ish area and sitting down, pulling up the new map in my mind.

At first, it wasn't that different, not really. The overall structure was as I saw it with my eyes, but with the wonders of the construction systems I'd gained with the Support tree had come design abilities that far outstripped my own.

I found the ability kicking in automatically as I peered at the map, allowing me to rotate and examine it from different angles.

Once I could do that? I stripped layers away. Sand was easily identified, quartz mainly, and once that and the other scattered and obvious rock particles slowly vanished, the actual remains of the ship became visible in black.

I shifted the angle around, finding tens of thousands of egg-like shapes. For a few seconds, my heart ramped up, wondering whether the fuckers contained aliens ready to come for a face-fucking, before a memory surfaced.

Manganese nodules—or noodles, as I'd thought they were called, to Ingrid's vast amusement. She'd looked at maps with Lars on our bed, arguing over the layout of the area, and where the ship most likely was buried, and he'd mentioned them in passing.

They were some kind of mineral deposit, and I'd never really gotten what they were beyond that people were trying to figure out a cost-efficient method of mining them.

Taking the mineral makeup of a handful, I used that, copying it across the ship, and then deleting them from the image...and wow.

It was huge, which I'd known, and I could only see a small percentage as it wasn't exactly ground—or sediment—penetrating radar, but still.

The ship was battered to fuck. Entire sections had been torn open on the side, and the water had made it in and had spread. Massive sections of the ship that I'd mapped out were probably well beyond repair, no matter what I wanted.

Hell, if I wanted to invest a decade, I'd probably never be able to fix this fucker up, and that was relying on both nanites and the efforts of people who were much smarter than me.

No, the conversation with the Erlking flashed back to my mind, making it clear that I could use things from the other ships, or locations that it'd shared, to repair and rebuild *one* of the ships. I squinted, thinking it over.

I couldn't remember exactly what it'd said. I'd been deliberately pissing it off, sending it along the edge of insane killing fury, and a determination to give me what I needed and to get rid of me.

From what I could remember, though? It'd made the point that I'd need at least one of the other facilities to make a working version of the ship, not to mention the equipment I needed to fix things up around the world.

Now, looking at the ship, I could see why. It was utterly *fucked*.

I mean, I knew he'd said both that it was usually set in place on Crete, and that it could be moved around, but this place looked as if it'd been smashed out of the skies by the fist of an angry god!

For at least a third of a mile, an entire section of the hull had been shredded, cut open as if a sword had been dragged through it. And in other areas? I had to guess at explosions.

That any of it had been intact and powered, let alone able to rebuild me, was a fucking miracle. I was seriously considering just cutting my way in, stripping out the medical suite as intact as I could, and dragging that out to sea, to wait for Ingrid and the others to arrive, when I saw it.

A single section where the ship arched upward. Identical damage ran through the hull sections on either side, at least a dozen meters that matched on both sides, as if that imaginary sword cut along in a straight line.

The middle bit, though? It stood solid. I looked at it from several different angles, before grinning. It must have been repaired and rebuilt! This section had been reconstructed, and clearly *after* the ship had crashed!

That got me thinking as I launched myself from the hull, twisting around and heading in the direction of Crete, closing on the identified section.

After the explosion, and the subsequent wrecking, there must have been limited materials and workers, I assumed, or else why not fix the whole place up?

No, they must have fallen back on some kind of emergency priority list, like an "in case of a massive fuck-up, do this" rule book. I squinted at the structure as I closed on it, bringing up the mapped section and the actual reality before me and comparing them.

No wonder I'd missed it. It'd been repaired, sure, but that had been a *long-*ass time ago.

It was covered in growths and sections of coral; sponges were everywhere in this bit and…and I grinned as I saw a bunch of fish swimming in and out of a gap in the middle that just wasn't obvious without the map.

The sponges had grown over it in overlapping, swaying patterns. I closed on it, then dove, sinking down, folding my arms and retracting my wings. My tentacles, in turn, extended as the nanites were repurposed, reaching out and latching onto the sides of the entrance, and lowering me, headfirst, into the dark tunnel.

CHAPTER SEVEN

The gap was narrow, with wide and flat, creamy sponges rippling and slowly flowing with the tide as I slid between them. I reached out and nudged them aside here and there, until finally, I came to the bottom, finding a shallow sandy coating over a reasonably clean air lock door.

I reached out, sweeping my hands across it, swirling it all up and reducing my visibility for a few seconds. It cleared, and the pitted, but distinctly artificial surface of the door was obvious. I grinned, because I'd found it!

I searched, dragging myself along, wings reforming into great scoops to shove and wave the sand aside, until I found what I was looking for on the right-hand side. It was grown over by a gray and black mass that looked more cancerous than spongelike.

My fingers edged under the sponge, not wanting to just rip it free in case there was a reason that the sponge was different—like it being an organic defense or something. I felt the soft, warm, and rubbery surface of the control pad. As soon as I did, I jerked my hand back. A powerful electrical surge discharged into the water around me, stunning and killing hundreds of fish, as I hissed in pain and anger.

As soon as I felt it, I reached out with my remote access systems instead of my goddamn fingers, and a familiar pop-up appeared.

Hostile system detected.

Attempt hack?

"Oh, fuck yes," I muttered, channeling myself into the attempt. The systems opened before me, infinitely more complex than they had been last time I was here, and I cursed as a dozen separate die appeared in my vision.

They were twenty-sided, each of them, and rotating: each face of the die required I spin it into the correct configuration before it'd open for me.

I split myself, pulling up the clone copies of my mind and spreading us out. The maximum 'conscious' versions I'd managed to summon in the past was nine, and when I tried for three more to exceed the spinning die?

Pain bloomed in my mind, slowing me to almost sluggishness.

I banished the three that were slowly starting to form. The pain was a warning, and I had no time to worry about why; I threw myself into the attempt with only nine additional mentalities.

The dice that hovered before me spun and flipped, as the security AI I could feel on the other side attempted to stop me. I snarled, directing all my minds into the effort.

The sides started to spin faster; here and there, a face locked inward. More and more slid into place, and I sensed the AI gathering itself, like seeing a malevolent cloud on the far side.

Last time I'd faced it, it'd been far simpler to defeat. Hell, I'd been a baby hacker, and I'd done it in seconds, so what the hell?

Contact. The thought bloomed, floating up from my subconscious as I flipped and spun, aligning more and more of the access points, getting ready for whatever the fucker was about to throw at me.

I'd had physical contact with the system before. The nanite tubes that had slid from the harvest tool hadn't been weaponized as the vast majority of mine were now.

No, they'd been active, and adapting, and they'd been physically plugged into the goddamn system! Like when I'd found I could easily hack the damn Greek air force fighters, because they weren't designed to counter a hack from an alien system when traveling at around Mach 2. Now I was finding that the seemingly simplistic goddamn security I'd faced before, was because I'd literally been bypassing most of the security setup.

They'd not just been shit at dealing with hackers; they'd had a hardened net to prevent the fuckers millennia before we discovered the concept! They must have been facing hackers when we'd been trying to decide whether hitting each other with rocks tied to sticks was a good idea!

I'd just been far luckier than I had any right to be. And now I was stuck in a battle for my life as whatever was left of the ship was not only aware of my presence, but it was also actively hostile.

I threw myself into it, blanking everything else. The die before me became all that existed, as I twisted and spun, flexed and locked.

Long minutes extended before me, and I gritted my teeth. More and more popped up, and instead of winning, I was being slowly forced out! Well, fuck *that*!

I triggered my time dilation effect. The world slowed as I aimed everything I had at it. Finally, slowly, the pattern started to reverse; the fifteen spinning die around me began to fall, instead of growing in number.

My counter ran like sand in an hourglass: the extra levels of die that had appeared as the AI gained ground slowly fell away as I fought on. I knew I couldn't keep this up, not for long. I had less than two minutes now, and I braced myself, plowing on.

Fourteen, thirteen…twelve!

The first minute was entirely gone, and I was halfway through the second when I hit ten; with four seconds to go, we dropped to nine. And then, wonder of wonders, another fell, making it eight before the world slammed back into regular speed.

I felt the fury of the security AI, and knew I didn't have long. No matter whether I managed to hack my way in here or not, that fucker would be rallying the sentinels by now, and I didn't have time to screw about.

With nine separate versions of me spread across my counterattack, and my own mind as well, now facing eight? They continued to fall. As each dice collapsed inward, the processing power of that mind was added to the others, and the assault sped up. What had taken long minutes dropped to less than a minute. Then thirty seconds; then ten.

When the final die spun, blurring as the AI focused all its efforts onto preventing me from advancing, I threw my trump card at it.

The authority that the Erlking had bestowed on me.

I was worried it'd not be enough. Hell, even I could tell that it was incomplete, that the data it'd given me was missing entire sections. But it was enough to make the AI back the fuck up.

This was a correctly encoded and viable password, mixed with a form of identification that was neither a physical key, nor a biometric. Instead, it was all of them at once, including goddamn alpha waves stored in my brain.

That I knew enough to throw something at it that complex and that close to being right? I really hoped it was enough to confuse the fucker.

For all of a third of a second, it was. It hesitated, examining the identity, before clearly deciding that it wasn't viable, and restarted the counterattack.

That third of a second, though, was all that I needed.

The collapse of the last dice opened the system to me, and I flooded it, forcing myself into the outer security grid. A million connections suddenly opened before me.

I did the only thing I could, and I released five of the spun-off versions of my own mind into the network. It weakened me for further fights, but with them inside? I had a chance.

The network flared; the door opened and sucked me in as the water roared down to fill it. A tall tube appeared around me as I fell, smashing into the floor, then bouncing off the walls, before the door above me sealed again, the current dragging me around.

I sagged for a few seconds, stunned, the world a blur as my brain rebooted. The other four of "me" sunk back into quiescence as I glanced around.

There were almost no lights, only a single red warning light above the door I was laid atop, letting me know that the facility under my feet was airtight, as I reached out, tapping the local "purge" button.

I didn't know how I knew it—it certainly wasn't in English—but the meaning was clear. And as soon as I hit it, the water was sucked from the room. Air bubbled up to fill the space as I shifted, bracing myself.

The door opened almost all at once, and had I not been ready, I'd have fallen. Instead, I swung through, tentacles lashing out and grappling onto a familiar design of a gantry, before I lowered myself onto it.

I shook my head as I stared out and down at a massive room, filled with long silent and dead machines. Some of them were still in place, built into the bulkhead along the left side, where the floor had once lain. But the majority?

Creations that could have revolutionized our understanding of the cosmos and repaired the world, machines that could create space stations—hell, things that I had no doubt were massive versions of my converters and things that looked as if they'd been designed to eat fucking asteroids…So much crumpled junk, torn free and hurled about in the crash, reduced to scrap.

I stood there, staring, horrified as I counted into the distance. Dozens of these huge factory-sized hulks, and not one was usable. Not one was repairable, not even close!

The ones that had stayed where they were bolted down? The passage of thousands of years hadn't been kind to them either. Add on that they were almost all stripped as well, presumably for tech that the rest of the facility could use…

I was jerked out of my reverie by the sudden knowledge that one of the "ghosts' I'd loaded into the security net had been erased. It'd been returning to me, a sudden encrypted burst of data showing a little of the local system architecture, and a sense of pain, of fear as the ghost was consumed.

It'd torn itself apart to prevent its core details being read, but the AI was chasing down the others, and it was *pissed*.

I turned, sweeping the room, and cursed when nothing easily identifiable came into view. A dozen other passages led off the main room below me, and gantries led here and there on the level I was on, but nothing let me know what or where I should be looking for.

Pulling up a new notification, as I searched, I sighed in relief. At least I had a chance.

Quest Updated!

Evolving Quest: Clear Out the Garbage: Level 3 has Evolved!

Evolving Quest discovered: Repair and Renovate: Level 1

Congratulations, Biological Weapon Variant #113782491603. You have regained access to Facility 6B, and as you have done so at the bequest of one of the Creators, you have begun a new questline!

You have been gifted a quest directly by one of the Creators, as well as authority to access the various facilities around this testbed world.

The remains of the security AI that protects Facility 6B does not recognize your right of access, and has therefore marked you as a trespasser. Eliminate or convert this security AI to reclaim the facility.

Part One: Secure the local area,
eliminating all active sentinels to gain the following reward:

- **+1 War Point**
- **+Access to Level 2 of this section of the Evolving Quest**

Part Two: Secure the local security net,
by penetrating and locking the security AI out of the local node to gain access to the next tier of the evolving quest to gain the following reward:

- **+1 Hack Point**
- **+Access to Level 2 of this section of the Evolving Quest**

I grunted, glad that at least it was giving me Hack points again, and that although I didn't dare use the one I still had right now, I would hopefully be able to soon.

Also, thank fuck the quest wasn't a single Hack point once I'd finished securing the entire goddamn facility!

Although I had no clue where the nearest security "node" was, or what the hell was actually meant by that, I had an easy way to find out.

Wherever the security AI didn't want me? I was fairly sure that'd be exactly where I needed to be.

I paused before doing it, thinking to keep my capabilities secret from the AI. But the medical area had been on the "ground floor" and, ultimately, with the size of this place, I couldn't afford to waste the probable days it would take to march back and forth, never mind climbing the goddamn walls.

My wings unfurled again, and this time I remembered to adjust them to the aerial mode—rather than the water version—before throwing myself over the side and swooping down toward the middle of the room.

I twisted, heading back on myself, figuring it'd be better to start with the area behind me and farthest from the island, for two reasons.

First of all, that seemed to be the most heavily damaged, and the least repaired. Using my questionable logic skills again, that meant that the area was likely to be abandoned by the AI, in favor of areas it could secure and maintain.

From the AI's point of view, that was a good plan, sure. But from mine, and adding in the tiny bursts of data I'd gotten from the clone mind that I'd sent into the local net? Well, I needed to find a security node. And if I chose the farthest one out, it was likely to be the least guarded, and the easiest to crack.

Secondly, if I started by attacking a security node in the middle? I'd be counterattacked from both sides, or hell, all around, depending on the architecture. Lastly, there was a chance that if I grabbed, say, the second link in the chain, that the quest would skip the other link, and I damn well needed to earn as many points as I could get.

That brought up a good point, though. I winged over to a tall section of broken machinery, landing and looking around quickly, biting my lip as I wondered whether I dared to do this now.

I still had a single...no, fuck's sake, I had *two* points to invest in Espionage. When the hell had I gotten the second one? I stifled the urge to swear long and loud, as I checked the options available to me.

I'd invested my single point into Internal when I'd gotten it last time, essentially making it easier to protect my systems, and to maintain them, to recognize external signals and to defend against them.

I'd chosen that, at the time, because they'd just taken Ingrid from me, and although the two sides of the Espionage tree looked identical, with Internal security and External security being both goddamn security, the difference was massive.

Internal was geared more toward finding threats and eliminating them. It was set up with the assumption that you were defending, so the suites of tools were more suited to my needs then, mainly because I knew that the encryption looked like the one the enemy were using.

I'd been looking at the overview of the systems that were spread across the city, and I'd needed a way to track a few similar signals, hence that path. Right now, though?

Well, I was the aggressor. The suite of tools that I'd unlocked when I'd taken Internal was definitely helping, but I was sure the External one, the path designed for breaking and entering, would have been more useful to me now.

I hesitated, flicking from one to the other. Internal broke down into the three subsections that were now open to me to choose from: Counterterrorism, Counter-Espionage, and Cyber-Espionage.

Counterterrorism was aimed at preventing damage, locking it down and protecting the overall system from danger from outside influences, including physical as well as cyber, economic, and more.

No goddamn wonder it'd hurt so much when I'd unlocked the tree. Hell, I'd barely looked at it since then, and that was a mistake.

Counter-Espionage was aimed at following an attack back to its base and using the attack to crack its own systems. Part of that was providing methods to set up an all-around honey trap, as I knew them.

It included effective ways to provide a method for the enemy to attack, and then enveloped them, attacking from a thousand prebuilt channels to enable an overwhelming DDoS-style assault.

Once the target was hammered from all sides, instead of killing the probe, it'd use it as a Trojan horse to roll back along and fight the attacking system. That could be a data breach, or a couple of professional "ladies of the night" to seduce the target, while I cracked their equipment and basically resorted to planting bugs and shit, or using blackmail and so on.

Cyber-Espionage was slightly different. On the External track, the echoes and bleed through of data suggested it was replaced with Physical Espionage, the real cloak-and-dagger shit. On this side?

It was a skill tree that went hand in hand with Hack, each supporting the other. Not for the first time, I wondered about that. There was so much crossover between the trees that it was insane. I mean, it was all a matter of perspective and specialization, but still.

I only ever used it to search for porn on my damn laptop a few years back, but I'd understood the basic premise of the internet, and roughly how it worked. I couldn't have built or maintained it, but I knew, when I was feeling a bit more serious, that it was all based on binary code and flashes of light along fiber-optic cabling.

That, just understanding that much, and the vague hierarchy of the way that search engines and so on worked, meant that I was basically low ranking in tech knowledge across the people who used the internet, and that was fine.

Over the entire human race that was currently alive? I was probably medium to high in tech ability at this point, when you considered there were places out there with no running water nor electricity, and a bunch of idiots apparently still believed that the Earth was flat.

Looking at it from the overall human race level? I suspected the downloads contained an absolute buttload of information, and a lot of it crossed back and forth simply because whatever I was communing with to select and use the upgrades process wasn't entirely sure what I knew and what I didn't.

If there was a system that was downloading the information directly to my brain, it needed me to understand what a data access point was, before it could reasonably expect me to hack one.

That was why the system was so automated and generalized in the beginning, I guessed, and now, as I got more and more knowledge hardwired into my brain, it was rapidly becoming less so.

It also meant that the more I adjusted to the system, the more personalized it became, building atop the information I had, and filling in the blanks.

That, in turn, reinforced my "broken" theory since surely I should have been getting less and less general data by now, right? I mean, the basic systems, like the general upgrades that had been wrought on my body, were there now, and the basics were all known.

Adding in more information now should be a lot less painful. But...

I stared at the Cyber-Espionage option, chewing my lip, not liking it, but seriously considering it after how close that fight with the AI had been...until a blurry movement in the distance caught my eye.

I focused in, zooming with the helmet and my own optical upgrades, seeing nothing, almost abandoning it, deciding it was a trick of my eyes...

Until I spotted another movement. A goddamn sentinel slowly crept across a mound of destroyed metal toward me. I launched myself on instinct, beating my wings hard as I shoved downward with the gravity inverter, feeding power to the system.

I barely made it up in time, as three blasts of coherent radiation carved through the air where I'd stood as the sentinels I'd not seen opened fire.

The world around me went white-hot with threat markers as the armor and my assault classes combined. My radar flashed out and mapped the area around me in blues and greens, grays, and oh so fucking many pulsing reds.

My fear that the system would have upgraded the sentinels was insanely on the mark. The things that scuttled forward bore as little resemblance to the class-one sentinel as the little circular thingies that swept the floor in posh houses bore to the Terminator.

Sure, they were both robots, and they both ran on energy, but that was fucking *it*.

I scanned one, twisting in midair and hammering my wings down, practically backflipping off the path I'd been flying down. The data popped up in my mind's eye, and more beams cut the air in the direction I'd been heading.

Security Sentinel	Robotic Minion
A Class-Three Security Sentinel. While the class three lacks heavy firepower, it more than makes up for this in versatility. Its power core is capable of running the primary unit for over four hundred revolutions, with minimal maintenance required.	
Capabilities:	
Laser: Class-Three Sentinels are equipped with Dual Gamma Laser Optics, permitting an 8-second burst that can cut through up to 30 inches of steel before requiring a recharge.	
Dispersal: Class-Three Sentinels are equipped with a thermobaric detonation device, and small aerosol storage canisters built in to effect different results. They are especially effective at crowd control and prisoner riot suppression in enclosed spaces.	
Maintenance: Class-Three Sentinels are equipped with basic repair and scavenging capabilities, enabling them to cannibalize damaged fellows in the field to maintain maximum combat effectiveness.	
Active Camo: Class-Three Sentinels have a limited active camouflage system that enables them to stalk their prey, as well as act as highly efficient sentries.	
Durability 150/150	Class Three

The air around me was suddenly alight with incoming fire. I cursed, darting left, then right, before flipping over and diving for the ground, weaving in and out of the crumbling and rusting equipment.

I landed, *hard*; my boots extruded claws that I dug into the metal below my feet. My wings stayed extended as I crouched, grabbing a stanchion; then I heaved hard as I threw myself back into the air, flashing across the distance in the new direction.

My arms and legs screamed at the strain, absorbing all the kinetic energy of flying in one direction, only to redirect it in the other, but I screamed silently back at them to shut the fuck up. My right arm blurred; the gravitational lensing effect of the gravity cannon dragged the power from the inverter, no longer enabling me to fly like I was weightless.

I plummeted on the far side of the piled debris. Tentacles snapped out as I pulled my wings in, converting them as more and more sections of the cannon spun up.

I limited it to three rings. I was damn sure that it was overkill if a stray shot hit the side of the ship, considering how goddamn old it was, but I wasn't sure it was overkill with these fucking sentinels.

The first of them clattered into sight on the right-hand side, and I fired just as it did, both of us missing.

Its shot carved two thin lines through a section of bent cowling I'd thrown myself behind; mine punched through the air about an inch from what looked to be its head, as the fucker had ducked!

They were four-legged, with a wide base, a leg at each corner of a slightly rounded square shape. The laser sat on a mount in the center that swiveled, tracking me.

Behind that were two stubby canisters that I guessed were the fuel-air bombs, and a pair of smaller arms were folded down atop the carapace, recessed into sections to keep them clear of the swiveling laser mount.

All in all, it was simple and straightforward enough: nothing overly complex, and nothing too insane.

Half of the cowling the fucker had cut through with the blast that had missed me creaked and collapsed sideways, making it clear that although it might not be hugely impressive and advanced-looking, it didn't need to be.

I triggered the time dilation combat enhancements, knowing it'd not had much time to recover, but fuck I needed an edge here!

Combat Enhancements: Active

Time has been slowed subjectively at a ratio of 2:1.
Time remaining: 17 seconds...

I rolled to my feet, sprinting back out into the open, knowing it'd be reloading, and I returned fire. This time the shot hit, and *damn*.

I didn't know what had happened to the one that missed, but this one? It cratered the fucker, literally. It looked as though someone had taken a crab and rammed it into a metal post at fifty miles an hour! The middle of its body just *disintegrated*. What was left of both sides tumbled away in a spray of parts, hurled in different directions.

I also heard a loud boom in the distance, and I winced, convinced that I'd just made a new hole out to the sea.

Fuck!

I cut the power to the cannon, dropping it to a pair of gravitational rings instead of the original three. I didn't want to win this fight, and have trashed the goddamn place I came to capture. A second thought came to me then, making me cringe. I also didn't want to be responsible for a gravity cannon shot carving its way through something easily breakable…like goddamn *Athens*.

The sides of the nearby mounds of crap—the huge, piled debris that settled over the long centuries—started to shiver as more and more of the enemy clambered up the far side of them.

"Well, let's fucking party…" I muttered. My desperation fell away as I realized that in dropping the rings from three to two, I'd also dropped the time it took to spin up.

I grinned unconsciously as I twisted the design, using the specs I had unlocked, and yet barely used, ages ago. The fluid shifting of details in my mind and into reality came easily.

The pair of rings blurred, compressing, as the first slid backward, shrinking and forming ten much smaller rings of makeshift ammunition, each ready to be fired. A central spike slipped into place with the rest of the ring, altering into a skirt at the back of it.

The skirt extended ten further tiny filaments, enabling the magnetic rings to hold them in place, and to make sure that anything they hit was severely fucked up. Then the main firing ring elongated, becoming a stubby spiral instead of a tight circle, even as the first of them came into view.

I lifted my right arm. The rings condensed into the new layout, laid across the outside of the arm and terminating just above my right wrist.

As I clenched my fist, extending my arm and dipping the hand, I lined up on the first of them. The dual laser shifted, aligning on me as the new cannon hummed, then fired.

The shot that erupted from the barrel barely made my arm shiver, let alone ruin my aim. I jerked my left arm up, quick as thought; two of the four tentacles I had deployed rippled back into my body.

They reformed on my left arm into a circular shield, bubbling up and over, solidifying, as the gamma radiation hammered into them. At the same time, the shot from my railgun punched into the body of the sentinel, tearing a line through the left-hand side, ripping one leg off entirely, and sending the body spinning from sight.

The burst cut off almost as soon as it started, but damn! A full quarter of the shield had been burned through in that time. Hundreds of nanite clusters cascaded away into a gritty, dead dust.

The shield reformed as the nanites flowed into the thin lines that had been etched into it, and I twisted. The combination of the radar, my combat systems, and my own hard-won instincts made me damn well run.

I was in the valley between two piles of crap, massive machines shattered long ago, and although they covered me from most of the sentinels, they also formed a kill box, if a sentinel was to make it to the top and fire on me before I could take them down.

I sprinted. The remaining two tentacles reached out and grabbed stanchions, pillars, outcroppings, and more, locking on tight and pulling, heaving me across the distance like I had a rocket up my arse.

As I ran, the combat system highlighted sections that it judged likely hid sentinels, be that lying in wait or about to top the ridges, and I fired over and over.

The air was filled with crackling beams of gamma radiation, and my systems flashed a warning as, despite my best efforts, I took hit after hit.

Lines were carved into my armor, making me scream as I dodged, ducked, dove, and drifted. I twisted at the hip, leaping into the air and kicking off structures, flipping myself here, there, and goddamn everywhere, as more and more shots came closer.

All the time that I was firing and reforming my armor, I was losing nanites…losing them in horrific numbers, and I hissed in fury as I realized that.

I couldn't win a battle of attrition like this. I guessed the ship couldn't have many of these machines. Or else why wouldn't it have repaired itself or whatever, and why make do with the shitty class one's back when I first entered, if it could produce these?

No, we were both limited here, but the difference was, the other side was defending and knew the layout, as well as…

The realization came to me, and I dissolved the gun, ripping my tentacles and shield in, and hammering the ground before me with the gravity inverter on three times its normal strength to enable me to fly.

I shot upward and back as if I'd been fired out of a cannon even as my wings reformed. I frantically pulled the gravity field this way and that, yanking myself in random directions as overlapping fields of fire tore through the air after me.

I flipped over and squinted back, then stared in horror, seeing the trap I'd nearly fallen into: four of the bastards hunched down at the end of the section I'd been racing toward.

I'd been reacting to the damn things as I would a human opponent—running, hiding, taking them down one by one—rather than thinking of them as being controlled by an enemy AI that could see the entire layout and would happily sacrifice units to kill me.

The fucker had been herding me! Literally giving up units to fill me with false confidence, weakening me as it set a trap, guiding and pushing me along to the real kill box.

If I'd not reacted when I had? I'd have been sliced into kibble pretty goddamn fast. There was certainly no way I'd have survived the trap. Even if my armor had held out from one or two, the crossover of all four slicing into me from all angles?

I'd never have been able to escape them.

As it was, I felt the burn of beams that hit and scoured my armor, even now, as I spun and flipped, diving and soaring as I desperately put distance between them and me.

I was rapidly running out of room, and I needed to make a decision. Either I tried to fly and fight it out, or I risked it all on finding a more defensible location and let them come to me…somewhere I could play to my strengths, as well as possibly using their fucking corpses myself.

I hesitated at that thought, wondering whether I could hack the fuckers. Then I shook that thought loose. No, it'd be awesome if I could, but realistically, I was practically nailed to the floor while I did that. It took all my concentration, and I'd barely won the last fight against the AI.

I fervently wished I'd risked it all and used either that Hack, or those goddamn Espionage points! At least I'd either be dead or…fuck. I'd not be dead, as much as I might wish I was. I might be *brain*-dead, though, and that was all I needed. I banished the thought, searching frantically as I dipped and twisted.

There was no way I could fight or flee at the same time as I tried to hack them.

No, I needed to find a secure location, somewhere away from these fuckers, where I could set up a defensive area, then fight them, reduce their numbers.

Do that first—then hack them once the risk was lowered to reasonable levels.

I remembered spotting a passage that led back out of this area, heading "forward" as I thought of it—away from the island and out into the ocean, toward the more trashed areas of the ship.

I'd head in that direction, I decided, literally go until I was sure that I wasn't going to get flanked, use my tool and start building a defensive area.

If I could? Once I'd gotten control of the area, I'd start reducing the dead fuckers to null blocks, and…

Null blocks.

Fuck, yes!

I dove onto a corpse of one of the sentinels I'd killed earlier, wings flaring as I reached out, grabbing the fucker, and sunk my claws into it. I beat my wings and adjusted the gravity tunneling so that I "fell" away from the ground.

If I could reduce these fuckers to null blocks? I could turn them into lead shields! A thick coating of lead on the outside of my armor would make a hell of a difference in this fight!

Sure, yeah, I'd be slower, but instead of my armor being cut like butter, I'd be able to take repeated hits!

I twisted as a distant laser clipped the very edge of my right wing, and I cursed, gritting my teeth and reforming it as I fell, then rose again. More of my rapidly depleting store of weaponized nanites were lost.

The entrance to the passage loomed out of the gloom ahead, and I adjusted, lining up on it. I furled my wings, dragging them in close and absorbing them as I landed in a shower of sparks, sliding sideways. The claws extruding from my boots caught and gave me enough purchase to kick off, running into the darkness.

CHAPTER EIGHT

The next ten minutes were spent in a mixture of panicked running and disbelief. I passed a dozen or more rooms in the first few minutes, all of them sealed so long ago that the doors would probably have to be carved out, making it clear that whatever was hidden behind them hadn't been accessed in living memory.

I was just glad that the doors I'd had to use so far had clearly been maintained.

The sheer size of the ship was intimidating, seeming far worse now that I was on foot to let my power stores recover.

I was awkwardly lumbering along, holding that half of a sentinel in my left hand, with the right playing the creation tool across it. Sod's Law, I'd not grabbed the section that included the laser projectors, as that would have been much more useful, now that I had time to think about it.

I could have set that up with a repaired power core and had it fire on anything that crossed its line of sight, although that might have been a big ask. I could have at least grafted the fucker onto my shoulders or something and have had a second method of attack, right?

As it was, all I had was half the corpse, and as it was utterly slagged, it wasn't even able to be repaired, or at least not for anything useful.

I could use it, though, along with a scary amount of my remaining attuned nanites, to make a converter. Thankfully, although it didn't have nanites, it was sufficiently dense enough with tech and high-end materials that I had enough to strip and rebuild it for that at least.

The overall structure twisted and warped in my hands, folding in on itself as I broke it down, some of the mass—as always—lost to the energy debt of the conversion.

As consumed with transforming the scrap into a converter as I was, I came to a skidding halt at the end of the corridor, when I found a massive airlock door, dully flashing red lights to indicate that the area beyond was sealed away for a damn good reason.

I hesitated, suspecting it might be the AI corralling me, making sure I didn't accidentally run into something useful, like the sentinel construction zone, or the armory. But I dismissed that as soon as it occurred to me.

The door had clearly been sealed for a long-ass time, and as near as I could remember about this direction, it made sense it'd be flooded.

On the bright side, the high-tech machinery that made up the sentinel had been enough to make a small converter, and in another fifteen or twenty minutes, I'd be able to start using it.

Admittedly, that was shit for me right *now*, but that was life.

I about-faced and headed back to the last corner, squinting around it and hesitating before going up the section. It'd cut left and right; the occasional adjoining passage that I could have taken, once upon a time, was now choked with debris, or with what looked to be emergency bulkhead doors sealed over them.

As I hurried along it, though, I felt the structure around me in an oppressive way I'd not felt before.

The AI was watching me, I was damn well sure, planning how and where to ambush me, while I, in turn, tried to counter it.

I wanted to upgrade the hack—fuck, I needed to do *something* to even things up—but I had no clue what. I made it to the next turn, one to the right. The joys of the twisted structure meant that stairs "up" and "down" as it once had been, now ran left and right, and I needed to leap down into yawning gulfs of blackness.

The whole thing freaked me out more than a little. After checking there wasn't anything in sight before the next bend in the passage, I turned around and headed back. I quickly found the nearest door, shaking my head at the weirdness of it all. They were in the floor and ceiling here, while before they'd been in the walls to me, making me wonder whether gravity was optional to the makers.

As it was, though, I slid the vorpal blade out, set the converter on the floor, and made a small incision in the door on the floor between my feet. As soon as I pulled the blade back, water jetted out, and I cursed, lining the creation tool up and wasting valuable nanites to seal the cut I'd made, before moving to the next along, one in the ceiling.

That one, when I cut into the door—an even smaller incision than the last—thankfully, water didn't come spraying out. Once I was sure, I carved a bigger hole in it, before releasing the gravity inverter and landing with a thump, quickly moving aside as some small discs and random broken scrap cascaded out.

I kicked the bits aside—there wasn't much, thankfully—then grabbed the converter, launching myself upward and through the hole, landing straddled in the carved-out section I'd just made.

The room was dark and silent. Piled boxes were scattered about, with sections that looked to have once been docks, like the kind that stored supplies.

Some still stood in place, but most had come loose, crashing about the room and crushing containers. I nodded to myself, damn glad to have struck a form of gold on only the second attempt.

This was a maintenance room, I was betting, or a supply one.

In my past, when I'd been helping Tommy out, welding mostly, I'd gotten used to the way he ran his repair shop. He had everything from a dozen different sizes of gaskets, to nuts, washers, and general crap stored in little boxes. They were meticulously laid out around the room, marked on the box, and always in some mystical order that meant he could lay a hand on anything he needed in literally seconds.

I'd never been able to figure out the layout, personally, but I understood the need for it. Here? Someone had been doing the same. Thousands of different sizes of discs or nuts or whatever were strewn around.

They seemed to be solid pieces of some kind of metal, stamped into circles about half an inch thick, by a full inch across. I had no clue what they were for, but I didn't give two shits.

It took me thirty seconds to use my creation tool to twist a handful into a scoop and another minute to form a bunch more into a funnel and frame. Setting the frame and funnel over the converter, and then scooping up a fuckload of the little bastards, I filled the funnel, letting them slide down atop the converter, sitting pressed against it, waiting as it continued the process of being rebuilt into a working unit.

I crouched as I heard a faint noise, and extended a tentacle out into the passageway below, scanning it as best I could. After a few seconds of seeing nothing, and just as I was about to give up and go back to working on the converter, I finally saw something move.

I froze, before sliding the tentacle out of sight...slipping it much more carefully back up to the edge again, then sending waves out to map the area.

There was something, a distortion at the very edge of my range, right next to the corner as it led around and into the next passage. But what the hell was it?

I had no clue.

It was smaller than the others, and wedged into a corner, clearly trying not to be seen.

Hell, I'd only spotted it because I was paranoid about the sentinels sneaking up on me again. So unless it'd just gotten here, I must have run straight past it at least once already.

I waited, watching it as it moved slowly along the floor...up to the door I'd cut before...and paused there.

Light flickered around the edge of the door, and I moved up, peering out and around. I grew the rail gun again, aiming, ready to fire and kill the fucker...before stopping, dumbfounded.

I couldn't see it, not really. What I could see, though? The door below it, thanks to some kind of stealth refraction field, similar to my own.

What I'd done was the equivalent of a rough weld slammed down across the cut I'd made, but what was happening right now? I could see the air was slightly distorted around it, with a bright light shining out in a few small areas where the cloak, or whatever it was, didn't quite reach.

Whatever it was, it was atop it. The bugger wasn't gathering itself to leap up here and fight me—or, at least, I didn't think so. What it *was* doing?

It was repairing the door, and it was nearly done. I waited, watching it finish. Then, as it started to move away?

I acted before I thought, reaching out with Hack, and finding a *much* more rudimentary presence hidden there, one that had nowhere near the level of security.

Three separate die spun up, each a twenty-sided one still. But with my augmented additional minds? I attacked from all sides, dropping them in seconds.

The little figure of what I realized after a second was a *custodian* shivered, then straightened. The active camo dropped away as it turned to look up at me, and I grinned, stepping back as it started to move.

It scuttled across the floor—eight limbs carried it at a hell of a speed—until it reached the section below me, stabbing a leg into the gaps that ran here and there in the walls; it twisted the end, using that as an anchor. It ran up the wall to the ceiling and along it, briefly vanishing from my sight, until it reached around the edge of the hole and dragged itself in.

It hesitated, looking up at me, and I stared back at it, unsure what the hell I was going to do with it. Hacking it had been an instinctual thing, considering if I started to lose the hack, or sensed others approaching, I could shoot it instead.

I'd guessed at what it was and that it might be useful. And given that the only other option was shooting the fucker? I'd gone for it. Now it shifted, torn between waiting for a command, obviously wanting to go and inspect the converter, and the look it was giving the cut section of the door that I'd done on the way in.

The fucker was *clearly* not happy with me.

It was much like the original class-one sentinels, in that it was smaller and considerably less lethal-looking than those class-three buggers that were freshly spun up to kill me.

This one looked as if someone had taken a disc with four limbs attached, then had flipped a second one upside down, using a bunch of magnets to keep them close, but seemingly not connected, and had then stuck a head between them.

There were four orb-like eyes, each on extendable arms, and they looked from the damage to me, to the converter, to me, to the damage. It stood upon four of the limbs, and the other four were apparently to be used for whatever it needed, as I examined it, reading the details that popped up.

Custodian	Robotic Minion
A Class-Two Custodian, capable of independent operations of up to two thousand cycles with only minimal maintenance required. The Class Two is capable of independent repair, recovery, and recycling, but is limited by the rules assigned. Where more advanced models may reason their way through a list of priorities, the Class Two is more literal.	
Capabilities:	
Active Camo: Class-Two Custodians have a limited active camouflage system that enables them to limit attacks and avoid subsequent damage by local flora and fauna.	
Repair: Class-Two Custodians are equipped with eight omni-tool limbs, each able to shift their configuration and loadout.	
Maintenance: Class-Two Custodians are equipped to carry out full maintenance of their assigned systems but require specific schematics to be assigned if set for long-term. Low-oversight roles.	
Warning: Maintenance will be carried out on an ASSIGNED, not PRIORITY basis. It is HIGHLY recommended that a Class Three is assigned to overwatch.	
Durability 50/50	**Class Two**

A sudden sound rang out from the corridor outside the room. I cursed, twisting around and pushing a tentacle out...only to have the tip of it carved off by a burst of gamma.

I snarled, jumping up and punching out with two other tentacles, stabbing onto sections of the wall; I braced myself and spun up the rail gun again.

I checked it, finding that even using much smaller "slugs" of nanites, I was running damn low already, and I had a hell of a lot more of the damn things needed yet, I bet.

My tentacle waved again, deliberately, then yanked back as the burn carved through a section of the door, chasing it, and wasting the shot of the fucker on the other side.

Then I dropped halfway out, my arm extended, and fired back. The recharge rate on these fuckers was better than on the smaller units, but I was ready to fire, and it'd just missed.

I took the first out with a single shot to the center of mass, deliberately aiming below the lasers, making sure to leave that section intact. The second caught the one that had sheared the end off my tentacle just as it was spinning up to fire again, tearing it into fragments. I winced as the shot went on, hitting the bulkhead behind it as the sentinel detonated into thousands of spinning and shredded parts. I cursed as the shot kept going, drilling a hole in the bulkhead that set a sudden spray of water flooding in.

I hesitated, then ordered the custodian back. It'd started to move, ready to try to repair the damage and prevent the flooding, but I couldn't allow that. Instead, as soon as I was sure it'd received my order and would obey, I sent it a chain of more complex commands.

It was to collect and feed the little disc thingies into the converter, then take the null blocks and create thick, gamma-resistant plates that could be attached over my current armor.

Realistically, I knew that it needed to stop the flooding—hell, *I* needed it to. The last thing I wanted was to lose this section of the ship to the sea, but…that was against whatever was left of the ship's AI's needs as well.

Something was guiding these fuckers to keep as much of the ship intact and unflooded as possible.

For now, if they decided to sacrifice this section, and let it flood? Well, I knew where the hole was and I could seal it back up later, if need be. There had to be a way to deal with this shit, a purge or whatever.

Gamma blasts weren't going to be as powerful under water—hell, I was fairly sure they would be fucking useless, in fact…as were the aerosolized weapons. So if I flooded this section? I could shoot the fuckers much more easily, despite the damage and risks that came with it.

I was betting that wouldn't happen, though.

More likely, the local custodian population—if there were any others left—would simply send another. If they did that? I'd kill any sentinels that popped up; then I'd let the custodian fix the hole, then capture it as well.

Win-fucking-win.

As it was? I needed to sort the damn sentinels out as they came along, and that was it. With the custodian here already, or this quickly, I was hoping that meant that there had to be more in the area, or I was insanely lucky. Either way, I was going to make the most of the situation.

Half-formed plans popped up as I aimed, waiting, and I angled a tentacle behind me, making damn sure that I wasn't being snuck up on. My rail gun steadily drained my internal batteries as I kept it loaded and spun up, ready to fire.

Five minutes passed, then seven…with me dangling there, seemingly ready to wait as long as needed…before the first plates were carried down by the custodian. The chest piece was solid, along with the back plate, and as it clamped onto me, reaching out and settling the sections into place, I grinned.

The biggest advantage, as I saw it, was that my nanite system was linked to my mind. In this situation, it meant that as my armor was primarily made from weaponized nanites—ones that had been corrupted originally, and then were stripped of higher, more complex functions—I could change its form whenever I needed to.

I couldn't, for example, make myself into a totally different shape, or have insane levels of tech built in, not easily anyway. I'd unlocked the power core tech ages ago, and although I only had the more basic levels, one as a perk and one as a genuine unlocking from the Support Creation tree, I still had access to them.

If I decided that I didn't want the power core, I could disassemble it, and absorb the specialized nanites that were required for it. They were fully unlocked and usable nanites after all, unlike the weaponized ones.

Or, I could make more power cores; it just took nanites and time.

What I couldn't do was just vanish them instantly. They took time to deactivate and slide into me in a restructured matrix. My armor, equally, was easy to alter in small ways. I could shift bits around, or as I was now, make the weaponized nanites reach out and link to the underside of the solid plate armor that the custodian was putting into place.

Big changes, though? Like unlocking the atmospheric cleansing and that level of tech? That wasn't something I could have made the nanites do without a really good understanding of the technology and the science behind it.

Instead, when I'd unlocked that, I'd done it partly on instinct, reaching out to the system with my mind filled with my need, and I'd basically offered up the points I had available.

They'd unlocked the abilities through the Augment trees that I had access to, both in the Traps and Augmentations and the Support tree Augment.

They sounded similar—again, like the Espionage tree was for Internal and External focuses—but I was now sure that due to the bleed-through of knowledge from one to the other, I really wasn't supposed to have access to them both as well as War, on top of the Support tree.

I'd be pissed if I had to unlock a section that I already "knew" everything about from the bleed-through effect for the knowledge, only to unlock something later.

For now, though, the big advantage meant that I could attach these armor plates easily, making the nanites form perfect seals and know that they wouldn't fall off if I tripped or twisted the wrong way.

I was forcing myself to hold on, trying to decide whether I dare make some structural changes to the rail gun, and possibly the power core, when, close to ten minutes after I'd killed the last one, I heard the oncoming clatter.

I grinned. Although the waiting was over, the fight sure as shit wasn't, and the security AI had clearly decided that waiting for me to run out of power wasn't the way to go. I'd been bouncing constant radar pulses off the walls, and I could just make out the shape of the first two incoming sentinels as they approached the corner.

I ordered the custodian back up and into the room, and I lined up the rail gun...then fired and released my tentacles at the same time.

A single shot tore through the air, literally punching a hole through the corner of the wall at the top, close to the ceiling, and through one of the sentinels just as it neared the corner.

An explosion of parts blasted all over. I fell, landing hard on the deck below me, legs dipping as I absorbed the impact, and I shifted my aim to the second one.

It'd just cleared the corner; the beam of the laser already cut its way through the air to where I had been, before tracking me downward.

I rolled to the left, planted a foot against the nearby wall, then straightened. I fought against every instinct, shifting to offer up my chest and trusting the armor, as I zeroed in on the fucker.

It took the offered target, thankfully focusing on the chest rather than my head or neck…and the end of its beam managed to get a two-second impact on the thicker plate, until my return shot took it down.

I winced, reloading the cannon and cursing as I saw how dangerously low I was on available and usable nanites. I had enough for five more shots…that was it. Then I was down to harsh language as my only ranged option.

I swallowed hard, then cursed again and ran at the corner, shucking my vorpal blade out of my left hand, while the cannon on my right arm reloaded. I reached the corner with a half second to spare as another sentinel closed. The edge of the body appeared before the beam weapon, and I threw myself down, skidding on my back.

I plowed into it feet-first, left arm dragging the blade up and over, hacking down and through the armored front, even as I lined the gun up and fired at the next in line, shredding it.

I planted my feet; the scream of freshly extruded metallic claws scraped across the ancient floor. I popped back upright, kicking the closer severed half of the sentinel back into its comrades, before dissolving the cannon and twisting around to the other half of the nearest sentinel.

I kicked it up, grabbing it, and braced it, using it as a shield and battering ram combined as I roared and ran at the remaining three that raced toward me.

Beams hammered into their former companion. Its own armor gave me a chance to close the distance, before I dropped it and leapt. My weaponized nanites formed tentacles that flashed out, grabbing hold of the sections of wall that were clearly designed for the sentinels' limbs to grip.

I used them against the fuckers, dragging and yanking myself from side to side, avoiding the last of the beams. The end of the third one's fire carved through the tentacle over my right shoulder, and I fell, crashing to the floor before rolling.

I popped back up, lunging forward, blade extended, and…

Base Environmental Assault Identified: Nanites Assessing…

Countering…

I hesitated, confused as I shredded the fucker before me, until I saw it. The back of the one I'd just attacked hadn't had the usual cylinders standing upright as ready. No, the fuckers were open. A dozen smaller nozzles on them, spiraling around, were jetting out something that it only took a second to identify.

The thermobaric detonation device went off just as I spun, trying to run. I made it less than a goddamn meter before I was picked up and smashed into the far wall, trailing flames and smoke, looking as if someone had shoved a payload delivery system right up my arse.

CHAPTER NINE

When I came to, hopefully only a few minutes later, I was crumpled against the wall, slumped on the floor. The corner was half submerged in the pool of seawater that had collected there, with still smoldering sections of debris farther up the passage, beyond the water's reach.

I winced, forcing myself up and looking around. The water was still streaming in, with no sign of another custodian, and I cursed, before contacting mine.

I'd ordered it up and into the room, out of the way, and since then it'd apparently been hiding and waiting.

As soon as I called for it, it appeared, half the arms full of armor pieces. It raced down the wall and then to me, splashing through the deepening water as it reached out, twisting the sections around and slapping them into place, before clattering away from me toward the hole that was still spraying water in.

This time I approved it, not being able to sense any other sentinels. And if there had been any nearby, I'd almost certainly not have woken up.

It grabbed some scrap from a nearby sentinel and pinned it over the hole, rapidly spot-welding it into place, before making a proper seal over the quick fix.

A minute later, it clattered back to me, pausing as I dragged myself up and forced myself to stand, before gesturing to the room again.

"You got more armor for me?" I asked.

It set off, blurring as it raced across to the wall—sinking one leg into the provided gap to stabilize—before running upward and vanishing into the storeroom.

Ten seconds later, it splashed through the water, rearing up and attaching the lower back plate to me, before additions to the helmet, shoulders, then upper and lower arms were complete.

I reached out digitally to it, getting an estimate that translated roughly to seven more minutes, or thereabouts, and I nodded, before sliding back down the wall with a sigh.

Pain flared in my head, my shoulder, my neck…I was all right, sure—I'd recover—but that had *hurt*. I'd been fired into the damn wall. Looking up, I could see dents where I'd smashed into it, practically headfirst. I must have been damn lucky not to break my neck and…

I winced as I reconsidered that. Considering the pain in my neck, shoulders, and head? I was betting that I'd not—in fact—been lucky.

I'd probably broken my neck at least, and a quick check of my usable nanites made me groan even more.

I had enough left for a single shot, and that was it, with this much smaller cannon. One thousand and forty-seven nanite clusters left beyond what I needed to keep going and run my usual systems, and most of them were involved in the cannon's structure.

It was time to accept that I was going to need to upgrade again. There had to be a goddamn reason that I didn't have something as basically important as ammo, right?

There was no way that warriors out in the field would be spending the nanites they were harvesting to build these devices, surely? Because if you've got to kill a hundred of the enemy to make bullets to kill more of the enemy, that was a stupid setup.

In fact...

I swore as more and more "minor details" linked up, starting a chain reaction that I just knew was going to end in the entire edifice crashing down in my mind.

You didn't specialize that far down into specific roles, not if you knew what you were doing—not for humans, anyway. And considering we were designed to be the way we were? No.

None of the other Biological Weapon Variants worked like that either, as far as I knew. Oh no, no, that was a game for insects, and much less evolved creatures.

No, the problem here was that when the creators had started the system? They'd been idiots, making it up as they went along. They'd tried to make us into set roles, which was fine, but they'd not considered real-world applications.

Looking at the nanites? I could get access to them, to harvest them from my enemies because I had the harvest tool, right? Well, that's great—and ignoring the little detail that I didn't have access to that anymore, it sort of made sense. If you were fixated on one-use classes? Have a class that was specifically designed to harvest, like the fucking ghouls, or the vamps.

The problem was that if the Harvest class was designed for one thing, and that was harvesting, *who* were they doing that to? I scanned the area absently, making sure I wasn't about to be dogpiled.

After all, *we* were the weapons, and from the sound of things, as near as I could remember from the Erlking conversation, we were also the only ones filled with nanites. If the enemy wasn't made for war like us, then where were the warriors supposed to get the nanites in order to upgrade themselves?

I knew we'd been locked down, to stop the nanites from making more of themselves, and I could understand that. The movies were pretty clear on what happened when nanites got loose. So, if they weren't letting us make the nanites ourselves, then I had to assume that those that were being used as harvesters? They were made for harvesting *our* side.

That made a certain cold sort of sense. Fallen soldiers who were damaged past viable "repair" or healing? If you didn't intend on allowing them the time to recover, which might take months or years?

Well, in the field, they'd be a ready supply of nanites to keep the army going. Looking at it as an emotionless controller, if I was using ten thousand ants to achieve an objective, and some died?

Yeah, sure, I'd want to be able to reuse those dead ones if possible.

Especially if the intention was that I could have more made up. Or failing that, when some "died" and they were more useful? I could have them revived by a nanite injection and sent back to the front line.

It made a certain kind of sense to be able to strip less successful units and reward more powerful and skilled ones.

This led me right back to my terrible realization about why this was all going wrong. I was making my own weapons as I went, and the reason that it was working out so well for me? It was because I wasn't supposed to be able to do it. The War class was supported—appropriately—by the Support class.

Two *separate* classes, not a jack-of-all-trades like me.

I'd made the gravity cannon, the original one that I'd used to smash my prison apart, when I'd used my own knowledge, along with hints and information that seeped across. I'd made it, crude as it was, but I'd repurposed several different things, such as my gravity inverter.

I had no real clue how the inverter worked, not really.

I just felt data starting to unfurl and had shied away from it. No, what I'd done was take a gravity gradient generator, and I'd doubled and tripled it, like I was making a slingshot, inside of a slingshot, inside of...well, you get the idea.

It wasn't graceful, it certainly wasn't efficient, but fuck me, it was powerful.

Then I'd unlocked deployable weapons systems. I got basic data for three kinds of weapons: a gravity shotgun, a better and much more efficient gravity cannon—or railgun, I supposed—and a deployable weapons platform.

I'd gotten access to the systems, the way they were built, etc., because I was expected, as a user of the weapon, to probably need to do things like replace a faulty section, or reload it, and so on.

I wasn't expected to *build* them with that data, though. That was why the data was frustratingly vague, and why there weren't things like designs for ammunition included.

After all, they'd not expect me to be making bullets in the panic of a battlefield. They'd be expecting the Support class to make them.

Add in that my system was a learning one? It was using my "unused neural capacity" as it'd once referenced it, to find solutions as I was alone in the field. Namely, in that situation, using my goddamn nanites.

I was betting that I was supposed to be using my nanites to improve myself only. All those options it'd been offering me to improve my stats by investing them? *That* was what they were intended for.

Hell, they'd probably been given out as rewards for missions from the creators, and they couldn't do that now because they didn't have ships full of the fuckers hanging around, watching over the wars we were supposed to be fighting.

Instead, the system was on "auto" and its aim of making me as powerful as possible meant that it was trying to guide me.

That was probably why the Erlking had been so unimpressed with me as well. I'd been firing the goddamn means to make myself into a living god, at people who annoyed me! Shit, I'd only been scratching the surface of the system and all I could do.

I knew there were set paths available—in the Support class, I mean—that gave you a solid understanding of the tech as you unlocked them.

I'd been *ignoring* that, just focusing on what I needed right then, like the matter converters, and leaving all the rest of the data "locked" away in my brain.

This was why my meat-based brain was freaking out. Why I was having so many problems. I was betting that one of the first upgrades the "real" Support class had were things like an improved brain. Hell, I was betting the reason I'd always been slow to learn and was crap with things like math and so on? It was because my brain was hardwired to work a certain way.

Shit, that explained why some of my systems hadn't worked as well when they were first installed, like the remote hacking tool. I wasn't expected to be running around in the field and grabbing the things I wanted to hack!

The connections between the Support package, and my natural tendencies? The best example I could give myself was a PC and a games console. If you buy a game on the games console, and then put it in the PC?

Well, there were ways to make it work, sure. Emulsions or something they were called...no, fuck it, emulators! That was it! So, you could make it work, there were ways, but they wouldn't work naturally or as well as they did on the system they were designed for.

That was what I'd been doing to myself. I'd been trying to run a Support-based system, in a War frame. It'd adjusted to the War system fairly well, I guessed, most likely because as a Support package, it was designed to interface and help the Support class.

The advantage was, though, that I'd unlocked things I damn well needed. It gave me massive versatility. And now? Now it was time to figure this shit out. I'd already upgraded my brain a little, but I'd probably not done it right, all things considered. I was betting that if I could get the medical suite operating properly, though? I could probably upgrade myself to the point that I could use the systems without the pain.

It was also why I had the modem-type-thing in the back of my neck, when I didn't actually need it thanks to the Hack tree. I had access to Hack through the synergy of the harvest tool, my mind, and the War tree. Thinking about it now, it seemed like the Hack tree should surely be part of the greater Espionage tree, not a separate one, right? Maybe Hack was like the dumbed-down version that War got access to as well, though?

Shit, I didn't know—I really didn't—but the one thing I was sure of was that whoever built this goddamn system was a mad genius and an utter bastard.

I checked and saw the skill trees shifting in my focus, as I pulled back the point of view, climbing from the section I'd last been in, and I slid all the way to the top of the trees. The view was very different, and I winced.

When I'd accessed things before, I'd done it with a thought, thinking that I wanted to spend a point in the War tree, for example.

Now, though, I was thinking that I wanted to see all the trees, and the pain starting to build was a hell of a warning. I quickly shifted it, making it clear that I only wanted to see the trees that I had access to. The pain faded, and after a few seconds, I could see again.

It was as if I stood in the center of a spider's web. On all sides, details glimmered as I stared from above. My War tree was front and center below me, the widest and clearly the most important.

To the right, and sweeping around to the top right, was Espionage. And between that and War? Hack. Silvery lines ran from one line that led from one section to another, indicating crossovers of information, or potential, and I shook my head at how little I'd seen before, as a handful reached across the middle and sank into Espionage from the War tree as well.

The left-most side and leading around to the top left was marked "Personal." And a quick glimpse at that? It showed the potential for personal development. It showed the costs for me to invest in *me* more: to unlock specific sections, like upgrading my elemental resonance, my ability with cybernetics, or improving my reactions.

Attached to both War and Personal, was Weapons Skills, which sort of made sense. I vaguely remembered it being mentioned, even if I'd never unlocked it, and although I wanted to look at it, the feeling I got was different from what I needed right then.

It had so much that I could use right now, as it was specialist choices, like sniper specializations, and I nodded. I'd come back to it in a minute.

Crammed in at the top, as if it were an afterthought, was Support, and I could see the madness it contained. Dozens upon dozens of drop-downs flickered as they tried to expand, instead constrained as if bound in a field of tiny silvery wires. They radiated out, crisscrossing over one another and binding to the other fields in a dozen or more places.

Worse still? Harvest was bound up between War and Personal, partially absorbed into the War tree, and again, confined and curtailed by compressing wires. It was then blanked off…dull, as if I were looking through a window at night, the details inside identifiable, but dark and dead.

I stared at the systems before me, and I saw the problem clearly for the first time. I wasn't even a jack-of-all-trades. Instead, I was truly a master of none.

I stared and stared. My mind reeled from all the random connections that formed, from the little details that had meant nothing and that had suddenly linked up to make everything clear.

Long seconds passed. My tentacles still swept the area for anything, any threat or possible issue, as the custodian clattered merrily back and forth. It added the final plates to my armor, before folding itself up and awaiting the next command.

I stared at it dully, unsure where to begin. I'd fucked it up, I realized. I'd badly fucked it all up. This was why, when I'd been looking at things like the Assassin tree, I'd been thinking that if you got Conceal and a few other skills, you'd be insanely overpowered.

It was because I had no real concept of the value of the points I'd been throwing around.

Looking back at it, how many Harvest points had I earned since unlocking the entire system? Three. War points? *Thirty-five.* Hell, I had four points outstanding in that tree, ready to be used. I'd been so desperately in the shit right before the fight with Shamal when I got them, that I couldn't risk the time and the possible loss of days if a download went wrong, not when I was urgently trying to reach Ingrid and the others to defend them.

There were more places to spend points if I had them, loads more. I'd just not looked, because I'd not had any. If I'd been a soldier in an army of creations like me? I'd not have been leveling like this, I knew. No, I'd have been getting points only for big events, for things that *mattered*.

Being one in a sea of grunts? I'd not have been an *officer*—I was too dumb and too much of a blunt weapon. I'd felt like points were easy to come across, and that was because I was getting them from several trees at once, all with no clue that I was damaging myself and filling up my limited neural capacity.

Worse still, the only way I could fix things right now? I needed to spend more points.

I needed access to things that I couldn't get any other way, and Sod's Law, I didn't think I could risk trying to do this on my own anymore.

I had two days left before the others would be here, maybe a day and a half, in the worst-case scenario, and that gave me just long enough to do a small, *small* number of upgrades...

Squinting at the little custodian as it raced over to me, seemingly awaiting the next command, I nodded, then sent it to the end of the connecting corridor, ordering it into stealth and to watch for anything approaching.

Then I pulled up the overview, and squinted, stunned at the sheer number of points I had available when I queried it.

Skill Upgrade Points	
WAR	4
WEAPON SKILLS	3
ESPIONAGE	2
HACK	1
GENERAL	1
HARVEST	0
SUPPORT	0
PERKS	0

I couldn't help but stare, stunned I had so many points, and confused. Hell, I didn't even remember some of them! I knew I had a few War points left over, sure, but this many other points? And of course, when the one thing I needed, and *wanted* to make was a weapons platform?

I had no Support points.

I shook my head, knowing damn well that was probably a good thing. If there was a single tree that I really shouldn't be investing in right now? It was Support.

I hesitated, then mentally added Espionage to that as well. I remembered just how damn painful it was when I first unlocked that tree, as well as the insane pain that I'd gone through when I was perched above Athens, upgrading the Internal Espionage tree to enable me to find Ingrid.

The Cyber-Espionage tree would be a massive help in dealing with the ship's AI systems, as well as anything else I needed to. But the thought of unlocking that?

That would be an enormous tree, I knew instinctively. Just thinking about the insanity that was hackers? All the "black" and "white" hat shit that the few I'd once known had talked about? Fuck no.

I shied away from that, knowing beyond any real doubt that if I unlocked that tree, I could be fucked for a good while.

Instead, I went to the Hack and Weapon Skills trees.

Weapons Skills were first. As connected and close to both War and Personal as they were, I hoped that they'd be a lot less devastating to unlock and use.

The first point, as always, was the general unlocking of the tree, leaving me two points to spend inside it.

This time, weirdly, I got four separate trees that I could unlock further, and only a slight buzz of pain, rather than the horrific brain-melting one that I usually got.

First was Melee, and then Ranged. They were fairly self-explanatory, and with a little thought, I could see that they would mesh damn well with the existing setup I had: the enhanced combat systems would integrate easily with anything I unlocked.

The other two, though?

Internal and External were a bit more puzzling.

Internal gave the impression of internal to *me*? That was pretty weird, all things considered. I mean, who the hell were those weapons designed to…ah.

I nodded as a bit of bleed-through made it all make more sense. It was a tree dedicated to improving weapons that I had built into me, and the skills that I'd develop with them.

So, if I went down that route I'd been offered when I lost my arm, and had a full-on large-scale rail gun implanted into my arm? This would improve my skill with it. I wasn't entirely sure how it'd make me better with it, not really, and I could sense a lot of crossover between Melee and Ranged, with both Internal and External.

Either way, though, I had two points I could invest in it, and it wasn't a killer headache moment to discover how the system worked, so that was a relief.

External, though? That was what I needed right now.

If Internal was all about the investment in systems linked to me directly, External was in operating remote systems. I felt the connecting wires that ran from External to Hack and Espionage, and I winced, knowing that this was going to sting—at the very least.

Then I spent a damn point to improve my ability to manipulate remote weapons systems.

I nearly blacked out. The world seemed to shudder around me, compressing. I hissed in pain; dozens of connections from different skills linked up and were slightly tweaked, targeting algorithms dropping into my mind as if someone had chopped the top of my head off, liquified them and poured them in.

Long seconds became minutes as more and more sections linked up. Finally, I started to come out of it. Spots of light danced before my eyes as I reviewed the data.

I'd done it, I saw. I'd managed to get the first level of the data download working, but more and more connective crossovers in other areas of the abilities meant that was as far as I was damn well going for now.

Although…there'd been no movement, no sign of any more of the fuckers, so maybe? Could I risk unlocking another level of Hack or Espionage? I knew it was a bad idea, I knew it. But…

If I could do this, then maybe I could take the rest of the ship faster?

I reached out to the custodian, finding it easy to connect to it now, and I hesitated; then I sent it on a fast loop. It raced out of its hidden niche to sprint to the end of the corridor, making it to the exit that led out to the main hold beyond.

Watching through a sensor as it skidded around, already dodging, the air nearby lighting with blasts as two concealed sentinels opened fire, I winced and ordered it back.

It scuttled behind cover, dodging this way and that, before making a break back into the corridor, tripping twice as legs were cut away, and the main body was hit again and again with glancing blows.

When it made it around the corner finally and into cover?

It was a mess.

I made my way over to it, extending a tentacle to keep watch around the corner as I looked down at the fucked-up little fella, where it sagged and sparks cascaded free to wash across the nearby seawater pools and floor.

It was down to three tentacles on the lower ring, and two on the upper, with sections carved out of it here and there. I winced at the damage, and felt I should apologize. Especially as it looked up at me with all the enthusiasm of a puppy.

Reaching out and triggering the creation tool, I grimaced at the levels of damage that were highlighted. Dozens of sections that didn't look too bad were suddenly glowing orange in the schematic that quickly built before me. And other sections?

Glowing red or just grayed out.

I shook my head and couldn't help myself. "Shit, sorry about that, little buddy," I muttered, scanning over it, and seeing additional sections that were highlighted.

"Okay, I really need you right now, and that was such a waste..." I admitted. I'd done it for a good reason. If there'd been nothing out there, I was going to invest in another level of a main tree, and accept that there was the risk, and just try to stay functional.

Now, though? I knew beyond a doubt that there were at least two out there, and that, at the very best, if they came in, I no longer had a really useful little scout.

I shook my head, trying to banish the voice that was cursing me internally, and checked the repair functions of the custodian.

It...it wasn't actually that bad, I realized after a few seconds.

Most of the general systems? Yeah, there was a load of damage, but the repair systems were more or less intact, and there were repair systems on all the fucked-up sentinels around me...

I reached out, gathering up one of the leg-tentacles it dragged along the floor, and focused on that with the creation tool. It gave me a barrage of data, which, with a thought, refreshed into a list of needed parts to repair it, and estimated times.

Most of it was still a mass of data, but the biggest advantage I had over a "normal" Support class trying to do this? I had access to the rest of the trees.

Support let me repair or adjust the design, rebuild it in a thousand different ways. As long as I could visualize it, and I had access to the tech? I could do it.

With Hack and Espionage as I had them currently? I was just guessing here, but they might be why I was so aware of the carryover between the different lines.

With War? I was massively geared around operating weapons.

So why the hell should I limit myself to rebuilding it as it had been? I smiled as I reworked the design before me in my mind.

There were five destroyed sentinels in here with us, two of which had intact laser clusters. And all five had at least one of their repair arms attached or intact still.

Sure, they were dead, but were the sentinels entirely dead? I suspected not.

I shifted the design for the little custodian around in my mind, still watching around the corner with a tentacle, as I started to play.

The custodian was made more for speed and to be able to get in and out of places. It could compress itself easily, rather than being as solidly built as the sentinels were. It seriously lacked armor, and it'd only survived as long as it had because it was so fast and maneuverable.

Well, it sure as shit wasn't that anymore, but…hey, fuck it. It didn't mean it was too badly broken either.

Looking at all the scrap around us? I quickly identified a fairly intact main shell from one of the sentinels.

More accurately, it was a full shell if I added two fucked ones up, and divided them in half. But that wasn't the point. There was a full shell there, and each of the five had at least one of those repair tools, so…

Half an hour passed with me gathering up the repair tools from three of the corpses, then attaching them to the custodian.

It seemed confused to fuck by this, and even more so when I injected fifty of my remaining nanites into it, with specific orders to literally just connect up the arms to the rest of it, integrating them.

To rebuild it properly, the metal all connecting and fixing, the various sections fitting like they were machined together? It'd have cost a thousand or so. Instead, I did as much as I could using a bunch of the little discs, two null blocks, and the parts that I *very* carefully stripped from the sentinels.

By the time I was finished, though? It had two sentinel legs attached to the lower ring, and three repair tools on the top, two "normal" walking tentacles on the bottom as well, and one of the weird ones that could attach to the wall and lock it in, so it could run around at any angle.

The top, with the three tools and two working tentacles on the upper ring? That was ready to work as well, and the first victim was ready for it.

I'd taken the stack of null blocks from the room above, and I'd brought them down, forming them into a rough square of solid armor plating.

Then I'd taken the two usable laser pods off the corpses, and I'd attached them to either side of the square.

The inside was filled with the systems that were found directly below the laser pod on the least damaged of the sentinels, giving it the ability to rotate and aim and so on. I'd ripped them out and mimicked them as best I could; then I'd set the now ugly as sin, but more or less working custodian the job of integrating it all onto one frame of the sentinels.

I ripped the power cores out of three more of the bodies, bringing them back and attaching them to the back of the Frankenstein's monster we were creating, using my creation tool to attach them, bypassing a staggeringly insane amount of safety limiters as I did so.

Once that was done, and the system started to power up? I reached out, ready as the sentinel began to come back to life.

Before it could fully boot, I attacked, enveloping it as my four expanded mentalities and my single, more or less meat-based one fell in to savage it.

I triggered the time compression and slowed it all down as far as possible, then tore the cyber defenses apart with overwhelming force.

The sentinel barely managed to get the most basic systems booted, before its allegiance to the ship was stripped away, and it was forcefully bonded to obey me instead.

I waited, ready with the vorpal blade, prepared to slice the fucker apart if it didn't work. But, wonder of wonders, it did. The security system welcomed me as its master, and I grinned, as the custodian started phase two.

CHAPTER TEN

It took the pair of us nearly an hour to get the "upgraded" sentinel up and running, and "running" was definitely a misnomer. "Staggering," or even "limping" might be more accurate. Sure, but what it lost in mobility, grace, and yeah, probably intelligence, it more than made up for in lethality.

My original plan had been that I'd unlock another of the Deployable Weapons Systems and then invest a few points in the Weapons Skills tree as well. I'd intended to set this fucker in the middle of the corridor, so as soon as anything came around the far end, it was ready and could carve it into shreds.

That was the original plan.

When the custodian accepted my "upgrades" so easily, and we managed to hack the sentinel so quickly? Yeah, I might have got carried away.

The end result was a much larger, and seriously heavy-duty version of the current sentinels.

It was also ugly enough that even Dave after fifteen pints would have refused to sleep with it, and that was saying a lot.

The new sentinel was still crab-like, as the last one had been, but it was also at least fifty percent bigger, with five legs on either side. It had a single tentacle that was formerly viewed as beyond viable repair by the custodian due to the loss of the end point.

Now it had a slab of armor attached to the end of it: null blocks reformed into three inches of solid circular mass and ready to be moved to catch incoming fire.

The top now had a *quad* gamma laser cannon on a swivel mount, and three power cores running at the very edge of needing to be scrammed.

That meant that sure, it was unstable, but it could fire the new heavy quad cannon every three seconds. It was armored, *heavily*, and had a fully functional security RI running it, rather than me remoting into it or setting it to fry anything it saw.

By the time it was finished—and by finished, I mean more along the lines of "minimally operational and slightly less likely to explode in the next ten seconds"—I'd picked up movement at the end of the corridor again.

I grabbed a single null block, the last we had, and quickly separated it into ten small darts using the creation tool. I gripped them with one of my tentacles, now modified into a loading mechanism, as I strode up to the edge of the corridor, waiting.

I made some adjustments on the fly to my gravity cannon, making it use them instead of the nanites it'd been using so far, and we waited.

We'd barely made it into place when the first of the fuckers sprinted around the corner, running full bore at us, clinging to the walls and ceiling as easily as the slightly canted ground.

Dozens of class-one sentinels blurred across the floor, feet clattering as they came, lasers already firing as we opened fire in response.

The first shot to hit was ours, thank fuck. Three of the smaller buggers were carved apart with a single blast from the powerful quad bore laser.

The others raced along the walls and ceiling and returned fire, splitting it between my weapons platform and me. Six hits landed on me, carving narrow lines through my armor and digging into the null block coating that covered my original armor.

The weapons platform used its shield to protect the more delicate optics, holding that in place as lines were torn in the thick plating that covered the majority of it, as it recharged the laser.

I returned fire. My gravity cannon was now converted to a much lower-powered rail gun, firing single-shot darts of solid and insanely dense null blocks.

The first two shots missed entirely, the self-correcting and perfection of the nanite shots making their absence known. The third one hit a sentinel head-on and shredded it. The central core exploded as it was sheared in two; thousands of tiny components scattered to the winds as if I'd shredded a biological.

The next thirty seconds were sheer madness: all of us fired, dodged, and were hit over and over. I might be the only one with a mouth, but I was damn sure if they could have spoken, they'd have been screaming swear words as well.

I took three hits to my left leg. One of the lasers etched a line across the knee and was stopped by the armoring, right up until it shifted across the side of the joint.

The lack of the armoring there definitely made its presence known as the inside of my knee and the ligament at the back were carved apart.

I screamed, falling sideways as my knee gave out, buckling under me. The damage was too fast to deal with. Fortunately, it helped me to roll sideways out of more fire, and the little bastard that had hit me was targeted by my massive protector.

The RI, or restricted intelligence that ran my sentinel companion, had three goals, as I'd uploaded them. First, protect and obey me. That was the primary. Second? If Ingrid and the others made it in? It was to protect and obey them, with her as the primary authority figure beyond me.

This was a "just in case" measure. If I truly died in the next fight? At least there was a chance that it could save her and the others.

Last of all? It was to fuck up the goddamn sentinels that got me.

That rule came into play as soon as I was injured. The orders I'd given it moving into this fight were to help me kill them all, but when I collapsed, it took that badly.

The shield was jerked aside and a fresh beam—or four, to be more exact—lashed out, dragging left to right and then partly up the wall, taking out seven more of the little bastards.

I came to a halt, leveling my rail gun and firing, hissing in pain as blood jetted out of the back of my leg. The hot, slithering sensation of the ligament as it rebounded under the pressure, cut free and squirming around under my skin and armor, made bile rise in my throat, but I kept firing.

More and more of the little sentinels closed the distance.

I snarled, leveling the rail gun and firing the last few shots off. The darts punched straight through the smaller figures, taking two and even three out with a single shot when they landed just right.

I was out of darts in seemingly seconds, though, and laid on my back on the floor was exactly the wrong place to be, when the remaining three on the ceiling—four on the left-hand wall, and two on the ground and right wall, respectively—threw themselves at me.

My sentinel protector was swarmed by three of the smaller units, which focused on the tentacle holding its shield, and then the quad cannon, using pack tactics to strip it of both defensive and offensive measures as fast as possible. It quickly shifted around, stomping and ramming into the walls, using them to damage its unwelcome passengers, while the remaining eight went for me.

I collapsed the rail gun. The nanites flowed back into a more basic configuration as I punched a tentacle down to the ground, bracing and flipping myself up, even as more nanites poured free to cover the back of the leg. Some rooted around and tried to fix the damaged section, while the majority simply closed the wound over, sealed the cut veins and formed a pliable coating that brought the knee back to more or less usable levels.

I slid the vorpal blade up and across, cutting one of the sentinels in half as it leapt at me. The tentacles clattered off me, but the second and third?

They landed, wrapping limbs around me. Laser optics glowed and carved into my armor, even as they unleashed blast after blast from their electrical attack.

My armor absorbed most of it, though the lines the fuckers were etching into me were getting deeper and deeper as I spun and struggled, trying to keep the joints covered and locked together to prevent burn-through in the weaker areas.

I stabbed a tentacle out, forming it from my chest. The nanites that made up the one that had helped me to my feet poured back into me, and pooled on my chest instead.

It hit the central core of the one that straddled me there, ripping it free before it could wrap me up; the first to land had done so on my left arm, and the second on my chest.

Now, as the one on my chest deactivated, the limbs falling loose, I twisted and rammed the other—and myself—into the left-hand side of the corridor.

It crumpled. Two of its limbs failed under the crushing impact. Then it twisted, trying to get its fast-recharging laser in line with the back of my neck.

Before it could fully recharge, I punched it, then ripped it aside, flinging it into the next that ran at me. I slashed my blade over and through another as that one leapt to take the last one's place.

I staggered, my leg still not ready for the pressure I was putting it under. The next bugger managed to land on my helmet, wrapping its limbs around me and unleashing a powerful electrical attack that sent me screaming and staggering.

Another of the damn things landed on my arm and tried to lock it up as well. Their arms and legs were like rubber-coated chains, and damn, they were surprisingly strong.

Both unleashed charge after charge of their electrical "crowd control" shite into me—and were shocked in turn by their compatriots—and I roared in pain and fury as I tried to rip the fuckers off.

My sentinel crashed into me from behind and to the side, ramming us all into the wall. Then I heard the roar of the ionized particles under assault as the quad cannon fired again, this time unable to see what was going on, as I fell to the floor.

The one on my right arm had four legs wrapped around my upper and lower right arm respectively, and it was hauling my arm straight, forcing the joint open as it prevented me from using that arm. The blade on my left arm was making me less than sanguine about trying to get the fucker off my head with it, and I triggered the retraction. It was already looping limbs down, wrapping them around my neck and attempting to strangle me, or haul off my head.

I snarled and triggered the kinetic absorbers. Each and every impact I'd taken in the last few hours or so of fighting charged up, as I rolled over, designated the generation point—my forehead—and yanked my head back, then slammed it into the floor.

There was a boom, accompanied by cracking and electrical shorting, as I crushed half the sentinel. My left hand came up and fingers frantically scrabbled for purchase on the damn thing.

I got hold of something and yanked, then shifted my grip when it wouldn't come off, and started to crush.

At the same time, I drew all my "spare" weaponized nanites in close, reforming them into a half dozen much shorter tentacles.

Then I rammed them out into the grainy radar-like images I could half see, and mainly sense on me. The tips plunged deep into the fuckers, thanks to the nano-molecular tip.

I expanded those tips into a star pattern with points outward, and ripped left and right, shredding the fuckers into a shower of parts.

All at once, apart from the sound of my heavy panting, the distant sound of rushing water—I'd apparently accidentally punched a few fresh holes in the far wall—and the tinkling of discarded metal, all was silent again.

I forced myself up, staring around, wild-eyed, ready for another fight. My right arm instinctively formed the creation tool as I searched for something to break down to use as darts...before I realized it was over, and the fight was won.

This time.

I collapsed back to the floor, chest heaving. Pain from my goddamn knee, and a dozen other places that had been cut, bruised, and fucking *lasered*, all screamed for attention.

Instead, I shifted and braced myself against the side of the corridor, squinting at all the damage and debris, as I brought up the data on my systems.

Four nanites.

Four fucking nanites I had left.

Not four million, not four thousand—hell, not even four *clusters*, which was how I was used to thinking about the nanites. No. I had four *individual* nanites left. That was it.

Admittedly, that was four after I'd taken off my operating "minimum" that were there to keep me functional and as strong as I was and so on, but still.

That was an insanely low number.

I reached out, mentally, to the custodian, sending it a series of orders, as I squinted down the corridor, trying to visualize the area at the other end.

Two minutes later, it reached me, four null blocks in its "hands." As soon as they were deposited with me, it sprinted down to the far end, off to seal the holes I'd accidentally punched in the ship.

I sagged back, playing the creation tool over the first of the blocks, then the second, breaking them down into the darts I needed. They were crap, genuinely they were, but they were all I had for now, and so they had to do.

I forced myself up to my feet, looking at the state of "my" sentinel, and winced. It was down to basically a mobile platform now. Its quad cannon was melted in three places, two of its legs were fucked, and as for the tentacle arm that had wielded the shield?

It'd been sheared in two and dumped.

I shook my head, forcing myself to move as quickly as I could. I gathered up the other lasers and more, grabbing the most intact and seemingly easiest repaired three sentinels, as well as their cores, and piled them aboard its broad carapace, hacking them as quickly as possible.

Then we set off, hurrying down the canted corridor, toward the main areas of the ship.

I spun up the rail gun again, more for show than anything else, as I marched along. The two of us were joined by the custodian after a few minutes. It'd sealed the holes letting water into this part of the ship, and that was apparently enough for it.

As we went, I gathered up more and more parts and loaded them aboard my little transport, moving out—hesitantly—into the main storage area, or whatever it'd been, and onward.

The next ten minutes were weird, and very uncomfortable. I started out expecting to be hit, that there'd be a dozen or more sentinels laid in wait, possibly about to launch themselves at me at any second.

As the minutes crept upward, I let myself feel a little hope, then more. Seconds stretched into a handful of minutes, before the distant sound of destruction finally rang out.

I cursed, expecting that the fucker of an AI was flooding the ship, as I hurried forward…then I slowed again, remembering that if it—he, whatever—did do that?

I'd be fine.

Yeah, sure the whole thing of gaining control of the ship would be annoying, but the gamma and crowd control weapons they'd demonstrated so far? They'd be much less effective, if they were at all.

I ordered my machines to move up. The sentinel "transport" passed along the "valley" between the hulking debris, as the custodian was to climb up high, to reach the gantry system overhead and follow from up there.

In theory, that'd give me a better view. After the sheer number of hits the bastards had landed on me with those gamma lasers, I'd not only used up almost all my nanites to heal myself, but I'd lost over a third of my weaponized nanites as well. That meant I wasn't flying again, or at least not anytime soon.

While the custodian raced for the nearest wall, slotting its attachment into it and ran upward, I started to climb the piled debris.

It didn't take me long to find the first of the sentinels, or at least the majority of it.

It'd been carved up and stripped of its core, as had the next.

I ran, searching, all my senses extended to their fullest, and after a few more minutes, I spotted them.

Three custodians, each being protected by two of the smaller class-one sentinels, hurried away in the distance. A door ahead, more intact and clearly better maintained than the others, was held open, waiting for them.

I hesitated, then swore. The fuckers were stripping the dead for parts—parts that would be used much as I had, to make more sentinels!

Lifting my right arm, the creation tool vanished, sinking back into the arm. Instead, the rail gun spun up; ridged sections of armor bent to form the lower rails and a bracing point.

The second system, the main coil, glimmered into being. The nanites lifted into the air to corkscrew along into a compressed, gleaming spiral; magnetic fields twisted them and forced them to hover, as if by magic.

Their own magnetic fields spun up as the tentacle fed a single dart smoothly into the back of the coil, and the dart lifted free as it was dragged into place.

I sighted down my arm. The targeting reticule zoomed in, in my augmented vision as I moved it slightly. My arm's own armor tightened up, providing stability unasked for as I made a million tiny mental adjustments.

The unlocked War and Ranged sections of my trees adjusted and assisted as I closed in even further. The target seemed to leap closer…and I fired.

Almost before the dart had left the spiral, the tentacle fed a second in. The smooth panning to the left and down two degrees would have made a staff sergeant weep with joy, and I fired again.

The first hit took out the leading sentinel; the second impacted the next in line.

As both scattered, blown on the winds of destruction into a million parts, I reoriented on the now sprinting and frantically dodging custodians. Their arms were full of parts, and I squinted, assessing, before firing again.

This shot took out the lower core of the middle custodian, a hairsbreadth off the target I wanted. It collapsed, the power ripped from its cells as life fled.

I shifted, tracking…and snarled as a beam reached out, scouring my left side.

I dodged, sliding down a short way on the unstable debris, reorienting, zooming in…and finding nothing. The fucker had run for it as well.

Squinting back toward the distant door, I cursed as it slid closed. Two of the custodians had made it through, their arms full of parts. I set off, running.

There was at least one of the sentinels in here, I knew; something had fired on me, and my damn quest to "clear out the garbage" was still live.

My custodian was above the fight now, scuttling across the roof. Its metal legs were nowhere near as subtle and quiet as the tentacles it'd enjoyed before I'd hacked it, but it readily provided me with a data feed of the site below.

I pulled it up, grinning over the advantage that would provide, and cursed half a second later. The fucker provided a view all right, but it was sod all use to me!

It was a mass of data and images, mainly on the systems that *should* have been in the room! The piled debris was marked up with cascading failures lists, priority repairs, component viabilities, and a thousand other details all warring for my attention.

I saw it all, and I saw the massive warnings and deep-seated orders that prioritized the custodian class.

These, these rotting and rusted hulks, these piles of fucking trash, were marked as highly important, as priority systems! They were full of valuable metals and more, and not a single goddamn one was available to be used.

They were marked as needed for whatever stupid goddamn mission the fuckers had been working on when the facility crashed. Or hell! It might have been abandoned millennia before, when the wankers who created us were booted out!

A truly insane amount of time had passed, I knew, since the systems that maintained this place had been checked on, and as such, in the way of computers, and other such stupid motherfuckers—like any member of a bureaucracy—they'd slavishly clung to the last orders given, despite its futility.

Thousands of years had passed as their main systems failed, as more and more of the ship they were designed to maintain crumbled around them. And instead of stripping and looting the components they needed from the trash that surrounded me now? They protected it.

A wash of cold fury filled my veins for all this place *could* have been. And then an evil smile crossed my lips for all it *would* soon be.

Fuck this shit.

I banished the images shared by the custodian and ordered it to route around and reach the one I'd just killed. We had power cores, half a dozen that were still viable. That was why I'd aimed as I had.

I ordered it to reach its dead brother and begin repairs, to use the power cores and parts that it had been carrying to repair it, as I set off again…hunting.

The best, and most sensible, method was to creep around, to use my stealth capabilities, to hide, and to lay in wait.

That was also the method that would waste the one advantage I had, and the most valuable commodity as well.

Time.

If the security AI was having to send out its finite units to grab any of the cores and viable units it could find, I was betting that my earlier guess was on the money. As limited as I was with nanites, it was the same with parts.

Some of the sentinels, I had to assume, would have been made from a security stockpile, or would have been in a vault or whatever, ready to go.

The rest? They'd need to be built to order. These bigger fuckers I'd been fighting certainly supported that logic. It had to be building what it could, and then sending them after me. After all, if it'd sent dozens of class ones along with the class threes, rather than spreading the waves out? I'd have been toast.

No, I was betting it'd made a handful of class threes after my first visit, thinking that was all it'd need, "just in case." Then I'd come back, and I'd scanned the damn ship. The hours I'd wasted searching for a way in? It had to have a way to monitor the outside, and that'd probably sent it into panic mode.

It would have manufactured as many as it could and sent them to face me.

I'd probably caused it some issues by going back and forth outside, swimming up and down, with the little bastards running around desperately inside. Once I'd found my way in, though? It'd sent everything it had after me.

I guessed that once the first wave of class threes had failed, it'd sent what it had left, gaining as much time as it could, as it made the class ones, using them as a "zerg," I think it was called. Basically, just making them all fucking run at me and try to kill me.

It'd damn well nearly worked. If they'd had three or four more? Have them hanging back and carving me up while I fought the ones that were on me?

It would have won.

The next three minutes were a pain, as I ran up and down the massive moldering piles of junk. Sections collapsed and slid out underfoot, making me use my tentacles as much as my arms and goddamn legs.

Eventually, though, as I'd expected, the temptation of me running about in the open proved too much.

The last of the sentinels burst from a pile of scrap as I ran past, legs clattering desperately, trying to maintain a viable distance, as the laser blazed to life. I dodged left and right; the beam tracked me unerringly, carving increasingly deep divots into my armor as I closed the meters that separated us, kicking up a sheet of bent and rusted metal and sending it spinning, right at the laser.

It dodged. The beam cut off as it reached the end of the charge, but it was too late.

Now that the little shit couldn't cut the tentacle free, I flung my left arm forward. A single lengthening tentacle flashed out to close the distance, latching onto the cylinder that sat in the middle of the suspension ring, powering and guiding the little machine.

Then I ripped it free.

It released a single burst of electrical energy into the tentacle, which totally ignored it, and I twisted it around, forcing it to face away from me. I hunched down in the nearest pile of debris, keeping out of sight.

Then I started the hack.

It was ready for me, but that made two of us. Before the firewalls were properly up, I'd triggered my time compression and augmented mentalities, swamping them as fast as I could.

This was a fight that I could afford to lose, which, paradoxically, made it easier to fight. If it won? If I sensed that I couldn't keep up with the die as they twisted and grew in complexity? I'd just smash it with the tentacle that clung to it.

With that in mind, there was less to lose, and I relaxed—or at least I wasn't as tense. I twisted and focused. The die before my eyes unfolded from a single, flat, one-dimensional square; sides lifted, forming three dimensions as they locked into position, the additional edges, side, and more becoming distinct.

It began to spin, but before it could build up speed, I was there. A touch of focus, a dash of determination, and a fuckload of mental gymnastics meant that my mind was as flexible as that blonde waitress I'd once knew who loved yoga, and that was more than enough.

Well, that and the sheer level of aggression that I threw at the problem.

I spun the sides...one at a time at first, then more, and more. I only realized my augmented mentalities were working on this one as well when I brushed up against the edge of one of them, our minds melding as the world was mirrored in our vision.

Ten seconds had passed from the start of the hack, when the last side of the die collapsed inward. The frantically struggling cylinder in my grip, that had been growing hotter by the second as the AI tried to make it overload its core, suddenly calmed.

The core temperature spiked, then dropped. Brief jets of pressurized air escaped as the bleed-off valves released, and the little sentinel welcomed me.

I grinned. The pop-up flashed at the edge of my vision as I slid it back into its housing. The legs that were slumped on the floor twitched and lifted it easily again.

The little optic spun, the gyroscope that housed it adjusting, then locked into place as it waited for orders.

I grinned, ordering it up to the top of the mound I was half buried in, and to watch the area for any enemies. While it did that? I pulled up the quest notification.

Quest Updated!

Evolving Quest completed: Repair and Renovate: Level 1 (a)

You have been gifted a quest directly by one of the Creators, as well as authority to access the various facilities around this testbed world.

The security AI that protects Facility 6B does not recognize your right of access, and has marked you as a trespasser. Eliminate or convert this security AI, and claim the facility.

Part One: Complete.

You have secured the local area,
eliminating all active sentinels and have gained the following rewards:

- **+1 War Point**

- **+Access to Level 2 of this section of the Evolving Quest**

Part Two: Secure the local security net, by penetrating and locking the security AI out of the local node to gain access to the next tier of the evolving quest to gain the following rewards:

- **+1 Hack Point**

- **+Access to Level 2 of this section of the Evolving Quest**

There was a lot left to do, and hell, I wouldn't call this area "secure," not by any stretch of the imagination. But fuck it—if the system wanted to reward me right now with a War point? I'd take it.

Hell yes I would.

I reached out again, this time to the hulking and fucking terrible-looking sentinel crab thing I'd made before, checking on it.

It'd reached the end of the debris field, and was now up and clattering across the end of it, sliding down the long slope of debris that led toward the door the fuckers had left from.

They'd used doors each time, and they'd grabbed parts from "dead" machines, rather than strip the machinery lying around, much like the custodians had, and I grinned.

I was betting that whatever was left of the AI running the security system *couldn't* trash the place. Sure, it'd set off the explosives before, but thinking about it? That'd done very little damage, all things considered.

Add to that, if the sentinels had said "fuck it" when I'd been in the pod, getting upgraded? Surely they could have just cut their way in, rather than sitting and waiting for the door to be unlocked, right? I mean, there were three of them, and they could have just cut their way through the goddamn wall. I could have, after all, and I was using a glorified fucking knife, not a gamma laser deliberately designed to cut things apart.

"Oh, I *like* this…" I muttered to myself unconsciously, as I reached out to the others. My little sentinel class one started to run immediately, doing a full lap of the area I found myself in, searching for any and all doors.

The class three set off, stomping along to take up station across from the doors the fuckers had escaped through, waiting patiently, as the custodian continued its work on its "dead" friend.

Minutes passed as I jogged back to the little cybernetic device, arriving just as it began to twitch. The powering-up cycle had been delayed until I could reach it.

In seconds, it was mine. Its defenses, again, were far more rudimentary than the sentinel's. It started to move less than a minute later, its "mind" locked to me entirely, refusing all attempts by the local AI to regain control again.

It moved to the class three, beginning its repairs on the laser, as the bodged-together first one I'd taken control of ran at the door. It didn't like the idea, that was clear, as I ordered it to start work, but it did it. Its welding, or molecular bonding tool, or hell, its magic-fuckin'-*wand* for all I cared, sparked to life, as it started to seal the doors.

I grinned as it continued. As soon as it was done, it moved onto the next, and the next. It performed a loop around the room, moving from door to door, sealing them all.

Three hours it took, and I expected at any minute to be attacked as it worked. But the security AI, I assumed, preferred me being "contained" as it didn't interrupt.

Admittedly, more than once, I reflected that all of this was born of my guesswork that the fucker wouldn't want to trash the walls. That logic was shaky at best, as most of mine always was.

Fuck it, though…I had to work with what I had.

Thankfully, by the time the little bodge job of a custodian reached me, having completed its loop? I had a lot more of a plan than I had three hours earlier.

CHAPTER ELEVEN

I'd been thinking—which admittedly wasn't my strongest skill, but hey—and I'd come up with what I hoped was a winning plan.

It revolved around my main strengths, as I saw them, in this situation.

First, I was me, with access to the full "jack-of-all-trades" setup. Instead of being a warrior, as the AI clearly presumed me to be, I was able to adjust much more on the fly than it could expect.

Secondly, I didn't give two shits about the ship overall, beyond that it was a means to an end. If I had to melt it all down to slag, but it meant that I could definitely get what I needed from another ship? Booyah, pass me the smelty-thingy.

To the security AI, I was a warrior variant that had somehow managed to break inside and gain control over the damaged sub-systems it was sending after me. I was also trapped in a large area, but one with limited resources.

After all, it'd been active for millennia, and if this room had been full of *viable* resources, it'd have used them, right?

The important word there was fuckin' *viable*. Because to me? All this scrap was a treasure trove of viable components.

I had almost no goddamn nanites available, and that sucked, but there were ways around that. After all, I didn't need the nanites to build things; they just made it much easier to bond systems together, and to essentially do everything faster.

It wasn't the only way—it was just the easier and faster one. Creating the shell of the boat, or redoing the outer hull of the plane? I could have done them without nanites, if I'd been willing to spend three times as long, easily.

I'd never had more than the bare minimum time to achieve my goals though, and now, for the first time, I had helpers, I had raw materials, and I had a burning fucking need.

I cracked my knuckles and reached out mentally, ignoring the building hunger in my stomach, as well as the thirst, as I started work.

First things first. I sent the bodged custodian to collect the converter, and while the other one finished up repairs on its larger sentinel brethren, I sent the little sentinel searching.

It took twenty minutes to find the first, and another hour after that to find the second, but as soon as it found the long-dead custodians that I'd been hoping would be scattered about—I'd run into enough in the first section of the ship, so I'd guessed they might be more around—it started to drag them back.

While that was working, and the bodge retrieved the converter I'd left behind—I mentally allocated him the ID of B1, and the working custodian C1— I started work with my creation tool.

It wasn't as good, nor as fast as working with nanites only, but it was literally a creation tool: it took whatever I had and adjusted its molecules into the patterns I needed.

With its help, and that of my vorpal blade, I worked on the scrap pile next to me, breaking down the large sheets into a frame that I could use. By the time B1 returned, I had it mostly done.

It was simple in the extreme: basically, a massive funnel, one that stood upright, with space for the converter at the bottom, underneath it.

We slid it into place and started to load the hopper, cutting the machinery scrap pile around me quickly and viciously, and chucking it all in.

C1 and B1 freaked out at first. Both jerked to a halt to look at me as if I'd punted a puppy into the middle of next week. But after a few seconds, they seemed to accept that their new loyalty was to me alone, and this was fucking scrap.

B1 started to repair the first of the fully dead custodians that the class-one sentinel had retrieved, and C1 and I got to work with the null blocks that were slowly being churned out by the converter.

The first step, as much as I'd have loved it to be something more fun, was a second converter, and then a third. As the second was completed, I made another hopper and loading system for it, then positioned it in place underneath, while C1 got to work on the third.

That meant that "soon" we'd have a much higher rate of production, or so I damn well hoped. The next half hour was spent alternately working on the nearby scrap piles, and standing upright, searching around, squinting as I tried to spot any changes around us, any signs that told of the security AI unleashing some super-secret ultimate deadly weapon.

Spoiler alert—fuck all interesting happened.

As the next hour or more passed, and both the third converter and the second custodian were brought online—named C2 because I was creative like that—our production speed sped up massively. C2 started work on a fourth converter, as well as the hopper design to feed it, while B1 got to work on the next long-dead custodian.

The bigger sentinel had moved off and squatted before the door that all the others had run out of. It was now even heavier, armed with a quad cannon and two smaller class-one sentinel beam optics.

It wasn't amazing, and I knew that, but it'd gotten heavier shielding as well, and was basically a fuckload better than it had been, so that was enough.

The next stage was making use of the four converters and the building abilities of the custodians. Without something to guide them, and certainly without orders to use the goddamn scrap, they were useless. But once you provided that? They were fantastic.

I left the converters to produce block after block, and re-tasked the class-one sentinel to keep the hoppers full. Then C1 and I, joined by C2 as soon as it was finished with the converter design, started work on two more jobs.

The first was a much, and I mean *much*, bigger converter. We literally printed parts, over and over, using the null blocks and making specialist factory units. They were similar to the ones that I'd made only a few days ago with Zac and the others in his engineering workshop, in that the null blocks went in, the finished parts were "printed" out the far side, and they ranged from about a meter to five meters across.

This time around, they were producing line after line of parts that C1 and C2 stuck together, pressing them like they were making a goddamn sandwich or something, but their additional legs were zipping back and forth like nobody's business.

Clearly, they were doing more than I could see, and I was fine with that. I hacked any of the units I'd not got to yet while B1 finished up soon with C3. As soon as it joined in, the power core from a damaged custodian granting it a new lease of life, I sent him off to gather up the rest of the destroyed sentinels.

The little area I'd claimed was fast becoming a hub of activity. The slag piles of crumbling debris were lit by reflections of welds and showers of sparks, with shadows cast by the multi-limbed custodians racing in all directions.

With them all busier than a one-legged duckling in an arse-kicking competition, I settled down, making sure I was hidden from view, half burrowing into the debris pile and lifting sheets of metal out to further hide me. I pulled up the trees.

I'd not wanted to do this, but every instinct told me I was being stupid. And with that in mind, I gave a few last orders in case I was "out" longer than I was hoping.

Yeah, I could wipe myself out, totally. This was a fucking terrible place to upgrade myself, especially when I had issues unlocking trees.

However, it was only the War tree I was going to work on. That was arguably both the least destructive to me personally, and the one I was "designed" to access.

It was also for a goddamn good reason.

I had five points in that tree available. And when I drilled down to the section I needed? I knew the risk was worth it.

I hit War, then Assault, dropping down the tiers and moving into more specialized sections as I went, pulling up the second tier of tactical upgrades, and then down to Ranged. From there, I hesitated. The three options that glimmered before me included Integrated, making use of my own body as part of the system—or, at least, my armor.

They could, for example, unlock the capacity to build a rail gun into my forearm, or my back, that would make the one I'd bodged together so far look like a popgun.

It'd take a few points, as I'd need to unlock specialist upgrades to lock sections of my armor together, and I'd need additional heat sinks and gravitational generators, not to mention a larger permanently integrated power core.

I'd also be able to take out shit in orbit, though.

That was tempting, for half a second. Firstly, as far as I knew, I didn't have any enemies in orbit. Secondly, I'd need a fuckload of nanites to rebuild sections of my body. I didn't have them, so yeah...And last of all? It wasn't going to be much goddamn use here and now.

Still tempting, though.

No, I moved past that, and pulled up the other two trees, Deployable Weapons Systems and Remote Ranged Weapons Systems.

They were, as most of the trees were, similar and yet oh so different.

Deployable systems were most likely designed to be built and used once. I could, for example, build a turret and set it up using this tree.

Well, that wasn't entirely accurate. I'd gotten basic access to a load of systems when I'd unlocked this section of the tree before, and it gave me some data on maintaining and more effectively using a turret. It showed me the best places to site it, the best ways to use it for maximum coverage and minimum losses…all that kinda good stuff.

It didn't give me the plans to make one, but in giving me the knowledge to maintain it? It was close enough I could bodge one together.

Sure, it'd never be as efficient and powerful as the real thing that was built by an engineer. And yeah, even with all the details, something that I made, I was betting Zac could still improve on, if he was given the same information.

Or hell, knowing him, a potato, a length of string cheese, and a fork, but that was life.

I'd already unlocked this tree though, and it'd wiped me out for a full goddamn day. Sure, I'd gotten much better access to things like the gravity shotgun design, the improved rail gun, and a basic weapons platform, but a full day?

I'd been using the details in here, in part, to help with the upgrades done to my bodged-together sentinel, making it a lot more durable and powerful than it had been.

This time, I dropped another point into the Weapons Platform selection. Before confirming it, I slid back up the tree, bringing up Remote Ranged Weapons Systems. This was what I needed to make both myself—and the others when they got here—as safe as I could.

Turrets, weapons emplacements—hell, I could make the recycling facility into a fortress with some of this shit, and I just knew it was going to sting. I winced. Then, before I could think better of it, I dropped the point in, and confirmed it.

It shuddered, then spread into a five-pointed star, one that led to more and more sections that unfurled second by second, linking to even more sections and…

"Arrrgh!" I growled, grabbing my head, even as the data store at the base of my brain flared up…and was overwhelmed.

Thousands of tiny details pushed up, joining additional sections. I felt remote access details, approvals and security features that linked to the Hack and Espionage trees; I saw weapons data that was both in War and Support. I sensed massive sections that were repeated in the Command and Control drop-down of War, as another point, and then another, was sucked from my little "store" of them, taking me from five points before I started this, to a single damn War point in seconds!

Right before the world vanished—everything already flickering like crazy, blood running out of my nose, my ears, and over my lips—I managed to load a counter into my augmented brain.

I deactivated three of the four remaining copies of me that were sitting pretty in my expanded mind, freeing up the space and setting the last to maintain the counter to keep track of the minutes as I went under, and to watch for any danger, hoping it'd help to wake me if there was.

Of course, when I finally awoke again, gasping as my brain seemed to reboot straight into panicked full functionality rather than the slow return to consciousness I probably needed, it was to a firefight.

CHAPTER TWELVE

I shifted, pressed into place, covered by sheets of metal and…I threw them off, realizing that when I'd passed out, I'd thrashed around and knocked over the crap I'd piled up to hide me.

It'd done its job, though. The three sentinels stomping through our little construction area hadn't seen me, until I started throwing sheets of metal about. *That* had certainly given my hiding spot away.

The secondary mentality was still there, and as I reached for a section of metal, a tentacle of weaponized nanites flowed out, grabbing it and tossing it aside before my hand could grasp it.

I rolled, planting my hands and feet, and kicked off, triggering the gravity inverter to power me up, making me light as a feather, and yet with the inertia of multiple tons of raging lunatic.

Beams sliced across the debris where I'd been, then closed on me, cutting into my armor even as I flew at them. The three were humanoid: two arms, two legs, and a recessed head deep between the shoulders. They strode forward in a small triangle formation: one in the lead; the other two were back and out to either side, right arms extended. Massive projectors took up the entire arm, even as the left ones were bladed.

Two small arms extended over their heads, coming out from their upper back, a smaller class-one style laser on the end. And all six of those slashed back and forth across the converters.

Behind them, I could see the carved-apart remains of the sentinels, both the class-three bodge job, and the little class one.

I landed close enough and ducked, projecting the gravity field into them. They staggered as they spun to track me, firing again and again, no longer "beam" weapons, but clearly multi-shot.

This time, even the null blocks were of limited use, and I instinctively knew my normal armor would have been cut like butter under a hot knife.

I screamed as part of my right forearm was cut apart. At least two inches were sliced inward from the outside, only stopping when it hit the creation tool and augmented bones.

Bringing my left arm around, I lunged forward; they staggered. I leapt onto one of the falling figures, ramming my vorpal blade into its chest, expecting to slice it apart easily…only to have it skitter across the surface. It caught a second later on a ridge and dug in—doing significant damage, sure, but I was used to carving the fuckers apart.

That its armor had been hardened to withstand my blade? *Fuck.*

I backhanded the laser aside as it tried to bring it to bear on my head, and screamed as the pain from my damaged arm made clear just how fucking unimpressed it was with my decision.

The one to my right pushed itself up as I ripped my blade free and blocked the blade of the one under me. I recovered first, yanking mine back on target, and stabbed down as hard as I could, punching the tip through the head of the one under me, before the one to my right launched itself at me.

I'd also not known about the fucking jump jets on its back, finding out about them when they triggered and hurled the fucker into me, lifting me and hammering us into the pile of debris behind, with it atop.

If not for my armor cushioning the blow? I'd have been dead already—and that wasn't including the fucker's weapons, just the goddamn impact. I struggled, trying to get it off me, while simultaneously fighting, thrashing, and gripping its right arm. The blaster, or whatever it was, was that hand—I'd had to retract my own blade or risk stabbing myself in the face in the fight—and my weaker, wounded right arm was pressed against the inside of its blade. The back of my wrist was against the flat of its weapon, shoving and twisting as we tried to avoid the other's weapons and still strike out.

It kept shaking and bouncing as I fought, trying to get my feet up to gain some leverage…when I realized why it was doing that.

The expanded mentality, Me2, was still there, and it was using my weaponized nanites! It formed them into a spear-tipped tentacle and rammed it out over and over again. The tip did little damage at first, but the smaller and smaller the tentacle's point got?

As soon as it found a chink, a flex point, or whatever? It drove in, then expanded. It was ripping great chunks out, and simultaneously massively limiting the fucker's ability to move. The next attack from the tentacle stabbed out, and I realized that since the thing had hit me, I'd not seen the back-mounted lasers, guessing that Me2 had made them a priority.

We fought, punching, twisting, and battering at each other. Insanely overpowered blasts from its blaster went off and carved great divots in the debris pile under us. Its sword got ever closer as I shifted my grip, pulling nanites from the tentacle and pooling them over my fingers.

I sent them racing up to the arm joint at my enemy's elbow, sinking them into it and then forming solid links, locking the joint straight at first, then expanding further. The shriek of spitting and tearing metal filled the air.

As we thrashed about, I saw out of the corner of my eye the other two, both rising to their feet and turning, headed toward us, blasters rising. And behind them?

The fucking custodians—C1, C2, and C3! They were fucking *sitting* there, half slumped as if they weren't happy, but they sure as shit weren't destroyed, or hell, not even damaged!

I reached out to them, ordering them forward, to attack, to…

They shifted, then settled back down. Something in their programming refused an attack order entirely!

I hissed in pain and shifted, kicking out, planting my foot and trying to turn us both. I released the blade arm, now that it was broken, and punched the damn thing in its armored head, even as I spammed orders over and over at the three of them.

I demanded they do something, anything, but the damn things refused any order that was violent, or destructive, or...

My fist impacted on the front of the head, smearing a tiny number of my nanites, dipping me under the "minimum operational threshold" by a hundred clusters. As I triggered the Trauma Burst ability, the front of the head—barely a head; it was a single eye and a bulge with sensors attached, but still—detonated, throwing us back away from each other.

It staggered, blasted almost fully upright, then collapsed, crashing to the floor. The other two locked their blasters on me, and I tried one last order.

The three launched themselves at the pair of sentinels, limbs frantically stabbing out as I threw my arms up, desperate to ward off the incoming blasts...that never came.

A few seconds later, I slowly lowered my arms, staring in shock as the custodians frantically and professionally disassembled the sentinels before me. Arms stabbed out, connecting to sections that I'd have sworn were as solid as the rest, only to have ports open up, connective sections popping as more and more slid apart.

The power cores were removed in a handful of seconds. The sentinels staggered then collapsed alongside their broken brother, as I gawked and mentally raced through the orders I'd sent.

It came to me after a few seconds, just as I slumped back into the debris with a crash, shaking my head in disbelief.

I'd ordered them to disassemble the sentinels. Not to attack, not to destroy, not to do anything "wrong" as they must have understood it—just to strip them for parts. I'd tried that before, but I'd sent it as part of a bunch of orders I'd been trying, clearly telling them that the sentinels were the enemy, that they were faulty, that they were...whatever.

They must have been checking my orders against an internal list of "okay" commands still, and each time it failed that "test"? They'd ignored the orders.

That they'd decided that was a valid order? Fuck me, it was blind luck...I mean, I'd been trying everything else, so, wow. I slowly pushed myself upright, looking around the destroyed production facility I'd had going, and clambered up the side of the debris I'd been sheltering under, squinting. I focused on the door on the far side, clearly seeing that as the way they'd gotten in.

Three custodians were next to it, and as I watched, they spun, racing back for the corridor beyond as the door started to close. I reached out, but the distance and the time it took me was too much.

I missed out on grabbing any of them, and I cursed as the door clanged shut. The dead bodies of two more of the humanoid sentinels on the floor between the door and me made it clear how hard my own had fought.

Well, we survived, and thank fuck for that, because it was time to even the odds.

I didn't know where the security AI was getting the parts it needed to build these waves, but it was clearly even more limited than I'd thought, as they were getting smaller and smaller each time. Sure, they were also getting more powerful, but I was betting it was having to justify spending more resources each time against some kind of scale inside.

I turned and headed back down, looking at the pair of sentinels that had been loyally serving me, chopped into kibble by the much more powerful weapons of the attackers, and the now neatly stacked parts of those same bastards.

I reached out to two of the custodians, C1 and C3, as they were closest to the intact bodies, and ordered them to put the "loyal" sentinel cores into the bodies they'd just disassembled, and reassemble them, but not to power them up until I was ready, just in case.

They shot off, happy to be working.

I turned to C2, and the remains of the sentinel I'd been fighting, as well as the converters and factories. They were cut apart, badly damaged, but...

"Hey, you! Fix that shit," I snapped, gesturing at the converters and factories, and shook my head in disbelief at the way it just leapt to obey. The damn things had just sat there, waiting for orders, when I was feckin' fighting for my life!

I hesitated, still catching my breath as my adrenaline gradually wound down. My hammering heart slowed, and I pulled up the notifications, quickly reading them over.

The Remote Ranged Weapons Systems tree was insane. So many of its systems linked to others; things like the remote control methods had, by necessity, methods to secure them. And those, in turn?

They provided data on doing the opposite, as you "had" to understand them, to protect against them. Entire swathes of data still unfurled, unlocking more and more as I tried to lock it away again, and to not think on it.

I saw hints here and there in the system on weapons platforms that were clearly available, or could be made so. Things like great mobile artillery sites, or massive weapons systems that could secure against planetary interdiction forces.

I saw details—barely anything that was clear, but clues and unsaid things, sections where data was redacted in specific ways—that hinted at more, at smaller, much more mobile sites, as well as much, much larger ones, systems that would make certain "moon" sized weapon platforms obsolete, as well as star-killers.

For now, though, I locked the data down to what I needed, managing to shove most of the bleed-through away, and focused on the systems that were revealed, and that I assumed were supposed to be there.

First was the design for a basic weapons system, along with the designs to maintain and operate the physical structure of it. It didn't have the weapons system attached but it was simple enough to see. It was literally a cradle system that would hold the weapon, and the ammunition if that was needed. The design and the maintenance dealt with the housing and moving parts of what was basically a turret: how to control it, how to fix it when it was damaged, likely issues...all that fun shit.

The next? The control system. That linked heavily into the Command and Control network, and that was where it'd used a second point, unlocking another command system upgrade to add in Remote Weapons Systems.

Here I could see more of the technical skills, things like interpreting the data, linking to it more effectively, reading the systems, and adjusting them to understand the difference between the various sub-systems, like lasers and their cooling times, the warp of the lens, range finders—fuck, there was loads. But it all boiled down to being in control of the system, as a commander.

I could give the system orders, and although it was far dumber than even the sentinels and the custodians, it could carry them out. I suddenly realized that was why I'd been able to bombard the custodians with a barrage of orders until I'd gotten the one I'd needed.

It'd included a section on controlling "dumb" systems as well as interfacing with more advanced ones. Glancing at the next steps in that tree, I could see subsections where I could invest in more advanced and specialized control abilities. With a little work, I could see myself controlling dozens, and possibly hundreds, of these little buggers.

Third, came weapons systems. I'd kinda viewed these as a priority at first, but as I knew now, they weren't. Sure, they were the point of the system, more or less, but without the will to use them, and the ability to aim them? They were fairly pointless.

No, in this section, the data was all about mounting, servicing, and using the weapon, covering things like firing arcs, drop-off calculations for both physical and energy weapons, attenuation, possible counters, the effect of weather, of vacuum—hell, of sustained fire and how to assess and maintain the most optimal firing solution as a battle went on.

I felt the linkage here to the second area that a point had been spent, as a separate tree, one dedicated to actually using ranged weapons, unlocked.

It felt weird that this hadn't been available before, considering I'd unlocked Ranged already, but…I groaned and retracted my helmet, rubbing at the bridge of my nose with a finger and thumb as I thought about it.

The reason it'd not been available before? I'd been focused on the need for other abilities.

Had I been thinking "I need a fucking rifle"? I was sure I'd have gotten a complimentary design. Hell, I'd gotten access to the gravity shotgun, and I'd still not made one!

Admittedly, I needed goddamn nanites and…and…*Wait. Did I?*

I turned to look back at the converters and factories, a small yet oh so evil smile on my lips.

Right.

Finish this, and get building! I decided.

So, the third option was weapons systems…the fourth? I pulled the system back up, and grinned as I saw the last two sections.

I had Basic Stationary Platforms and Basic Mobile Platforms.

They were pretty self-explanatory. I'd not put points into either of them, or any of the five subsystems yet, so I'd only gotten the basic data that was unlocked by the overarching tree to date, but it was obvious what they were.

Stationary was turrets, emplaced weapons systems and, thanks to two lines that led off it, they could be linked to traps, and to deployable weapons systems, gaining me a little extra data from both fields. Essentially, I got the basics on a shitload of things, like knowing that there had been turrets on this ship. The fucker had them on the outside once, it seemed, designed to keep the flora and fauna away.

It gave me a very limited overview on those systems, and a subset of even more restricted info on armor.

A tiny bit of data unlocked against the armor designs I already had, letting me know that I could invest more, or even just work on it myself, to make the armor much more resistant to weapon damage.

I put a pin in that. I'd need to check it out later, and I moved to Mobile, the fifth and final section.

So, where Stationary Weapons Platforms was—surprise, surprise—all about weapons systems that were put in place and didn't fucking move, Mobile was all about the opposite.

For the first time, I got usable data on the sentinels, as that was, at heart, what they were: mobile weapons platforms.

Sure, they were a little more advanced, as they had a rudimentary RI or low-level AI maybe, and they roamed the ship looking for threats. They were there to identify them and—at least, in theory—fuck them up.

I got a fundamental rundown on them, including the more basic details on how they were put together, mainly because my current experience included them.

I took a deep breath. The enormous mass of data, its branching paths and more, all seemed to settle more comfortably into a brain that felt insanely stretched.

It was, however, pretty much what I'd been hoping for.

I had enough of an outline that when I started to scan and check over the parts that made up the damaged humanoid sentinel, I could see a shitload of usable parts.

Ten minutes after that, my two new sentinels, christened S1 and S2, were up and moving, burying themselves in debris and out of sight, while watching the doors, ready to attack.

Now that their repairers weren't taken up with that job, they got to work on fixing the factories. The damage with two of them was significant enough that it was better to load them into the freshly repaired hoppers and have the converter return them to null blocks.

Twenty minutes later, the first of the factories was back up and running, this time working to churn out armor plates with specific connection points on the back and sides.

The next machine worked on turret systems, running a hundred off in short order of the simplest designs. As each of the factories came back online, they churned out parts...parts that were then set aside, ready for construction.

An hour later, we had seven factories running and the only bottleneck on our side, now that we had access to the abundant, if fucked, equipment around us to trash and recycle?

Power cores.

I could only make them if I had spare nanites, and I had absolutely fuck all.

Searching the local area, I'd found B1, my bodge rendered down to slag by the attackers in their last assault, and three more power cores that could be repaired. That, along with four of the attackers' cores, and the others I'd found lying about—either stripped out of dead sentinels, custodians, or who knew what—gave me eleven in total.

Five were set out as power cores for the turrets we were building. In short order, they were ready, missing only usable weapons systems.

The remaining six were set aside, ready to power my counterattack.

Once the construction machines were finished, we went back to the drawing board. There were three "corpses" left over from the new sentinels, and I intended to get two of them back up and running, but this time serving me.

To do that, I took the last one and tore it into pieces, scanning each and every section, making sure I could reproduce it, and fed the design of each individual intact component into the factories.

I had them churn them out ten of each for every part I'd scanned. The weapons systems, those powerful single-shot blaster thingies? Yeah. Eight were made over the next few hours: five for the turrets, three for the next generation of sentinel.

These wouldn't be the assholes that I'd faced—neither would they be as nice, nor as well constructed. I barely understood what I was doing, and I sure as shit didn't understand the insane intricacies that governed the RI that ran these things.

I could grasp some of the basics, though, and as soon as the turrets were up and running, each atop three-meter towers, spread around our little factory? I set to making a skeleton version of them.

Not in the "I just dug this fucker up" mentality, though. Oh no, it was more in the "bare bones and fuck all frills" version.

They were tripods: a single simple pillar served as the chest, heavily armored and with the weapons pod attached, and the power core hidden inside.

The legs were spaced out around the base, attached to a ring system that let them slide when needed, adjusting the layout. The turret could move in a wide arc, and although it wasn't hugely fast, nor accurate, it was heavily armored and armed.

It was also simple as fuck to direct.

The other three power cores were set aside for me, to power three little toys that I couldn't wait to get some use out of.

The first was what I was tentatively calling the Cracker.

Essentially, as a power core held, yup, you guessed it, power, it could in theory be used to provide that power wherever I needed it.

I figured that I didn't need to hack the door to make it open, if I could simply ignore the controls and plug the battery into the relevant section.

After all, the power circuit on the door was the issue when it was locked, right? When it was locked, there was a break in the circuit. When power was applied? The door did what it was designed to do, and fucking opened. Take the power away? It sealed again.

I guessed that in this case there was also a secondary power route that supplied power to the closing mechanism to make sure it stayed that way. But for me? I liked straightforward, and I was fairly sure that provided I carved the connections out of the wall with my vorpal blade, then I could simply apply power to the bits left over until the door opened.

The best bit?

There was fuck all the security AI could do about it, as it was left with either carving its own doors up, or leaving them be, while I forced them open.

If it had them welded shut, which I wasn't sure it could do, with its programming and all, but if it did? Well, I could cut them open as easily as it could seal them.

The doors were hardened, so although I could carve my way through them, or the walls, it'd take a lot of time, not to mention weakening the overall structure.

Jez Cajiao

This left me a simple solution, in my Cracker.

The second "little" invention was another simple one, although it was designed to deal with multiple "problems" all at once. Essentially, I set two connections onto the power core at either end and a tight bundle of spring-loaded copper and gold wires in the middle, set atop a laser projector. Compress both ends with a hard smack, then throw the fucker as far away as possible.

The sheer electrical energy contained in a mobile fusion core was insane. And as soon as both connectors were smashed into place on the output points? Power started to flow.

As soon as the power flowed, it hit the laser projector, triggering it, and the laser hit the compressed copper wiring. Those wires were less than a molecule thick, coated in gold, and when the laser hit them? The tightly compressed bundle of wires straightened out under the charge, flung in all directions.

The laser would burn out in half a second, leaving the remains of the power core to flow through the copper wiring, essentially providing a massive electrical shock to anything touching them.

It was my version of the electrical shocker that the little class-one sentinels used. Had I had it before? I could have taken most of the fuckers down when they bum-rushed me in the corridor.

The third and last one was for my weapon, which was currently being printed, a dozen pieces already skillfully assembled by C1.

I could create the rail gun myself—the design was integrated into my armor and my mind already—but I'd decided it was time to really go for it, so to speak, and create the first weapon that would be available to my people as well.

That, I'd decided, was the fléchette shotgun.

It used a shorter, but still insanely powerful gravity gradient and would throw the metal fléchettes at the target, ten at a time, with a variable distribution pattern that was set by a dial on the grip, going from three inches apart for all ten—making damn sure that whatever you fired at was going to have at the very least a three-inch hole *all* the way through it—all the way up to a meter dispersal pattern from around five meters out.

The fléchettes were attuned by a secondary magnetic gradient that was designed to keep them at that range. Although it wasn't perfect? It would seriously fuck up someone's day.

If I'd had the chance to make some of these bad boys before? Shamal would have had a very different reception at the recycling facility. Not least because he'd have been trying to regenerate his fucking head.

Even if I'd had the chance to make a few of them before, though, I'd not have had the time to make many, and certainly not much ammunition. But that was the point now: there was no way I was going to let the others be at risk, not in the way we had until now, and certainly not when I had the capacity to do something about it.

C1 assembled the weapon as parts came out of the factories, and C2 worked on the magazines. They were weird, cubes of monomolecular fléchettes that were compressed together, making it possible to carry a seemingly solid rectangular "block" that, when it was hit with the correct charge, split off ten darts, allowing them to be loaded with a single "pump" of the mechanism.

The gun was short, by rifle standards. Its grip was in the middle in what I vaguely recognized as a bullpup design. The dispersal and magnetic guidance system was in the front half, extending about half a meter ahead of the grip.

The back half meter running to my elbow was the magazine and primary launch cradle.

Each magazine held ten shots of ten darts, and I had ten underway, making me feel a lot more ready for the next fight, especially as there'd been one last addition to our arsenal, and that was the shields.

The custodians carried one each, and I had a big fucker, much like the tower shield I'd made of nanites back in Copenhagen. But this time, it was solid null blocks. And as well as being heavy as fuck, it was *substantial*!

Another hour passed as final assembly was completed. Checking on the timer, I swore. In the worst-case scenario, I had about two hours until the yacht would reach the area. In the best? Twelve.

Fuck.

It was time to go to work.

CHAPTER THIRTEEN

I organized the group. The three skeleton systems, A1 to A3—short for "Asshole One"—were to lead, as they were the most disposable.

The main sentinels, S1 and S2, were to run with me, on either side, and two of the custodians, C1 and C2, were to follow. We were bringing a single converter and a factory, allowing us "in the field" repairs.

C3 was to stay behind, loading the remains of the debris fields into the converters and essentially getting us as much usable material as possible for later. It was, in turn, protected by the five turrets, so that gave me hope that if the shit hit the fan, at least we'd have a base we could retreat to.

That left eight of us heading to the door, with C1 cracking it, then getting the hell out of the way, as the laser fire started.

The custodians slid in from the sides, once the first barrage was over, shields held up high and at the ready, soaking up shot after shot. Beams cut through the air with the sizzle and zip of ionized debris.

S1 and S2 marched forward on either side of me, their right arms extended. The blasts that leapt from the projectors killed with each hit, as the smaller class-one sentinels that stood against us attempted to hold us back.

I strode forward in the middle of the group, shield in my left hand, shotgun in my right. A tentacle extended from my forearm to grab the charging lever, pumping it back after each shot.

My first shot missed the sentinel I was aiming for, literally by an inch, if that. The second? I'd had it dialed up one notch by the tentacle, and when it *would* have missed again? Instead, it shredded the fucker; fléchettes tore through the air to rupture anything else that moved nearby.

The corridor we advanced down was cleared in seconds, with C1 and C2 pausing long enough to strip the surviving cores from the dead sentinels.

Of the five we faced, we recovered two, and that was more by blind luck than anything else.

"Let's pick up the pace!" I called out, not needing to say it. I knew as soon as I had, but it'd felt right.

We sped up to a jog, shields at the ready, and dropped to a slow creep a minute or so later as we reached the end of the corridor. Taking a turn to the right, we ignored the steps that rose sideways along the wall on the left-hand side. We searched, decided there was no threat, and set off again.

The next clear section had us running again, before finding that the end of the next corridor was only a hundred meters ahead. As we closed on it, we slowed, not wanting to run straight out into an ambush, and *damn*.

A1 was the first to move out, me not being stupid enough to risk my damn life, and a barrage of shots hit him about a third of a second later. One impacted center of mass, right above the core, punching into the armor, and sent the powerful creation spinning to the floor, a burning crater clear to see, as it fought to rise again.

"Fuck! Bum-rush it!" I snapped at the rest, using my Conceal for the first time. I'd deliberately not used it before now, hoping that it'd work against the damn AI, and knowing that if I needed it as a surprise, then I'd probably *really* need it.

I didn't know whether it was working, or whether the AI had decided the others were better targets and wanted to save me for last, but as I slid forward, trying my best to keep my Conceal active and efficient, the others were hit over and over again.

I gritted my teeth, torn between the need to run like fuck, and knowing that my stealth would only hold if I kept my movements slow and steady.

The security office or station or whatever lay just ahead. One wall had collapsed, showing some of the interior, and that looked to be full of frantic movement.

Inside the office, there were a dozen smaller units, some things like smaller custodians, but…but they were weird, like they were only half the size of the normal ones, and with massive fins on their back for some reason.

The others were four-legged and clearly designed to operate machinery of some kind. They scrambled around, bringing parts to assemble a second turret, while an already completed one fired at us repeatedly.

Sweat poured down me, even with my armor keeping the temperature inside perfectly matched to my body as I crept forward. Enemy shots hammered the walls and units all around me.

My creations continued to fall, one at a time, taken out by the turret as I moved forward, teeth gritted. The damaged A1 collapsed to the concentrated fire, quickly followed by S2.

The remaining skeleton systems, A2 and A3, had held their fire as they clattered forward, lining up their shots. I split my focus, torn between trying to "remote" operate them and keeping myself alive and going.

I let S1 take and return fire, while the custodians soaked up most of the barrage, then split to either side when they couldn't take any more. It was like watching lava pouring, right at the end of its life, cooling to form rock, but in *reverse*, as the black, solid null blocks shields gave up, splitting as glowing materials tore and dropped to the floor, exposing the machines cowering behind them.

C2 was hit in the core and blown apart. The fucking shot took out the pair of additional cores as well, before I finally ordered A2 and A3 to open fire, their friends' shields no longer able to protect them.

Where the blasters whose design we'd copied were insanely powerful originally, I'd toned them down in my version. They were less than a quarter of the power of the "proper" sentinels' version, but what they lost in fire*power*, they gained in *rate* of fire.

They fired over and over, more like machine guns than single-shot blasters, and the little bastards racing around the turret fell in droves.

The mobile turret collapsed as its operators were cut down, and I grinned, lowering myself slowly to the floor and triggering the gravity inverter.

I extended it as carefully as I could, letting it take all my weight, before extending it ever so slightly ahead of me, then reversing it, so I "fell" forward, weightless.

I skimmed across the ground, flying almost, as I picked up more and more speed. A handful more of the little bastards, like four-legged spiders, similar in upper body to my own skeletons, popped through the gap again, only to be cut down by the overlapping fire.

Reaching out with the inverter, I aimed carefully, hoping I wasn't about to pile-drive myself into a wall, and I triggered a twist in the gravity field, flipping it from low down, close to the ground…to up close to the ceiling.

I spun, my Conceal ability rippling as I suddenly moved much faster. The last two sentinels, crouching behind the ruined wall of the security station, twisted in response, clearly seeing me at the last second.

It was too fucking late, though. I planted my feet on the ceiling—or floor, as it was to me for a brief second—and kicked off, canceling the gravity inverter.

I flipped around and dove to the ground between the pair, spinning and slicing out low. I dragged my blade through them at core height to hack them apart, even as the last shots from A2 and A3 splattered into the walls around me, missing by inches as I threw myself down.

"Memo to fuckin' me, stop the idiots firing *before* I attack!" I snarled, reaching out and summoning the rest of them, as I grabbed at the controls for the turret.

It was fairly big: a triangular layout with an angled front, a dual cannon design that fired heavy bolts of laser or plasma—no fucking clue which. I'd been too busy dodging the blasts to give two shits, but they glowed and burned, so I guess plasma was more accurate?

Either way, though, there was a section on the back for an operator, albeit one a lot smaller than me.

I dragged the turret around, pointing it out through the collapsed wall into the next section directly below this one, and I aimed it downward. A half dozen of the little bastards ran at me, one arm locked to the wall to help them run up the vertical surface.

I grinned, twisting and having to half hold the turret up, but able to angle it around, before grabbing a lever and opening fire.

It was like shooting ducks in a barrel. They had nowhere to go, and hell, they didn't even try to dodge as I walked the fire across them, blasting them free of the wall, and then moving back to fire a single shot into the machine that was assembling more of them already.

I hit it where a thick power cable, or something that looked like one, was plugged in. The resulting explosion, both in terms of the shower of sparks and the way that the machine shut down instantly, was satisfying as fuck.

I couldn't help but grin, shifting the turret around again, squinting. I tried to make out any more targets, before growling in irritation as the surviving C1, S2, A2, and A3 joined me in the security office.

I got them to help as I moved the turret around, lining it up so S2 could control it, and ordered C1 to repair the damage I'd done to it and finish building the other turret, getting it ready, just in case.

Once that was done, and I'd checked the corridor that led on from the man-trap that the security station was clearly designed to be, from the middle of a nest of three corridors, I deployed A2 and A3 to the other corridors, leaving the one we'd just come along as a safe avenue of retreat.

That meant, as the ship was lain on its side, that that one was stationed pointing straight up at a distant wall ending in an air lock above us, and I just hoped that the security AI didn't open it and let in the ocean.

I gave them orders to fire on anything that came along; then I started to look around the actual station.

It was a square-ish room, two walls given over to storage that had seemingly long ago been plundered, or collapsed—a diamond-hard, glass-like surface that had fallen out of the wall into the room or cavern down to the level below us at some point.

I could see it, still intact and atop a pile of debris. I was impressed, despite myself, at just how hard it must have been to survive a crash that shook it out of the fucking wall.

I stood in the middle of what had once been a wall, and the way the place was laid out? Despite the damage, it was clear that gravity had been an optional point to the people who had once lived here.

The main system in here seemed to be a single black tower that led from the wall to my right out into the middle of the room. A dozen small ports were clear on the sides, and I winced as I wondered whether I was about to make a horrific mistake.

It fairly hummed with malevolent energy. And I knew, I just *knew*, that trying to hack it remotely was a mistake.

The AI had made it clear that it was able to fight me to a standstill with remote access, and only my time compression had allowed me to beat it so far.

This was a part of the actual security infrastructure, clearly massively different from the tech that covered the walls around me.

I stared at it.

I knew it was the literal seat of the goddamn AI; it was there, watching me, waiting, and I had anywhere from a matter of minutes, to a few hours to…

Then I stopped, and I grinned to myself. I'd forgotten one very important point.

I wasn't alone. I was worried that I desperately needed an edge in this fight, that I needed to do something to give myself a chance against the AI, here, on its own grounds.

I also knew that I was having massive problems with my brain when I downloaded additional data and skills, and I was terrified that I'd fuck things up if I did more.

I'd been in pain before, though, and even though it was the War tree that I'd been using? I'd still been wiped out. I knew this, and I knew I couldn't afford to use the Hack or Espionage points I had.

I also knew that I couldn't afford to risk being knocked out, because I had Ingrid and the others incoming.

What I'd not been considering, though, was the custodians.

Okay, yeah, I was down to one, and I damn well needed it right now. But I was surrounded by dead units, and it looked as if they didn't have cores, for some reason…

I examined them, checking them over, scanning them with the creation tool and building up the schematics as best I could, until I finally found it.

The long spike that extended out of the back of them, like a fin almost, which I'd seen during the fight, wasn't a goddamn fin. It was something like a remote control and transmission point, both for data, and for power!

I'd moved up into a more intact part of the ship here, something that was clearly viewed as more important than the medical wing I'd been in before, because it had so much more power available.

The AI had gotten around the power core issues and their presumable cost to produce by sending out drones that were receiving their power and orders through some kind of wireless transmission, and that meant...

As soon as I'd figured that out, I had the custodian running back to reach the other one, dragging its body back up and starting repairs.

I couldn't risk the control method that the AI was using being part of the signal, so I couldn't just use their methods to connect it all up and get it working, not until I'd secured the area.

That there was a working power grid in the ship, though, and that up until this point, I'd been in the unpowered sections, as well as only dealing with the few things that could reach me out there?

That was both terrifying and awesome.

It meant that if I could take over the power grid from where I was and lock the security AI out? I could *really* secure the area.

I agonized over pulling my little tools apart, considering that I'd made them for a damn good reason. But in the end, I reluctantly handed over the power core for the Cracker, hoping that I'd be able to loot another soon and replace it.

I just knew that if I didn't? I'd desperately need it soon. But if I kept it? I'd never get the chance to use it.

Fuck it.

I had C1 get C2 back up and running using that core. Then I created a very simple program, which was to say I knew what I wanted, and thanks to the Command and Control, as well as dozens of other upgrades, I just about managed to share it with the pair.

One immediately got to work, constructing a rail support for the turret, so that it could be easily moved from side to side, letting us use it wherever it was needed, while Two finished assembly of the second turret, that I'd interrupted One in working on.

On examining the turret that had been tearing us all a new asshole earlier, I found that it had a cable leading into the underside that provided power. I started to shit myself that when I needed it, it'd be cut off, forcing me to order S1, my last "real" sentinel, to power down.

Fifteen minutes into the process of rebuilding the turret and getting it all "properly" online? A dozen of the smaller remote-powered and remote-controlled sentinels sprinted out of a door on the far side of the storage area below us.

They barely fired on the security office: a handful of desultory shots slammed into the area around the window to drive us back and that was it.

Instead, the vast majority fired repeatedly into the massive machine that was clearly designed to produce more of them!

The goddamn AI had spotted that the real threat, if I claimed this area, was me using its own systems against it, and the fucker was trashing them first!

I opened fire, ordering A2 and A3 down to back me up, as most of the little bastards continued to concentrate fire on the machinery.

They fell, literally seconds apart, but the damage was done, and most of that machine was trashed. By the time the last of them was down, I was cursing, glaring at the far exit, and determined that as soon as I could feasibly do it, I'd be coring that fucking AI out of the system.

The custodians, now two of them working together, inserted S1's core into the turret, mounting it in just under an hour, onto a mobile gantry that was locked to the wall and floor of the security office.

It let S1 traverse back and forth on powered guide rails, locking the now dual turret into place wherever it was needed.

With that done, I got C2 to make up a small plaque and an antenna that could be mounted on the yacht, and then sent it off to weld that goddamn door shut. Once that was done, I gave it orders to get to the surface, with images of the crew, as well as the yacht, burned into its memory module.

It was to hide until I saw one of them; then, provided there was nobody else about, make itself known with a light or a noise, and depending on the situation—I'd given it a dozen scenarios—it was to deliver the plaque and antenna, and do as Ingrid ordered until I gave it other orders.

There had to be a way to remotely control it as well, rather than giving it if/or missions and sending it off, but even with the remote data I had, I just couldn't figure any way.

I'd need a lot more control over the situation and the surrounding ship, and right now I just didn't have it, so it was time to trust the orders.

As soon as I secured the local area? Yeah, sure, then I'd be able to reach out and remote it, but right now, I had to trust.

That done, and with A2 and A3 back on guard duty, C1 working on sealing up the security station and making it as impregnable as possible, and S1 safely mounted in our new turret?

It was time to do what was starting to actually scare the shit out of me. It was time to spend some points.

The danger, I reasoned, was down to my meat-based brain. Essentially, I was overloading it to an insane degree, and although part of the reason for doing all of this was to get the medical suite to repair my brain, and possibly upgrade it so that this wasn't an issue in the future, that wasn't helpful right now.

The thing that *was* helpful, though?

I already had an expanded mentality.

I had extra space built into the suit, into my helmet, to control the suit's power core. If I wasn't doing anything, the power core was essentially sitting there running on low-power mode, no need to balance equations or zeroes from the zero-point whatnot.

Currently, the extra space basically acted as buffering for the additional mentalities. And when I'd slid a copy of myself into a more primary role, and I'd told it to monitor the time until I woke up and keep an eye out for danger? It'd done it.

It'd been able to interact with my suit at a basic enough level that it could control my weaponized nanites to drive them out as spears and seriously help in that fight.

That it'd had that level of access was a bit freaky, but it was also seriously impressive. Because, normally, when I spun up copies of myself for a hack or whatever? It was a much shorter time thing. Like seconds to a minute or two, that was it.

This time around, I'd been able to spin nine up, and I'd sent five of them into the system, causing trouble for the AI.

One had died straight away, and when I focused on it, I instinctively knew that three more had been killed while I was fighting and unconscious.

The last one? Absolutely no clue, except that it was out there, somewhere in the system, roaming.

If I came across a screen full of porn? I'd know I'd found it. Until then, though, I had four copies left. And all of them, rather than being reabsorbed, had been shifted sideways into the armor's neural capacity.

Reaching out, I erased three without thinking about it, just doing what needed to be done. They were copies of me, after all—it wasn't as if they were actually alive.

Each of them simply went dark, and a portion of the processing power freed up.

The fourth, though? The one that I knew—with no clue how I knew, but that I *knew*—had been the one that had helped me before? When I reached out to it, I got a…a sensation back.

It wasn't begging to be left "alive" or afraid—hell, it didn't feel anything, just that it was ready for the next task, whatever was needed to protect Ingrid and the others, and fuck up those wankers who had started all this shit.

No, what I felt was curiosity. A brief spike of *what-if* as I considered the hacking data.

I was here, in part, to try to get my brain fixed. To unlock whatever doors I needed to in my own mind—my mere meat-based brain—to make sure that later on I could upgrade as much as I needed to.

What if, the sudden thought went, *what if* the changes I needed weren't ones that could only be done by the system?

What if they weren't needed from anyone else at all?

I was learning to do well with the hacks, after all, and I'd spun up additional versions of myself to achieve those aims, when I needed to. So, what if, instead of spinning it up and scrapping it when I had to, I made and kept a dedicated sub-mind for hacking?

Hell, I could do it for all the other bits as well. But, more to the point, there was space in the neural strata for an additional four copies of me, even if only in the short-term.

What if instead of scrapping them, then trying to do everything myself, spinning up more and more based off the current me, and then shutting them down each time…what if I kept one, and dedicated it to Hack and Espionage, then just gave it targets?

Give it a dedicated space in the helmet, and instead of me spinning up copies of me each time, I spun up copies of *it*? Shunting them sideways into additional storage I could upgrade to later?

The more I thought about it, the more I liked the idea.

The problems I was having were coming along because of the sheer amount of data I was trying to deal with, cramming in master-level degrees in subjects I'd never even hit someone with a textbook for, never mind studied.

If I could dedicate a copy of my mind to that, and have it "live" in the neural strata? I could get an overview of the subject, and the basic understanding of the how and why things worked. But instead of the download coming directly to me, it'd go to that sub-mind.

It'd still be me, hence why I "knew" I could do this. And my brief thought about "what if it tries to take me over" was dismissed instantly. The sub-minds weren't separate entities.

They were all me. Their goals were mine; we were all one, so there was no risk, not in that sense.

I could see issues with the project building pretty quickly as I increased their knowledge base, and certainly if I spun up one for Support, another for Hack and Espionage, one for Harvest and...

Hell, I could spin one up for goddamn Ranged Remote Control Weapons and shit if I wanted to, eventually.

The governing issue was *capacity*.

I'd had enough capacity for four basic clones of my mentality to sit there, merrily watching and mentally cheering, while washing down their popcorn with cold beers.

If I dedicated the space that wasn't being used by the system to balance the power core, to instead run a fully expanded copy of myself, with all the Hack tree's and Espionage data unlocked and integrated fully?

I sat for a few minutes, wondering about it, considering it from every angle, before making myself as comfortable as possible, and reaching out, as well as in.

This was going to be complicated, and it wasn't something I could do for long, not least of all because I was going to need the space in my suit to run the power core properly sooner or later.

But if this test worked?

I'd not be constantly on the back foot with the security AI. I'd be attacking it as an equal. Or, hell, I'd have the equivalent of an actual hacker, one that understood the system and our goals, in ways that no outsider ever could.

It'd be like I'd freed up a year or three to go to college and study cyber security, hacking, data in all its forms; then I'd be able to use those systems in ways that my new experience dictated, rather than blundering through the systems, smashing around like a trash panda on coke.

I cleared the space I needed, setting a small amount of space aside for the armor's systems, and mentally marking up a hell of a lot more as potential to improve for later.

If this worked? I could foresee a massive investment in my armor again, and very soon.

That goddamn harvest tool was getting put back in, and I was going hunting again, I silently vowed, as I moved my last sub-mind into position, and looked at the Hack tree. I had a single point available in it.

I hesitated, then gave in to temptation, and pulled up all the trees, focusing on them. Not only did I have a point available in Hack, but a General one left over as well. That was one I'd never assigned to anything. Then I had one War point that was left over, the two Weapon Skills, and two Espionage.

Deciding quickly, I pulled the Hack tree back up, determined that if this worked?

I'd be building my sub-mind up with the Hack point, and both Espionage points to kick this AI's fucking ass.

For now, though? I'd just be using the single Hack point I had available. I hoped that'd get me the most bang for my buck, without too much risk of a shutdown or brain aneurysm if I was totally wrong about all this.

It wasn't a hard choice, really, considering what I was dealing with, and the current situation.

I moved straight to the Control sub-tree, and then down to the one I had in mind. Looking it over, I unconsciously nodded to myself, seeing that it was exactly as I remembered.

Where the other choices were generally more subtle, Assimilate wasn't—not at all.

It was the nuclear option, basically rewriting every branching node of a technological system to make damn sure it had one master, and that master was me alone.

Any system had its own seeds of destruction coded in, no matter how complex—even those systems that were built around reading brainwaves and more, shit that the system's creators was utterly sure couldn't be copied by anyone else—they *all* had a single weakness. For it to check your response, to decide whether you should be let in? It had to know whether you had the rights to it.

The only way it could tell that was by holding a copy of the correct answer inside itself, then checking your presented answer, identity, or token against the one it held.

What Assimilate did was provide the question with an answer, all right—it grabbed the extended handshake protocol, and it overwrote it. Every system linked to it, in checking to see what was going on? In being connected in any way to an infected one? It was fair game, and would eventually be subsumed.

It reached out, and everything it touched became part of it. It spread like a slow inexorable tide of tar, enveloping everything before it, encasing it, and leaving behind more of itself. Every single node behind the spreading wave was coded to me. There were no security questions for another to attempt to answer: the only key was me. And when I attached to the system, it was mine...there was no way it could be anything else.

The operating system that was left in there, running everything, I realized now that I was more familiar with the concept, was a sub-mind. It was one that was dedicated to the system, which was how it didn't need anything to check against the intrusion request.

It knew me, because it *was* me, and nothing else could be. In accessing the system, the sub-mind linked to mine, forming the key and challenge all in one.

The Assimilate package was a horrifically powerful tool, but it was also slow as shit. This was the basic level of it, after all, but looking deeper? I saw that I gained more options to build atop with it.

Where the Plague tree had advanced with Contagion, a spreading infection that claimed all of a system, twisting it to serve me, but staying hidden until it was needed?

There was also the option to essentially envelop the system, using a newly unlocked sub-path of Assimilate.

It was called Tsunami, and although it wasn't exactly what I needed, as it was still fairly slow, it had a massive advantage over the Contagion path.

Contagion needed me to hack the system first, then slide it in, like a Trojan horse, getting it inside, and then activating. Tsunami swept through the target system and enveloped it. It acted as a combination containment and attacking program. Like a moat made up of plague victims, it surrounded the target. Any system that was linked that wasn't as secure? It'd take over and spread through it.

It'd find, map, and cut off secure areas, surrounding them, then extend handshake protocols and wait.

If the system accepted the protocol and reached out? It'd start eating the system that touched it, using that as a path to get inside. If the system sacrificed that extension and somehow cut itself off from the encroaching attack? It was isolated instead.

It was an accumulation of all the shit I'd learned so far, including the new access protocols for the Remote Control Systems, and the data I'd gained from Support, for creating communication pathways. It was built atop the foundations of Hack, and of my own experiences, and it was the baseline level.

It'd evolve with each skill I gained. I couldn't help but grin; if I invested points into the Stealth-based tree next, the options that would come up would be based off this, but with more subtle applications.

There would be ways that Tsunami could be hidden, making it into an even more terrible system, one that could eventually evolve into something that no system could stand against.

It was insane the versatility that could be gained from all these abilities, especially when more of them linked up. That gave me at least some hope for the future, considering that I had yet to figure out some way to deal with the Old Ones and more.

For now, though, I needed to find a way to cut this fucking AI out and roll it back from me.

This was the best chance for that, I decided, selecting it and focusing on my sub-mind, instead of letting the data download into "Me2."

There was a second of Me2's hesitation, as if the system were deciding whether this was allowed, whether I could designate something else, before the nanites seemed to accept that yes, this was still me, and it was simply an extended version, like when I'd done work on my brain before, speeding up the connectors.

This was still attached to me, after all, and as such? The download started.

I felt it still, a cold sensation, as a dozen new connections were opened up. Data streamed in, but not being the focus of the data dump, it was different. It was more like watching a download into a system on your PC, observing a buffer getting filled as more and more data slid in, then seeing the program starting up.

It wasn't entirely like that, unfortunately, as I was still attached to the sub-mind, but the experience was no longer painful. Now it was more…overwhelming.

The sheer insanity of the data was a terror to behold. It felt as though it'd never stop pouring in, until finally, it started to slow, breaking up and reordering as the neural buffers were used, absorbing the data in great swathes of understanding.

I checked the timer I'd created with this sub-mind, and found it'd taken nearly fifteen minutes, but that was all, and...

And it'd worked! I could feel it! The data was there, ready for me. The sub-mind knew what I knew, and although it'd grown in size, the download increasing the space taken up by the sub-mind by about ten percent overall, it was stable!

I grinned to myself and pulled up the Espionage tree, feeling the slight hesitation that came from both me and the sub-mind at the thought of what we were about to do.

"In for a penny, in for a pound..." I muttered, before selecting the Internal path of Cyber-Espionage.

This time, I felt the pain all right, even buffered, even set aside and funneling the data dump into the dedicated sub-mind. The sheer excess? It was insane!

Cyber-Espionage was on the Internal tree, its opposite being Physical Espionage...literally the art of sneaking around and doing whatever was needed to achieve your aims.

Rather than sneaking around James Bond-style, seducing random models who were shagging the bad guy and then acting totally surprised when they were killed by said bad guy, this was the digital version.

It was heavily built around, and included—even here in the absolute most basic version—breaking into secure systems, and raiding them or installing programs.

The shining filaments that spread out from the data and its subsequent trees were insane. Dozens of strings became hundreds, reaching out and tagging more and more, until almost all the skills and abilities I'd unlocked were touched in some fashion.

Assault trees were adjusted with methods to include attaching tracking or hacking devices to the target; drones were upgraded to allow sneaking in and dropping off of signal repeaters or methods of hijacking transmissions. There were methods of injecting data into networks using harvest tools, key designs that could be attached to controllers and data devices to variously work them, protecting or breaking in.

A million different potential changes spread out, little touches of data that changed only a minor spot here or there, but fuck me.

By the end, I was laid on the floor, shaking, a migraine almost blinding me. I tried to focus, shifting as much of the data sideways as I could.

The buffers were holding as much as they could. Still, more tried to unfurl as space became available in there, with more and more being lost to fuzziness as additional data was unable to fit.

I lifted one hand, reaching up to rub at my eyes, blinking in confusion as my gauntlet hit my helmet, and I barely stopped myself from banishing both instinctively.

Not only would it be a terrible fucking idea, while an ancient ship was literally trying to kill me, but if I didn't fully absorb the data into the sub-mind, and I tried to banish the helm?

At best, it'd all be lost.

At fucking *best*. Most likely, it'd roll out and into my brain, erasing and overwriting it, reducing me to a mumbling fool—more so than when I last caught a glimpse of Ingrid in the shower and she invited me in to join her—and that was the best I could hope for.

More likely, I'd be utterly brain-fucked, and then, when I was unable to respond, the AI would march its drones in and I'd be chopped to kibble.

I lifted my hand back up, staring at it out of my right eye. The left twitched constantly and was almost totally blind from the bright-white line that was super-imposed across my vision.

My hand shook like a shitting dog. Hell, I could make martinis like a god right now, and there was sure as shit no way I was stealing any tambourines, I reflected. My own stupid sense of humor bubbled up, even as my innate stubbornness rose as well.

I wasn't losing the game to a goddamn textbook, to a bunch of stupid goddamn details about the best way to stick a spike into a goddamn data store!

Fuck, no. I'd fought Athena, I'd fought Shamal's pets, I'd fought Cristobel and goddamn Beowulf! I'd torn those fuckers a new asshole, and I'd used their corpses to build my home!

I snarled and forced myself back up, pushing my back against the walls. I dragged myself up to a sitting position and huffed out a breath, snorting out the congealing mess into my helm that let me know that I'd had another goddamn nosebleed.

It was insane that these goddamn things gave me that, and even more so that they still did it, even when the vast majority of the download had been caught in the buffers and installed into the sub-mind.

All of this? It was from the connective details, the little touches, and I winced as I checked on how the sub-mind was coping.

The feeling I got back was like it'd had its brain scrubbed with bleach, then it'd been rolled in salt and vinegar and was currently getting a million dirty great needles jabbed in over and over.

It lasted a few more minutes. But with the space in the neural network that was available? It actually worked! A download that, just looking at it, I damn well knew would have left me brain-fried for hours at the very least, was over, and the pain was dying away in a matter of half an hour or so. Even the sub-mind was recovering already.

As I watched, it slowly settled back down, the data processing being sorted time and again as it reconfigured itself. Additional clusters came online as it spread out slowly.

In the end, as it adjusted to the new data and the abilities, I checked the overall space, chewing my lip when I realized that the fucker had taken over nearly sixty percent of the available space. Space that had held four of the sub-minds before, as well as providing enough space to run the armor's power core and more, was now barely able to hold *one* of the sub-minds and the armor's systems, with maybe one of "me" spun up as well.

I shook my head, wondering whether it was worth it. But as I did, I couldn't help but stare at the black spike of the security tower that extended into the middle of the room.

The gleaming black mass of the spike, the numerous ports that could be seen here and there across it, filled a third of the room. And where before it'd seemed to almost loom malevolently…now? Now it seemed weak…and *worried*.

I knew it didn't feel that. It was ridiculous, like I was imposing human emotions on things that couldn't have them—and this was totally different from the way I'd apologized to my fucking bike before I'd ridden it off the cliff and into the sea.

My bike was a *motorbike*—it'd had a soul.

Either way, though, I was no longer feeling like the security station was beyond me. Instead? I reached out and started to gather up a handful of the spare null blocks we'd brought with us.

I'd been planning to use them as ammo, breaking them down when I needed them, for the shotgun, the rail gun, or the gravity cannon. But I now had a fucking far better use for it.

It took twenty minutes to craft. The overlapping layers of crystal and connective latticework required a shitload of effort to get absolutely perfect. But when it was done? I had my first Spike.

CHAPTER FOURTEEN

The Spike, as I named it, was a mixture of three different techs that I'd gained access to. First and foremost, it was a nanofilament blade. The tip was insanely sharp, and, unlike my vorpal blade, I couldn't retract this fucker into my arm when I wasn't using it.

Instead, I created a special sheath on the outside of my right thigh. The dagger's grip stood upright from there, ready to be grabbed and torn free.

The second tech was a nanite-based one, which, yeah, they all were in some respects. But in this case? It was a fuller that ran the length of the blade.

Instead of being used to channel blood away and to enable you to rip the blade out of your victim easier, or being impregnated with a specialist venom or suchlike, as I knew I could do, it held a single strip of reactive cells.

It was made in mimicry of the nanite surge ability, the way that the nanites could connect to one another and spear out, forming structures one atop another to achieve their aim.

In this case, it was an adaptive link. Far less effective than if it was made of real, attuned nanites, this was a pale imitation, and I knew it. But it meant that anything technological that I stabbed this fucker into? The fuller would drive the reactive cells forward and into the target, forming a bond that would in turn connect to the third bit of tech.

That was based on human tech I'd seen before, namely the little device that Dan had given me to plug into the police station right back at the beginning of all this weirdness, further augmented with the Contagion system. It was like a modem, but one that worked against the system it was plugged into, forcibly hacking it. It connected directly to any system to grant me access that just wasn't possible coming in through a more acceptable method.

It formed a link and spread my control into whatever device I'd just stabbed. And as I had absolutely no intention to use the ports it provided? That would nicely bypass the first layer of any security system.

Once I was connected? The sub-mind would attack the system, linked remotely through the Contagion system, burrowing in, as the beachhead was established by a single-use deployment of nanites.

Or it would, once I had some goddamn nanites to spare.

For now, the attack was going to be a lot harder, but at least it could only get better. I sure as shit wasn't putting any more goddamn nanites into anything, considering I'd lost another three hundred and seventeen to the repairs needed to my neural clusters after that fucking download overspilled.

Either way, though, it wasn't long before I was holding my Spike, admiring the gleam of light from the blade as I twisted it, catching the dim light that reflected up from the buzzing and damaged machinery below.

Then I flicked it up, caught it in the air, and stabbed the fucker into the security system.

My sub-mind surged as soon as the connection was made. A good dozen individual die appeared in the air before me, twisting around. More and more of them materialized in a wave, stacking high atop one another and low, rolling as if they floated on a sea all around me, hundreds of them and...

And then they started to wink out.

They appeared as red twenty-sided die. Each of the individual faces spun; a secondary layer beneath that spun counterclockwise to the upper layers' clockwise.

And as I focused on them, they blurred, flickering out. Like a creeping tide of black and gold, it rose all around; the reds darkened all the way to black as the sides spun furiously, and in a distant wave, the blacks slowly turned to gold.

As more and more gold nodes appeared, I felt the change. The sub-mind wasn't doing this alone. Oh no—each of the nodes it took over, it converted into another sub-processor, adding its strength to the assault.

A handful became dozens, and as there were hundreds of reds, slowly the rising tide of gold grew. With each red that fell to the black, I sensed the change, that the security AI was being cut out of the system, losing that node as it was locked to us, slowing it infinitesimally.

As the black turned to gold, though? No longer was the processing power of that node simply lost to the overall security AI—now that node fought for us!

The wave of claimed territory surged and grew second by second, until, in less than a minute—a minute in which I'd barely even tried to help—the fight was won.

Literally, the final lockouts fell, and the system around me unfurled, accepting me.

I drew in a deep breath, stunned at the power of the sub-mind, and I grinned evilly. The tables had fucking turned all right, and it was time to pull my finger out.

Searching, I detected the local nodes welcoming me. I fell inside the system, finding branching paths of system architecture. There were billions of systems, but only a few, despite being "available" in the system overview as I looked at it, actually responded.

I reached out, feeling my way through, as the sub-mind continued to work, cataloging, sealing, and securing.

The local power systems were...*fuck*. They were powered elsewhere in the ship and then fed here. And regardless of the reason the security AI hadn't pulled the plug on us, yet?

I didn't see it leaving the power up for long once I started to produce my own waves of mini sentinels, and I mentally marked that as one of the first things to sort out.

The ship was shown in a wireframe drawing. Some sections were grayed out as unresponsive. Others were red and gently pulsing, showing that there were issues there, like flooding, or solid red, indicating I was blocked from there by additional security systems that were forming a physical break.

Still more were a pale blue, including the area I now stood in, showing that I had control, but that it was weak. As I watched, a slowly spreading tide moved out from where I "stood" in the image, leaving behind its gently glowing golden nodes.

As these came on, it displayed just how many sections were dead in the network as well. Even here, where the ship still had power and some operational systems, it was perhaps one in twenty of the nodes that responded, that was all.

I focused, looking around and bringing up the various accessible and responsive systems, finding three points where systems were currently drawing power.

One was the security station here, and that had its own dedicated emergency internal battery farm, one that was gently humming away at 76 percent. That was the maximum it could manage, I saw, the degraded symbols clear as they pulsed over the power nodes. More points around the room below lit up as I searched, showing that there were still usable connections here and there, but only a small number.

The machine that had been producing the sentinel "drones" was marked as orange and red in places. But nowhere was it black, I was pleased to see.

It was badly damaged, though, and although I got a general clue about the machine—it was literally a factory, just a much larger and more complex one than I had access to—I couldn't check for any information on what it could build.

The third and final system was what I could only guess was a transport link of some kind. It was clearly fucked up: sections were totally blocked, and the rails that led up and down it were buckled and twisted. The doors were marked as sealed, and non-responsive when I queried them, but for whatever reason, the section still drew power. I cut the fucker off, recognizing a section that was being powered for literally no reason beyond a program said it should be, "just because."

I searched the local area, spending a few minutes to make sure that no fucker could get to me from either of the corridors that led from the AI's end of the ship to the security office, nor the transport link, and sent C1 to weld them shut. I got it to add a layer of null blocks across the outer mechanism for the doors as well, making it very clear that the only way they would open again was if they were entirely cut through with a powerful laser, or if it was done from our side.

That done, I moved A2 and A3 into the room below, setting them up to cover the entrance that the security AI had used until now. The rooms around this one were either showing as entirely lost—in the case of one on the far side, and underneath, which I assumed was simply smashed into the bedrock of the ocean— or badly damaged.

The rooms leading back toward the areas I'd already been in were marked as intact in two cases, one buried and destroyed and flooded in the last one, but all damaged.

Looking over the markers, as near as I could tell from the sensors that still functioned, they were pretty much in the same condition as the rooms we'd passed through. And the corridors?

Battered to shit and full of scrap.

That was fine, though, because a little careful examination showed that only the very basic repairs had ever been done in here as well. That might not have sounded like "good" news to anyone else, and certainly not to anyone who had seen the ships before now, back when they were marvels of tech and design.

But for a scrapper like me?

They were more than good enough.

I hesitated, my thoughts on the skills I'd learned with Tommy, making me wince as I realized that I'd never actually returned his damn bike...I'd gotten so distracted with Ingrid, and then the fighting, the hunting, and finally being, you know, kidnapped and tortured for *three fuckin' years*, that I'd just never gone back.

The best he had to think of me right now was that I'd taken his bike and fucked off. The worst? Well, he'd have been guessing all the shit I'd done had been a front, to make him open up so I could steal from him. He probably hoped I was dead, and I silently cursed myself for getting so distracted by my own life that I'd never gone back.

Tommy was a miserable old bugger at times, and when he'd taught me to weld to earn a few euros with him, he'd been at a really low point.

His ex had fucked off with a younger guy, a *much* younger guy, and she'd taken their savings with her. She'd even taken the ring he'd planned to propose to her with, and he'd seen it a few days later in a pawn shop window.

That was how bad it was, and just how rock bottom he'd been. And when I'd gotten to know him a bit more? He'd once admitted—while in his cups—that he'd been planning to take his bike for a last ride, then go out in a blaze of glory against a mountainside pass we both knew.

He'd denied it afterward, said it was all a joke. But now? As I looked at the fucked-up systems and trashed areas, and I saw it with eyes he'd basically beaten and drilled into me? I saw value here that I never would have before.

I owed him the effort to go and make things right, and more, and I silently vowed I'd go to him and make sure he was all right soon.

I blinked the sudden burn of shame-filled tears away, taking a deep breath, and forced myself to get to work. No matter what he'd taught me, if I didn't pull my finger out of my arse and get to work now? I'd not get a second chance.

There was no way that AI was sitting back and twiddling its ones and damn zeroes, or whatever they did.

Reaching out, I summoned C1, tracking the power conduits, and mentally marking them up.

I could see the minimum and maximum range markers on them. With a little searching through my general construction details, I soon found what I was looking for.

Energy, like light, sound, and more, could be beamed from one point to another, rather than needing cabling.

The technology wasn't even that complicated, all things considered. Looking the details over, it was basically a laser, which I had plenty of, thanks to fighting the security AI's units, and a photo-voltaic cell, like I'd made for the solar panels.

The laser needed a bit of tweaking, so that it broadcast a level of energy that could be collected, converted to electricity and rebroadcast, rather than just burning a hole in the cells. But that was just fiddly bits.

It took all of ten minutes to plot out a path that would get power sent back toward the converters and the little turret system that I'd built before. I got a rough estimate of seven hours to do the work, if I sent C1 to do it all now, or fourteen, if instead of just making each unit to order, I instead built a couple of converters, then several factories to churn out the relevant parts.

I chose the fourteen, gnashing my teeth as I did it. But if I had C1 do it all one at a time, although it'd be quicker, each part I needed after that?

I'd have the same issues: make a single part, then another, then another. With this setup we were building? It'd churn out the parts I needed constantly, stacking them ready for the next phase, or whatever else I told it to instead.

A little part of me pointed out that if I pulled C3 up, having it join in as well, that would massively increase the production speed, but I had another job for it.

I'd gained access to the security node, and with it, not just the rooms on the way I'd come up to the security station, but three more on the way "forward."

The first thing I'd done, as soon as I saw that those sections were slowly converting over to me and my golden control nodes, was make sure that if anything started along the corridors toward me, I'd know, thanks to a series of sensors on the roof, floor, and walls. I also realized that the only reason my Conceal had worked before? It was the gravity inversion.

I'd been doing it so that I presented as small a target as possible to them if they started firing, essentially lying flat and floating along, "falling" toward the enemy. If I'd done it while creeping along? I'd have been spotted as soon as I was too close to one of the sensors on the floor. No wonder they'd been firing randomly in all directions: they'd known I was there somewhere, but not exactly where, so they'd been firing blind.

If they started to come? I'd wait until they were nearly to me, and then I'd shut off the power broadcasts in those rooms. Hopefully that'd send the drones clattering to the floor, and I could retrieve them one by one, powering them up and converting them to my side.

Either way, though, for now, the power was coming from farther "forward," so I didn't want to draw the attention of the AI to it, as it was basically powering my section now.

I had options, though, and that was a relief. I turned and started to jog, then snorted at the stupidity of it all. I reached out, manipulating gravity to make myself fall toward the far end of the corridor.

A little twist, and I slowed as I approached the farthest wall, then "down" shifted sideways; I was falling along another corridor, then another.

Only a few more minutes, and I landed with a grunt, catching myself and half running as I tried to keep myself upright, before plowing shoulder-first into the wall with a curse.

I'd totally missed the point I should have flipped over there, and trying to do so at the last second, I flipped it too far, essentially jerking myself into the wall.

I laid there, literally slumped against the floor, blinking, glaring up at the dent I'd made with my shoulder, head, and hip, and the subsequent shining scratches I'd left sliding down it, as I muttered to myself.

"Well, that's fucking embarrassing."

Forcing myself to my feet, I set off, limping this time, into the room and over to C3, where it was happily stacking more of the null blocks into a pile.

The hoppers were full on all the converters, and I checked them over, giving C3 a series of new orders, before using my gravity inverter to lift twenty of the null blocks as if they were almost weightless.

It was a bit of a waste of power, but as near as I could tell, the zero-point module in my power core was able to make much more than I needed for now. Using it for this?

No great issue. Sure, if I wanted to use it on a hundred different things at once, or to power something much bigger and so on, it'd run out pretty quick. It was a small power core—hook it up to the ship? Nope.

However it worked, it generated constant power, and if it wasn't used, it just stopped, more or less. There was a hard ceiling on how much power the system could generate and how fast, but as long as I used it just under the top limit? I could use it as much as I wanted.

Hook it up to a car? Fuck yes—it'd run it for years, if not centuries. It was all a matter of scale. The core could only generate so much at a time, which was the point.

I jogged back along the corridor, holding the null blocks and half expecting at any second to be attacked somehow. But, wonder of wonders—this time, at least—I was left to it.

While I was doing that, though, C3 used a handful of null blocks to form up and place a series of small repeater stations, heading up to the hull of the ship. Then it was going to move from there back along to the security center and lay them every hundred or so meters, making damn sure that the signals overlapped, so I could easily communicate.

Working from the security station side back to our little production center? That was C1's job, bringing the power.

In theory, this provided us with communication with the surface, as well as a protected fallback position, and with the turrets being there already, it was reasonably secure. Best of all, with the factories having already been set up to make those turrets? Once we had the area powered, I'd be able to start repairing, rebooting, and hacking the little drone units.

They'd be sent to recover and run the factories—leaving some there, just in case we lost the security station—but most of them would be shlepping the factories up here, and setting up to build us a real center of power.

I pulled up the notifications as I neared the security station again, nodding to myself in satisfaction as I read over the latest one.

Quest Updated!

Evolving Quest updated: Repair and Renovate: Level 1: Completed!

Congratulations, Biological Weapon Variant #113782491603! You have eliminated the local security forces rallied against you by the security AI that protects Facility 6B. As it does not recognize your right of access, and has marked you as a trespasser, you must eliminate or convert this security AI, to claim the facility.

~~Part One: Secure the local area, eliminating all active sentinels to gain the following reward~~: **Complete!**

- +1 War Point
- +Access to Level 2 of this section of the Evolving Quest

~~Part Two: Secure the local security net, by penetrating and locking the security AI out of the local node to gain access to the next tier of the evolving quest to gain the following reward~~: Complete!

- +1 Hack Point
- +Access to Level 2 of this section of the Evolving Quest

*

Quest Updated!

Evolving Quest updated: Repair and Renovate: Level 2: Unlocked!

Congratulations, Biological Weapon Variant #113782491603! You have established a beachhead in Facility 6B, but beware! The security AI will now be reawakening long-dead emergency systems to deal with your incursion. Prepare for an extended assault!

Part One: Secure the local area and survive the incoming assault, eliminating all attackers, and establishing a secure and defensible perimeter to gain the following reward:

- +1 War Point
- +Access to Level 3 of this section of the Evolving Quest

Part Two: Increase your control over the local security net, by penetrating and locking the security AI out of a secondary node to gain access to the next tier of the evolving quest and gain the following reward:

- +1 Hack Point
- +Access to Level 3 of this section of the Evolving Quest

"Always gotta love being rewarded for shit I was doing anyway," I muttered, shifting slightly and grabbing at a block in my arms as it slid sideways, almost dropping half a dozen others as I caught it. Muttering over my own inability to make two trips, and the need to always do it in one, just like I used to with the damn grocery shopping, I hurried into the security office, before dumping them all on the floor, and looking down through the old "window" at the room below.

If the AI was, as the quest suggested, waking older units up, and resurrecting "long-dead security systems," then I was quite possibly fucked.

Then again...I did have a team up above, in the yacht, didn't I?

I checked the timer, finding I still had twelve hours until the communication links were done, and again, for a nice change, I cursed.

I didn't have time to do it the "right" way, and I didn't dare leave and go up to the yacht myself. If I did that, I had to bet that as soon as I left, it'd launch a full-scale assault and find ways around my security.

It'd also, no doubt, send something up after the yacht if it could see that it was linked to me. It'd be fair game, and regardless of the risk of exposure, it'd probably have a go at sinking it.

That meant that I had limited time here, and I'd better make the most of it.

I was betting that the reason the AI hadn't taken the power down was the same reason it'd not swamped me with dozens more sentinels already.

It needed time to make them, and it had limited numbers when it came to the cores, which was why I'd only faced a few at a time. I was betting the fucker had been, or now was, scouring the ship for them.

If it was waking up "long-dead" units? I bet the fucker was digging through trash piles and more, trying to find anything it could lay its grubby little...*digits?*...on.

Whatever.

The point was that if I was it, I'd either keep the power on and rely on being able to out-produce me with drones and swamp them over my defenses, or I'd keep the power up right until the beginning of the fight, and then I'd take it down.

That way, if I'd spent all my effort on making drones, I'd be fucked when the power transmission that they needed—not having their own individual cores—cut out.

That's what I'd do, anyway.

There was a chance that it'd been programmed that it couldn't cut the power, and that was it—in which case it was going to be really pissed when I did.

I didn't know how long I had, but the basics of a plan were there already. First of all, thanks to the simple gantry system I'd already had built in here, the turret could be fired in any direction to cover the security station. I'd only installed the core in there after the fight was over, though, so I was hoping that it didn't know that the turret was running under its own power, and its own limited sentience, rather than needing a drone to manually aim and fire it.

There were three possible avenues of attack from where it was to get to me and retake the security station—well, four if I counted the corridor that led up from the turrets as well...but I was fucked if it cut me off in that direction, so to hell with it.

The three possible routes were: firstly, in through the flooded section, and flood the ship. I gave that a low chance of being used, mainly because it'd wipe out most of their weapons' effects, massively giving me and the vorpal blade the advantage, and it would damage the ship, which was the opposite of its entire reason for existing.

Second, the corridor ahead of the security station and leading to it. I gave that a low chance. Yeah, they might take it, but the sections leading to it also led to the third option, and I'd already had this corridor sealed with null block coating. Also, well, there was the turret.

It was now a quad, having originally been two separate turrets that were now joined together.

The real limitation on the weapon was power, as each barrel fired separately, so you could fire essentially continuously, without a concern of it overheating too much.

That was also the problem for the section below, where the factory that had been making the drones was housed.

It was badly damaged now, but I bet it was something that could be fixed up in only a few hours by the custodians.

That, I was betting, would be the main target for any attacks—or at least it'd be mine, if I was attacking.

Take down the power, take down the opponent's ability to make replacements by totally fucking the factories, rather than the minor damage they'd managed to do so far, and only then attack the security station.

That's the point when I'd send in a secondary wave from the corridor that lay straight ahead, if it had it.

When the fight was close, but could still be won, I'd send them then, to break my opponent and force them to panic and fall back.

Then I'd…I shook my head. Then, *if* my opponent had repaired the goddamn power relays, *as I was doing*, I'd use that, and the power that was now available in the old powerless areas, to send drones in and make sure I killed the fucker.

That made me think.

What were the chances it knew what I was doing?

Because if it did, and it was a little brighter than I had been originally thinking, then it might have realized that the things that were holding it back, namely the rules about not trashing the place and so on, were also rules that were stupid.

If so?

Nice easy solution: wait until I'd provided power to those sections, and I'd built up a nice store of repair materials from the old machines that were trash anyway, but that it'd be banned from "damaging."

Then turn off the power, roll over me and force me back. If I survived long enough to run? No worries. Retake the security station—somehow, considering my tech that was in there now—then turn the power back on, and use the drones to overcome me.

It'd be able to make the most of the situation and fix itself up a load more.

That was a lot of what-ifs, but the important details were clear. If they weren't attacking me right now? It was for a good reason. That reason was almost certainly resources. It'd thrown as much at me as it could so far, and I'd survived. If it was following anything like a common sense or logic-based approach, it'd have to scale up each attack.

That meant that the next attack? It'd be at least double the enemies I'd faced already, either in power and lethality, or in numbers.

I needed to plan for double that, just in case.

Mobile heavy weapons, and a fuckload of little bastards zerg-ing, I guessed, frowning now as I considered how I'd deal with that.

Well, the turret up here would make short work of them, so their first priority would be to take it down.

Either heavy weapons, or a mad rush to overwhelm it, I imagined.

I had control of the sensors now, so I was betting against stealth; it'd be too easy to spot.

The first priority was definitely power, and to get our own power systems up and running here, I needed to fix those goddamn factories.

I reached out and checked on C1—C2 was already outside of my range—and I changed C1's orders, as much as I hated to do so.

It was now to install the signal repeaters in place of C3, along with the power relays. That was a pain in the arse, as it increased the time to finish the power project from twelve more hours to fifteen, but it freed up C3.

I ordered that bugger to run to the turrets as fast as possible, and to take three of them down, leaving two with overlapping fields of fire, and it was to bring the turrets, rough and ready as they were, to here, setting them up in the corridor that led forward to the enemy from the construction facility below me.

It was also to set up two of the turrets on the other side of the door—not on my side—but ready to whittle down the enemy as they approached along the corridor.

That was the plan anyway, and I marked the third one to be set up outside of the security station, facing the other corridor that headed forward as well, just in case.

Beyond that? Well, we had a few converters working on null blocks back there, and we also had a bunch of factories working on the parts for more turrets.

We'd just not been doing anything with them, because we had no power, nor cores for them, so even if I could power it, it'd be brain-dead.

Well, that wasn't a problem anymore, because I also had a sub-mind that was ready to work, and that I bet could handle the job of directing some turrets.

That was a massive advantage, now that I thought about it. There was no way that the AI could know I had sub-minds, let alone that it could be used to take over a gunner's role.

I checked the power relay stations. They were still in production, with at least an hour to go before the first could even be laid.

That made me swear, a lot.

Then I forced myself to grow up, and got to work.

First job was the factories. As much as I wanted the drones, and hell, anything else that might give me a load of weapons to watch my back, the sooner I got the factories back up and running, the sooner I could get a power facility working.

The sooner I got that? Well, fuck it, you got the idea.

I grabbed a handful of the null blocks, and leapt through the open window in the floor, falling toward the factories, and caught myself with the gravity inverter, slowing. I landed, crouching to absorb the impact that now felt like I'd barely jumped off a table.

The grin that had started to form at the fall, and how much better I was getting with the inverter, was wiped away when I looked at the lines of damage carved into the device.

There were a dozen places where the outer cowling and housing had run like butter under a blowtorch, rehardening and spot-welding sections together once the beams had been shut off.

The overall device was maybe six meters wide by twelve long, and although it was more or less solid at my end, with a hopper for materials, the far end was circular and ran around a roller system that was clearly designed to deposit the fresh creation out of the far side.

I hesitated, frowning as I looked over it, and wishing that I either had the nanites to spare to upgrade my armor to spin off a sub-mind dedicated to Support and construction tasks, or that I could get Zac down here.

Neither was an option, though, so instead I scanned the damn thing.

It took twenty minutes, examining it from one side to the other, to build up a complete picture of it in my system. After a minute or ten of puzzling crap out, I had the beginnings of a plan.

First, there were a few sections that had been damaged that were totally useless, as near as I could tell, including backups for the power supply in case the main power was cut off, and it was needed.

Yeah, great—hell, *wonderful* even—considering I'd blown the main power connection apart for it, and I was going to have to replace that.

The problem was that, as near as I could tell, the backup generator for it hadn't worked in at least a thousand years.

It had one, though, and although it was damaged, I could see how it worked, and why it was knackered now. I saved that part of the plan for later, and moved on.

A materials sorter was slagged: three arms that were a bit like insanely high-tech 3D printers and a memory module were all knackered as well. The rest was more or less cosmetic damage, and I didn't give two shits about that.

Ten more minutes passed while I scanned a working arm, and then got to work with my creation tool, melting down the three damaged arms and rebuilding them.

The hopper took maybe five minutes, and then I was up through the hole and into the security station, gathering the rest of the null blocks and back out again.

Half an hour later, I had everything bar the memory module fixed. The factory was powering up; the "draw" for the power that I'd been able to replace the original connection with was lower than the old one had probably been, as I only had basic levels of that tech unlocked, but fuck it.

Pulling up the factory and scanning through it, I double, then triple-checked it, then stood there, head bowed as I tried to maintain my cheerful fuckin' disposition.

The memory module was slagged, and clearly that'd been deliberate, because the secondary module was happy to house orders, but didn't have *designs*. That meant that although I could program it to make things for me, provided I had the materials, I also had to have the design unlocked.

The ones that had been stored in it? They were a collection of melted exotic metals, alloys, and silica now.

Forcing myself to be calm, I instead brought up the plans I had access to, sorting through them and pulling up designs I knew I could make and would be helpful in this situation.

I'd even scanned the coffee machine a week ago, when it looked like Scylla was going to smash it up. Although I'd *love* a cup right now, there was no point in making a coffee machine.

Instead, I loaded the hopper with smashed-to-shit drones, and after half an hour of scanning the various surviving and intact parts of around fifteen drones, I finally had a completed blueprint that should work.

I fed it in and ordered the factories to produce one of my own design.

Clambering around to the far side, and holding my shotgun ready, I waited, watching as the little bastard was assembled in a matter of minutes. It was heart-stopping when it first powered up, the limbs shaking gently as it ran tests.

The drones I'd faced here were much smaller than the normal sentinels. Only half of them had fucking weapons, for a start, and they were less powerful. The arms and upper bodies were replaced with simple laser systems much like mine had.

The difference was they were about a quarter of the size of my "A" models, partly due to the lack of a core, and probably so they were a fuckload cheaper to produce.

I used similar designs to produce the new drones like the ones the enemy had, with the same lasers that the enemy drones had been armed with, but giving the offensive units a bit of basic armoring that the original drones had lacked.

There was one that was armed, to actually fight, and another that just had arms, but no weapons. Like before, they had four legs: three that were more or less solid, bending only at the "knee," and the other a tentacle that interlocked with the wall. I reasoned that gave them decent mobility, but I removed the armoring from the ones that were to have actual hands and be used to carry shit.

Any reduction in cost here was welcome, and considering I'd been half expecting that as soon as the first one powered up, it'd attack me? I was just pleased the bugger didn't.

As soon as I knew that they were working, and I confirmed in the local cybersphere that it was actually being guided by my sub-mind, and not just biding its time, I started the main production run.

I ordered five of the models with arms, sending one up and through the window to the security station, one that was to act as a runner from here up to that unit, and three more that were to work in here.

The room was still full of scrap, after all, and although the factory that produced the units currently had been maintained and even repaired on a fairly regular basis, it seemed, the rest of the machines certainly hadn't been.

I ordered the three to collect the scrap and load it into the hoppers. The one that was a runner for this room was to carry completed sections up the wall to the security station, where it would hand them over to the unit I'd sent up there.

Once the five of them were done, and were working? It was time to get the basic power plant up and running.

Looking it over, in the designs and data I had, the best method I had to generate power, and without complicated regulation systems that would require dedicated AI, RI, or sentient controllers, or hell, even nanites, which were a form of RI?

I needed to go to fusion.

It struck me for a second how ridiculous it was that I, a man who should never be allowed near anything even vaguely breakable, and certainly not near anything complex, was shrugging off the creation of a nuclear fusion plant as part of my daily life.

Especially as I guessed that I needed water for it, in a place that was underwater and pretty much doing everything it could to keep said fuckin' water out, and that to make use of said water, I needed to create from scratch a literal fusion generator.

Something that the scientists of the world had been frantically trying to do for years, I was considering as more of a case of was it worth bothering with or should I step over that level.

I reviewed the tech I had available, and for a second contemplated spending my General point on upgrading the Support tree to allow exotic storage. Then I shook that dumb-ass thought out of my head.

No, nuclear fusion was simple and reliable enough that it'd do for my needs. For now.

I reviewed the data, grinning and nodding to myself when I saw that the best idea didn't even need the damn water—I could just convert some of the null blocks into liquid tritium and deuterium. Then I needed to set up a second converter on the far side of the power plant to collect and convert the helium that would be generated as a by-product.

I decided that the converter option was a much better one than fucking around with processing seawater. Although it'd burn through my blocks, it'd also create additional oxygen on the other side, and I was a fan of having some of that around.

The converter that I'd need to collect and process gases was slightly more advanced than the standard one, but I still had the plans, and so did the factories now.

I also decided that making use of the helium like this was a better idea as I didn't think attacking the enemy while sounding like a cartoon duck was really the way I wanted to go out.

C1 was dispatched up to the security station above, and began setting up the first of the three sets of relays that had been completed so far, while G1, the first of the gophers—go-fer this, go-fer that—was tasked with running back and forth to it with the kit as each section got access to power.

When G1 and G2 weren't running those parts about? They were carrying up the sections for the fusion plant and setting them out to be constructed up there.

The plan was that if it was done up there, instead of down here? The enemy was less likely to be able to take it out, and if they wanted to take it at all, they'd have to hammer through my defenses to get to it.

I was also conscious that I'd need C3 to actually assemble the power plant, as soon as it was finished with the turrets.

It was still setting up the first one, so I got back to work as well, pulling up the next stage in my master plan, while damn well hoping the security AI didn't kick the door in at any second.

CHAPTER FIFTEEN

"I know what it says, James, but this is ridiculous." Ingrid sighed, sitting back in the cabin on board the yacht, gesturing to the plaque that the little custodian had delivered.

It stood there now, silent and calm, as Zac attempted to do…*whatever* he was doing. He was certainly cursing a lot as he tried to plug a cable into the thing.

Ingrid reached out and picked up her coffee cup. She smiled her thanks at Casey as the steward suggested to Scylla that she make the coffee "this time" while the ancient warrior focused on the fight ahead.

"This is best," Scylla grunted after a few seconds of silence, most of it spent glaring at her nemesis, which sat there in all its chrome-plated smugness.

"I understand how you feel, Ingrid. In truth, I feel the same way, knowing that even now, Steve may be fighting for his life, far below us. We're just sitting here, relaxing, but we have to be realistic." James sat across from Ingrid, wearing an immaculate "yachting" outfit made of crisp whites and pale blues, looking far more likely to be the owner than she or Steve ever did, Ingrid silently admitted to herself.

"If we go now…" The older man started, before holding a hand up imploringly as Scylla started to rise. "My lady Scylla, please, let me finish." He waited as she growled, before sliding back into her seat.

"Thank you." He inclined his head. "Okay, *if* we were to go to him now, against his clear orders, then what? We have no way of entering the ship without violence and destruction. We don't know where the entrance is, what the control systems look like, nor how to communicate with the ship to request entrance. Think of it as a sunken submarine. Should we force entry? We may flood it, ruining anything that we intended to recover." He lifted his hands in a "what can we do" gesture as Jonas spoke up.

"It's true, I'm afraid." The rangy big American twisted his mouth, as if displeased to admit to it. "Believe me, I want more than anything to get in there and take advantage of the ship's gifts—" He held a hand up as if imploring patience. "I know, I know, we don't know if it can 'upgrade' us like it did Steve, or if we'd even survive the process. That man's a hell of a stubborn bastard. I can imagine he died on the table, and simply refused to stay dead, getting back up and forcing his body to play along.

"The point is, we all want to get in there, and to be very clear, even if I am upgraded, or I'm not, Steve could have killed me easily, and after my actions, I had no reason to expect anything else from him. He didn't. That simple action, not to mention saving my goddamn life, that of my team, and healing me of advanced cancer? I'm his man now, regardless. If he chooses to upgrade me? I'd surely like that and be appreciative. If he decides it's not for the likes of me? I'm still loyal."

"And thank you, Jonas. Steve and I appreciate that." Ingrid forced a smile as she reminded herself to not take offense at the fact that everyone, *everyone* else knew and respected that she and Steve were an item, and that they were equals.

She ran the recycling site, and as much as she loved him, he generally just hit things *very* hard. Still, some of the team made her feel like she was there as the entertainment for "the boss," a secretary kept around for her body rather than her skills and mind.

"But as I was sayin'…" Jonas went on, nodding at her comment and showing absolutely no sign he'd even spotted her subtle point. "If we were to go in there? The damn thing is *miles* long. At least half of it is flooded. If it's only a hundred meters, or even two wide? As you said he described? That's still enough space there for thousands of rooms.

"If it's say, two hundred meters, by two hundred, and then 'only'…" He lifted his hands, making air quotes as he spoke, clearly still coming to terms with its size. "Say *three* miles long? Because Steve said it was miles long, plural? That's around a hundred and twenty *thousand* square meters. That's what, a couple hundred soccer pitches in length? Pitch black, with limited air, limited light, and crumbling architecture?

"We could spend a year searching for him, and not find him, walking past each other in connecting corridors and never know it. And that doesn't even include the enemy," he pointed out, gesturing to the little custodian robot thing that had brought the message to Ingrid, as she sat working on her laptop on the upper deck only ten minutes earlier.

Her scream, as much as it embarrassed her to admit it, had carried enough that it roused the entire crew in seconds, when it had clambered up over the edge of the railing to stop a matter of inches away.

Worst still was that she'd been so engrossed in her studies that she'd totally missed it, until she looked up, thinking it was James to remind her to get some sleep.

Instead, she'd stared into the gleaming "eye" of the thing as it stared at her. She'd screamed in a way that she'd never admit to Steve, and she'd hit it with her empty coffee cup as she scrambled backward, falling off the end of the bench seat and yanking her laptop off the table when she'd caught her foot in the charging cable. She glanced at it again in dismay, the shattered screen making it clear that it was well beyond repair.

"I know what you're saying, Jonas, and I understand your other, none too subtle point. Again, we appreciate you, and your advice. But honestly, the notion of sitting here, relaxing with coffee while he fights for his life against an army of these machines?" She shook her head. "It's not that I don't believe Steve can win. I'm sure he can. I love him for who he is, and I know him better than any of you. If he decided he wanted the day to last longer? I wouldn't put it past him to reach up and drag the sun back a few hours.

"As much as I joke about how stubborn and unstoppable he is? He also has weaknesses, ones that could ruin everything he's hoping to achieve. Steve destroyed half of Athena's island base when he lost his temper. He tore the roof off the building. He smashed a cell that was deliberately designed to hold the

Arisen. A cell that was *literally* made to hold his kind, that he'd been tortured to death in a hundred times.

"He lost his temper and he tore through it, killing all the Arisen who stood against him. *That* was impossible, and everyone knew it, until he did it. Now he's fighting for the ship, and while I don't doubt he'll win? He might destroy everything to do so. I love the man, but to him every problem is a nail, one that he has to hammer into the wall."

"And you have another option?" James tried to hide his smile at her description of Steve.

"We send this thing back to him with a reply. He said he's working on securing an area, and then he'll push forward, claiming more of the ship. As soon as it's secure, he'll guide us down. I understand why he's doing what he's doing, but he's leaving his greatest strength up here."

"Look, darlin'—" Jonas held a hand out as if to mansplain the situation in terms she'd understand.

"I'm not your 'darling,'" Ingrid snapped, glaring at him. "And if you feel the need to interrupt me every time I speak, you can go downstairs and leave the adults to talk. Are we clear?"

Jonas froze, then nodded silently.

"Now, as I was saying, he's leaving his greatest strengths up here, wasted." Ingrid turned to look over at Zac, who was on his back now, half underneath the robot, squinting at the almost organic panels that covered it. "Zac?"

"Yeah?" he answered distractedly, before cursing as Casey kicked the bottom of his foot. "Fuck's sake, Case! I...owww!" He grabbed his head, having jerked his head up and smacked it into the underside of the robot.

"Well, thank you for making my point so eloquently, Zac." Ingrid sighed, laying one hand over her eyes, and trying not to swear. "So! As I was saying, he's leaving his greatest strengths up here. Namely our diversity, and Zac's engineering abilities. While I understand that Steve is able to take the fight to the enemy in ways we can't, he says that he's establishing a production center to make more of these, and that we're to wait here."

"But you think that we'd be of more use there now?" James asked. "His reasoning is clear. He could lose that area, and if it's overrun, currently all he'd lose is materials. While he doesn't say it, he makes the point that with us there to defend as well, it would limit his offensive options."

"And it would, in his mind," Ingrid agreed. "He's focused on defending us, on splitting his focus, because so far, he's the only one who can do these things. The difference is that he's already demonstrated that there are other ways to do this. He created the devices to produce the solar panels and left them with Zac and the team. They work so long as they're loaded and set to work. I can't believe that these robots are less capable. Surely there'd be a way that he could order them to obey Zac or—"

"That's a point," Zac chimed in, grinning suddenly. "Why's it still here?"

"What?" Ingrid growled, frowning at the irrepressible Aussie in confusion and irritation as, once again, she was interrupted.

"The robot," he clarified. "Why's it here? I mean, it gave us the message. Why didn't it fuck off back to him? Surely he needs it. It's one of the construction thingies, right? It can make anything, so why's it here?"

"Because..." Ingrid whispered, her eyes widening as she saw it. "Because he's sent it to help us! It'd have returned to him otherwise! Robot, can you hear me?" She sat up straight and looked at it.

It stayed as it had, since handing the plaque over, utterly stationary, watching her. Since the others had come running, the only reaction it'd had to them all was to look when one of them moved to join the group, and then to return to watching her.

"It's a machine," Zac pointed out.

"I know that, thank you, Zac!" Ingrid replied, trying not to roll her eyes.

"Yeah, sorry. I mean, it thinks as a machine. It can't talk—at least as far as we know—so asking it questions is pointless. It needs orders, like..." He cast about the deck, before grinning and scooping up her laptop, setting it down on the table next to her. "Ask it, I mean, *order* it to fix that."

"Fix this." She pushed the laptop forward, then winced and added "Please," her innate nature and upbringing refusing to let her give an order, even to a machine, without being polite.

The response to the order was immediate. Two of the arms lunged forward, stabbing out and plucking the laptop from the table. Jonas's team leveled weapons, and Scylla dragged a short, evil-looking hammer around, ready to attack.

The custodian ignored them all, as it flipped the laptop around and around, scanning it, examining it, then reached out and plucked the null block that Zac had tried to offer it earlier—like he'd been bribing a puppy to play with him—from his hand.

One of its tentacles split a dozen times at the tip. Tinier and tinier filaments broke free and latched onto the laptop screen, and the null block was shaved of minuscule amounts of materials. It dug into the screen, somehow weaving the glass back together, adjusting the various sections that made the screen into a "screen" rather than a pane of broken technological glass.

In less than a minute, the laptop was handed back, along with the block.

Ingrid took it, staring at the gleaming screen in stunned amazement. When she pressed one finger to the power button, the laptop awoke again easily, unlocking as it recognized her fingerprint.

"It works." She shook her head in disbelief.

"Will it only obey you?" James asked, getting an inviting look from Ingrid as he smiled, cleared his throat, and spoke up. "Robot, please sharpen this blade." He handed a penknife over to the custodian, who took it, carefully examining it. It ran the tips of the tentacle across the blade, then handed it back, seemingly done.

"Did it do it?" Zac crowded forward.

"Let's see." James frowned, and looked for something to cut, and Zac leaned in.

"Here...Ow!" Zac jammed his thumb into his mouth and sucked furiously on it. "Ith's harp!" he mumbled around his thumb.

"You're an idiot." Casey sighed, shaking her head in disgust. "He said it's sharp, for those that don't speak 'idiot.'"

"We guessed." James stifled a smile. "So, we've established that it can understand us, and accept orders. Zac, how many null blocks do we have aboard?"

"Ten." Zac squinted at his thumb as it started to bleed again, then scratched at the cut with an oily nail. "Damn, that's tiny…"

"That's what she said," came the muttered comment from Paul, one of Jonas's team, who stood off to one side with his wife Courtney.

"So it can follow orders." Ingrid straightened. "Can it make something we can use, though? Does anyone have a gun?"

"I do," Jonas offered, setting his handgun on the table. He frowned as Ingrid reached out and took it, as if every instinct in him fought to take the gun from her inexperienced and untrained hand.

"Robot…"

"I think Steve called the repairers 'custodians,'" James pointed out quietly. "With the War class as sentinels."

"Thank you. Custodian?" Ingrid said, thanking James, then turning back to the squatting machine. "Upgrade this weapon to a level that would be effective against the sentinels in the ship you came from."

"Uh…I think that's too vague." Zac winced when it didn't respond.

"Do you want to try?" she asked, and he nodded, stepping up.

"Custodian, triple this weapon's effective damage while maintaining its integrity," he ordered, holding the gun out, and offering the null block as well. "Use as much of this as is necessary."

There was a slight pause before the machine started to work. Two tentacles flashed out to claim the weapon and block.

The rest of the group stared, unable to look away as the handgun was disassembled, clearly scanned, then reassembled. The null block was halved in size by the time it was done, but the individual bullets that filled the magazine were stripped out and reconfigured. And as to the gun?

When it was handed back, it was markedly different: lighter, streamlined, and considerably more peculiar-looking.

The original gun had exuded a certain level of threat, as all such weapons did, while the updated version seemed to be more like a child's toy gun.

It went from a compact metal creation, to a plastic-looking and longer one, looking more like a plastic water gun than a weapon of war.

The heaviest part of it was the small coil battery system in the grip, with the bullets of the magazine held in the upper form, ready to be dropped down into the receiver.

"Is that it?" Jonas asked, seemingly unimpressed as it was passed back to him.

"Does it work?" Ingrid asked, and he shrugged, looking around for something to test it against.

"Give me a minute." Casey suddenly grinned as she set off, running down to the cabins. Two minutes later, she was back, holding up a bright-yellow rubber duck wearing, of all things, a kilt. It gripped a longsword, propped up on one shoulder, and glared at the world with an eyepatch and ginger beard.

"Here, see if you can hit that," Casey suggested, throwing it to Jonas, who snagged it out of the air, and then nodded, before underarm tossing it out over the side and to the sea.

"Case!" Zac cried out, betrayal clear in his disbelieving voice as he shook his head. "Fuck's sake, not McDuck! What am I gonna use now?!"

"Do I want to know?" James asked Zac, fixing him with a wary look.

"Fuck's sake, James, it's not a sex toy or anything…it's a rubber duck!" Zac groaned. "I swear, you've all got the wrong idea about me. You never heard of the rubber duck method?"

"Like in programming?" James asked Zac, and he nodded, as James went on. "Ah, I see. It's an old trick to clear the mind when searching for problems. Essentially programmers and in this case, engineers, keep an inanimate object, usually as ridiculous as possible, and they explain the process they're trying to carry out to it. In the act of explaining it, in as detailed a way as possible, they often find the issue that's vexing them and solve it. My apologies, Zac. I thought the worst."

"It's okay, boss." Zac sighed, shaking his head. "I'm used to being misunderstood." Then he grinned evilly. "Besides, I see Case didn't bring *her* duck up in public. It's got batteries and—"

"You shut up right now, Zac, or you'll regret it," Casey warned him, creeping redness staining her cheeks as she lifted her head, glaring at him.

"Yes, dear…" He grinned back, unrepentant, as Jonas lined up on the floating duck.

"Might be an idea to move the boat back…" James started to say, when Jonas fired.

The crack of the miniature rail gun discharging was sharp, but the cratering of the water as the bullet impacted was anything but subtle.

The group stood there, mouths open, shocked, as seawater rained down on them all, and Jonas stared at the unassuming weapon in his hands.

"Fuck me!" he growled, shifting his aim to a point much farther out, almost as far as he could see in the dark, before pulling the trigger again.

Another explosion of water erupted in the distance, and Jonas grinned at the others.

"Ladies and gentlemen?" He held the gun up. "We have a new winner!"

"Custodian, make me a sniper rifle version of that," Courtney said quickly, stepping up and holding out her rifle.

In seconds, all the security team clamored for new weapons, Zac begged for tools and new toys, and Scylla glared at the hammer she held, clearly unsure whether she trusted the machine to alter it.

Ingrid and James looked at each other. The pair of them recognized that they finally had a viable alternative to just sitting there, as Courtney snorted at some comment of Paul's as the custodian started work on her rifle.

"Don't be more stupid than you already are," she said. "My good rifle is in storage. I'm not exposing that to sea air without a good reason. That's just my spare."

"Then I guess it's time to start preparing. James, let's get our equipment out and the null blocks we have," Ingrid said after a second's thought. "We're unlikely to have enough to upgrade everything for everyone, so let's see what we have, and what we can get."

"With an eye to heading to the ship, when?" James asked, straightening.

"Tomorrow," Ingrid said. "We prioritize breathing equipment and weapons for the security team. The custodian should be able to get us in and take us to Steve's fallback position."

"I don't like that we're going against his orders," James admitted quietly, moving in closer to Ingrid so that only she could hear. "But..."

"But things have changed with us getting viable weapons. And as much as he's trying to do everything? There's a reason we agreed to a team-based approach rather than it just being him and me," Ingrid pointed out. "Steve gets fixated on the problem. He's great at multitasking, but Zac will be able to create things he can't imagine. With your organization and the rest of the team to hold and develop the base? We can do this. Tell me honestly, James. Do you disagree?" She watched him.

"No, no I don't, Ingrid." He sighed. "I think Steve has focused too much on the fact he needs to protect us all, that he's missing an opportunity."

"Thank you." Ingrid's heart felt lighter as she drew in a deep breath and looked around. "Then let's get moving. Tomorrow, we board a sunken alien ship."

"And there's an order that I never expected to get, even as a butler." James sighed, shaking his head at the strange turns his life had taken.

CHAPTER SIXTEEN

The power plant was up and running for all of three minutes when the attack began a dozen rooms away, with the custodians still working on laying the power transfer back toward the other end.

Of the three turrets that had been slated to be stripped from the previous position and reassembled, only one was working, and that was the one that secured the security station from the other corridor.

That was the one that I was fairly sure was the least likely to be goddamn attacked, as well, but fuck it. At least I didn't have to worry about it.

I grabbed my shotgun, sprinting for the doors leading from the main construction area and into the forward areas of the ship, cursing that the second turret had literally just begun construction. The doors had to be unsealed for that, meaning that it was the perfect time for the bastards to attack.

I didn't know how it knew, but it damn well did.

I flung orders at the factories as I raced past, ordering ten of the small fighting drones to be constructed. They were to be built, then sent forward to the next section, there to hold the line against the security AI's systems.

I sprinted ahead, cursing myself as I remembered that not only did I only have eight shots left in the goddamn shotgun, but I'd not brought any null blocks or ammunition with me, beyond a single spare mag. All the rest were on the desk above and behind me in the security office.

Eighteen shots—that was all I had, and the sensors were showing the incoming sentinels as a fucking wave!

They swarmed forward, maybe forty or so of them, when I gave up counting, and just started fucking hoping.

They were drones...I was fairly sure of that. There was no way they could have produced enough "real" sentinels—even class ones—in that time.

I hoped. Fuck, I hoped!

If they'd made forty plus proper sentinels, then my options were down to fucking run, or stand and die.

A momentary relief that I'd gotten Ingrid and the others to stay away from the ship surged, and I let that comfort me, as I ran.

The ship ahead was black. Even my enhancements could only see so far, and the system's sensors filled in the rest with wireframe images that did little beyond distract.

I was about to blank them out when a nearby section of cowling shifted. I spun on instinct, unloading a blast with the shotgun into it, even as a trio of darts smacked into my armor, shattering and falling off, but flashing warnings about "biological poisons" in their wake.

I banished the warning. It was assessing and countering it already—adding the poison to my repertoire—even as I was thankful for the armor itself.

The little bastard didn't get a second barrage off, shredded as it was by the shotgun, and I skidded, glaring at the sparking, shattered form.

A second barrage opened up. A half dozen darts slammed into my armor from my right, and then more from ahead. I spun and returned fire, dodging behind piled scrap and rusting, long-dead machinery.

More warnings flared, and I cursed the secondary warning that was provided this time.

Advanced Venomous and Acidic attack Identified: Nanites Assessing...

Countering...

Nanite Prioritization Request:

Venomous Regulation: Yes/No

Acidic Counteragent: Yes/No

I spammed the acid regulation, knowing that regardless of that dumb-ass phrasing, what was happening was that the little darts that were slamming into me and shattering? They weren't intended to kill me—or at least, not at first.

The fuckers were weakening my armor, setting me up to be easily killed by the swarm!

Add to that, the bastard AI had managed to sneak ninjas in? I swore as I returned fire again, this time dialing the dispersal up another notch and shredding one of the legs of the damn thing as it ran from cover to cover.

I could barely see the ninjas, as I mentally tagged them. Clearly they had both some kind of stealth and they were avoiding the working sensors! It was literally a case of me firing at movement and noise, and that had to be wasting my goddamn ammo.

I snarled and slapped my shotgun onto my back. Nanites clung to it and held it in place as I sprinted out of cover, shucking my vorpal blade out of my left arm and triggering the gravity inverter.

Jumping, I shoved upward with the inverter, flipping myself into the air, before ripping myself downward again, blade extended.

Landing right behind the cover that it'd dragged itself behind, I whipped the blade sideways, unable to see anything, but feeling it as the edge caught.

Instantly, the Conceal effect, a more advanced version of my own, and clearly entirely cybernetic, was broken, as pressurized systems burst. Liquids jetted free, and I leapt back as the little body sparked and burst into flames. Acrid smoke and bright-blue sparks filled the air.

I darted backward, then leapt, triggering the inverter and my own stealth field at the same time, bracing myself against the underside of a passing gantry. I stared downward, trying to figure out what was going on.

That the enemy had been able to sneak the ninjas around the sensors was clear, but was it still in the system?

Unlikely, I decided after a moment's thought, squinting into the dimly visible holding area below me.

The fucker had been here forever, though, and being a machine, it didn't forget things the way a human did. It knew where the working sensors were, and it'd simply guided its drones around them.

That was a much more likely situation, I realized, and it made sense. I was fairly sure the security station couldn't be retaken by the AI, short of rebuilding the entire system.

The sensors were the same.

The sub-mind had reached out, and I'd been dimly aware when the security AI had attempted remote hacks of them several times, with insanely obvious results.

There'd been no more since the last attack, as the sub-mind had counterattacked and claimed a borderline defense system from the security AI. The other side had immediately taken the system offline—and they hadn't just switched it off, either. The sub-mind had reported that it'd registered a surge of heat, then signal degradation; then the freshly claimed system stopped reporting.

Clearly the other side was taking us more seriously now.

I hung there, my gravity inverter ticking over steadily, the charge well within manageable levels, as I waited and watched.

Ten seconds, thirty…At a full minute, I reached out and checked the roster, summoning one of the armed drones from my side, and sprinting it forward into the room.

I waited. Sparks cascaded from both the damaged drones nearby that I'd managed to take down—one was still smoking and frying; clearly my blade had mangled the reactor and it was fucked—and the distant entrance back into "my" territory.

Over there, back near the doors, the custodian was reassembling the second turret. Every second that it got to work brought our defenses closer to being enough to stop the oncoming wave.

The only enemies in this room, as far as I knew, were the ninjas, and I knew there had to be at least one more, after that last barrage. Also, considering the flashing warnings I was getting from the suit, I was going to be seriously fucked soon, if my nanites didn't develop a counter to the acid.

My right shoulder pauldron was down to twenty-seven percent viability, and my back? Fifty.

That wouldn't normally be a massive issue. Hell, I could swim in the goddamn ocean and make it all right, wash it off, probably—but for me to survive down here?

I needed the armor.

I needed the atmospheric processing units built into it, I needed the physical protection, and I needed the damn suit's regulation and pressure protection!

More than that though, I needed…*There!*

The drone that was sprinting into the room was hit from a pile of debris below—or to my point of view, above—me. I triggered the inverter, restoring the hold of gravity and fell, blade extended, and ripped the shotgun back around into my right hand.

I fired three fast blasts into the pile. A nanite tentacle snaked forward to grip the lever and crank the action between shots.

The debris pile to my left erupted. Three darts smashed into my chest, before the pile to my right and ahead exploded as well.

The fuckers had been baiting me!

I stabbed out. The one ahead of me appeared damaged, sections of its armor torn up, and it clearly couldn't fire, judging from the way it flung itself at me.

I caught it. The blade punched through its chest and sunk deep, the scrawny build just enough to set off another burst of acrid smoke. And this time? The bastard exploded.

I crashed into a pile of debris behind me. More of the rotting metal and crap cascaded down on me, as my notifications flashed. Two of them came in at almost the same time, with a third flashing as I saw them.

Advanced Acidic Compound Identified and Countered

That was the first one, and a goddamn relief that it was dealt with, considering how low the viability on my armor was now. I could feel the changes, though, as the nanites shifted, altering at an almost unimportant and undetectable level, until the acid was no longer an issue.

Advanced Venomous attack Identified: Nanites Countering...

That was nice as well, when it popped up. Clearly the nanites were done with the first one, and now they were working on the venom. Coolio.

The third one, though? That made me smile.

Fusion reactor boot process complete. Fusion reactor is providing 1/100th of maximum power, climbing...

I saw it instantly, as the power from the fusion core flooded the nearby systems. Golden nodes around me were suddenly surrounded by dozens, then hundreds of black, unknown nodes.

As power was returned to them, the ship went from emergency power conservation mode, to boot-up. And although most of the long-powered-down nodes flickered and failed—or hell, many didn't even do that, simply staying dead—for every ten or so that failed, one actually responded.

The world around me slowly came back to life, and I grinned. The sensors in the floor nearby slowly flickered and registered movement.

I kicked off, hurling the metal that covered me aside, shotgun rising and firing toward one that was deep in stealth.

It took the hit dead-on, shredded by the blast as electronics, solid-state components, and pressurized containment devices were sent flying.

The last of them turned and ran, only to run into a blast from the damaged drone I'd used as bait. The shot punched through the head and took it down smoothly.

I skidded, twisting around, and searched the area, expecting another attack, but finding none.

The clatter of incoming drones could be heard distantly, and I couldn't help but grin as I ran back toward my area.

They'd used the sensors, or the lack of them in certain areas, as a trap for me, because the AI could remember where they were.

Now that there was power flooding the level, though? Its systems would be trying to assess the changes, and what this meant for it.

That made it the perfect time for me to play a little trick of my own.

Arise: Reclaimer

I didn't know whether the fucker had any spies left in here, hidden and watching. I know I'd have held one back if it was me, so on those grounds, I deliberately ran as if returning to my area.

Then, as soon as I was in the corridor and out of sight?

I triggered Conceal and my gravity manipulation ability, jumping back toward the room I'd just left, and falling at speed.

I rose into the air, clearing the piled materials, and hurtled toward the open corridor at the other end that led to the far entrance, just as it opened, disgorging a mass of sprinting drones.

They'd been fooled by my amazing acting, I guessed, as they raced forward. On the spur of the moment, I decided to try to get behind them. That way, I could catch them when they got close to the base, and my hopefully working turret. They'd be caught between the crossfire of my powerful shotgun, the turrets, and the few working drones I'd managed to get built.

I grinned for all of three seconds before they opened fire, filling the air with overlapping laser fire. Jerking myself sideways, I crashed into the wall of the corridor, then down toward the floor as sparks flew, with me powering the inverter with sudden random bursts to keep me out of the firing line as much as possible, while my shotgun hammered out return fire.

I scraped along the floor, still "falling" toward them, and I twisted my foot, stomping it down. Clawed tips erupted from the underside of my boots, catching and digging into the metal floor, popping me upright. I triggered the inverter, flipping around and landing on the ceiling; laser blasts ripped through the air below me.

Two more shots rang out; then my shotgun ran dry and I snarled in frustration. The fléchettes had punched through multiple figures before failing.

I reached for the spare magazine, the tentacle already flipping the chamber open...and found it gone.

I blinked, distracted for a second, then cursed as more shots lanced out nearby, carving lines in both the corridor and my armor.

Flashing warnings, damage indicators, and fucking integrity failing markers appeared in my mind, as if the pain of burning lasers carving their way into my flesh wasn't enough to make the fucking situation clear.

I reached out, doing what I'd only managed to do a time or two before, and instead of using the gravity field to manipulate gravity for me, lifting or throwing myself into the air, I did it for them.

Of the sixty or so that had made it into the corridor, I'd taken at least thirty down, and I needed an edge, if I was going to survive this. Fortunately, I had one...one that could only be used once, admittedly.

I shoved the entire corridor downward, gasping as my power core went from full and ticking over, to redlining in an instant.

It was enough, though, as we all crashed to the floor.

I fell, because I no longer had the power to defy gravity. And them? Well, they'd just found out what fifty times gravity felt like, for half a second.

It was enough to smash them to the floor, considering most of them were running at the time. Arms and more were jerked down, sensors mashed into the floor, bodies were pinned atop each other, and the entire lot, smashed downward, lost sight of me for a brief second.

In that time? I triggered the power systems here to shut down.

They were linked to it, the power transmission protocols keeping them upright and running. And as soon as I pulled the plug, cutting off the incoming power?

I knew it wasn't coming back on.

In the distance, I heard more units approaching, which meant that at least some of them weren't powered from the grid…and I still had a fight on my hands.

I cursed, forcing myself back up to my feet. The units before me twitched and jerked, switching from external power to, I guessed, some internal battery reserve.

I swore and ran forward, slashing right and left, frantically beheading as many as I could, before the sounds of approaching units got too much, and I turned and tried to run.

Seven of the first wave rose again, and I hissed and snarled as I hobbled, blood running down my left leg inside my armor. Dozens of injuries screamed for my attention as I tried to get away.

The gravity inverter was offline, too little power to bring it on, and my armor was damaged beyond belief.

Sweat ran down my face—at least I hoped it was sweat, considering how many injuries I'd taken—and there was a smell like moldy socks and burnt plastic, along with the coppery tang of blood.

That wasn't good.

Obviously the whole "fuck me, I'm bleeding" wasn't exactly happy making, but the fact I could smell it, and the outside world?

My suit was breached, and I was breathing ship air again.

Last time I was here, I'd been too fast at running to really have any issues with the atmosphere, but I was betting that was a situation that'd not last long.

There were cracks all around me, electrical hisses and worse as the damaged units powered up on what *had* to be internal batteries, which I'd totally fucking discounted!

I'd thought about the main power cores, and the transmission-based power systems, but I'd never even thought about short-term battery backup!

Mainly because *my* drones didn't have one! The bastard AI had outsmarted me again!

I screamed as an impact smashed me from my feet, hurling me to the floor. My upper right chest erupted in a spray of blood. Something flashed from sight as I fell, and I heard the *chunk-clunk* of a reloading system somewhere behind me.

"Get up!" I snarled at myself. It was only the blind luck of my uneven limping gait that had meant the shot punched through the upper right of my chest, rather than dead center through my heart.

Or my damn head.

I triggered the inverter. There wasn't enough power to run it for long, and for whatever reason, the "magic" of technology in the core meant that when it was fully depleted, it took longer to refill.

The boost was enough, though, as I "fell" sideways, and forward.

I was less than an inch off the wall of the corridor, and hurtling along in a matter of seconds, when I flipped myself upright again.

Arise: Reclaimer

As I did it, a second shot hammered into my left thigh. The impact of the solid slug on my metal bones reverberated through me. I desperately wanted to throw up as a second hit shattered my left forearm, the vorpal blade registering as heavily damaged in my mind.

Bile rose in my throat as a new warning flooded my brain.

I was out of nanites, for my healing.

I was too low on weaponized nanites to be able to fully form my armor. And without the armor being intact?

I couldn't take any more hits.

I couldn't even form a proper tourniquet to stop myself bleeding out!

I stripped my armor away from my arms, waist, right leg and lower left leg, my shoulders, and my desperately needed crotch protector. I stripped it away from everywhere bar my chest, my upper left leg as I needed it to hold the lower section of my leg to the rest of me, and my helmet.

I even sacrificed the vorpal blade, ripping the damn thing apart in a desperate orgy of need, using the materials to repair as much of the arm as I could. I used the few nanites I had left, forcing them to be building blocks to keep me going.

I couldn't afford to lose the power of the core, which I needed to form the inversion fields, nor could I lose access to the sub-mind.

With some of my weight, a lot of it actually, now discarded—the null block additional armoring fell free as I retracted my armor—I was both lighter and found it easier to move, thankfully.

I jerked around from side to side, just in case, before burning the last of the power as I flashed out into the main room from the corridor. I hurled myself up and over the first of the piles of debris, and I made it over the top before the power failed entirely.

Then I fell, smashing into the piled metal and crap. Bones that were unable to break instead lost connective tissue, torn free of ligaments and tendons. I howled in pain, bouncing and falling down the far side, leaving a smear of blood and the remains of my clothing behind.

The last thing I remembered, as the world around me grew dim, and a looming carapace of solid steel sat right in my path, was reaching out to the sub-mind and ordering it to rescue me, to get me out of here.

The last thought I had as I smashed into the metal?

Home.

CHAPTER SEVENTEEN

I woke sometime later—how much, I genuinely didn't know—but it was the warm rush of water that did it.

I distantly heard voices. Pain rolled through me as I alternated between sweating, shaking, and lapsing into unconsciousness over and over again.

The world rolled around me; sensations flared and faded away, as my body burned and melted, and terrible cold warred with it.

Gentle hands rubbed soothing cream into me, and I laid there, unable to…to *anything*.

There was a block, something that stood between me and that melted, broken thing that had once been my body. And I was fucked if I knew, or cared, what it was.

It was like I stood on the outside, staring in, emotionlessly, as my body lay there, slowly dying. Hours became days. The heat of the sun tracked across my body as I lay on crisp sheets, as hands tended to me, cleaning me.

I could feel, even in the worst of my pain and delirium, the comfort of the remains of my armor, where it gripped me, holding me tight on my chest and head.

Over and over, a distant voice begged me to retract the armor, to release it, and over and over, I ignored it, knowing that while I wore the armor, I was still connected.

The sub-mind was there, functional, battling wave upon wave of intrusion attempts, somehow still able to keep going, despite it all.

It seemed to my frenzied mind that days, and possibly years, had passed—centuries even. But when the time finally came that I opened my eyes, and saw not the insane swirl of madness, not the colors and the creatures that flew and gibbered, but instead saw the simple white of the ceiling above me?

I drew in a deep, shuddering breath and stared at it, trying muzzily to make sense of it.

I'd been aboard the alien ship, and now, I wasn't? I was…I didn't know…it *looked* like…"Ingrid?" I mumbled, blinking, as I turned my head to the side, to look at her pillow.

She wasn't there, but this *was* our cabin! I was aboard the yacht, and I could distantly hear seabirds and conversation. Could feel the softness of the silken sheets beneath me. The warmth of the air was almost stifling.

I blinked. I was still covered in my armor, but…I lifted my hands, staring at them, seeing the battered condition, the still healing scabs, bandages…I turned my hands over, then sat up, thinking to look at my body, when the world spun and I sagged sideways, slipping out of the bed and smacking the side of my head against the bedside table.

It crumpled; the solidity of my helm smashed it easily, combined with my weight. The voices outside broke off in panic, the door bursting open seconds later.

Then she was there, hands reaching, my name on her lips as she slid under me, helping to take my weight, to get me back onto the bed.

I shook my head when she said something about the armor, and instead I stared at her, seeing the stress, the worry that she'd been dealing with. Her hair was a mess, her eyes red-rimmed and puffy, she wore little makeup—I'd always said she didn't damn well need any, but she liked to wear more than she was now—and combined with the clothes, and the way that she and Casey were helping me back into the bed?

It was obvious I'd been the source of the worry.

"Wha...what happ...ened?" I managed to force out.

"Steve! Oh, thank the gods!" Ingrid groaned, reaching out and clinging to me.

I reached up, wrapping my arms around her, and I pretended not to notice the way that Casey delicately and discreetly slid the blanket across my crotch.

I was naked, I realized, and I'd been flashing the poor woman.

"Are you all right?" Ingrid pushed me back, staring at my helmet. "Can you...Steve, can you pull back the armor? It's still half on and..."

"No," I said softly, shaking my head, then coughing and wincing at the raw pain that ran through me at that. "Damn..."

"No?" Ingrid shifted and tried to see through the visor. "Steve, are you—"

Whatever she was going to say, she broke off as I cleared and retracted the front of the armor, freeing my face and making me look more like I was wearing a partial motorbike helmet instead.

"I need the space for the neurons," I explained, before wincing as data started to pour back into my brain. "Fuuuuuck." I groaned, reaching up and covering my face.

"Steve?"

"I'm okay," I lied. "It's just...What happened?"

She started to speak, while trying to get me back into bed. For the first time in my damn life, when a stunningly beautiful woman was determined I should be laid in her bed, I refused.

Instead, I forced myself to my feet, cursing as I accidentally flashed Casey again, who promptly left the room to give me some privacy as Ingrid helped me to stand.

She tried repeatedly to convince me to go back to bed. Then, when she saw that wasn't going to work, she helped me dress, before guiding me out to sit at the table on the deck.

Ingrid explained that they'd all been making ready to assault the ship, and to give me backup, when a pair of custodians had breached the water nearby, bringing me to the yacht.

One had left as soon as I was in place and safe, returning to the wreck below, while the other had stayed long enough to synthesize some medicine from the few null blocks at hand, then had taken what was left of those blocks, and had dove into the water.

They'd used the medicine on me. I'd been hit with a bunch of small darts at some point—a goddamn surviving ninja had gotten me, I realized—and I'd been both poisoned and eaten alive by the acid when I'd been brought aboard.

Clearly once the armor was off, the protection I'd gained against the acid had gone as well.

I'd apparently died four times, the last one being for about five hours, and the shortest of my dirt naps.

The only reason I was alive now, I realized as data piled up, rolling over and over, the sub-mind trying to bring me fully up to date at the same time Ingrid was, was because Scylla had given me a blood transfusion.

Her blood was shit for nanites, considering the long centuries she'd spent in death, but the ones she had that were active were only a tiny fragment of the ones that were corrupt. My systems, fully active and working, could do what hers couldn't, though, and they wiped and reset the corrupted into active and attuned.

Those nanites, combined with the ones that my body was naturally producing—we were designed to have a certain number at all times, after all—had been enough to reboot my brain and heart. From there, my body had started to repair itself. The poison shut me down again a few times, as had blood loss and trauma, but I was back. And after that transfusion, I had almost a thousand nanites available on top of the bare minimum I needed. That little nugget made me swallow hard as I reflected on how many nanites that meant Scylla had.

I'd lost all my armor, save the chest, back, neck, and helmet, the rest being cut away over and over, struck with nanite-destroying gamma radiation repeatedly.

In my wounded, semi-sentient state, I'd seemingly redirected all my armor to those priority points, and then I'd ordered the sub-mind to get me out of there.

A fleeting memory of wanting to be with Ingrid, and that home was wherever she was? That'd been enough for my orders to the sub-mind to have redirected me from where I'd thought I needed to be—back behind our defenses—to instead be taken to Ingrid.

Now I was back on the ship, and the rest of the crew were...

"How?" I asked, stunned.

"We discussed it, and realized that if you'd taken a beachhead, and it was worth you fighting this hard to protect? It was worth us defending it. We'd already used the custodian you sent to give the security team some weapons that would work against the sentinels, and you tend not to leave many enemies alive, so—"

She broke off with a half nervous smile.

"So you retook the base?" I asked, stunned, seeing the data from the sub-mind, and shook my head as it suddenly made sense: the new combatants it'd registered, the counterattack that drove back the AI...all of it.

"We don't know. We stayed here, the three of us. James is asleep. He was working all night, trying to make sense of the transmission we were getting from the ship."

"Transmission..." I muttered, reaching out and checking the local area, and finding a constant stream of data from the wreck below and the sub-mind. "It's not a transmission, not like that. It's a control signal and feedback. The sub-mind is...okay. I'm going to need to explain a lot." I broke off, seeing the look on her face. "So..."

Five minutes later, I'd been stopped by Ingrid, and Casey had made coffee and woken James. We'd moved so that I could sit in the sunlight in my shorts, feeling the warmth of the sun invigorating me, as I returned to the beginning—for James's benefit—and I explained everything.

"So," he said several minutes later, frowning at his cup of steaming coffee and turning it around in his hands, playing with the mug and not really seeing it. "You're saying that the fight is ongoing, but that the sub-mind, a sort of truncated clone of your mind, is currently remoting into the wreck and is controlling the defenses? And that the others are alive?"

"I think so," I said slowly, squinting into the distance as I pulled up the details that I could see. The connection was intended as a comm-link so I could reach out and call the others down, that was it.

I'd never expected it to carry heavy traffic, so it was a bit like trying to stream a movie on a copper telephone line from the sixties. The signal was getting through, but the compression, encoding, and decoding algos on either side were playing hell with it.

"So we go to them," Ingrid said, and I jerked around, looking at her. "Don't look at me like that, Steve! I may not be a soldier, but I can fight if I need to!"

"I know you can…" I lied, searching for the words. "But…"

"I swear to God, if the next words that come out of your mouth are something like 'but you're a girl,' I'll murder you in your sleep," she warned.

"HA!" I barked out the laugh. "Fuck, no. Athena was a 'girl,' even if only a lot of centuries ago, and I've fought vicious and deadly women enough times. No, I mean, we, uh, can't leave the yacht unmanned."

"Casey and I will maintain it," James said, and I glared at him, with absolutely no effect. "As much as I'd much rather explore the ship—preferably once it's pacified, I'll admit—a single person, male or female, on a multi-million-dollar yacht sitting a little way out to sea is a bad idea. There are few pirates in the Mediterranean Sea, but with the recent disturbances in Africa, there are a constant stream of people smugglers and small boats crossing in the night. A verifiable, legitimate, and powerful vessel such as this would be an ideal target for them."

"So you think that you should both stay here, just in case, but that Ingrid and I should return?" I asked. My first instinct was to refuse, that I'd be putting Ingrid at risk, as much as I loved her. But even as I thought it, I banished that idea. I didn't like her being exposed to the risk, and I'd never forgive myself if something happened to her, but…

But she was the love of my life and my partner, not my possession.

"Yes," he said simply, and before Ingrid's thundercloud frown could break into a storm, I agreed.

"That works a lot better then."

"Steve, I…wait, what?" She broke off, confused.

"Look, Ingrid, I agreed before, and yeah, I don't like it—I genuinely don't. One of my concerns was leaving the yacht abandoned, and another was the risk to you. You've got the right to go wherever you want, and I need to get used to that, but…" I fixed her with a look.

"When we're down there? I'm running on fumes. I've got barely enough nanites to keep myself alive. They're rebuilding me as we speak. I can't form my armor, nor my weapons. We're going to be in the middle of the base and running things in the short-term, claiming the area, making sure that the AI can't counterattack, and that's it, all right? No wandering off to explore, no demanding to help on the front lines of the fight...none of that shit, okay? Jonas came along and brought his people because we needed a dedicated security team. That's what they're for."

"I agree," she said, smiling gently, and I relaxed, for all of a second. "Which is why you'll be doing the same." Her smile widened. "You're our leader, and my partner, and you're the one who needs this the most. You've just admitted you've got no weapons and no armor, so you'll not be needed on the front lines. Instead, you'll be with me, helping to get the base up and running."

"Right..." I winced. "Sure!"

"Steve, this is a very deep dive. You need me..." Casey started, only to be shut down by James and Ingrid, as this was apparently a conversation that had been had before.

"So, when are you planning on going back down?" James asked, after making it clear that Casey was staying with him aboard the yacht.

"Now?" I broke off at the look I was getting from them all. "Look, I know you're thinking I just woke up," I said, and all three nodded.

"Well, that's true, but Zac is currently trying to explain to the custodians and the base systems what he needs from them, to make it more secure for everyone." I looked around at them all, making the point as I went on. "At least, that's what I *think* he's trying to do. He's nearly triggered the defensive programming three times now. The sub-mind keeps stopping the turrets firing on him or the others."

"Why..." Casey started to ask, and I held up a hand, speaking over her.

"It's because the signal you were trying to figure out was just for me to essentially make a call to you, nothing more, and it's being used to transmit the situation down there, to the sub-mind here." I tapped my chest and helmet. "And then it's relaying its assessment to the systems down there. It can barely register what's going on, and while it's dealing with Zac's pestering, it can't deal with the counterattacks by the AI."

"Zac, you stupid bastard..." Casey groaned, shaking her head. "I'm sorry. He just..."

"No, it's okay. He's trying to help. But the signal that's getting through is being taken up with dealing with him. We need to get down there. The closer I am to the base, the less data transfer there needs to be, and the less lag in the decisions.

"Currently we're being counterattacked, and the sub-mind is roaming drones against the enemy. But it's losing three or four of them to each enemy they kill, because they're firing where the enemy was, and might be in a few seconds, by the time the signal gets to them. They're remote drones, and controlling them is hard enough, without that mad Aussie bastard pestering the custodians."

"You have my permission to smack him across the back of the head regardless then, sir." Casey shook her head as she looked at James. "Did we really have to bring him?"

"We did," James said blandly, stifling a smile. "Although next time, perhaps we could leave him at home, with a coloring book."

"He'd only eat it." She sighed, before smiling as I stood, still a little unsteady on my feet. "So, do you need diving gear?" she asked, and I hesitated, checking my systems.

"For Ingrid only," I replied after a few seconds. "And I'll get us to the ship."

My power core was fully charged, and what was left of my armor was registering that it was able to form an airtight seal and provide clean air, so that was a relief.

What I hadn't expected, and hadn't even occurred to me, was the technical issues that went with diving to the wreck from here with a "normal" setup.

The maximum safe depth for normal scuba diving was too shallow, so to reach the wreck, the others had gone, not in typical scuba gear, but in special saturation suits.

They were cutting-edge, I'd been told, meaning that instead of the hours to days or more that everyone would need to spend in a decompression chamber from diving to a depth of just under two hundred meters, they'd instead breathe a special air mix before returning to the surface.

They'd also need to stop for four hours at a time, at three different depths, as they swam back up. They'd all need to pause to let their bodies adjust, and let the various gases equalize.

We'd discussed it, and although I could equalize the gravity with my inverter, the fact that the ship might be pressurized appropriately to the depths meant I couldn't just do that all the way. We had to adopt a hybrid approach; otherwise, if I lost control over the local field, it might cause much worse side effects.

Casey, who as one of her yacht jobs was the divemaster, was desperate to be in the sea, leading us as we did this, but again, James, Ingrid, and I refused.

"The ship is at pressure." Casey sighed. "Hopefully, it's the correct pressure for the depth and the differentials for nitrogen narcosis have been taken into account. But if they haven't? Watch for tremors, for confusion and unexpected pain. I know you can heal, Steve, and you probably didn't even notice it, but…"

"But my body, with the nanites, adjusted," I finished for her.

"Exactly," she agreed. "When you were brought up by the robot thingies, you didn't just suffer from the injuries you'd taken, there was so much going on, but I'm pretty sure you had the bends as well. If anything, you were lucky you died— and how wrong is *that* to say—but it stopped you breathing in, so there was less nitrogen to mess with your cells."

Ingrid winced. "I won't have that."

"No, you won't," Casey agreed, but smiled as she went on. "But you're also in the best suits I've ever seen. These things are so cutting-edge that I don't believe the details and service advice, so diving to that depth, and then accessing the ship, moving to a pressurized environment? It should be fine, especially with Steve's ability to manipulate gravity. But if it's not? You need to know what to do, so…"

"Shit, of course, my gravity manipulation." I grunted, shaking my head. "I'll alter a bubble around Ingrid. That'll prevent the issues, or it should. We'll still play it safe, but when the time comes to come back up? I'll create one for everyone."

I hesitated, focusing, then sighed, relieved. The gravity manipulation was still easy for me; the loss of the rest of my armor didn't affect that, as it was housed primarily in the chest unit.

Twenty minutes was lost as I helped Ingrid to suit up. My own armor left me unable to play it safe and wear the same stuff as she did, so I settled for a dive bag with jeans, boxers, and shoes in it, electing to swim in a pair of shorts.

"It's going to be a lot colder at that depth," Casey warned me, and I shrugged.

"I can't wear anything else, so I'll make do."

"Well, if you're sure," she said, having been clearly trying to figure out how the hell I could get one of the suits on and only half wear it, without losing it to the depths.

I moved around Ingrid, helping to close her suit and lifting the various sections into place, then spoke as Casey went to retrieve the helmet.

"You know, usually when I imagine you diving, I think of you either naked, or in a really tiny swimsuit…" I whispered in Ingrid's ear. "Or, if we're talking about you just 'going down'…"

"Shut it, you." She elbowed me in the chest, then rubbed her elbow, glaring at me, as if it were my fault she'd hurt it.

I grinned, then gave her a quick kiss, before stepping back and moving over to James's side as Casey sealed Ingrid's helmet.

"If you need to pull back, do it," I told him. "I'll be in touch, but if the shit hits the fan, I genuinely don't know how far this AI will go to secure the ship, so be ready."

"One of us will be on deck at all times. The sonar picked up the custodians coming and going, once we knew what to look for. If there's suddenly a lot? I'll get us out of range."

"Good luck, my friend." I smiled at him, then gave him an awkward hug as he reached out and gripped me. "What's that for?"

"You're a good man, Steve, despite your protestations to the contrary, and I just spent two days watching you die and rise again. Be careful. All this falls apart without you."

"I will." I forced another smile before sealing my helmet and moving up to the edge of the yacht. "Are you ready?" I asked Ingrid, and then Casey, who'd be remotely adjusting her air mix as we sank.

I got a thumbs-up and a worried smile from Ingrid, and a distracted nod from Casey as she worked on the dials and details.

Then we stepped off and sank into the crystal-blue waters of the Aegean Sea.

CHAPTER EIGHTEEN

We plunged down. My armor was plenty heavy—and to be fair, so was I—and Ingrid's suit was weighted, with a buoyancy tank on it to help her, so the issue certainly wasn't swimming downward.

In fact, although I was slightly concerned about the depth—okay, more than slightly—I was banking on the fact that the ship was under pressure. As long as we were damn fast in getting to the ship, and in? There was a lot less chance of any of the crew needing to spend much time decompressing.

If the ship was pressurized, we'd simply walk to the higher areas as we took more and more of the ship over.

As we trekked the miles toward the shore at Crete, we'd stop and take frequent rests, and that'd hopefully sort the worst of the symptoms.

Add to that, these suits were rated for depth work, with an expectation that the wearers would be working for eight plus hours at a time, deep in the ocean, rather than swimming down and straight into a hatch?

Well, I had hopes, put it that way.

Add in that I could literally adjust gravity, and yeah, I was reasonably confident that we'd be okay. I also wasn't going to speak those hopes aloud because that utter bastard Murphy was always watching and listening.

We sank through the water. The crystal-clear upper stretches over our heads showed the underside of the yacht as we submerged, and the depths below gradually became clearer as we fell.

"Are you okay?" I asked Ingrid, having reached out and scanned for her signal, connecting to it with barely a thought, after the complicated shit I'd been hacking of late.

The sub-mind, now getting closer and closer to the ship, was getting better access. It'd barely acknowledged the hack order, when it was done, and I grinned.

When I got the chance? When I wasn't constantly fighting for my goddamn life? I was going to make the most of this, starting with my damn music that I'd lost access to ages ago.

"Steve, oh thank God!" Ingrid whispered. "Sorry, I was going mad in here trying to figure out how I could talk to you!"

"What's up?" I asked.

"Nothing, but, you know, we're sinking in the sea, we're miles from land, and this suit is heavy! There's no way I could swim back up, not if something goes wrong, and there's sharks and all sorts of creatures out here!"

"There's not many, though," I assured her.

"Many what?"

"Sharks."

"There's sharks!" She gasped.

"Well, yeah, you know, we're in the sea. What, didn't you know?"

"I knew they were, well, out *there*..." She made a vague swirl of her hand in the direction of the wider ocean. "Not in *here*...you know, close by!"

"I think that one's checking out your ass, actually..." I joked, and she gripped my hand tighter.

"Please, don't," she whispered, and I winced.

"Sorry," I apologized. "Honestly, don't worry. In that suit, you're literally a random mass to him. I'm all free flesh. If they come for us, it'll be the first time anyone ignores you in favor of me."

"Oh gods..." she whispered, closing her eyes and reaching out desperately for my other hand.

I grabbed it and pulled her around so that we faced each other, rather than side by side, and I almost banished my faceplate to smile at her as she opened her eyes. Then I remembered what a goddamn monumentally stupid idea that would be, and I didn't.

Instead, I just watched her, staring out fearfully, and yet entranced and excited. She was lit from behind the squared-off glass or plastic that made the front of her helmet, and I watched the trickle of sweat that ran down one cheek, the lock of blonde hair that always seemed to escape even the most carefully tied ponytail or immaculately styled ensemble, free again, as she stuck her lips out to the side and blew at it.

It fluffed up slightly, twisted, and settled against her neck and cheek again, and she puffed at it, still lost in staring at the undersea world, as we sank.

Fifteen minutes into the dive, using the inverter to equalize the pressure more or less, rather than making us sink faster, and I was starting to get a good idea why there were so many problems for divers, as the first signs of the wreck began to show in the distance.

It was well beyond Ingrid's human eyes, but I could make it out. I shifted us around, holding her in close as I pointed things out, waiting until they grew closer, and drawing her attention to the details I'd picked out.

Everything from shattered rooms, sunken and collapsed sections, and more importantly, the airlock, drew gasps of wonder from her. By the time I twisted us around, and managed to direct us to land close enough to the airlock that we could reach it?

Ingrid had forgotten about minor issues like sharks and gory death, nitrogen narcosis and alien machines that were out to kill us.

She was lost in the wonder of the ancient wreck.

Something that had once cruised the skies, landing and working atop both ancient Crete and Thera, and who knew where else—it was built by hands that we'd never know, long before the first humans learned that trees were great and all, but this fire stuff? That's the shit.

We were apes, and possibly not even that, when they'd come for us. And by the time they were finished? We were fighting wars in deep space.

We were warriors tasked with patrolling the galaxy, protecting the little guys, and essentially being the law and order for a place that was clearly in fuckin' need of it.

I'd dismissed the mission as it was explained to me, when the Erlking had shared it, but since then? I'd found myself thinking of it again and again.

It was to serve and protect. The way those coppers in America claimed to do. Ignoring the few bad apples who stood out, who always fucked things up for everyone, that call appealed to me.

I didn't know whether it was genetic, something that had been instilled by long-ago programming, or whether it was cultural, or just my shame for the things I'd done in the past reaching out. But that mission resonated with me.

Add in that the Erlking had basically ordered me to fuck off into deep space and see whether any of my kind were still about? That we'd set up pirate empires, plundering the space-lanes, and that our makers had to devote insane resources to stopping us? That just made it all the more needed.

I didn't know whether there were others like me out there, but I was going to damn well find out.

And, if they were bastards? I'd rip them a new asshole.

I'd had to find a reason to be "me" after I found the nanites. Something to guide me, because I knew myself all too well. I could quite easily have gone to the dark side, beating the crap out of people and worse.

Knowing that these fuckers were probably out there, or more assholes like the Erlking, or hell, whatever reason had driven that bastard and his kind to weaponize a fucking monkey in the first place?

That gave me hope.

We landed atop the sponges and coral reef, with me guiding her in, and then lowering her down through the gap, to land on the sandy bottom. Her suit lights illuminated the control panel. She reached out, pushing and prodding at it, and got nothing, while for me, a light press was all that was needed.

I braced her, letting her know what would happen, then I triggered the opening cycle, holding her against me. We both clung to the rocks as the door slid open. The water crashed past to fill the chamber below us.

As the frantic pull faded slightly, I jerked us both free, diving in, and we plunged down. The door above us closed literal seconds after we were inside.

We sank, bending our knees to take the impact. The thuds as we hit the entrance reverberated through our feet, and I moved us over to the side, bracing us both again, before triggering the purge, followed by the internal door.

This time the water was sucked out, and the airlock was pumped full of air. And for the first time in ages, I remembered just how fucking cold the damn ship was.

I wiped some of the water from me as the cycle completed, and the sub-mind, now in control of this area, took over, opening the door. I'd felt its approach through the data fields I could sense around me, but still, it was nice to see the custodian there, ready to help.

Even nicer was that the pressure felt "right" instead of higher than expected here. Although it meant that the others who had gone ahead might be suffering from side effects—I hoped they weren't, but it was a possibility—it meant that Ingrid wouldn't.

I reached out, and I assured Ingrid it was all right, as it helped her down to the gantry. I jumped down after her, still lugging my dive bag along with me.

A custodian, in addition to coming to help Ingrid and me in, had brought me a shotgun, and two magazines for it, and damn I felt better being armed again.

I had them wait a minute, as I stripped the rest of the water off myself, then the swim shorts, and redressed in the clothes and shoes I'd brought.

No longer basically running around in budgie smugglers, I was a lot happier, and made a mental note to get some new shorts at some point that were resized to fit my much larger frame.

I had no clue what had happened to my clothes that had been on the yacht, but I was guessing that they'd ended up in the Sudan, and James's pants were a lot smaller than I'd like.

We set off again, jogging along the gantry, and then I triggered the gravity inverter and jumped over the side. Ingrid stifled a scream as I carried her with me, and we fell.

I caught us, of course, bending my knee and adding a little bounce as I set her on her feet.

"Are you okay?" I asked her absently, already scanning the area, noting how many sections were outside the reach of the working sensors. I almost missed her response, squinting as I wondered whether that was a ninja hidden in one pile, before recognizing it as a defunct custodian, one beyond all hope of repair.

I reached out, manipulating gravity until I felt like John Carter, picking Ingrid up and running forward, leaping over the piled debris and flinging myself ahead with abandon.

"I'm fiiiiiine!"

Ingrid held onto me for dear life as I leapt, the end of the word trailing out into a scream.

It didn't take long, bounding and running like that, until she was clinging to me, but also gasping in pleasure and grinning as I flew us around. The gravity field fluctuated so rapidly that she must have felt like she was on a personalized roller coaster.

It was a bit more terrifying for her, given the circumstances, than it was for me, both because I was in control, and because even with the lights on her suit, she barely got to see the walls before they blurred past at speed.

She trusted me, though, and relaxed into my arms.

Not much later, I adjusted gravity again to form a more gradual tilt. The pair of us floated to an almost perfect halt, as we landed at the security station.

We'd been passing lasers and receivers, not to mention the power plant and the turrets, all of which had whipped past too fast for Ingrid to really make out. But now that we were there? The distant zip and sizzle of laser fire, and the echoing boom of solid shells impacted.

"What's happening?" Ingrid asked, and I frowned, reviewing the data, before shaking my head.

"It looks like we're winning. Well, they are. Zac is below us, working, while the rest are off—"

Three more shots rang out, and I sensed more of the enemy winking out, before I cursed, realizing that I'd not had time to explain the differences, nor the value of the cores!

I straightened and moved over to the hole, reaching out to Ingrid, who stepped into my arms—and onto my feet—trustingly.

We plunged down, landing a handful of meters from Zac, who jerked around, fumbling for a gun, before swearing.

"Fuck's sake, boss!" he snapped. "You know how close I came to shooting you in the face there?"

"Considering you couldn't get the gun out of the holster?" I grinned. "Not fucking very!"

"Bah, I was being nice," he muttered, then shook his head. "Damn, it's good to see you on your feet, though. You gotten even uglier than you were or something? That why you're hiding your face in that helmet? Ingrid, you okay?"

"It's more complicated than that, but sure, let's pretend I'm almost as ugly as you," I murmured. "That'd make me want to hide, all right. Are the others on comms?"

"Yeah, but Jonas said not to bother them unless it was important." Zac shrugged. "No idea why he told *me* that. I know when not to pester people..."

"Sure," I agreed, grinning as I reached out, searching the air nearby and finding the encrypted comms channel easily enough.

Ten seconds in, and the encryption was broken, military grade having barely slowed me, as Ingrid distracted Zac from asking me more questions.

"Jonas, this is Steve," I said into the link. "Sitrep."

"Pinned down by the little fuckers," he replied tersely. "There's a few snipers on the other side, and they're making Court's life hell. They can stealth like you."

"Reaching out," I assured him, as I settled on the floor and focused in, scanning the area where they fought. It didn't take long to find them, and then searching, another ten seconds or so to find some possible locations.

"Courtney, back left, there's a red light, low on the wall. Find that...track down and left three meters. Pile of debris there...think that's one of them," I sent, getting a terse reply.

"Acquiring..." She paused, and there was a solid boom in the distance, as a spray of debris showed on my sensors. "Negative."

"Keep watching," I ordered. Three seconds later?

"Targeting." And, "Dead."

"Good. Track down and right six meters, pile of debris, long sheet of solid steel...you got it?"

"Acquiring."

"Look for a break in the cover, somewhere something small could fold up around—"

I didn't even finish before the shot rang out, and I blew out a relieved breath as another small explosion marked the death of a ninja.

"Leaving you now. Good hunting," I sent to her, before switching back to Jonas. "Jonas, I've not got any more likely sites for snipers on my sensors. Doesn't mean they're not there—just that if they are, I can't see them."

"Got that."

"Try to take them out with head shots," I said. "If they're in here, they haven't got access to the ship's power grid, meaning they've got an internal core instead. Those fuckers are valuable to us."

"Will do. Team Actual, out."

I shook my head, not used to their internal comms rules and I didn't give a fuck to learn them. That was the awesome thing about being the boss. *They* could adjust to *me*.

I turned back to Ingrid and Zac. He'd started to tell her about the plans he had.

I listened for a few seconds, then shook my head, stepping up.

"No, I know what you're looking at here…making a full-scale factory, right?" I asked, having heard the grand plans he had.

"Yeah! Once we've got that up and running, we can run off hundreds of these little sentinel bastards and—"

"And they can't take the other side, as they don't have access to the power grid," I finished for him.

"What?"

"They're drones, not full sentinels. Okay, look…" I squinted around the room, looking for anything I could use as an example, when I spotted a familiar-looking leg dangling out of a hopper for the factories. "FUCK!" I swore, running over and jumping up.

I landed on the top and yanked the leg up, finding it wasn't attached, and that the core and the rest of the "good shit" was already half converted.

"Dammit! Okay, fuck, you know the sentinels?" I waved the leg around. "The ones that have these legs, or the bigger ones?"

"The ones with the shark fin on them or not?" Zac squinted up at me in the dim light.

"Without the fin…how many do we have?"

"Maybe a handful?" He shrugged. "They're the most efficient for us to feed into the converters. We get more of the little guys out for them than anything else, so that's what we've been focusing on. There's some still out there that Jonas and the team just took down, I think."

"Steve, what's wrong?" Ingrid asked, seeing the way I stood, reading my body language, even when I was hiding my face in a helmet, better than Zac could with a goddamn map and a translator.

"The ones you've been prioritizing, because they're denser with high-tech shit?" I tried not to snarl at Zac.

"Yeah?"

"They're the ones with sentient cores and include energy storage. Basically, they can go anywhere, and are like low-level AI, or RI. Tell them what to do, and they do it. The others, with the fin? They're remote-controlled. They can only operate where the power grid is solid and the controller has access to it. I'd bet that these ones with the fin haven't been getting far in their assaults?"

"No…" He winced. "They've basically gotten into the first room, and they've been holding the line there, like they're daring us to go and take them on."

"And the rest?"

"Without the fins? They've been advancing, like the fin ones lay down the fire, and they swap out regularly, but the others march in and fight and try to drive us back."

"Yeah," I muttered. "And you've been trashing their bodies because they're easier, and because they're closer, with the cores."

"Yeah," he admitted. "The little fin guys, the drones? Sometimes when they're fighting, they just collapse. We thought faulty components, probably because the place is so old, but more likely…"

"It'll be the power. They have a little battery in them. Ours don't, or at least the originals I designed off their ones didn't, because they didn't have a battery in that version. The ones I fought at the end, that fucked me up bad? They had a battery that lasted a few minutes of fighting time and let them get a few shots off at me when I was trying to escape."

"Okay, so what do we need to do, Steve?" Ingrid asked in a calm and firm voice, and I took a deep breath.

"We need to feed only junk and the drones into this. Any cores we can salvage from the dead can be used to build into a new class of sentinel. I designed some quickly before…"

I looked about, trying to think of anything I could use to show it, then dismissed the idea and moved to the factories instead. I accessed its remote link and pulled up the queue, seeing that it was literally just full of drones, nothing else.

"Where are the drones?" I asked. "The ones that were already made?"

"They stopped being produced, mate. They were churned out regular like, then they fucked off. Get up once they pour out of the end, and then march off to join Jonas and the others…or they did."

"And now?" I shook my head. "It's okay, I can see it."

As soon as we'd returned to the ship, the sub-mind had cut off controlling the factories, and had focused on the drones it had, making them patrol and defend.

It'd been producing them like crazy before, because they died like damn flies, being on a lag for the remote. Now it was able to control them in real time, but it was still crap at it, with everything it knew being dedicated to hacking.

I roamed through the interface, flicking details aside, until I had three things I needed.

The first was a touch screen, the second a memory storage, and the third was a bridge I could use between those two and the factories itself.

I ordered them to be built, getting an estimated time of eleven minutes for the lot, and I jumped back down, turning to the other two.

"Okay, I've ordered a screen and memory system. As soon as they're built—and the connectors to link them up—you should be able to use it," I said to Zac and Ingrid. "It's going to be about ten minutes, then probably another ten for me to fix it altogether. Our plan here is, first of all, to get the local area secure. That's a must. Once we've got that, we need to make sure we've got a secure atmosphere. I rigged the power system above us to convert null blocks into liquid tritium and deuterium. The system uses them to—"

"You created a fusion plant?" Zac groaned, shaking his head, and staring up. "Fuck, I need to get up there! It works?"

"You're breathing the air it converts," I said dryly. "It's literally shedding helium as a by-product, and a second converter is changing that to oxygen and nitrogen to keep the air in here breathable."

"Damn! You get the plans for that, boss?" Zac asked, and I nodded.

"All that and more, buddy." I gestured to the memory module that was even now rolling off the end of the line. "And that's going to house it. I'm going to spin up a sub-mind, one for Support tasks, and I'm going to run it into there, have that attached to the factories. Bear in mind, this one will be dumb as a brick. It won't be able to give you advice—it's brain-dead, essentially. It'll store all the data I have access to. That's going to then be plugged into the factories, and a touch screen attached. That, I think, should give you a way to access it, and to run it safely. Then you select and build what you need."

"Oh hells, yes!" Zac grinned. "Don't you worry, boss, I've got your back and—"

"And you're going to work on the things I tell you to," I finished, cutting him off. "No wild shit, no flights of fancy and creating things because you want to. This isn't going to be the main site either, or at least I don't think so. Most likely we'll capture the next section and then claim a few more areas before we decide where to set up."

"Why not here?" Ingrid asked.

"We're at least a mile, if not two, from where I found the medical capsule," I said. "It makes no sense to build everything here and keep sending back and forth for shit. I need you to come up with a plan that gives us some flexibility. I'm thinking there's at least one more of these, or something similar, left working up ahead." I gestured at the large factories.

"Something needs to be making the drones and sentinels," Ingrid said, a half second before Zac could.

"Exactly. So what we need to do is secure this area...I'm talking seal the area in from the damaged sections, so if the fucker decides to cut its losses and drown the entire ship? That's its problem, not ours. We need gravity inverters to make sure it doesn't increase the pressure until we're all flat, air recycling...all that good shit.

"Best of all? We need it planned out so as we claim new areas, we can start rolling this out into those sections. That means we need to factor air locks into the design. This is a hell of an ask, I know, and this is only the physical conversion. We need defenses...I'm thinking turret emplacements, drones that we can command, and sentinels to patrol. We need food and a secure area to rest, as well as..."

I went on for a few minutes as I plugged the memory module in and got it connected to the existing equipment using my creation tool.

I covered the need to replace the sensors in all areas, install cameras, repair the walls, doors, floors, and ceiling, not to mention the factories, and defensive improvements, like positions to fire from cover, weapons emplacements...

It wasn't long before I'd run out of ideas, but damn it'd lit a fire under Zac, knowing that he had access to all of this.

I spent, not the next ten or fifteen minutes as I'd expected, but the next four hours redoing the system over and over until it matched the lunatic Aussie engineer's needs.

By the end of it, though, I had to admit it was impressive.

He had remote access to few custodians through it, and could order them, or the drones that I'd built as gophers, to carry out any of the work he needed, and damn, he had some impressive plans.

The local area was to be rebuilt to a condition that it'd probably never been in, considering the thickening of the deck, the overheads, the walls—hell, there were going to be turrets on the walls and ceiling about every twenty meters.

One of the first things he was making was a new set of drones, though, in response to my request that we needed to get this done today, and maybe tomorrow, not in ten years' time.

"Don't you worry, boss man," he assured me, cracking his knuckles and staring at the screen before him. "Trust me, I've got this."

Never had five words filled me with such terror.

I was put to work while Ingrid examined the local, and more or less secure, areas of the ship we had.

My time was taken up running back and forth doing assembly, most of which I had literally no clue about. The download of the sub-brain to the memory module had gone well. It wasn't as complete as the Hack module one was—hell, it was a quarter of the size, if not smaller, and it definitely couldn't do things like the Hack one could, in running semi-autonomously.

I had no clue why, but it was essentially a dumb variant. I, or in this case Zac, could give it parameters—like, I needed a power module to transfer the power from x to y, and it needed to carry this level of charge—and it'd provide the options that I'd unlocked.

It couldn't, though, say, create a power core production line, or more custodians.

Or, more accurately, it *could*, but they were brain-dead. They'd follow very specific orders, like the drones, and not in a good way.

To get around that, Zac took a few existing designs and created a new class of custodian, then tore the core out of C1 and installed it in the new version.

Where C1 was similar in design to an octopus, and about a meter across and another high, at the most, the new construction bots were scary motherfuckers.

Three meters long, six-legged and about two meters across and high, they were a heavy version of the original, closer to spiders in design, but with a multitude of secondary limbs tucked up underneath the main body and atop it at the back.

The butt—or what would be an abdomen on a spider, Ingrid laughingly informed me, when I asked why the thing's butt was like a spider's—was a storage compartment.

It could hold small parts, with a dedicated set of arms to remove and place them in and out of there. There were connectors on the back to attach heavier or larger parts, and a set of tools underneath, including arms to position things—welding attachments, laser cutters, and more.

The fucker even had some decent armoring, because it was Zac's intention that these would form the backbone of our units to retake the ship.

They could carry things, like turrets, forward to the areas we needed them, then emplace them and return, while the "dumb" drones could carry sheets of armoring and extra parts, or power transmission devices.

They were armored enough that it'd take concerted effort to take them down, and they were big enough—not to mention scary-looking motherfuckers—that they could assemble at a terrific speed.

Each of them would take about fifteen hours to produce, having to be built in sections, as they were too big for the factories.

That was my job, along with C2, while C3 continued making converters. There were plans for an assembly line to be done up, literally, to carry the null blocks from the main conversion plant—the original area I'd built the turrets and so on—all the way to here, and then for a second line to be built as we moved forward.

By the time the new C1 came online, powering up and scaring the shit out of everyone bar Zac, the others were back, resting in bunks and maintaining weapons and so on.

The areas I'd taken such a pounding in before were still held by us, but they were very much "contested" zones, with both our side and the security AI battling it out in attempts to move forward.

Few of the sentinels were involved in the attacks now, and almost exclusively the drones, with the new versions carrying some kind of signal and power generators as they came.

I wanted to grab one to copy it, and then return the favor, but as Jonas pointed out, take the fucker down and the enemy drones fell back quickly.

It was that or have them run out of power, and be easy pickings for us to collect and recycle. I'd hoped to make them into our own drones, simply capture and hack them, but the other side had come up with a plan to prevent that, much as with the ninjas.

They had a goddamn *bomb* implanted in them, and our five attempts at capturing them intact all ended badly. The last almost killed Scylla, who was meditating right now, while her flesh literally regrew over half her body.

The new plan was to take down the generator, and as many of them as possible with chest shots, detonating the bombs and destroying others nearby.

They were churning out units that had superior firepower and better aim than ours, presumably because they were being remote-controlled by a dedicated security AI, and ours were being controlled by a sub-mind set up to hack enemy systems.

We had considered trying to create a War sub-mind, but there were a lot of concerns on that part. First of all, if it was even possible, why the hell hadn't the creators done that, instead of creating us?

Secondly, everyone, bar Zac, had fairly specific worries about it, mainly starting and ending with a robot holocaust caused by our own version of Skynet.

That argument ran on long and loud as I worked on the new C1, connecting up sections. Ingrid and Jonas made it clear I wasn't joining the front lines, and we needed another solution, while Paul and Courtney argued over who would be best at fighting the Terminators.

I eventually agreed that the sub-mind was something we would test under very, *very* controlled circumstances, including us taking the time to pull a couple of the sentinels apart first. They were RIs, I was reminded, and as such, might be able to teach us a lot.

Specifically, restricted intelligences had to have subroutines that told them, "Go here, do this, and if this happens? This is your response," and they hadn't gone out to start world domination yet.

Something had, after all, kept them inside the ship for millennia, when people had been literally swimming and fucking about in the water directly over and around the water processor intake valves that the ship had active.

People—or, more importantly Biological Weapon Variants as well as Support Variants—had touched the rocks on a regular basis for centuries, and they'd ignored them. That the current had stopped being drawn in when I'd slapped my hand, covered in my blood and with my inactive nanites suspended in it, on those intakes?

It had to have happened before.

I couldn't have been the first person to have done it, surely? But if others had done it, and perhaps over the centuries it'd happened dozens of times, what would people have thought? Was it the blood? Hell, what would medieval nutjobs have thought when someone died here and the waters all stopped?

Did they start sacrificing people to the stones? Thinking it was appeasing some mental god of the sea?

I shook the thoughts free. It wasn't important. What was important was that for now we sort of had a plan, we had a chance, and the team was getting good at this, even if it couldn't last.

Over the last few days, they'd pretty much all grown to be great with the new weapons. Jonas was a terror with that handgun, and even more with the assault rifle version that the custodians had made.

They were expensive, though, like a two-hour print run, per gun—no clue why, considering the shit that could be made in that time, or that a giant spider-construction bot was only seven times that, but hey. Something to do with not needing a dedicated core in them like my one had, I guess.

Some things were in the hands of the gods, though, and I just accepted that was it.

Courtney had her customized sniper rifle. It was her "cheap" one. The special and insanely powerful one she kept in its case, ready for special occasions, and she'd given her normal day-to-day "working" rifle to the custodian.

By the time it'd finished with it, she had a weapon that could have castrated a fly, from the fucking *moon*.

It was essentially a rail gun, but with a variable power setting. She could crank it right down to a normal sniper shot's damage, or up to a level that would shatter the sound barrier. Normal bullets traveled at around 2000 mph, I'd been told, and "broke" the sound barrier, making the crack of the gun's firing.

This thing?

She had it cranked waaaaay down to make sure she didn't accidentally hole the side of the ship, and still, it was deafening.

Paul, on the other hand, had gone all out. Showing his Marine Corps roots, he'd opted for an assault rifle, like Jonas, and was lethal with it, even if Courtney apparently outshot him on a regular basis.

It was the melee weapon that he'd started to carry that was the most intimidating. He'd been carrying a massive battle-axe when he'd had his arm almost ripped from his shoulder by Davos, a vampire.

His new weapon, though, was a tomahawk and long hunting knife combo, and he was terrifying with them.

Now, I'd tear Davos's head off his shoulders and barely notice, but back then, freshly Arisen? It'd been a hell of a fight.

Davos against a "regular" human, even one as skilled as Paul or Jonas, was no real contest.

It'd taken eight months of rehabilitation and four separate operations, not to mention cutting-edge medical tech, to get him back on the front line, and damn that man had earned it. I'd had conversations over the last few weeks with him and Courtney. She barely spoke to me, wide smile if she was in the mood to talk, and friendly, but kept a noticeable distance.

He was a bit grim, but once he started to talk, he reminded me of old army buddies, all self-deprecating humor and "I'm nothing special," while being able to kill the average man with a teaspoon at a half mile.

The three of them made up our little security team on this mission. With Amanda midway through her pregnancy, she'd been relegated to planning and research tasks with Marie.

Dave? Well, he'd gotten some training over the last year, and although he was still a dick, he'd actually graduated to a level of being more than competent with most weapons.

As such, when Dimi was flying to places that we really couldn't show any of the Oracan? Dave was the ostensible security team. He'd been seen publicly around the insanely high-tech plane, while Ronai or one of the other Oracan would usually be hiding inside, enjoying the air conditioning and advantages of modern life.

They were apparently fascinated by a program about beautiful people who met up with their ex-partners on beaches for some reason.

Either way, it meant that the small security contingent for the mission here was made up of those three, and they looked like shit.

They'd been wearing body armor, decent stuff as well, but it'd been shredded by the sentinels' weapons. And as to the ninjas? The acid and poison darts were a serious risk.

So far, we'd been lucky that they had been able to strip out of the armor and discard it, then print up a new version each time, but sooner or later their luck would run out, and they'd be fucked.

Normally I'd have been able to heal them—literally, just stab the fuckers with my nanites and rebuild—but not anymore.

I didn't have the nanites to spend, simply put. I had just under a thousand nanites, and they were about half attuned now, thankfully. They were given to me by Scylla, but I didn't have the harvest tool to get more. And by giving me some of her nanites, she'd weakened herself.

Not hugely, but still, where Jonas, Courtney, and Paul were ostensibly the security detail, she was our hunter.

They fired from a distance, while she used centuries of fighting experience and her body's insanely high levels of nanite saturation to recover from anything that the sentinels could dish out.

She stalked the battlefield, hiding and hunting the ninjas, as they did the same to her.

Jonas had taken me aside not long after they returned from the latest assault, to warn me that they couldn't keep this up for long.

Sooner or later, she, or the rest of the team, would take a direct hit, and they'd be dead. The short-term solution to the problem was that we scaled up the drones on our side, as well as the defenses, and we made sure that nothing could move inside of our "territory" without being captured by some kind of sensor.

If the door opened at the far end, and "nothing" appeared, it wasn't a fault with the doors: it was a stealth motherfucker coming to play.

That meant that the turrets went active and fired a low-power, but steady barrage across the corridor. When they hit something? High-power kill shots.

Hopefully that'd give us some time to get things in place for the rest of the plans, because although I had backup here now, and Zac and the others were making a hell of a difference, I was also exposing them to levels of risk that were insane.

Without my armor, I couldn't fight on the front line, and that the others were doing it without the benefit of nanites at all?

I felt like a hell of a coward.

I knew what Ingrid and the others were saying—that if I died in here, they were fucked. If the AI recovered my body or used gamma lasers on me enough, I'd not recover. If I didn't recover, they couldn't claim the ship, and even if they somehow fought on and figured out how to control the systems, they'd almost certainly never be able to get the ship to work with them.

Lastly, if they did manage to do all of that, and supplied the right equipment and more to the medical capsules, and survived the procedure?

They'd be, at best, right back where they were before all of this: with one Arisen...and a much weaker one than me, if it was anyone bar Scylla who was chosen to be uplifted.

Nobody had said so yet, but there was a definite feeling of "not fucking Scylla" going around as well, as she was at best unpredictable, and at worst psychotic.

For now, she followed my wishes out of a sort of wary alliance, and general good feeling attributed to me killing her mother. Ingrid had set her free and provided someone to talk to in her own language, gave her food and explained things in terms she could generally grasp.

That wasn't going to last forever, though, and when she decided she wanted something, or we disagreed? I needed to be there. I needed to be her equal at the least, to ensure that things stayed civil...more or less.

She was from an age where might equaled right, and was raised by Athena. As much as she was trying to come to terms with the new world, it wasn't coming easy.

All of this came out in a conversation between Jonas, Ingrid, and me. And when it was done? I knew what I had to do.

There was one solution here that got things back on track. One solution that gave us the strength and depth we needed, not to mention the ability to fight on and face these risks, without it being the end of the world if we failed.

I needed to replace my nanites.

I needed to get the hell back to the level I'd been when I first entered this goddamn hellhole, at the very least, fully armed and armored. There was only one way that I could see to do that, considering that the ship was trashed and was fucking unlikely to have a massive vat of nanites waiting for me to chug.

What I needed was my harvest tool back, and I needed to get out there, doing what I did best: slaughtering the assholes who preyed on humanity.

CHAPTER NINETEEN

The argument was predictably huge. Ingrid and the others were totally on board with me needing to recover the harvest blade, or tool, or whatever. They were also totally on board with me needing to recover my nanites, and get back up there, fully suited and booted, and be a fucking terror for the creatures of the night and the asshole "mere" humans who preyed on people.

They weren't, however, overjoyed about the plan I'd come up with.

Yes, they accepted that I was the only one of them who could find the medical suite.

Yes, I was the only one who could interface with, and possibly take over the system, and force it to give me what I needed.

Nope, they did *not* like the plan.

Admittedly, calling it a "plan" was a bit grand.

More of a concept.

A feeling.

Or, as Jonas so eloquently summed it up: a complete spur-of-the-moment "yank it out of my pants and helicopter it around, and see what happens" kind of situation.

They, however, couldn't come up with a viable alternative, which meant that I won the argument, in my book.

I did agree, after a lot of arguments, to take one person with me as backup. The only one who could possibly keep up was Scylla.

Overall, it was still a shitty plan, even I admitted, as a day later I dragged myself, hand over hand, along the outside of the ship, hoping against hope that the distraction was going well.

We'd held back as long as we had, because that gave Zac the time he needed to build new drones, and to get the turrets and sensors in place.

Now twenty drones were flying forward at speed, much simpler than the ones I and the AI had been throwing at each other. He'd basically strapped a laser to a quad copter, and sent them tearing ahead.

I'd never even thought of adding in flying ones, and it was insanely obvious now, when I thought about it, that the AI hadn't either. Zac had suggested that it meant it was used to operating in environments without air, as the design he used would be shite in water or vacuum. But here?

They were fast and agile enough that they were fucking up the other side's defenses to an insane degree.

Jonas, Courtney, and Paul advanced behind the drones, and the C1 "spiderbot" carried turrets forward, ready to lay the advance base's foundations.

The distraction might actually succeed in breaking the damn deadlock, and so Scylla and I moved as fast as we could, knowing that every additional meter they covered and claimed left Ingrid and the others in more danger when they inevitably counterattacked.

Scylla swam past me, and I shook my head at the insane Greek woman. For all that Ingrid had tried to teach her about body modesty, it'd been a losing battle.

Her point that the armor slowed her down in the water, and had very little effect on the beam weapons, was a good one, as was that waterlogged clothes would only make her less stealthy.

We'd managed to convince her to wear a swimsuit, which was as far as she'd compromised. It was clear that she didn't see the point, but was willing to go along with it to shut us up.

Zac had practically had apoplexy when she'd walked out of the small private areas we'd had for changing and for the bathroom, and she'd been wearing only that, and carrying her spear and rifle.

The clothing was made of a graphene variant that we'd gained access to from the General download I'd received in the Support tree. It was strong, supple, and stretched well, as well as temperature regulating and water resistant. The plan was to design a new form of armor with it as a base layer for everyone, it was that strong and light, and it was even available in multiple colors.

It was also thinner than a hair, and that resulted in Ingrid and Courtney immediately clapping hands over Paul's and my eyes.

Zac had a grin that could be seen from orbit, and was in severe danger of being skewered by the ancient warrior woman. Jonas had coughed and suggested that perhaps a thicker outfit would be more appropriate.

All in all, it'd taken three attempts to make one that, when stretched, was more or less decent, and Scylla had been furious over the delay.

She'd also, much to everyone's surprise, made her intentions clear regarding Jonas.

"You have a problem with my clothing," she'd said to him, and he'd coughed, trying not to look anywhere he shouldn't, maintaining eye contact as he explained that it was a little too revealing.

"The problem with my body is not mine—it is all of yours. I would prefer to do this fight without clothing, but to settle your minds, I will wear this thing, for now. Once we have claimed this ship, you and I will discuss this again. You have seen me fight naked, and as such, wearing this? It should be no issue."

"Well, yeah, I can see your point, my lady Scylla. But still, it's not right that—"

"It's not right that you have seen me naked and that I have not seen you?" she suggested, then shrugged. "Very well. This, I understand. Should you survive being raised, you shall come to me, naked and in private. If you please me, then perhaps you will stand by my side at day and night...for a while."

That'd shut the fucker right up. He'd blushed bright red and stared at her for long seconds, as she waited.

"Perhaps I have this wrong then? You do not wish to come to me and serve me naked, in a more private way? I will not offer a second time."

"I do!" he blurted, then coughed and cleared his throat, before going on. "I will come to you, my lady, once this ship is taken, and..." He'd done his best not to look at the rest of us when he stood there, facing her and basically making it clear he wanted to play "hide the sausage."

"If you survive being raised," she replied flatly. "Else you will not survive the experience either, and I have no desire to dispose of your body." With that, she'd gathered up the bag that had been printed up for her, and I did the same with mine. Both of us put our guns, spare magazines, and shoes in them. All the while, I tried not to grin at the look on Jonas's face.

I'd kissed Ingrid goodbye, and she'd threatened me with both unending torment if I died, and a seriously good time when I won and came back to her.

Then I'd carried Scylla and me up through the gap in the ceiling and out, using the gravity inverter.

We were crawling and swimming along outside in the hope that the damn AI wouldn't be able to tell us from fish or whatever, without the disturbances in the gravity field I usually left everywhere I went.

That meant that I was back to swimming—properly—and grabbing onto rocky outcroppings and dragging myself along.

I didn't realize just how damn much I'd gotten used to my abilities until I couldn't use them anymore. If I could have formed my wings? This would have been easy. Or hell, flippers!

Anything would have been better. Instead, I wore the remains of my heavy-ass armor, thrashing and pounding the water as I tried to swim.

Scylla, on the other hand, swam ahead and came back to check on me, looking annoyed at how slow I was, with her tiny little rebreather puffing out the occasional silvery bubbles that fluttered away toward the sky so far overhead.

I snarled in my helmet and kept going, forcing myself not to listen to the team comms. I could, I could so easily, but considering the mission here? I couldn't allow myself to be distracted, nor let myself distract them.

Minutes passed. My heavy breathing rasped in my ears as I thrashed and fought with the sea, my own tiny goddamn swimming shorts recovered on the way out, and my clothes in the bag.

I kept going. The outline of the scans I'd done when finding the entrance I'd used last were enough to guide me along to where I guessed the one I'd used to exit the ship after my first visit was hidden.

Now, I found it.

It was well hidden, a cliff-edge drop-off, one that led down to a sandy bottom that was surprisingly clear of any debris, literally just being a stretch of blank sand.

This time, I wasn't concerned about hiding the fucking place from others. I was far enough out—nearly a mile from shore—that anyone who found this area and noticed the disturbed sand deserved to find it.

I landed in the middle of it, kicking up puffs of disturbed sea bottom, drifting sand, and sending fish flitting here and there, as Scylla landed with barely any reaction from the marine life.

I grumbled to myself, searching around until I found the panel, hidden artfully under an overhang that made me imagine a moray eel clamping its jaws down on my hand as soon as I slid it in.

Fortunately, either the eel was out to dinner, or it had better taste than me, and I was left unmolested. The warm, pliable rubbery surface gave under my hands, and I pressed, then turned.

The hatch under us slid open. A collection of panels glided apart like an iris dilating to let us in. The chamber below was already filled with water, presumably from my last visit.

I led the way. The same feeling of instinctual terror that had filled me on exiting rose again as I swam through the open area between the panels of metal.

Scylla followed. The pair of us were barely inside before it sealed again; the mechanism jammed and juddered as disturbed rocks caught in it.

Sinking to the bottom, bending our knees as we settled, I reached out to the panel before me, and I couldn't help but grin.

I'd hacked this control panel on the way out, and it still merrily accepted me, pumping the water out and letting the air whoosh in to replace it.

I hesitated a few seconds as the chamber filled, a sudden thought that the AI, again, could be fucking with us, and that the air could be a mix of knockout drugs—or hell, anything, really—only to let out a long, relieved sigh when Scylla dumped her rebreather into her bag with no ill effects.

"We are ready?" she asked me, her accent smoother than it had been, speaking to many long hours of practice with the language, and long centuries of speaking other tongues.

"Let's go," I agreed after dressing and readying my gun. Scylla did the same with her weapon; then I reached out and ordered the door to open.

As soon as we stepped out, a small sentinel, with its arms wrapped around a nearby stanchion, opened fire—the beam at head height, tracking across and downward—drawing a cry of pain from Scylla and a snarl from me, as I returned fire.

The little fucker had been waiting, set *perfectly*. The gantry that we'd stepped out onto was laid on its side, as was the rest of the ship, making it seem more like a metal cage that was missing one side. The little bastard had been hanging from the upper section of the gantry, laser aligned on the opening door.

Scylla barely got off a single cry, before she was down, her head almost entirely severed, and the beam was cutting into my upper chest, tracking upward and across, aiming for the throat.

I fired three times. The first shot missed, the second caught the side of the sentinel and ripped a leg free in a shower of sparks and shattered metal, and the third tore the core apart, with one ring of the fléchettes catching it.

The little sentinel was torn free, spiraling out over the edge of the gantry and into the open air in a spray of metal, even as the gantry itself shuddered.

The shots I'd loosed had punched holes farther along. Hell, the gantry was barely hanging on anyway, having collapsed in more places than it'd stayed together, and now?

The tearing sound of shifting metal made me swear, as my chest seemed to tighten.

I looked to Scylla, collapsed to the left, inside the airlock still. Blood pumped free, the walls liberally coated and slick with her blood, and I cursed.

There was no saving her, not now.

Her eyes were filming in death already, and the last thing she did was look at me, eyes wide, staring, as if to beg me to make sure she woke again.

I moved to her side, kneeling, reaching out to where she slumped on the floor, and settled her head more or less back in place. I swallowed, willing my helm to clear over my face, and I stared down at her, taking her hand in mine and waiting.

"I'll come back for you," I promised her. "I'll be here when you wake."

The terror in her eyes faded slightly, and I forced a smile, waiting, as the last light left them. I shook my head, straightening, and forced down a lump in my throat.

Scylla was a pain in the ass half the time. I was never sure whether I was going to be met with her gutting someone who failed to show her "the proper respect" or whether she was going to be naked. Probably beating the crap out of someone who wasn't sure whether they'd be stabbed for looking, or for not paying attention to the lesson.

She was terrifying for all the wrong reasons for everyone around her, and yet...she risked her life for us. She fought alongside us. And now? That she'd been on my left, rather than the other way around, was the only difference between her or me being dead.

If I'd taken the full force of the beam to the throat, as lightly armored as it was, I'd have been drowning in my own blood at best. Because it'd targeted her first and had moved steadily enough to be sure of her before moving onto me? I was alive still.

And she wasn't.

I'd seen real terror in her eyes as she'd died, fear that once again, when she awoke, she'd be locked away, that she'd be doomed to awaken time and again, trapped as she had been, only to die repeatedly, until her nanites were no longer able to free energy from her cells, and shut down as well.

I wished I'd taken the hit, for a few seconds, and then for a lot longer I felt even worse.

I didn't wish I'd taken the hit, I knew, because I genuinely didn't know whether once I'd recovered—*if* I recovered—I would have awoken to her standing over me and protecting me, or to her rising into godhood as an immortal Arisen with centuries' worth of nanites attuned and unlocked.

I didn't know for sure that she'd have supported me, or whether she'd have set me aside and have ruled instead.

I felt terrible wondering that, but it was still true. I crouched again, and this time I crossed her arms, settling her hands on her chest, one atop the other, and I closed her staring eyes.

She might be down for an hour, or minutes, or days. There was no way to be sure, not really, and while I stood here, the others fought for me.

I had to move on.

I settled her spear by her side, then—slightly freaking out about how "wrong" this was—I wrote "I'll be back for you" on the wall, in her blood.

I also forced myself to turn away from that blood, knowing just how full it was of nanites.

It'd be an easy thing for me to help myself to some, even to just clean it up from the floor and walls. She'd not necessarily be recovering that, would she?

It'd make my chances of survival a lot better, and...and those nanites were slowly making their way back to her even now I saw, shaking my head.

And I'd be stripping her of her strength for when she awoke, as well as violating her. It'd be no different than if I touched her, when she was like this. It wasn't with her consent, and although I was a horrific asshole in a lot of ways, I certainly wasn't like that.

I checked my rifle and moved back out onto the gantry, looking about and drawing a deep breath. I mostly remembered the route I'd taken before, and as the AI certainly knew I was there now, there was no reason not to use my abilities.

I stepped off the edge of the gantry and plunged down. The gravity field around me flexed and formed, catching my weight and lifting me, even as a handful more sentinels sprinted out of the corridor I was headed toward.

They flowed forward, their four legs carrying them at a hell of a speed as their lasers started to glow, and I opened fire.

The first shot was wide, again. The dispersal pattern that I'd used on the shotgun no longer adjusted as easily, and I'd not yet formed the nanites into a tentacle that I could use to change things like that pattern, not yet.

The second shot, though, as I dragged myself left, the gravity field flipping me around, tore through one of the five.

It was sent spinning, clattering in death back along the corridor, as I dropped like a stone, my mind now so thoroughly enmeshed into my gravity inverter that I moved by instinct.

I chambered another round as the beams tracked me. The sizzle and crash as they missed and tore into weakened metal behind me filled the air. I fired back, hitting another in the core, shredding it entirely as I snarled my frustration with the limited accuracy weapon.

I should have brought a goddamn rifle!

I rolled and hammered myself upward, doubling the pull of the planet on me, ripping me upward…

And then they fell silent, ten seconds of fire already expended, time in which I'd flipped and dove, rolled and fired back.

I soared into the entrance to the corridor again, landing hard and running to absorb the impact. I pumped and fired at one, blowing it apart, and threw myself down.

One of the surviving two flung itself at me, legs spread wide, clearly intending to grab onto me and release its electrical attack.

I was already sliding under it, though. My skin screamed in protest as it was dragged across rough surfaces at speed, when usually it'd be safe inside my armor.

Regardless, though, I stomped hard, planting my foot and twisting, half flipping myself to my feet. The one that had passed me overhead landed, took two steps, and launched itself at me again.

The one before me?

I did what I'd done seemingly ages ago, and I'd grabbed it, ripping the core cylinder free, then dropped it.

The legs and lower body were connected to the core by some magnetic ring, something that kept the main core floating and helped it to do whatever technical crap it needed it for.

It didn't matter to me, though. What did?

If you were ballsy and stupid enough to get in that close to one of these fuckers? You could take them down, and *hard*.

The body collapsed, and I twisted, grabbing the lower nearest tentacle of the reaching fucker, as I triggered my time compression.

I needed this crap for the hack I had ahead of me, I knew I would, but for a few seconds?

Hell yes.

Time slowed to a glacial crawl. I gripped the tentacle and yanked hard, triggering two fast bursts from the gravity inverter. One was atop me as I limbo-ed under the reaching arms, and one behind and below the main core of the creature, pushing up and forward.

With my body acting as a fixed point, I whipped the fucker overhead in a parabolic arc, smashing it down atop its former friend's corpse.

Then I dropped my gun and ripped its core free as well.

I reached out and triggered the hack protocols. The sub-mind struggled for a brief second as it clearly tried to do multiple things, and I grinned. Despite everything, it was still me.

I was always crap at multi-tasking.

I didn't release the slowed time capacity yet, keeping it running for a few more seconds as the hack took hold, cracking the defenses of both sentinels in seconds, and making me feel as if I'd used a sledgehammer to break a soft-boiled egg, it was that much overkill.

That didn't mean I wasn't taking advantage of the situation, though.

I reached out, sliding one of the cores back into the nearby body. It twitched and flailed, as the now obedient system flickered and tried to make sense of its new world.

The second one?

Well, looking at it, I knew I'd trashed the body a little too much, so I gathered up the other corpses nearby, and started to run. The corridor didn't go far before I came to the first gap in it, seeing the long faded, and yet still visible marks left from my bloody footprints so long ago.

They'd sunk into the metal, staining it, but seeing them made me nod grimly to myself, as I followed them.

A minute later, I jumped off the side, plunging down into the depths of the cross corridor. The gravity inverter helped me to land smoothly, before I snorted and tossed the armfuls of metal and dead sentinel into the air, catching it with a second bubble of force.

I relaxed, a little, as I brought the gun around again. The single operational sentinel clanked along with me, staring up and then racing ahead as I ordered it.

I remembered these corridors, and the way they'd seemed endless—the horror, the fear, and the sheer mind-numbing panic, the blood loss, then exhaustion, and the terrible cold.

Now I strode them in jeans and half an armored suit, an alien-designed shotgun under one arm and a sentinel of my own keeping pace.

Madness.

Following the footprints, I picked up my pace, starting to run again, hearing distant clatters as something, presumably more sentinels, started to give chase.

Panels blurred past on all sides. Long-dead custodians that I remembered seeing on the way out were noticeably absent now, the corridors stripped clean of them. I snarled, seeing the proof that the security AI was doing the same as us: stripping anything it could justify, and using it to build its forces.

Another minute, then two passed; three came and went, before I finally saw it just ahead, and my heart dropped.

The sizzle and zip of lasers flashed in the distance. I cursed. The AI knew what I'd come for! I dropped the remains of the sentinels, keeping the core in my bag and the mobile class-one sentinel with me, but sprinted now, desperate to reach the medical suite before the fucker could do any more damage!

The door irised open as I approached, and one of the bigger, crab-like fuckers opened fire, clearly expecting me. Two smaller, class-one versions behind it continued to work on carving the medical suite up.

"Motherfucker!" I screamed, raising my gun, then snarling. If I used it in here? I'd trash anything they hadn't already.

The class three opened fire. Its dual gamma laser seared its way through the air. I frantically threw myself sideways, twisting, yanking myself downward with the inverter, even as I reached out, frenetically thrusting upward, trying with all my might to shove the beams that were closing on me off target. I triggered my time compression again, desperate for any kind of an edge.

And...I failed.

I failed, and the dual gamma lasers carved into my lower chest, arcing around...and then lifted.

I knew what was coming, and what it meant. Despite every instinct, everything that I wanted, everything that I knew that raced through me—despite it all, I somehow managed to do what I knew I had to.

I retracted the armor over my chest, keeping only the helmet, as I shunted the sub-mind into a new path. Instilling one order above all others.

Protect and serve Ingrid.

Then?

It wasn't even pain. Not really.

There was a sudden feeling, like the absence of a ticking clock, as the beam carved its way up into my chest, destroying my heart.

I collapsed, fell to the ground, impacting and bouncing, and came to a halt on my back.

My eyes were wide open, seeing the world all around me, but not. None of it made sense, as if I watched the events unfolding from the other side of a glass panel, one that stood between me and my body.

I saw my corpse on the floor, the helmet still on me, but the rest of my armor was gone. The sentinel clanked forward; its gamma optics died back to a glassy sheen, as the eight-second burst was exceeded.

The class one that was following me went *mad*. It sped up; the legs flashed over the walls as it opened fire. The little laser, feeling almost like a popgun against a howitzer, opened fire, dragging across the optics of its much larger foe.

They melted into slag, and the back of the unit opened, my last thoughts of horror as the gas contained in the "crowd control package" dispersed into the area, clearly to make goddamn sure of me.

Then the room vanished in a white-hot bloom of rolling flames, and my eyes, like the rest of my skin, crisped, and ran like butter beneath a blowtorch.

CHAPTER TWENTY

Death.

It wasn't like a waiting room in some mystical train station, with important people from my past coming out to greet me. Nor was it the much more likely, personally earned alternative, where there were hot pokers and manacles, or chains and whips.

Shame that, really, as a little kink never hurt anyone…permanently.

No, death for me was pain, then silence. Everything had stopped, and I mean everything: no thoughts, no pain, no fear. If anything, it was like as soon as I died, that was it. When I'd been standing on the other side of the pane of glass, watching my body collapse? It was like that, except that after a few seconds it all just froze, and then it was gone.

I'd heard sleep referred to before as "the little death," and it was true. That step, right between being awake and the dreams and paranoia and all that crap your subconscious flung around like a monkey at the zoo?

That fraction of a second, when all stopped, when the world took a breath and it's all silent?

That was death.

I didn't expect to wake, not at all—hell, when I died, I didn't expect anything…it was too damn sudden. But when I did wake again? It was to a cold metal floor, with distant noises ringing and clanging, and a constant whooshing noise nearby.

I laid there for seemingly ages, the left side of my face pressed against the metal of the floor. I stared at the minute grains that made the panel before me up, the scratches and scrapes, the battered, absolutely fucked-up floor.

It was green, I realized, my brain slow at first as it picked out details.

The panels of the walls and floor that I'd thought were some kind of dull blue or gray? They were a metallic *green*, mixed with the blues and chromes to make an overall color that was just a little weird. Where a recent scrape had been made on it, it showed brassy undertones, and…

I was grabbed from behind suddenly. A metal clamp gripped me by the back of the head and lifted, my body limp and numb.

It hurt, the grip, as did the fact I was literally being carried by my fucking head, but…but it was distant. Really distant, as though it happened to someone else.

I could suddenly see more of the room around me, as I was lifted and carried by something huge.

Trying to move, I found that I couldn't, that there was something wrong, really wrong, as my body refused to respond. I flexed and shifted my arms, clenching my fists, kicking out—hell, wriggling and letting out a fart even. None of it worked!

Starting to panic, my eyes rolling as I tried to move my body, I froze.

I could move my eyes. Testing it, I could move my jaw, yeah, and one of my ears was being crushed against the side of my head, the clamp having squashed it.

The pain was distant, but I *could* feel it.

My body, though? If it wasn't for the feeling of the gently swinging weight on my neck, and the glimpse I'd gotten as I was picked up? I could have been a disembodied head.

There was nothing, but I could feel from the top of my head down to my neck, and…and my head. My helmet was gone.

FUCK.

The sub-mind! Shit, I had to hope that it was still contained in the nanite neural clusters somehow, but fuck, I didn't know how, nor why the helmet had gone. Had what was left of my armor gone too? I just didn't know.

It felt…my head felt stuffed full, like I had a horrific cold and the aftereffects of a migraine at the same time. I just had to hope that was something to do with the sub-mind, and not just me being headfucked right after death.

Focusing in, as I looked around, I forced my sluggish brain to action. I was being carried by something, something huge, and it was moving on multiple legs. All I could see was the occasional flicker of them as they came down, the way I was being held. I was pretty much being carried ahead of it, and those flickers were all that I was getting.

They were metal, though, looking like wide tapered oblongs that rose and fell, connected to a piston that vanished back out of sight.

Ahead of me, and all around, was a cleared space, one that I instantly recognized as a hold on the ship.

One that was much more intact than the ones we'd seen so far, though—one that was maintained, and even lit by what looked like a massive furnace at one end.

Dozens of smaller machines moved back and forth, busy as fuck. Some moved equipment into the room, depositing it in massive piles to be assessed and dealt with. Others gathered it up and carried it forward, feeding it into the furnace, or setting it into a section to be worked on by what looked like a small legion of custodians.

Not a furnace, I realized, stunned. It wasn't a goddamn furnace—it was a smelter!

The radiant heat of it reached me as I was carried closer. Inside it, I could see debris breaking down, melting and being formed into a pool of glowing metal.

That, in turn, was being floated—fucking *floated*—through the air to a set of converters. They were separating it out, feeding it, still glowing, into access points.

On the far side, they all churned cold blocks that looked more like the discs I'd found when I first started this fight.

They rattled and jingled along, rolling into each other, as they were lifted by a clear gravitational field, and carried onto the next stop. More converters and construction machines were being built by custodians. Hell, there were at least a dozen in various stages of being produced.

They were all new, and even the smelter was gleaming, clearly freshly finished.

What the hell had changed?

Genuinely, I didn't understand. If the ship had been running at this level when I found it? I'd have been scooped up and fucked up in seconds.

206

There were machines being finished that would soon be able to churn out dozens of sentinels, I was betting—not just drones, but *sentinels*.

They could churn them out over and over, production-line style, and we'd have no damn chance.

Masses of equipment were brought in, almost all trashed, but here and there? I spotted things like the medical suite that I'd been "fixed" in, or at least it looked like the remains of it.

Burnt, blackened, and cut into several sections, it was being moved along to be dumped into the furnace soon. And up ahead?

The still body of Scylla was laid on the pile as well.

I stared at her, stunned, seeing her eyes still closed, her unattuned nanites clearly slower to reawaken her than my own.

What I saw, beyond that she was dead and broken still, though? A collar.

A circular collar that ran around her neck, a thin band that was pressed tight against her flesh.

I concentrated as I swung gently. And yeah, knowing it was there? I thought that I could feel something slightly warmer pressed against my neck. It might be my imagination, though, just as easily.

If it was there, though? That meant that there was a physical reason that I couldn't control my body. And I was betting it was because the fuckers that gave us the abilities in the first place? They'd have to be idiots to not have a way to restrain us once they decided to get rid of a weapon that could regenerate.

I pulled up my nanites, finding I was down to two hundred and thirteen, after Scylla's gift, but they were all attuned.

I closed my eyes, reaching out, and in.

My nanites pooled in my mind's eye atop my Adam's apple, flowing like tar and extending a single tiny tentacle downward.

As it touched…*something*, the nanites failed, crumbling to dust, and I yanked them back, frantically trying to save as many as I could.

A hundred and eighty-seven. That was all that was left. Not knowing what else I could do, I tried again, slower this time.

The first time, I'd pooled them on my skin, then I slid them down, reaching out. Now, as I thought about it, there had to be a reason that it was pressed to my skin, rather than being simply a gun they pointed at me or a field that filled a room. That, logically, meant that there was likely a projector of some kind, and that it was around my neck to cut off the body below, extending a field of interference into my neck, so the signals I sent down to my body were instead being blocked or broken.

Right. That made sense.

That would mean, though, as surely you'd not want anyone who tried to put them on the prisoner losing the use of their hands and so on, that it'd be, first of all, something that you could handle, meaning it either had an on/off switch, or a safe place to touch it.

With that in mind, I extended the pseudopod outward, standing proud and straight from my neck, and then looped it around. Slowly, oh so slowly as the machine carried me, and blood ran down my skin from the grip it had on me, I extended the nanites.

They came into contact with a warm surface—solid and crystalline, I realized—as I forced myself to stay as still and "dead" as possible.

The surface was smooth and made of overlapping layers, hundreds of them, that pressed down atop each other. I focused, sensing a current, but not an electric one...something organic, and...

As I mentally explored it, I'd extended the tendrils into the structure, and as they passed each layer? They grew less and less responsive, in a recognizable way.

The crystal in the cave—the crystal weapons!

It was the same feeling, the creeping failure, but much weaker, and more intentional. More guided.

My mind raced as I thought, evaluating it, remembering and comparing the feeling.

I drew back and thought for a second. The layers, the feeling...I'd seen a woman who converted slowly into a living crystal, and the band around my neck? I guessed that it was the refined and high-tech version of her.

The layers? I bet that each of them, crystalline as they were, and slightly curved, arcing inward, were identical.

They were microscopic layers of that damn crystal laid over and over, and projecting a field inward, across my damn neck.

That was why my helmet had failed, I thought, and why even now I could feel the nanites crumbling and losing functionality. A hundred and fifty-four nanite clusters were active now, and even as I checked, the counter ticked down one more.

I had no time, no chance to get this wrong, to figure out a better way.

The one thing I had was a burning need to fuck some shit up, so I went for it.

The outside of the collar was safe to touch, more or less, and I slid the nanites under the edge of the first layer, cutting like the thinnest of razor blades, to slit the top layer loose and flick it away.

It slid out easily, dangling loose, and I sent the nanites flowing, carving layer after layer free.

They came loose like string, no longer compressed, and almost joyous in their release, unraveling and rolling down my back, as sensations started to return to me.

One of the first, of course, was pain.

Whatever the effect of that thing around my neck had been on the rest of the body, it'd also dampened the pain that came from the goddamn metal clamp on my skull! I forced myself to stay still, and to show nothing.

Blood ran down my head and across my body from the clamps, where they dug in, and I knew that if I gave away that I wasn't dead?

This machine could fix that in short order.

A single squeeze and my skull would pop like a spot. And seeing the way that Scylla was laid in a pile, before the furnace? I was betting that all the "rubbish" was to be fed into it.

That would have included us, I guessed. And, more to the point, the only reason I was alive right now was because the machine was probably programmed to not crush things when it carried them, just in case it lost components or whatever when it carried shit that was valuable to places that weren't a smelter.

The collar was unraveled at speed now, and feeling returned to me as I made another discovery. When the nanites accidentally cut too deep and penetrated the layer, connecting to a severed section, rather than cutting and flipping it free, like a long apple peel? The sudden feeling that flooded me? It was like I was poured into a high-speed data link.

It was similar to the way I'd followed the links when I was hacking in the casino, tracing out lines, making connections. But here? It was insanely fast.

Like comparing driving one of those hairdryer-like powered worker motorbikes, or an electric scooter with a dying battery, to the feeling you got when a plane first took off, the g-forces pressing you back, the lift, seeing the ground pass too fast to focus on a single detail, and…

I was back.

I was out, I was…I was confused to *fuck*.

It'd felt like I was poured along a data connection, but this was a restraint device intended to stop people, surely, not just…

I saw it then, not entirely, but the similarities. The structure of the crystalline layers and the superconductors that I had access to, and hell, the data connections.

They were all so similar it was insane. And best of all? If the pulse was fed along the "cable" or whatever it was? It stopped generating that suppression field.

It was an if/or situation.

A high-speed data transfer line, or a suppression field, and my biggest problem with hacking things myself? Getting access to their systems.

The vanishing suppression field sent waves of pins and needles throughout my body as sensation returned, along with under a hundred more nanite clusters, spread out across my body.

I sent the tip of the nanites that had unfurled the "cable," spreading out along its length, then triggered my time compression ability, as the machine came to a stop, extending me farther out ahead of it and dropping me atop the pile of crap.

I slammed into Scylla's corpse, legs buckling, and I slid sideways, trying to keep myself from reacting. I stared at the rest of the room and the behemoth that had been carrying me. Something attached to my back jabbed me painfully behind the already injured ear.

I rolled, seeing it, staring up as it slowly—oh so slowly—started to turn. It stood atop six legs, each needle-like, three meters tall, about half a meter wide at the center where the pistons attached to it, and narrowing to maybe ten or fifteen centimeters wide and deep at either end.

The next section was a simple oblong where the legs attached, clearly heavy-duty, and a storage area on the back, like a flatbed truck. The "body" sat almost centaur-like at the front, rising high with four arms attached: two that were massive, clearly intended for digging or mining, and two that were smaller, more agile and dexterous.

One of those was folding back in toward its chest now, and I guessed by the blood on it that dripped and reflected the furnace light, it'd been what had held me.

The head was an oval. Two fins atop it suggested it was remote-controlled, rather than sentient. A dozen orbs gleamed on the head, either cameras for eyes, optics for lasers—or hell, both for all I knew.

Either way, though, I twisted as I reached up and grabbed the end of the cable, whipping it out. The bundle of crystalline cells, layered over and over, unfurled like a whip, snapping out and smacking against the leg of the four-meter construction as it turned away.

It clearly saw my movement and turned around. A central, much larger eye blazed to life, glowing with an unholy inner light. I had no time to dodge, no chance to run, and so I threw myself into the one possibility I did have, and poured my mind along the connective link to the metal that made up my enemy.

The world around me vanished, as I released Tsunami into the link, forcing myself to make the most of the brief seconds as the end of the connection flowed down, slithering against the metal and falling to the floor.

With the time distortion cranked *waaaaay* up, I had just long enough, thanks to it being made of metal, and it clearly accepting its orders through the fins atop its head, to force the Tsunami into the connection.

It flowed out, cutting off the security AI's control as the outer shell was locked down. I grinned, seeing the eyes shut down. I cut the time compression, saving it for later…if I lived long enough.

I rolled, sliding down the mass a little as I twisted, feeling torn metal and rust slice into my skin, knowing damn well I'd be in serious danger of infection if I were anyone else. I clawed my way to a halt, and I frantically threw myself into the climb, shoving my way back up toward Scylla.

She looked peaceful, if a little paler than normal, probably thanks to the blood loss. I reached out and drew my fingertip across the back of the collar, pressing out a tiny blade of nanites to slice the top layer free, then pulling her upright as I desperately unwound it.

Ten seconds it took, ten seconds in which the distant noises picked up massively, as a handful of sentinels started to roll off the production lines nearby.

I was practically gibbering by the time I got to the end and ripped it free, tossing it all aside, before dropping her back. She was still dead—the most use she could be right now?

Probably as a meat shield.

Instead, I forced myself up and clambered across the pile, staggering from side to side, heading for the nearest factory.

It was hissing and whirring. Sections of a crab-like class three sentinel slid out, while the two class ones it'd already dropped went through a powering-up cycle.

I swore and started to run and jump, my body responding sluggishly.

Crashing across the uneven pile, I slid, setting off a cascade of rubbish, hitting the ground and rolling, as the first class one opened fire.

I threw myself sideways, landing on my shoulder and rolling as the beam carved a line into the floor by my head, before cutting off. Then I was up, sprinting, a dozen meters, ten, eight, six…I was two meters away when the second sentinel came online, spinning toward me, and I threw myself into a sliding tackle as the beam lit, passing over my head after nicking my left shoulder.

I kicked out with both feet, slamming them into its legs, and sending it toppling atop me. I grunted at the thing on my back that jabbed into the back of my head again and…and I twisted, frantically reaching over my shoulder and ripping my bag free.

I'd forgotten about the damn core, but now that I'd realized what was jabbing into me? I had a goddamn powerful need for it right now!

The sentinel twisted, the core rotating and aiming for me; I grabbed its core with my right hand, ripping it free and flinging it away. The one that still stood turned its optics on me.

It was clearly recharging, as I ripped the core I'd dumped into my bag free—finally, tearing the bag half apart as I did so—and shoved it in the direction of the other active sentinel.

It opened fire a half second before the other could, carving a line through the enemy sentinel's core, killing it, as I held it out, like a can of goddamn spray paint.

Sagging back, I let out a groan, stunned that I was still alive, before half rolling on my side and dragging the empty "body" of the first sentinel close, then jamming the core in my hand into it.

It spasmed. The legs flared as if I'd jammed a 240V battery up its arse, before twisting and standing, coming to its feet, as the clatter from the one it'd just killed died away.

I didn't know how long I had. Hell, for all I knew, there were a thousand sentinels all racing for me right now, about to come around the corner and slice and dice me.

But the class three was rolling out of the production line now, and I hastily shoved myself back to my feet, staggering and then running to it, leaping up, while I frantically sent orders to the class one.

It set off at full speed, rushing across the ground to snatch up the long strip of crystal cells, the connectors, or whatever it was, then speeding back toward me, the end fluttering in the air behind it.

I dragged myself up and across the class three, grabbing at the dual gamma laser, and twisted it, making damn sure it was pointing away from both me and the incoming little dude.

It didn't respond at first. The section turned smoothly; then it clearly started to awaken, as the mechanism suddenly jammed, before starting to crank back.

Noises started in the carapace below me, clearly chemical ones, as the canister on its back extruded nozzles. I winced, remembering how I'd damn well died.

A second passed as I clung to the back of the thing, being slowly dragged around by the laser. Then another, and a third, as the first hints of a gas started to hiss free of the nozzles. Then the sentinel was there, dropping the connectors, and I released the turret, grabbing the data links, and jammed one end flush against the core that I could just make out.

The result was electric as I was ripped into the digital world again, savagely crushing the machine's defenses as it came to life. My time dilation spun up frantically...and the sentinel under me shuddered.

The nozzles clicked, then slid back; coverings slid over them with a satisfying *clunk*. I grinned, twisting around and staring at the room, desperately searching for anything else coming.

The construction machine that had just churned out the unit I was straddling gave off a clang, and then shut down, as did others around the room. The smelter seemed to give up as the liquid metal fell suddenly, hitting the ground with a solid splat. Globules flew in all directions as the gravity field powered down.

It was the AI, I guessed, my mind racing feverishly. It'd seen that I had a powerful sentinel here, and that if it lost the fight, it lost what might be its last line of defense. Instead, it was pulling back.

All around the room, the systems shut down, and I grinned. I'd rather have taken control of a hundred or so more sentinels, sure, but forcing the AI to shut down the power and their factory instead? It was a good consolation prize.

I'd not permitted myself to worry about Ingrid and the others, not yet—too much was going on—and I desperately shoved down my concern again.

My helmet wouldn't form when I tried it, too much damage, and the weaponized nanites were almost nonexistent, literally—making me hope and pray there were enough currently holding the neural structure of the sub-mind together still.

What I did have, though, around the room, were dozens of custodians. And unlike the sentinels, they were still here.

Some of them, anyway. They were spreading out, separating and clearly heading off onto other tasks, as I started to search the rest of the room.

Many of them were headed for the far end of the room, toward a corridor that looked pretty heavy-duty. The "door" was clearly an air lock, and shit, it was armored.

Thought was as good as action, and my new trusty steed set off at its top speed, racing to cut them off.

The class-one sentinel with me started to open fire at my order, carving the legs off one side of as many of the custodians as possible, as they headed away.

I rode the other one after the majority, cutting them off as they picked up speed. Leaping from the back of the class three, I landed hard on one of the custodians, sending the small machine clattering to the ground. I rammed the connector against its core, holding on as it tried to buck me off.

Ten seconds it took, to claim it; then I struggled to my feet, the custodian setting off, running at another of its former fellows, launching itself at it, and wrapping its arms and legs around the other.

They both tumbled to the floor. And the big fucker that had been carrying me to dispose of earlier? Finally, Tsunami kicked in with it, as it came to life, twisting around and heading in our direction.

Three of the custodians had made it around us as I claimed the last one, and the class three had managed to grab another. The class one had cut two down, and I was closing on the next, when the air lock between the corridor ahead and the room I was in triggered.

It slid shut with terrifying speed, clearly an emergency response, as it caught a custodian midway through the door and crushed it. I winced, then grinned as I jumped, landing on the custodian I'd been chasing, catching it from behind.

It was mine in short order, but the room we were in now was sealed, and clearly I wasn't getting out easily.

All the doors, I saw as I looked around, had been sealed, and the various custodians and smaller, presumably drone collectors and so on had stopped.

There was a brief pause, as I wondered whether they were just going to turn themselves off or blow up or something, when instead they all spun, and started to run at the now silent factories.

"Fuck!" I snarled, setting off running as well. "Stop them!" I yelled. "Fuck them up!"

The units with me—the sentinels, at least—opened fire, targeting the limbs of the others at my order, while the custodians ran at their counterparts, leaping and tangling their legs, unable to fight, but able to lock onto and stop them.

Two more of the converters and one of the smaller factories were damaged, half torn apart and "disassembled" before I could get to them. But fifteen minutes later, a total of nine custodians, one large as shit heavy-duty collector—that shut down as soon as the power was cut—and after a few repairs, a single class-three and two class-one sentinels stood ready.

The power to this section was gone. And even with the large-scale construction machines we had here, there was no way that we could get the place into a defensible condition in short order.

The power plant, which I'd need to get the place running properly, needed power to the factories to be made, so that was a nonstarter. I cast about desperately, gritting my teeth as I tried to figure out a solution.

Fortunately, a wonderful one presented itself to me.

CHAPTER TWENTY-ONE

Six of the custodians set off running as soon as the thought occurred to me: two to each of the doors, latching onto them and welding them shut. It'd not hold in the long-term, no way, but for now? It'd do.

The other four were moving as fast as they could with one of them to tear two of the converters apart and rebuild them in the transport section of the big fucker.

I'd noticed that the bigger factories needed power, but the smaller ones and the converters didn't. I'd had only a vague understanding as to why—something about the energy release from molecular conversion tried to rise up and wave at me. I stomped that fucker back down, hard.

The details could suck my balls. What was important was that the converters could generate their own power, and so, being a sneaky bastard, I reasoned that if they could generate enough power to run the conversion process, well! Plugged into the big fucker, if they were connected up, and you provided trash to shovel into it?

The converters could be set to produce much smaller null blocks, or the disc things they'd been churning out. And the excess power? It'd hopefully be enough to run the big bugger.

If it did? It'd be able to run around the room, gathering up the crap, and feed it into the converters. That made sure we had plenty of bits if we needed them. The smelter clearly made the entire process more efficient, but regardless, we knew we could do it without that, so we would.

The other three custodians?

They were *much* busier.

I'd seen the wreckage earlier, in the pile, ready to be disposed of, and damn was I glad I'd spotted it now.

The medical suite had been entirely stripped out and brought here.

Most of it was trashed, including, unfortunately, the tube that had held pretty much everything.

The base and top of it was intact, though, and I was seriously hoping that any system that designed multiple emergency backup medical suites in a ship would make damn sure that the system required to run said machinery was secure.

If you had it in a central location, the system might break, so when I considered it, I was placing a pretty heavy bet that the medical AI was still here, probably in the machinery and protected.

If it wasn't? Well, I'd be fucked, basically. But hey. Sometimes you have to live on hope. That was the basis of the fight against the security AI so far as well, as I had to believe that if it was the main AI that had been around for millennia, I'd be rendered down to a smear of fats by now.

Instead, I was betting that this was a backup and/or broken security system I was facing, which was why it was so shit that I'd survived this far.

The two custodians had happily stepped up and started repairs on the tube when I'd ordered them, and I, not really being able to add much anywhere else, shlepped piles of the discs around in my arms, trying not to panic too much over the state of the others, despite everything.

I piled the discs up near the medical equipment, and the custodians took them from the pile as they needed to. The tube seemed to regrow its gently glowing glass as I watched.

A few minutes became an hour, then two.

As soon as the doors were sealed, I started the custodians on making some defenses for the tube, and I carried Scylla over, laying her by my side as I sat, waiting.

I scrapped another of the custodians after a little thought. Two more joined the first two, and were working on the medical equipment, rebuilding everything from the recliner-type massage chair to the screens and more. The last two were working on loading and repairing the various units around the room.

The scrapped custodian had its core inserted into a modified factory, and with a pair of converters built onto the side of it, and the core's power, we managed to jump-start it.

The smaller ones were already producing a new rifle for Scylla and me, as well as more ammunition, and I had plans for armor on the go, when Scylla finally twitched.

I twisted, frowning as I looked at her, unsure I'd really seen what I thought I had, when she bucked more violently.

"Scylla!" I grunted, sinking to my knee by her side, then jerking my arm up into an instinctive block as she lashed out, seeing me there.

For a second, it was a blur. I slapped her strike aside, and she rolled, jabbing out with her other hand, striking me in the nerve cluster at the top of my left bicep, numbing the arm. I grabbed her wrist and yanked it back.

I rolled onto her, half pinning her as my arm spasmed, and she snarled, baring her teeth…before blinking as she finally recognized me.

"Steeeve?" She drew my name out, her accent heavy, before she cleared her throat and visibly composed herself. "Steve, why do you press against me like this?" she asked, her voice clearer, even through gritted teeth.

"You attacked me." I released her and forced myself up, before offering her my hand. "Are you okay?"

"I…yes." She closed her eyes and took a deep breath. "I am alive, again. Thank you," she said in a softer tone, clearly getting hold of herself.

"It's okay." I smiled despite my aching arm, as she took my hand and I helped her to her feet. "I'm sorry about before."

"Before?"

"When you died," I clarified, reflecting how weird some of our conversations must sound to outsiders.

"It happens." She sighed, then forced a smile. "You stayed with me. I remember that. My thanks to you." She looked around, frowning as she took in the new area, so different from the one she'd died in. Then she looked me up and down.

"You have lost your armor, that you claimed you must keep, and now, despite your lectures on modesty, you are…not?"

I looked down, seeing the damn state of my clothes, and snorting in amusement. Basically, my shoes were intact. Mostly.

They were a little charred and the soles were a bit melted, but beyond that, they were okay.

My jeans were pretty trashed: coated in blood, crisped to buggery, and melted in places. And yeah, I was practically hanging out of a rip in them.

"Yeah, it was a hell of a fight," I admitted, hesitating and trying to decide what to tell her first.

"It seems so," she said after a few seconds of silence, and misinterpreting my silence, she spoke up again. "You have made it clear you have issues around your body. Do you wish me to disrobe? You may wear my clothes, if this means we can move on with the mission."

I covered my eyes with one hand as I tried not to burst out laughing at the conversation that would have triggered with Dave. The whole "I made her strip so I could cross-dress" would never end.

"I'm good, thanks," I assured her, then went on quickly, adjusting myself so I wasn't quite as obvious. "I died as well. There was a lot of fire."

"An unpleasant way to die," she offered, nodding enigmatically. "You do not wish me to disrobe, so what is the next step?"

"I…you know what? It's all good," I said after struggling for the right words. "So, I've got us new weapons coming, hopefully not much longer, as these factories are more advanced than the ones we had access to. Once that's ready, we've got three options."

"Yes?"

"We were brought here when we were killed, I think to dispose of our bodies. Something's changed with everything, though. It's no longer concerned about keeping the ship as it was. The AI is making the machines strip the ship for parts. They're building new machines, like that." I gestured up at the hulking drone that was slowly clearing the junk away and loading it into converters.

"It is impressive."

"It's just big, that's all."

"This is what she said?" Scylla asked haltingly, and I squinted at her.

I sighed. "You've been talking to Zac, haven't you?"

"And Paul," she confirmed. "Is this not the correct use of the joke?"

"It is and it's not. Don't worry about it." I shook my head and mentally marked down a need to kick them both in the dick when I saw them next. "So, either we cut our way through and lead an assault on the AI now, or we stay here and consolidate our gains. Wherever we are? I have to bet that we're definitely not supposed to be here, especially judging from the thick doors and heavy-duty machinery.

"This is the best maintained, or brand-new, equipment we've seen in the ship, and I'm betting that we've been brought here to be rendered down to make sure we didn't come back. I think this is where the security AI was making its drones and attacking forces. Now that we've taken it, we've got a few options." I held up my thumb.

"First, we can get the custodians to cut their way through into the next area. They were damn adamant about shutting that off when I tried to advance before, so I'm betting it's a control center of some kind, or at least a local security node. Capture that, and we gain control over a lot more of the ship.

"Option two." I added my first finger. "We secure this area as best we can, and we head in the other direction, either leaving this as a secure point to come back to, or after we trash it. We lead the sentinels and everything back and we try to find our way to Ingrid and the others."

"Why?" she asked. "I mean no offense, and I understand that she is your lover, but leaving a section that we must capture for victory, to go in search of reinforcements? It is unwise."

"Good point," I agreed with a sigh, lifting my middle finger. "As much as I don't like it, that's what my own training and experience says as well. We don't know for sure that they're in any danger, and there's more of them, with a lot more resources than we have here. They should be okay. Option three, we secure this point. We wait for the others to reach us, while we build our forces to attack the next area, and…"

"And?"

"And while they're built up, I try to activate the medical AI and do my best to get us both upgraded."

"Upgraded?" She frowned, then paused. "You mean to make us both like you are?"

This time, I was the one to hesitate. "Yeah, more or less. Look, we know, or think at least, that we're not designed to be multiskilled like I am. We should be one thing, like the War class, right?"

"Yes."

"I think we need to try and 'fix' ourselves properly. You and the others, like Jonas, Courtney, and Paul? I think you should be War class only," I explained. A pit opened up in my stomach at the thought of how fast they might outclass me if they did that.

"I'm already multiskilled, and while I might have found a way to fix this, it's not a great solution. And it's going to mean that I need to dedicate a lot of my armor to it, to maintaining the sub-minds. You don't need to do this, so I think you could get a lot stronger than me that way."

"You would permit this?" she asked bluntly. "For now, our enemies are one, but this will not always be so. I do not offer to swear myself to your eternal service."

The look she gave me was challenging, and I forced myself to take a deep breath and respond deliberately, well aware that the ancient warrior was translating my words and weighing them carefully, searching for meaning in every casual fuck-up.

"Scylla," I said, "you know that I'm not good with words. You know that I'm doing my best to save people and this goddamn world. We've got the same enemies, for now at least, and I hope it stays that way. I really do. But as long as we're not enemies? That's enough for now."

"You do not seek to rule me, nor the world?"

"Honestly? No, not really." I shrugged. "What I really want? I want to sail on my goddamn yacht, screw Ingrid's brains out, and look after my friends. Oh, and eat and drink some really damn good food and booze. That's it. But that's not really an option, is it?"

"Then you are weak." She stepped up and turned to face me full-on, glaring in challenge.

"I killed your mother," I pointed out, well aware that this was possibly the only situation where that could be said as a good thing, and knowing this day had been coming for a while.

"You faced her in open combat?" she asked, and I nodded. "And yet Shamal and his lesser servants bested you."

"They did," I agreed. "After I'd fought a small army, flown across the fucking ocean and back, and fought my way through a second fucking army to face them. Oh, and that was right after I'd killed Beowulf, Cristobel, and some freshly Arisen shits, wasn't it? Yeah, I lost my fight against Shamal after killing over *three fucking hundred others*, while you were hiding in a secure room, one that *I'd made for you*."

"You made it as a prison," she growled, shifting slightly, clearly getting ready.

"Yeah," I admitted. "I fucking did. I made it as a prison for someone who might have been my enemy. And then what did we do? We gave you food, clothes, and nanites. We set you free, and we offered to help you."

"I fought for you."

"You fought for yourself!" I snapped. "Shamal would have killed you as happily as me, or any of us. You defended yourself, and I helped you then as well. You say you'll not swear to serve me? Fine. Did I fucking *ask* you to? No! I just saved you, gave you a chance, fed you and fucking protected you. Even here, what did I offer? To help you to be the strongest you could be, and what's the response I get from you? That you'll not swear. You're a fucking greedy child. No wonder Athena—"

I was cut off by a punch, one that cracked my jaw and sent me flying, hitting the ground with a spray of blood.

I blinked, stunned, staring down. I was laid on my chest, facedown, crimson blood smeared across the floor, blood, bone, and teeth seemingly massive in my vision.

I tried to make sense of it, as horrific pain tore through me, and the sound of retreating feet rang out. "Muuuurgh," I managed to force out. More of a gurgle than a word, pain filled and unintelligible, considering that when I managed to get a hand under me to push myself up, I reached up with my other hand to find shattered bone and gory, exposed flesh.

She'd torn my fucking jaw half loose!

The pain screamed through the shock, hitting me like a freight train. I tried to focus, knowing goddamn well that I didn't have the nanites for this shit, to waste them in repairing myself in a fight with a literal monster from the Dark Ages.

The room swam as I stared at her retreating back, seeing the way she snatched up the freshly finished rifle and ammunition, then strode off without a backward glance.

She was heading from the room, leaving me as I bled out. I reached out, frantic, knowing that once she was gone, so was any protection I had. I also knew that unless my nanites did something—and fucking soon—I was going to black out, and that'd be goddamn terminal in here.

The AI had brought me here to dispose of my body, and that had been a stupid mistake on its part, but I couldn't hope that it'd make the same one again.

It now knew that both Scylla and I had died—that was beyond reasonable doubt—and that a short while later, we'd been fucking up and screwing with its charge again.

It'd make damn sure of us the next chance it got, I bet, so I did what I had to do. I reached out and I summoned all the custodians I could, ordering them to me, except for the two repairing the medical chamber to keep doing it. But the rest?

They were to get the largest factory running however they had to. The factory unit was to assemble the class-one sentinels, as many as it could, and split them between defending me and this location, and Ingrid.

Ingrid. For all I knew, Scylla had decided that it was time to take care of any loose ends and was off to kill her. My stomach tightened and twisted even as I coughed.

Blood ran down my throat, half drowning me as without my jaw, the ruin of my face was pouring my life out in vicious sprays of claret. Again I coughed; the world around me dimmed as the nanites fought to cut off the arterial jet.

I ordered the custodians to get me into the medical tube as soon as it was finished and operational. For the two that were building it—and that were nearly finished already—they were to maintain it and provide whatever was needed from the converters for it.

I was blacking out, the world going dark as my brain stuttered and lurched, starved of blood, of oxygen. I slid in and out of shock as the insanity of a single punch being the thing that killed me, after all that had happened, reared its head.

Power! Fuck, I needed power…a power plant! My mind was dim, as I tried to lay the details out, seeing a miniature power plant in my mind, the thousands of possible permutations offering themselves to me, as I sagged forward.

I mentally demanded "what we did before" and then hit the deck with a splat of wet flesh, congealing warm blood, and distant pain.

Then I was gone, sinking down into the depths of death, all over again, mentally hurling abuse at Scylla as I went, until a distant sound rang back to me, one that I knew.

Gunfire.

When I swam back up from the depths next, the world around me slowly sliding into place, it was to a distant argument. The sharp tones and clear utter fury that was on display made me goddamn glad it wasn't me getting a tongue-lashing.

I forced one eye open, focusing blearily and trying to make sense of what I was seeing.

I was upright, more or less, and looked down at a scene that was very different from the one I remembered, and I was in a shitload of pain still.

The room before me was a mass of mad movement: sentinels, custodians, and more raced in all directions, as Zac swore and kicked at a factory unit, Courtney fired slowly and steadily, kneeling with her new sniper rifle braced against a rough barricade of junk, and Paul and Jonas stood ready.

Faintly, I could hear the zip and crack of gamma lasers and more. Occasional detonations shook the room, and I shifted slightly, feeling the restraints that held me in place.

Before me, in the middle of a small, cleared zone of piled scrap, stood Scylla and Ingrid—and fuck, Ingrid was going to town.

The words were distant, almost utterly unintelligible, but here and there, one filtered through. I blinked muzzily, realizing that I was floating in the medical tube, laid on the chair and restrained by bands that gripped me like steel.

Distantly, I felt a surge of fear. Memories rose, as the last time I was in this fucking thing came to mind, and I started to struggle, weakly.

"Honor...coward...he...owed...thief..." Ingrid was snarling at Scylla.

I desperately tried to free myself, jerking my mouth open and—

My mouth! I felt it, half formed, soft, like warm plastic, and something was clamped over it...a mask of some kind.

I swallowed. A liquid filled my throat, my lungs...It sent me into a panic of convulsions, as I instinctively tried to drag myself free, tried not to drown.

I needed to get free!

I needed to escape this fucking prison, to reach Ingrid before Scylla hurt her, before she killed her!

I shook and tried to shout, my mouth not fully formed yet, but that didn't stop me. I thrashed from side to side, desperately reaching out...

And my nanites responded.

The tube was hit by a panicked multitude of spikes driving out of my flesh. Nanites formed spears and lanced out to hit the glass, scratching it in a hundred places. Over and over, they stabbed out—short spears, maybe, but they were driven by fury and a determination to save Ingrid.

The glass started to break. Cracks radiated out from the impact points as I desperately hammered on it, feeling the structure of the tube, whatever it was, sure as fuckery wasn't goddamn glass!

I dragged the spears back, curling them around myself, readying for a last attack, as a distant sound got my attention. I looked up from the glass.

It was Ingrid, standing before and below me, flapping her hands frantically as she tried to get my attention. I froze, staring at her, seeing the fear as she shook her head, and waved her arms.

I couldn't make out the words. Even shouted, there was just too much distortion from whatever the fluid and the tube was. But she was there, and although Scylla looked pissed off—and sullen, like a child who'd been smacked and had their toys taken away for bad behavior—she also wasn't stabbing anyone, nor was she leaving.

Ingrid shook her head again, trying to make sure I got the message, and pointed to the tube, holding her hands and moving them slowly, patting the air as she mouthed "It's okay" to me.

I flinched, my nanites gathering, ready to attack again. I looked upward as a sudden shadow loomed over me...only to relax as I saw a custodian. Its legs somehow attached it in place as it extended tools and started to fix the damage I'd wrought on the tube.

I glanced back down. Ingrid and the others stared up at me, even as Courtney straightened from her firing position, calling something to Zac, who responded, as far as I could see, but I was buggered if I could make out what was being said.

Ingrid waved again, and I looked at her, my heart hammering, still panicked as I found that yeah, I could breathe whatever this fluid was.

It was still alien and fucking horrible, though.

A shift out of the corner of my eye got my attention. A screen unfolded, flowing up to position itself before my eyes, like so long ago.

I instinctively tried to rear back, but as restrained as I was? I was going nowhere.

I managed to catch a glimpse of Ingrid, looking to one side. And when the screen flowed to that side, I flicked my gaze back to her, seeing her for about a second as she nodded that it was okay, that she was safe. Then it was there before me again, moving to ensure I had to see it.

This time, with my heart gradually slowing, I focused on it, and read the message that filled it.

Biological Weapon Variant #113782491603

State reason for access to Facility 6B

Have you been sent to assume control?

CHAPTER TWENTY-TWO

I didn't hesitate this time. Whatever the system was—medical AI, the original AI, a coffee machine that had gained sentience—it could read my mind, to the level of detecting lies…last time, at least.

This time, I focused on the conversation with the Erlking, with it bequeathing me authorization to command the ships, with it giving me command access, and I responded.

Reaching out, I dismissed the screen and focused my hack to provide a link to the controlling sentience.

Instantly, I felt it, and damn was it different from anything I'd ever experienced.

It was exactly like I thought interfacing with a machine would be, and nothing like it at the same time. There was no emotion, no interest, no humanity.

It didn't care, not even slightly, that I was there, and unlike the security AI, which I was grimly sure hated me with a passion and was determined to cleanse me from the system, this one was uninterested and somehow stunted.

RI, I mentally identified it, seeing the difference straightaway.

Biological Weapon Variant #113782491603, command access request accepted. State reason for access to Facility 6B.

"I'm here to take command," I mentally sent to it, getting precisely fuck all for a response. "Shit, right, computer, okay, try this. I'm here to assume control. I need to be upgraded and repaired."

Secure Facility 6B has been deemed irrevocably damaged. Communication has been lost with Primary Facility. Argus Protocol has failed. Upgrade process unavailable.

"Identify Argus Protocol," I tried.

Biological Weapon Variant, Argus Protocol baseline download is unavailable. Recommendations:

1) **Repair global security net**
2) **Repair interdiction system**
3) **Repair facilities #1-4**
4) **Regain access to Facility #5, ensure termination of BWV and BSV breeding program**
5) **Terminate extant BWV and BSV, and ensure blockade renewed**

"Blockade...? Interdiction? What the fuck?" I shook my head. It wasn't important, not right now.

"Security systems! The security systems are trying to kill me. I need a way to shut them down."

Silence.

"Upgrades?"

Secure Facility 6B has been deemed irrevocably damaged. Communication has been lost with Primary Facility. Argus Protocol has failed. Upgrade process unavailable.

"Fuck's sake!" I snarled. Goddamn computers! "What about repairs? Healing? Help?"

Biological Weapon Var—

"Fuck's sake!" I cut it off. "Steve! Change identifier from 'Biological Weapon Variant #113782491603' to 'Steve'!" I snarled, finding the identifier had been used for me so many damn times that I could rattle it off without difficulty.

Identification marker upgraded.

"Thank fuck. All right, I need help! You responded to that last time. Help me!"

Request for aid approved. Command access recognized.

Systems are damaged, reducing operational options to five.

Select one of the following forms of assistance:

1) **Nanite Reboot**
2) **Weapons System Realignment**
3) **Support Package**
4) **Main system override and install**
5) **Command Access Protocols**

"Explain the options," I demanded, wincing as a sudden icy-cold spike of knowledge was rammed down the data link between us.

The nanite reboot was clear. Literally, it was a full wipe and reboot. Useful, certainly, but the accompanying data said that it was an iffy prospect.

Basically, the more corrupted nanites I had, the longer it'd take to wipe and reboot. As this was a computer system, and time was fucking meaningless to it, it'd essentially put me, or anyone in it, into a forced hibernation. Then, nanite cluster by cluster, it'd work its way through, wiping and repairing them, before rebooting.

At first glance, that was the choice for Scylla and Hans definitely, but the limitations were clear as I looked at it.

The work it'd done on me originally had used the last of its stores, and it had fuck all available right now to start the process. It was somehow blocked from providing nanites themselves, as well. That meant that it'd be a damn slow process, probably one that took at the very least, decades, for someone like the older Arisen.

For me, even as I was right now, it'd take weeks.

That was out.

The weapons system realignment was a lot higher tech. Essentially, the War upgrades I'd been doing as I went along? They were repairs to my system to bring me into line with what I should be.

I'd take a massive leap up in capability, and lethality, if I chose that; my DNA would be paired back to the genetic ideal that I was designed to be. Broken links and failed replications would be culled, original lines reinserted, and my original "Ursus class" would be brought online.

I got a partial image of gaining several inches in pretty much all dimensions, of my bones being reformed to allow additional weapons systems to be grafted on; my "skeletal load-bearing system" would be entirely upgraded. Organs would be replaced with higher functioning ones, muscles would be replaced, nerves...

Hell, I would be entirely upgraded, everything from subdermal armoring to retractable claws, shoulder-mounted weaponry, remote targeting links, the lot— all would be possible further in, once the basic system was installed.

I'd be made into a weapon that could eventually scour the planet of anything that pissed me off.

I could go toe-to-toe with the older Arisen, and given a few months of additional upgrades, I'd have a good chance of rocking the Erlking on his ass if he tried to stop me.

The only issue?

It'd take at least a year, probably two, and I'd need to unlock a shitload more nanites to fuel the upgrades. Meaning I'd need to complete quests—which I had to hope would be provided—and I'd need to return to my "controller" to have the nanites integrated.

The controller was clearly meant to be the Erlking or whoever, and although it accepted me as having command access, it also kept defaulting to me coming back to report...to me. Clearly a weaponized monkey wasn't supposed to have command access.

Basically, I'd need to pair up with someone with a harvesting kit to get the nanites from the targets I killed, and they were supposed to provide them to a controller, who was to dole them out to me sparingly.

Fuck no.

Option three was the Support package, one that I'd already received, and one that I was gloomily sure was going to be what I needed, despite the newly unlocked options, and I skipped it, looking at number four.

I winced as I checked it out. It was a full brain wipe and reset, all the way down to a genetic level to ensure that basically I'd just be a weapon.

I'd not be me, in a weaponized body—no, I'd *just* be a weapon. One that was exactly what the creators had intended: mindless, directionless...everything that was me, wiped clean.

That was part of the plan they'd been working on, I guessed. Their solution to the problem of humanity, before they'd been booted from the ships and sent into exile.

They'd come up with a "BWV Mk2" and that was what we were. Upgraded beyond the original design, but with a mind that was capable of being entirely wiped and reset to "factory default"?

We were the next generation, the counter to the originals, and as far as I could make out, we'd never been deployed. We were still in beta, being tested, ready to be upgraded to the next stage, and then they'd been exiled. I could be reset to what I was designed to be, and I'd be insanely powerful...but I'd be dead.

What made me, me, would be torn away and discarded. I'd be a soulless killing machine, and as soon as I was released, I'd basically be deposited to the floor below, ready to receive my orders.

Without them, I'd probably just stay there, standing dumbly, while my friends were slaughtered around me. Add in that I got the sense that although it could use the discs to "pay" for the upgrade, covering the cost in terms of materials, it'd take about a year or so.

That'd be a hard pass.

Option five, though?

That was more interesting.

That was a class I'd not seen before, presumably because as a BWV, it wasn't supposed to be offered to me.

Structurally, there was little difference—at least, not to me. My body wouldn't be upgraded much: a few baseline changes, nerve impulse upgrades, slight improvement in the speed of reactions, and a significant improvement in the actual brain itself. Much higher processing capacity, higher data access...

No, the real change was in the links. A commander, a much rarer version than the BWVs and BSVs, could reach out and maintain contact with their subordinates. They could control the battlefield—hell, they were designed to be ship commanders—or...

No, I had that wrong. They weren't the commanders, not in the way I was thinking about them, and despite the way they were named in the system.

They were more like an augmenter, or an advanced Support class. They were designed to be the link between the weapons—like me—and the creators.

They were there to reach out and control us, to help the Support class to achieve greater things, to keep the weapons in line, and to act as sub-commanders on the ships...on *space*ships!

I had a vision of the creators giving the orders, like the old-style military admirals aboard ships at sea. Some old walrus-mustached fat bastard sitting there in a tunic that could barely cover their belly while they barked orders and the "lesser" men ran to obey.

The Command class was misnamed, that was for sure, because they were essentially slave controllers, the second-in-command in each situation, the link between our masters and their weapons.

The Command class, or "BCV" as the system identified them, could boost their minions, granting them temporary bonuses, with the subsequent costs to be paid later.

They could make their weapons faster, at the cost of burning fuel—our food and fats—faster. They could "remote" into us, a bit like the way I could hack some systems, and they could help us identify targets.

They could help Support classes work more smoothly, and establish better design controls, direct harvesting teams, help to maintain and guide starships and orchestrate battles...all of it.

They were a great upgrade to a team, and they were totally fucking useless to me.

Well, no, that wasn't entirely fair. A Command class could be awesome for us, but it wasn't *me*. First, I'd need to be spread out across the team—mentally—and trying to fight on the front lines when that distracted?

That was an invitation to die.

Secondly, the Command class needed its own line of upgrades, ones that would need to replace some that I already had! Things like internal modifications that I needed to be able to carry weapons systems, like my heavier bones and generally upgraded form.

Nope.

I'd need to remove the storage lacunas in my bones, have them reformed into data and range specific systems. Attachment points for weapons? Replaced with integration points for ship, vehicle, and factory systems.

The harvest tool that I desperately needed? Replaced with a storage system for nanite connectors to integrate the commander into the surrounding equipment.

All in all, it was great, and utterly fucking useless to my "build."

I slid back up the tree of options, tagging option three, marking it up as my choice, only to feel my balls shrivel in fear as a new message arrived.

System repair and Support package selected. Be aware, Biological Weapon Variant #Steve, stores of anesthetic have been replenished from additional stores—

"Oh, thank fuck…" I sagged in the restraining harness.

But are insufficient to affect a fully active BWV for the time required. Please choose from the following options:

1) **Receive partial anesthetic, slowing integration and time to completion to 1.9 revolutions.**

2) **Proceed without anesthetic, time to completion 1.1 revolutions.**

My first instinct was to tell the system to go fuck itself and to give me the goddamn drugs, right fucking now, thank you very much.

Then I thought about what, and where I was. More to the point, I thought about who I was with.

I opened my eyes again, having not realized I'd even closed them, and saw that the screen had been removed.

I looked down, full into the eyes of Ingrid, and I knew what I had to do, and why.

She saw me, saw the look in my eyes, and—I trusted—the love. Then I triggered the system, just hoping that it wouldn't be as bad as last time.

I was fucking dreaming.

I tried—holy shit, did I try—but the system was a computer program: it wasn't sentient, and it couldn't be reasoned with. My argument that I didn't need the rest of the package, that I just needed the nanite recovery tool, and a bit of healing maybe? Nope.

It couldn't accept it. My choice was take it all, and just hope that some of my upgrades would be left as is—they'd damn well taken a hell of a lot of pain to achieve, after all—or accept that I'd lost access to my greatest strength.

I'd never again wield the harvest blade, if I didn't do this, and that was no choice at all.

I forced myself to stillness. My heart slowed, faltering, then being forced into a steady beat, as I grimly made myself stare at what was coming full in the face.

Then I approved it.

Commencing basic Endoskeletal strip and integration...
estimated time to completion: 1.1 revolutions.

Prepare yourself, Biological Weapon Variant #Steve.
Stores of anesthetic have been denied.

With that simply wonderful message, the system flowed back from contact. I couldn't help but look up, seeing the blades, the drills, and more sliding out. My gorge, and my panic, rose.

The gasps of horror, from the others watching outside, made it through the tube, and all the fluid.

I managed to keep my own screams internal, or at least muffled to groans and whimpers that couldn't make it through the fluid.

It wasn't down to any machismo bullshit. Mainly, it was down to fear that if I didn't, then Ingrid and the others would never allow it to be done to them. And that was the main reason I'd refused the anesthetic: so it was there for her to use.

Also, the tube in my throat helped to keep me fucking silent. I could barely make any sound around it as it dug deeper into my lungs, clearly working on them as well.

Hours passed as blood sprayed. The primary strip was less painful than I remembered, which only served to draw attention to how fucking terrible some of the tortures I endured were since I escaped here.

Thankfully, the system apparently did check some things, evaluating them against existing details. My brain and my left eye were mainly left intact, as were my bones.

My right eye? Well, that was rendered down to soup stock—again—and a fresh implant made into the optical nerve. No fucking clue why, but the system evidently didn't like the one that it'd put in last time.

The system at the base of my brain that was designed to allow remote access, and that I'd upgraded before—unsuccessfully, to help me deal with the data downloads—was ripped free and replaced.

The only consolation, for me at least, was when my right arm was torn apart, the creation tool removed, and the nanite recovery tool inserted instead, sealing the gap between the bones and filling the majority of that arm's internal structure.

Hour after hour, the process continued. Some of the changes made no sense to me, like when the skin on my left arm was replaced. I allowed myself a little hope that for that limb, at least, the worst was over.

Then it was stripped away, inch by inch. It wasn't cut, even—instead, it was peeled! Like I'd peel a fucking banana.

My fingernails were removed; fresh ones were inserted—which was a horrible sensation all its own as they were jabbed into place—then coated with a liquid that melded them into the rest of my body.

By the time my eye was replaced, and my skin was fully attached again—even my goddamn hair was replaced, for fuck's sake…I mean, *why?*—I was exhausted and the tube was a mess of red fluid.

It'd been drained and refilled a dozen times over, and I had only the vaguest understanding as to why it'd done that. The data was leaked, as so many things were, thanks to the data spike, but I knew that somehow it helped the healing process, as well as ensuring there was less biological matter wasted.

That wasn't really helpful to me, but at least I sort of had a clue now.

Fuck it.

When the flashes came, some kind of mask being pressed over my eyes to spark a full rise to consciousness through the light, I stirred despite myself.

When the restraints released? I almost fell from the seat, managing at the last minute to grab the side of the armrest and half swing myself forward.

It meant that I landed on the floor in front of the capsule, the top and bottom of the tube sliding back together as I landed—in a three-point hero landing, thank you very much—before the stunned rest of the group.

There was a long minute of silence, before, predictably, Zac broke it.

"Fuck's sake, boss, put yer todger away. We don't need to see that!" he managed, as I straightened.

"Speak for yourself…" I heard Courtney murmur.

I deliberately didn't respond to what had clearly been unintentional, considering the black look that Paul—her husband—gave her.

"Steve…" Ingrid cried, stepping into my arms and clinging to me, much as I held onto her.

"What the shitting hell was that?" Jonas asked, his voice a rough whisper, and I looked at him over the top of Ingrid's head.

"You want to be like me, mate?" I asked him, before jerking my head back toward the tube. "That's how you do it."

"Are you serious?" Paul asked. "You…you died, right? I mean, I saw your *heart* get taken out!"

"Not to mention your cock! Fuck's sake, boss, it cut your cock off and replaced it!" Zac groaned. "Man, I'm gonna have nightmares about that…" He paused, then licked his lips, clearly nerving himself up to ask a question when I beat him to it.

"Sorry, mate, you get the same length back…no extras added. So if Casey's already disappointed, it won't fix that." I forced the joke out, trying to lighten the tone, as the others stared at me with varying degrees of shock.

"Did it work?" Ingrid asked, her voice husky and rough from what I guessed were a lot of tears.

"I think so…" I lifted my right arm, focusing as I did.

The twin ports between my knuckles were the first to open. The nanotubes flexed and flowed out, extending up to a meter, hanging in the air like an insect's antennae, before flowing back into my arm. The second exit point in my wrist was next, and they extended from there instead, hanging for a second before returning.

I grinned as I checked my systems.

228

Sure, I only had literally a hundred nanite clusters, and that was entirely it—not a single nanite more or less—but I also had access to the full range of my old upgrades still.

The transmission box, whatever it was supposed to be called, at the base of my neck was active, and for the first time, I could see what it was supposed to be like.

For whatever reason, the original one hadn't worked properly, partly because I was a War variant, I understood, and so I shouldn't have been trying to use it, and partly because the system when it was installed had been failing.

No, I could feel the world around me again, full of signals, even here, but I no longer felt as open to them, as unshielded.

I snorted, realizing that the reason for that was that I was supposed to have had firewalls and more that protected me. Until now? I'd been doing most of that work personally.

No more.

I felt a "dumb" presence contained in the stack, something that gazed out passively, but that could be upgraded. It had potential, I could see that, certainly.

Unfortunately for it, it also "lived" in a layered system that was considerably more high tech than the data storage and neural node that my armor had held.

As soon as I had enough nanites to reactivate my armor—and providing the sub-mind had somehow survived—I'd be moving it out of the goddamn armor, and into the stack, fuck its current resident.

I let out a long breath, realizing that the pain, all of it, was worth it. I looked around at the others, where they were standing, seeing the directions that they were watching, and who.

"What happened?" I asked quietly, while staring into Scylla's eyes.

She stared back at me, something different there, but nothing that I could be sure of, until Ingrid spoke.

"We fought our way through most of the enemy," she explained. "We'd stopped, making it clear we were gathering ourselves for the next step, but…"

"But we weren't," Jonas said into the silence. "We'd advanced as far as we thought we could, and we were making the point that we were going to keep going, keeping the AI fixated on us, when we ran out of enemies. The fight calmed for a few hours, and we gathered more drones and shit, repaired the sentinels, and we were trying to figure out if we could keep going, or if we should hold the ground we'd taken.

"We were hoping you'd succeeded, and that was why there were no more waves incoming, but it also could have been that they were setting a trap. We tried scouting, knowing that we were well past when we should have heard from you, one way or the other, when all the sentinels and custodians went nuts. Half the sentinels abandoned their posts, ignoring all orders to group around Ingrid. The rest ran off, the custodians following them." He glared at me.

"Seriously, Steve, if you're going to take the troops we're relying on anytime you feel like it, can we rely on them at all? You're the boss, but please, give us a little warning if you can, all right?" he asked grimly.

"I…was dead," I said. "Or I think I was."

"That's what I said," Ingrid admitted, hugging me again. "We followed them…I did, anyway…"

"And we followed along, boss, and not at all just because if we let anything happen to Ingrid, you'd have fucking slaughtered us!" Zac added helpfully.

"Yeah, well, we followed her, making goddamn sure we kept together and covered each other's backs. What we found was this one in a pitched battle with a shitload of sentinels, and once we'd rescued her?"

"You did not rescue me," Scylla shot back, acidly.

"You were in a firefight, low on ammo and pinned down. You were about to fucking die, and we killed your enemies, saving your life. Sounds like we rescued you to me," Courtney replied blandly. "But sure, you say it however you like."

I noticed a massive difference in the way the others were all talking and acting around Scylla. I frowned, wondering what the hell had happened.

Before this, Jonas and the other two were always respectful to her, and not just because she was strong and fast, enough that she could rip their limbs off and beat them to death with them. Now they seemed to be almost baiting her.

"Anyway, we rescued Scylla—"

This time it was obvious. Every other time he'd spoken to or about her, it'd been "lady" this or "lady" that. Now she was just plain Scylla, and she was pissed, judging from the look she gave him.

"And she refused to speak about you. We didn't know if you were alive or dead, but considering the robot thingies that had plowed through the battle on their way somewhere? We followed them."

"And we found them loading you into a huge tube, blood and bone everywhere," Ingrid finished for him. "Scylla wouldn't speak about what had happened, and we didn't know if you were alive or dead, and…"

I wrapped Ingrid in my arms again and pulled her in close, feeling the wetness of her tears on my chest.

"What happened?" she asked after a few seconds, pushing back and looking up at me.

I looked over at Scylla, waiting, and she bowed her head, speaking, literally a half second before I was about to.

"I lost my temper," Scylla admitted, stepping forward. "Words were said, on both sides, that should not have been, and I reacted as my mother would have. My shame is great."

"You did this?" Ingrid hissed, gesturing to the ground off to one side, where it was covered in blood and shattered bone. "You're why he was in there, instead of fighting?"

She shoved herself free of me, and I let her go, knowing it was a mistake, but also knowing it needed to be done.

The next ten minutes or so was painful, for all of us, and especially for Scylla, as Ingrid laid into her.

It was verbal, which was a relief—I don't think Scylla could have controlled herself if Ingrid had done it physically—but considering most of it was in a mixture of ancient Greek and modern Danish, it showed just how furious she was.

Three times we tried to break it up, before we finally managed to get Ingrid to calm down. It was Zac who pulled it off in the end, asking me where my clothes were.

Ingrid glared at him, clearly about to ask whether that was really important, when I seized on the opportunity to break off the verbal flaying.

I was pissed at Scylla—of course I was. And would I have shot the bitch? Yeah, probably. A little payback would have suited me just fine.

The thing about the torture I'd just encountered, though? It was more than enough to clear the mind of any minor details.

It was like being pissed at someone who had broken my nose in a bar fight, after I'd been run over by a truck. It just wasn't in the same league.

Add to that, I had a very clear feeling of what was to come, and I knew it was going to get me more than a little payback.

"It's not important," I said firmly. "What happened, happened, and we need to move on."

"You!" Ingrid snarled. "She—"

"Trust me," I said. "There's a lot that we need to do, and no time to do it. First, though, we need to address this." I reached out and laid my hand on the tube.

"You want to smash it up, right, boss?" Zac took a step back from it. "I mean, surely you don't want to—"

"We need to address who wants to use it," I corrected. "As they're going to be in there being sorted and upgraded while the rest of us attack the security AI."

"Yeah, I don't think I want a go anymore, boss..." Zac said quickly. "I mean, you know, just—"

"Zac."

"Yeah, boss?"

"Shut the fuck up."

"Yeah, boss."

"We've got two choices here," I looked around the room, "and only one of them is ours to make." I stared hard at Scylla.

"What does that mean?" Jonas frowned.

"He means that one is mine." Scylla stepped forward. "One of the choices, and the cost that goes with it, is mine."

CHAPTER TWENTY-THREE

"It's true," I agreed. "The options that we have with this, they include unlocking your nanites, and making you massively more powerful."

"But?" Scylla asked when I paused.

"But it'd mean you'd be trapped in there for several decades," I finished. "You'd literally be there, at the mercy of anything—or anyone—that found you, and the medical equipment would be useless to anyone else."

"Or?"

"Or, you get to start again," I said softly, watching her eyes. "Understand this, Scylla—this isn't me having revenge, or wanting you to be weaker. Am I pissed at you? Yeah. Yeah, I fucking am, but I'll get over that. Right now, for the short-term, it's much more valuable to me and to the rest of the world to have you as strong as possible, but that won't help us in the long-term."

"What do you mean, 'start again'?" she asked dubiously.

"Your nanites," I said. "To perform the full upgrade, they'd be removed. A small number will be reinstalled, but they'll be wiped, reset. You'd be a bit stronger than a regular human, and that's it. The nanites that are taken from you, though? They'd be wiped, broken down and reset by the systems in there, and then a small number would be available to upgrade others."

"And…" She paused.

"The pain?" I asked. "You'd feel it." I shifted and drew a deep breath, looking around at the small group. "There's a small supply of anesthetic that the medical capsule has managed to create. You'd need to refuse it, just as I did."

"Why?"

"Shit, you refused it?" Paul grunted, looking at me with new respect in his eyes.

"It wouldn't make much difference to us," I explained. "It'd be less painful, but the nanites would clear it quickly, meaning it'd be wasted. We'd still be in horrific pain, but it'd be half the time or so, instead of all of it."

"And you wanted to save it for us, didn't you?" Ingrid sighed, knowing me too well.

I nodded, reaching out and pulling her close. "We need to talk about the options. We all do, but you and I need to as well."

"And if I do this?" Scylla interrupted.

"You'll be little more powerful than a regular human, for the short-term." I looked at her.

"And the longer term?" Jonas asked for her.

"I have the recovery tool again," I said. "From here on in, we'll work together, as a unit. At the end of the fight, we identify our personal kills, and we share out the nanites. We can all help each other that way—when one of us needs something, we can pool our nanites to help if need be, and we can 'buy' upgrades."

"Such as?" Jonas frowned.

"Such as my armor." I shrugged. "You can unlock things, if you go down that route, abilities that are made available through completing quests that the system gives you. Some of my first were to gain War points, and they required me killing my enemies. Unlock a War point, pick an upgrade, such as the ability to slow time, subjectively."

"That's why you're so fast?" Paul asked, and before I could respond, Zac covered his mouth as if to cough, and forced out a sentence under cover of clearing his throat.

"That's what she said."

"Fuck's sake, Zac!" I groaned, covering my face with one hand. "Okay, yeah, but there's more. I built my armor and weapons using nanites…that's one use of them. Another is to spend them on yourself. And honestly, I think that's what the system was originally designed to do. The strength, the speed, and more that Scylla and the rest of the Arisen enjoy? It's a pale imitation of what they could be.

"For every unlocked, attuned, and usable nanite cluster the average Arisen has? They've got at least five or ten that're corrupted. Still, it's those attuned nanites that grants them that strength, even in their relatively small numbers. The corrupted ones? They're actively holding them back, blocking up their bodies, and I think that's what happened to the Elders that Hans talks about. I think what happens when you get too full of corruption, you literally shut down.

"Imagine, instead, that you spent those points on yourself. That you unlocked the various things, like your body, and 'spent' those nanites there. It'd take you centuries of 'rising' to be able to face Shamal or another like him. Officially, I did it in three and a half years, but three of those? I was being tortured to death daily and experimented on."

"Six months," Jonas whispered, shaking his head. "In six fucking months, you became more powerful than monsters that had spent millennia growing in power."

"And so can you all," I said. "The only difference? If you do this, if you take this step with me, don't expect to be able to stay here, on Earth. I know some of you wanted to come to space with me, once we've got Earth sorted, but view this as a red line. You do this? The Erlking will come for you if you stay."

"And then we fuck him up," Paul said grimly. "That motherfucker never faced a US Marine!"

"Paul?" Courtney said.

"Huh?"

"Quiet. The adults are talking," his wife said, getting a glare from him, but he settled back, missing the quiet smile she shot his way.

"Seriously, Paul, as much as I like the gung-ho attitude?" I forced a smile. "You have no idea what it was like. I fought and killed Athena in single combat, and the Erlking took me apart like I was nothing. I'd have probably been able to take on Shamal at that point—maybe I'd have won, maybe not—but I can tell you for sure, the Erlking slaughtered me with an ease that was terrifying…"

"Fuck."

"So...we'd need to get a hell of a lot stronger before we kill that old fuck," I finished, getting a grin from the ex-marine.

"We can do that," he agreed quietly. "Nobody beats a marine. We regroup and come back. Marines always win."

"Well, you remember how I tore that fuckboy of a vampire apart in the salt mine?" I asked, and he nodded.

"I'd been 'active' at that point for a few days. I'd been draining werewolves and asshole enforcers, that was it. My plan now? We get our systems active, we get this ship taken, and we start cycling some of our people through here. We get the process started, and we begin making the equipment we need to sort the planet out.

"While all that's going on, though? We have a harvesting team on the prowl." I couldn't help but grin at them all. "I've got a quest from the Erlking to go hunting in the underground. To fight the creatures that were hunting the Oracan. I'm thinking that we go hunt those fuckers, and more."

I turned to look at Jonas. "You remember the lie you recruited me with?" I asked him.

"It wasn't a lie," he replied, clearly a little uncomfortable, but sticking by his words. "I told you, you'd be hunting monsters."

"Well." I smiled, and I meant it. "How about we start doing just that? None of you are ready to fight vamps and shit face-to-face yet, and frankly the things that go bump in the night and attack and kill the Oracan? They'd kill you as you are..."

"You mean...?" Paul straightened up, an excited look on his face.

"Oh yeah," I assured him. "All those fuckhead rapist, murderers, and bastards out there? It's time they contributed to society again."

"They can contribute for the last time!" Jonas agreed, grinning. "Lord Steve?" he said formally, making me look at him askance at the formality. "I'd just like to point out that the goal for my original team was *always* to make the world a better place by removing scum like that. I can't fuckin' wait to get started."

"So," I turned back to Scylla, "what do you think?"

"I have a choice?" she asked, and I nodded.

"Of course. Look, Scylla, you're stronger than me right now. I'm almost drained of all my nanites. Hell, I don't even know where I got enough nanites to damage the tube—"

"I gave you my blood. Again," she admitted.

"I—wait, what?"

"I was leaving the room when I was attacked by a small team of the sentinels," she explained sourly. "After killing them, I saw that you had not come to help, and that you were laid still. I realized that I had, perhaps, hit you harder than I intended, and—" She took a long breath and blew it out, as if embarrassed. "I gave you my blood in payment of the debt between us. You were right that I owed you, that you saved me where another would not have."

"It wasn't just me," I pointed out, and she snorted.

"I mean no offense, but in this world, much as the one that I lost, might is right. If you decided that I was not to be permitted to reawaken, I would not have. While I owe Ingrid, as your woman, and the leader of your settlement, both respect and gratitude for her kindness, her decision stands because you permitted it," she said flatly, and I tried not to wince openly.

"Well, thank you for that," Ingrid replied brittlely. "Steve, that conversation we need to have?"

I nodded. "In a minute," I agreed. "So, you gave me your blood, and my abilities cleansed and attuned some of your nanites. That makes sense. Thank you. It also reinforces what I'm saying. When I woke up the first time, I had a small number of nanites, a hundred to be specific, that were in me and running my 'basic' systems, allowing me to heal faster, making me stronger and so on.

"With the nanites I had before going into the capsule, and the ones you gave me? I should have had a lot more than that. Instead, I'm back to the hundred for the baseline. So, Scylla, you need to decide here. If you refuse to be reset, if you refuse the cleaning and to be upgraded like me, then you can enter the capsule and use it. Right now, you're too strong for me to stop you outright. You'll be in there for decades, but when you leave, you'll be far, far stronger than you are now."

"And yet, I could achieve that strength in mere months if I stay out and fight alongside you?"

"You could," I agreed. "Don't get me wrong—you'll be stronger than a baseline human, faster as well, even if you lose all your nanites." I thought back to the massive number of nanites I had that had bonded to my body, that were no longer "free range" and that granted me the strength that I now enjoyed. To the difference between when I was captured by Athena, and when I escaped. The force-feeding of the literal pureed people to me had made an insane difference, as terrible as that was.

"There are differences that are made, and that will stay with you. But the majority of the changes the nanites make? They'll be lost. For the next few weeks, and possibly months, you'll be weaker. Overall, though? If you do this, you'll grow to be a hell of a lot stronger."

Scylla stood there for long seconds, clearly thinking as we all waited for her, until, eventually, she spoke.

"I tried to fight my mother. Did I ever tell you that?"

"No," I replied, watching her.

"I would have won." Scylla straightened slightly, throwing her shoulders and head back. "I trained for decades to ensure that. And this body, as it is now? It is weaker than I was then. I challenged her, as honor demanded. She agreed, then laid a trap and betrayed me, laughing about how foolish I was. It took dozens of her sworn followers, her pets, to stop me, and far more of her humans. But in the end, Athena took me, wrapped me in chains, and imprisoned me." She paused, taking a deep breath, then nodded to me.

"I will never again be weak. I will never again be taken advantage of. I will do this, in the knowledge that I will grow stronger. But I warn you, Steve, if this is a trick, you will regret it."

"It's no trick," I assured her, before looking around. "Okay, if Scylla is going to be reset, and realigned as a weapon, then most of her nanites will be stripped and lost, but a few should be ready for integration into the next users. That would be all of you, if you want to go ahead."

The others looked at me as if I were fucking mad.

"Look, I know the damn process looks bad, and yeah, it, well, it fucking hurts, sure." I shrugged, ignoring the incredulous looks I was getting from them. "But, and this is a big point, people, if you do this, you'll be unconscious, with the anesthetics that were designed by the creatures that built us originally. Not shit we found by experimenting with random fucking plants...actual tailored drugs. As far as I know, you'll go to sleep, and wake up fixed. That's it. You'll also be immortal, more or less."

"When do we start?" Scylla asked bluntly, interrupting me, and I paused, sighed, then went on.

"We've got a fuckload more sentinels than I expected us to have," I admitted, gesturing to the mass of the little bastards around the room. "So, I think we start by checking out what's around us here first. If we can find a security node and claim it, then we do. Either way, we give ourselves some breathing room. I don't want us getting pushed back while you're in the capsule.

"Once we know the area is secure, more or less, then we move you all through the medical capsule and get you upgraded." I looked around, checking that they were all on board with the plan. "Unless, of course, you don't want to," I finished.

"'Want' is a subjective word," Ingrid said softly, before forcing a smile. "So, you wanted to talk to me?" She pressed one hand to my stomach and shook her head. "How about we find you some clothes first?"

"That might be a problem." I snorted, before looking at the nearest factory unit. "Or not, actually," I added, smiling.

Ten minutes later, the first of the under suits rolled off the end of the factory unit, still warm from the printing process. I snatched it up and grinned.

It was a one-piece—with a zipper, because fuck having to get naked every time I needed a piss—like a wetsuit. That was where the similarity ended, though. It was figure hugging, and yeah, a little snug, which hadn't been part of the plan, I'll admit, despite how amazing Ingrid would look in one.

The suit was made, essentially, of tens of thousands of tiny, tiny metal scales, woven together. Individually, they weren't that strong. But collectively? They were flexible like a normal wetsuit, feeling almost rubbery in the way you could bend and squat, but they could also take a short-range shot from a Colt Magnum.

There'd be a hell of a bruise, admittedly, but there wouldn't be a fucking hole through and through.

Thirty seconds after it'd rolled off the end of the production line, I sealed the zipper, feeling a little better about not flashing everyone anymore.

I'd also had the time to make Zac an interface with the main factory unit, and he was now happily adjusting the suit design to make one for each of us, while getting glared at by both Courtney and Scylla, as he asked personal questions about their dimensions.

"Look, I'm not being a fucking pervert!" he pointed out in annoyance. "I need them to make sure this fits. You want it to be tight, or too slack? Be my guest and do it yourself! And hell, you're naked half the damn time!" He glared at Scylla.

"That is for training, not to allow you to fill your eyes," she replied.

"Fuck's sake, I'm married! You have any idea what Case'd do to me if she caught me looking? Seriously, you want to do this, be my guest," he finished as Ingrid and I drew off to one side.

236

"I'll admit I'm not looking forward to that," she said to me in a low voice.

"To what?" I asked.

"The tube. You're literally hanging there right in front of everyone, naked, with only some little straps and tubes on you, and none of them cover you in those ways. I know it's stupid, considering the things that will be done, I mean. It removed your skin, you were literally skinned alive, and there's nothing sexual about the process, not at all, but still…"

"But it's undignified for you to be hanging there naked in front of everyone," I said. "I understand, don't worry. We can get a drape or something to go over it." I shrugged. "We can sort something."

"Thank you." She took a deep breath and blew it out as she looked up at me. "I-I know it's ridiculous, but it means something. Anyway…Steve?"

"Yes?"

"I…I don't know if I can do this," she admitted in a small voice.

"It's like the dentist," I told her after a few seconds of thought. "Getting a filling or having an operation. It's crap knowing you need it, and a little scary, but you'll be asleep for it, and afterward? It'll all be worth it."

"I've never had a filling."

"Lucky. I have, and the damn tube snapped my teeth to get them out, then replaced those teeth with new ones."

"That's really not making me feel better!" She groaned.

"Sorry." I smiled. "Well, what I need to talk to you about…"

"Yes?"

"There's a system I managed to unlock that wasn't open to me when I was here last. It's only available because the Erlking unlocked things for me, because they gave me command authority."

"Go on."

"It's literally a Command class," I said, moving on quickly. "I don't know entirely what it entails, but it's like being an admiral at sea, that was how I saw it, or a general. The Command class gets orders from our creators, and then gives the orders to the rest of us. They can also help people on a more specific basis. I think this would be great…for you. You could reach out and 'remote' into me."

"Into you?" Her eyes widened.

"It's not something that I could do," I explained. "First of all, I'm a fighter. You try managing the battle when you're on the front line? You're not paying enough attention to either job, and you're going to fuck at least one of them up.

"Add to that…well, I'm shit at details. I'm good at the specialist level. You want a building cleared, or an objective taken? I'm your guy. You want a small squad to take something? I can probably do that, but I'm better off letting Jonas lead it, if I'm honest. Moving forward, if we form a real team? I'll probably have him as the NCO, maybe even the team lead.

"You, though? You could be at the back of the party, or even back aboard the ship as I understand it. You could guide us all, improve us, boost our strengths, and make up for our weaknesses. It's like a support role, but one that'd let you help us all a lot more, and it'd help you to lead. Your upgrades wouldn't be like the ones most of us, as War units, would get. Yours would be around learning more, around interfacing with systems, like when we get our own ship. You'd be able to physically tap into it.

"It's called the Command class, but it's almost like a supercharged Support class. Remember that *we,* as humans, were never supposed to be in charge. This class was designed—I think—to be the step between the grunts like me, and the creators. So they'd give you the orders, and you'd guide the rest of us to carry the objective out."

"It'd help me to help you, and everyone," she finished for me. "Rather than me just being another of the generic Support classes, that would specialize however I needed to, my 'tree' would be for the Command class?"

"I think so." I shrugged. "I don't know, though. I get hints and leakage of data, mainly because I'm broken—and I still am, by the way—and I have access to several trees. Hell, there might even be an Archaeologist or Researcher tree that you get offered, I don't know. But before you go in there, I wanted you to know that this was an option, that's all."

"If I get offered this, would it help us all?" she asked after a few seconds of clear thought.

"I think so," I admitted. "And it's something that I think I'll have to add for you from the outside, though I'm not sure."

"Then I'll take it if I'm offered it," she said determinedly. "What about the others?"

"Scylla, Jonas, Courtney, and Paul will take the weapons system realignment. With Scylla's nanites stripped and them not being wounded already, they should be fine with that, and it'll mean that they can start from a healthy base level. Zac, well, he's Support class all the way. He'll probably be offered some kind of engineer specialization, and then we're all fucked, knowing that crazy bastard." I shrugged. "There's only so much the galaxy is ready for. And a true engineer gaining access to thousands of schematics, and a factory that can make anything? It'll be even odds if the universe still exists next week."

"Ordinary people think a product is fine, if it works. Engineers think it doesn't have enough features, until it's broken," Ingrid quoted, shaking her head in memory as she smiled. "Far always says he hates working with gifted engineers as much as he loves it. They can always find a solution, he says, but usually, the problem they're fixing is one they made happen in the first place, because they were bored."

"So we make damn sure that Zac doesn't have the chance to get bored," I agreed. "So, you're going to do this?"

"I am," she assured me. "Buuut…" She drew the word out, looking up at me as I waited.

"Yes?"

"This is your last chance to escape me, you know?" She bit her lip, staring into my eyes. "After this, well…if I'm going through this, and I'm immortal, you know you're never getting away, right?"

I gazed at her, hearing what she was saying, and the meaning behind the words.

"Are you insane?" I asked her slowly. "If there was ever one of us who would be leaving the other, it'd be you leaving me," I whispered. "You're amazing on every level, you're smarter than me, you're kinder, you're a hell of a lot better at leadership, and you're certainly more attractive. Ingrid, I'm punching well above my level with you, and I damn well know it. I'm in love with you, and I'm never letting you go."

"Well, now you won't have to." She cleared her throat and smiled up at me, her cheeks pink and her smile wide. "But I'm an old-fashioned type of a girl, so you'll need to put a ring on it one of these days. And to do that? You'll need to have a conversation with Far first."

She stood on her tiptoes, and I leaned down. The pair of us shared a long kiss, before she dropped back onto her heels and rested both hands on my chest, catching her breath.

"Right. Now that I've said things aloud that I shouldn't, I'll say one more, then we need to get moving."

"Right?" I replied, nodding in agreement but still confused.

"We need to get this sorted, all of this, and then we're getting back to our cabin, or to a hotel, or to a cubby hole in private as soon as we can find one, because you were gone a long, long time in Russia, and I have needs! We've been back together since then, and while that's actually a long time in our relationship, it's not been enough! You are going to take care of all of this"—she gestured at the room around us—"then you and I are finding somewhere private!"

"Yes, Commander!" I agreed with a wide smile, before ripping off a textbook salute.

"Right, let's go back to the others." A little smile quirked the edges of her mouth, before she reached for a second kiss, and then a long hug. "Honestly, you've got no idea how terrifying it was to see you in there." She stepped back, searching my face to see whether I understood.

"I bet," I said. "Look, I know the process in there"—I jerked my head in the direction of the capsule—"is terrifying when it's still to be done. I do. But right now? The thought of having to see you go through that? Even unconscious? It's terrifying me."

"And me," she admitted, interlacing her fingers in mine. "It's me who's got to do it yet."

"True." I smiled. "But at least you know there's a positive outcome, and you'll be asleep."

"Yes, but…wait, when it happened to you the first time?"

"I didn't know what was happening," I said. "I'd grabbed at what I thought was my only chance at life, so I'd made a choice, sure, but I had no clue what it really meant. And as the blades started cutting? I honestly didn't think I'd survive. Pretty sure I died a few times in that damn tube, actually."

"That's not filling me with confidence." She groaned, squeezing my hand tight. "Okay, here we go. Hey, everyone!" Ingrid called, raising her voice. "Steve's made me aware of a few things, and I need to make you all aware of them as well, so…"

CHAPTER TWENTY-FOUR

An hour later, I was under heavy, if sporadic, fire again.
Lasers carved lines through the metal all around me as I raced from cover to cover, firing back at the sentinels on the far side, even as they chased me, and my own sentinels chased them.

All in all, it was a fucking terrifying mess, but it was the best plan we could come up with. And I'd known it was going to be bad when Jonas suggested that he "had a plan."

When he went on with the magic words "…well, depending on your point of view, this is the easy bit…" it just got fucking worse, mainly for me.

Basically, we'd agreed that, for better or worse, the security AI was fixated on me, and would probably remain so now.

I'd done the most damage, I was the first to board it, and I brought others here. I was seen as the one who claimed its sections, and yeah, I had come back from the dead when it finally managed to put me the fuck down.

I was pretty conclusively the primary threat, as well as a major annoyance.

That meant that logically, the system would focus on me to a certain extent. That was fine, and yeah, we all agreed it really had a bit of a hard-on for me.

The problem was what we did about that.

Jonas's solution was both elegant and evil, and I was at least a little convinced that this was vengeance for a certain job I may or may not have had him do in the literal bowels of the recycling plant.

I'd "heard" that something had been seen in the sewage system, and I didn't want to send someone defenseless in there to check it out.

I was too busy, personally, and well, there was only room for one person in there; it was a tight fit, too. So, as Jonas was arguably the most lethal after Scylla and me, and nobody was going to ask Scylla to wade and slither through shit-smeared pipes, I asked him to do it.

That'd been about three days into him joining our side, and yeah, maybe, *just maybe*, there'd been an element of payback involved.

And if I was honest, although I had genuinely "heard" that there might be something in there…it was because I'd said it aloud to myself that morning when the idea had come to me in the shower.

So although I had technically "heard" it, it was a bit of a shitty—heh—thing to do.

This, I was goddamn sure, was retaliation for that.

I was to charge with a small number of sentinels as if I were the entire attacking force.

The rest of the group would wait until the other side committed, and then they would take them in the rear, while I ran like fuck around another of the big cargo holds. They seemed to be everywhere in this damn ship, and in this case, it was in another of the adjoining rooms from the one that we were originally in.

That way, hopefully, the AI would stay fixated on me for long enough that the others could slaughter its forces, and then we could go "for gold" and bum-rush the next section.

I had no doubt there'd be traps and shit as well, but regardless, that was what the sentinels were for.

Now, though, I sprinted from cover to cover—lumbering might be more accurate—as I was hammered again and again, and fire rang out on all sides.

I was in pain from what felt like a hundred different places, sections where the armor that Zac had come up with had burnt through already.

I felt ridiculous, both slow as shit and heavy as all hell, and I wondered whether this was how sumo wrestlers felt when they had to run, like if they turned it wouldn't matter because inertia meant they kept going in the original direction.

Because I'd lost access to my armor for now—and although it'd been tempting to see whether I could strip Scylla's nanites away myself, I knew that doing that, growing massively stronger at her direct expense, would have been too much for the proud woman—it meant that I'd been forced to rely on good old-fashioned methods instead.

Namely the kind of plate armor that had been so beloved of knights of old.

The first version had been a nightmare, falling apart as I tried to wear it. The second version had been better, sure, but I'd lost half of it while running.

If the others hadn't been using my distraction of the enemy to pick them off, I'd be dead already, and I swore as a fresh burn-through carved a section out of the back of my left thigh.

I staggered and fell, crashing to the floor and rolling—or flopping—out of sight behind the remains of some ancient crap.

I actually slid—slowly, thanks to the force of the landing and the angle of the floor here—and had to grab at the floor to stop myself from slipping back out of cover and into the line of fire again.

Before I could, though, a solid crack filled the air as Courtney's rail gun-based sniper rifle rang out again. She was goddamn lethal with that thing, and not for the first time, I was damn glad she and her idiot husband Paul were on my side.

That lunatic had changed up his armaments, going to a heavy machine gun-style rail gun. Basically, the goddamn thing could probably put a hole in the *moon*, and Zac had deliberately lowered the power on it to more reasonable levels.

He'd also upgraded that goddamn tomahawk and his massive bowie-style survival knife as "essential equipment" for this fight. And when I'd asked him when he thought he was going to use either, considering we were fighting fucking robot bastards in a sunken ancient alien ship, he'd shrugged and claimed it was a cultural weapon.

And then that I was oppressing him.

The fucking dickhead.

I'd just walked away, and as I lay there now, facedown, the floor on the other side of my crappy and insanely heavy helmet—blurry thanks to the sheer amount of old mold, crap, and sweat that stained the glass after my slide—I heard him shouting something about "kicking their ass."

I sighed, resting my head for just a few more seconds, before groaning and forcing myself to a sitting position, as I started stripping the armor off.

"You sure you want to be doing that?" Jonas asked me in his slow Southern drawl as he slid into the space next to me, squatting behind a misshapen bit of metal, then lighting a damn cigar.

"What?" I asked.

"Your armor—you sure you want to be removing it? I mean, there's going to be more of them, right?" He grinned at me. A plume of cobalt blue and gray smoke slid free to gently rise to the ceiling far overhead.

"Then you can fucking wear it," I growled at him.

"Ah hell, boss, you don't need to be like that…" He shook his head sadly. "It was downright brave the way you drew all their fire, racing ahead, throwing armor this way and that to make sure they kept focused on you. Brave as hell."

"Stupid," I said flatly. "You mean stupid as hell."

"Well, I wasn't going to say that, sure, but come on now, did it work? I think it did."

"Whatever," I growled, forcing myself up, then bending at the waist and shucking the massive breastplate free to hit the floor with a clang. "God, I want my *real* armor back," I muttered, reflecting that although this might not have looked much different, big and black for a fucking start, my armor increased my strength.

My armor was attached to me and moved with my body.

This fucker had been made exclusively of null blocks, and without my armor for it to go over and be carried in part by the enhanced systems, it'd weighed a literal fucking ton.

As it was, I was knackered, and even with the many enhancements to my body, and it being "refreshed" by the medical system so recently, I was nowhere near my usual peak condition.

I straightened, retrieved my rifle, and looked around the room, squinting as I picked out Courtney and Paul in the distance clambering down the side of an unstable mound of debris. Sections slid like they were about to cause an avalanche at any second.

I glanced about, frowning. Jonas was with me, and Paul and Court were there…so where was…?

A second later, sudden laser fire rang out, followed by the crash of heavy metal hitting metal, and ancient Greek swearing.

Peering around the edge of my cover, I made out Scylla then, a massive hammer in one hand, and the remains of a ninja-style sentinel being smashed into literal scrap at her feet.

Jonas and I stood there as she slammed the hammer into it over and over. The bang and crash echoed around even the massive hangar before I spoke.

"No offense, mate, and I'm sure you know your own mind, but are you sure you want to get into bed with that?" I asked him, and he snorted, before looking at me.

"Son, you might be an all-powerful Arisen now, and hell, a biological weapon in your own right, but take out the fact that she's an immortal warrior of myth and legend. Not only is she one of the smartest, most interesting, and probably *the* deadliest woman I've ever met? She has an ass that makes me straight up praise the Lord for its existence. That she's interested in me, even slightly? That's a miracle. That we're going to be put on a level playing field and set off to grow as strong as we want? That's a dream come true for people like her and me."

"I still think you're fuckin' mad," I muttered, shaking the last of my armor loose, then setting off toward the distant doors that were even now closing.

"Yes sir, I am," he replied, and I ignored the grin, as I mentally summoned up a handful of custodians, sending them racing forward to stop, or repair the door, depending on the state of it by the time we got there.

I also, because I'm such a trusting fella, sent a handful of sentinels ahead of the custodians.

The first of them detonated less than ten seconds later, hit by a beam weapon that was hidden in the wall off to one side. Half a second later, the next vanished in an explosion of tiny monofilament shards.

We were goddamn lucky that we were passing between some debris at that point, or we'd have been seriously goddamn inconvenienced.

As it was, it meant that we had to hold back a little and re-task the sentinels and custodians.

That, in turn, meant that it was a little more than half an hour before we reached the door. And by then? That AI bastard had welded it shut.

Twenty minutes more passed as four sentinels cut the damn door free, and while they did that, the fucker managed to pull up a few more defenders.

It was annoying as all hell. Personally, I'd have much preferred a massive, pitched battle, both our sides screaming and running into each other, rather than a million little fights, but this was what we got.

I'd have even taken this happily, if I still had my armor, as I'd have won easily.

As soon as the door opened, lasers lashed out at the space in the doorway. One of the custodians and one of the sentinels were caught in the blast and were shredded.

Our side returned fire. Then I ordered our last six sentinels forward, their multiple limbs clattering as they charged headlong into the withering enemy fire.

Courtney knelt way back from the door, her rifle propped on a small pile of debris, while we stood on either side of the door, and she fired through it.

The *crack-bang* of her rifle overwhelmed the sizzle, zip, and crackle of the lasers the sentinels were exchanging, and with each shot, another of the enemy was no more.

Less than a minute passed, with Paul and me on one side of the remains of the door, Jonas and Scylla on the other, and we waited impatiently as Court fired steadily.

"That's it!" she called ten seconds later. "I'm out!"

"Attack!" I roared.

All four of us raced for the gap and piled through, only to find a single sentinel at the far side being shredded by three of ours.

By the time I'd leveled my goddamn gun, it was over, the enemy core melted to slag.

We were in a corridor, and this time, as we reached the end of it, passing over the remains of a dozen small class-one sentinels, it bent to the right, and our destination was finally in sight.

The security office up ahead was clear. A pair of drones in the middle of the corridor out in front tried desperately to seal the entrance, as we closed on them. Jonas lifted his rifle and took two fast shots, taking them both down.

They looked as if they'd been hit with a hammer from a moving car, their tiny forms simply detonating in a spray of metal, fluids, and electrical parts.

Ten seconds later, and we were there.

I kicked the scrap out of my way, swinging through the remains of the window and dropping to the ground, before reaching out to the gleaming black spike that filled the middle of the room.

This time, now that I had the harvest tool back, and a way to feed active and attuned nanites through my body and into the spike, the fight was a hell of a different affair.

I even chose to use that over the Spike dagger I'd made, keeping that fucker for another time.

It wasn't easy, though—fuck no.

Had I had access to the sub-mind? It'd have been over in seconds, and I knew that. Instead, I had to activate my time compression and throw everything I had at crushing each and every die as they appeared.

With my time compression dialed right up, though, and my nanites forming an active and controllable bridge that I unleashed Tsunami into?

The wave of unrestrained contamination that Tsunami brought with it washed around the die as they appeared, each frantically trying to remain sealed as I spun and flexed them.

They couldn't respond to me in the outside world, defend against the Tsunami envelopment, and react fast enough…and in six seconds, the security AI made a decision.

It abandoned this section of the ship, fleeing as fast as it could, deeper into the system architecture.

I followed it, racing as quickly as I, in turn, could go. I felt the difference in the system up ahead a second before the section cut loose and I lost contact. The world seemed suddenly to end, literally right ahead of me, and my digital self raced in a dozen different directions before I figured out what the hell had happened.

It'd physically partitioned itself from the system that I was in, I realized, and as I reached out, bringing more and more of the ship under my control?

I laughed as I found the physical edges of where it'd run to.

The security AI had seen what was coming and had fled, all right: it'd fled to the digital equivalent of a sealed fortress, right in the heart of the new section I'd gained control of.

I needed to secure my control over the system properly, but it was looking like the AI had fled to a secure storage area, like a last-resort panic room or something, one with a physical break so I couldn't follow it.

Not in the digital realm, anyway. And in the physical? I could feel it was hiding in a not-too-distant but heavily armored room, the cheating little shit.

By the time I'd secured the area, though? I'd be able to hunt that fucker down happily.

I'd probably use a fucking hammer on the bastard when I found it.

Regardless of everything else, though, we'd done it, I realized, as I started to run searches. We'd secured the ship, all of what remained—save the section the AI had retreated into—and although most of it was unresponsive?

That was down to damage, and needing to actually hack the remaining systems, to lock them to me and to fully integrate them, not to any enemy action.

I slid out of the system, leaving Tsunami to work its evil tech magic. I turned to look at the others, drawing a deep breath and smiling.

"We've done it. It's ours," I told them, before sagging to sit on the floor and close my eyes as a wave of exhaustion and relief washed over me.

"Now what?" a voice asked, and I forced one eyelid open, glaring up at Paul.

"Now we fucking have five minutes to catch our breath, and we start work," I explained grimly. "The security AI ran for it. There's a secure storage area ahead, but we've got control of all the systems around it. It can't reach out, can't take the systems back, and it can't contact the outside world."

"So what do we do with it?" he asked again, and I shrugged tiredly.

"We make damn sure the systems around it are secure, we check out what it looks like in the real world, and we put some security units around it. As long as the area it's got is too small—it looks like it is from inside the system, anyway—then I don't really give a fuck."

"You're going to leave it?" Jonas asked, surprised.

"Jonas, it's a secure system. It's built with physical breaks, so it's meant as a last-resort fucking digital fortress, as near as I can tell. If it's in there and we control everything around it? It's not secure, it's fucking trapped.

"I'm not trying to hack it until I've got full access to my sub-mind and the Hack abilities I need, and I'm sure as shit not killing it."

"It tried to kill us," Paul pointed out, hefting his machine gun and shrugging. "I say make sure it's dead. Anything else, and it's got a chance to fuck us over later."

"Sure, there's always that chance," I admitted, before sighing and forcing myself to my feet and looking around. "I don't like leaving it in there, which is why we make sure it's not got room for a factory unit or anything in there with it. I don't want to face more fucking sentinels when it's had time to make more. But I'm not goddamn wasting this either! This is an AI, or at least an RI—it's a security system that maintained shit here for centuries.

"It's gotta know stuff we can use. And even if it doesn't? If we can hack it, make sure it's loyal, and then clone it? We could have the damn thing running any of our systems we need, like the recycling facility with ten thousand of the sentinels buried in the sand as backup."

"Heh, that'd be a nasty surprise." Jonas grinned. "Next time anyone comes looking for us and they all dig themselves out of the sand and cut them up? Hell yes."

"And with better weapons, better sensors and armor? Hell, we make ten thousand Terminators and give them great big fucking lasers? See how well it ends for the Arisen when they come to pick a fight next."

"Pull back a bloody stump with no body attached," Paul murmured, his eyes alight as he stared at something only he could see.

"Damn right." I nodded, arching my back and twisting, making it crack, before I swept up my gun. I reached out mentally to the sentinels and custodians, gathering them up.

By the end of the fight, getting up to here at least, I was down to one of each that was operational, and about a dozen broken and dead ones of each scattered about.

"The custodian is going to repair the other custodians…" I explained. "Once it's gotten three working, the other two will keep on repairing them until they're all working, then it'll start on the sentinels. We need to gather all the cores, so I can hack them. Then we go make sure the enemy is definitely trapped."

"Then what?" Scylla asked, and I looked over at her, forcing a smile.

"Then?" I asked. "Then, once Zac is set up and working here, getting the rebuild and repairs on track, and you're all upgraded, we're fucking off."

"We're going hunting?" Courtney asked, and I nodded.

"I think it's time to make use of someone we've been neglecting," I said with a smile. "Time to get Marie involved."

CHAPTER TWENTY-FIVE

The next week passed in a blur. Although some of it was good, and hell, some was downright interesting and exciting, some of it was sheer fucking nightmare fuel.

For me, the worst point, by a massive margin—hell, the worst thing that had ever happened to me in my life—was the upgrade process for the others, and definitely Ingrid.

Scylla, being Scylla, showed absolutely no outward fear, and when she entered the capsule, I took control, managing the options, just in case.

She was identified as an Acinonyx class, where I was identified as Ursus, and I felt terrible making sure that the anesthetic was refused.

I'd asked her again before she entered the tube whether she was sure she wanted to do this, knowing that when she left it, she'd be healthier and stronger than a regular human, but that was it, until she could harvest nanites.

She'd confirmed it, and I'd triggered the "close." Minutes later, with a ring around the outside of the capsule, hidden behind a shielding wall of metal—for modesty and gore's sake—the sounds began.

Unlike my system, which was thoroughly human when I'd first gone in, and practically drained of nanites the second time around, Scylla was filled with nanites.

I'd been sensing them more and more as the days passed, as more of the little machines became active again, recovering from their long centuries of disablement.

As they came online again, even with nine in ten of them corrupted, she had been growing in strength daily. Now, as I stood there, staring up into her eyes, Scylla stared back at me desperately.

She'd been stripped of flesh as the first step, literally, from her hair to her toes; then the blades had focused on little details like her toe and fingernails, ripping them out.

The muscles and tendons, fatty deposits and more were next, carved loose and lifted free, slid into recesses in the capsule that I'd never been able to see from the angle I was held at.

As the hours became a day, she was rendered down to a skeletal form, organs replaced by tubing and attachments to keep her functioning as the removed section was worked on, and then the tube's manipulators replaced them.

Sections of intestine were extended out, cut apart, and reworked, then reinstalled. Everything from the heart to bladder, lungs to sexual organs: all were removed and meticulously repaired and upgraded.

I'd seen some of it, from the inside anyway, but watching it from this side? It was horrible. Literally sections of her were rebuilt until they practically glimmered.

Parts like the nails were replaced, this time with gleaming metallic-looking plates that made me think of knife blades more than anything else.

I watched as new sections were inserted into her skull, the eyes being removed and operated on, sliced apart, then rebuilt and reinstalled.

Metallic and carbon-based systems were installed, then muscles and fatty tissues were reinstalled over again, this time looking...cleaner. The process of removal...well, it was obviously messy. The fluid that filled the capsule seemed to draw the blood away and leave the body pristine. But even with that, the sections as they were cut free were battered.

Centuries of them being used and abused, then more when she was in stasis or dead, had resulted in her body being beaten to all hell, no matter how you looked at it. Then, although the nanites had repaired and kept her going since she awoke, the majority of them were non-functional as well.

The "parts" that were stripped out were visibly worn out, as much as we all were, I had to assume.

The ones that were installed, though? They were perfect.

Literally.

She gained several inches in height overall—her genetic ideal having been tweaked, apparently—and when she was finally released from the capsule, she was weak and confused, slow and sluggish as she tried to move.

It didn't take long for her to get control of herself again. But damn, the difference in who and what she'd been, from what she was now? It was massive.

Ten minutes after she'd been released, she challenged me to a fight.

Knowing what she needed, knowing that she needed to test her body, and to experience the changes to it, I agreed. But damn.

She was a skilled warrior; she'd literally fought in battles weekly, if not daily in an age known for insane levels of violence. She'd also been used to the fact that she could use her greater strength and speed to win those fights, and as we sparred, she grew visibly enraged.

Kicks that she snapped out were too weak, too slow, or off target; blocks were poorly timed, and I could see why.

She was used to exerting a certain amount of force, compared to the maximum she had access to, to achieve a set aim, such as to catch the back of my forearm and to slap it aside.

Now, the amount of effort she had to put in meant that her innate muscle memory was totally off.

Add in that she'd grown several inches, and that the ground was no longer where she felt it should be, instinctively? The result was a mess.

She stormed off after a handful of minutes, furious as near as most would be able to tell. The group down here with her, though? We could tell the difference between anger and fear.

Surprisingly, it was Paul who was the best at dealing with it, taking her off to one side and speaking quietly to her.

When he'd almost lost his arm, it'd needed to be rebuilt from scratch. And add in a hip injury, well, he'd been left using a crutch for a while, it turned out.

That the arm and leg injuries were on opposite sides of the body meant that he'd developed a twist in his spine, one that resulted in a buildup of muscle on one side.

That, in turn, meant that he had to stop everything. Weeks of enforced bed rest had been the first step, making sure that the injuries were properly healed; then he'd started with the basics.

Weights and walking, something he'd done all his conscious life as far as he could remember, were suddenly a challenge for him, and he'd forced himself to do it *right*, instead of fast.

He'd spent more time moving slow, doing Pilates, yoga, and moving through stances of non-contact martial arts in the next few weeks than he had in his entire life, but it had worked.

He'd taught himself to adjust to his new body, and then, with a solid foundation, he'd pushed harder and faster than the physioterrorists ever believed was possible.

He explained it to Scylla, and the explanation, coming from a muscled mountain of a man, got through to her.

The pair went off to one side—followed by a distrustful Courtney; Scylla had a habit of being naked a lot and had no modern sexual morals—and started to train.

While they were doing that, Ingrid and I talked.

I'd spent most of the time that Scylla was undergoing "work" in there with her. I'd been there, where she could see me, knowing that even a little comfort was worth my time a hundred times over.

Now, though, that it wasn't another warrior, and one who annoyed the shit out of me and concerned me to equal measure daily? That instead it was the woman I loved?

I was almost more nervous than Ingrid was.

Three times I nearly asked her not to go through with it.

That was insane, it was selfish, and it was cowardly. I knew that, for her, the best possible thing that could happen here was that she would be borderline immortal. She'd be able to grow to the point that she'd have been able to not just stand toe-to-toe with Athena, but surpass her, then bitch-slap her into the middle of next Tuesday.

Ingrid would be able to learn, to see history pass, and most of all, she'd never be sick, hopefully never die, and be—in my eyes, at least—physically perfect forever.

What she'd gain was insane compared to the level of risk, and I knew that, at a mental level. At a visceral level, though? The woman I loved was about to be carved up before my eyes.

We talked, deliberately avoiding the subject of what was to come, instead focusing on inconsequential things: details around us, places we wanted to go, the mission, our friends, who we should offer the upgrade process to next…all of it.

We spent hours talking about everything and nothing, until she finally blew out a long breath and walked back to the capsule, before stripping off.

She'd said her goodbyes to everyone earlier, even linking up to the yacht, and from there making a call to the recycling plant and speaking to her parents.

She'd not wanted to worry anyone else, bar Lars, who was frantically wanting to be here, both as support for Ingrid, and to explore a veritable alien spaceship from the dawn of time.

Now, though, after I'd helped to lift her up, the capsule closing around her, and the look of forced bravery on her face as the fluid flowed up, pouring into her lungs?

I shook, doing my best not to show it.

Seeing her body spasming as it fought to eject the liquid was painful, like watching her drown. She coughed and shook; her arms and legs, the rest of her body as well, were strapped into place by tethers as she convulsed.

Her body fought against the fluid instinctively, and by the time it accepted it, I could see how traumatized she already was.

I'd reached out to the system, selecting the Command class, and as she half drowned, accepting the fluids and being bound into place, the capsule and medical AI assessed her.

She was accepted, approved even, and a dozen small recommendations were marked up and greenlighted by me. Once she was in there, we'd both known that she'd not be able to communicate, and the system menus provided so many options, and so little clarity, that she and the others had agreed to trust me to do it all.

As the first of the blades slid out of their recesses, and I saw the fear in her eyes ratchet up a notch, the anesthetic finally started to pump in.

The fluid that we'd all been enveloped and contained in was mainly clear—a little touch of blue to the color, if anything…when it wasn't stained with copious blood, anyway—but now, for the first time, I saw a sea-green shimmer start to fill it.

I watched her, holding her gaze as it grew distant, confused, and vague, before her eyelids slid shut. And when, literally, a second later, the first blades reached her?

Well, I waited to make sure she didn't wake, before turning away.

I forced myself to stay there, to be here, as she was stripped and rebuilt, as dozens of bits of tech that I could barely guess at was installed in her.

Organs were removed entirely and replaced with smaller, more space-efficient systems, and technological components were put in their place.

Bones were worked on, but mainly left alone. Her skull, though, once her beautiful eyes had been removed and replaced? It was carved apart and rebuilt.

For long hours, her brain was worked on, and I panicked silently, wondering whether the woman who awoke would still be Ingrid, as sections were installed. She was partially released from the webbing and restraints, rolled onto her front, and sections were laid in along the back of her neck, down her spine.

I watched as they were placed and the movement of her body tested. Sections were adjusted, and tests run; then they were buried under muscle and flesh.

As she was rebuilt—everything, all the way up to her skin, re-layered onto her skeletal structure—the heartache of watching her being operated on slowly receded, and was replaced with a terror that she'd not be *her* when she awoke.

Her hair was the last to be laid into place, the scalp being re-laid and the edges sealed, before she was adjusted and held in places, as the fluid began to change again.

It'd gotten to the point it was literally blood-red in there for a while, with the fluid leaking from her open wounds as blood was pumped back into her, until it was finally filtered away.

In seconds, it went from deep red all the way back to faintly blue, and a minute after that, she started to stir, blinking slowly.

As she came around, the fluid was sucked free, leaving her dangling from the restraints. Her skin pebbled with the cold as the capsule opened, lowering her to the ground.

I took her, feeling her arms wrap around me as I lifted her in a princess carry, holding her to me as I sat down on a chair Zac had made for me.

"Ingrid?" I reached up and lifted her chin, making her look at me.

"Yes?" she managed after a few seconds, staring past me as much as at me.

"Are you okay?"

"I…I think so?" she whispered groggily. "The world around me, around us? I can see…I can see so much!" She shook her head, and visibly forced herself to focus on me.

I blinked in shock as I felt something, a presence in my mind, and a question being asked. None of it was verbal—hell, there wasn't really a question, not in that sense…it was more an injection of intent, and wonder.

It was her, I knew instinctively, like when I was lying in our bed with my eyes closed, I knew it was her who lay by my side, and no other, despite not seeing her.

I could tell by the sound of her breathing, by her scent, the feeling of her body, the knowledge that she was there when I slept, all of it, and now I realized, I'd been sensing her as well.

I could feel that sense of her, her presence, at the border of my mind, standing there, reaching out and offering her help. I accepted it without a second's doubt, and she gasped involuntarily.

"Your stats, your capabilities, the choices you have?" She frowned, clearly seeing the tangled mess of my "jack-of-all-trades" build. "It's…magnificent," she finished, surprising me, as I'd been expecting censure.

"You can see it?" I asked, and she nodded, smiling.

"I can, and your outstanding choices, as well as the prompts you've been ignoring."

I shrugged that off, getting a look from her, before I drew a deep breath and accepted them.

I'd not been ignoring them for a particular reason; it was just the notifications that I'd finished the last two sections of the quest, and a notification for the next one. It'd not been important enough to do anything with, not right now for my War points. And I sure as shit wasn't going to spend my Hack points until I had access to the sub-mind again.

Quest Updated!

Evolving Quest updated: Repair and Renovate: Level 2: Completed!

Congratulations, Biological Weapon Variant #Steve.

You have eliminated the local security forces rallied against you by the security AI that protects Facility 6B. As it does not recognize your right of access, and has marked you as a trespasser, you must eliminate or convert this security AI, to claim the facility.

~~Part One: Secure the local area and survive the incoming assault, eliminating all attackers, and establishing a secure and defensible perimeter to gain the following reward:~~

Complete!

+1 War Point

+Access to Level 3 of this section of the Evolving Quest

~~Part Two: Increase your control over the local security net, by penetrating and locking the security AI out of a secondary node to gain access to the next tier of the evolving quest and gain the following reward:~~

Complete!

- **+1 Hack Point**
- **+Access to Level 3 of this section of the Evolving Quest**

*

Quest Updated!

Evolving Quest updated: Repair and Renovate: Final level: Unlocked!

Congratulations, Biological Weapon Variant #Steve.

You have established a beachhead in Facility 6B, the security AI has been beaten back and has retreated into a secure fallback position, and must now be removed, eliminated, or converted to your side.

To gain full control over the remains of Facility 6B, establish control over the surviving control nexus and secure the remains of the facility to gain the following rewards:

- **+1 War Point**
- **+1 Hack Point**
- **+1 Point of Specialization**

I nodded to myself. It was literally what I'd been expecting, and sure, the War and Hack points were useful, but I wasn't going to make use of them right now.

I needed to get myself back on my goddamn feet first. And more importantly? I needed to make sure that Ingrid was all right.

"Are you okay?" I asked her, and she nodded slowly.

"I am. I'm just…I don't know, not really," she admitted after a few seconds' reflection. "I feel amazing in one way, like I'm full of energy. And the room? I can see so much better. The world is full of details I'd never noticed before."

"And on the other side?" I asked, and she hesitated.

"I feel weird…I was at a party once." She looked a little embarrassed as she pushed a stray lock of her hair back behind her ear, folding her arms around her body. "I—can I get my clothes?"

I snorted.

"I'm sorry." I grinned, letting go of her as she stood, then hunched slightly, clearly aware that someone could come in through the little gap we'd left for access at any time and find her like that.

"There." I nodded, pointing to her clothes.

"Oh, thank God!" she muttered, half sprinting to them and quickly pulling her underwear on, torn between getting it on comfortably, and actually just getting it in place so that she could get her top on as well.

She gave up on comfort and yanked that on, and stepped into her jeans, half jumping to pull them up, and looking stunned at how easily she did it.

I gave her a few seconds to rummage and adjust herself, before speaking.

"So, you were at a party?" I prompted.

"What?" She winced as she caught herself with a nail, then finished dressing. "Oh!" She grinned, her cheeks flushed pink. "Sorry, yes, I was at a party with some friends and one of them had some, umm…"

"Drugs?" I guessed, and she nodded quickly.

"I wasn't really interested, but you know, I was away at university, and I thought, why not? Why not try it? So…I did, and while I ended up being really, *really* sick a bit later, until it went to that point? It felt like this."

"Hmmm," I murmured, admiring the view, as she twisted this way and that, trying to adjust her jeans to sit right. She'd apparently gained a few inches in height and whatever the augments she'd had in her back and elsewhere, she'd gained a fraction here and there as well.

She actually looked better, if that was humanly possible.

"Probably all the energy. What did you take?" I asked, and she shrugged.

"No clue. They told me, but I'd not heard of it before."

"Did you smoke it?"

"No, I wouldn't smoke. It's nasty."

"Fair enough. In your nose? A vein?"

"Ummm, I rubbed it on my gums?"

"Probably coke." I shrugged. "Or speed." I used the local names I'd known such drugs by, then dismissed it as I realized that as a rich Danish girl, she'd probably been offered much better shit than I used to have access to, not to mention it'd have been in a different language. "Made you feel good, and full of energy, but a bit twitchy?" I tried, and she nodded.

"Was this what it was like for you?" Her lips quirked as she actually danced a few steps.

"Ha, no!" I barked a laugh. "As soon as the capsule opened, I was dropped onto the floor and three sentinels were waiting for me. I had to fight them and escape from the ship, with the AI trying to kill me."

"And then you swam to shore, naked." She winced, remembering what I'd told her.

"Yeah, I was just glad that fucker Dave had left his bike there. I mean, I'd hidden the keys, but anyone besides that cheap bastard would have had it towed away, at least."

"I'm sorry." She dropped down from her tiptoes, where she'd started to dance, looking mortified. "I'd forgotten that for you…" She looked around, presumably remembering the way the ship had appeared to her before. "You were lost in here, when you couldn't see?"

"Lost, freezing to death, and with my feet cut to ribbons by the gangways," I agreed. "Don't worry about it. Considering the shit that Athena put me through, it barely registers now. Anyway!" I grinned at her. "Are you glad you did it?"

"I am," she said after a few seconds.

"Did you feel anything?"

"No…" She drew the word out, frowning. "At least, I don't think so. I've got memories, like when you've had a really weird dream, and then you remember something about it the next day, you know?"

"Yeah?"

"It's like that. I don't remember anything but there's something...?" She hesitated for a second, then shrugged. "I don't know."

"But you're okay?" I pressed, and she nodded.

"I am."

"Are you up to seeing the others?"

"Of course!" she assured me, then clicked her fingers. "I need to call Mor and Far and...oh."

"What?" I asked, as she stared into the distance, eyes wide.

"Ingrid?" I took a step closer, then felt the backwash of a connection as she reached out.

I frowned, searching. A sensation like the wake of a ship on the ocean pushed out around the connection she was making. As I reached out, though, I instantly knew that I could probably hack the communication, but that she'd likely sense it.

Instead, realizing that it was her first fledgling use of her abilities, I pulled back, granting her the privacy to do it herself.

Taking her hand, I led her to the chair, settling her down as she smiled distractedly at me, before staring off into the distance again, then starting to speak quietly in Danish, with tears shining in her eyes.

I moved off, passing through the narrow gap we'd left in the metal curtain we'd erected around the capsule, finding the others talking and resting.

"How is she?" Jonas asked before the others could, but it was barely a fraction of a second ahead of them.

"She's good," I assured them, only now realizing that once again I was damn well shaking. But instead of it being through fear, it was with relief!

I moved to a chair quickly, settling down on the edge, glad all over again that Zac had taken the time to make them.

"She's calling her parents, or I think that's what she's doing. I felt the connection as she was establishing it."

"She's got access to what? Calls?" Jonas frowned.

"Great, all of that to save on a cell phone bill," Courtney muttered, looking unsure.

"She can remotely access a data device in fucking Sudan from the bottom of the ocean in the Med," I corrected. "Bit of a difference from a fucking text, all right?"

"Point," Jonas said, before forcing a smile. "So, who's next then, boss?"

"Who wants it?" I looked from one to another. "No offense to you all, but I'd suggest Zac next, then Jonas?"

"Fuck yeah!" Zac crowed, jumping to his feet. "Okay, boss, I'm ready."

"Settle down." I gestured at him to sit back. "First, Ingrid is talking to her parents in there, and the last thing she needs to see is your naked ass streak past. Secondly, I need to know what you're doing in here, and where you're up to. What's the plan with the production line and..."

That was it—we were off again, working on plans.

Zac's master plan was surprisingly similar to my old one, in that we were basically securing the area, primarily. First, he'd built and repaired more sentinels and custodians; then came a new fusion plant, a bigger and much more powerful one.

That would be finishing production in about three hours, and the assembly would take two days. Once that was up and running, the ship would have sufficient power to basically bring all the surviving systems, and then some, back online.

That there were almost none of the original systems intact was a minor detail, but fuck it.

It did mean that we could get access to the remaining sensors, the doors and the various tertiary systems that were somewhat responsive.

That included the water processing plants at the very rear of the ship.

As I reached out to them, I realized that the reason they were so slow, so inefficient and yeah, caused a goddamn riptide where they jutted from the seabed, rising near to the cliffs where I'd first met Marie and Amanda?

It was because they were designed to be lowered into the sea from above. Either from a stable platform, or from a ship that cruised past.

Where they remained, of the original ten, there were four shattered versions left. And three of those four were actually jutting out of the water, worn down by millennia of wind, rain, and crashing seas, coated in probably solid meters of bird shit, not to mention that the original forms had been broken down by oxidation as well.

I winced, accessing the systems and evaluating them. Across the four units that responded, there was a grand total of three percent viability reported.

That wasn't three percent per unit either, or all in one of them.

It was total.

Fuck.

I pulled up the designs in the ship systems, or I tried to, finding that they were restricted to "Command personnel only." When I got Ingrid to try?

We found that we then had the authority, and hit a break in the line, as the repository was—of course—stored where the fucking AI was hiding.

We'd found it, of course. It was one of the very first things we'd looked for, and when we'd found it, there'd been an argument.

Most of the others wanted to try to hack it, and when I explained that wasn't possible, not until I'd gotten access to the armor and my sub-mind again, the next solution had been to burn the fucker out of the ship.

It was in a heavily armored chamber deeper in the ship, a room similar to the storage areas we'd passed through, or the production facilities in that it was high and wide, but it was also clearly fucking designed as a last-ditch safe room.

The area it was in was dark, seriously so, the only light in it coming from the crackling discharge of the repulsors.

It hovered in the middle of the room, a square base with a pyramidal structure above it that floated some three meters off the ground, encased in a crackling sphere of naked energy.

Worse still, the generator keeping it powered was clearly on the inside, and the structure itself was made of some black, glossy metal that seemed to suck in even the light of the sphere.

I tried to reach out to the structure and felt nothing. When I mentioned that to the others, Zac had grunted and casually remarked that it was probably a Faraday cage of some kind.

Apparently, that was where a current was run around the area you wanted to protect, blocking anything that was trying to come in, or go out.

It was a counter to an EMP, Zac helpfully noted, and Paul immediately took the piss out of him, pretending to have a nuke as a weapon, and how relieved he'd be that there was a nice cage to protect his phone and his porn stash, while he was being reduced to a number fifty-seven, extra crispy by the fallout.

I tuned them both out, reaching out again and again, trying to feel the structure with my Hack capability.

Nothing, unfortunately. It was as if there were a massive black hole in the room. After ten minutes of trying, I gave up.

The best I'd been able to sense was that I was being shifted around the outside of the sphere, like water drawn around the vortex going down the plughole.

Our solution was to make sure that the fucker couldn't do anything to us, by shipping null blocks up here and having a pair of custodians assemble a box around the fucker.

It took them four days, but by the time they were finished, Zac assured me that the AI would have to either cut the power soon, or risk frying itself in the backwash of radiant heat the process generated.

I had no clue how or why, and just accepted that due to the way the Faraday cage worked, that once the AI tried to escape, it'd be fucked.

I'd hoped it'd be enough to get me the quest complete notice, but apparently not. Dicks.

Zac had been "upgraded" in just under a day, the Support package realigned for him, and an engineer sub-specialty selected, getting him access to a creation tool in his arm, instead of a harvest tool unfortunately, but fuck it.

That massively sped up the process, as he started construction of the power plant, then worked on more of his giant spiderbots.

He called them all-terrain construction bots, but fuck it. It was a six-legged giant spider as far as I was concerned, and it really annoyed him when I called it that, which meant that was rapidly becoming its official name.

James stayed aboard the yacht at first, Case swimming down to an access point closer to the shore and joining Zac as Ingrid and I returned to the yacht in her place. Scylla and Jonas went with us, Paul and Courtney staying below as a security force.

The next three days were spent remotely accessing the facility, and working to get it as repaired as possible.

James chose to get "upgraded" as part of the next wave, with the medical facility warning that it was almost out of nanites and anesthetic.

The decision was made that although we'd love to get all the team upgraded, right now we needed to pull our goddamn fingers out. Hans still hadn't turned up, and Marie—along with Amanda and Dave—were ready.

CHAPTER TWENTY-SIX

"Oh, she's good," Ingrid whispered, shaking her head as she glanced over the details on a tablet screen held in one hand. She was laid back half against me, turned away and resting her back against my shoulder, long legs stretched out on the yacht's seats, sipping her coffee.

"What's that?" I frowned at her, before realizing it was the data that we'd gotten from Marie that she was referring to, not the sounds that were rising—again—from the cabin that Jonas and Scylla were now sharing.

"She's really worked hard…" Ingrid shifted and smiled up at me. "Sorry, I didn't mean to disturb you…"

I shrugged, grinning, before nodding a touch sourly in the direction of the ladder down to the lower decks. "It's all right, I was already disturbed, and yeah, it sounds like she is!"

"What?" Ingrid frowned, then laughed. "Sorry, I filtered out the noises from below. I'd forgotten about them!"

"How'd you do that?" I asked, impressed.

"Command privileges." She winked. "If I need to focus on something, I can choose to block out details. I just create a bubble of sensory negation around me, and then anything that the filters judge to be coming from outside that? They block."

"Damn," I muttered. "I need to get the Command tree as well."

"Don't you dare." She tapped the end of my nose with one finger. "This is my role…go find your own."

"Yes, dear." I grinned at her. "So, if you weren't commenting on Scylla trying out for the bedroom Olympics, what were you meaning?"

"Marie." She shook her head, clearly blocking the noises from below out again. "She's good."

"Because?" I prompted.

"She's located three groups of people on the island who nobody will miss," she clarified, reaching out to me and offering a link. I accepted it—of course—and she pulled up a satellite image of the island that Marie had helpfully included in her report.

"Here…" The map rotated, showing the party center of Malia, and I couldn't help but grin at the memories of there.

"Malia, eh?" I nudged her. "I met a girl there once…"

"It was a long time ago." She snorted, before leaning around and giving me a quick kiss. "I'd not change it for the world, though," she assured me, before focusing the map and showing me the island as if I were aboard a drone, flying in from the sea.

"So, in the three and a bit years since we were last there, there's been some changes. One of them is a small but growing organized crime gang. They're paying off the local police, as near as Marie can tell, which is why word doesn't get out, but there's been a marked increase in 'accidents' there this year so far."

"Accidents?"

"The kind where drunk tourists fall from balconies and are either maimed for life, or die," she clarified darkly. "It's noticeably richer, younger guys, and they all happen around this location."

The drone view flashed up from the beach to where the road hit a crossroads, heading off to the left and passing a few smaller hotels, before coming to some very nice, newly built models.

"Five in this hotel, four next door, seven across the road," she said. "The only common point, beside the terrible accidents, and the perfectly good barriers on the balconies that should be preventing it, is that it's always men, and they all have their accounts emptied. Frequently, one of the last transactions before they clean their account out for cash, supposedly to spend in the local area, is in this place."

The view changed, flashing a little farther along the street to a small building that I vaguely remembered.

"That's—" I frowned. "That *was* a twenty-four-hour bar," I rephrased. "I used to go there…not a lot, but about once a week or so."

"It was bought out by the same group that own the hotels, according to Marie's digging. Now it looks like it's a strip bar, and that's a front for a brothel. It looks to be the main link between them all."

"So, they go to the brothel, get a lap dance or whatever, spend on their card?" I scowled. "Seems a bit stupid. I mean, if you're going somewhere like that, you're not going to want it on your card, right?"

"It's illegal in Crete, but the police don't seem to be doing anything about it," she agreed.

"Okay, so we've got corrupt coppers, a knocking-shop that's finding the targets…then what?"

"The accidents happen after the tourists withdraw all their cash. They tend to vanish for a few days. They message their friends saying they've met someone, that kind of thing, then they return to the hotel, just before they're due to go home, and fall off the balcony."

"So someone's keeping them out of sight after they clean out their accounts, probably in a basement or something, making it so the police—if they check it at all—can say that they spent it all on holiday. Also makes it look like the last place they went wasn't the knocking-shop." I nodded.

"Exactly. It's also happening, as near as I can tell, every few weeks, somewhere in Malia, and I'm betting that these are just the ones that the local thugs think they have to keep quiet."

"Sounds about right," I agreed. "Okay, let's go check them out. Then we've got two places to visit while we're there."

"Oh?"

"My friend Tommy," I said. "He loaned me his bike for a few days—that was what I was riding when I met you—and I never went back."

"Ah…" She winced. "He must have thought you stole it!"

"That's what I'm betting. I got Marie to check out the address, and he still owns it, so I got her to get a bike on order for me, shipped from Germany, and it's making its way to him now as an apology."

"But you want to see him?" she asked, and I nodded. "Okay. Can I come, or do you want to go alone?"

"You're damn right you're coming," I assured her. "I'm damn well showing you off to him."

"You idiot." She laughed, shaking her head, but I noticed the pleased smile that I wanted to show her off to an old friend, and the way her cheeks pinkened slightly. "So, that's one place. Where else?"

"We need to visit Val at the hotel," I said. "I think he deserves that, right?"

"Definitely," she agreed, smiling widely. "I was going to suggest it, if you could hack the cameras in the area?"

"I can do that easily enough. While I'm not going to be able to get my armor back anytime soon, even if we find there's a lot more of these fuckers involved in the scams, I'll still be able to do that."

"What's that about your armor?" Ingrid frowned.

"About getting it back?" I asked, and she nodded. "This won't do that. Humans don't have anywhere near enough nanites to be worth heavily harvesting, not the baseline variant anyway. We'll get between a few hundred and a few thousand if we're lucky. This is more for them—and you—to get used to your abilities, and yeah, to get us some nanites. Once we've got as many as we can, we'll start hunting the variants like lycans."

"Good," she said, before moving on. "So, that's the first target, and the two places you want to visit, but what about the rest?"

"Go on."

"Marie said that there have been disappearances in this area, and that they match the pattern from the werewolves that you met the last time you were there…" She pulled up the map of the island again and zoomed into the area around Heraklion, and I grunted.

"That's an issue then," I said slowly, looking it over.

"Oh?"

"The creatures I saw there were massive fuckers, and they were guarding a door that led somewhere else." I scratched at my cheek as I tried to remember the details. "I can't remember the name, but they were big, like ten meters plus, glossy black skin like they replaced their flesh with onyx, and their faces? All their fat removed just on their faces, the flesh seeming to be vacuum packed. Great big white eyes like those angler fish you get down deep…"

"The lures?" she asked, and I nodded. "There was a mention of them, or something like them somewhere…" She started to sort through the files on her pad, before laughing and focusing her mind instead, reaching out and accessing the file she'd been wanting with ease.

"Okay, so are these the things you saw?" She pulled up an image, one that made me nod.

It was a photo, clearly old, and looked to be of a wall image somewhere hot. The colors that had presumably once been painted on bright and vibrant were now peeling and covered in sand, or flaking away. Sections of the images had crumbled and fallen, and only a small fragment had survived with any clarity.

"What's this?" I asked.

"It's from the temple complex at Karnak, or nearby anyway." She frowned as she looked over some of the details. "It was uncovered last year, which is why some of it is clear, and some lost. It was buried for a few thousand years, most likely. Lars heard about it and sent it to me, trying to get me to interact with him so he could figure out what the hell was going on."

"And?"

"I was being held by Athena's thugs." She sighed. "I was allowed to respond, but it was carefully read over and searched for any alternative meaning. He knew something was wrong, but not what, or where I was. He tried to find me, again and again, despite his own family Arisen—you were right, he has an ancestor who rose—stepping in and ordering him to leave it alone."

"The Arisen stepped in personally?" I frowned.

"Well, I think it was someone who wanted to be sponsored." She shook her head. "Lars didn't know any details but he said they acted like they were the rulers of the world and they made it clear that unless he wanted his family to have an 'accident,' he'd better forget about me."

"And?"

"And he made sure the family was safe and kept looking for me," she said, clearly proud. "You know Lars."

"I do," I admitted, unable to keep from smiling. "That fucker's getting an upgrade soon."

"I think he should," she agreed. "But anyway. Lars sent this, and while I couldn't exactly discuss it with him, it matches some images that Athena had on a wall, ones that were hermetically sealed in a display case."

"Photos?" I asked, and she shook her head disgustedly.

"You think she'd make do with just a photo? No, it was torn loose from the site at Karnak, and preserved."

"I don't know if I should be pissed or pleased," I said after a few seconds. "On one hand, Athena, and the shit bird that she was—on the other? She might have saved priceless relics once we find them."

"Pissed," she said. "We'll never know where they were taken from, nor if they were all that was found there. Also, Athena was a bitch, and when I tried to ask her about it, she beat me to within an inch of my life for daring to speak to her, then had me rolled in salt to make sure I 'knew my place.'"

"Fuck," I groaned, wanting nothing more than to resurrect Athena somehow, just so I could fucking slaughter her again. "I'm sorry…"

She laid her fingers over my lips. "Don't you dare apologize for what that evil witch did," she growled. "You were far more of a victim there than I was, so don't you *dare*. I remember you signing your life away, literally, to the council, to let them experiment on you, just to make sure I was safe. I mean it… don't you dare apologize for what was done to us."

I reached up, taking her hand in mine, and kissed her fingers, not knowing what to say, and she went on with her tale.

"So…the details I found called them the Xi-Ma, and they were linked to the pharaohs of old, like the first dynasty ones."

"Right?"

"Karnak was a middle kingdom site, and I asked her because she was laughing to someone about how little we knew, that we thought the colossi were just decoration."

"Right," I said, and she smiled.

"What do these look like?" She pulled up a few pictures of the pharaohs sitting in their giant chairs at the temple of Karnak and elsewhere.

"Like the big fuckers that are sitting on a giant throne. They're about the right size, sure, but they're human-looking, if a bit dodgy around the eyes."

"And the head—there was a fashion to make their skulls longer, but that's for another day," she said almost absently. "Now, ignore the face of the colossi. Instead, look at the thrones and the size."

"That's right." I nodded. "But the figures…"

"There's a theory that the figures were added *after* the thrones." She smiled, her eyes twinkling. "It doesn't get much traction, because most of the images show them with these figures sitting in the thrones. But some of the very oldest? They show the thrones as empty, waiting for them to be occupied. Some archaeologists say that's showing that they had their inhabitants swapped out, following a change in the local belief structure, but I don't think so, not now."

"Right?"

"Remember that there's almost no writing of normal life that survived from those days. Sure, there's stuff about the glory of this pharaoh and the magnificence of this or that, but of normal life? Not from then. There's records of stories kept even, because that needed to be noted down, but the normal world around them? Almost nothing. When Hans told us that the pharaohs of old, the very first ones, were Arisen? It got me thinking."

"Right," I repeated, settling back and nodding for her to go on.

"We know the Arisen like using creatures and more as their servants, the other humanoid races, so with that in mind, I started looking at the legends and myths of those days. Most of the records of the 'gods' of the various animal-headed creatures that ruled the afterlife? The records that later generations built their myths on, came from then."

"Okay, so—"

"I'm not explaining this very well." She cut me off, then smiled at James, who'd come up to join us, bringing a tray of coffee for us all.

"May I?" he asked, and we gestured for him to take a seat.

"Always," I assured him, before winking. "Well, when I have pants on at least."

"Steve, you're naked more than any man I've ever known." James sighed, acting as if it were a terrible thing, and hiding a smile.

"Yeah, well. What can I say, I'm just that nice to you all," I replied.

"*Anyway!*" Ingrid interrupted, drawing our attention back to her as she linked to the tablet and passed that to James so he could keep up as she pulled up images. "So you see the original Egyptian 'gods' here?"

The images were of jackal-headed people, birds heads, and more.

"If we look at these, and consider that we know there are creatures out there that are both similar to this, such as werewolves in the middle of the change, and no doubt there are a great many creatures that we've just not yet seen?" She shook her hair back, then cursed and reached up, freeing it from the ties and starting to braid it with a speed that was incredible.

"So…" she said around a few hairpins she stuck between her teeth, "if the creatures are possibly real, and they probably were then—remember this is happening at least a thousand years before the Minoans' and Therians' warrior culture of exterminating the monsters really got established—then there could have been these things walking the earth. In those days, the Minoans were a much simpler people—this is the Bronze Age, after all. And the biggest and most impressive culture in the area then? Definitely the Egyptians."

"And the other Arisen?" I asked.

"Mainly in Eastern Europe, and what's currently Iran, or farther north as near as we can tell." Ingrid shrugged. "Hans said that the schism sent some of the various Arisen to the south to Egypt, and they founded the early dynasties of Egypt, remember."

"Uh-huh," I agreed noncommittally.

"If we assume that the Egyptian early pharaohs were Arisen, and they had access to these creatures, and then as they moved on, or died out, or whatever happened, the successive generations would have stopped seeing them around, right?"

"It is logical," James said. "If they were still around, we would have seen them in popular culture a lot more, at the very least…not to mention fossil records and more. At some point, they had to vanish, and while the Minoans were an industrious people, I can't imagine that they were exclusively the monster hunters of the ancient world."

"Exactly!" Ingrid agreed excitedly. "At some point, the Arisen left Egypt. Something happened and they vanished, leaving behind more regular pharaohs. Maybe they just decided to move on, maybe they were killed somehow, maybe their creatures rose up. We'll probably never know for sure, but we do know that there are legends of these creatures in the underworld."

"Underworld, or underground?" I frowned.

"That's my point." She smiled. "If these creatures moved, maybe disappeared and continued protecting their masters underground or in a remote location instead? You'd be left with occasional sightings, anecdotal evidence and stories. You'd maybe have some corpses, but most likely, if they all left with their masters? You'd just have a jumble of stories left over, and the artifacts."

"From the ships?" I asked confusedly.

"No, I mean real artifacts, sorry…like the Colossi of Memnon, where there were massive figures found seated in huge thrones."

"But you think the figures were added after?" I guessed, and she nodded quickly.

"Successive generations that had myths of earlier times where these things were genuinely around would have tried to make sense of the past, just like we do, but they would have had things left over, like the statues and the thrones. We know that the thrones were likely older than the figures that are seated in them. If instead of accepting the standard theory that the thrones' original occupants were replaced with a new more socially acceptable group? The old pharaohs' guards or gods or whatever being supplanted by the new generations' beliefs?"

"If instead of the pharaohs of that time saying 'Hey, get rid of that statue of Bob and put one there of me,' you mean?" I asked.

"More or less." She smiled at me. "It didn't make much sense. Most people just accepted that the original occupants were probably damaged and needed to be replaced—it happens, after all—but this is a culture that made the pyramids, the sphynx, and more...massive, truly mind-boggling constructions of stone. I never understood why they'd cut corners by replacing the figure and reuse the thrones, rather than simply make them fresh overall."

"You think that the thrones were possibly there for creatures such as the ones that Steve saw underground, and that the thrones themselves may have had some religious reason for being kept as they were?" James guessed.

"I think so," she said. "If we consider that these creatures were real, and that they literally sat in thrones this size? It's logical that they'd have survived the ages, while the smaller thrones that their masters sat in would have been stolen, melted, lost or whatever. If these things were protecting their masters, and then left? The impact on the local populace would have been huge. They'd have scattered for an explanation as to why their god-kings just vanished, and why the creatures that served them left as well.

"A sudden surge in religion that explains all of this, that the gods returned to the heavens, or the underworld? That fits! Then, if and when the gods—or their creatures, anyway—are occasionally seen again, it'd create the upwellings of belief and fervor that these times are notorious for.

"It'd also explain why the later generations were so desperate to make their pharaohs into gods. They'd believe that the originals *were* gods, and that they left. The new pharaoh could never accept that the older ones were better than them, not if they'd stopped coming back by this point, and so they'd be desperately trying to rewrite history over and over again to hide the early wonders and make it so they were the best pharaoh of all. They'd be trying to earn their way into the next life with huge gestures and—"

She broke off, eyes widening, as she turned to me. "Steve, the area you saw the creatures in...what was it like? Not the caves leading up to it—you said that they were ancient caves and passages, like a catacomb, right?"

"Yeah, all rough stone and shit," I agreed eloquently.

"But was the room they were in the same?" she asked quickly. "Was it a cave, with just thrones in it, and the door or..."

"No." I attempted to remember the other details. "I was just fixating on the big fuckers at first. Them and the dozens and dozens of werewolves, the vamps, the cats, all that shit, but the room wasn't the same as the rest."

"Describe it." She pulled a notepad out, clearly preferring the act of writing to simply making some kind of recorded digital note.

"Umm, high ceiling?" I said slowly, struggling with it. "The floor was filthy, covered in dirt and stuff, but I think it was flat. The passage I came out of was high up, overlooking the fuckers below, and there were massive thrones with the creatures in them, braziers about the room. Stairs led up to the door at the back, and it was between the thrones, and more or less human sized..."

"Anything else?" James made notes as well. "Was there a way in for the creatures? You said they were big...could they have made it along the passage you used?"

"No, definitely not," I said firmly. "There was a pool in the corner, a big one, one that I think probably led out to the sea, and they had massive spears...no, tridents. They sat on the thrones, watching over the door, protecting it."

"So we've got a method of entering and leaving, a location that's protected by these creatures, and dozens more?" James asked, and I nodded. "Interesting."

"Where was this?" Ingrid asked, and I took control of the map, spinning it and zooming in on the area from above.

"This is the entrance we used." I pointed, before shaking my head. "Jonas was with me, and while he didn't reach that section—I went back after he and I had our little falling-out—I bet he'll have had the place monitored or something."

"James?" Ingrid asked, and the older man nodded, getting to his feet.

"I'll see if they're available," he said, heading for the stairs.

"Scylla might know something about them," I said.

"Hopefully," Ingrid agreed, looking at the map. "Any idea how far you went out?"

"Only that it was a few miles," I said with a shake of my head. "It could have been in any direction, though—it was a cave system that went in all directions."

"Damn," she murmured. "Okay, well, while we wait for the others, the third group of people Marie identified who nobody is going to miss?"

"Yeah?"

"Human traffickers who are set up in a small island to the south of Crete called Kastri, off the southwest coast." She pulled up the location, showing it to me, and I nodded, checking it out. "Marie said that there's a sudden upsurge of small boats landing and leaving from there, and they coincide with the times that the local forces, both the border patrols and the coast guards, are away, so it looks like they've got a spy in there making sure they don't get caught."

"How many of them?" I checked out the small island, seeing the recent signs of building on the island at the tiny port—literally three houses and a pier stood there—and yet, I could see a ship in the harbor there that every instinct cried had no business in such a small port.

It looked like a fishing vessel, but one without nets, cranes, or the capacity to hold lobster and crab pots. That wasn't usually a big thing; after all, fishing tours were popular in the area, renting out to tourists to let them sea fish in comfort. This, though? The boat was filthy and battered, and for that to be clear from a damn satellite pass, you knew the fucker was filthy indeed.

"The traffickers?" She flicked through the details. "Ten or so—human, it appears—but they're also involved in various crimes, from drug dealing to murder, modern slavery and providing drug-addicted men and women to brothels in northern Africa, as near as Marie can tell. She thinks the group are smuggling people out of Africa and into Europe, then kidnapping people in Europe and selling them in Africa on the return journey."

"Industrious fuckers then. Fine, I think— Scylla, Jonas, nice of you to join us!" I greeted the pair, before going on as Ingrid added them to the link.

"So, we've found two groups of criminals—or, more accurately, Marie has," I said. "The first group is here, trafficking people across Africa and Europe, kidnapping and murdering as they go. Looks like they're also involved in the slave trade, and probably rape, as I can't see people who kidnap women and sell them to brothels not lowering themselves to that as well."

"Looks like the perfect target to me," Jonas said. "These are the kind of scum I hate. Tell me...we can make it painful?"

"Feel free," I said. "If this is what it seems to be, then I've no issue with it. Feel free to get as much information from them as possible. And we transfer their money to the company coffers as well—no need to waste it—but we make sure once we've got boots on the ground first."

"Sounds fun," Jonas said with an evil grin.

"I like this," Scylla said, and I nodded to her.

"The second group are a bunch who are killing and crippling tourists in the north, around the Malia area." Ingrid moved the map to there and spun it around, showing the others in the link, while James continued to follow along on the tablet still. I explained what they'd been doing, and where, as well.

"So, we hit these two, and then we've got some choices." I took a deep breath, focusing and forming an image from everything that I remembered, of the big fuckers I'd seen underground.

To my surprise, it formed clearly, and I showed it to the others, getting grunts of astonishment and gasps.

"So these I found at the far end of the catacombs we explored, Jonas. You have any ideas about them...?"

"I've heard of something that might fit," he muttered, looking at them. "But, honestly, it might be something else. There was a reference to the 'Great Ones' and their servants the colossi, or giants. That mentioned something like these, and there was a warning to avoid them. But it was in an old manuscript, and I mean *old*. I just assumed it meant some particularly high up Arisen and not to piss them off. It mentioned giants, or colossi anyway, but Zeus..."

"Zeus?" I said. "Fuck, I'd forgotten he was one of us."

"The Greek god Zeus?" James asked, as Ingrid winced.

"I forgot to mention that," she admitted. "I heard he was one of the Blessed, one who was generally avoided."

"He's a...what was the word? Shit?" Scylla said. "An utter shit, and cannot be trusted."

"You know him?" I asked, and she nodded, refusing to elaborate further when I asked.

"Okay, so Zeus...you were saying?" Ingrid prompted Jonas.

"Yeah..." he said slowly, watching Scylla and clearly wondering about her past with Zeus. "Well, Zeus was apparently notorious for killing colossi. It was one of the ways he made himself popular with the Greek people."

"So these fuckers were around back then, and now we've got them sitting on thrones underground," I grunted. "Great. Don't suppose you know how Zeus killed them?"

"Thunder and lightning, supposedly," Jonas said softly, and when I glared at him, he grinned and shook his head. "Sorry, boss, I'm not being a dick. I mean that's literally how they said he killed them. Now that we know a lot more? And that it's tech, not 'magic'? We all overheard the Arisen commenting on artifacts, and they made it sound like they were mystical things from their past. Now I'm wondering if it was something that he found—or stole—that's tech from way back?"

"That...would make sense," I said. "If he found some tech from the ships, and used it in front of people, they'd have called him a god, especially if he used its power to kill colossi with lightning."

"And how many of the older Arisen would have such things?" Ingrid asked me slowly. "Not the lower-level ones, but the older, much more powerful ones?"

"Athena had several artifacts," Scylla admitted. "She went nowhere without at least one of them, so when you killed her, it was unlikely she did not have one at hand."

"She didn't," I said after a second's thought. "There was nothing that she used that was anything beyond a spear and shield. I mean, they were crystal weapons, but still..."

"You said you attacked her ship. How did you fight her?" she asked, and I explained, going over the attack on the ship, over the impact and the effects it had, and the subsequent fight on the dock.

"She probably had several broken bones at the very least from the impact," Ingrid pointed out, and I quirked an eyebrow at her. "I'm not saying it wasn't impressive you killed her, Steve. I know you fought hard for that, but I'm thinking that if she was sitting on her throne, and that boulder hit the skylight and punched through it? At the very least she'd have been smashed from her throne into the deck above and then back down. With the yacht rolling and bouncing, is it possible that she lost whatever artifact she had?"

"It is," I admitted sourly, not wanting to think that I beat her at anything less than her best. "She was carried from the yacht, stunned."

"So you might have been luckier than we know. We need to ask Laia." Ingrid nodded. "She was highly placed in Athena's service...she'd know."

"You knew her before she came to work for us?" I had forgotten that they might have known each other when I was a prisoner.

"No, but I heard of her. She was trusted...for a human." Ingrid snorted. "She was relied upon by the Arisen, and she was trusted by us humans as she tried to keep her people safe from the Arisen's rages."

"I can check with her," James said quickly, and Ingrid and I exchanged a look, trying not to grin.

Laia and James always seemed to be on the verge of a huge argument. James was our butler originally and then our go-between; he was nominally in charge of our people, where Ingrid's father Anders was officially in charge of our facilities.

Laia had been in charge of people for Athena on her yacht, had sworn fealty to me, and was insanely organized and competent, but had been badly injured and I'd had to heal her. I'd not had many nanites to spare at the time, so I'd done it in a way that would take a lot longer to heal her, but that was much cheaper for me.

That meant that she'd basically spent the last few weeks in the recycling plant trying to establish that she was useful and to keep busy.

That, in turn, had morphed into her and James bumping heads practically all day, every day, and we were all convinced that as soon as she was healed and back on her feet, the pair would be bumping uglies as well.

"Okay, so, we're going off on tangents here." Ingrid shook her head. "The important thing is, we know the colossi were real, more or less. We think they were used by the first pharaohs to guard things, and the pharaohs themselves, and they're guarding a door down there now. Do you think we could fight them?"

"Not a chance as we are," I said firmly. "I didn't have my armor then, but I had a fuckload more nanites than I do now, and the system picked up that they were a threat and basically told me to run like my dick was on fire, and that I had no chance against them."

"I will face them." Scylla straightened up.

"The fuck you will," I replied. "You're not used to your new body yet. Give it a few weeks, or months, and sure…but right now? They'd probably kill us all." I saw the glare that she gave me, backed up by Jonas, who clearly, now that she'd started sword-swallowing practice, had decided he was more on her side than mine.

"What Steve means to say," Ingrid hurried to point out, "is that we all need to train first, and then we can face the colossi. So, you were saying we should attack the criminals first, Steve?" she prompted, and I growled, not liking the whole "be nice" way of doing things.

Still, I took a deep breath and forced myself to go along with it.

"Right," I said. "So we hunt the criminals, rip their nanites free, upgrade ourselves, and move on. Do that for a while, and then we hunt the colossi."

"For how long?" Scylla asked. "You say that humans have little of these nanites in them. How many are the colossi likely to have?"

"A fuckload more," I admitted. "But they're the fucking guards at the door. What do you think is on the other side of that door? What's going to happen once we kill its servants? You think they'll just wave us off? No."

"Then we waste how long doing this? Hunting humans who give us nothing?" Scylla growled at me. "Do we have the time for this? Time to waste here…or are we hunted? Pursued by enemies who are now stronger than both of us!"

"What the hell's your solution then?" I snapped back at her, matching her glare for glare. "What do we do?"

"We hunt!" she snarled. "You found prey, lycans and other real enemies far to the north in the steppes! We go there, fly on the plane of Dimi, and we hunt them!"

"Fuck's sake!" I snapped. "You think it's that simple? That we can just go slaughter them all and feed on their corpses? We need to get strong enough to do that first!"

"Steve—" Ingrid started, and I cut her off.

"No! You don't understand this, Ingrid. I know you want to go—fuck's sake, I know you want to see these places. And Scylla, Jonas? You feel like you're invincible right now. You know that you'll come back from death, and yeah! You will!" I got up from my seat and took a few steps, staring out over the wine-dark sea.

"But in that case…?" James started, and I spun back to them.

"But when you die, to come back takes either nanites, or fucking *time*—and we've got neither, all right? If we go straight after the Stelek, they'll kill us."

"The what?" Jonas frowned. "What the hell is the Stelek?"

"Shit," I muttered, gripping the bridge of my nose between thumb and forefinger and rubbing slowly as I gathered my thoughts. "Right, look. I know where there's a bunch of things for us to hunt, all right?"

"Where?" Scylla asked, before glaring at me. "Are you seeking to control us? To force us into weakness while you hunt alone?"

"Oh, fuck off!" I snapped, pulling my hand free and glowering at her. "You can fuck right off with that shit! I was saving it because I damn well knew you'd want to go straight there, all right?"

"And we shouldn't because…?" James asked.

"Because they're the species that are displacing the Oracan," Ingrid said softly. "I remember you mentioned them. Is that right?"

"Yeah, and you all know they're good fighters, right?" I pointed out. "They're losing their homes and being hunted by the Stelek. They're some kind of hive species, and they're deep underground. Something was driving them up, according to the Erlking, and they were in turn pushing the Oracan out."

"So we hunt the Stelek," Scylla said. "You wished to recruit more Oracan. They are excellent warriors, so we save them and extract oaths of fealty as payment."

"Again, you can fuck right off," I said. "First, if they can kill a warrior race like the Oracan—which are stronger than you right now, remember—then how do you think we can kill them?"

"With your new weapons," Scylla said.

"I— Fuck." I'd been so fixated on fighting them in my armor and with the harvest blade that I'd not even considered the new guns.

"Steve," Ingrid said softly, and I turned to look at her. "You know we need to take risks, if we're to survive this, right?"

"I do. Look, I'm sorry," I apologized, looking at them all as I said it. "I know we need to take risks, and I know you all can. You're all strong enough to survive most things, and I know we get rewards when we risk everything, sure. The issue here? We need to get as many nanites as possible, as fast as possible, all right? Add to that, we can't spend weeks away. We had a month offered from the Old Ones, and that's literally what I offered them as well, so they're clearly giving us the time to go to them, but if we don't?

"Fuck, we've been here for almost two weeks now. Let's say they go off weeks instead of months—I mean, do they even know what month it is? Do they use our calendar? Either way, that gives us about two more weeks. That's not enough time to do this, not properly, and—"

"So we need to take the risk." Ingrid cut me off, reaching out a hand to me.

I took it, and let her draw me back down to sit, as she spoke.

"So, we need to get as strong as possible, and we need to be ready in case the Old Ones attack us, or try to stop you leaving, right?"

"Right," I agreed, begrudgingly.

"So, we hit the criminals here and maybe here." Ingrid spun the map back up for us all. "We kill…" She paused, clearly having issues with the fact that we were going to go ahead and execute them all, but moved on. "We kill them, and you strip their nanites. Then we get Dimi to pick us up; we take the weapons and armor we have Zac make for us, and we go straight to the Stelek. We hunt them, using their nanites to grow as strong as possible, and we kill them using those weapons."

"Do you know where they are?" Jonas asked.

"Roughly," I admitted. "I got some details from the Oracan, and the Erlking. I know a rough location where at least one of their 'hives' should be, and the cave entrances to them should have Stelek nearby. They can't stand sunlight, supposedly, so that's why they've not spilled out of the caves, but they've driven lycans and Oracan from the caves out, so their villages should be reasonably near."

"Okay, so how about this?" Jonas suggested. "We hit the criminals, the four of us—kill them. Then we take the plane and go find this hive. If there's lycans nearby? We kill them, strip them of nanites. Once we find the Stelek, we hunt the upper cave system, kill them as we can, and retreat once we're tired or if there's too many to fight. Take some modern toys with us as well."

"Like?" I asked.

"Claymore mines, lasers—fuck it, we take a few sentinels with us to guard us when we sleep." He shrugged. "That way, we should be able to do this as safe as possible. Then we go as far as we can, keeping an avenue of escape ready. When we find the hive, if we can, we take it out. If not? We tour around the outside, pick them off one by one, strip them of nanites, and we grow stronger with every kill, as they get weaker."

I watched him for a few seconds as silence fell, and I thought, forcing myself to really consider it, instead of listening to the fear that rose in me at the idea of diving into the depths of a fucking cave system, unprepared, with Ingrid.

"You all want to do this?" I asked them, taking the time to look at each of them, one by one.

"Yes," Ingrid said simply.

"Of course," replied Scylla.

"It's the safest way." Jonas looked at me. "I know it's a risk that you don't think we need to take, but trust me, Steve, if we've only got a few days to a few weeks? We can't risk doing less than this. Consider the alternative. We take the safer path—we hunt human criminals, make the world a better place. It takes us what, fifty kills, *each*, to get some armor?"

I snorted. "I wish. Hunting humans, it'll be a hell of a lot more. I think my armor cost me about two million weaponized nanites, and in regular humans? That'd be anywhere from fifty to several hundred, depending on how many they naturally had. Add in that it would be just enough to form the armor? That's nothing to upgrade yourself...that's just your armor."

"And if we hunt the Stelek?" he asked, and I sighed.

"No clue. But if they're like the oracan and lycans, humans bring in a fuckload less."

"So...?" he prompted, and I nodded, unhappy but accepting it.

"So we need to arrange a flight with Dimi."

CHAPTER TWENTY-SEVEN

It took a lot more than a single call, of course. We needed to arrange a place for Dimi to touch down to collect us, and we needed to hit the criminals first and get those important initial supplies of nanites.

Dimi was given a list of kit that could be bought in regular places and could be brought along by Ingrid, and then was booked to land at Heraklion Airport for us the next day at midday. We'd picked that mainly because if we had him land anywhere else, the local government and that of other nations would descend on the area and start trying to figure out what we'd been doing.

Picking up a known member of our group from her home? Fine. Him landing and then taking off again from a random location? Nope—expect it to be hammered by spies inside the hour. Zac was also contacted. Specifics of what we needed were given to him, and an agreed collection arranged for an hour before we were due to meet Dimi tomorrow.

Then we set off, sailing to the west, heading straight for the small port on the tiny island to the south of Crete.

"Port" was a bit of a grandiose term for it when we dropped anchor an hour later. Half a dozen small buildings all blended into each other, and save for the supposed "fishing" vessel that wallowed at anchor between us and the shore, there were six or seven small—and I mean *small*—boats.

Most could just about fit two people in, if you didn't mind the water coming over the gunwales and if you were happy to sit on your friend's knee.

The only exception to that was the large and well-maintained Zodiac that was pulled up on the beach with a frame over the top of it, camouflage-style netting concealing it from any satellite reconnaissance.

We pulled up into the cove, and I took a deep breath. My worry about Ingrid fell away as we clambered down into the little shore boat we had.

At the end of the day, as much as I was shitting myself over the future, Ingrid was with me, and we had Scylla and Jonas along as well.

Although I didn't have my armor, I'd not had it when we first met, not properly, and I'd still managed to keep her safe.

I had my harvest tool back—there weren't enough nanites yet to form a blade, but there would be soon—and we were ready.

Add to that, with Ingrid showing her planning skills were better than mine already—which wasn't saying much, admittedly—she and Scylla wore tiny bikinis, and Jonas and I were just in shorts.

That meant that we were also visibly unarmed, which was going to hopefully make us an insanely tempting target for the local gang.

Ingrid had a single bag—which held Jonas's hand cannon and a long, leaf-bladed knife, in case we needed them. But honestly, we didn't expect to.

Instead, we beached our boat next to the Zodiac, and we made a point of looking it over, and the covering, before wandering—all unconcernedly—up the beach and onto the poured concrete path.

The sun was dipping at this point, and the little beach and surrounding jetty looked idyllic, if you ignored the shitty quality of the construction of the new buildings and the smell of shit and unwashed bodies in the still air.

We headed for the only building that had lights on *and* real windows, a small restaurant and shop, where a greasy little man stepped out and waved to us, inviting us in.

We did, ignoring the fact that the state of his overalls suggested the fucker should never be permitted near food, and we made small talk, sitting at the table he recommended—at the back of the building, the wall behind us and clearly nowhere to go to once we were sat—and I did my best not to snap the little fucker's neck as he leered at Ingrid, naked hunger in his eyes.

We ordered drinks and food, apparently confusing him when we asked for a menu. He seemingly didn't expect to have to bullshit to this degree, and Ingrid again took charge.

"We'll have whatever you recommend, no need for menus," she assured him, smiling widely, and managing to ignore the look he was giving her.

We made a bit more small talk for about thirty more seconds, before the door to our right, marked "private," opened, and four men walked out, each of them visibly armed.

The little greasy fucker moved off to one side, grinning, clearly used to this dance, as the leader of the newcomers spoke in a loud scouse accent.

"Right, you lot, anyone still on the yacht?" he asked, and Ingrid smiled up at him.

"Just James, our butler," she said in a happy tone.

"Butler, eh?" He snorted. "Fucking posh bastards! You rich then?"

"We've got a few million," I admitted, looking at the first guy who'd now moved toward the bar. "You going to get us those drinks then?"

"Na, e's not." The leader snorted, spitting on the floor, before drawing a handgun and showing it to us all. "Ver' kind of yer to wander in like this, but yer picked the wrong bar."

"Did we?" I asked mildly. "Looks perfect to me."

Looking at the group from his perspective, I was at the back left of the group, with Ingrid to my right, and Jonas next to her, closer to the newcomers, with Scylla across from him.

It meant that the four men—the little greasy one had moved off behind the bar by now—were arranged in a semi-circle between us and the door. The closest was less than a meter from Scylla, and boy was he about to regret that.

The leader waved his gun and grinned at us all, showing two gold teeth gleaming out from between numerous gray and furry monstrosities.

"Yer fink? Yer a dumb fuck then, aintcha! Why you fink we've got these then?" He showed the gun again, in case we'd missed it.

"Money, now!" one of them growled, waving his shotgun.

"An' yer gold 'n stuff!" the greasy figure behind the bar added, staring, again, at Ingrid.

"Steve?" Ingrid smiled, looking across at me, and I nodded. "Do you remember the incident with Yanni, and the smugglers?"

"I do," I said.

"Do you remember what I asked you to do?" she asked, and again I nodded. "Make it quick, but make sure that one..." she pointed one finger at the figure behind the bar, "regrets leering at me, please."

"With fucking pleasure." I smiled. "Scylla, Jonas, time to play," I invited.

All hell broke loose, as they demonstrated their enhanced reactions.

Scylla was the fastest, unsurprisingly, flowing to her feet and attacking the man in the middle-left of the four, from their perspective. She slapped his shotgun aside, then rammed a thumb into the eye of its wielder. The gun bucked in her hand as it discharged into the leg of the figure next to him, and on the outside of their group.

Jonas was the next quickest, grabbing the barrel of the handgun and twisting it out and around as the leader opened fire, snapping his finger, thanks to the trigger guard, before hitting him with a throat strike. A rising scream broke off with a gurgle of pain and panic as Jonas's enhanced strength almost crushed his windpipe.

By this point, I'd lifted the table and flung it at the little guy behind the bar, who'd screamed and dove for something concealed there.

Jonas tore the handgun free of their leader, snap-kicked the remaining guy in the stomach hard enough to double him over with a strangled wheeze, and shot him in the back of the head, as it came down.

Scylla jerked the shotgun free of her first victim—who was now permanently blind in one eye—and spun it, before using it like a baseball bat and spreading the contents of his skull across the rear wall.

In less than ten seconds...probably closer to four or five...two were dead, one was struggling for breath, fingers frantically scrabbling at his windpipe, one was bleeding out on the floor, half his leg missing from a close-range shotgun blast, and the last of them?

I'd taken three quick steps and planted my right hand on the top of the counter, vaulting over the bar and landing behind it as the pretend proprietor dragged a second shotgun out from where it'd been hidden.

He twisted, trying to bring it to bear, and I seized it, ripping it free of his hands and tossing it over my shoulder toward the front door.

Then I grabbed his right arm and twisted it, locking the elbow out into a full extension, and called out to Scylla.

"Scylla?"

"Yes?"

"You probably know this one, but I'm not sure, so can I show you something?"

"Yes?"

"You see, if you twist like this, how the arm is locked, and he can't do anything?" I pointed out, gesturing with the arm I held. "And the way his only real option to escape here is to either dislocate his own shoulder, or elbow?"

"Yes?"

"Well…" He kept struggling, and I snapped out a stomping kick downward into his left kneecap, almost ripping it free and driving him to the floor, screaming. "It means you've got control of him, so you can do things like that, or this." I struck the elbow joint hard, hitting the "outside" as it was normally arranged, and the inside as I held him now.

He screamed as the lower and upper arm hinged destructively open in ways it was never meant to; sinews and the joint broke, ripping and popping.

"Ah, we had a similar strike." Scylla nodded, reaching out and snagging his wildly swinging left arm, then wrapping her forearm under and around his, pressing the back of her hand against the inside of the arm, and straightening her arm into a secondary lock.

The way she held him meant that his shoulder was popped upward, and he was forced to try to keep himself up on his tiptoes—hard to do with a smashed knee—or he'd dislocate his own shoulder.

"You see?" she asked conversationally, and I nodded.

"What would you normally do from there?" I asked, before glancing over and saw that Jonas had delivered a second strike to the throat, and the leader of the group was now dead as well. "Oh damn, looks like he's the only survivor now…"

"You wish him to survive?" She frowned.

"Oh, gods no, but we need information from him."

"I'll tell you anything!" he screamed desperately.

"Oh, I know," I assured him, patting his shoulder, then punching him in the stomach as hard as I could.

Scylla held him in place, making sure my blow was as effective as possible, and we all heard the lower ribs breaking.

"Now, you were looking at my partner in a very disrespectful way," I pointed out to him. "So, to make our situation here very, very clear? Personally, I want to torture you to death right now, then offer your blood-soaked body as an apology to her, for letting you do that. Understand me? So, the only chance you have…" I made sure he was listening. "And I want to be clear here, the only chance at all that I won't kill you personally, slowly and fucking painfully, is if you tell us all about your little setup here. Where you go, when and where you deliver the people to and whom, and where your money is. You understand?"

"Plu-ease!" he whimpered, and I smiled happily.

"That's not telling me what I want to know." I nodded to him, before taking him by the throat and lifting him into the air, as Scylla released him. I spun him around and drove him down into the table top I'd flung at him before, where it rested at about a seventy-degree angle against the back wall of the bar.

I used his body to break the table in half. Several of his bones broke with the force of it as well. He tried to scream, while one of his lungs apparently started to fill with blood.

He started coughing it up, and I released him as he vomited more up, begging for mercy.

I reached for him again, and Scylla stepped in.

"Steve, he must answer, remember?"

I shrugged. "Better talk fast," I warned him, and the idiot did.

He babbled out all the details of their little setup. The bubbling and coughing as blood filled his lung only made him more desperate to share, seemingly. After a minute, I picked him up and carried him back around the bar, dumping him into a chair near Ingrid, who sat calmly, hands clasped demurely in her lap, one knee atop the other, listening.

What he couldn't see, slumped and whimpering, bleeding heavily as he was, was that she was making notes in her system, comparing details he gave and more.

"Steve," she said when he mentioned his laptop, and I nodded, before moving off and starting to kick open locked doors. The office turned out to be behind the bar, and the laptop was there, while Jonas—now armed with his hand cannon—checked out the other buildings.

Fifteen minutes from us walking in the door, we were walking back out. Ingrid walked between Jonas and me as we headed to the larger of the two buildings. Aboveground, it looked like a storage and boat maintenance area, with the smaller building as an ostensible "smoking shed" for preparing the fish that the pretend fishing vessel presumably caught.

Move some of the equipment, though, and the passage that was revealed led down to the holding areas underground.

Dozens of men, women, and children were kept in cells that were barely large enough to hold a quarter of that number, and these were the people they were being paid to smuggle.

The ones they were planning to sell?

They were under the second building. More were chained up as well, alongside what looked like heroin set up to be pumped into them all intravenously.

He'd admitted that was their business plan: kidnapping people, forcefully addicting them to high-grade heroin, abusing them, and making them fully dependent and broken, then selling them.

They made their "bread and butter" money, by people smuggling from Africa into Europe. On the way, if they saw women—or men—they liked in the crowd, they were separated out and taken aside, being channeled into the "for sale" pool.

Drugs were shipped at the same time from Africa and the Middle East to Europe, and their contacts in Europe kidnapped and targeted people there. Some were ransomed off and returned, but most were sold.

Those who did pay the ransoms usually didn't get their people back, either—they just got to be poor *and* lose their family members.

By this point, Jonas had to step in and do some magic with a ballpoint pen to drain the lung, gifting him a valuable few more minutes of hope. But once he'd finished giving us the broad strokes of their business model, including the locations, times, and their bribed officials—where he knew them—any last-minute sympathy that Ingrid had started to feel for the way that we were questioning him had thoroughly evaporated, and she was fine with it when I handed him over to Scylla to work out some of her frustrations.

He'd screamed something about me promising to let him go, as we headed for the door, and I'd snorted in disgust. I casually pointed out that I'd promised not to kill him myself, that was all, and Jonas had added in that all things considered, he should have been holding out for a quick death at my hands, not Scylla's.

He'd looked like he was about to beg for that, when I'd raised my right hand, and extruded the nanite harvesting tool.

The last time he saw me, I was grinning at him as I dragged the nanites out of the bodies of his friends.

Jonas and I checked out the rest of the building, calling James and getting him to come across and help as we freed people and cut off the heroin feed, and Ingrid worked on confirming the details we'd been given.

Half an hour after that, we were on the yacht again, laptop cloned, then dumped, ready for the next visitors, and we all sailed back out of the little port.

I'd gone into the main building and drained the little guy's body as well—no sense in wasting the nanites, after all—but one look inside had told me that it wasn't something that Ingrid needed to see.

As much as she was becoming harder in some ways, like being happy to make it clear that we needed to kill and harvest these scumbags, she was still far from needing to see someone actively tortured to death as an object lesson about their behavior.

"What was it that Ingrid asked you with that Yanni guy?" Jonas asked me as we settled back into our seats aboard the yacht, James sailing us north and west to loop around the island.

"Hmmm?" I frowned, before laughing as I remembered. "Oh, sorry! He kidnapped her. Then he was a dick, and she was facing them all down, a bunch of Albanian gangsters, talking like they were idiots, and keeping their attention until I crashed through the window…"

"He wrapped his wings around us and they opened fire. The bullets bounced off as he held me, and I was really upset with them, thinking they'd killed James and knowing they'd killed our guards, so I asked him to hurt them all."

"And I did," I said. "Killed them all, fed on them, and dumped the bodies— then found they'd had about a hundred million in their account, so that was a nice start for us."

"A hundred and forty," Ingrid said. "And we already had a million or so by that point anyway."

"James was the butler the hotel assigned to look after us. It was how we met. Good times," I murmured, remembering that penthouse pool, the food and drinks, the fun, and my god—the sex.

"Speaking of feeding on them…" Jonas said slowly, and I nodded.

"We harvested a little over seven hundred nanites in total from them, about a hundred and forty each. Most are corrupted, and I'm processing them now. I'll wipe them, render them totally blank, and we'll lose half, unfortunately. That's the breakage, really. I can attune and cleanse them, breaking them from the corrupt ones and making them perfect for my system, but then they're linked to me, and they'd have to be wiped again to be any use to you."

"So we'll get…?" Jonas prompted.

"About seventy nanites each." I sighed. "As much as I don't like it, you were right. We need to go Stelek hunting."

"I got a quest when you said that!" Ingrid exclaimed suddenly, and we all looked at her, as she frowned, staring into the distance. "Steve, can you also share the quest for the Stelek with me? With us, I mean?"

275

"I don't know," I admitted, frowning.

"Just…focus on the quest and see if you can share it?" she suggested.

Fuck all happened with that, but after a few minutes of trying, I shook my head. "Right, I'll try this again in a minute. First, we need to do something else, then I can focus on this. Are we all happy that as much as we want to hunt the criminals right now, and with four of us, to get nanites it's just not worth going to the group who are robbing people in Malia?"

"Yeah," Jonas said. "I don't see the point when we're getting seventy each."

"So we all need a lot more to drain, basically," I said. "We need to hit a bigger group, right?"

"Right."

"Yes," Ingrid said.

"I agree," Scylla added.

"James?" I called to him. "Set a course for North Africa, please. Destination will be in the system in a minute." He nodded, and I focused, accessing the yacht's rudimentary systems and marking the destination as an island off the coast of Libya called Jazirat Barda'ah.

"We're going after the people smugglers?" Jonas asked, and I nodded.

"We had Dimi picking us up from Heraklion Airport. If instead we get him to pick us up from…" I hesitated, then nodded my thanks at Ingrid as she sent it over. "From Bombah Airport, that gives us time to hit their little base on the island nearby."

"What about the European side of their operations?" Jonas asked, and I grinned at him.

"We've already got a little bit of a contact with Interpol. They can't do much in Libya, or if they can, they'll be hampered by getting passes and shit, but we won't. I'll use that contact to direct them to the island back there…" I jerked my thumb over my shoulder, pointing at the rapidly vanishing land mass behind us. "They'll go, find those people, and hopefully give them help."

"I'll put together a list of the details he gave us, and tease them with it," Ingrid said. "I'll make sure there's enough in there it's clear who they were and what they were doing, and that there's locations in Africa and Europe in use. Once we've done what we need to in Africa, we can send them the local details for there, and the exact details for Europe."

"Better to send them the European targets now," Jonas said after a second's thought, scratching at the few days' growth of stubble on his chin. "Damn, I need a razor. Anyway, if we wait until we hit Africa, word might get out from anyone we don't know about, and they'll go to ground. I know we're risking being interrupted in Africa, or worse, them all running, but the alternative is we lose the European groups. We've got no clue how many victims they might have at this point, so I'd say that needs to be our priority."

"James, how long to our destination?" Ingrid called to him.

"About five hours." James set the autopilot and headed over to join us. "As near as the records have it, though, that island is uninhabited."

"It was," Ingrid agreed darkly, popping up an image for us all, with James sighing and reaching for his pad again.

"I really need to get that upgrade," he murmured good-naturedly as he tilted the pad, trying to get rid of the glare of the sun, while we all saw the image in perfect clarity projected before us.

It showed a small, deserted island, a handful of sun-blasted ruins scattered about here and there, and at the head of a narrow path, leading up from a tiny inlet, was a section of suspiciously regular ground.

Looking at it from several angles, it was obvious that not only was it a square, but that it had slightly sloping sides—not a pyramid, as it was flat topped, but one of those weird shapes that they insisted you needed to learn when you were in school, like when they insisted you study algebra. Nobody ever remembered what they were called, either; it was just a waste of brain space.

Ninety-nine percent of the students would never need the fucker, but the schools loved to waste your time, just so that when, say, the tax deadlines rolled by, you were totally fucking unprepared.

Weirdly, the taxman, with all his arcane fucking phrases and papers, didn't accept the circumference of a fucking circle as a valid response.

Bastards.

"It's an isosceles trapezoid, isn't it?" Jonas asked after a few seconds, and I glared at him, unable to bring myself to respond.

"So, specifics of the shape itself aside, what are we looking at?" James asked, before nodding. "Ah, I see, the frequently trodden path that leads up to it gives it away."

"As does the rubble in the shallow water nearby." Ingrid shifted the view with surprising dexterity. A small area of water, just off the coast, where what looked to have been centuries of coral and sponges had lain, was now mostly obscured by a mass of scattered and shattered rock.

"So, you think they use that as a base, and the crap is the rubble they took out?" I asked, getting a nod and a squeeze of the fingers as she took my hand in hers.

"It looks like it's probably underground," she pointed out. "There's enough stone there to have covered a fair size area, and the shape, judging from the satellite feed, is big enough to be a small building or large single room. I'm betting that they dug down and compacted the area. There's not enough stone to have been many rooms there, or at least not that I can see."

"You're getting good at this," I complimented her, and she blushed prettily.

"Thank you," she whispered, before going on. "As an archaeologist, you learn a lot about structures, and especially the kind of mass it takes to obscure and fill one. Looking at this, it's either, as I say, a small building, or..."

"Or?" Jonas asked.

"Or it was a buried house or something. An old one that they uncovered."

"Likelihood?" he asked.

"Low." She shook her head. "I've never heard of a historical site there, and—"

"It was a colony," Scylla interrupted. She'd clearly been having problems getting her head around the view and the reality of the world as it was now, compared to her past—not least of all because although in the last few centuries the sea level hadn't risen, much, the world had grown noticeably different.

"From Carthage to the west, there were three colonies," she whispered, staring back across the ages. "This one was for the lepers, a place to hide them, to pretend they were dead."

"A leper colony?" Ingrid frowned. "I've never seen any records of that."

"They were the secret shame of Carthage, so it is no surprise," Scylla growled. "The chief temple of Ba'al Hammon was infected. A leper died in the second well. Their corpse was found too late, and the majority of the upper priesthood were infected. Weeks it'd been there, with them bathing in and drinking the water.

"Hanno, the shofet, tried to use it as an excuse to reclaim the power the priesthood and nobles had stripped his father of, and failed. They couldn't kill the priests, not and escape the wrath of Ba'al Hammon, so instead they exiled them, built a colony there, buried in the island."

Scylla said it while staring at her drink, grim fury on her face.

"One of my people was one of them. When I found out? It was too late, and he was infected. I tried to raise him, to save him, and he—" She shook her head and drew down a deep breath. "He was special to me—a grandson, pure and of my direct line—but still, when I gave him my blood, he fell apart, screaming."

"Fell apart?" I frowned.

"Lepers do that," she said grimly, forcing herself to sit up straight.

"No, I mean like lepers do, or did he break apart?" I asked. "Like into little bits?"

"Steve!" Ingrid said, shocked. "It's okay, Scylla, you don't have to answer—"

"No." I cut her off. "Scylla, I need to know. It's important, please...did he fall apart like lepers are supposed to, like a nose falling off or whatever, or did he dissolve?"

"He became dust and ash," she admitted after a few seconds. "It took days, and he screamed the entire time."

"I'm sorry." I nodded to her. "Thank you for that."

"What did we learn that was worth that?" Jonas asked grimly, glaring at me, and I waggled a hand back and forth.

"For sure? Nothing. Look, I'm sorry for asking—I really am, Scylla—but it's important. When I took the Support path, I got access to healing information, and using that and the Assassin trees, I've kinda learned a lot about our bodies. Add in some guesses about the way that the nanites work, and what I think happened was a replication issue.

"The nanites rebuild us, right? They take the code that's stored in our cells, and they make a billion copies of all of it, everything from the fact that I've got a fucking haircut, to if I shave my damn balls, it's all stored in there—" I broke off at the look from Jonas, and I snorted.

"Seriously, when your nanites rebuild you, they rebuild you exactly as you are. I have no clue how, or why, but your hair regrows to the right length. You're not bald, for a start. Add in that if you, as I say, shave your balls? You come back with shaven balls. It's weird, but awesome."

"You know, of all the conversations I reasonably expected as a butler to have aboard a yacht, at sea, with a group that's essentially comprised of a demi-god, an archaeologist, a monster hunter, and a skilled immortal warrior of legend? That you shave your nether regions wasn't one I expected, Steve," James pointed out calmly, and I snorted again.

"Well, just another little treat for you, mate," I said. "So, you think there was a leper colony here?"

Scylla nodded. "There was."

"Until when?" Ingrid asked, clearly making notes.

"Until I left," she snapped.

"What?"

"I killed them. Carthage's rulers had a fear of Ba'al Hammon, but I knew better. The priesthood was a collection of evil old men, and they'd forced my grandson to serve them, infecting him with their diseases. I killed them all and burned their keep to the ground."

"Okay…and this?" Ingrid pointed to the shape that she'd picked out.

"It could be anything," Scylla growled. "An entrance to the wine cellars, the dungeons, the remains of the living quarters for the priests…anything."

"So it could be a single-story building that's half-buried to keep it hidden," I said with a nod. "Or it might be a full underground complex full of people."

"It is possible," she agreed. "I burned their temple and their homes. My servants and warriors stripped the local area of anything that would burn, but underground things might have survived."

"Roughly when was this?" Ingrid asked, and Scylla named a date from a calendar I wasn't familiar with. A little working out, and Ingrid nodded in satisfaction. "About 340–330 BC, I think. That works out as it fits with Hanno the Second, a shofet of Carthage as well, though I'll need to check the dates when I get the chance."

"What's a shofet?" I asked, and she hesitated.

"It's a little like a king, but not…more like a chief judge, from a noble family. He was the ruler of the city, because he could judge most people, but in practice the nobles and priesthood were systematically taking away his power, and that had begun with his father. He still held the most land and wealth, but the other families and the priests were steadily stripping them of whatever they could, trying to pass the mantle of shofet to another."

"You knew of Carthage?" Scylla asked, and Ingrid blushed again, shaking her head.

"I studied it as part of my training. I was interested in the area, all of it, but so much of the information was lost with the fall of the Library of Alexandria. So what survives? It's often wrong."

"History is written by the victors." Jonas shrugged. "Like us enlightened Americans know that the English were all bastards. None of them helped to develop the country…they were just there to rape it."

"Weird that, because I was taught you were a bunch of ungrateful colonial thieves," I replied blandly.

"Yeah, well, I was taught—" he started, only to be cut off by Ingrid.

"And as an outside nation, we kept accurate records, or as much as we could. You were both terrible to each other, and deserved what happened. And the French only made it worse for both sides, regardless of what anyone might say. Which is the point here, though, as Jonas was trying to make. I hope it was, anyway, not just to take an opportunity to start an argument. That being said, Scylla, you refused to discuss much of your past before. Would you talk to me now?" she asked, clear hunger in her voice.

"I will, though there will be little I know that you did not learn," Scylla grumbled. "Better that we get you access to study the records."

"The records?" Ingrid asked.

"From the library."

"The library?" Ingrid gripped my hand hard enough it almost hurt, and considering the life I'd had, that was saying something.

"The records of the Library of Alexandria," Scylla growled. "Some were lost when the city was sacked, of course, but the rest were moved to the Library of Pantainos."

"But...but..." Ingrid practically spit feathers as she tried to get her words out. "But the Library of Pantainos was lost in the second century! It was around the time that Alexandria was lost!"

"It was rebuilt." Scylla frowned, staring at Ingrid in confusion. "The libraries were rebuilt, one for the commoners, and then the Library of Pantainos had copies of most of Alexandria's scrolls, so it was rebuilt in Athens. My mother was involved. Her pride that her city was the home of it was obscene."

"It was in Athens? Where!" Ingrid begged, and Scylla shrugged.

"I know not. It was in the mountains, somewhere in the Forest of the Giants. I never went."

"You don't know!" Ingrid practically screamed. "It's still there, lost, and you don't know where?"

"It was built and buried, a safe place for our kind to study." She frowned. "You humans kept burning the libraries, so it was needed." She shrugged. "It was somewhere for the factions to have as common ground, somewhere that any could go to study, to learn of the past, so that nothing was to be lost again. But you are no longer human, so you should have access, with a sponsor to vouch for you."

"But you don't know where it is?" Ingrid whimpered.

"It was not for me." She shrugged again. "I lived then, and I remember the past. It was common that records were shared with the human libraries, so that they would learn of the folly of their past, but that was it."

"Oh my God..." Ingrid broke down, alternating between swearing in half a dozen languages and practically weeping, before pushing past everyone and storming down the steps into the main deck below, slamming the doors behind her.

"I think we need to give her some time," I suggested.

"She is strange." Scylla sighed. "Jonas, you wish to share my bed again?"

"Why yes, yes I do!" Jonas said quickly, and I grunted, before holding my hand up to stop them from fucking off.

"Just wait a minute," I told them, activating the Emergency Wipe for the corrupted nanites I held. It took only a few seconds, but the sight of the number of nanites I had, almost halving, was a painful one. Normally the nanites I'd claim were all mine, and it sucked ass to have to share them.

I reached out, focusing, and formed the nanites into a small cube, carefully leaving them blank and not allowing them to access my own form, imprinting to me.

I passed a cube to each, shaking my head at how small and unimportant the damn thing looked, before waving them off. I set Ingrid's down on the table before me, watching as they stayed in the same shape, as James shifted to sit at the table with me.

"So, that went well?" he said.

"That went like a fucking train wreck," I corrected grimly. "Ingrid is pissed and upset, we got hardly any goddamn usable nanites, and those two are off screwing again. Fuck's sake, it's like they're teenagers," I complained as the first noises started to echo up already. "Close that fucking window!" I bellowed over the side, hearing only laughter from their room below.

"I swear, I'm getting a fucking hose and spraying it in there," I growled.

"I think that you're a little frustrated, Steve," James said delicately. "I know you're typically a man of action, and as such, the changing nature of plans and leadership seems to be somewhat of an issue to you. Do you want to talk?"

"Honestly?" I reached up with both hands and scratched my head roughly. "What I want is to hit someone really fucking hard." I shrugged.

"I'm certainly not volunteering for that, but perhaps an ear to listen would help?"

"Thanks, James. Truthfully, I miss when it was just us, you know?" I said. "When I had the responsibility for killing fucking monsters and that was it. Making the nanites available for the others...it's a nightmare."

"Why?"

"I can cleanse them myself, and we don't lose half," I said. "But if I do that, the nanites are locked to me, so then they need to be wiped anyway for everyone else. If they could harvest their own? They'd be so much stronger, it's unreal. They'd literally earn twice as many nanites and be—" My eyes widened.

"Yes?" he prompted.

"I need to call Zac!" I said, then I grinned. "No! I need Belle!"

"Ingrid might not be pleased to hear you say that," he said, and I looked at him, seeing the smile he was trying to hide.

"She's a Support class."

He nodded. "And she's very supportive." He nodded seriously, still trying to hide a grin.

"Sure, she is, but she's a *greater dryad*," I said. "She's already a species that's focused on taking in and giving out. Admittedly, usually it's seeds from any male in the damn area, but she's essentially stockpiling that to enable her to create greater trees, huge things that can help to rewild the planet."

"Right?"

"Right. So what if we get her into the medical capsule?" I asked. "What if instead of us using the nanites to improve ourselves, we use my command access, and Ingrid's Command class, to make Belle into a Harvest class? I mean, she's Support already, naturally, and if she was to be a Harvest class? She could keep a percentage of the nanites she strips for herself, to aid in her mission. The rest? I've gotta think that as a dedicated harvester, the creators would have had a plan to enable them to get and manage the nanites, right?"

"It makes sense," he said. "Two points, however. First, would Belle be willing to do this? And secondly, you mentioned quests, and Ingrid did earlier, saying that she'd received one. You were going to try to share that quest with the others, yes?"

"Fuck, yeah." I groaned. "Right, James, while I figure this shit out, can you go interrupt Ingrid and get Belle on that flight from the base? We need to get her out to the ship as soon as possible, but I need to explain to her what I want, and…"

"And you don't want to interrupt Ingrid yourself because she might explain why she's so upset and you really don't see the big issue?"

"Well, yeah," I admitted, grinning. "Plus, I'm the boss. It's gotta be good for something, right?"

"Sure, keep telling yourself that." He sighed, before standing, then pausing and looking at me. "And I suppose you'd like some more coffee?"

I smiled. "Well, that's damn kind of you to offer…" I ignored the loud fake sigh he made as he walked away. "Maybe being the boss isn't so bad after all," I mused, before diving back into the system and searching for my quests. "So, first we message Interpol, and then there's got to be a way to do this…"

CHAPTER TWENTY-EIGHT

I strode up the path from the little inlet on my own, the others spread out a little more: Jonas off to my right, hidden and armed, and Scylla hiding somewhere to my left. That woman could vanish into the brush like nobody I'd ever seen.

The path before me was worn by the passage of feet. Old marks made it clear that months, if not years, ago there'd been machines used here: deep gouges left by knobbed tires had been carved into the sides of the path. For a minute, I wondered what had happened to them, and how the hell they'd gotten them out here in the first place.

Then I dismissed it as unimportant, instead focusing on the building coming into sight.

Are you okay?

I gave her a thumbs-up, lifting my hand to where I could see it. That was Ingrid, and her voice in my mind was a weird experience, to say the least.

She and the other two had taken a little time to get used to their systems, Scylla most of all. But when they'd all managed to get full access to their notifications—they'd been suppressed in the other two for some reason; Ingrid's had been open, but there'd been so much in the command system, it'd taken awhile for her to find it—they'd all found that they'd gained at least one point of specialization.

I'd gotten fuck all, so far at least, but then I'd "spent" dozens of points by now. And I had to admit, even if only to myself, that if I had gotten points for the pathetic fight back there, it'd have been a bit weird.

The others, though? As far as the "system" was concerned, they were baseline units, and so they deserved points just for surviving.

Ingrid had gained two separate points, one in her Command tree, opening up a more advanced link to her "subordinates" and one that had gone into Espionage.

That she had both of those trees was annoying to me, considering how painful Espionage had been for me to unlock, but she'd winced a little and that was it.

A bit like me with my War and Hack trees, so yeah, clearly, they were complementary ones.

She'd taken External as her choice with Espionage, and got a basic education in all things spying. That, added to the Command Systems Upgrade, meant that not only could she now see through my eyes if I gave her access, but she could manipulate my vision.

Details were highlighted, and I tried to ignore it as she examined old goddamn stones in the corner of my vision.

344

Scylla and Jonas had gained two War points, and on my recommendation, they'd both taken the Assault Tactical Systems Upgrade, and the Infiltration Stealth Systems Upgrade as well.

They were general ones, and they'd both be able to gain a lot from here in, but those two systems would make a hell of a difference to the trained warriors.

For me, I'd spent my nanites, and Ingrid had generously donated hers to me as well, enabling me to more or less form my harvest blade again.

It wasn't the full-on mass weapon of terror it'd become after a while, but it was back to being a decent-sized punch dagger, and that was enough.

I strode up the steep incline, watching as the building before me became clearer in the dark, smiling to myself as I made out the figure sitting under an awning on "watch."

His head bobbed, chin resting on his chest, back braced against the wall behind him, as he snored and filled the air with a reek of cheap cigarettes and sweat.

I didn't even bother to sneak up, as Scylla materialized next to him, standing over the sentry and looking down at him with undisguised disgust.

Jonas appeared next to the tent as well, and I silently reflected on just how fucking lethal a real ninja would be with these abilities.

I'd been able to see them slinking up, but that was partly because I knew what I was looking for, and more so because as we were in the same team, a bonus of the command net that Ingrid now used meant that we were all highlighted for one another.

Scylla drew a small needle-pointed dirk and drove it into the back of the sleeping sentry's skull with a faint crunch of bone. Jonas braced the body, his lip curling in disgust at the smell.

He'd not made a sound as Scylla killed him, and the loudest thing from the entire encounter was the creak and scrape as she dragged the blade free of the bone.

Jonas dragged him out of the entrance and held him while I formed my harvest blade and drove it into the corpse.

The heart had stopped, but the blood was still moving, slowing rapidly, but that was the way these things went.

Less than a minute later, Jonas lugged the body off to one side, and I was processing the nanites, as I walked over to the door that led inside.

It was laid backward at an angle, like an American cellar door in those old movies, rather than flat to the ground as cellars generally were in Europe. I paused, letting Ingrid get a good look at the stonework around the edges of the door.

The swearing told me that at least some of it was definitely ancient stonework, and she really wasn't happy about the desecration of it, judging from the language she was using.

"You open," I whispered to Scylla. "I'll lead. Jonas brings up the rear."

She nodded and reached for the door. A gentle tug, followed by a harder one, made it clear that it was locked from the other side. I had to extrude the blade again, slicing slowly through the hinges all the way around, shaking my head at how idiotic it was to lock a door, with the hinges on the outside.

I mean, seriously, it was easier for me to cut them off, but a hammer and a spike and you could knock the damn hinge pins free. Then you lift and, boom, doesn't matter whether or not the door was locked when you lifted the whole thing out of the frame.

The inside was a bit noisier than the outside. Distant sounds, cries, and clattering made it clear that yes, it wasn't just a single room below. And the stench made it even clearer that there were plenty of bodies inside.

Scylla led the way, and then I stepped in, activating my stealth and fading from sight. I slipped along behind her, trying not to curse as I made slight noises—the whisper of cloth, the soft sound of my boots on the metal steps that led down.

Scylla was insanely stealthy, and I made a mental note to ask for her help at some point.

The Oracan had taught me some of it, but their skills were better suited to forest and steppe than metal. But still, even they were better at it.

I was annoyed with myself until the first loud footfall on the staircase behind me announced Jonas's entry and the hiss from Scylla in response. Then I felt a lot better.

The steps led down a single level. Roughly assembled pipes as railings on either side and the metal grate steps themselves made it clear this wasn't an expensive operation.

The room ahead was old, seriously so, with stonework that reminded me of the castles and remains of the Roman camps I'd grown up near. A second door ahead was simple wood, rather than the thick steel of the outer one, and I paused, checking the other side and making sure it was empty, before speaking in a low voice, primarily for Ingrid's benefit.

"Either they're fucking idiots and they've not considered anyone finding them, or there has to be a secret way out," I whispered. "If the local navy or coast guard or whatever found this, they must have considered an escape route, so watch for it."

Will do.

The other two nodded as well, and we were off again, opening the door into the next room. More sounds echoed out, louder this time, but clearly not in the next room or two either.

The walls were rough stone, with occasional carvings here and there. And as I passed a large slab that had been braced as a table, covered in the remains of a meal, I heard Ingrid's strangled exclamation that it was "Ahlat stone," whatever that was.

It was apparently important, or at least fucking old, and she was growling to herself—forgetting that we could all hear her—as she swore in Danish over what should be done to these people.

As far as I could see, it was just more of the local stone, a kind of dusty orange-yellow, rougher than a badger's arse and old as sin. If it'd been marble or something, with a carving in it, I'd probably have been impressed. I'd seen marble carvings, and they were expensive-looking, but this?

I couldn't have told the difference between this and other rocks if I'd been given a second set of eyes.

I moved on, sliding up to a doorway with no door, with light from old-style miners' and builders' lamps—a lightbulb with a cable for power and a metal cage around it to protect it from being hit accidentally—and I peered through into the next area.

There were two ways to go. One led into a darkened room that snoring drifted out of, and another led downward, a ramp carved into the floor, going to the lower floors.

I gestured at the ramp to Scylla, moving to the darkened room as quietly as I could.

The room beyond?

It held three figures, fast asleep, the heat inside practically an oven as they all farted and sweated. All three were laid on rough camp beds—six legs with a frame and a cloth stretched across the top—holding their weight. They had pillows, blankets—which was insane considering how warm it was in there, but still—and guns laid within easy reach.

My first job as I stepped into the room was to gather up the guns, passing them silently to Jonas, who took them and set them out of reach. Then I went from body to body, my harvest blade driving into their brains, via a closed eye.

I'd rather have gone for the heart—faster and more sure, I always felt—but the crunch of bone as I penetrated the rib cage made that a no.

Instead, I killed and drained each of them efficiently, despite the feeling of revulsion I got from Ingrid.

I'd have to speak to her about that later. I didn't know whether it was because we were as close as we were, or whether she was sharing these details with the others, if it was intentional or accidental, but she needed to knock it off.

She'd grown harder, much harder than the woman I first met and fell in love with, but in some ways, she really needed to grow up. Killing an enemy like this might be seen as dishonorable by the civilian populace, I knew, but fuck it.

Hell, some "warriors" would probably curse me to hell for it, but at the end of the day, the mission was all that mattered.

If they died with a gun in hand, or farting in their sleep, dead was dead. The only difference here was that they went out painlessly, and that nobody else was alerted to it.

Personally, I'd kill the entire base like this if I could.

Fuck honorable combat. I always remembered the guy with the sword who tried to threaten Indiana Jones, then got shot. He'd been honorable, challenging the guy to a duel and all that, and he got shot dead.

Fuck that shit.

I shucked the last of them off my blade, leaving the room as the stench of loosening bowels rose. I crossed the dusty stone floor and out into the passage, following Scylla downward. Jonas fell in behind me, the three of us moving as silently as we could.

The next area below was clearly old, and seriously so. The upper section had been as well, but it'd been dug out more recently, and had been worked on by modern hands, making it into a crapshoot.

Now the buzzing of electric lights filled the air. The cable that ran between them dipped and hung in uneven loops, nails and hooks driven into the stonework to hold them, and burnt sections of walls showed just how battered the place was.

The ground was more or less clear here. The passage of many feet had kicked the dirt and sand clear, piling it up to either side as we carried on.

Openings were dotted from time to time on either side, leading into smaller chambers. Several of them were full of shattered stone, the floor above having apparently fallen in and buried them, but where the rooms were clear, they were used.

We passed storerooms, more quarters, what looked like a break room, and a small communications room that had cabling vanishing into the roof overhead. It'd been drilled through, as had a stovepipe out for a kitchen. All were abandoned, silent, as late at night as it was. But the deeper we went, the worse the sounds ahead became.

Jonas slipped into the comms room, taking a few seconds to remove fuses from the equipment and pocket them.

"No need to trash the gear, it's not bad," he whispered, and I nodded, seeing his point. Once we'd cleared the site, it might be usable. But if it wasn't, at the very least, archaeologists would want to use it once Ingrid spread the word.

At the end of the passage, we came to another door, this one propped open. A ladder led down. I paused, taking a deep breath at the sounds that rose from below.

"Ingrid," I said softly. "You'd be better off not watching this, I think."

I'm okay.

"I know you are, but that sounds like a fighting pit, and worse. Considering the kind of people these are, maybe you'd be better not," I suggested, knowing she'd almost certainly refuse, and knowing damn well that I had to at least try.

I've seen fights before, Steve, and I have to get used to this if—

"They are raping below," Scylla interrupted, her voice low and hard. "I can hear them, above the sounds of fighting. Ingrid, I judge you not, but if it is possible not to see what is to come, I say you should avoid it."

"Yeah, we need to see it," Jonas murmured, "but believe me, there's shit I've seen that regular people have done to each other, and it's given me nightmares. If you can avoid it, I would. We won't judge you for that, and I wish I could avoid it."

"I'll call for you if we need you," I promised, and after a few seconds, Ingrid responded.

Thank you.

That was it, but the mental voice that we all heard was full of relief, and I was glad that she, at least, didn't need to see what was to come.

I felt her leave us. The feeling of coordination and always knowing where the others were massively decreased, and I nodded to myself, seeing that as a team of BWVs, we still had advantages over regular humans.

The next thirty seconds, as we slid down the ladder, made it clear just how much of a bonus that was.

The area below was much larger than the one above, and the first section had cells filling one side of the passage, every few feet along. They opened into small rooms, ones that had metal bars sealed into place over them.

The first two rooms had women in them, the third a young man, and all the occupants were curled up and staying as far from the door as possible.

The fourth room was unlocked, and two men were inside with its single occupant.

Scylla didn't wait for a signal, and Jonas and I flowed past it, moving to the next cell, as the woman's screams ceased...and the men's started.

A large man leaned against the wall in the next cell, standing over a sobbing figure on the floor, one that begged him for "just a little fix...I need my medicine" as he grinned down at the man before him.

My harvest blade made almost no sound as it slid into the top of the big man's spine, severing the cord at the base of the brain, and I caught his body before it fell.

What I'd not planned for was the meth'd-up fucker, who'd been on the floor begging, suddenly screeching in abject fury and launching himself at me, hands crooked like claws and going for my eyes.

My hands were full with the body, unfortunately, and my instinctive reaction…well.

My nanites extended a slim tendril from my chest. Fully active nanites formed the tentacle rather than the dumb weaponized variants, and they stabbed into his eye, piercing deep into the brain.

He jerked to a halt, twitching, and for a half second, I cursed, thinking I'd killed him, until I stopped.

The eye was a write-off, sure, but the rest of him?

My thought had been more "stop that fuck" than "kill him" and the nanites had responded to my will. They'd formed the tentacle because I was used to using them in that way, from when I had, well, a fuckload more nanites.

The end result was that my nanites had essentially hijacked his brain. They'd slammed through his eye, then had branched into a dozen tiny filaments that were spread across the brain. Some interacted with the front, others layered throughout the back and hindbrain, and several interwoven with the spinal column.

I flexed a linkage, and he twitched, letting me know that yeah, the fucker was still alive.

He was also, unfortunately, practically catatonic, his brain hijacked by the instinctive attack. I slowly removed sections of my nanites, peeling them back, attempting to repair as I went, then cursed.

I'd not intended to kill the guy, but for all intents and purposes I had. A section of the brain I'd shredded then repaired was clearly a crucial section, considering his upper brain activity had dropped to zero, and I winced.

The hindbrain, that was working fine, and my medical knowledge—sparse though it was and limited to "hit this hard; don't hit this unless you want to kill"— was enhanced by the Support information.

I ran through the options, before settling on one.

He was essentially brain-dead, and so I did the only reasonable thing, and I used the harvest tool to drain him, then simulated a brain aneurysm, and repaired the eye and stab point on the way out.

It left his corpse more or less intact for when we passed information on the location to Interpol, and it didn't leave his family with a living but brain-dead shell that had once housed a loved one.

I regretted it, but it was life. Nobody got out alive.

I turned, only just now realizing I was holding the other corpse upright still. I set him down, finding I'd stripped him of his nanites without thought.

Jonas had checked the next room, finding another pair of figures locked in there, men this time, and he was engaged in a low conversation with them, while Scylla was threatening the women with dismemberment if they didn't shut up in their cell.

They were thanking her over and over, and begging to be let go, while Scylla ordered them to be silent.

I stepped out of the one I was in and moved to their cell, reaching down deep and pulling a simulacrum of my helm up, only as thick as paper. But it flashed across my face, eyes lighting with an unholy blue light and seeming to smolder from within, as I spoke.

"Be silent!" I hissed at them, and wonder of wonders, it worked.

It also might have been helped by the way I grabbed the first of the two men's bodies and it started to shake as the skull cracked under my palm.

I'd used the majority of the nanites that were responsive in my mask, just to shock them, and as such, I'd been forced to extrude the filaments from the ports in my wrist to drain the body.

I'd slapped my hand down atop his head, and the filaments had broken into the top of his skull, setting off the occasional neural signal as they dragged the good stuff free, his body spasming.

Ten seconds later, I did the same to the second corpse, and we were off again, ignoring that the women we'd told to stay in their cell were now out of their cell and racing back the way we'd come, fighting to get free of the place.

At least they were doing it quietly, so fuck it.

"They say there's a gambling ring below, bare-knuckle fighting, and more private rooms. Up here, it's a pick-and-mix."

"A what?" Scylla asked, confused.

"Well, more of a pick-your-own," Jonas admitted. "These cells are where they hold people they're selling off, or renting. The 'premium' ones are kept below. These ones are generally ones they've had for a while and they're not as concerned about.

"They say that a lot of the customers like to get violent, and that's limited 'by management' to the ones that they buy, or the older, less popular ones. These were moved up here tonight, as 'fresh meat' were brought in earlier today, and they were given the lower rooms. It's busier than normal because there's a party for their supporters going on."

"How many?"

"At least ten to twenty, possibly more. The 'regulars' have bodyguards, and they'll be working below, making sure their masters aren't interrupted."

"Fucking sick bastards," I growled.

"How?" Jonas said after a few seconds.

"How what?" Scylla asked.

"How do they get here?" Jonas shook her head. "There are no boats outside, no ships, no planes…How do they come and go?"

"I…" I frowned. "I don't know." I glanced about. "This section's a lot cleaner, right?"

"It is?"

"Why?" I asked. "If the upper levels are filthy, why make the lower areas nicer? I mean, you've still got to pass those sections to get here, right?"

"Although…maybe not," Jonas said softly. "What if the upper areas are something like 'staff only'?"

"What does this matter?" Scylla glared at us, and I held a hand up for a second's quiet as I reached out to Ingrid.

"Ingrid...Ingrid, can you hear me?" I asked, cursing when there was no response. "Fuck, she's not listening!"

"What is wrong?" Scylla growled. "You told her to go, to not see this. It was right to do."

"Yeah, but if these fucks are getting here another way?" I said. "It means they're probably getting in from below! That means a way in and out we don't know about. And if they use a sub or something? They'll fucking see the yacht!"

"Then we need to move fast," Jonas said. "They've got no reason to go looking for her, but every second we delay increases the chance of her being seen."

"Fuck it—all out." I gritted my teeth, as the other two grinned darkly. "Hit them fast and hard, quiet as we can, but speed over stealth."

And just like that, Scylla was off.

We'd been trading off leading the way because of my stealth and experience in these situations, but as much as it annoyed me to admit it, she was the most lethal of the three of us.

Especially when I was without my full range of abilities.

She tore off, feet barely seeming to touch the ground as we followed. Each branching of the passage, each room we passed, we peeled off, checking. We found dozens of empty rooms—some with signs of recent habitation, others with dried blood and bone, stained sheets and worse left behind.

We passed rooms that looked like they were from some kink's favorite fantasy—all manacles and dripping benches, braces and spikes—and in other rooms, we found work that had clearly been in progress—a ceiling braced here, a wall that was being repaired and pointed there.

The next level down, as we continued at speed, was far better maintained, making it clear that as the people Jonas had spoken to had said, the uppermost sections weren't for the clients to see.

Presumably the figures we'd killed had been staff or something, rather than clients, because as we reached the next floor, it changed again.

Where above it'd been dusty, dirty, and presumably freshly excavated, the deeper we went, the more maintained, repaired, and polished everything became.

We passed under old stone archways, and into a wide room with a vaulted ceiling. It had heavily carved sections of the walls that depicted religious shit: rows of people marching, spears lifted to the heavens with bodies dangling from them, and monsters like dragons without wings crunching figures in their jaws.

A figure sat in the middle of a relief, atop a throne, an older man with curling ram's horns, and a weird-ass hat. All around him, figures marched inward and out, some bearing platters of food, others riches...still more, the bodies of the dead. A second character, a woman with the head of a lion, stood by his side, blessing the dead, and they rose up, marching away to stand as soldiers in the army. And then, as the figures flowed around, they took the place of the soldiers who fell, and carried still more bodies back to the figures in the center.

"Ba'al Hammon and Tanit," Scylla noted with a grunt. "Ignore them."

Regardless of how impressive it was—the artwork, I mean; not that Scylla was utterly unimpressed and we were literally running through a building she'd burned down centuries ago—but that it stood where it did, casually in the wall still, meant a lot.

That kind of ancient shit would have been looted and ripped out, then installed in some rich asshat's private collection normally. That it hadn't?

It worried me.

Either this group had money to burn, they were idiots, or they had access to so much of this kind of thing, that they didn't need to worry about leaving millions on the wall like this.

Here and there, there were tables, chairs, and the signs of refreshments on offer. A modern refrigerator stood in one corner. A gentle hum came from it, and the sounds of laughter and screams rose louder from below.

Leaving the main room, we passed two more smaller rooms, one on either side. One held the remains of a meal, hastily abandoned, while the other held a small office, one overflowing with piles of paperwork, a small laptop, and sets of keys and more.

I took one look over it all and turned away, feeling sick to my stomach.

One of the folios I'd seen was marked as "broken" and I made a mental note to get that, and other files, and have Marie and her small research team pour over it.

We didn't get much from "regular" humans we harvested, but there were other reasons to make sure we fucking reached out and touched some people.

Any "client" of this fucking island hellhole who we could trace, and who wasn't already here?

They'd be getting personal visits soon.

We moved on, taking a final set of steps, wide stone ones, polished and black, that led to a massive door, all black iron banding and heavy nails, age-blackened oak and more.

Jonas grabbed the ring handle and looked back at us both, getting nods, before he twisted and pulled.

CHAPTER TWENTY-NINE

The wall of sound that hit us made it clear we'd reached the "main floor" as Jonas pulled the door open. And beyond?

It was madness.

Music that had been faintly heard, but ignored in favor of the occasional screams and cheers, was now a low, throbbing beat. Strobe lights flashed, and as we stepped out, we found ourselves on a spherical balcony that circled a pit.

The bottom of the pit was at least ten meters down, and bodies were strewn here and there.

I froze, staring down and feeling my life had come full circle as I saw the figures that fought and killed down there, for the crowd's baying approval.

This time, instead of the pit being rough stone, surrounded by men and women wearing tattered clothes and practically drooling over the fight as they waited for their turn at the fun, the room was dressed, ancient stonework, and men and women in suits and expensive fabrics watched in their place.

The sound of bets being placed, or cheering as a dagger ripped through a screaming fighter's stomach, made my heart freeze.

The sight of these rich fucks laughing and cheering, united in bloodlust, made fury rise in me.

I could feel it in the air, the presence of the nanites below, and not one of the figures down there, not a single fucking *one,* was Arisen.

They weren't lycans, they weren't mindless beasts—they were humans.

Every one of the rich, useless fucks were cheering on innocent men and women who wept as they fought for survival.

I saw a man who looked as if he'd been dead ten years at least, judging by the sunken, wrinkled skin, offering a dagger, hilt first toward the bars, as a young man, barely out of his teens, frantically begged and reached for it.

Then he laughed and pulled it out of reach, throwing back his head, howling in amusement with his friends.

"Kill them," I hissed in fury. "Kill them *all!*"

Scylla and Jonas needed no more encouragement than that, and I took three quick steps up to the edge of the balcony, before vaulting off and plunging to the floor far below.

I hit hard. My legs flexed as I took the impact. The sound of laughter and cheering suddenly cut short as I slowly rose to stand straight, the fighters around me cowering back.

I reached down deep inside, my fury bringing the nanites up in waves.

Some were attuned—hell, many were now—but not enough. Not enough to form my armor, let alone to supply us all.

There was enough to do two things, though: enough to form my harvest blade, from my "cut" of the harvest so far, and enough to form a mask that made it clear that I was anything but human.

It was all sharp angles, glowing fury, and blank-faced terror, and the people in the pit got the fuck out of my way as I leveled my blade at the wrinkled old fuck who gaped at me.

There were at least a dozen of these rich bastards, maybe fifteen or twenty in total, I saw as I cast my gaze about. Each of them had at least one bodyguard. Those had been standing against the back walls at attention: feet braced, hands clasped, looking every inch the professional, unjudging of their masters.

Now they were moving, faces showing surprise, fear, and determination.

That I stood on the inside of the pit gave their masters a few seconds of security, I guessed, as I saw the sneering and confident looks return to their faces.

Then they drained off, eyes moving slowly as they turned, looking up as the screams from above started.

The floor rolled around and down in a great spiral, circling the pit as it went, providing plenty of seats and spaces for clients to see the "fun," with regular small sections of level ground, followed by a decline that ran to the next flat spot.

Scylla sprinted down, a blade in either hand, already dripping blood from a guard who she'd passed, while Jonas stood stoically on the upper floor, aiming carefully.

When he fired, the *crack-boom* of the upgraded hand-fuckin'-cannon going off was loud, but the screams that rose as the figure he'd targeted detonated as though he'd swallowed a grenade made even more of an impression.

I strode forward and slashed my blade around in a wide arc. The ancient, blackened iron and bloodstained bars of the cage crashed free as I leaned back and kicked them, hard.

They fell on the old fucker who'd been scrambling, trying to get up from the recesses of the luxurious leather seat he'd been buried in.

He screamed as the metal crashed atop him. Papery-thin skin tore; blood gushed and brittle bones snapped under the impact.

Before his security could cover half the distance, I was through the gap, triggering my time compression to allow me to twist and bullet dodge as at least one of the bodyguards thought rather than reacted.

He had leaned back, bracing himself; his handgun barked as he fired in a two-handed grip, looking like he at least knew what he was doing. Most of the others raced forward, trying to get to their charges, ripping guns out, but putting themselves within my reach too.

I leaned to the left, then ducked as the bullets tore through the air next to me—not truly fast enough to dodge bullets, but fast enough to see the angle that the barrel was at, and to use that to guide me.

I punched down with my right fist as I stepped through the gap fully. The harvest blade speared through an opening between the bars, and into the old bastard's heart.

He gasped, eyes jerking wide in pain and terror as I ripped nanites free. My other hand grabbed the dagger he'd been holding as he dropped it.

I underarm flung it at the guard who'd been firing. The blade buried itself in his crotch and cut off the spray of bullets.

He screamed, dropping the gun and grabbing at the hilt of the blade, and I grinned as I ripped my harvest blade free. I'd not been aiming for the crotch, not consciously—I'd been aiming for the stomach—but clearly the gods of luck were taking a hand, all things considered.

I grabbed a figure to my left as she scrabbled to get away, tipping a table full of expensive drinks over as she tried to get out of the seat, moving in slow motion to my eye.

I grabbed her by the wrist, yanking her back. The harvest blade dripped blood as I whipped it around and rammed it into her throat. Her scream was cut off as the blade punched through her windpipe, while the *crack-boom* of Jonas's shots rang out, dopplering as I raced between the seconds.

From where he was, he could only see about a third of the room, and he clearly decided it was time to test out his new body, as he took a quick few steps, then jumped, following me down.

Scylla was in the thick of it now. Apparently, the door they all wanted to get through was about halfway down the spiral, on the far side from the one we'd used to enter. The bodyguards were all trying to get their charges to it, and had found a woman, grinning at them, wearing a strange-looking one-piece, and dual-wielding long knives.

Some had thought they'd have an easier time facing her than Jonas and me, and they screamed in horror and disbelief as she hacked them limb from limb.

I had over a thousand nanites in me now, thanks to the levels above, and although a good portion of them were in use, I slid another two hundred from the "pile" and weaponized them.

The rush as they flowed out, pooling on my skin, was insane.

They bought nothing to the fight, not really, but the feeling of having them back, after so long without? I sent them coursing to my right hand, pooling as they formed a chain that I gripped, and the harvest blade lengthened and detached.

It shrank in width and length, becoming a single finger wide and long, but razor-edged, and attached to a chain of nanites a meter long, coating the rest of the harvest blade's nanite length.

Then I dragged it out of her throat and flung it into the small of the back of another figure, a much younger, and drunker man who was trying to flee.

His guards had realized that as they'd waited as long as they had to draw their guns, they could no longer fire without risking their principal responsibility and instead grabbed ornamental weapons from the walls.

I noticed the tags attached to them and rethought that. They were price tags; presumably you could "buy" one of them and pass it through the bars for "your" chosen fighter.

Now *that* pissed me right off.

The first of them to step over the screaming form of the drunkard, now writhing on the floor below him, as the harvest blade did its work, leveled a glaive at me and stabbed out.

I dropped the now dead woman and grabbed the glaive behind the head. My increased perception of time made it child's play, and made it appear to those watching that my reflexes were faster than any snake could dream of.

I triggered my combat overlay for the first time in seemingly forever, consciously, and for a second, the room was washed out in a pulse of white light.

Then, before I'd even started to register the loss of vision, everything was back, and clearly marked.

Figures that still held guns were highlighted, as the predicted path of bullets, judged by the angle of the barrel, were shown as faint blue lines.

Red lines flashed as the path crossed me, and I stepped to the left as one went off; the bullet rushed past my face, half an inch to the right.

I couldn't help it. Just like when Ingrid crouched down, for literally any reason and I had to say it immortal 'while you're down there' line, no I felt the words rising and I let them free.

"Get over here!" I boomed out, channeling the greatest line of Kombat.

I pulled, both dragging the glaive wielder into the path of another shooter and the harvest blade from its latest victim. The blade and chain retracted to my hand, and I whipped them around, ramming the narrow length of pseudo-metal up under the fucker's chin and into his brain.

He released the glaive, eyes widening, and reached for the blade as blood gushed from the underside of his chin, and I flipped the glaive, throwing it overarm into another shooter.

I dragged the weaponized nanites free of the chain. The harvest blade reformed into a punch dagger jutting from my knuckles, and I pulled it free of the dead man before me.

As I stepped to the left, the nanites flowed up my arm, across my chest, and down my left arm, forming a thin band of void-black mass on the outside of my forearm.

The sword that was flashing around from that side hit it...and snapped.

I saw the counter counting down in the corner of my vision. A hundred and twenty-seven seconds to go. I grinned. I could easily do this, and clear my section of the room before the timer ran out.

The blade of the sword—thin, badly made, and clearly intended more as a "statement piece" rather than a weapon—spun as it passed my face. It flashed end over end, broken into three pieces that reflected the light as they went. I stabbed out, plunging the blade into a man's chest, ripping it free, and stabbing again and again, driving him backward with each blow.

He gasped and gurgled, dropping the hilt of the sword, and grabbed my left arm with weakening fingers, as I took him by the throat and lifted him, using him as a meat shield.

Crack-boom!

The figure on the far side of me, on the left, backing up protectively between me and another woman in a long red dress, her skin midnight black as she screamed for help, vanished.

Blood sprayed the walls. Half the body sagged to the floor; the rest painted his charge as she screamed again, spinning and grabbing another figure, then throwing them between her and us.

Her reprieve was short-lived, as she spun back only to jerk to a halt. One of Scylla's blades tore her a new, much wider, smile.

Two more were in close with me: one with a knife and a gun in alternating hands, the other swinging a mace.

I stepped back. The mace whistled past and dragged the wielder off-balance as he tried to recover. I retracted the harvest blade, backhanded him, breaking his jaw, and staggered, as the other fucker shot me three times in fast succession in the stomach.

I looked at him. The look of relief on his face that he'd "got me" poured off as I extended my left arm, palm raised flat to him. Anger filled me as my nanites slid back into a familiar pattern.

The gravity invertor had been tied to my armor, but as long as I'd used it now, I had enough of an innate understanding to form this much cruder version.

He hesitated, then shot me again, this time in the chest; then he raised the gun to aim at my head, before screaming.

His body collapsed inward: arm snapping down and in, spine cracking, legs lifting from the ground. The look on his face of utter terror as his heart became the center of an insanely powerful gravity gradient—only a small bubble, but intense—was satisfying.

As were the pops, snaps, and crunches that rang out. Even the bursting-free blood, falling back to swamp his remains, made it clear to everyone that if you shot *me*, you better use something better than a fucking 9mm.

The screams hung in the air for a few seconds more, as Jonas fired twice more. And then, apart from the drip of blood, the frantic panting of the former "gladiators," and the panicked moans and sobbing of the dying, it was all over.

"Well, that was fun," Jonas muttered, stepping up and looking at me as I lowered my arm. "How long you been able to do that little trick?"

"About five seconds," I said. "Don't worry, I'll make sure you all get your cut of the spoils."

"I'd rather learn that trick," Jonas said. "Seriously, if you can bend fuckin' space and time like that, ain't no way that motherfuckers are walking away after a fight. How'd you do it?"

"It was linked to my armor, and the way I unlocked other skills. Not sure if I can teach you, but I'll try."

"That's all I ask."

"I need the blade," Scylla cut in, striding over and looking at her own blades then at me as she flicked them, splattering the blood free with a practiced motion. "When we fought Shamal, you controlled my weapons, making them reform, grow and shrink. I need that."

"I'll teach you," I said, "but it's not easy, and you'll need a fuckload of nanites."

"You managed it now," she said, and I hesitated, before shrugging.

"Fair enough." I'd been thinking that they'd need armor, and that they'd need to learn to control their nanites, but fuck it...I could do it like this, so I had to guess they could too.

I looked around, the walls covered in dripping blood and torn entrails. A single survivor of the bodyguard contingent was laid in the corner, eyes wide and staring in horror. A section of what looked to be small intestine dangled from his left ear.

He shook like a shitting dog with an electrical cable jammed up its arse, so I doubted we'd get much that was coherent from him.

I gestured to him, nodding to Jonas, who sighed and stepped over, crouching and trying to question him anyway. Scylla and I moved to the next set of doors, opening them and looking through into another corridor.

"Do we go on, or question these?" Scylla gestured to the group of gladiators, who were now giving one another degrees of medical aid, and trying not to be noticed by us.

"Jonas, deal with them next," I called to him, jerking my head in their direction, and getting a flat glare from him. "We should have brought Belle."

"She would have been breeding with them by now," Scylla grunted, before taking the lead.

"Maybe, but they'd be smilin'." I sighed.

The passage that led off branched in a dozen ways, each leading into cells, and each of them occupied by traumatized people. Men and women were locked in there, their price marked on the wall by the entrance—a fucking card reader installed and ready. Thankfully, there were no children. But everyone there either stared in shock, were unresponsive, or wept, terrified and trying to hide as we passed.

By the time we knew that this was all that was down this way, we were passing a new wall frieze on the way out, as at last, Ingrid spoke to me excitedly.

Look to the left!

I spun, my harvest blade extending as I dropped low, ready for a fight, and saw a fucking stone wall, before cursing under my breath.

"Ingrid!"

I...Sorry. I didn't mean to scare you. Are you okay? Sorry, that frieze, it's—

"No time for that," I snapped. "Get James to move the yacht. Get a mile or two offshore and start sailing around—keep moving!"

After a second's hesitation, she agreed, making me sag in relief.

What happened?

"We found...we found some rich fuckers' playground," I told her. "The people here are gonna need a fuckload of therapy and help. Get Dimi to fly Belle out here. When we've checked out the rest of the site and we're sure it's clear, I'll finish draining and we can leave. Fuck it, I'll hack the satellites and try to remove the yacht or something...I don't know."

What about the people?

"We'll call in Interpol. I know they're probably on their way already, but they'll need to hurry the fuck up." I sighed, then shook my head. "You might want to look away as we pass through the rest of this section."

Steve, I've seen you in action before, and—

She broke off as Scylla pushed open the door ahead of us, and a second later, another section of intestine fell from the roof to land on the floor with a final, wet splat.

And again, you've been busy.

"Very," I admitted.

How bad was it?

"Very." I broke off as Jonas moved over, leaving the group in the fighting pit, and I glanced over. The bodyguard he'd been speaking to before had come down with a noticeable case of "dead."

"What did you find out?" I asked him.

"There's two more levels below, and a handful of guards. They'll have heard the gunfire, no doubt about it, and there's a sub-pen as well. Depending on how experienced and trained the guards are, they might be coming this way. They might have left. No way to be sure."

"How many guards?" I asked, and he shrugged.

"The bodyguard was adamant this was his first time here. He claimed to have seen two guards on the sub, plus the pilot, and there were three guards left below. He wasn't sure if there were two guards plus those three, or if the two from the sub were included. He was dumb as shit, frankly, so I did the gene pool a favor in removing him from it."

"Anything else?" I asked, and he shrugged again.

"His boss has been coming here for about a year—off and on, he said. Usually it's a different guard who comes with him, but he was sick. I think it was bullshit, trying to play the 'wrong time, wrong place' card for sympathy, but it might be true. Regardless, I think we need to be careful as we finish our sweep."

"Then let's go," I said.

I'd already extruded the bullets I'd been shot with, and the wounds were healing steadily. But it itched like a motherfucker, and I was in no mood to hang around here.

"Listen up!" I called to the former gladiators. "You're on a small island, off the coast of Libya. It's uninhabited, officially at least, and the sea has sharks in it. I don't recommend swimming to shore, as you'd be illegal immigrants, if you survived the swim. Free the people in the cells, find somewhere to rest and wait. Interpol is aware you're here and they're on their way. So rest, recover, and get on with your lives after this."

"And forget what we look like," Jonas said when I finished. "You really don't want the people we work with to come and remind you to keep quiet. So, as far as you're all concerned, you saw nothing, understand?"

They nodded quickly, and Jonas gestured back to the cells where the others were still held.

"There's a few more up above, and a lot of dead bodies, as well as a little food. We're not going to lock you up, but if we take a corner and find you standing there with a gun? It could end badly. Stay the fuck out of our way, and preferably altogether," he added.

The three of us moved off, following the slowly spiraling path to the mid-level, and then exited through the door that Scylla had been guarding earlier.

The door was heavy, and although on our side it looked similar to the one above, all aged wood and black iron, on the other side it was anything but, making it clear that it was an aesthetic they'd leaned into.

The far side was a modern steel door. The passage beyond was in excellent repair, clearly well maintained, and with oxygen masks and more hidden behind a door marked Emergency as we passed it.

There were two rooms farther in. One was clearly abandoned in a hurry: the monitor and more for a desktop still in place, but the computer itself smashed open and the drive ripped free.

The second room looked to have been a duty post, or break room—again, empty, and with a cooling bowl of something spilled on the floor.

It looked like porridge, and I shook my head at that. All the food in the world, and if someone was choosing to eat that crap, death would be a mercy for them.

At the end of the corridor was a set of wide stone stairs, and leading on from there, a final hallway. A single room on this level was a security office. The gun rack was stripped bare, a safe emptied, and the hard drive for a wall full of cameras missing.

I cursed. They were definitely running, regardless of who "they" were, and they most likely had video of us all.

I'd not been thinking of cameras, the idiot that I was, because of the look of the place higher up. I'd been lulled into a false sense of security. The rough stone walls and more had been left at the top level, I was betting, as they were an emergency exit only, and mainly designed for the on-site security.

The real security detail had been down here, protecting the clients—we'd still killed them, but at least they'd not been asleep—and down here.

Now, as we started to run, me triggering my nanite flux concealing ability and shimmering out of sight, and Scylla using her natural stealth, we heard a distant claxon going off.

Picking up more speed, we reached the end of the corridor. A massive steel door had been built across the entrance to the sub-pen, one that, through the small porthole, was clearly being opened to allow a surprisingly large vessel to leave.

I reached out, focusing, and snorted a laugh as the single die appeared in my mind—a four-sided one, the encryption was that weak. It'd barely finished forming when the locks disengaged and the door started to open, while the main doors that led out of the sub-pen, and presumably to the greater ocean beyond, ground to a halt, before reversing.

As they closed, the sub picked up speed, clearly hoping to make it out, despite the doors already being too close together, and I swore.

If that fucker hit the doors, the very least that would happen would be that they, and the sub, would be fucked.

Since I'd opened the door here and the pen doors were open, the water had started to rise as well, and I had to think there was some kind of pressure lock forcing this.

I darted through the door with Scylla and dragged it shut. Both of us winced as the overpressure made our ears pop as I sealed the door, spinning the crank to lock it.

Then I reached out, focusing and hoping I had enough strength for it.

I couldn't lift and move the sub, not with my gravitational abilities, but what I could maybe do was force a bubble there that would interfere with it.

Creating a bubble of twisted gravity behind the rear of the prop, I increased its pull again and again. The water around it swirled as I grunted in pain.

My brain felt like I was trying to drive it out through my ears with the strain, but as I forced the water away from the bubble, literally creating a field of reversed gravity that I moved to encircle the screws, the sub slowed, and then drifted, its planes waggling as it tried to direct itself.

Unbeknownst to the pilot, the reason it was going nowhere was that as the screws spun, they were doing it in a bubble of empty air.

With nothing to push against, the sub drifted slowly, then crunched into the side of the stone berth that it normally sat in. The rubber and plastic barrels that floated there, placed for exactly this eventuality, took most of the impact. But the screech of metal on stone still rang out, as Scylla sprinted for the dock, leaping from our side to land on the walkway that crossed to the far side, then jumping from that and landing on the sub itself.

It was a strange design—no conning tower as I'd always seen in the movies, but instead closer to the design that Athena had been using, which made me wonder what the hell had happened to that thing.

It was rounded on top and bottom, longer like a cigar than circular, and with an all-enclosed glass front that looked to be made from a single piece.

It was eight or ten meters across, and perhaps fifty long, as well as clearly insanely expensive.

A hatch in the top cranked open. Water washed across it—it was nearly at water level now, as it'd been trying to dive before—and a panicked-looking figure in a smart white dress uniform, the kind that was worn aboard yachts and in the navy, leaned out, bringing a Steyr assault rifle around.

It was one of their variants, I saw straightaway, futuristic as fuck looking, bulky yet maneuverable, and probably lethal even in close-quarters combat...provided you weren't fighting someone who had been in more battles than I'd had wanks.

Scylla ripped it free of him, slit his throat, and dropped into the hatch atop his falling body before he could get off more than a gurgle. Ten seconds later, the engines stopped.

I dropped to my knees, hands barely managing to catch me, as I coughed and gasped. Blood ran from my eyes, ears, nose, and mouth. I collapsed sideways, my entire skull throbbing fit to split.

Steve? STEVE!

I couldn't speak; the words wouldn't come. Instead, I forced myself to stare at one hand, shaking as I lifted it, and coerced my fingers to curl until I gave the bloody ground a thumbs-up.

Are you okay? Gods, no, that's a stupid question...Are you dying?

I shook my head, making sure it was clear as I coughed and wiped at the streaming blood.

You've strained yourself too far, haven't you?

I nodded, shakily offering a thumbs-up again, then forcing myself to a sitting position, closing my eyes as I tried to get control. I didn't know when the nanites forming my mask had vanished, when I'd released the pattern across my face I'd been holding, but at some point, I'd let it go. I sat there again now, clearly visible as Scylla brought out the two from inside. The body of the third was left below.

"You want it?" she called to me, and I nodded, unable to speak.

I looked up as the other two were marched across to me. One looked terrified, the other furious.

"You don't know what you've done!" the angry-looking motherfucker snarled. "The work you've ruined! You have no idea how many of society's highest are my clients! They'll make sure you vanish, and in a week, we'll be back in business. The only difference is that it'll be you and your loved ones in the pit! You'll be raped, daily…your wives, mothers, and—"

I straightened. My right hand lashed out. The conduits from the harvest tool punched into the body of the second man, the one who'd been terrified, but dressed as an employee.

I triggered System Replenishment, from the Harvest tree, and bugger me sideways with a double-ended dildo dipped in donuts did I need it.

Not only did it rip the nanites from him, his body collapsing as I dragged in a deep breath, sucking it down as pain and a terrible pleasure raced through me, but it also tore away just about everything else that made him, him.

Everything from nutrients to genetics, bone marrow to hair follicles—anything and everything that could be used to return me to a pristine and perfect version of myself was ripped free. The remainder of his body collapsed into a gray and red mush of torn, suppurating flesh.

The process even damaged the DNA of the victim, making it impossible to identify him, as the body began to break down at a truly horrific rate.

In ten minutes, all that would be left of him would be a mass of gloop that looked more like it'd been vomited up by a sick animal—half mold and half sloppy mess, but certainly not identifiable as fucking human.

I drew a second deep breath as I stood over the now white-faced figure who'd been berating me before, and who now wore piss-soaked pants.

"Now…" I growled, licking a film of my own blood free of my upper lip. "I've got some fucking questions about those clients."

CHAPTER THIRTY

It wouldn't be accurate to say that Interpol was overjoyed to get the information I sent them. Not really.

In some circles, it'd probably be classed as a "career bust," considering the sheer level of fuckery I'd exposed. But as there were one or two in the upper echelons of pretty much every nation implicated, as well as a sitting president of a small nation, and two prime ministers—one former and one who'd only been in place a week—not to mention a member of Interpol's own leadership?

I guessed it was also going to be problematic.

I'd used some nanites and a bit of hacking magic to show myself in full—*paper-thin*—armor and "avenging angel" persona as I contacted the second-in-command of Interpol directly.

It had to be the second-in-command unfortunately, as the top banana was mentioned on the list I'd gotten from that now very, *very* helpful individual.

I called her, interrupting a morning review she was leading. The TV screen that stood at the foot of the table where she was being briefed suddenly flickered and changed to show my armored form, as I stared at them all.

There were dozens of them, all dressed in suits and staring at me, pretending interest as they waited for the next section to begin.

Their boss frowned, asking someone why they'd skipped to "that section of the briefing early" when I spoke.

"Francine Amanda Deena, I am the one you know as Steve. I have limited time, and much to do. All save Bartholomew and Minas, get out," I ordered, my voice flat and cold.

To her credit, she'd stared at the screen with hardly a change of expression, before she sighed, passed her now-empty coffee cup to someone to her side—I'd not bothered to learn the names of most of them; I'd just checked that those two, as her aides, were clean—and then she'd shooed the rest out.

"To what do we owe this pleasure, Steve?" she asked. "Or should I call you Steven Barr?"

"You can refer to me by any name you wish. It matters not," I replied formally, internally cursing that they'd dug that fucking detail up. "The nominal identity of the previous inhabitant of this shell is of no concern to me," I repeated to her, prompted by Ingrid through our link.

"Previous…?"

"You were provided information on a smuggling ring, both drugs and people, some eleven hours ago."

She frowned, before one of her aides passed her something.

"Ah yes, it was to be part of the morning brief, but…"

"Here," I said. The screen that showed me split down the middle, showing a map of the Mediterranean, with over a dozen sites highlighted.

"This site currently houses several dozen who were being smuggled north into Europe, as well as victims who had been kidnapped and were being abused prior to being sold into slavery." I made the island of Kastri off the coast of Crete flash.

"These locations are brothels that are currently holding your citizens, kidnapped and sold." Ten more sites flashed, then remained on the map.

"This site is the main client-facing headquarters of the group, and is both an ancient site that was being used as a combination brothel and fight pit, but is also, I have been assured, of great cultural significance to the city of Carthage." Again, a flashing icon appeared.

"Carthage?" She frowned.

"You know it now as Tunis," I clarified. I'd known it as fucking Tunis as well, but that little extra detail should muddy the waters about who and what I was nicely, Ingrid had pointed out.

"It also holds some fifty people, currently, many of whom are your citizens, and are now addicted to mind-altering substances, and have been forcibly used by their captors."

"I…I see. Thank you for your assistance. Can I ask why you're involved in this?" she asked, clearly making notes on her tablet, then showing them to her companions.

Because I see all.

I printed it across the tablet screen she was using and over her own words, making her freeze.

"Also, because I was investigating your organization, and others. You will be pleased to know that I found you, and those two with you, to be clean of corruption…so far."

"Well, yes," she replied dryly. "I am pleased that in the headquarters of Interpol, we're not too corrupt for you to lower yourself to deal with. So—"

"Unfortunately, President Matthias De Gosselaar, your master, was not found to be so pristine." I picked slightly wrong words deliberately, knowing that every goddamn thing I said would be pulled apart later as they searched for the most minute detail.

"What?" she snapped, glaring at the screen. Her body language changed entirely.

"He is involved in this ring, and is a regular client." I sent her a dozen files I'd found on the island site when we'd recovered the hard drives, and after unleashing Tsunami into their supposedly "secure" remote server.

Considering it included video, showing him with others she knew to be criminals as well as politicians, I had the pleasure of watching naked fury pass across the features of Vice President Deena.

I'd had to do a little digging into Interpol to find the right person to pass this to, and in doing so, I'd learned that the group consisted of a single president, three vice presidents, and then a group of delegates that formed the executive committee.

That there were three possible vice presidents I could have gone to had slowed me slightly. But considering one was a matter of days from retirement? I figured she'd not want what was coming. The other? He would have been fine, but to have this conversation I'd have needed to learn another language, and frankly I couldn't be fucked with that.

I knew he spoke English, but the nuances I'd have to deal with were more hassle than I needed at this point, and he was apparently cordially detested by most of the other committee members, so, as the person I was handing this to was about to become a star?

Well, I'd picked Deena. She was already notorious for being a hard ass. Ex-military, the only complaints that had ever been made against her? She was too efficient, and too uncaring of the political landscape.

Considering those politicians who were involved? That made her the perfect choice.

"As such, you can, I'm sure, understand why I have chosen you."

"Chosen?" she snapped, clearly seriously unhappy right then.

"Yes. You care not for the supposed invulnerability of your political masters. As such, you shall be my tool."

"I'm nobody's tool!" she snarled. "Listen, Steve, or whatever the hell you are, I'll examine the evidence, that's all. *If* I find that it's worth following, then—"

I shared video evidence taken from the hidden security cameras around the island site, ones that the owners had apparently been keeping as potential blackmail material for the future.

The scenes it showed—of rape, murder, beatings, and more—shut her up fantastically. The image shifted to the owner of the site on his knees, frantically babbling out names, tears and blood streaming down his face in equal measure, before the cameras changed, and rooms full of freed prisoners and the walls dripping with the results of our slaughter replaced them.

"I am not bound by your laws, Deena. I shall not be here on your world for long. And when I leave it, I shall leave it in a better state than I found it on my arrival. If that requires me killing every tenth human—or more—to teach you honor and humility? I accept this as a valid cost, although my human allies have pleaded with me to show restraint.

"I offer you a choice. Prove yourself to be an honorable human, one who can be used as a tool of justice, and I shall use you as one. No tool is demeaned by being used for its purpose. As *my* tool, you shall scour the corruption from your leadership, and more.

"You shall find files, each containing the evidence I have recovered, stored on your personal device. Use these. Clean your own house of corruption first, then seek out and destroy all others. In one of your weeks, data packets will be unlocked on the servers of several of your major media companies, and evidence, including some of this, will be made available to them.

"I do this not to force your hand, as should you choose not to deal with the corrupt? I shall simply pick another. No, I do this, so that should they eliminate you, should one of their agents have escaped my sight, then no matter their actions, your world will still have its chance to judge these people."

I sat back, waiting, and she stared, eyes flicking at desperate speed left and right, as she read over the files that I'd just given her. She opened some at random, clearly testing them, hoping to find anything but what she found.

Presenters of daytime TV shows, celebrities, news anchors, politicians, and more…judges and regular people, coffee shop owners, and goddamn cat lovers. People who the majority believed could never be guilty of anything beyond a speeding ticket were shown reveling in the depths of sadism.

Locations of buried bodies, identities of the unidentified corpses recovered, and hidden offshore accounts all wove a web that drew Deena to only one inescapable conclusion. After a long minute, she lifted her head and spoke three words.

"I'll do it."

Those words released a knot I'd been holding in my chest. I forced myself to remain impassive, as inside I celebrated. At least not all the police were corrupt. At least some would do what needed to be done.

"Then I shall be in touch. There are many people in these sites who require your assistance right now, Deena. Prove yourself, to me and your world."

With that, I cut the call off and blew out a long breath. The nanites dissipated back into my skin as I ran my fingers through my hair, glad that was over.

This step, I knew in my bones, was as important as rewilding the Sahara, or cleaning the oceans. Cutting out the cancer that had crept into government, that squatted, spiderlike at the center of media corporations and blogs, that posted anonymously with thousands of accounts to change the worldwide narrative, to fit their corrupt masters' will?

It had to be done…although, being the bastard that I was, I still saved one of the group for myself.

He was a politician, one who had done incalculable harm to my homeland, and he was growing in power, manipulating the narrative in the Houses of Parliament. I'd decided that should I survive all that was coming?

He would be my little treat to myself.

I was going to use my abilities, once I was back to the peak of nanite-infused glory, and I was going to take him. I was going to use him as the example for the rest of them. I'd take him from the place he felt most secure in his power, "live" in the weekly question time that the politicians used to beat their chests and pretend to serve the public.

I'd appear then, and I'd break him, force him to confess, releasing the evidence I had on him, and I'd show the world that none of those fuckers were safe from me…make it clear that no matter where they skulked, they would be dragged out into the light.

I was no innocent, and I was no "good man."

Fuck's sake, I'd killed before I was reborn as the man I was, and I'd kill again and again. Only hours ago, a drug addict who had leapt at me, desperate for their fix, addicted through no fault of their own, had died at my hand.

I didn't like it, but it was what it was, and I was fucked if the people who abused kiddies and did the things that I'd seen in that place were going to go free.

What made it even worse, in my eyes, was that as high-tech, sophisticated, wealthy, and goddamn professional that operation had been? There was no way that at least one or more of the Arisen didn't know about it.

I cordially hated them all, sure, and even now I was waiting for those cocksuckers to show up and for it all to kick off into killing one another again.

They were immortal. They'd had centuries, *millennia* to grow the fuck up and to see what was right and wrong, and even those mentally degenerate fucks should have seen what was happening and stepped in.

For them to have ignored it? I'd find out which fuckers had known, somehow, and I'd make an example of them, I silently swore.

"How was it?" I asked Ingrid as she slid into the seat next to me, smiling proudly.

"Perfect," she assured me, as James and the others moved back to their places around the small table. We were in the yacht's main cabin, and with the eight of us all shuffling around one another, I started to see just how cramped it was.

It wasn't so much the size of the yacht, although now that Belle, Oxus, and Lars had joined us, that was seriously becoming an issue.

More so, it was a case of the sheer size of the people involved was getting insane.

Oxus had already put half a dozen scrapes and holes in the ceiling overhead with his horns. And the way that Lars essentially sat there, in the middle of all this madness, was hilarious to watch.

He was, from his perspective, in absolute heaven.

First and foremost, he was an archaeologist, one from an exceedingly wealthy family who had essentially been able to indulge his "little interests" without effort.

That meant that when he'd discovered he liked archaeology, they'd sent him to the very best schools, the best universities, and had arranged little trips where he could meet "real" archaeologists and pester them.

The difference had been, that rather than ending up being some useless rich kid, he'd actually learned, studied, applied himself, and fuck me had he earned his place as one of the preeminent archaeologists of the age.

He'd used his insane wealth, and the access that gave him, to actually make a difference, increasing humanity's knowledge of the past to an incredible degree.

He'd gotten his masters, and a doctorate, and then he'd started to *really* work. As he'd been when I met him three years or so ago, he'd been a major "mover and shaker" in the world of archaeology, splitting his time between giving speeches or attending dinners and running entire museum's decades-long plans.

That he also had a young family and was actually, according to Anders, an amazing father as well? It pissed me off.

Well, no, it didn't, not really. But fuck me, how little effort had my father put in, that this guy managed to do all this and still be a great dad, while running around the world and doing all that?

I shook my head, looking at him, and yet I couldn't help but grin at him. He was one of those genuinely likable people you just couldn't say no to, about average height, fairly muscular and good-looking, with a shaved head and a few days' worth of stubble, but a smile that never stopped.

He currently sat with a seriously good cup of coffee between Belle, a greater dryad who had seen thousands of years pass while learning at the feet of one of the creators of humanity, and Scylla. A woman who had literally been such a successful pirate of the Greek ages, that even now she was mentioned in myth and legend as a sea monster impossible to escape.

On the floor nearby, on about his tenth can of energy drink—and soon to be off his tits, if I was any judge—was a Minotaur. And by my side was Ingrid, one of Lars's oldest friends and his wife's best friend, who'd recently been aboard an alien craft from the dawn of recorded human history.

He was literally filling the air with questions, barely able to let anyone respond, before he had another, and the top of his head was at risk of falling off if his smile got any wider.

Add in that Jonas and Oxus were both so-called "alpha" men—big, muscled, and rangy? Then that Belle, being Belle, was bare-ass naked, and Scylla and Oxus had been sunbathing with her so both were naked as well, and none of them had any concept of personal space?

It meant that poor James was trying to thread his way around everyone with drinks and snacks, while half the available space was filled with private parts and greasy with sun oil.

I couldn't help but laugh to myself, while admittedly enjoying the view a great deal as Ingrid slid in closer in her white bikini.

"What?" she asked me, and I snorted, shaking my head. "Seriously, you were thinking something and it wasn't about the call, so what was it?"

"We need a bigger yacht," I said, and she smiled her agreement.

"Well, we've got Athena's to sort out yet. Last I heard, it was still being worked on, right?"

I nodded. "Any plans for this one?" I asked, and she shrugged.

"Not really. I was thinking we'd just sell it, or maybe keep it as a spare?"

"Sounds good." I smiled back at her. "Maybe see if Scylla wants it?" I suggested, and she nodded. We'd mentioned this a few weeks back, when we'd been relaxing one night after working on the recycling facility.

Realistically, I'd claimed anything and everything that belonged to Athena when I'd killed her. I'd also split that with Hans, on the agreement that he cover all the costs for the superyacht's repair, and that it was mine.

He'd known damn well that he was getting a good deal, and when I'd finally found the time to hack the computer systems that had survived the destruction I'd unleashed on her ship, I'd realized just how much I'd agreed to share with him. Her personal accounts—the ones I'd been able to find so far, anyway—were ten-figure sums.

I didn't have to share any of that with anyone, not really, and certainly nobody had suggested I should. But there was also the minor detail that Scylla's booty—not the one that Jonas was making the most of, but the treasure she'd been amassing for centuries—had likely been absorbed into Athena's trove.

We'd decided that we needed to make sure that Scylla was set up right. And then, if she chose to move on without us? At least we'd done the right thing.

The yacht was another example of that. We could keep them both, or...

"Yeah, once the other one is finished, we'll give her this one," I agreed, before grinning. "In fact, let's get that worked on sooner rather than later."

"You've got a plan?" Ingrid asked, before putting her lips to my ear and whispering as she went on. "Besides screwing me in a bigger bed?"

"I do." My grin grew. "You know how Libya were cool with us, but Egypt's representatives were assholes?"

"Yes?"

"Well, we were saying that we'd allow access to the lake we're going to make in the desert, right? And it's much easier to get things to places by ship, when it's bigger things, right?"

"Yes…" she agreed, frowning and drawing the word out.

"How about we make a channel from the lake out to the sea?" I suggested. "We need a bunch of machines to dig the sand out, and to lay a stone basin, right? We're going to make sure it's sealed so the water we pump up from below doesn't just sink back down."

"Go on."

"I think we need Zac and Casey in on this," I said as I gathered my thoughts. "And maybe your parents…hell, a full team meeting maybe."

"In that case, how about we hold this for a few hours?" Ingrid suggested. "We're, what, three hours from the ship?"

James nodded. "Three and a half."

"Well, considering how much skin is on show here right now, I think we all need to get dressed before we hold any calls with the rest of the group, or we might have some heart attacks going on. Let's get to the ship, get Belle into the capsule, and then we can hold a full team meeting."

"We need to give the others an update on your plans now in any case," James pointed out. "We gave them a very truncated brief when I arranged for Belle to join us, so I think that needs to be done regardless."

"Okay," I agreed, drawing a deep breath, then kissing Ingrid. "That gives me time to figure a few things out, I guess, and time to do this…"

We'd agreed that as we needed to "upgrade" Belle, we'd donate a full quarter of the nanites we'd gained in the assault of the island to the medical capsule.

That was sufficient to restock it enough to do her, hopefully, and the rest was going to be split between the four of us. I'd already assimilated and attuned my own, and the rest, thanks to finding the "disposal pile" of "used" bodies on-site, meant that we all had, after the Emergency Wipe, about four hundred nanite clusters each.

We tried to talk about things for a little, but it was obvious that most of the group were broken, both by the things we'd seen, and in the case of Lars, Belle, and Oxus, the sheer hours they'd been functioning.

Our call to them had meant that instead of going to bed last night, they'd prepared for the flight here, and Oxus…well, he wasn't a good flyer. He'd made sure that none of the three had been able to get any sleep, and as he'd been genuinely convinced he was dying, they'd taken pity on him and distracted him.

In Lars's case, that meant he'd sat with a pillow wrapped around his head, trying frantically to drown out the noises and the view as Belle "distracted" the massive Minotaur.

Lars had only arrived at the recycling base a few days before, and he'd been running around trying to learn everything, so hadn't fixated on who and what Belle was so much, as there were so many others to talk to up until then.

Now he made the most of the situation, while trying to keep awake on stimulant drinks and coffee.

We all broke up, drifting apart after I'd filled them in on how the call went; some went to the cabins, others ate or drank, and Ingrid and I moved out to lie on the front deck area of the yacht.

There were comfy loungers, sun lotion, and even a bit of privacy, more or less, which meant that the two of us could relax a little, just the two of us.

The breeze as we sailed was nice, but broken by raised barriers, so it wasn't too much. And the blistering heat of the sun overhead was lessened by a gentle and constant misting of spray thrown up by the bow.

All in all, it was goddamn wonderful as we relaxed, both of us falling asleep and passing the hours between the call and the arrival on-site at the sunken ship in the second-best way I could have imagined.

CHAPTER THIRTY-ONE

Several hours later, I sat, again, around a small table, looking at a screen as I explained my plan, while Zac shared details with Ingrid, and Ingrid, with the command net and more, sliced and diced those details, before projecting them in front of us all, and on the screen for those who needed it there, remotely back at the recycling plant for the others.

I'd given Zac an hour to come up with the details I needed, as well as a list of the various gear we'd require for our mission; he'd shrugged and worked his magic. The passports he'd made up were especially good. I'd explained the plan to him and Ingrid, then I had the childish edges of my plan rubbed off, and the entire thing tweaked, polished, folded, and mutilated. Now I was explaining the *new* plan for the benefit of the others.

There'd be some polishing to do, plenty in fact, but the direction it was going in was more than a slight improvement.

The original plan called for a huge lake in the middle of the Sahara, with our recycling facility and more, at the eastern edge of it. I'd agreed that the desert tribes could have access to the waters for free. When the politicians from the local states and countries had begged and blustered, I'd agreed that yeah, giving them some form of access to fresh water, especially in the quantities that we were going to have, was a reasonable request.

The new plan—again, somewhat polished—kept the lake, but expanded it…slightly.

It also added in a river that ran due west, crossing lower Libya and into upper Chad. That river would terminate in a new lake on the border of both nations, half on each side, giving them a massive amount of fresh water that would essentially jump-start their local areas.

For both, all they had in those areas was a nominal border, a few small souks, and a scattering of desert tribes. Beyond that? It was utterly worthless desert, unable to even be mined, considering the constant sandstorms and the naked heat.

Our basin lakes would be lined with smooth stone, forming a solid barrier to prevent the water from simply soaking back into the sand, and then, as the constructors that Zac had designed worked, they would lay soil atop it.

Essentially, in the Sahara, the rock and minerals, soil and more of the area over millennia had been aggressively overgrazed by cattle, in the deep past, and the combination of ferocious heat, constant winds, and the lack of any large vegetation to maintain the area—not to mention the loss of rain—had broken all that down into sand.

That sand would be dug up and fed into converters, with the construction machines Zac was creating, literal terraformers, digging out the channels we needed, laying the stone—coming from the converted sand—and moving on constantly.

Behind them would come the second wave of machines—smaller and faster. They would chew up even more sand, hundreds of tons of it, and it would be converted into fresh, mineral-rich soil.

While two of the terraformers—each the size of an average four-bedroom house, and that would need to be assembled at the recycling plant—worked to dig out the basin, another would dig the secondary river and lake on the border of Chad and Libya.

Two more would work their way steadily north from the lake, carving out what would be a river eventually, all the way through Libya to its northern coast, passing the small town of Al Jaghbub, on its western side.

Several of the group laughed as they followed the predicted and planned path, noting that in a direct line, as I had pointed it out, it'd reach the sea by the little town of Lukk.

There were two reasons for that. One was entirely sensible: a straight line was easier to navigate, and I intended that we'd be able to ship things in and out, noticeably masses of sea mud and crap harvested from the bottom of the ocean.

That would provide all the bacteria and so on that we needed for the bottom of the lakes. Although seawater bacteria and freshwater bacteria were obviously different, we'd add in whatever else we needed from the converters, and more. If need be, I'd arrange massive tankers to drive across the desert filled with river mud from the Nile, or wherever basically, pumping it all in and leaving it to settle.

That was enough to get us started, Casey had assured me, and it also brought us to the second point, which everyone, by now getting a fairly good idea of who I was, had sort of guessed.

It would ensure that the river, which would be navigable, and of fresh water, both insanely valuable as they were to a desert country, would be firmly several miles out of even the most optimistic reach of Egypt, mainly because they'd annoyed me, and I was being childish about it.

Libya would have a brand-new source of billions of gallons of fresh water, and the banks of the river would be declared as free land belonging to Libya, provided they protected it and made damn sure that nobody tried to interfere with our movements on it.

Beyond that, it was theirs.

They'd be gaining roughly half again the sheer arable land mass that they currently had across the entire damn country, by a four and a bit hundred-mile river appearing. And the best bit?

Once the machines were constructed and they set off, they could chew up and relay around ten miles a day. They were each thirty meters wide, and one would run slightly behind and to the side of the other, ensuring an overlap in the middle.

The sides were angled, meaning that at the deepest point, the river would be ten meters across and thirty deep, with fifty-five meters as the width of the river.

A slight change to the plans at that point was raised by Anders, who, as a seagoing man for most of his life and an ex-navy captain, almost had apoplexy at such a narrow beam.

It was instead changed to three terraformers, one to create the base, at thirty meters across and thirty deep, and the other two to work on an angle, creating a much more reasonable eighty meters across as the full width.

He wanted more, commenting that the Suez Canal was just over three hundred meters wide.

I pointed out that this wasn't for general commercial traffic, and that if people wanted it wider than this, they were welcome to find a fuckin' shovel and get to work.

I agreed with moving it to the eighty meters width, as it was primarily going to be for our shipping and yachts, both for Ingrid and me personally, hopefully at some point, but also for our people. Although a few would no doubt come with us when we left Earth for the stars, most wouldn't.

This would provide them somewhere to bring in supplies and more. There'd been all the fuckups not long ago from that ship crashing in the Suez Canal and blocking it off, and I didn't want that happening here, so that was enough of a reason to hit the eighty meters.

The unnamed superyacht that was undergoing repairs still, formerly owned by Athena, was twenty meters at the widest, and nearly five in depth, giving it plenty of space, in my mind.

Apparently, the best plan, if that was the main size of vessel to be sailed down it, was to have at least half again its length as the width, in case of bad weather— and again, I pointed out that either a maritime pilot who knew their shit would be sailing it, or said pilot would be outside with a fuckin' shovel.

Moving on from that, now that my feelings were understood, we discussed the second stage for the area.

The lake itself was to be roughly circular, with the deepest section fifty meters below the surrounding land, which, in turn, would be twenty meters below the average for the area.

Great awnings would be buried into the ground and extended inward toward the lake, angled at forty-five degrees or so, creating a solid area of shade, and yet plenty of light still, for the plants.

The plants, it was decided, would be a mix of trees, hardy, quick growing grasses, and small shrubs, all enhanced with Belle's aid, and hopefully that of her sisters.

The land they'd be planted in would be, again, soil converted from the surrounding sand and rock, and churned over to a depth of about ten meters.

That meant that the ten meters of "dead" sand on the top, basically rock and silica, and the next five meters of "medium dead" ground below the top level, but not totally fucked by centuries of baking heat and scoured by sand, was to be entirely converted.

The next five meters of pretty dead, but not totally fucked ground was to be mixed in, giving it some of the local bacteria and bulking it up a bit. This still meant that the surrounding area would be at least a good few meters above the average for the land around the lake, and a section was to be built atop the awnings.

That would funnel windblown sand into channels that would, in turn, be fed directly to converters.

Those converters would work to create dense blocks of nutrient-rich fertilizer, and they, in turn, would be fed to the plants.

This, combined with the sudden presence of billions of liters of water, would essentially jump-start the local water cycle, I'd been assured. And Belle had earlier added in that she and Par'a—once they awoke—would be able to increase the growth rates of any and all trees and plants in the area by an order of magnitude.

It'd take awhile, admittedly: the entire plan would take about a year, thereabouts, and the terraformers, once they'd finished their own specific sections, would be set on a permanent rotation.

The lake's ones would be the first to finish, despite it being several miles across, as machines that were automated and with restricted intelligences running them— once Zac earned access on his own quests to create them—didn't need sleep.

They'd also have their own onboard custodians to repair them, so there was that.

Once they'd finished the lake, and they were established, they'd move around the outside of the awnings, working in greater and greater loops, converting the sand back to soil.

Hopefully, by that point, we'd have at least one of Belle's sisters helping to ensure that the grasses and more grew quickly, forming a solid mat that would resist the destruction of the desert.

Then, once the second river up to Chad and across Libya to the west was finished, those terraformers would create the second, smaller lake, and repeat the process of converting the surrounding ground.

The trio that would head to the northern coast would return along the length of the river, chewing up and regurgitating usable, arable land behind them as they worked their way back to the recycling plant.

Once they were there?

Well, we'd pick a second area, and start its conversion.

Rewilding the entire Sahara, I was coming to realize, would take decades, not the handful of years I'd first envisaged. But that was fine, because once we were ready?

We'd make more terraformers, and speed that right up.

There was also a need to get the forests up and running. Although Belle had assured me prior to starting her "upgrade" that she could do it herself, literally flash-growing miles of forests to maturity over only a matter of months?

I needed it to be faster, and more efficient.

To that end, Marie had been switched from criminal hunting, with her little team of Dave and Amanda helping her, to dryad hunting.

Dave had looked pissed off at that, seriously so. He'd not been happy about the criminal hunting, until he'd gotten into it and found he was surprisingly good at spotting the patterns, and had been enjoying it.

Once he realized that it might well result in a group of sex-crazed, beautiful women—or greater dryads—wandering around, though, he perked right up.

"I mean, this is for the planet, not for me," he added, trying to hide his grin, until Amanda did something out of sight and he whimpered a bit.

The locations of Belle's lost sisters were described as best as she could, and although Marie now had rough areas that she suspected matched up, there would be days to months of work needed yet to confirm.

Jamya, the youngest of the sisters, according to Belle, was "buried in the mountains far to the west. A landslide had long ago consumed her valley, leaving only small fractions of her exposed."

Considering the mountain ranges and the location I'd found Belle, most likely that meant the Alps, in Spain, Norway, or Sweden.

Annai was described as "on a small island far, far from here, south and east, almost the entire world between us." We were looking at that as possibly being somewhere in the Galápagos Islands.

Belle had said that wherever she was, it'd be lush and wild, with few, if any, humans, pointing out that if there were many humans about, they'd all be playing "hide the sausage" with her a lot, and over the centuries, word would have to get out.

The Galápagos Islands were both beautiful—lush and overgrown, a paradise by most people's standards—and had suffered relatively recent volcanic eruptions that had killed off a lot of the life on those islands.

That the plant life grew back so fast and so vibrantly pointed to a caring hand, and one that might well have been lost from human memory thanks to the volcanoes' activity.

The last of the three lost sisters was Barishka, and she lived "in a hidden valley far to the south," which pointed to somewhere in the Burma, Vietnam, Thailand, and Bangladesh area, although admittedly, that was a pretty vague location.

There were a fuckload of legends of a mother earth goddess situated in those lands, though, and some truly wild places that were insanely hard to get to.

My bet was some little valley in the mountains there, almost impossible to reach, and when the explorers did manage it, they met a woman who was their ultimate ideal, and a lush verdant paradise.

Dryads weren't evil, but they sure as shit weren't "good" either. They saw the world as their responsibility to heal, to pour their plants across, and as the greater version, they were insanely powerful.

That only four still survived was probably down to maniacal pogroms in the past, as I couldn't imagine people being too happy about finding their loved ones disappearing in a certain location, then finding them moldering under trees, literally fucked to death, pleasured until their hearts gave out, and then being used as fertilizer.

Again, though, who fucking knew. That was guesswork on our part, and Belle genuinely didn't know. She just knew that there were once many of them, and that now, well, there weren't.

Some were eaten, some died in volcanic eruptions, or fires, earthquakes, meteor strikes, floods...you name it. The planet had a go at using it as a pest control method, so we'd probably never know.

What we did know was that we had a plan, and after carefully examining the options that the medical capsule offered, I'd accepted the Harvest selection and Belle was even now undergoing the upgrade.

Her status as a greater dryad had caused a few hiccups in the system at first. It saw her as complete, after all, not broken or failed versions like the rest of us, needing repair.

It'd accepted the command authority though, and it'd installed a harvest tool in her right arm and gave her access to the Harvest tree.

Now, as I finished talking over the plans, with Ingrid's help to make the images, maps, and designs clear, the others were onboard with it. I settled back, knowing that we'd gone from rough plans, all the way to a solid one in a remarkably short period of time.

Anders added in two more machine requests. First and foremost, as we'd already agreed, a massive new factory unit was to be built at the recycling center, in a giant warehouse, basically.

That factory unit would be where the terraformers would be put together initially. Then, as soon as they were out and working, there would be a new, smaller, and more specialized machine constructed.

It would be roughly the size of a small truck, five meters across and ten long, and it'd "chew" up the sand and ground from our base, heading all the way to the city of Dongola, in Sudan.

That'd provide us with a link to the city, as it laid a substantial mass of solid stone and train tracks as it went.

That, in turn, would make damn sure that not only could materials that were needed for recycling be delivered to us quickly, easily, and cheaply, but we'd have fast methods of travel should we need it, and it'd be a lot easier to move bulk to and from us.

The second machine he wanted?

Well, he might be a titan of industry now, but he'd started in the navy, and he'd seen and lived through the damage that prick Shamal had inflicted on us.

He wanted a second factory unit that could be used to make more constructors which would be, in turn, used to make a *fortress*.

It would look like a hotel, he'd explained when he unveiled the design. He'd apparently been working on it with Freja on their "downtime" as a family project, before roping Zac and his team in.

It would be modeled after the ancient Hanging Gardens of Babylon. First, because it was a stunning design that made the most of water and plants, and in a location like this, that would be insanely impressive. Secondly, the gardens, flowing waterfalls, and plants would make it much harder for anyone to see anything from orbit and any real distance, which meant that anything could be hidden. And thirdly, the world deserved something wondrous out of this, and frankly, so did we all.

It would be armored to fuck, and as I nodded at the design they'd made first, he grinned and showed me the second version.

It looked much the same: a bit wider, a bit squatter, and with plenty of bulbous protrusions here and there that made it look like domes for who knew what. Probably stargazing or something.

Then they stripped away the plants and the water, and extended the cannons.

It was a fucking fortress, all right. Literally, all the way around, it had batteries of cannons, both smaller laser versions that I guessed had been scaled up from the sentinel class-three version, all the way to stuff that I recognized as incorporating gravity and rail gun technology.

315

They'd be able to clear the *skies* with this once I was gone—tear missiles apart, including the most powerful nukes that the human nations had—and they'd be sitting pretty.

I saw shield generators marked out, fusion plants, construction areas, and housing...Then I looked at the size markers again.

The original had been three hundred meters on a side. A big building, all right. The new one?

Two fucking *miles* on a side.

It was square, and that converted to *three thousand meters* on a side, nine *million* square meters, and it went down four stories, and up five, stepping inward with each level.

Zac had put an estimate, even with everything we were doing, of having it finished to the point that it was livable and usable, of six months, and two years to have it "properly" complete.

That included the weapons emplacements, the walls being coated in a special armor that would prevent lasers from doing much damage, and more.

I took one look at Ingrid, and I approved it on the spot. This would be the home for our people regardless of what happened to us "out there" in space.

The rest of the meeting was more or less a catch-up event, and a fairly subtle feeling out on both sides as to who wanted to be upgraded, and when.

Lars's name was on the list, but being Lars, he'd made it clear that he would like it, yes—it was fucking immortality, after all—but he'd only accept it if his wife and children, and immediate family, were included.

That was, his parents, not the rest of the clan, as they were apparently the "poor relatives" of an Arisen who had their servants come and warn him off inquiring into me and Ingrid.

He'd played along, but since then, he'd been quietly separating himself and his parents from their clutches, realizing exactly what they were like.

Ingrid and I agreed, but on two conditions. First, we had no way of knowing what would happen to children who were inducted into the realities of life. We refused outright to do it until they were at least eighteen. For all we knew, it'd cease their aging process, leaving them as six-year-olds or whatever, literally forever.

The second point was that I'd do a deep dive on the parents and the entire clan, making goddamn sure that we wanted them having immortality, and that because it was at least seven damn people—he had both parents, him, his wife— she'd lost her parents—and three kids—he'd be waiting awhile.

The rest of the group were on the list as well: James, Anders, Freja, Ingrid's sister and the rest of her close clan, Jay, Paul, Courtney, Amanda—after the baby was born—Marie. Hell, even Dave was getting in.

Unfortunately a few details came to light with Jack, our previous cabin boy, including him taking liberties that weren't his to take. When I was told that he'd also told his parents some of what was going on and they'd gone ballistic with James, unsure if the story they were getting was accurate or not, that decided it.

As part of his contract was an insanely strict NDA, and he'd breached that, even though it was to his parents? When they asked he be released from the role, well it wasn't a hard decision.

I agreed with Anders's assessment when he asked, and asked that he be paid off and sent home asap, with an understanding that he wasn't to discuss anything that he knew, and would be "under observation" for a while, just in case.

Some of the locals had proved themselves as capable members of the project, and would have a chance at inclusion in the future, while others had disagreements and were let go.

One had apparently taken badly to this, being used to pushing people around and getting what he wanted. He'd threatened that he'd sell the information he had, and then had tried to steal a converter.

The Oracan had dealt with the incident in their own inimitable way.

As they saw it, he was a member of the tribe, who had attacked the tribe. The worst kind of transgression—not to mention betraying me, their new master.

They might not show me a great deal of respect outwardly, but that was a serious fucking no-no in their eyes.

He'd died hard, before Anders could intervene. And in truth, he wasn't that concerned.

The hippies were settling in well. Annabeth had apparently decided that all of the group being equals didn't really extend to the fact that she didn't want to run the washing room, and had palmed that off to the boy-band wannabes, making them do it instead.

Surprisingly, after one of them had seriously fucked up some of Freja's underwear—nothing perverted; he'd just put it on far too high a temperature and for too long—she'd taken the group to task, and they were now taking to the job with dedication.

Another hour was spent going over the last few details, before an alert went off in my mind—a signal sent from the capsule to let me know that the upgrade of Belle was done.

For a second, I had to stifle a snort of laughter. The sound that was associated with it wasn't intentional, but it sounded like the beep of my old microwave, letting me know that it was done reheating whatever abomination that was pretending to be my dinner.

That Belle was now ready, and hopefully wasn't either piping hot nor microwaved, made me smile as well, as I left the meeting at that point.

Oxus had refused to leave Belle's side while she was in the capsule. Although he would be a hell of a resource to us in our mission if we could have taken him, the simple truth was that after this, he'd be staying to help protect the ship.

He wanted to come with us, but he was huge, and the sheer number of nanites we needed to be able to reboot and restart his system just wasn't viable, not at this point.

That meant that if he came, he could die on the mission, and be lost forever, leaving Xous, his son, as an orphan. I'd not liked that he'd already left the boy behind. He was at the recycling plant, but the hippies were looking after him. Also, the Oracan were apparently loving training him to fight, as he was stronger than most of them, and they liked a challenge.

Belle, when I reached her, stood free of the capsule—Oxus had helped her down—and she stared in wonder at the harvest tool in her arm as she extended its tendrils.

With her, they looked more organic than my own did. I frowned, before realizing that it was her dryad heritage. She could adjust her body easily, instinctively becoming that which the males around her found most attractive—Oracan and Minotaur women were fuckin' scary-looking, as a side note—and that malleability served her well here, as she could extrude tendrils already that could hold the harvest tubes.

A little questioning as I checked that she was okay, and she reached out, laying her hands on mine, and asked for permission to "recover" the broken nanites of the others.

I hesitated, then told her that as long as she got that individual's permission, and it wouldn't hurt them, then sure, go for it.

She smiled brilliantly, before turning to Oxus and whispering something that made him grunt. Then she kissed him, growing even as she reached out to wrap her arms around him.

I thought for a second I'd misunderstood, and she was about to get "busy," when she pressed her right hand to the center of his broad, well-muscled chest.

He gasped, eyes opening wide, but held onto her, lowering his head to nuzzle at her neck. She groaned, tendrils like vines spreading out from the palm of her hand below his skin.

He let out stifled moans. A rivulet of blood seeped from under her hand and ran south, down his chest, making me go from slightly embarrassed, to concerned, and then back to embarrassed as the fact Oxus was enjoying what she was doing became apparent.

Ten seconds later, she stepped back. Oxus panted a little and looked at her with glazed eyes, as she removed her hand.

His skin looked disturbed, and there were two bloody entry wounds. But as I frowned, the blood stopped running, and he rubbed at it, glancing down as it started to heal over.

"What did you just do?" I asked her, and she smiled, even as Oxus, apparently having been told about modesty, or at least "please don't go swinging a giant horse cock around when you've got a hard-on" tried to hide it.

He apparently decided it was best to hide it behind her back, and she grinned as he "accidentally" prodded her with it.

"Down, boy," she murmured, glancing back at him, winking, and then turned to me. "I have some control over the feelings of others, as you know, and when a being is in the later, almost final stages of extreme sexual gratification, pain is felt significantly less.

"I suspected the process of removing, cleansing, and returning Oxus's builders—sorry, *nanites*—would be uncomfortable, so I helped to maintain him in that condition instead."

"Uh, yeah, I think you managed that," I agreed, sarcastically, before going on as a thought occurred to me. "Anyway, I know you can affect humans easily. We're going to need to get access to the airport, and keep people from searching the plane and so on. Can you help with that?"

"I can, but I'll need to be close to those I target. It's pheromones, I think you called them, the scents I can control. It makes most beings like me, and want to agree. I can force them to obey, but only for a short time, and only when I'm in contact with them. As soon as I stop? They'll recover, and they'll know I did something."

"That's no good. Any way you can make them just be happy with us and let us pass?" I asked, before hurrying on. "Without screwing them, I mean."

Oxus was clearly trying to hide his wood, while looking at me and giving me a hopeful "how about you fuck off for a bit, please" look.

"I can, but it works best if they want to do it anyway. So convince them of something, and I'll push them over the edge maybe? That way, they help to keep the illusion intact themselves."

"Okay, I'll think about it, and thanks. Ten minutes, then we're out of here," I warned the pair as I turned. "And keep the damn noise down!"

I knew, even as I started to walk away, that was a wasted request, but fuck it. I had to try. The damn place already echoed to buggery.

CHAPTER THIRTY-TWO⊙

The trip from the ship, up to the shallow area of the beach, where James had arranged a coach to meet us, was a bit boring…basically just a walk-and-talk situation, and the large and heavy suitcases that Jonas and I were carrying with the three sentinels, our equipment and weapons for the mission.

James had also arranged for a dozen other coaches to be moving around the island, as a sort of complicated shell game, just to confuse people if anyone checked out where we'd been, so that was fun too.

We'd agreed that as soon as I was settled on the coach, I'd reach out and add a recording of us all on the coaches—remotely, again—to fuck with any surveillance attempts.

All in all, I was damn glad when we dragged ourselves out of the steady surf on the beach several hours later, timing it so nobody was about, thankfully.

We all wore swimwear, our armored one-pieces in the bags, as five people striding from the sea, who hadn't entered it here, with waterproof suitcases—and seemingly buff as fuck, in my and Jonas's cases—had to be remarked upon.

Add in that once again, we'd had to explain the need to both Scylla and Belle to wear swimsuits at all, and Zac, being the filthy pervert he was, had provided them with essentially less cloth than was needed to floss with?

Ingrid was the most unremarkable of us all, and considering that she was a stunningly beautiful Nordic blonde, that was insane.

The coach waiting at the end of the beach was warm, the air sweltering as we boarded it. The look on the driver's face as the girls climbed past him was laughable.

He tried to insist that he didn't want sand on the coach, and that we'd better get dressed before we boarded, only to have Jonas pause and glare down at him. Then he changed his mind and decided it was fine, really.

Jonas, Scylla, and Ingrid had wiped and attuned nanites now, which apparently disappointed Belle slightly, but she'd assured them that she'd "help them to cleanse themselves later if they needed it."

I sat holding Ingrid's hand as we bounced along the dirt road back up to the main parking lot, and then to the highway, wondering whether I needed to understand exactly what Belle was doing to the others. Maybe just a little cleansing? I mean, sure, I was capable of cleansing myself a lot faster than the others were, but still. It'd be more in the nature of expanding my understanding, right?

I was certainly looking forward to Belle "cleansing" Ingrid's nanites at some point, if that was needed, though. Just for "scientific" curiosity, and not at all because I was a filthy pervert wanting to watch the woman I loved and…

I choked that thought off, and forced myself to reevaluate the area, as we passed through it, before leaning forward and speaking to the driver in Greek.

I'd picked up the basics before now, and when I'd seen how much easier people responded to their own language, I'd made slightly more of an effort there of late.

It helped that I was connected to the internet and just had to repeat the words I needed as I fed them into a translation program, then adjust with regard to the modern Greek language, over the ancient I'd already learned.

"Which way are we taking to the airport?" I asked him, and he glanced at me in the rearview mirror, clearly unimpressed with my butchery of his language.

"We go here…" he said, his heavily accented English clearly better than my Greek as he described the route.

"Great. We'll need to stop at the old bike repair and general store near Karteros Canyon…you know it?" I asked, my Greek flowing a lot better as I worked in the changes.

He glanced back at me in the mirror and frowned at the difference in my words, and I smiled. I'd been using a lot of the accent and phrasing that was in use around two thousand years ago, so yeah, he'd barely understood it at first.

My abilities, my access to the internet, the language download, the experience with swearing in Greek, as every worker learned quickly…all of it was coming together to make it much smoother.

"You mean Tommaso's place?" he asked in Greek that was—deliberately, I thought—so fast it was almost unintelligible.

"Yeah. He still there?"

"He was last month." The driver settled back, splitting his gaze between me and the road equally. "You got Greek family?"

"Just friends. Been awhile since I spoke it, though."

"You're getting better," he admitted, grudgingly. "We can stop there for gas. Needs a top-up anyway."

That was it, it seemed, as he went back to watching the road, and occasionally the girls, as I settled back with Ingrid.

"So, Dimi should be at the airport in a little over two hours," Ingrid whispered. "We've not got long—to stop and see your friend, I mean."

"It's—" I winced as I realized that yeah, she was right. I'd been thinking of the distance from where we were to the airport as about fifty minutes' drive, which it *was*…on a motorbike. Coaches always took longer, and not just because they were naturally slower.

The length of them meant that a lot of sneaky side roads were off-limits, roadworks meant that they were trapped on the main roads, and as to top speeds?

I was betting that a random coach rocking up to the private airfield side would draw a bit of attention. Especially when the plane that'd be landing around then was probably on just about every watch list around the world, and noticeably had a fucking mini-gun built into it, so we really needed to factor that in as well.

"Five minutes," I offered. "Give me five minutes, just to make sure the old bugger is all right, and then we can go."

"Dimi won't take off without us." She smiled. "It's our plane, after all. I just wanted to remind you, that's all."

"Thank you." I raised her hand, held in mine, and kissed the back of it, before smiling as she shifted around to squeeze under my arm and against me, pulling up the link between us, and starting to assemble a new file.

There were constant changes every time I saw this system. The command one wasn't something that I had access to unless Ingrid shared it with me. And even then, it was more like watching as someone shared their screen remotely on a laptop, rather than having access yourself, but still.

Ingrid was learning, and had apparently had a few more quests completed and rewards since we'd raided the people smugglers' base.

The system as she showed it now started with a map, an orbital view of the area we'd identified as most likely the rough location for the first hive.

It was in northeastern Russia, north of Mongolia, and about a hundred miles to the east of where I'd tentatively pegged the Erlking's domain as.

That fucker had done something, I was sure, as every time I tried to find its valley on a map, or mentally, my mind wandered, picking on some random clue or detail.

I'd blink and realize that I was looking at a city somewhere else, and when I tried instead to explain it to Ingrid, so she could find it?

Nada—my words were crap.

I just couldn't explain it, like when you were drunk and you lost track of a conversation halfway through…it was like that.

Instead, I'd worked on marking out where the Oracan villages I'd visited were, and then I shifted along the line from there, picking out the lycan camps, until I found what I guessed was the village I'd accidentally set Eto up as the leader of.

Ingrid was working things out, sharing them with me as she did so, and I was amazed as she went at it.

The map expanded outward, all the way into orbit, to show where we were now, a line drawn from here to there, with a parabolic arc to account for the plane's capabilities.

The engines didn't need fuel, so there was no need for a stop for refueling, but the flight itself was still going to take several hours. It was around five and a half thousand kilometers, or three and a half thousand miles, I roughly worked it out as.

The top speed of the plane was over three thousand miles an hour, so in theory we could do that distance in about an hour and a half. But even as I thought that, Ingrid popped up a small box on the side of the image, and a dozen different designs of missile and fighter jet showed up in it.

Zooming out, and showing our plane in comparison…yeah, we could easily be mixed up for one of those.

So instead, she routed us around the southern edge of Russia, taking us through mountains and more, deliberately figuring a route that would make the most of our radar invisibility, and make sure we passed as few inhabited areas as possible.

Her notes made it clear that the initial thought if anyone saw us was that we were a first strike-capable fighter or missile in flight. They'd scramble counters to us if they were even slightly paranoid. And considering how cheerful and trusting Russia was at the best of times?

That was a problem.

We tried the route a dozen different ways, until we finally picked the best one, a path that flew out south by southeast over Saudi Arabia, out into the Indian Ocean, and then northeast once we'd done half of the journey.

We'd pass over Bangladesh, staying low and using the heavy forests for cover from ground-based systems, then up through the mountains and across Tibet into Mongolia, then finally into Russia.

It was longer, taking about three to three and a half hours all told, and would need Dimi to be seriously on point to keep us out of sight, but it was the best possible route. It also didn't require us flying all the way around Europe and to pass Russia to the northwest.

Once the route was plotted, the next stage was worked on, with everything from possible food in the area—she was pulling up foods that were known to grow wild in a rough area—and the kinds of things we were likely to find, then cross-referenced that with what kind of foods we were likely to find underground and more.

She'd already arranged a list of supplies that were on board with Dimi, and I stared in amazement at it, as well as amusement. She'd basically have us all being pack horses with that much gear, and I winced as I saw the effort she'd put in.

I started to sort through the list, marking things like the four tents as not needed, one would do, when a sad face appeared in my vision, followed by a sexy image.

I grinned, then moved on.

We'd be hitting a pair of sites, both the upper and lower hives, and then killing the queen, before getting the fuck out of there and heading back.

I compared the masses of gear that we had on the plane, to the literal small backpack I'd taken to survive crossing Russia with, and snorted.

We'd be going for a hard, fast hit, not a bloody protracted hike, and at least eighty percent of this crap would be staying on the plane.

I reached out to the others—with Ingrid's permission; it was her system, after all—and I tied them in, getting everyone's attention on the list.

Ten minutes later, it was down to a small backpack each, the rest being left behind, and Ingrid feeling a bit annoyed, considering the effort she'd put into the list, when I started to explain.

We weren't human, I reminded her.

Not anymore, anyway, and as such, we didn't need a lot of the things that humans needed.

Shelter? It was a military-style operation—we didn't have a need for shelter in the traditional sense. And, most likely, we'd be underground for most of the time we were there.

A bedroll would do, at the most, and probably, we'd not even need that. We had two small sentinels with us as scouts and watchdogs, essentially, so we could sleep, or at least rest. But as strong as we were, we didn't really need to sleep for a few days.

Night-vision goggles? Nope. Our augmented vision was already better than they were. Firestarters? Sure, we'd take a few, but that was it, and we'd probably not need them. A flint and tinder would be scroungable, if I remembered the rocks in the area right.

Food? Not really much needed. We had enemies, after all: we'd eat them if they were edible. And if not? Well, a few days was all we'd be there for. Two days of emergency rations was more than enough, each. I'd damn well forgotten supplies on my first trip to the ship, and besides being a bit annoyed and hungry, I'd been fine.

Changes of clothes, replacements for damaged clothing, and toiletries? Just…no. At the very most, a single change of clothes and a few small details, like some toothpaste and soap.

Lights, tents, emergency flares, camp beds, folding chairs, a pop-up table, a mini-stove…The list went on and on, and as much as I loved her for it, things like black bags to clean up our rubbish as we went?

Nope.

We'd be deep in enemy territory, fighting for our lives against giant insects that could kill and drive out Oracan tribes. I wasn't concerned about leaving literally a turd in the passageways.

Wipes? Yeah, I suppose I could see the need, and hopefully there'd be underground water sources…but if not, two flasks of water each.

Jonas and Scylla went through the list in a matter of minutes, scrapping most of it and Scylla, being as subtle as she was, burst out laughing at some of the items.

The rest of the journey to Tommy's place was spent with me trying to cheer Ingrid the fuck up.

By the time we got there, I was damn glad to get out of the coach, even if I was a bit nervous about what I'd find inside.

Tommy was there, I saw straightaway. The big bugger had his back to me as I walked in the door, arguing in English with an older woman I'd never seen before, and who glared at him as he tried to explain that he'd always run his shop this way, everyone knew where his stuff was, and there was no need to change it.

Her response was simply that was the point. People who went to buy just a bottle of water, got it, then paid and left. People who looked around a little first might spot other things they wanted, and they'd buy more.

He was swearing about how he didn't want people hanging around, that he liked the shop being empty, for fuck's sake, and she started in on how much time he already wasted "on those damn bikes," as I cleared my throat.

She pushed him out of the way as he turned around to look, and as she marched past him, putting a wide and obviously fake smile on her face, his eyes widened.

"Steve?" I saw the word on his lips as she shifted into halting Greek and asked if she could help.

"I'm here to pay a debt." I smiled, and she frowned, before clicking her fingers.

"The bike!" she said, and as I nodded, she went on, clearly picking up speed and anger. "You're the one! You rode off yesterday without paying for the fuel…Well, someone saw you on social media and shamed you into coming back, didn't they…"

"Marina…" Tommy said slowly, stepping up and putting a hand on her shoulder.

"No, Tommy! You're too kind! You'd let them all off with a warning, but he—"

"He's not the thief!" Tommy said more forcefully, giving her shoulder a little shake. "And I think he's the reason I got that bike out back."

"What?" she said.

I grinned at him, stepping up. "Hey, Tommy," I said simply, pausing and surprised at the nerves I felt inside. "I...I'm sorry, man."

"You're alive!" he snapped, stepping forward and enveloping me in a bear hug, squeezing hard enough to hurt a normal man.

I laughed; I couldn't help it. I hugged my friend back.

"I am!" I grinned as he gave me a rough kiss on each cheek. "Ah, get off, you horny old goat!" I snorted, and he shook his head in amazement.

"I thought they caught you," he said softly, before frowning as he clearly started to wonder where the fuck I'd been for three years, and why I'd not been in touch.

"They did. They caught me, man, and well, it's been a hard few years."

"You look good," he admitted, shaking his head as he looked at me. "Even in whatever that is."

I grinned again. We'd all taken the time once we'd gotten aboard the coach to change into our one-pieces. I had to imagine that was why the driver had nearly crashed into oncoming traffic twice. Ingrid, Jonas, and I had taken turns changing in the tiny onboard toilet, or on the back seats out of sight. But Belle and Scylla had simply stood in the middle of the gangway and had gone for it, totally unconcerned.

Tommy frowned as he looked at the all-in-one outfit, its figure-hugging material, and the obvious armoring here and there that I'd had Zac add.

Ingrid and the others had followed me into the shop, and she was picking out T-shirts and overalls and more from the small rack of clothing that had been added, while they grabbed essentials, like energy drinks and chocolate.

"We've got access to some good gear." I shrugged. "Can we talk?"

"This is Marina." He introduced the woman who he'd almost knocked over in grabbing me. "She is my..."

"I'm his partner," she clarified as he seemed at a sudden loss for words. "Both in the business, and at home."

"Congratulations!" I grinned, looking from one to the other, before she glared at me, and I took a step back reflexively.

"You're Steve?" she asked, suddenly putting the name and details together. "The one who stole his favorite bike?"

"Yes."

"No," he corrected.

"I did." I said, "I meant to bring it back, but..."

"I gave it to you." He shrugged, looking embarrassed. "I knew you'd probably not come back, but—"

"As long as I've known you, you've gone on about that bloody bike," she said hotly. "Now you're saying he didn't steal it, and he says he did! So what happened?"

"I borrowed it, and promised to bring it back in a few days, then I got kidnapped," I said. "It took me awhile to get free, and now, as I'm passing through, I wanted to make sure you got my apology."

"Kidnapped?" She frowned, being totally ignored by us both.

"The bike?" The edges of his lips turned up into a smile.

"Yeah."

"I got it," he said, the smile going full blown. "You know how many of those there are left in the world? How'd you get it?"

"It was the one you always said was the best Harley ever." I shrugged. "It was the best apology I could come up with."

"They're *expensive,* man! How'd you find it? There's no 1943 Knuckleheads about, none, not for real money and...?"

I turned, finding Ingrid close by, looking as if she were examining a stand of tourist crap, but clearly trying to listen in and be ready if I needed her.

"This is Ingrid." I waved her over, introducing her. "She's my partner, in our businesses and our lives." I mimicked the way Marina had laid claim to Tommy.

"Be welcome!" he said quickly, forcing a smile, while stepping back a little, and I winced.

"Tommy?"

"Yeah?"

"She's good...it's all right," I said firmly, knowing how much he, as a shop owner, should be great with people, and instead was the opposite, hating to meet anyone new. "You can trust her. And she helped me to get you that bike."

"Ummm, thank you." Ingrid frowned, not understanding but trusting me, as the coach driver walked in, calling that we needed to get moving if we were to make the flight.

"Look, Tommy, we've got a flight to catch, but we'll be back soon, I hope. I just...I needed to come and see you, to tell you I'm sorry."

He shrugged. "It's all right. You've been busy. Kidnapped?" He flicked his gaze to Ingrid, then to me and tried to smile as if to suggest she'd dragged me off.

"Like I said, it was a hard few years," I admitted softly. "Ingrid, could you get everyone on the coach, please? I'll pay for this."

The coach driver shrugged and moved off, clearly not about to refuse an idiot who wanted to pay for the fuel.

Ingrid kissed my cheek, thanked them both, and said it was nice to meet them, that they'd hopefully see each other again, and then directed everyone out of the shop, even as Marina complained she'd not had time to count up what we'd grabbed.

"I'll take care of it," I assured her again, reaching out and plucking the card machine from the table, and inputting fifty thousand euros.

I made it look as if I was pressing my card to the machine, despite not having one, and did it all through my Hack capabilities. She shook her head, complaining that even if I was his friend, I shouldn't be touching the card machine, when she saw the receipt that started to print off, and the money I'd just put through.

She showed it, eyes wide and staring, to Tommy, and he nodded, as if it were nothing.

"That bike was a quarter of a million euros, easy," he said, and I nodded.

"A bit more," I admitted. "Those are the original parts, and she had to be shipped, but yeah."

"The one I loaned you was worth maybe eight, ten at most."

I smiled, unable to help myself.

"I needed a bike. I had nothing, and I got a change of clothes, a helmet, a bike, and no questions asked from a friend. That was fuckin' priceless, Tommy. The least I could do was get you the bike you'd always raved about. Money isn't really an issue."

I took him off to one side. I didn't have long, but also, a damn minute more here wasn't going to make too much of a difference.

"I told you they were hunting me, right?" I asked, and he nodded. "Well, they found me, and they hurt me, man, a lot. Torture and worse. I won't say more, but Ingrid? She risked her life for years to protect me, to help me. And when I say she's good? I mean it. In the end, I killed them all, man—all that I could find, anyway—and now I hunt them."

"The government?"

"Them and others," I said, unable to say much. But he'd believed me to be hunted by the government in the past, and the rich fuckers who had turned out to be the Arisen. "All that matters, my friend, is that I'm alive, and free now, and I took their money from their corpses, so why the hell shouldn't I send you a little gift, to say thanks?"

"You didn't have to." He looked embarrassed.

"Tommy," I said, "you knew I was being hunted, and that helping me might cost you everything, and you still damn well did it. You'll never know how much that meant to me. And I'm sorry it's taken me until now to come back and tell you thank-you."

"You helped me enough," he mumbled, before glancing at Marina. "Met her a year or so back. Friends for a bit, then…you know."

"Yeah?" I smiled. "Life good?"

"It is. It'd be better if she didn't keep changing things, though."

"That's what they do, mate." I snorted. "The best of them change our lives around, and we're better for it. Look, if you ever need me, there's a hotel, on the other side of the island, in Agios Nikolaos…"

I described it, and Val, and told him that if he needed me, to get word to Val, and he'd be able to get word to me.

The coach honked the horn again, and I gave my friend a last hug, before leaving, feeling like I'd had no time with him, no chance to do anything but drop unsubtle hints and fuck off, but also?

I felt lighter, relieved, and fuck me, I felt a lot happier in some utterly stupid way.

I'd not got the chance to say anything really, but the little I'd said, and knowing that he didn't hate me? It was worth it.

CHAPTER THIRTY-THREE

"Do you feel better?" Ingrid asked, and I nodded, smiling at her, surprised by how much better I did feel, even as the coach bumped across the little curb. The whole thing swayed from side to side as the crappy suspension and the massive curbs made themselves known.

"I do, thank you. I bought the...well, I probably bought the store," I admitted, knowing that Tommy's entire stock was probably worth a quarter of what I'd just spent there.

"We need to see Val when we come back as well," Ingrid said, nodding. "We need to make sure he's okay, and check in...let him see that we're still okay, and still together."

"And stay in that room again." I nudged her with one shoulder.

"I'd like that." She winked, a little blush rising in her cheeks. "I remember our first room there as well."

"We broke the bed, as I recall," I murmured, and she shot a tight-lipped smile at me, nodding.

"Then you made me spend hours on that bike the next day...I could barely walk," she pointed out, and it was my turn to wink.

The conversation went nowhere after that, breaking down into in-jokes about the bedroom and reminiscences, as well as things we'd like to do, ranging from sailing the superyacht up and down the Med, screwing each other's brains out the entire way, wearing nothing the whole time—and presumably either telling everyone to stay out of sight and give us privacy, or somehow work it so that we could manage the yacht alone—and having romantic dinners.

We talked about having her family with us—not for the sex-capades bit—and she asked whether I wanted to reach out to any of my own family.

She pointed out that as much experience as she was getting with the systems now, if she couldn't find them straightaway, she'd be able to do it soon, certainly.

My mother had abandoned us when I was a kid, moving on with another guy, presumably—or girl...who knew. She'd gone out for cigarettes and just never came back. Her room had been stripped of anything of value to her, and our family bank accounts cleaned out as well, as I'd heard it later.

Either way, I certainly wasn't going looking for her. And my father? He'd married again, pretty quick, and he'd made it clear I was an uncomfortable reminder of his earlier life that he'd rather do without.

I had step-siblings, and a stepmother, and they, like he, had made it clear I was about as welcome as syphilis in their new life.

I'd moved out at sixteen, and aside from occasionally going to see them out of a sense of obligation, like when I was with the ex and she'd force me to try to "mend bridges"? I'd basically fucking left them alone.

No, the only reason I'd reach out to them was if I figured out a way to fuck with them. And I was honest enough with myself to admit that I'd thought a few times about hacking their banks and making their mortgages and so on be marked up as defaulting, just as petty revenge.

There was no need, though. That part of my life was over, and had been long before I'd left humanity behind as well.

Now I was free, and fuck them all.

We joked and laughed, flirted, and I made a point of looking down Ingrid's top, whispering utter filth in her ear and getting her as frustrated as possible—all the things that you do to pass the time on a coach journey—before finally we rocked up to the entrance to the private section of Heraklion Airport.

There were smaller, private airfields dotted around the country, but fuck it, Dimi had insisted on using this one. Ingrid had agreed, knowing that, regardless, the plane would be watched for, and it'd have been seen landing and taking off.

If it was seen taking off from the main government-owned airport on the island, then it at least cast doubt on anything that the Cretan government said about not knowing we were there to others, and further muddied the waters.

Now we were slowing at the entrance to the airfield, a barrier across the road, as two bored-looking security guards stood watch, and a pair of local armed backup squinted out of the hut, where they were sheltering from the sun.

I reached out, focusing on the local area, and found the signals I wanted only a handful of seconds later. Their radios used a repeater signal in the little hut, and I sensed machines in there, computers and more.

I hacked them, the struggle barely worth noticing as I took them down, killed the air conditioning, and passed control of them over to Ingrid, who took it like a pro.

Ingrid looked up at me, and I nodded, climbing out of my seat and twisting around to get Belle's attention, making sure she was dressed and that our body armor was covered by the long-sleeved T-shirts and jeans. I also made damn sure that the armor plates were subtle, and that the dagger that sat behind my back was hidden. That was the last thing I needed, after all.

She stood as well, moving up to join me. The two of us climbed down the stairs, stepping out of the air-controlled minor discomfort of the coach, and into the full, late-morning heat of the summer, as the guards in the hut started swearing about the local power company.

The pair before us strode up, watching us impassively from behind their sunglasses, before demanding passes and passports.

I stepped up to them, smiling widely, staring down at them from at least a foot of additional height and probably half again their weight in solid muscle, as I started to speak.

I could already feel Belle working. My nanites perked up as they worked to counter the unintentional backlash from her pheromones and abilities.

The guards slowed, seeming to relax a little, and I smiled happily, handing the new fake passports over.

"We're here to catch our flight," I told them, deliberately being as unthreatening as possible. "The plane just landed, and it's hot out here…"

"It's summer," one of them replied grimly. "Papers."

"Papers?" I asked. "No. You were supposed to have this all sorted out."

"We were?" The other frowned.

"Well, yeah, the guards…" I acted confused. "We left this morning and were told that we just needed to come back through this gate? The guards who were on at the time said they would make sure everything was dealt with…some issue with the power going out and they had no computers? Ah crap, dammit, what were we told your names were again, uh…"

Yanni and Georgiou…

I smiled as Ingrid sent me that, and I dutifully repeated the names, getting a start when they heard them, mentally marking down which was which from their startled movements.

"And who told you our names?" the less happy of the pair asked, and I frowned.

They came on shift an hour ago.

"We left this morning," I repeated. "A quick visit to town, then back to the plane to continue on. Your shift changed, what? An hour ago?"

Francis and Constantine were on earlier.

"Francis and…ah, man, I forget the other guy's name…Constantinople? He told us your names."

"Constantine," the guard grunted, relaxing slightly.

"Yeah!" I smiled. "Sorry, always been bad with names, me. Anyway, they looked at our passports, said there was a problem with the system this morning. It kept crashing…something about the power," I repeated.

"Again?" The guard glared, shaking his head as he reached up to trigger the radio, getting only static. Then he cursed in Greek.

The one I'd marked as Georgiou glanced at the passports, popping open the first two, seeing myself, then Belle, and squinted in the windows of the coach.

He grunted, moving past me and climbing onto the coach to check the images of them against the people he saw before him.

"Constantine and Francis said they'd mark down our passports and fill out anything that was needed for us, when we came through earlier," I pointed out to the lone guy—Yanni—now. "They said that as we'd paid the handling fee, they'd sort it all out?"

I saw that wince all right, and I pressed on, resisting the urge to say something like "These aren't the droids you're looking for" and wave my hand.

"Do we need to go to the main security desk?" I asked, and again, the wince came back. "I mean, we can if need be. It'd probably delay our flight, though…and when we lose our takeoff slot…"

Greek islands, or at least the ones I'd traveled, had no more issues with corruption than anywhere else that I'd been. Surprisingly, they were just more concentrated at the lower levels. They certainly weren't corrupt to the level that the UK Parliament was, or any other "banana republic," as I'd heard them called.

No, the issue with the Greek islands, and its corruption, was primarily forced upon it by the infrastructure.

They'd been a victim so long of the "ah, fuck it, minimum investment now, and we'll fix it later" mindset that everything broke down regularly.

That, in turn, led to a system that was full of backhanders and minor corruption because nobody ever knew for sure whether the system they were working on was genuinely broken and whether the guy on the last shift had been, in truth, accepting a bribe or not.

The only way to know was to directly ask them, and that would lead to awkward questions. The alternative was to pass it higher, in which case an investigation would be launched, and certain details that might lead back to others could then be raised.

Such as if the guard in question had been accepting the occasional "gift" himself.

No, it was best to ignore it as much as possible, play it cool, and as long as there was nothing screaming that it was out of the ordinary? Don't dig too deep. If it's someone else's fuck-up? It's someone else's problem.

The other guard stomped down the steps, looking at his companion and nodding that it all looked normal.

Right now, that meant that they needed to take us to the main building, which meant getting more guards over here first, then arguing with us, and possibly pissing the rich foreigners off.

Once we inevitably complained and the "handling fee" was brought up, they'd possibly get their colleagues screwed over with a bribery investigation, and maybe end up being looked into themselves.

Not to mention, if the others got fired for it, what that'd do to the situation in the staffroom...No, these people were clearly rich, stupid, and they'd shown him their passports happily enough. A quick look at the coach, and nothing stood out...plus, the driver was a regular local, so fuck it.

Nod and smile, nod and smile, and get rid of the rich idiots. The air conditioning breaking down was clearly a much more important issue.

Five minutes later, the coach rolled to a halt at the small terminal five building. The driver peered around curiously, but didn't see anything interesting as we climbed out and waved him off.

Two minutes later, we were all staggering back as Dimi brought the plane in fast and hard, the local air traffic control screaming at him for jumping the queue, before shutting the hell up as he presented his plane ID.

Archangel One was the ID that air traffic control was given for this plane, and fuck did they shut up when they'd had the chance to examine it, setting off who knew how many markers from the government that came complete with "do not fuck these people off" warnings.

Five minutes after the plane had landed, we were strapped in, with Dimi climbing again, not bothering to taxi into position, or really listen to the local air traffic control.

"Why did we have to come here again, instead of picking us up on the beach?" I asked him, braced against the door into the cockpit as he grinned maniacally back at me. "I mean, I get fucking with the locals so they argued over us being allowed to use the airport or not, but..."

His fiancée was nowhere to be seen, and the dog was happy in his little cubby, so I slid into the copilot seat and squinted at all the tech around me, before shaking my head.

"My ex works here!" he called, his headphones making him shout a little louder than needed, and I frowned.

"So?"

"So I wanted to see if she'd recognize my voice!" He laughed. "Maybe I should buzz the tower?"

"You mean we sat on a fucking coach across half the country, getting our arses beaten numb by shitty seat leather, just for that?" I growled at him, and he blinked, then forced a nervous smile.

"Uh, I needed somewhere to land?" he tried.

"It's a fucking VTOL! You're gonna be landing in a goddamn clearing in Russia in a few hours!"

"Uh…yeah, but you know, um…fuel?"

"*I* made the changes to this plane," I said through gritted teeth. "Do you even know what the fuel is?"

"Ah." He chewed his lip for a few seconds, then shrugged. "Perk of the job?"

"What?"

"A perk of the job. You know, you get an awesome pilot who'll fly through a city under fire for you, and I get to do things like that, now and then?"

"Once a year," I growled, impressed by his cheerful madness if nothing else.

"Twice a month," he countered, grinning maniacally.

"Twice a year, and I won't tell your fiancée that you diverted to see your ex in Crete."

"But—"

"I'm a bastard, remember?" I asked, and he glared at me before sighing and offering his hand.

I took it to shake on the deal, and he spoke quickly.

"Quarterly it is then!" Then he released my hand and started flicking dials and switches. "Now, sorry, boss, but I need to concentrate. Maybe you should go back and sit with the other…passengers?"

I didn't want to know what he was about to call the passengers before he stopped himself, but "cattle" would have probably been the nicest bit. I sighed, then gave up on it.

We could look for a new pilot, but they'd be presented to us by some enemy agency. Hell, they'd probably be bribed by at least a dozen of them at the same time. At least I knew that Dimi hadn't started out that way. And he, in turn, knew that I could fuck with the systems of pretty much anyone, and the only way he got to fly the absolute cutting-edge of planes was by flying for me exclusively.

Two and three-quarter hours it took, as he'd loved hammering the ship to higher power. By the time we came in for a landing outside the Oracan village, the sun was setting, a riot of reds and golds dappling the trees and lengthening the shadows. I leapt free, landing with bended knees on the ground below, not bothering with the rear ramp, nor the ladder. I looked about, seeing half-grown and seemingly abandoned crops all around us, making me wonder what was going on.

I strode forward. The filthy faces of Oracan guards squinted at me over the walls as I neared, lifting both hands in the air.

"Eto!" I called in the Oracan language. "It's St—"

I was cut off by a hail of arrows. I swore, dropping down low and swinging my arm overhead, focusing as my nanites formed a sharply slanted—if thin—shield.

"Quit that, you dickheads!" I screamed at them. "Or so fuckin' help me, I'll kill you all!"

Arrows slammed into the shield, over and over, shattering and deflecting to the sides. I glared at the camp as the Oracan readied a second volley.

A harsh voice barked out orders, stopping them.

"The Steve?" Eto shouted back, and I stood as the last of the arrows clattered to the ground.

"Who the fuck else is it going to be?" I shouted back, striding forward.

"Kim…he is with you in the silver bird?" Eto asked hopefully.

I hesitated, wondering why…before snorting and shaking my head, getting a growl of anger and disappointment.

Kim had told me, since he'd joined my "tribe," that for the Oracan, leadership was a position of power, but also responsibility. It was in most cultures obviously, but in the Oracan they took that to extremes.

Everyone respected the tribal leader, but that respect resulted in them needing direction for just about everything. Or, instead, they were *dis*respecting them.

That meant that although being the chief looked great from the outside, as you got to do whatever you "wanted," and everyone else did what they were told?

In practice? You became a virtual prisoner of the job. As you could neither complain about it—that was seen as weakness in the Oracan people—nor quit, you had two options once you learned the truth.

You could take on a sub-chief, like he'd tried to do with Kim when we'd been leaving, essentially forcing the old chief he'd displaced to do the job he'd just escaped for none of the bonuses and all the grief. Or you could let yourself be supplanted by a new chief, and either fuck off into the wilderness…accept you're now a nobody in the tribe…or fight to the death.

Eto didn't want to give up the position, and seemingly, nobody was appropriate to lead as sub-chief.

Kim had laughed his ass off about it, as apparently the best of those Oracan who were suitable were forced out of the tribe with me, because Eto hadn't wanted competition for his role.

He was left with great warriors and skilled crafters—loyal members of the tribe, one and all—but nobody suitable to lead in his place.

Eto would also be finding out that he wasn't suitable to lead about now, Kim had declared, sniggering around the edge of his cup when we'd discussed it. He was too bull-headed and too immature.

Kim had suggested we wait another month or so, and then we'd go visit, and he'd recruit the best and brightest from the clan to join ours.

When I'd asked him about the rest of the clan, he'd looked at me like I was an idiot and he'd said that if they worked harder, he'd try to recruit them, and if they didn't, why would we want them?

It reminded me of an old joke, that basically went that "vegetarian" was an old name for a useless hunter, mainly because they couldn't catch anything, so they were forced to eat veggies instead of real food.

I doubted it was true, but it still amused the shit outta me.

Now I was reminded of the shit that Kim had warned me about, especially as I saw the haggard and stressed look on Eto's face.

"What do you want, the Steve?" he asked, and I stifled a growl.

"It's just fucking *Steve,* Eto!" I snapped.

"Fine! What do you want, fucking Steve!"

I reminded myself stabbing him to death would be a bad thing for cultural relations. I took a deep breath before going on, and made myself be as subtle as possible, even as I felt Ingrid and the others watching.

"Where's the Stelek hives?" I forced out, and I got a minute of silence.

"Why?" he growled. The gates opened and he strode out, noticeably in full armor that no longer fit him, with a belly that was somehow already forcing the seams apart.

"Why the hell do you think?" I snapped back. "I'm going to invite them to a party, with blackjack and fuckin' hookers!"

"What party?" he asked after a second. "Hunting party? You hunt Oracan?"

"What? No, you fucking idiot. Why the hell did you think that? I'm going to kill them!"

"Why?"

"Because the Erlking asked me to!"

"Good. I order you, too—go do it!" He grunted, turning away from me and starting to walk back into the camp.

"Where the fuck are they, Eto?" I repeated. "You want them dead? You need to tell me where they are!"

"The caves!"

"WHAT FUCKING CAVES!" I roared at him, starting to follow; I got a glare from him, as half a dozen Oracan stepped up, drawing their arrows back and aiming at my heart. "Where are they?"

"One more step, and we fire," he growled. "Idiot, leave now!"

"I need to know where I'm going, Eto!" I snarled, frantically trying to control my temper as every instinct screamed at me to punch the fucker. He had to be deliberately making this into a confrontation.

"LEAVE!" he roared at me. "Leave or we fire!"

"You fire, and it'll be the last thing you ever do," I replied coldly, glaring at him. "You know me. You know I'll kill you all if I have to. I gave you that village, and I can fucking take it away!"

"You dare!" he snarled, staring at me, fists clenched, eyes wide with fury.

I took another step forward.

"Oh, I fucking dare all right, *Oathbreaker!*"

Silence rang out, and I stood—my fists shaking, they were clenched that tightly. A mixture of fear, wild abandon, and fury filled me as the damn word had slipped out.

"What did you call me?" He marched forward, dragging his sword from the scabbard on his hip, and making me curse internally as I remembered that it wasn't a normal sword.

It was a gift from the Erlking, and the other reason that Ronai, the first of the Oracan to join me, was so pissed off generally.

He'd been "given" to me in payment of a debt by the tribe, and basically banished through no fault of his own.

Eto had also taken the opportunity to strip him of his sword that the Erlking had given him, keeping it "for the good of the tribe."

That meant that he had two of the most powerful weapons in the tribe's history, and they belonged to him alone as chief.

Aaaaand I had basically fuck all in terms of armor these days. That was, after all, the entire point of coming up here.

"I called you a fucking Oathbreaker," I snarled. If I backed down and walked away right now, I'd get a dozen arrows and a sword in the back for my troubles.

I strode forward until the pair of us were a handful of meters apart, close enough that nobody else could hear us, and far enough out of each other's range that either side still stood a decent chance of surviving, if the other struck.

"You agreed to teach me, Eto, and I obeyed! I followed the tribe, I fought in the line, and I killed the lycans your way. I agreed to do it all, to be taught, and you fucking abandoned it! As soon as I agreed you could have the camp, you broke your word!"

"No!" he snarled, eyes darting as he quickly thought. "I sent Ronai!"

"Did you tell him to train me, or to serve me? Was it his place to train me when it was you who agreed?" Sensing weakness and hesitation, I pressed harder. "Or did you abandon your post? Did you break your word because you saw an opportunity?"

"I gave you Ronai!" he repeated, before speaking quickly as a new thought occurred to him. "*And* you left!"

"You banned me from the village and ordered me and the others to leave," I corrected, and he glared at me, his breath coming in fast huffs. "You started this, Eto! You made this happen!" I warned him in a lower voice.

"*You* did this," he snarled back. "Now I must kill you to save face!"

"You know you can't," I said softly, seeing the look in his eyes. "I was ordered by the Erlking to kill the Stelek. If you attack me, you attack the servant of the Erlking. Not only will the Erlking kill you, but instead of killing the Stelek, I'll have to kill you. You'll doom your tribe, all because you're an idiot out of your depth in a fucking puddle!"

"I will kill you," he growled.

I shook my head, seeing the rising panic in his eyes as he realized that he'd maneuvered this into the wrong place. He'd been trying to show that he was in charge, and that I'd not given them the village, but that I instead obeyed him, I realized now.

Whatever hold he had on the tribe, it wasn't as strong as Kim's had been, and he was teetering on the edge. He'd bluffed, and it'd come crashing down, all because he'd tried to dismiss me and to make my life harder to prove he was in charge.

I saw it suddenly: the state of the village, the fields that were barely sprouting that should have been overgrown with crops, the filth that covered the walls. Instead of it being cleaned and set right, they looked like...they looked like they were squatting in the ruins of the old village, with a new building half built and towering over the rest.

My eyes widened as I stared into his, and saw not the proud Oracan chief, who was a bit of an idiot but had stepped up from the troop leader I'd known. Instead?

I saw a man, be he human or Oracan, who'd seen a job he thought he could do, and that "should" be his, and he'd taken it.

Now he was out of his depth, and he was floundering desperately.

The village that I'd left was one that'd been frantically fighting for its life, but it'd been full of Oracan working to do it...to survive, to achieve something. They had a golden opportunity—a village that was perfect, their own village, long lost—and instead?

They were failing. The entire village was failing, and just looking about, I could already see it.

The Oracan who had fired upon me?

The troops I'd met when I was last here would never have fired without orders. Fuck's sake, I'd never have known they were there until they struck, they were that good.

Now the walls were covered by the Oracan equivalent of scruffy kids.

"Where are they, Eto?" I asked, my voice hoarse. "Where have they all gone?"

"Gone," he snarled. "Gone, and now you come to make it worse!"

"Gone where?"

"To fight the Stelek!"

"Why the fuck did they do that?"

"I..." He deflated suddenly, looking smaller, grayer and weaker, and the rage poured out of him. "I sent them to kill the Stelek."

"Why?" I asked, stunned. There'd been so many of the tribe lost in the assaults by the lycans that Kim and Ronai had been worried that they'd be too weak to defend against another Oracan tribe, should they try to expand.

To have sent their best fighters away was madness, unless...

"Because of me," I said suddenly, and I got a spark of the old fire back in his eyes. "You sent them because I led the war party that crushed the lycans. You had to send them to kill the Stelek, because otherwise..."

"I lost face," he agreed grimly. "Already my warriors spoke of the time of Kim like a gold mine that was played out. Always things were better when he ruled. They would have rebelled."

"So instead you sent them to fucking die?" I asked, aghast as I realized why he'd been such a dick about telling me where they were.

If I went and killed the Stelek? I'd save the tribe and do what he couldn't. If I went and managed to rescue the rest of his tribe? He lost, because I'd have done it, not him. The only chance he had was for him to order me, and for me to obey. I'd refused that, demanding information—that I'd needed, to be fair—but I'd not been properly respectful, and he'd been forced to come out and show me he was a threat.

Now he was fucked. If he backed down, he was finished as a leader, and he knew it. If I saved the rest of the tribe? The same. If I didn't? They'd not have enough people to defend themselves.

There was only one way that he came out of this, and that was if he could kill me and somehow turn this around, and he hadn't a clue how to do that.

The only thing he'd ever been good at was fighting, and he was finding that leadership was much, much harder.

I saw it all in a split second, and I understood. Fuck did I—hell, that was why I was so damn happy that not only was Ingrid naturally good with people in a way I wasn't, but she actually liked to lead.

I liked to hit people and get laid, that was it.

She loved the minutiae of making a job run perfectly.

And now, I saw the decision in his eyes as he made it, the peace that came over him, the determination, and I shook my head.

"Don't do this, Eto," I begged, my voice low, as he responded, drawing his lips back in the first true smile I'd seen on his face.

"For the tribe!" he declared.

Then he attacked me.

CHAPTER THIRTY-FOUR

He led with the sword, ripping it free of the sheath on his hip, whipping it around in an arc, and extending the blade out ahead of him, lunging and aiming for my stomach.

I twisted; nanites flared and rose to coat the back of my left wrist, forming a thin bracer that barely managed to deflect the strike.

I felt a vibration, almost a scream inside me, as the nanites that hit the blade crumbled, and I panicked, realizing that the Erlking's gift to Eto had been at least as powerful as the goddamn crystal blades were, and just as deadly.

Eto was, like all the Oracan, a warrior. Literally bred for this. So my only chance against a weapon that powerful was to get in too close for him to use it.

I darted forward, even as he backed up, flourishing his blade and hacking sideways across the space between us, aiming for my chest.

I jumped back, then closed again, reaching behind myself and pulling the dagger from behind my back. I took it in my left hand and held it in a reverse grip, ready.

He licked his lips, starting to circle me. The sword weaved a figure eight, and for a second, I was damn glad that it was a sword. If it'd been a goddamn spear like the Oracan usually used, I'd be dead already, I had no doubt.

The bastards were practically born holding one of those, and this in comparison was a long knife, which meant I still had a chance.

Do you want Jonas to kill him?

I heard and felt the words, not so much having to pay attention to them as just knowing that they had been sent by Ingrid. I shook my head. If he did? The rest of the tribe would attack, as we'd have proved ourselves honorless, to have killed their chief by trickery.

No, this one was all mine.

He took two quick steps forward, slashing from high right to low left, then spun, leveling it at head height and swinging hard enough to decapitate me. I jumped back, frantically backing up.

"Fuck's sake, Eto! You even attack like you have no honor!" I shouted, hoping to rile him a bit.

He snarled, stabbing out, high, then low, and I sidestepped, dragging my dagger across, blade down from my hand, still in a reverse grip. I slapped it against the flat of his blade, shoving hard and stepping in, trying to close the distance to inside of his range.

Before I could do it, though, his left fist swung for my face, and I backhanded it aside.

The distraction was enough as he rolled his wrist, backing up, and tried to bring the sword across my chest. I shoved against the blade again. The pair of us were now in close. His sword twisted backward, him grabbing at me; I took hold of his shoulder, getting a grip before he could get one on me. I dragged him forward and my nanites flared to form a mask for a second, one that took the impact as he shifted his forehead down, robbing my own headbutt of any real force.

Thanks to the cut-rate helm, I managed to avoid stunning myself, but that was about it.

He twisted his left leg around the back of my right, shoving into me, and I staggered, then dove aside, releasing him as he slashed down at me. The blade literally tore the air close enough that I felt its passage.

I hit the ground and rolled, coming up and diving again as Eto stabbed down, driving the blade, tip-first into the soil where my face had been a split second earlier.

I twisted as I came to one knee, grabbing at the soil and dirt, flinging it into his face…and staggered to my feet, backing up, as he ignored it.

It wasn't broken up enough, nor wet, nor dry enough for that trick, really. The best he'd gotten was a little grassy dirt, and it'd even missed his damn eyes.

No, I needed to fight better than this, or I was fucked.

He hissed at me, "Fight!" before lunging in and trying to stab me again. I blocked with the sword, shoving it off-balance, and backed up, trying not to worry about the fact the dagger—one made of null blocks and formed with a goddamn molecule edge, no less—was looking battered to shit, while his sword still appeared pristine.

"Fight me!" he screamed, almost frothing at the mouth and hacking at the air.

I dodged a wild swing, before lunging in and stabbing at him. I barely missed as he twisted, rolling his wrist, and kicked me in the stomach, driving me back.

He paused, though, gesturing at me to come at him, panting, and I hesitated, staring at him.

I'd seen Eto fight before.

He was fucking merciless, fast, skilled—hell, he'd led the training when I'd had any from them, with all the other warriors trying to emulate him, and only Ronai exempt as he taught me.

Now, though?

He fought crudely, leaving opportunities for me to escape, to dodge, and I groaned, as it all made sense.

"Eto…we don't have to do this," I ground out.

"Fight me!" he screamed again, thrusting wildly in the air and at me, rushing me, forcing me to face him.

I backed up, watching the swings, seeing the way he rolled his wrist, reading the flow of the muscle in his arms, and I triggered time compression.

Eto seemed to slow to the point he was moving through molasses, and I stepped in, seeing the way his eyes widened at my sudden speed.

I was behind his blade as it swung wildly, and I dragged my blade up, smacking the back of his sword across the flat from underneath, speeding it up as it slid out of my way.

Then I struck.

My harvest blade was damaged—*again*—although this time it was simply that I didn't have enough nanites to form the blade to a real length after using them as the bracer and having them collapse.

Instead, I formed them into a short poniard design, needle-like, thin and short, and I drove it into his left lung. The tip crunched through the armor.

He panted, his eyes widening as I pulled on it and dragged nanites free, even as I stabbed the dagger into the meat of his right shoulder, cutting across the top of the bicep. His arm flopped weakly, the blade tumbling free to land on the grassy overgrown field.

He gasped, grabbing at my shoulder with his left hand and staring into my eyes as I released the time compression.

I saw it then, as I knew I would, all the little hints falling into place.

He coughed. Blood bubbled in his voice as he spoke the words. "Finish...it..." he gasped, holding onto me.

I lowered him to the ground, staring into his eyes. A mixture of sadness and regret filled me.

I knew why he'd done it, and seeing that look, I had no doubt. Hell, he had a dagger on his hip on his left side—he could have easily fought two-handed, but he'd not even drawn it.

And as soon as he'd realized what it meant, me being there, it'd been the only outcome he was going to accept, short of me bending the knee and fucking off.

He was too proud for anything else. And this way?

This entire fight was on his terms, and it was his choice.

I stared into his eyes as I drew the blade back, altering its shape. I stabbed it forward again, piercing his heart, and pulled, hard, as I watched the light die.

Seconds passed. He seemed to wither. His natural form was an Oracan, not like the human crossbreed lycans, so he remained as one, but yeah, he sagged a little as I took a deep breath, feeling the nanites rushing into me.

I straightened after a few seconds, the last of his nanites now mine, and began their cleansing. I took two small steps and reached down, picking up the sword.

Rolling my wrist, I sent it through a figure eight, then tried one of the flashy moves I'd seen on TV, barely avoiding cutting my own foot off.

"Right, play with that later," I muttered, before striding forward, facing the Oracan village. "Who was your second? Who was Eto's right hand?"

"Nishka," one of the figures called, stepping out of the village and standing in the middle of the arched doorway inward.

"That you?" I asked, and he shook his head. "Where's Nishka?"

"He went to fight the Stelek," the figure admitted, and I started to swear. "We fought together, against the Retan'nu'orr."

I squinted at him, vaguely remembering his face, and the Oracan word for the lycans.

"I remember." I wondered where this was going.

"For honor then, I warn you now. None not of the tribe may enter," he said.

I frowned, before cursing.

"You're warning me that if I try to enter the village, you'll have to try to kill me?" I asked, and he nodded somberly. "You know I just killed one of your best, right?"

He nodded again.

"Fuck's sake…" I muttered, reaching up and rubbing at my face, before speaking as another thought occurred to me. "What if Kim, or Ronai was to come here? Could they enter the village?"

"They are of the tribe," he agreed slowly.

"Great. So how about this—you have your people just, you know, keep their distance, leave us the fuck alone, and we'll leave you alone. Send one of your tribe with us to show us the way, and we'll kill the Stelek for you, see if we can rescue the others? While we do that, I'll send for Ronai or Kim, have them come and help here?"

"Where are they?"

"At my…village," I said lamely, before shaking my head and turning to look back at the plane. "Fuck this…why the hell am I dealing with this? Ingrid, a little help here?"

In a matter of seconds later, she was there, jumping down and staggering slightly as she caught herself, still not used to how much more powerful and graceful her body was now.

She strode up, the pair of us still linked, and I felt the pull from her as she reached out to me. I didn't know what she was doing, but I accepted it, and a few seconds later, she started to speak.

It was halting at first, but clearly her Command abilities let her access information from me somehow, enabling her to access the language matrix I'd apparently been building.

She spoke to them, assuring them that we were friends, that Kim and Ronai were honored members of our tribe, and that they would come here, to see what could be done.

She pointed out that as I was not Oracan, I could not claim the position of chief, but that as I ruled the lands that Kim, their ex-chief, lived in, and that Kim and his family had sworn fealty to me, that there was a wonderful solution to all of this that might be possible.

I was already on my way back, with Jonas stepping up to stand by Ingrid's side, and Scylla and Belle unloading the plane. I hurried up the ramp and found Dimi dragging a case off.

"Dimi, I need you to make a flight," I said, and he straightened, frowning.

"When?"

"Literally as soon as you've dropped us off at the caves," I said. "I know you just flew here, but I need Ronai and Kim here, as fast as you can, and I need them yesterday."

"Well, I mean, I can fly there…it's like three hours or so from here, but—"

"But you just finished a flight." I cut him off as he started to nod. "Dimi, you're used to flying long distances, so crank the speed up, and use all the tricks you can, full stealth coating and whatever. Rest when you get them back here. Hell, pack a bed and have a sleep when you land, I don't care. You need to get them back here in six hours."

"Six…" He groaned. "Boss, I mean, I can, but those speeds? As low as I have to fly to keep stealth, to make sure nobody can see what or where…?"

"Dimi, how much do I pay you?"

"Not enough," he grumbled.

"Double it then." I shrugged. "Do you think I give a fuck about money? If you can get Kim and Ronai back here in six hours, we might be able to save this village from failing, and even more, we might be able to recruit them all. An entire *village* of Oracan. Hundreds of them, who are dying, or surviving on how fast you fly. Get them back here, then sleep as long as you fucking want, all right?"

"I...ah, for fuck's sake!" he snarled, before kicking a bag in frustration, then yelping as he clutched at his foot, swearing.

Ten minutes later, the plane was unloaded. We'd figured it was better that we have anything we needed here, and if it gets wasted? Well, fuck it.

The harvesting and experience plan had become a system-generated rescue quest, and just like that, we'd all gotten even more of a reason to do it.

Quest Granted!

New evolving Quest discovered: Rescue the Oracan war party: Level 1

The Oracan war party ventured into the underground to face their ancient enemies the Stelek, but have not been seen since. Scout the Stelek hive and the old Oracan underground fortress, and find out what happened to the war party. Complete the following prerequisites to receive this reward:

- **Discover the fate of the Oracan war party**

- **Rescue any surviving Oracan**

Reward:

- **+1 War Point**

- **+Access to Level 2 of the Evolving Quest**

We'd all gotten it, although there were several different versions, it seemed. Ingrid's was to lead her war party to recover and rescue the Oracan—which we took to mean that they were likely still alive—and Belle's was to harvest the enemy to provide support to us.

Belle was gaining two Harvest points, Ingrid a pair of Command, Scylla and Jonas two War points, and I was getting one, which I guessed was down to the fact that I'd had a lot more experience in this vein.

Ingrid used a satellite phone to provide a link as Dimi took off, explaining the situation to her parents and filling them in. They arranged for "our" Oracan to get their fingers out and get ready for the flight.

Annabeth was detailed to help the Oracan, as she'd already proved that—as much as she annoyed me, by basically breathing and not apologizing to the trees for wasting their hard work in producing oxygen—she was also really good at distracting people.

Not to the level that Belle was, admittedly, but that was a different story.

An hour after that, and we were off, headed north, as Dimi flew south at a hell of a speed, enjoying the excuse to push the plane. Realistically, there was no emergency here, beyond that people were barely surviving, but there wasn't much that was going to change in a few hours.

My concern was that every time I damn well turned around, shit hit the fan. And I damn well knew that if I told Dimi to take his time?

There'd be a fucking earthquake, or a lycan invasion, or Martians…who knew really. The truth was, though, if Dimi pushed hard and was back here in six hours or so? Kim and Ronai could look after these people. They were ex-tribe members, and the less time there was for a new chief to claim the slot, the less chance there was that the Oracan village would fail.

They were people, regardless of species, and they needed a home. And given that I'd even accepted the hippie fucknuts into our community, there was no reason to turn away from a chance at recruiting people who weren't insane and actually were capable of being useful, instead of just annoying the shit out of me.

I'd had it in my head for some reason that the caves with the Stelek were miles away, like a huge distance from the village, but when Ingrid had asked the Oracan warrior—Belar was his name, apparently—it was less than ten miles.

That was why they'd been forced to send out a group to "deal with the Stelek," apparently, despite the fact the fuckers hated sunlight in a way that vamps were supposed to, and for some reason sometimes didn't.

I'd asked whether the Stelek had come out of the caves, and Belar had looked at me like I was an idiot. But when I tried to explain that if they couldn't come out of the caves, even at night, then there was no need to have gone to fight them, he just stared at me like I'd been recommending a sex act involving a small chicken and an anteater.

There was a lot of disgust and some confusion in that look, and I basically left it as the Oracan were just unable to accept a threat in their territory and not deal with it, and moved on.

Belar set the pace, with us leaving most of the gear outside the village, taking only a basic loadout and the two sentinels, still in "sleep mode" attached to my and Jonas's backs. We managed it, although by the end, both Belle and Ingrid were staggering and the remaining three of us had their packs spread out on us.

An hour for ten miles wasn't great timing, certainly not for a group of post-humans, but considering it was also through the forest and up and down hills? It wasn't bad.

Belar was dressed in his armor, a mixture of metal plates and leather that should have made it impossible to make anything like good time in the forest, but he'd managed to make all of us look bad, as well to be the quietest.

He stood there, cheeks slightly red, barely breathing hard, as he pointed down the valley we stood at the head of. His spear pointed at the overhanging cave entrance in the distance. Jonas and I tried to look as if we were fine, and Scylla glared at everyone.

Ingrid was bent over, hands on her knees, panting and clearly trying not to be sick after pushing herself so hard, and Belle was sucking down great lungfuls of air.

We were all drenched in sweat. The air here was surprisingly humid, even for late summer, and I couldn't help but eye the river that wound past the entrance to the caves longingly.

It was a glacial melt, that much was clear. The mountain behind it fed it and kept it both crystal-clear and icy-cold, thanks to the speed of it.

Belar hesitated as we started off down into the valley, and Ingrid paused, gasping for breath, as she explained that it was all right, and to return to the tribe, that they couldn't afford to lose him.

He clearly wanted to face the Stelek. The damn Oracan were fearless in battle, but he also knew that the village had only a small number of fighters left to defend it now, and that was the priority.

He vanished into the dense undergrowth, and we continued down the side of the valley, amazed by the lushness of it all.

"I'm not saying we should move the group to here," Jonas started, before shaking his head as he reached out and pushed a large leafy branch out of the way. "But damn, the thought that we could be living here instead of deep in the devil's asshole in the Sahara?"

The valley was literally lush and overgrown, and Belle was obviously loving being somewhere like this after the desert.

Everywhere I looked, the forest was filled with life. The cacophony of birds overhead filled the air with their cries; monkeys, voles, spiders, snakes…fuck's sake, wolves and even evidence of bears were all around us. And the more I looked? The more I realized that this place could be a paradise in truth.

For an Englishman, no matter where we went in the world, we wanted and expected to see green. Green grass, hills, forests—all that shit.

The desert was nice and all, and the Greek islands were great, but there was too much scrubland, too many twisted stunted bushes and too little green grass for any Englishman to be entirely at home.

Here, though?

The world was full of life, and it was obvious and overwhelming.

We walked down the hill, pausing at the base of the valley and the fast-racing river. We took turns, leaning down, getting a drink and relaxing for a few minutes, watching the world around us, making sure no fucker was about to attack.

It was becoming second nature, and here and there, Ingrid's new abilities made themselves felt.

She didn't just direct us and provide a secure comms link—she augmented us all, in a load of little ways. Our senses were sharper, the world around us seeming to share its secrets easier, and best of all?

We felt it.

Not in that way, although I had to wonder what sex in this expanded mentality was going to be like. No, I mean we felt the world.

I sensed the approach of a small animal, four-legged, furry, like a wolf but sneakier, that was hiding behind me on the far side of the group.

It inched closer to the water, watching us as it came, clearly wanting the water but not willing to come out of the concealing brush until we fucked off.

That it was on the far side of the group, where Scylla was watching it, and yet I still knew about it as if I'd seen it myself? This was going to be a hell of an improvement in a fight, especially in the damn depths of the cave system.

It was also fucking obvious that the area had once been important to the Oracan, if you knew them at all.

There were signs that the overgrowth had been managed once, areas that were once cut well back. And although the plants now ran up to the water's edge, and even over it, the thickest and older growth had a clear delineation a little way back.

I was betting that the cave system, and the Oracan "fortress" that had been mentioned in the quest were a fallback point or something. There were older sections of stonework here and there, and although more were covered in moss and vines, there had once been a formal archway into the caves, even if it was hidden.

Moving closer, it was obvious a large group had passed through recently, as even one as skilled as the Oracan couldn't hide their passage entirely, not here.

There were sections where a recent heavy rainfall had left at least one of them scrabbling for footing, and boot prints left in the soft earth, and occasional twisted sections of grass and plants.

We moved closer, climbing along the valley, passing abandoned and clearly old fishing areas, sections where if you looked, you could see the signs of tools having been used to expand a small section into a deeper pool.

Here and there, we found more signs of occupation, but we also found bones.

Lots of old bones, a veritable pile of them, and obvious masses of corpses that had been seemingly pushed out of the way, dumped into the pool.

"What happened here?" Ingrid asked me in a low voice, and I shrugged, all of us watching the entrance to the caves.

"I don't know. Most of the Oracan wouldn't talk about it, but they told the Erlking they were at war with the Stelek and the lycans. Maybe they were driven back by the lycans, and they tried to retreat here?" I gestured to the piles of long-dead bones, and the signs of more nearby.

"They mentioned that the Oracan had a load of villages up here. Hell, Hans said that the Russians needed to bomb the area to kill them all. But now? There's just little tribes scattered about—no real groups—and they're on the verge of being exterminated."

"You think that when the Russians did that, they fucked the balance of power here?" Jonas asked, and I hesitated, then nodded.

"Maybe," I agreed. "If there were groups keeping each other in check, and then suddenly one gets wiped out, the others would expand faster, taking the territory."

"And looking at the bones, they were overrun," Scylla said. "They're by the entrance, so they were either stopped from entering and slaughtered there by a foe that wouldn't come out, or they were driven out and killed by something here."

"You think the Stelek drove them up and pushed their bodies out?" I asked. Of all of us, Scylla would be able to read the situation far better.

"Unlikely. You said they were insects—they would not waste Oracan meat, surely. If they cannot leave the caves, though, they might eat all that was inside, and leave the rest outside."

"Well, only one way to find out," I said after a few seconds, moving closer to the entrance and drawing the sword I'd looted from Eto.

I'd taken the scabbard for it as well, and the others had their guns, as well as a spear and shield for Scylla, a hammer for Jonas, and a spear for both Ingrid and Belle.

They'd looked at them a bit bemusedly when I insisted on them, and had brought a dozen magazines each, but I was damn well determined that they'd have a fallback weapon, even if it was just a short, five-foot spear.

Zac had designed them as collapsible, meaning they could be pulled out to their full length from just one foot long, then twisted and locked; pins slid out to keep them extended until they weren't needed any more.

"Do we use the sentinels?" I asked the others.

For a second, we all thought about it; then Jonas and Scylla shook their heads at almost the same time.

"Better to keep them as a surprise," he suggested. "I don't know if they can see us, but set them up and deploy them when we need a break, and hopefully they'll ignore them."

I shrugged, not really bothered either way, and wanting to vent some frustration on the insects anyway.

The river ran down the side of the valley. The slope of the grass and the well-worn banks made it clear that once it'd run by the entrance, probably as an extra security feature. But now? The distant heavy rains we'd seen as the plane had landed by the village had caused the river to burst its banks, leaving a solid inch or two of water rushing across the worn stone of the entrance.

Even this had been planned for, I saw, as I stepped up, ducking my head under the moss and vines that dangled from the entrance of the cave. We were looking at clearly carved steps that rose up and back. And the way that the ceiling in here, rather than a naturally occurring cave roof, was carved and vaulted, with two areas to either side of the entrance that looked to be funneling away the water that made it inside?

Damn. It was a thing of beauty.

Scylla moved up, reaching out and laying a hand on my arm, then lifted a finger to her lips, watching me to be sure I understood, before she took the lead.

I frowned, realizing that when we used the command link, we actually spoke out loud normally, and I'd not noticed. Focusing, I tried projecting my voice to the group, without making a sound, and I failed miserably.

Something for another day, I decided, following Scylla. Jonas brought up the rear, while Ingrid and Belle were in the middle.

There were a dozen or so steps, leading steadily upward, and the decades and centuries of usage were clear as soon as we saw them.

The middle was worn down, not hugely, but the edges of the steps were rounded. The center gently dipped inward while the outermost side, apart from being covered in dust and the detritus of the ages, was sharper and better formed.

Great tattered banners of spiderwebs drooped from the ceiling, the center-most in a line torn free, the sides dangling, and the outmost, again, looking as if they'd been coated in dust and dead flies for millennia.

Oh my God...

The horrified thought that seeped from Ingrid made me shake my head and smile.

I didn't like spiders...sure, I mean, who the fuck actually does, besides edgy teenagers looking to piss off and horrify their parents? But here and there were massive, fucking horrible specimens, and I couldn't help but compare that movie I'd seen as a kid, with all the spiders in it, to this passage.

Ingrid was practically stepping on my heels as I moved, and I made her stop, reaching up ahead and brushing the thinner, much more recent spiderwebs that survived Scylla's passage down.

Ingrid wasn't afraid of spiders—she'd made that very clear on numerous occasions—but she didn't like them very much. And here, in this cave, with a steady breeze flowing out past us and making the walls of cobwebs wave?

She was getting more and more freaked out.

I wasn't much happier, to be fair: the multilegged bastards were on all sides now, and every itch of the skin across the back of my neck made me imagine some monstrosity from the dawn of time sliding its way down there.

I literally couldn't wait to get my goddamn armor back.

The path rose and fell, at first seeming a bit strange, but that was it...until after the third rise and fall, I started to count the steps, curiously.

Fifteen.

Fifteen up, a narrow platform, maybe three or four meters across, then fifteen steps back down.

I frowned, wondering at it until I considered the usefulness of it. Running up and down the steps would be a hell of a workout. And a few traps here and there? Hell, a tripwire alone would do some serious damage.

If you were defending this area, splitting your team and having half at the top of one flight, then half at the top of the next?

You'd always have the high ground—because fuck you, Anakin, it does matter—and you could leapfrog back each time you retreated.

That way, you'd rest your teams, while the attackers would be bled for every meter they took.

Add in that if you trained on the steps regularly, you'd be able to take them fast and hard, without being broken by them, but an attacker would get worn out quickly.

The top of the next set of steps was narrow as hell as well, with space on the far side for a group to shove spears through small gaps in the walls, while on the attackers' side? No more than two men abreast could enter.

Sneaky fucks.

The roof was the next section, a carved artificially-lowered section that would make anyone passing through duck. It wasn't ridiculous—most Oracan were in the five to five-and-a-half-foot range, wider than the average human but about the same height, if not a little shorter. Eto had been unusual at six foot.

The passage here, though, dipped down at around five foot. And considering that lycans were typically at six to six-and-a-half foot? It was a clear way to slow those fucks down.

There were offset sections in the passage that made you jink to the left, then right. Looking at them, I blew out a long breath, impressed all over again at the effort that had been put in.

Even a full sprinting lycan on all fours, that would get through the last section easily enough, would run headlong into the walls here.

On either side, there were more slots for spears or arrows. Scylla crept ahead, spear held low as she stared through the gaps, making sure we weren't walking into a trap, before whispering that the sections behind there were long abandoned as well.

The cobwebs were left behind here. The Oracan who had come recently—they'd left footprints that had dried but were still clear—had only partly cleared them away with their passage. And unlike where the mass of webs had been, some of the spiders here had clearly not bothered to replace them fully yet.

That meant that when the roof went back to normal height, being the tallest, I got an occasional face full of spiderweb, which put me into an even worse mood: I'd feel like they were gone, and then there was another, like police speed traps when I let it rip on a bike.

Five minutes farther on, though, Scylla dropped to one knee, waving a hand slowly.

I looked at her, then the others, then slowly crept up to her, getting a frantic "stop" gesture when I got closer.

I did, getting a glare from her, and for a few heartbeats, we all stayed silent and still.

Then a minute, then five, until Belle finally asked what we were waiting for, quite cheerfully.

That, of course, was when the ceiling overhead moved, and the mass of eyes blinked open, the hiss of challenge escaping the watchdogs that had been left in the tunnel.

CHAPTER THIRTY-FIVE

The first to move was a lizard, which was something of a relief, considering that it was at least six meters long and looked like the bastard offspring of a moray eel and a fucking dragon.

If it'd been that size and a *spider,* half the team would have noped the fuck out right there and then. As it was? The fucker lowered its face from the ceiling where it'd been hiding, its chameleon-like skin keeping it from being noticed, and it hissed again, this time in pleasure.

From all around us, more hisses sounded, and I cursed, hearing the *chunk-click* of charging levers being pulled.

I ripped my new sword free and reacted to a blur of movement out of the corner of my eye, hacking sideways and dragging the blade down the back of a creature that had been clinging to the ceiling only a meter from me.

It screeched, tumbling loose, a line carved deep into it from shoulder to rear legs. Blood rained free as the white of bones were exposed, organs and more.

It hit the floor and writhed, bucking wildly in agony; I spun, lashing out at a second, before stabbing the first one in the skull, ending its frenzied, painful panic.

All around us, the others were facing more.

Belle had been unable to sense them, geared and evolved as she was to humanoids, and Jonas was already firing, even as Ingrid clumsily fired her rifle, cursing as the bullets tore through the lizard and ricocheted off the wall behind it.

Explosions filled the air as Jonas fired again and again. The overpressure wave made us all shout in pain as our ears were assaulted, and the lizards counterattacked.

For whatever reason, they weren't overly concerned about the overpressure, and that gave them the advantage as we flinched.

I could sense them all around me; I realized it was their nanites I felt—much stronger in the injured ones than the rest. But as one snapped at me, sprinting forward, I leapt back and hacked down, opening the large lizard's skull from the top to the mouth, sending a spray of blood shooting free.

They had wide mouths filled with teeth. Again, they looked like moray eels: long, flexible necks, rear-facing teeth that I instinctively knew would be a bastard to escape once they sunk into something, and a frill of bone spikes that ran around the upper section of the skull, a line that ran down to the nose and a hooked horn or egg-claw on the tip.

The eyes had a double ring of pointed scales around them. The body was more or less sinuous, as if a god with serious issues and plans for the evening had simply slapped some legs on a snake and called the day done.

They were fast, vicious, and they totally ignored their friends that screeched in agony, interested only in getting at us.

The one whose skull I'd just carved a line down whipped its head from side to side, hissing in pain. Before I could get another strike in, I dodged to the side, a feeling of warning from the command sense and my own nanite senses alerting me just in time.

I didn't want to use my time compression capability, not again, not so soon after the fight with Eto. But I snarled and did it, worried I'd need it, but also worried about my friends.

As everything slowed, I twisted, following as the one that'd just leapt at me started to turn. I stepped in closer to it, dipping the sword in almost delicately, behind the frill at the top of the skull, and felt the crunch as the skull gave way beneath the point of the blade.

It sank into the brain. The lizard stiffened, and I dragged it free. The body convulsed as it hit the floor, twitching wildly.

I turned and slashed, opening another lizard's maw far wider than nature intended, then taking the top of the head off.

Bullets streaked past me. My sped-up senses were still not fast enough to see them, but certainly fast enough to sense where they'd gone as bodies quaked and shivered.

Ingrid stood next to Jonas and Belle. Belle used her spear, keeping the lizards back as Ingrid fired on them. Jonas picked the creatures off that tried to creep along the walls and roof.

Scylla was spinning and carving, her rifle still secured to her back; the weapons she knew best, her spear and shield, flickered and spun.

It might have been the influence of the fight earlier with Eto, but I unthinkingly shifted into the stances that he and the others, Ronai especially, had taught me.

Flowing from one to another, my blade flashing, I felt almost like I was dancing, as all around me teeth flashed and eyes rolled, blood sprayed and screeches echoed.

I punched out right-handed. The punch dagger flowed out to form just as I sank it into an eye; tendrils extended into the brain of my victim on instinct. And for the first time, I realized I'd swapped my sword to my left hand.

I'd been so in the flow of the fight, that I'd been almost somewhere else, and I blinked as it all crashed back. Ingrid killed the last of them with a triple burst of fire that rang out, the echoes hanging heavy in the air.

Two minutes and four seconds.

Two minutes and four fucking seconds was all I had left in the tank now, and I cursed as I pulled up the stat screen, checking how long it'd take to refill that, and cursing again as I remembered that wasn't included in the details.

For the first time, I saw that my actual name had replaced the numerical designation on the screen, and I let out a long breath of relief—it was stupid, I knew, but it meant something to me—and I glanced about, making sure everyone was okay, before returning to the details in front of me.

Identifier: Biological Weapon Variant #Steve					
Species: Human			**Nanites available**: 10,411		
Threat Level: Kappa			**Corrupted Nanites**: 1,297		
			Weaponized Nanites: 800		
Stat	**Current points**	**Description**		**Effect**	**Cost to Upgrade**
Body	5.3	Physical strength and capacity to absorb damage		+43 resistance to damage	530k
Reactions	4.3	Mental and physical reactions		Time Dilation= 4.3*3.9*10=167.7 +50%= 251.6 seconds	430k
IQ	4.9	Intelligence and the capability to utilize it in the real world		+39 to Assimilation of new technologies and capabilities	490k
Nimbleness	3.9	The capacity to utilize tools, weapons, and small devices		+29 to success with devices	390k
Dexterity	4.3	The ability to dodge and utilize larger items/devices		+33 chance to dodge	430k
Karmic Luck	5.1	The likelihood of an action to spawn an adverse/positive reaction		+41 chance to gain a favorable outcome in games of chance	5.1m
Perception	4.1	The ability to differentiate between details and spot threats at a distance		+31 likelihood to spot concealed items, details, or traps — see Reactions	410k
Control	3	The ability to control external systems			300k
Cybernetics	4	Integration of Cybernetic and Biogenetic augmentations and how likely they are to work			400k
Resonance	5	The capacity to use and integrate devices that require elemental resonances			500k

I'd lost a few levels of threat, it seemed, sinking all the way to kappa, whatever that was, and I'd gained a point here and there, mainly in nimbleness, perception, and I thought control, unsure whether I gained a point in cybernetics or not.

I thought I had, but honestly, it was just a fuckin' blur at this point.

The important details were that I was up to supposedly two hundred and fifty-one seconds of compressed time dilation now, and I'd still had to use more than half of it to win that fight.

Roughly, if I was remembering right, it took about five minutes to regain a single second, so maybe twenty seconds an hour I'd get back, and that made me wince.

It'd take roughly six and a half hours to recover it all, and by then? I had to guess I'd have used the rest.

Looking around at the piled bodies, I dismissed the screen and spoke aloud. "Okay, people, reload and get ready."

"Anyone else down here had to have heard that…" Jonas called, barely below a shout, and I winced, nodding.

We were all partly deaf from that barrage, and we damn well all needed nanites.

"Belle!" I called, then gestured to the corpses.

"Of course!" she said, as Ingrid, Jonas, and I moved up to stand by Scylla.

This time I sheathed the sword, drawing the rifle instead, as we all stood, staring into the dark, waiting.

Belle was quick, moving from corpse to corpse. Her harvesting tool punched down into the bodies, making them shake as she ripped their nanites free. But before she was done, we saw the first distant signs of the Stelek.

I'd not checked the lizards for a marker, too busy fighting, but as soon as I saw these, and wondered, the system provided a designator.

Stelek Hive Warrior	Biological Weapon Variant
One of several early and semi-successful BWVs that were granted further augmentations, the line designated as "Stelek" spawns various greater strengths that warranted expanded investment, including hive mentality and simplified hormonal aggression controls.	
The hive warrior is an extremely simple creation, but cheap to maintain, requires very little direction, and can be deployed for extended periods with only minimal maintenance.	
Capabilities:	
Hibernate: The Stelek warrior can enter a limited form of hibernation to enable extended periods of inactivity without detrimental effects on the unit, self-generating a useful cocooning facility.	
Ferocious: Stelek warriors have highly limited pain receptors, and when they scent damaged nearby units, they will attack those that carry the scent markers without mercy, enabling fast and efficient responses to territorial incursion.	
HP 200/200	Stelek

I relayed the details to the others, and Jonas lifted his handgun, squinting down the barrel as he aimed.

"Let's see just how accurate that scent marker thingy is then," he suggested, firing a single shot downrange.

One of the front runners practically detonated, and the warrior behind it caught what was left of the round, collapsing to the floor. Its carapace and more cut into those around it, as the first one's shredded body tumbled end over end.

The Stelek around it were liberally bathed in ichor, but showed no interest in each other, making us all curse. Clearly it was just other species covered in it they didn't like.

That would have been a nice solution. Instead, they raced toward us. The creatures seemed to flow from side to side as they ran in perfect unison.

They were clearly insectile. Even if the detail hadn't said so, I'd have known that: six limbs, four lower grouped around a central thorax, a short rear abdomen, and an upper body like a centaur, with the head atop that, and the last set of arms extending from the upper body.

I now knew some of the right terms for this, thanks to Ingrid laughing her ass off and taking the piss out of me calling it a 'butt' so many times.

The upper arms ended in chitinous blades. The top and bottom looked as if they were serrated, and the tip viciously pointed and sharp. And the head?

It made me think of a wasp: all bitterness and anger, mandibles clacking as they raced, compound eyes glittering in the darkness of the cave. Basically, everything that they were broadcast a single message: namely, "I am a twat, please exterminate me."

"Happy to help," I muttered, focusing as I lifted my own rifle and took aim.

"Single shots! Aim for the head!" Jonas called out.

I squinted, lining it up, timing it...and fired!

The first shot was wide, more or less. It passed a hairsbreadth from the side of the head I'd been aiming for, but took the one in line behind it, slightly behind in the sinuous snake-like run, full in the face.

Its head was torn apart. The body collapsed like a puppet with its strings cut, and the one behind stumbled over it.

On either side of me, Jonas, Ingrid, and Scylla fired as well. The four of us, in a line, took aim and fired. The echoing crack of the miniature rail guns made the air shudder as the rounds flashed through it.

Zac had "toned down" the rifles, out of fear that we'd accidentally hole the ship when we were on it. Here, the fear was more of causing a cave-in, with each of the slugs, literally a solid mass of titanium, ripping clean through their targets and into the figure behind, then traveling onward.

I winced, lowering the rifle as I saw the damage. And in the distance? Booms echoed as the rounds slammed into the far wall, an entire section of it shattering and falling free.

"Fuck!" I grunted, stunned.

"Cease fire! Cease fire!" Jonas cried out.

The Stelek were closing, but behind them? The wall was literally tumbling down. Cracks radiated outward from the impact points and streaked across the walls nearby, making us all back up a little on instinct.

"Get ready!" I called, flicking the safety on and releasing my rifle to hang free. The cord on it retracted, keeping it close to my chest, and I didn't have the time to slide it into its place with the webbing on my back.

Instead, I drew the damn sword and stepped forward. Ingrid moved back to stand with Belle, who was still harvesting, as Jonas pulled out his spear, cursing as he frantically tried to get the pins locked back into place.

Scylla was already moving to cover one side of the corridor, and I the other, spreading out to give us some room, as the survivors closed.

There were eleven of them, out of maybe twenty that had come running. One of the survivors was well behind the rest, staggering drunkenly with half its head missing, where a round had evidently clipped it, the impact doing that much damage.

"Zac needs to tone those guns the fuck down!" Jonas growled, and I nodded.

He gave up on the spear and started to fire the handgun again, each impact far less powerful than the rail gun rifle's, and yet still a kill every time and stunning for the rest of us.

They exploded on impact. The massive handgun barked as the Stelek covered the last few meters, before he stepped back, slamming it into the holster, and dragged a knife free.

I was relieved, and not just because the thought of explosions that close wasn't happy making. The goddamn echoing booms were horrific, and with the command link making it easier for us all to see everything?

I could see the way the pressure waves shattered the walls even more.

The closest to me reared back, arms spreading wide, and leapt at me, legs fanning out, clearly intending to land on and bear me to the ground.

Fuck that.

I stepped into the jump, turning the sword sideways. The tip extended out to my right, the hilt held in both hands, and carved the fucker in two. I ducked under the reaching arms and pivoted on my left heel, flicking the blade around and lopping a stretching arm off the next in line on the left. Then, spinning and ducking down low, right leg extended out to the side, my blade hacked through the next in line's legs.

I had so little experience with the sword it wasn't funny, and the experience I did have? It was almost all with my harvest blade. I'd absorbed some knowledge as I'd gained points in the War tree, and yeah, I'd seen some shit on TV and in the movies.

The only thing that kept me going right now, though, was that I was much stronger than a baseline human, had far faster reactions, and a blade that was literally forged to be a weapon against this kinda shit by one of our creators.

It was the equivalent of being gifted a god-tier sword, and I snarled at myself as I used it.

I needed to learn to use it properly, not to flail about with it at random like this. But for now, it was working.

Scylla was using her shield and spear in tandem, literally using decades of tricks to make up for the loss of her inhuman strength. She took the first of them full on the shield, legs braced and leaning forward, having run a few steps closer to them as they closed.

She hunched behind the shield, slamming it into the first and ducking. Her spear, drawn back, then stabbed out through a small carved divot in its rim.

The blade, created by Zac again, carved through the Stelek's carapace like a hot knife through butter. Then she twisted it to make sure, dragged the blade sideways and ripped it out, stepping back as the next tried to bull into her.

This time the shield rocked; the spear lashed out again, dipping almost delicately into the section between what would have been the clavicle and throat of a human.

Another twist, pull back, step to the right and back, and she moved her shield to catch the next in line's attack, even as the one she'd just hit tried to follow, only to have its body collapse out from under it.

Thick orange ichor burst free, and the head, almost severed, bounced on the ground as the rest of the body fell.

I had one more ahead, and as I switched the blade to my left hand, I heard and felt Jonas behind me dispatching the badly injured ones I'd left on the ground with his blade.

Stepping up, I swung the blade in a figure eight, giving the Stelek the choice of running into it and being carved into sashimi or stopping. It straightened its legs, scrabbling on the floor and lowering itself like a horse did when it tried to stop suddenly, and I struck.

I didn't use the sword—no, fuck that. I lunged forward and punched the fucker in the face.

It helped that just as my punch landed, I'd extruded the harvest blade in a punch dagger combination, admittedly, but fuck it.

It slammed into me, arms flailing and legs twitching on reflex. I grunted, forced back a few steps, before I could twist and shove it to the floor, dead.

I turned, needing to see it with my own eyes. But yeah, Jonas was cleaning up the last of them now, lifting his heavy bladed dagger free of the top of the head of the one whose legs I'd hacked through.

"You know…" he started, pointing at me with his dagger, ichor dripping off the end. "You're absolutely fuckin' useless with that thing, right?"

"Fuck off," I snapped at him, looking at Ingrid, then the others, making sure they were okay.

"No, I'm serious," Jonas growled. "You're the boss, I get that, and you earned my damn loyalty, so don't go thinking I'm being a dick, all right?"

"Right?" I frowned, looking at him.

"You can create goddamn weapons from your nanites, right?"

"Yeah?"

"So why the hell are you, the only one of us who can create them like that, also the only one of us who's carrying a fucking magic sword?" He shook his knife. The mess flew free as he glared at me. "Seriously, for fuck's sake…sure, you own it, all right…I'll not try to keep it. But if this is payback for me giving you that silver dagger back in the goddamn catacombs…?"

"Dammit." I grunted, realizing that I was screwing up massively here, then shook my head and stepped up closer to him. "You've trained with the damn sword, haven't you?"

"Of course," he said. "It's part of the standard loadout for anyone serving the Arisen. You never know what you're going to fight, and they, well, they like to have us fight each other a lot."

"Here." I forced myself to try not to sound bitter as I passed the blade to him. "I was using it because I've not got enough nanites to form a proper blade yet. Plus, I didn't think about it…like we didn't with the guns and the fucking walls down here."

"Seriously?" He seemed surprised, but a smile broke out as he took the blade. "You're giving me this?"

"Loaning!" I snapped. "It's a loan…for now," I muttered, trailing off as he stepped to the side, making sure he was clear of everyone, before rolling his wrist and sending the blade flashing through a complex dance that made most Hollywood fight scenes look amateurish.

I really disliked him.

"You can have my nanites," he said after a second's pause, still staring at the blade in his hands as he checked it for weight and balance. "Until you've got enough to make your own sword or whatever? Straight trade."

I glared at him. "That's a sword made by one of the creators of our species, to kill practically anything, and it fucking destroys nanites," I pointed out. "I think saving me from a few hours of waiting and collecting nanites is a bit of a shitty deal."

"Says the man without the sword." He grinned. "Seriously, though, boss. How about half of everything I'd have collected for the rest of the day then? I need this."

"You need the fucking nanites as well," I grumbled, but I pulled the scabbard off and offered it to him, shaking my head. "I'll not take the nanites either. As much as I *should*…we all need them."

"And this?" He held the sword up, despite promising he'd not try to claim it literally seconds ago.

"You can use it until you die or I find someone better," I grunted, looking at the others.

Belle moved from corpse to corpse, her face a mask of concentration as she worked. Her harvest tool clearly evolved totally differently than the way mine had, in that she now looked like her right arm was a mass of vines. They broke down into tiny tubules that dug into the bodies from a dozen angles, then shuddered, even as blood—or ichor, depending on the species she was harvesting—was ejected from holes along the thicker "vines."

Ingrid was focused on something, presumably another upgrade for surviving the wave of enemies, as she shook slightly. I couldn't help but wonder whether I'd looked like that when I was unlocking things, because with the flickering eyes and shivering body, she looked as though she were on the verge of a fit.

Scylla was making sure of the bodies, moving from one to the next, stabbing the fucker in the head and moving on. Jonas sheathed the blade after shaking it clean—nothing seemed to stick to it—and then started to reload his handgun.

I shifted to the rifle, pulling it back around and checking it, making sure, again—even damn well knowing that there wasn't, but needing to look—to see whether there was a way to crank the power down on it.

There wasn't.

They'd been made less powerful by Zac, and we'd all just accepted that it was done, and that was it.

Now we were paying for that complacency.

"So," I said, as Ingrid drew a deep breath, seeming to wake at my words. "We know the rifles and the handgun are last-resort weapons."

"Definitely the rifles," Jonas agreed. "My handgun, though…"

"Is loud as fuck and nearly deafened us all," I said. "I mean it, Jonas—that thing is as dangerous to us as the rifles. Whatever the hell it does, the bullets explode, and that's bad enough in here. Look at the cracks in the walls. We don't need a landslide, or a cave collapse. So, for now, it's rifles away, and that fucker too. We do it with steel…or whatever the hell the sharp shit we have is made of," I finished a bit lamely, considering I was using nanites, he was using whatever the sword was made of, and Scylla was using something different again in her spearhead.

It took Belle another ten minutes or so to drain all the corpses. I was tempted again and again to step in and help, but she needed the experience, and was the one of us literally designed to do this.

By the end, she went from one of us to the next, giving us each a thousand nanites that were "cleaned and ready to be used" as well as assuring us that we'd get more as soon as she'd finished stripping and unlocking the rest.

A thousand nanites, plus the three hundred I'd ripped from the Stelek that were instantly usable, was a massive help. The rest, and the majority I'd gotten from the warrior, were currently being stripped and cleansed by my own system.

Either way, though, it left me with about three thousand seven hundred and change to use. It was nowhere near what I needed to form my armor again, nor to begin upgrading myself, but it was a start.

Add in that my armor had been almost entirely weaponized nanites before, and really? I needed to come up with a better solution, as well as some upgrades.

I'd made it that way because it was the best I could do at the time, but now? I had access to real tech, and there was no reason to go all out and waste so many nanites.

I'd have weaponized ones still—sure I fucking would. Although they were less usable than the "normal" ones in many ways, they were also faster to respond, operated on an instinctive level, and as I couldn't use them up, they stayed with me.

It'd taken a running fight through the bowels of an alien spaceship to rob me of them, and I was damn well determined I'd get them back.

Just, this time? I'd be making it a hell of a lot better.

For now, though, I reached out and converted the rest of the nanites I'd gotten from the Stelek warrior straight into weaponized ones.

Two and a half thousand.

That was all I had, but damn. Holding my right hand out and feeling the way the nanites flowed again? It was just so good.

"Steve?" Ingrid said, and I blinked, turning to her.

"What?"

"I asked if you were ready?" She smiled.

I nodded, holding up my right hand, flowing the jet-black, thin layer of nanites around to form a glove, then a dagger, then back to a long-bladed dagger.

This time, the attuned made up half of the blade, forming the outer edge, a dedicated tunnel in the middle to pull the nanites to me, and the tip, while the weaponized made up the rest.

It was a hell of a lot smaller than the weapon that Jonas was handling now, but I refused to think about that.

It'd grow, after all.

I set off with the rest, falling into our previous pattern again: Jonas at the back, Scylla ahead of us, scouting, Ingrid and Belle behind me in the middle.

I mentally cursed again, having meant to have a word with Scylla before she darted ahead, about the stupidity of having a scout who used signals the rest of us didn't understand, and who tried to communicate using them, only to have her vanish around the corner, with the rest of us having to hurry to catch up.

The passage cut left and right, running for almost a full minute solid before coming to an area that had clearly been a resting or holding area for the Stelek warriors. Twenty tattered and veined things, like deflated balloons, were attached to the walls nearby.

"Pods," Ingrid whispered, looking at the mess. "Jonas, have you fought these before?"

I mentally cursed myself for not thinking to ask him about it.

"Never," he said. "I'd have said if I had any experience with them, but as far as I know, they're a rare one. There's some species that are common, like the Oracan and the lycan, and we all know them. Others?" He shrugged. "Some things are in the records, but they have only little descriptions, like those Xi-Ma things you said about under Crete. They won't deal with us, only the more powerful Arisen, and they'll even kill them if they get too close."

"Hans knew about them…" I offered, and Jonas snorted.

"Hans is a lying sack of shit who likes to make himself seem more important than he is," he corrected. "Sure, he's Arisen, and yeah, he's been around for a while, and he's fun to drink with. But seriously? He might have claimed to be controlling the vamps when you met them, but if they serve the Xi-Ma, then, at best, they were obeying him while their orders matched…that's all."

"You think he was bluffing?" I remembered him giving the first vamp I'd met orders and the way that it'd called him lord, and had obeyed.

"I think he was probably watching us all already," Jonas admitted in a low voice as we set off again, following Scylla.

"I unlocked mental linking. Think at the group and we should be able to hear you," Ingrid interrupted, and I grinned, glad she'd thought to do that with whatever points she had.

The link could carry our voices to each other, clearly, over the sound of anything happening around us before, but we still needed to say it out loud.

"Thank you," Jonas said.

The tell-tale sound of his voice echoed around in my mind, and yet his lips no longer moved and risked anyone else hearing us.

"So, I think Hans was probably watching us, or having us followed. Once we killed a bunch of the lycans and were bugging out, he probably saw the vamp and the ghouls following, guessed what you were, and wanted to recruit you. Much easier to do so if he looks all-powerful, rather than simply following along and snatching up the scraps the bigger ones leave behind."

I snorted, unable to help myself as it made a hell of a lot more sense suddenly. Hans had always been an opportunist, and knowing him—and his loose sense of any morality—he'd probably been using the catacombs to dispose of people who annoyed him, hence knowing, and having the vamp, in turn, know him.

The sneaky fuck.

It also explained why he'd claimed his territory was far away, and yet he'd been there, following the vamp when it'd come after me and the others, as well as being able to order it about.

The only thing that still stood out as weird for me about the whole thing now, though?

"Is sunlight and vamps a real thing?" I asked the others. *"I mean, I've fought some in daylight and..."*

"Really?" Jonas asked, his mental voice conveying surprise. *"The ones I've seen all burned in direct sunlight...something to do with the UV waves. Oh, and ghouls, although they're a bit weird as well."*

"Yeah!" I replied, still watching the corridor, splitting my gaze between the ground and the ceiling, making sure there were no more goddamn lizards about. *"I faced some up here that were out in daylight."*

"Damn, that's not good. Did they look like normal ones?" he asked. *"I mean, maybe they were a variant or..."*

"Shit no," I said, having forgotten about that. *"The vamp was a weird one, like really weird. Ran on all fours, hissed a lot, really hairy...and the face was wrong, like someone grabbed it by the nose, then smoothed it out to the ears. No normal cheeks or rounded face, more straight lines and..."*

"The ears pointed up and down?" Jonas asked. *"Curved, like an axe?"*

"Shit, yes! Exactly like that!"

"Heard about them...mostly exterminated as they're the buggers who got the usual vampire legends started. Remember, the Arisen like to keep this shit hidden. There's a feral breed that were pretty much wiped out in the records, though...can't remember the name, something Oriental..."

"Will you be silent!" Scylla cut us off; the anger and venom in her voice made us all flinch. *"We hunt, inside of our enemy's territory and to rescue their prisoners, and all you do is yap! BE SILENT or leave! I cannot track with all this noise!"*

"Sorry..."

"Sorry Scylla..."

"Sorry..."

The only one of the group who seemed neither pissed off nor embarrassed at the talking was Belle. She just followed along, barely paying attention as she clearly did something internally.

Thinking about it—sure, nobody else could hear our conversation now, which was a relief, but us all talking like that? We'd been drowning out other sounds, especially as the command link made sure we could all hear each other clearly.

I winced, and I was sure Jonas would be doing the same.

As experienced soldiers, not to mention hunters, we'd just massively fucked up, and we'd done it because we'd placed pretty much total faith in Scylla to find anything ahead.

We stayed silent as she padded ahead of us, the anger practically rolling off her in waves.

I started to pay more attention to the passages around us as we went again, noting the carvings on the walls, the patterns and the depth of the dust covering them. There were torn cobwebs, footprints in the dust, and occasional patches of scuffed earth, where cracks in the walls had disgorged dirt long since.

Now, as we moved as quickly and quietly as we could, we passed across ancient sections of polished stone, moving around cracked and broken bones and long-abandoned armor and discarded weapons as often as broken stone.

More and more as we went, we came to small areas that made no sense—widened areas of the passage that held great slabs of stone on either side. Ingrid paused at one, resting her hand on the slab and looking sad, but when I started to ask her about it, she just shook her head that it wasn't important.

Scylla dropped to one knee again, a hundred meters down the passage from us, and held up a hand. Then, distantly, we heard noises. She fell back; Jonas and I fell in on either side of her as we caught up.

"More coming," she said aloud, and I nodded, flexing my right fist, only to be shoved back by her.

"This time, Jonas and I will take the charge. He needs room to use that sword, and you may kill the injured."

I opened my mouth to tell her to fuck right off, then shut it with a click.

She was right, and it fucking galled.

She was a warrior of legend, so yeah, she got her slot on the front line, and he was now the guy carrying the "sword of God," basically.

I had a posh punch dagger.

Of the three of us, if one was standing behind the other two, it should be me, despite how much I hated that. I consoled myself with the promise that it was only for now, and it'd been Jonas who did it last time.

What really galled was that as the corridor was as narrow as it was, it meant that when the Stelek came into view this time, they were only two abreast.

They raced forward, and Scylla and Jonas killed them easily.

It was literally a case of stab out, deflect the incoming sword arms of the creatures, then stab to the chest and kill them.

They looked like terrible foes, but honestly, they were crap, and...

And then, between and behind two more of the warriors, something else moved.

CHAPTER THIRTY-SIX

W here the "warriors" were fairly simple creatures, the next in line was anything but. For the first time, I realized why the Oracan had been pushed back by these fuckers, losing their homes and clans to them.

Stelek Hive Guardian	Biological Weapon Variant
One of several early and semi-successful BWVs that were granted further augmentations, the line designated as "Stelek" spawns various greater strengths that warrant expanded investment, including hive mentality and simplified hormonal aggression controls.	
The hive guardian is an entirely different evolution of the Stelek queen's drive for specialization. Where the warriors can be identified as the more basic of the hive's members, used mainly as a "quantity over quality" design, the guardian class is deployed only to fight.	
Capabilities:	
Sleep of the Dead: The Stelek guardian's main defensive method, beyond its significant mass, armoring, and speed, is the "sleep of the dead": a gaseous attack that renders most creatures insensate within seconds. Any damage done to the outer carapace that cracks or otherwise pierces it will result in the membranous layer beneath extruding a fluid, that, on contact with the external atmosphere, vaporizes.	
Hunter-seeker: Stelek guardians have highly advanced scent receptors, and when they identify those that carry the scent markers of Stelek killers, they hunt them down, enabling a fast and efficient response to territorial incursion.	
Crush: The Stelek guardian uses its segmented exoskeleton as an additional weapon to flex and compress its prey, literally reducing them to broken and shattered remnants of their former selves, enabling more efficient ingestion by the queen upon the guardian's return to the hive.	
HP 900/900	**Stelek**

The fucker was huge, and where the warriors—that I now guessed were the equivalent of fucking worker bees or ants, in comparison to the actual "soldier" class of the guardian—were rushing forward? It flowed.

It was longer and bigger than them, about three meters across, and more like a centipede, a dozen legs pulled in tight that propelled it along at a hell of a speed.

It was segmented, section after section covered in a thick armor plating that reminded me of a woodlouse or pill bug. The head was bigger—hell, it was twice the size of the warrior variants. And the jaws?

A half dozen sets of smaller mandibles flexed and clacked.

Its eyes were a long band that ran left to right across its face, easily twenty eyes set side by side all seeming to glow with an infernal sickly gray and green light. Last of all, the head itself was topped by a thick plate of armor that stayed in place as the actual head dipped and bobbed with its movement, making me think that the damn thing could retreat into it at will.

"Nope." I retracted the blade I'd formed and reached over my shoulder for the rifle I'd reattached to the webbing. "Fuck, no," I said, before making sure I was between the other two, tracking its progress.

"Watch for the gas," I called. "The big fucker gives off a gas counterattack when it's injured."

"You can't use that," Ingrid warned me, seeing the rifle and knowing me too well.

"Fuckin' watch me," I replied grimly, knowing that the corridor was narrow, but that the damn creature was both long and solid, more or less.

"Steve…" Ingrid warned again, and I ignored her, firing.

"Fuck it up!" Jonas snapped, having clearly seen it at the same time as I had, and coming to the much more reasonable—in our eyes—reaction that something *that* size had no business living.

The titanium bullet hit it about three inches above one of the center-most eyes, smashing the nearest two eyes inward as the impact cratered the chitin, popping a half dozen of them, and radiated shattered segments in all directions.

It continued onward, digging through layer after layer. The impact and kinetic energy worked together to both burrow through them and cauterize them as the titanium fragmented and began to convert to both gas and liquid.

Ichor caught by the blast front was rendered into gases as well, flash-boiling in a split second, then erupting outward in all directions, forced by the speed of the hit to create a crater throughout the body in a straight line from impact, down.

Where the bullet was about half the size of my pinkie finger's nail, the wound left by its impact was at least six inches across, and ran most of the length of the creature.

It fell to the ground like a sack of shit and skidded. The gas that the description warned about poured off it in waves from the wound, looking more like low fog than anything else.

"Steve!" Ingrid snapped at me, and I looked at her, grinning over the kill.

"What?"

"We agreed not to use them! The risk of a cave-in—"

"Was less than the risk of that bastard smashing into the walls and ceiling as we fought it." I glared at her. "With the size of it, it absorbed at least most of the impact in its body, right? If we'd fought that? We can't take the hit; it'd have chewed through Scylla's shield, and probably ignored the spear. Jonas could cut his way through it, but then what? He'd have to literally walk inside the fucker to do that, and it'd be giving off gas!"

"He…you…" she fumed, as Jonas stepped back, his new blade flashing as he cursed, finding me there.

"I need a little room!" he snapped, and I quickly backed up, as he and Scylla fought the handful of warriors that had led the charge.

"I didn't have time to discuss it," I half apologized, and half stated as I moved backward with her, all of us retreating to give Jonas and Scylla space. "Fighting that would have been a goddamn nightmare!"

"I know that, Steve," Ingrid replied, clearly forcing herself to speak calmly. "But we can't use the rifles without consequences! What if it ricocheted? Hit the roof? It could have brought it down and buried us all!"

"If that thing's armor could ricochet a shot from this?" I said, seeing but disagreeing with her concern. "Then none of our weapons would have stood a chance against it. Seriously, Ingrid, I didn't just toss aside that we weren't using the rifles for nothing. You need to trust me when I say that we needed to break the rules for that fucker."

"Okay," she muttered, shaking her head in annoyance, clearly not wanting to give up, but seeing my point as well, especially when the second started to try to work its way past.

Where the first had collapsed pretty much as flat as it could on the ground, the second was awkwardly clambering atop it, scraping against the ceiling as it started to drag itself forward. The carapace of its dead fellow creaked and cracked as it piled its considerable weight atop it.

"Fuck, now what?" Jonas asked, straightening as he dispatched his last opponent.

"We wait," I said. "It's climbing along the top, so it can't dodge. Wait until it's halfway, and we shoot the fuck...deals with the problem and—"

"And wedges the passageway," Scylla pointed out, making me wince.

"You got a better idea?" I suggested. "If we wait until it's halfway, then at least there's a good chance the body will absorb the rail gun round. We just fire randomly, and it might end up taking the passage out."

"Can you open this?" Ingrid asked, and I frowned, looking to where she pointed.

"The wall?" I asked, and she shook her head.

"I think it's a passage," she said. "One that was sealed off."

"A passage?" I stepped over to look at it, only to be cut off by Jonas.

"Boss, we need to decide what to do about that fucker," he reminded me, and I cursed, sighted, and fired at a slight angle, aiming into the guardian as it worked its way closer.

I'd angled it slightly down, from the front of its head, hoping that it'd stay more or less inside the body, before wincing again as a muffled and distant boom echoed back.

"Steve!" Ingrid growled, and I shook my head, stepping up next to her.

"Fuck it, we're not going that way now anyway," I told her. "What's this?"

"Well, we're not now!" Belle agreed with a wide smile. "Give me a minute..." She stepped up now that the passage was blocked and started to drain the corpses as I moved to the wall where Ingrid glared at me.

"I think it's a passage the Oracan closed off," she said slowly, still glaring at me, and pissed.

"It's a wall." I pressed one hand against it and shoved, hard. There was no give in it, and I looked at her in question.

"We've been using this passage for what, half an hour?" she asked me, and I nodded.

"About twenty minutes," Jonas corrected.

"Okay, so the average walking speed of a human means that we've probably traveled about a mile in that time," she pointed out.

I shrugged. It sounded about right.

"Well, what kind of a refuge, a fortress or village or whatever, has an entrance a mile long?" she asked. "There's choke points all along the route, but a mile long? The effort that would take to cut out the stone is insane."

"It's the Oracan." I smiled despite myself. "They're not exactly sane."

"No, Steve, they're perfectly sane," she corrected me. "They're literally a soldier caste, bred for war, so think about it. The effort they'd put into carving a solid mile of a passage into the mountains? They could build almost *anything* with that. Certainly a real fortification. So why would they just make choke points and leave it at that?"

"I...don't know," I admitted.

"It's because we're not traveling *to* their fortress, Steve...we're in the middle of it," she said sadly. "I think these were crossing points, like the way Americans make straight streets and blocks in the cities, rather than winding streets the way we do in Europe, because our cities grew over centuries to be the way they are, but American cities were planned.

"To make a place like this would take decades, possibly centuries. You'd have entire generations dedicating their lives to it, and it'd be planned perfectly. It'd be like Derinkuyu! It'd have to be planned out, and that includes the doors."

"Derkin-you-you?" I asked, confused.

"Derinkuyu," she said. "Steve, your tentacles! Can you form them still?" She stared at me.

"A little." I nodded, lifting one hand and showing her a small one. "But I need a fuckload of nanites to form them the way I did before..."

"Can you send some under here?" She pointed to the ground where the massive stone slab vanished into the dirt, and I shrugged, getting down on one knee. "See if you can see anything?"

I dug my fingers into the piled dirt and dust, finding after a few seconds of work that there was a definite edge to the slab that I'd assumed was part of the wall. Instead, I found that it was sitting atop the carved and once polished stone floor.

I moved to the sides, forming a claw and using it to drag along the edges of the slab. Where it rested, there was a definite groove, which meant...

"Fuck, I think you're right," I whispered, extending a finger and reforming the claw, focusing and forming a tiny spike. I dug it into the gap at the bottom of the door, wiggling it deeper and deeper, having to shift it like water, holding my hand still and instead inch the nanites forward.

It took long seconds, the little line absorbing and breaking down material as it went, burrowing in the depths, until suddenly it pushed a section of dirt aside. Beyond it, I could sense an open space.

"There's air," I said unconsciously.

"Fresh?" Jonas asked, and I snorted.

"Dude, seriously, I have no clue, all right? It's like radar. I can sense an open space, that's all, what feels like probably walls on either side, and an open space in the middle. But yeah, I think it's probably a passage. You're right," I said to Ingrid, smiling. "How did you know?"

"I just thought about how far we'd come, and what was probably behind there," she said sadly, and I frowned.

"What's wrong?" I asked.

"It's a fortress city, right?" she asked, and I nodded. "Well, when the fortress fell, they were still fighting their way out, right?"

"Yeah?"

"So, usually when you make a fortress or a city, it's because you've got a lot of people, and while there'd be a lot of people who managed to escape, or Oracan, I suppose, the majority? They wouldn't. They'd be either driven out if they were lucky, or they'd be killed."

"Right?"

"Well, that's unless you had really strong walls and ways to seal off a section of your city. Then, well, you'd have your people wait, and wait, hoping for a rescue."

"Oh fuck," I muttered, finally seeing what she was getting at. "It's a mass grave?"

"I think it might be." She gestured at the dead Stelek. "They're insects, and unless their queen is a lot brighter than they are? They'd have no reason to go looking for a way through the walls. They might sense something, but after a while, sniffing around the edges and unable to find a way in? They'd just stop."

"And the people inside would starve." Scylla stepped up and reached out, laying one hand on the wall before her in reverence. "Another one."

"Another?" I asked, and Ingrid twisted to look at her in question.

"When a city falls, its defenders and citizens die, usually painfully," Scylla said softly, the closest thing to tears in her eyes that I'd ever seen. "For long ages, we tried to find ways around that. We made rules, and we punished those who broke them. We made stronger and stronger defenses, and here and there, we built hidden cities. There were dozens that I know of…great cities that had a small area aboveground, and the rest hidden below."

"Where?" Ingrid asked, and Scylla shrugged.

"Thessaloniki, Naours, Petra, Anatolia, Roma. We made many, until they failed."

"Failed?"

"Like this," she said softly, drawing one hand down the wall before her, then looking around. "They failed. They were refuges, but when the defenders couldn't come back? Their people withered and died, or they opened their doors and were punished.

"Some conquerors poured naphtha into the breathing holes and burned them out. Others simply waited, knowing that no matter the stores, eventually they had to come out.

"Snakes and more were fed in…poisons, acids. Some were smoked out. But wherever it happened, rather than the hiding citizens being safe? Their conquerors punished them even more harshly. For every city that survived and was retaken, ten were destroyed utterly. The invading armies had time to rest, to recover, and for the hatred to fester. When their victims were taken, they died hard."

"Well, fuck," I muttered, shaking my head and staring at Scylla, reminded again that for me what was ancient history, dry and meaningless, beyond the immediate concerns it might have for me, was her past. She'd known people who died in these kinds of places. Hell, knowing what a psycho she was? She might have been a besieging general or fighter. I stood, not sure how to ask, or even if I wanted to.

"I don't know if I can lift it. If I had more nanites? Sure, there's a block..." I told them, as I found it, half buried and making sure that the block stayed exactly where it was.

"A wedge?" Ingrid asked, and I nodded.

"Yeah. It's driven into the ground on the far side. There's what looks like a chain or something—it's attached to the block, and the wedge keeps it in place."

"They'd have needed a way to raise and lower the blocks," Ingrid agreed. "A pulley system, most likely. They could haul it up, a group of them, then they'd have punched a wedge into place, holding the blocks up. When they needed to close it off? A hammer and a couple of blows, that was all that was needed."

"Fuck," I whispered, not sure what we could do now. Maybe we could cut our way through? Or go through the corpses?

"Steve?" Belle called.

"Yeah?" I turned around, relieved to have the distraction.

"Do we need to leave soon?"

"Yeah," I said. The longer we were here, the shittier the situation would get, and judging from the look on her face, as she stood in the damn fog, she was suffering from trying to harvest the first of the guardians.

"Then I think...I think I will need help..." she whimpered, sagging sideways, as she tried to hold onto the head of the corpse.

I ran to her, barely making it ahead of the others, and before covering my mouth as I grabbed her, dragging her backward.

The others darted in as well, picking her up, and we carried her back. Ingrid was affected the worst by the mixture, staggering as if she were drunk after only a few seconds in it. Jonas and Scylla dealt with it better, but for me?

There was an unexpected bonus.

Highly Advanced Anesthetic Compound Identified: Nanites Assessing...

Countering...

Compatible baseline detected! Substance may be synthesized and artificially boosted using Mavka Queen Acidic Venom. Continue?

"Fuck, yes," I muttered as an insanely complex formula grew in my mind's eye.

Design Schema Complete!

Name: ?

Description: A highly potent acidic-based anesthetic, this compound is unique to date, and as such awards the following reward for its creation:

- **+1 War Point**
- **+1 Weapon Skills Point**

"Death's Kiss," I whispered, getting a strange look from Jonas, as I shook my head and read the next prompt.

Warning! Chemical weapons production offline. Emergency synthesis available, at a cost of 5:1. Confirm?

I forced myself not to curse, instead refusing it as I banished the screen. Of course I couldn't fucking produce it! The systems that I had inbuilt that could have done it? They were inbuilt *in my fuckin' armor!*

I didn't have my goddamn armor, just like I no longer had the ability to fly, just like I could barely use the gravity inverter, and had to make it from scratch each time—when I had enough nanites—to use it.

I couldn't use the vorpal blade, I couldn't...

Fuck, I couldn't use any of the shit I'd gotten used to having. All the things that made me a virtual god among men had been lost thanks to the fucking fight for the ship and now...

Nanites.

I needed nanites, desperately, and there were nanites nearby. I dumped my backpack; the slumbering sentinel twitched but stayed as it'd been ordered to remain.

Turning my head slowly, my eyes tracking like the searchlights of a fucking warship cannon, I fixed on the dead guardians.

Belle was broken by the effects of the guardian's gas attack; she couldn't get the nanites for everyone. But me?

I was immune to it now, or at least I thought I would be.

I pulled the nanites I had up, sealing them over my face and ordering them to filter the air, not even thinking about how I knew they could, just that I'd unlocked the capacity before, and I was damn well using it now. How they did it was their problem.

Striding forward and into the low, roiling cloud of fog that seeped from the cracks of the corpses, I ignored the cry of alarm from Ingrid, extruded the harvest tool, and stabbed it deep into the wound that Belle had been exploiting.

It was sluggish at first. The nanites were there, all right, but there were nowhere near the quantities I'd get from an Arisen. There were a decent amount per pound of converted human-to-fucking-monster flesh, though, and by weight?

These bastards were *big.*

Belle had drained a lot of the immediate area, though, so that meant I needed to go deeper. I formed the nanites into thin claws on either hand, not even aware I'd done it until I was cutting, the need guiding me as much as any conscious desire.

Instead, I cut and I dug, carving my way inside the corpse. The distant calls and demands from the others that I back away were ignored in the face of my determination.

We needed the fucking nanites, and they were here.

I burrowed deeper. The harvest tool opened all four ports. Tendrils of active and attuned nanites flowed out to punch into the flesh all around me, forming a net that twisted out around me, feeding, as I let out a feral growl.

More.

I needed fucking *more!*

Every time I thought I was strong enough, every time I thought I could do it, that I could protect them, they got goddamn hurt and I lost them.

I'd lost them for weeks, *months* even in Russia, when I'd been unhinged enough I was losing my mind. I'd lost Ingrid for years when Athena and the others had captured me—three fuckin' years I'd been tortured and broken. And the only good thing that had come out of that?

The nanites.

I'd gained millions of nanites. I'd formed my armor. I'd grown. I'd become the dark crusader in truth, a protector of the innocent and a fuckin' nightmare for the guilty. The things I could do had been worth the suffering, the pain.

Then I'd lost it all. I'd lost my armor, I'd lost my strength, I'd even lost my goddamn abilities and my damn blades! Now here, with a team again, all of them growing, all of us ready to be more, and my former enemies—or at least, reluctant allies—were better than I was! They were stronger, faster, and certainly goddamn smarter.

They had experience, they had training, and what did I have? Skills *I* was teaching them, and sheer bloody determination. That was it.

I reached out and pulled. My weaponized nanites flexed and stabbed, churning the flesh around me...the muscles, the organs, the bones, *all* of it.

I needed this fucking thing out of the way. I needed the nanites. I needed...

What I needed? It was to get rid of the corpses and the shit to get at the nanites, and to get at more of the enemy. What I had? Well. What I had was *System Replenishment.*

I felt it triggering, called up by need, by the demands of the user. I felt the nanites in the two corpses sluggishly responding, deactivated, corrupted, lost.

They shifted and were dragged to me as more and more of my own nanites went active.

My corrupted nanites, and the majority of those around me, were being torn free, dragged inward and converted, even as more started the process of breaking down the guardians' dead bodies.

Thousands of the nanites were weaponizing, called to fulfill a need. A new pattern that I'd never known before—but one that they'd always been capable of—swam in front of me, and more and more flowed out to coat my skin.

The surface rippled as designs that were partially unlocked shifted, matching up. Ragged edges of technology, long lost, locked away and simply never used in this manner, were suddenly twisted, as the key of knowledge was made to fit the lock perfectly.

I felt the cascade effect as my new armor formed. A thousand idle thoughts, curiosities, *needs*...all of them were examined, evaluated, and accepted, as the template was adjusted and found acceptable.

System Replenishment was a simple thing, something so minor and weird that I'd almost ignored it. Hell, it'd saved my life, and still I'd been looking at it as one thing, and nothing more—a single-use tool—and I should have known better.

Nothing in all of reality was one-sided, not even this.

I hissed as the nanites were pulled in faster. The catalyst picked up speed, as the first corpse began to collapse inward. I blinked, realizing that I could see— no, that I could *sense* the strands of nanites, the webs I'd extended around me.

They drank down their corrupted cousins in great quantities, pouring them across my skin as I dragged myself forward. The flesh and ichor, the armored plates, muscles, bones, chitin...all of it failed before me as structural weakness flowed out like a terrible plague.

On all sides, the matter simply failed, massive quantities of it being dragged inward. Anything that could be used was fed into the forge that I was becoming, rippling black skin like the event horizon of a black hole flexing and expanding to cover more and more of me, as the gray, unidentifiable mass of broken chemical and biological links piled up at my feet.

My classes were responsible, I knew distantly. My knowledge of the Support class granted me access to converters, to constructors and factories—and what was a converter but a housing that held a nanite's conversion field?

They shifted the atomic blocks from one form to another, making glass into gold, or sand into steel.

Well, now they made more.

They fed the best of the matter all around into me. I felt the massive influx of...*everything*, and I pulled harder.

My nanites reached the far side as I stepped free of the second corpse. The two warriors that had stood there launched themselves fearlessly at me, and they died, carved apart as I stepped into them, their bodies hacked in roughly equal halves by the harvest blade, now regrown to a sword, and the vorpal blade, reconstructed and reborn.

Their bodies hit me, bouncing. But rather than falling free?

They stuck, held there as I stared forward. My mind roiled as my new armor worked, stripping their remains of anything it could get.

They collapsed into mush, and I continued forward. More of the hive awoke to the threat even as I distantly heard the others speaking, calling to me.

I ignored them, feeling the fragile bubble I was in and knowing that I couldn't afford any distraction, any thoughts. I buried my mind, my consciousness below the level of need, and I saw them.

The warriors raced forward, literally pressed side by side in the passage—mandibles clacked hungrily, antenna twitched, ropey drool hung free of their maws...

I saw them come, and I smiled.

They were bringing me what I needed.

I could feel the nanites they were bringing me, and I hungered for them. I felt the need, the way that I could reach them faster. Nanites were repurposed, flowing inward. Organs that were assessed and found to be wasteful were culled. An appendix? Pointless. Liver? The nanites did its job better. Intestines? Far longer and less efficient than were needed. More and more was culled, replaced with smaller, more graceful designs. And the freed-up space? A new gravity inverter spun up again; the system rebuilt fast as thought, no longer a part of my armor, no longer a system that would need to be summoned, nor designed and rebuilt.

Now it was a part of me, and it twisted space at my will. I fell forward, faster and faster. The passage ahead became a pit that I dove down, arms outstretched, as the Stelek raced up toward me.

Chitinous blades were lifted, and we hit one another with a great crash. They dug their blades into me, shredding the thin armor, tearing the flesh beneath and then stripping it away , erupting into the dark passageway and sending great gouts of blood spraying...before they started to dissolve.

Their serrated terrible ridges, the sharp blades, the muscles that drove them and the bone that reinforced them, all smoked and crumbled, strength ripped free and dragged into me instead.

My blades, though? They carved through them effortlessly. I twisted, slicing, dicing, and fucking julienne-frying, gasping as my body was torn apart, rebuilding visibly—flesh knitting, bones reattaching to muscles almost as fast as they were severed.

Nanites formed webs, tentacles, spears. They flashed out, stabbing into the enemies on all sides, skewering them, drawing their nanites free and pouring the black, glossy surface of my flowing armor across them.

Where it touched, it ate. The bodies beneath its covering torn apart as their nutrients, genetics, and cells were repurposed. They were shredded, adding fuel to the rebirth. The stronger my enemies were, the more they gave me.

The warriors broke free of the fight...or they tried to. Of the original dozen that had closed, five turned tail and tried to flee, and spears of nanites, attached to chains, ripped free, lancing across the gap and stabbing deep.

The heads of the spears shifted—spikes extending, growing, anchoring.

Then the chains rippled backward, dragging their frantically twisting bodies back to me.

More and more tentacles flashed out. The nanites grew in number: a few hundred becoming thousands, becoming tens of thousands.

Most broke down, their higher functions abandoned in favor of new coding. But laid atop them? Atop the armor I was regrowing? A fully functional attuned and repurposed layer. The same thin, glossy black layer that rippled in anticipation, that poured across my enemies, and that fed me.

At the end of the passageway was a room, a much larger one, and there, in the distance, I could see the remnants of the hive gathering.

As I stepped out and into the new area, I stared around. My mind was deliberately not active, kept below the threshold, dismissing the centuries of carving that ran across the stones, the high ceiling, and the throne that sat in the middle of the far wall, atop a raised dais.

I saw it all and brushed it off as unimportant. The only thing that mattered: the three guardians and thirty or so warriors, as well as the dozen smaller creatures.

They looked like grubs, or maggots, if they were supersized to the size of Dobermans.

All of them tore and dug at the far wall, and the various supports that protected the vaulted ceiling. I saw them all as the walls shivered, and I knew what they were doing.

The queen had decided to abandon the hive, the maggot things being carried from the room atop the backs of warriors as the passage they escaped down was attacked.

The guardians and warriors that remained were going to bring the roof down. They were going to kill, or at least slow us, in exchange for their lives.

No.

Time dilation kicked in. I flashed forward, leaping and diving, landing atop the nearest guardian as it reared back, lifting its bulk and clearly intending to crash itself into a pillar.

Instead, I hit it with the power of a semi, smashing into it. My blades extended and ripped, tearing my way through its upper segments, my nanite flesh eating its way through.

It twisted, driven sideways and falling, and crashed to the floor with a boom of crushed carapace, killing two warriors and injuring a third, the back legs reduced to splinters.

I rode it down, half inside its body and continuing. Tentacles punched out; webs of nanites speared from the tentacles, connecting to each other, forming a latticework that ripped and ate, tore and absorbed.

I saw carapace ahead, and I reached out, stabbing the blades into it, shifting them. They reformed into blunt extensions, crowbars of unbreakable force. I heaved, ripping the carapace apart as I emerged into the throne room again. Steam rolled off me, the fuckers' internals dripping and slithering down my armor as they were eaten.

The others went into a frenzy as I launched myself at the next in line, another guardian spinning as I jumped. Rather than try to fight me, it latched onto the pillar and twisted, using its strength and weight to slam into me like a Louisville slugger hitting a headlight, and I flew through the air, crashing into the far wall.

I fell, momentarily stunned, hitting the floor as rifle fire rang out. I shook myself, planting my hands before me and shoving myself back up. Tentacles reached out, securing themselves and lifting as well as I rose into the air.

The inverter rippled, and I hovered there, staring in cold, emotionless fixation at the fucker that'd just sent me across the room.

It was my turn.

Ingrid and the others knelt by the entrance, firing over and over. Warriors and the two remaining guardians totally ignored them as they continued to try to close off the access routes that led deeper.

I formed a new gravity well, a tunnel of twisted space that led from me to the guardian, and through it. I looped it, arcing to where the second guardian was attacking the wall, and then to the warriors.

I formed it like a water slide, all loops and flowing motion, and then I poured power into it. There was a slight pull as I began to move, before the speed picked up exponentially.

The pull doubled and redoubled for every inch and meter I covered, falling faster and faster. I extended my arms before me, the blades reforming. Behind me? Tentacles, ridges extended, lines forming from nanite webs, until I looked more like a fuckin' shuttlecock than a man.

I hit the guardian almost too fast to see. The impact juddered up my arms. Pain erupted in me as bones were twisted, hairline fractures in the damn metal I'd made them into reverberating through me as I ripped free of the far side of it.

Ichor, chitin, armored carapace, and more erupted out of the far side, dragged behind me as I tore into the next. The massive guardian snapped in half, its upper segments collapsing.

I hit the next almost before the outside world had registered, then the warriors.

The world around me erupted into a blossom of ichor and flying, broken armored plates.

Pain rolled over me as my body was shattered, the impacts alone enough to render a normal man dead. They went on and on. And, despite lasting mere seconds in total? The time dilation dragged it out into far, far longer for me.

I twisted and spun, the end of the loop ahead; the gravity inverter flared and dragged insane amounts of power to counter my speed.

I landed, claws extending from the front of my boots, digging into the ancient stonework with a squeal like a chainsaw meeting flint, great arcs carved into it.

Stone fragments flew, cracks radiated out, and I roared in pain. The sound was distant to me as all around the room, Stelek parts rained down in a great cascade.

Waves of fog rolled off the shattered forms of the guardians, and for a long second, I almost launched myself after the fleeing members of the hive, knowing I could kill them all.

Then her voice reached out to me, and I hesitated. All around me, I could sense the changes, feel the pain I'd been ignoring, the alterations racing through me.

I felt them, and I knew this body couldn't continue, not as it was.

I needed to repair, to reload, and to absorb. That last attack had been sheer insanity. Using my own body, even cushioned by the nanites' armor and the gravity field, as a projectile?

It'd broken most of me, and it'd take time to fix. Ingrid's voice was calling, and despite being deep in a red fog of rage and insanity to make the words out, it guided me.

It calmed me, and slowly, grimly, I arose from the pit.

The world around me rolled back in. My rage subsided, and the pain rose.

I lifted into the air, unable to bring myself to respond to her, and almost unable to focus, the pain was that bad. Every bone in my body, every joint, the cushioning cartilage, the tendons and gristle...fuck, the veins and skin...

All of them were damaged, and the nanites were rebuilding at a frantic pace.

They expended themselves now, no longer able to draw from the enemy, and I snarled, reaching out as I floated through the air. A second, a third, and more gravity wells formed around me as I rotated, slowly lowering and landing atop the throne.

I collapsed back onto it, my body unable to support itself. Nanites latched to the wall behind me, keeping me upright as the gravity wells dragged the remains of my enemies closer, tentacles leaping out to sink into them.

I gasped in relief. The nanites flowed across the bodies and settled in, begging to break them down. My System Replenishment went into overdrive as more and more of the bodies were consumed.

Rebuilding and refueling me, replacing nanites and flesh lost, nefindium bones that were covered in cracks were forged anew, and I settled back. The autonomous needs of my body took precedence as my mind, the fulcrum that had kicked the rest of this into action, shut down.

I was burnt out, but I was alive, and so were they. That was all I needed to know.

Cocooned in my new glossy black armor, I lifted my gaze with difficulty, at a sound, and stared across the mass of flagstones at the others, where they stood by the far passage.

"What the fuck are you...?" Jonas whispered, and in the command link, I heard it, even dozens of meters away.

"A weapon," I whispered.

As the word left my lips, I felt it slam into the world around me, shaking it with its power, and I sank into unconsciousness.

CHAPTER THIRTY-SEVEN

BEWARE — A DEVOURER HAS BEEN UNLEASHED UPON THE COSMOS — FLEE ITS WRATH

That was the prompt that they'd all been given, and even now, more than two hours later, as I sat there, staring into the distance, the ancient throne of the fortress city of Bashanti-Ulm cradling my ass, I still didn't know exactly what the fuck it meant.

The Oracan war party was free, and it was they that had supplied the name of the place at Ingrid's request. Eleven of them had survived out of forty. The rest died in the fight, already stripped into meat for the queen, or having been taken deeper. They knelt before me, heads bowed, right fist pressed to the ground, left held to their heart as they awaited my response.

They'd sworn fealty as soon as we'd freed them, based on the sight of me in full-on rage berserker mode, carving my way through the local forces of their feared enemy; the Stelek guardian leapt at me, only to find me diving through it…literally.

Its most potent weapons—the bite, the crushing ability, and its good old trump card, the gas: all fucking useless when facing something that the very touch of its flesh burned through solid carapace…not to mention that I'd hammered myself through it like a rocket through wet paper.

Add in that I was using swords with an edge a molecule thick, and yeah.

I was back, baby, and the fucking Oracan knew their master when he walked the earth.

"Steve?" Ingrid whispered.

I turned, the motion of my head almost inhumanely smooth as I stared at her, seeing a mixture of images, her flesh and bone, the mental images I always had of her, the memory overlay, and now?

I saw the nanites, the outline, the sheer numbers of them that shifted beneath the surface.

I blinked, banishing the sight, burying the hunger that had arisen at the sight of her…and the need to take her nanites.

"Steve?" she said again.

I realized that she'd been talking, that I'd lost it all, totally ignoring the sounds in favor of contemplating…*no*. No, I'd never hurt her.

I cast out the thoughts and focused, swallowing hard and pulling the armor back.

For the first time, it seemed to resist me, as though the armor wanted to be there still, as if it wanted to be on the surface, not inside of me.

It went though, dragged back beneath my flesh, and I pulled in a long, shaky breath of warm, foul air.

The bodies were disposed of. Their internals had become externals for a short while, though, and yeah, the pillars, floor, walls, and ceiling were still coated in congealed ichor.

"Are you okay? Can you hear me?" Ingrid asked softly, and I nodded, feeling weak, as if I'd just woken from a long illness, as she sagged in relief. "Steve, what the hell did you just do?"

I couldn't answer. I didn't know, and I certainly didn't understand the prompt she'd gotten before, nor the one that she shared with me now.

BEWARE — A DEVOURER HAS BEEN UNLEASHED UPON THE COSMOS — NEW QUEST UNLOCKED!

Eliminate the Devourer:

Devourers are the most feared of all the legions of the ancient enemy. A new one has arisen, and all efforts must be made to eliminate it before it grows in power. Every last trace must be destroyed, and the corpse fed into magma.

Reward:

- **X10 Specialization Points**
- **X1 Greater Perk**
- **X5 Lesser Perks**

I'd not gotten it, but the others had, apparently, and as I reached inside myself, I could feel it. My armor, which was usually just there, like my hand or my hair or whatever, part of me, but not really anything else?

Now it was...*more*.

I could feel the hunger in it.

I could feel...I focused, searching for anything I could identify, looking for traces of sentience, and finding none.

The armor wasn't alive, nor was it aware in the way that even the nanites were. It was a part of me—like my skin, definitely—but it wasn't like it had been before.

Before, it was layers of nanites, ones that flexed and shifted to form the armor, growing thicker here, thinner there, cupping my goddamn balls in silk here, and forming a solid mass of pseudo-metal there that could shrug off gunfire like rain.

It was all those things, but it was also almost dead. The armor responded to my needs and wants but it did nothing more. Now, though? It felt alive and a part of me, as if it were living.

I shook my head, knowing that was useless even as I tried to explain it to Ingrid, accepting the others as they moved closer, watching and listening.

"The armor isn't complete," I whispered. "It's at its most basic. It's barely millimeters thick, not if I want to use the tentacles as well. I've got a fraction of the nanites I need to return it to its former size and strength, but it's more than it ever was before. Belle, in your options, is there one called System Replenishment?"

She hesitated. "There is, but it's grayed out for me. It says I'm incompatible." She sounded confused.

"I used that," I admitted. "I don't know why it'd be removed from your system or how, but I used that, linking it to my armor, feeding it into the nanites, teaching them to form it, and to form across me."

"What does it do?" Jonas asked, and I frowned, still searching inside myself.

"It breaks down organic matter," I said. "Stripping it of the building blocks of life at a cellular level. It literally snaps them apart, taking what's needed to repair you, to make you into the best version of yourself you can be."

"You used it when you fought the Reta Variant, in the catacombs," Ingrid whispered. "The bodies that you broke down."

"I did. What's left of them afterward? It's a mess, nothing really usable or identifiable. Now, though, somehow I used it to supercharge my healing, using my nanites to strip more nanites free of the bodies around me. I then used them to extend the net further.

"Every organic bit that I touched was broken down. Every cut I got, every injury—they were stripping the enemy apart as we fought to repair me."

"The Devourer," Ingrid whispered. "It's you. The system is warning us about you."

"I think so," I admitted, still stunned and brain-fucked. "But I don't know why."

"You said that the creators used us to fight their wars and we rebelled, right?" Jonas asked, and I nodded. "Okay, so the prompt says that we should kill you— don't worry, I'm not gonna try—and it names you as a new Devourer, saying that it was 'one of the most feared of all the legions of the ancient enemy.'"

"Right?"

"So, what I'm wondering is who the fuck the ancient enemy is?"

"Well…" I paused, as I thought.

"Exactly!" Jonas growled. "You said that we were created as a counter, as a kind of police force, space army and peacekeepers, right? You don't make a fucking army unless there's a need. Either that's what we were, or? Or they fucking *lied*! Are we the ancient enemy, or are we the counter to it? Are we supposed to be the ancient enemy? Because if we are? We're fucked."

"How?" Scylla asked, confused. "They are long dead, yes?"

"No," I whispered, seeing his point. "The phrasing…either this ability is something that some ancient enemy could do, and somehow I found out how to do it as well, or…"

"Or there's someone out there right now that views humanity as the ancient enemy, and the system is accepting them as having command access." Ingrid's eyes opened wide. "The Erlking?"

"Could be," I agreed, feeling sick. "Could be that fucker, or…"

"The Erlking said it had abandoned all access to the ships and systems," Belle added. "That it transferred to you the access codes, the authority it had. It wanted nothing to do with any of it. And when it gave you that, it cut itself out of the last remnants of the system. It was why it was determined that if you ever returned, it would kill you. It didn't want to be tempted to retake control."

"It…when it gave me that access, the authority, it failed. It was incomplete…I couldn't take it all," I said.

She shook her head, looking afraid. "The authority was limited," she said, clearly trying to work through it in her mind. "Only one can carry each authority, so when the Erlking gave it to you, even if it broke down, it meant that it was done with it. So unless you can somehow repair that authority, it's lost."

"I can't just, I don't know, get it to fix it? Maybe we fight, and I get it to do it again? To give me some advice?" I asked, even as I said it knowing that I was being stupid.

My meat-based brain was too small, too immature, and too fragile to hold onto the full pattern. And now? After I'd convinced the Erlking, a being that had been banished from and had in turn turned its back on all that technology? I'd lost its authority as well, hanging onto only a fraction of it, in the form of a broken and fragmented BioScan.

"That means…" Ingrid whispered, her eyes widening. "The others!"

"What?" I glanced up at her, where she and the others stood before me, arrayed around the throne, and then cursed, forcing myself to my feet as I looked from them and down at the Oracan, still fuckin' kneeling on the floor below.

"The others!" Ingrid repeated. "You said there were three of them, three creators, and that two of them you'd been warned to stay away from, right? That one of them sank Atlantis?"

"Uh…" I thought back, focusing, and then spoke. "The Erlking mentioned that one of them was 'deep underground' or something. It'd continued with the experiments that had gotten them banned from the collective—whatever that was—and to stay fucking clear of it. The other one was yeah, from Atlantis, and they changed or something, and sank the island, pissed off with people. It warned me not to approach them until I'd proved myself by repairing a ship, and then also told me that if I approached them with a stolen ship, it'd end badly for me."

"So…we're damned if we do and we're damned if we don't?" Jonas frowned, folding his arms.

"Yeah, don't get me started. Seriously, that fucker had a head full of spiders." I shook my head. "Not even slightly sane, and it's one of our creators…so I suppose that explains a lot about us, really."

"Great…mad gods, and at least one of them is still here and pissed at us?" Jonas finished, and I shrugged.

"When's life fair?" I asked, before staggering slightly as a wave of exhaustion flowed over me, followed by—weirdly—a feeling of incredible strength.

Ingrid was there; even as I straightened, she burrowed under my arm and helped me to stand. I smiled, wrapping my arms around her, hugging her, as Jonas coughed, then scratched the back of his neck awkwardly.

"So, you're the Devourer then?" he asked.

"I guess so?" I muttered, wondering whether he or Scylla was about to make a play for the points.

"Well, it makes sense." He looked away from me.

"Why?"

"You looked at your clothes recently?" he countered.

I looked down, from Ingrid's beauty and at myself, before starting to swear.

"Motherfuc—where the hell are my goddamn clothes!" I cursed, finally seeing why it was goddamn uncomfortable on that stone throne when I'd retracted my armor.

I was bare-ass fuckin' naked.

I'd also dumped my damn pack, when I'd gone mad and had dived into the enemy, "wearing their insides like a fucking lunatic," as Jonas put it. Most of my stuff, bar a little food and the sentinel, had been ruined by the mess. But, fortunately, he at least had some spare underwear in his pack.

That was it, though. The rest of the clothes were too small, and obviously Ingrid's spares and Scylla's were useless to me, considering the size disparities. And Belle? Well, she wore so little and even that with considerable distaste, that there was no point in asking.

So instead, I was dressed back in my armor, more or less.

I stomped down the steps to the Oracan, still frozen in place. I spoke clearly to them, as I recognized the figure in the lead.

"Nishka?" I asked, and he nodded. I remembered fighting by his side, or him at mine—whichever way these things worked—in the line with the other Oracan, against the lycans when we took the village.

He was a hell of a fighter, and unlike most of the others, was happy to talk to me and give me advice, viewing me as a fellow warrior.

"Yes, lord?" he asked, his voice a respectful rumble.

"You remember me?" I asked, and he nodded.

"You fought with us in battle."

"I did," I agreed. "You didn't fucking swear fealty to me then, though?"

"We weren't trapped, captured by a terrible enemy that was almost impossible to defeat then. Then you fought with spear and shield as a battle brother, not flying through the air and smashing the Stelek to shattered pieces."

"Point," I muttered.

"Will you accept our oath?" he asked, and I stared at him, before nodding.

"You know what? Yeah, yeah...I fuckin' will. Get up. I accept your oath. I've already summoned Kim and Ronai back to take care of the village. You lot swearing to me just makes this easier. We're going to see how many of your village want to come with us and live with the other Oracan in our home."

"Eto will not like this. He will fight you," Nishka warned me, standing and looking me in the eyes.

"He did," I agreed. "You see that sword that Jonas is carrying?" I pointed to it, and Jonas waved it a little to make sure they could see it.

"The Jonas, he killed Chief Eto?" Nishka frowned.

"No, that was me."

"Yet he carries the sword of the chief?"

"Do I look like I need it?"

Nishka hesitated, before nodding his agreement. "What do we do now?"

I jerked my head in the direction of the passage. "Fuck off back to the village...help Kim and Ronai to get things sorted out. Tell them what happened here, and that we're going to kill the Stelek queen, then we'll come back."

I half expected a comment, something along the line of "The queen? Oh my God, that's amazing," or "She'll be so strong, we should aid you," or some shit.

Instead, he just nodded as if I'd said "I'm going to have a nap, and maybe a beer, then I'll come along as well," and he turned to the others, barking orders.

They gathered up what was left of their weapons and headed out of the passage, making me again stare after them in consternation.

It just felt fuckin' wrong that the Oracan didn't say things like "bye" or "good luck," etc.

Screw it.

I turned to the rest of the party, seeing the mixture of looks on their faces, ranging from curiosity, pride, hunger—on both Ingrid and Belle's faces—and what I was damn sure was a desire to fight me, on Scylla's.

It wasn't a need to kill me. Hell, if anything, Scylla was back to looking at me like she respected me. It certainly wasn't a desire to jump on me like I was getting from Ingrid—or a need for my seed from Belle—it was a desire to fight. To prove herself, to show me that she was lethal as well, and that my cheating and leaping ahead like that didn't mean she was weak.

"Are you all ready?" I asked, and Ingrid quirked an eyebrow at me. "What?"

"Are we ready?" she asked. "We're fine. Belle just needed that smoke stuff to wear off. You're the one who was flying and glowing black and shiny. You're also the only one who was practically catatonic. Are *you* ready, Steve?" she asked grimly, and I allowed myself a smile.

"You know what?" I said. "I am."

I pulled up the flashing notifications as I walked in the middle of the party, feeling a bit weird as I did so. The others fell in around me. Scylla took the lead again, Jonas the rear.

"I'm sorry." I banished the screens and told myself this was more important. "When I did that, when I attacked and when I lost myself in the...in everything? I didn't mean to claim the nanites," I admitted, and despite every instinct in me, I went on.

"I can strip the nanites that have bonded to me. I can't fix the weaponized ones, but I can strip the rest and share them out between you all, and..."

"Don't be so bloody stupid," Jonas grunted.

"You keep what you kill," Scylla said from a few meters ahead.

"We'll share them when it's a battlefield or where we all play our part, but that was...that was all you," Ingrid added.

"Besides," Belle spoke up quite happily, "I already shared out the nanites I'd recovered, splitting them between the others and me."

"Oh." I couldn't help but smile. "Fair enough then, I guess."

I pulled the screens up again. I'd flicked through them before when Ingrid had shown me the last one, the Devourer notification, but when I'd seen that I'd not had one of those, I'd dismissed the rest. Now I pulled them up, reading quickly.

Evolving Quest Updated!

Evolving Quest unlocked: Cull the Interlopers: Level 2

The Stelek have been driven up from the deep places of the world, claiming higher territory and displacing the Oracan people. Cull their numbers to receive the following reward:

- ~~**Eliminate Upper Stelek Hive**~~
- **Eliminate Lower Stelek Hive**
- **Eliminate Stelek Queen**

Jez Cajiao

Reward:
- **+5 Support Points**
- **+5 War Points**
- **+Access to Level 3 of the Evolving Quest**

*

Quest Completed!
Evolving Quest completed: Rescue the Oracan war party: Level 1

The Oracan war party ventured into the underground to face their ancient enemies the Stelek, but have not been seen since. Scout the Stelek hive and the old Oracan underground fortress, and find out what happened to the war party. Complete the following prerequisites to receive the following reward:

- ~~Discover the fate of the Oracan war party~~
- ~~Rescue any surviving Oracan~~

Reward:
- **+1 War Point**
- **+Access to Level 2 of the Evolving Quest**

*

New Quest Discovered!
Evolving Quest unlocked: Rescue the Oracan war party: Level 2

The Oracan war party was defeated and captured by the Stelek defenders. Some of the party have been freed; perhaps there are more beneath? Either way, complete the following prerequisites to receive the following reward:

- **Search the lower hive for any additional survivors**

Reward:
- **+1 War Point**

That was another War point added to the list, and I grinned at that. Five War points and three Weapon Skills. I was saving them for now, until I picked a real weapon that I wanted to keep using. I also had a point of specialization that could be used on anything, something I couldn't help but think of as a "free range" point. Two more Hack, and last but not least? An Espionage one.

I couldn't risk the Espionage, and I certainly wasn't wasting the free range on a War slot. I'd keep that for whatever I needed further down the line, but for now, fuck it. War point investment it was.

I explained quickly to the others what I was going to do, and why. The others could invest their points easily now, and the only way I could be a hundred percent sure that the pain was from my widespread skills was to test it.

I'd do a single point and let it "settle." Then, if I was all right? I'd do the second as well.

I rolled through the options, knowing what I needed, knowing that I needed to be better with my nanites, to know more, to be able to do more. At the same time, I damn well knew it was going to be the most borderline dangerous to do. In for a penny, in for a pound, though.

379

I selected War, then Infiltration, Stealth Systems Upgrade, Assassin, Personal Equipment, and finally, there at the bottom of the tree?

Nanite Manipulation. It had a single sub-tree, which was Armor, and inside that? Armor Design.

It was basically what I'd used to create my armor before. I'd worked with the Nanite Manipulation skill to form the armor, and everything that I'd built from there? It'd all been based on that.

Now I was investing in the tree again, not the Armor Design section—instead just the Nanite Manipulation section, focusing on it, and just...sort of hoping?

There wasn't a second level to it, there wasn't more to unlock, but there was...

It accepted it. Nothing else unlocked: no more sub-trees, no links to another area...or, at least, not yet. I could feel it though, the potential.

Other areas were there, ready to be unlocked, ready to link up, once I learned them. And then? Then there'd be more here to work with.

Or I thought so, anyway.

What I knew was there, though, was enough, as more and more unlocked in my mind. It was the path of War, not Support, not the minutia of the nanites themselves, nor harvesting, where you, I guessed, learned more about the collection and purification of the nanites.

No. Instead of all that, I learned more about using them as weapons.

I could feel the adjustments, the way that they seemed to twitch as more data was unlocked. I knew instantly, even as I bit my lip and tried to keep my focus, to keep putting one foot in front of another, that they were faster now.

I sensed tiny, and I mean damn tiny alterations, as I tried to figure it all out. I felt the way that they shifted in links, becoming slightly faster, more efficient and pliable.

Again, none of it was a massive change, but as the throbbing of my skull and the hard hammering of my heart subsided? I knew it'd been worth it.

I also knew that the War tree was safe to use again.

I flowed back up it, shifting through the options to one that I'd thought about a few times. I'd also thought that it was unnecessarily evil, and that besides the desire to use it on Shamal, I didn't really need it.

I had Trauma Burst, an ability that let me essentially make my nanites explode if I stabbed someone and forced the nanites out of me and into them.

That was great and all, but it was incredibly wasteful. The most important resource I had were my nanites—and my time with Ingrid, but that was a separate thing—and using them to blow things up? Insane.

The nanites were tiny machines, though, and if they could be made to explode, they could be made to do other things.

I already knew how to hack, and I knew how to cleanse nanites when they were in my body. Logically, there was no reason I couldn't cleanse them outside of my body as well; it was literally a command line order that cascaded through them, after all. When I did it in my system, I mentally designated them, and ordered them to wipe or whatever. I'd not really considered that was what I was doing, but it was simply that the nanites were responding to me mentally. The new information that I'd unlocked made that clear.

So, there was no reason I couldn't force the nanites to unlock, not really—besides stupidity, of course. I didn't want them bonding to an enemy and making them more powerful, after all.

If they were corrupted and unattuned, then they were just floating around, augmenting the body they were in, but only a fraction of the way they could.

If I unlocked them? They'd bond to the body and then that person would be much stronger.

Again, fuck that shit.

What if instead, though, I did the opposite? What if I made the nanites in them *mine*?

Could I do it?

I'd be essentially hacking them, after all...something that, in the middle of the fight, I couldn't do. Fuck no. That'd be madness as well.

What if, though...what if I could create and encode a small number of nanites with Tsunami?

I stumbled. That thought sent my brain racing off in an entirely new direction.

Logically, I could, right? I mean, there was no reason I couldn't. They were machines. Tiny ones, admittedly, but they were machines, so why the fuck couldn't I make them into weapons?

I'd been thinking of making them produce the chemical and biological weapons templates I had access to, like that Death's Kiss I just created. That was unique to me, and I'd been thinking that I could use the nanites to deploy it. Instead of them detonating inside my enemies and sending their guts all over the place?

I'd been thinking cut them, back the fuck up, and wait. The nanites would spread through them, picked up and dragged through the bloodstream, reaching the heart and brain, and as they were carried? Synthesize it.

It'd drop people damn fast, after all.

That was what I was planning to do with it. But what if there was a new option? A third way, and one that was far more effective?

Why make a poison, when I could instead make a virus? One that hijacked their bodies?

I could control my nanites, after all, and hell, in the fight with Shamal, I'd even been able to control them when they were separate from my body, reaching out and making them shift their forms, even at a distance.

Could I do that with the enemy? Cut them, pour in Tsunami, give them a few minutes to back up and let them give an evil villain monologue, and then just, what? Click my fingers and stop their heart? Rip them apart? Make their nanites pour out of them, flowing straight to me and joining me, and shred their brain on the way out?

Hell, I could have made Shamal's nanites pour out of his eyes and fucking stab him in the dick.

The potential was insane. Thinking about it, I could feel that there was no reason it couldn't be done, nothing beyond that it'd never been done before, that's all.

As far as I knew, there'd never been another like me, a jack-of-all-trades and a sick and twisted puppy all rolled into one.

Did that mean that I was really unique, though? Could I do this?

I reached out, and I tried, focusing not on a single tree, but on what I wanted to do.

I felt it, the changes as they became viable, as they became options I could select. Biological Weapons, the tree under Crafting, and again in the Assassin tree, unlocked a second option, one that contained a dozen links, and I frantically stopped, mentally shoving the door to it shut, or trying to.

It failed. The links reached out: Hack and Support sections responded, and I absolutely freaked and began to pour the nanites I had that were unlocked into the one thing that could help me now.

I summoned the helmet again. Not the physical structure that had been the secure mass around my skull—oh no. I'd have loved to pull that armor back, but I couldn't afford it. Not for the level I'd had it at before.

What I could afford though, was the neural net augmentation that I'd been using. The space that I'd released the clone of me that had grown into the Hack sub-mind.

It took a hundred thousand, basically more than three-quarters of the goddamn nanites I'd managed to loot so far, but it worked!

The sub-mind flowed free of my own mind, decompressing, and as it did? I gasped in relief, not having known the fucker was even there!

It'd been at the back of my mind, layered over my subconscious, taking up space in the buffer layer of my mind and essentially squatting, and keeping silent, running in "battery saver mode" or whatever.

It had been there all this time, taking up space, and essentially clogging up my memory.

Now, as it unpacked, I staggered, blinking, squinting against the blinding pain that was building. It started to take some of the load for me. It expanded outward, unlocking more and more. Data lines seemed to expand as the links were made, and I bit down hard, trying to keep going, as I lost the sight in my right eye.

"Support," I muttered to myself, focusing, desperately mimicking the Support sub-mind I'd made and poured into the factory unit for Zac. I repeated it now. There wasn't enough room to make it as comprehensive as the one I'd made for the Hack tree, but anything was better than what was coming.

I poured it out, and the data started to unlock, even as I staggered to a halt. The passage around me seemed to twist and spin. Ingrid and the others closed in around me, reaching out to help me, to protect me. I sank to one knee, screwing my eyes shut and cursing myself for my stupidity. Of my five War, my two Hack, and my "free range" points that I'd had a minute ago?

All but a single one of the War points was used.

I saw the new total flashing, pulsing weirdly as the image twisted, warping...Then the world collapsed, and I fell into the depths of my own mind.

CHAPTER THIRTY-EIGHT

Sight was slow to return, or so it seemed to me. The first thing that registered was sound. It was distant and it warbled in and out: some of it nonsensical, others seeming familiar and somehow important.

I reached out blindly, feeling solid stone under my hands, by my back…and I was alone. I blinked, squinting as the world came back into focus, and I cursed as I heard the rustling, and the distant zap and crackle of laser fire.

I twisted, forcing myself to focus, and saw them: the two sentinels that we'd brought. One was still pretty much intact—the other damaged, beaten up, but still going.

All around me were branches, woven around and around, forming a solid barrier with narrow gaps to see through. On the far side were the two sentinels, patrolling. Their lasers fired over and over, steadily, not frantic, but in a controlled "we can do this all day, motherfucker" manner.

A dozen meters ahead of me, I saw what had drawn the others from my side, even as I felt the presence of the Hack sub-mind, and realized that it'd done, again, the thing I'd told it to in the ship earlier.

When I'd been rendered insensate, it'd monitored the area, and when it recognized a valid threat, it'd booted me back to the real world.

I blinked and focused in on a dead warrior. And behind it? Dozens more coming.

I forced myself to my feet, extruding my blades, glad beyond belief that I had both the vorpal and harvest blades back now. I hacked my way free of what I recognized to be Belle's Forest Fortress ability, my balance wavering as I forced myself to function.

She'd used it before, growing a massive interwoven bramble and thorny patch to help when the Oracan and I were fighting the lycans, and the difference between then and now?

Massive. This was the enhanced, polished and improved version, compared to her early steps—a painting compared to "kiddie trying to draw with a crayon."

I pushed free, staggered and began to run. Or I tried to, anyway. I took a handful of steps and fell to my knees, then vomited. My inner ear roiled as some changes finished working their way through.

The clacking and tapping nearby dragged my head around, revealing itself to be not one, but both of the sentinels, following me now. Clearly Ingrid had set them to watch me.

I blinked, seeing the last of their targets collapsing in the distance and realized that I'd forgotten about them. They'd been so bloody useless so far, but clearly the others had been forced to leave them guarding me. And for them to have moved on without me?

What the hell had I done?

I reached down inside, feeling both empty from the sudden loss of all the space fillers in my brain, and full, as I saw the new neural latticework that ran around my internals.

I'd basically demanded it be "there" so that I could fit the damn sub-minds in, but I'd also had no clue what I was doing. As such? My nanites had responded to the vague direction and demands in the best way that they could.

I was a big guy, always had been. I was seven foot, easy, deep chest, and yeah, broad shoulders, and all the crap that came with that. But now?

I'd replaced my bones with a form of nefindium, basically stronger than titanium, and as light as aluminum, then I'd built in a latticework of storage lacunas into them.

This time? I'd taken that a step further.

My lungs were big; they needed to be for a man my size, but they'd been natural, more or less. Not anymore.

Now they were a third smaller. The tubules and more still rolled through the changes, as each breath that I took dragged down more and more oxygen into my bloodstream.

I felt the changes as my body adjusted to the new capacities: filtering the levels and settling them down, adjusting to make me slightly stronger, faster and smarter, without the dizziness and basically oxygen poisoning that would come otherwise.

That wasn't the real change, though, I knew as I lumbered to my feet, trying to get my brain back in gear.

No, the real change? The thick band around the inside of my rib cage, reaching from top to bottom.

My ribs were no longer in the typical shape. They looked it, from outside at least, but now?

Layered nefindium, two overlapping forms, one that moved as I breathed, expanding and contracting. The second held steady and took "chest armor" to a whole new fucking level.

I reached out and scooped up the pair of the sentinels. Each of them reacted to my silent command, clinging to me as I started to run. I moved faster and faster, searching for the others, as I mentally dismissed the fucking look I could imagine on the TSA's face if I went through customs now.

The x-ray would be fun to read, that was for sure.

I could feel them, though, the pair of sub-minds—the Hack considerably bigger and more sentient than the Support one. Regardless, they were there, and there was room for the others now, plenty of it, and all I had to do was upgrade the storage.

A mental twitch informed me that I was at two out of five possible upgrades to the chest. I banished that, determined that although I'd look at it later, I didn't have the time to fuck with it right now.

Passages blurred as I ran faster, then launched myself into the air, gravity switching comfortably as the last of the inner ear issues faded, and I picked up speed.

Here and there were sections like in the earlier passage, crossing corridors, and although most were sealed, occasionally I passed ones that weren't. Invariably, these were coated in the desiccated pods, making me think of the warrior Stelek in their hibernation.

More and more, though, I passed bodies.

Most were drained, or at least partially so, making me think that the others had time to work as they pushed forward. The closer I got to the sounds of fighting, though? The more frequent the intact and full bodies became.

Side corridors, low passages, and massive halls flashed by. Groups of dead were piled here and there, and frequently I passed more. There were humanoid bodies in the larger halls that were raised up, attached to the walls, drained and broken. Collapsed pods, similar to the warrior pods, held them. But instead of looking like they were there to help them sleep or whatever? These looked like prison cells.

Arms and legs were cemented into place, necks encircled by something that kept the head up, and the lower body? The lungs, stomach, heart, and so on?

Ripped free, looking like someone had shoved their way up under a blanket to get at something, leaving the blanket all rumpled and messy.

It was a stupid comparison—fuck, it really was—but at the speed I was going? It was what flicked into my mind.

I'd been going down for ages, I realized, suddenly noticing that as I'd been passing left and right, there'd been bridges, sections of flat, level ground, and then ramps that led sharply down again. I passed choke points, passages that led up and across into the distance, passing over huge chasms, and stairwells that dug down, deep into the dark places of the earth. All the time, though, I followed the bodies. Cursing, I picked up my speed, swooping down closer to the ground, pulling my arms in tight as I passed through a doorway, a thick wall that had long since lost the door itself. And finally?

I burst out into the main hive.

All around me were massive pillars. Some displayed the majesty of the huge cavern: gemstones and striated marble patterns, precious metals. Others were of fully armored and celebrated figures, statues of some mighty and unknown warriors.

I saw the others ahead.

Ingrid was in the middle, barking out orders as she waved her arms. A small number of warrior Stelek close to the group wheeled on their companions and attacked them at her command.

Scylla danced and snarled, spear flashing and throwing blood in all directions as she clambered higher atop a veritable hill of corpses.

Jonas was hacking and swearing, kicking and punching. A square of nanites on his left fist blocked a stab from the nearest warrior; his own blade sliced across the front of the square, hacking its arms free.

Belle spun in place. Thorny trees raced upward, reaching for the sky; tendrils from her buried in the mountain of bodies that lay around them, draining them, even as she poured more and more of those same nanites into her abilities.

A veritable forest surrounded them on all sides, narrow paths all that was left to reach them as the trees wove fronds, vines, and branches together. The warriors and guardians tried to forge a path through, even as the milky-white mist rolled off the guardians' bodies.

Two were down, three more fighting to close on them. A dozen warriors easily raced around the outsides, fighting to tear their way inside. And the grubs?

They were laid here and there—dead, torn apart, something having burst free.

As I fixed on them, though, I heard it, and I rolled on instinct, as both sentinels on my back opened fire.

Something flew close by, with massive wings and a small body. It screamed as it fell, cartwheeling from the sky to burst as it crashed into the stone floor far below.

More were coming, I felt: the nanites in them screamed at me as they closed. I snarled in frustration, twisting in midair; a tentacle reached out and snagged onto a pillar.

The tip grew claws, claws that gripped tight and tore free a shower of stone chips as I whipped myself around to a new trajectory.

The sentinel on my left shoulder, clinging on tight, fired again, even as I reached out, grabbing the one on my right and plucking it free.

I dove; the gravity well flared behind to provide power, and ahead to drag me down. A handful of warriors turned at once, even as I felt *it*.

Or *her*, I suppose was the more accurate identifier. Fucked if I cared. I just shoved out and down, flaring the gravity well again. The warriors flung this way and that; my armor poured across my skin, the glistening, gleaming wash of nanites flowing out to coat me.

A single warrior hadn't been quick enough to jump, and it'd taken the full brunt of the gravity shear.

Half of its body had been fucking pancaked, literally—shattered into the ground, crushed under a hundred gravities of force. And the other half? It'd been under the normal level of gravity.

The line was night and day, and the fucker died messily.

I landed. Nanite tentacles stabbed out, sinking into the corpses closest and ripping nanites free as I underarm flung the sentinel over to Ingrid.

It landed atop the branches that were woven over her head, staggered and twisted, then grabbed on tight and fired, her control asserted over it as it changed its firing pattern and started to carve the Stelek from the sides of the refuge.

I launched myself into the air. My shoulders and back flexed on instinct as the ghosts of nerve impulses, the memory of wings, plagued me.

Fliers swooped in: long legs and even longer wings, narrow bodies and sharp, vicious talons flashing as they closed on me.

I sneered, reaching out and designating them as targets.

Gravity wells bloomed, opening and twisting for a split second, then collapsing shut again. Tiny ripples in the fabric of space that told the furiously beating wings that they were about to have a very bad day. Then, that was it, and they were flexed in exactly the wrong way.

They crumpled, twisting and snapping, their fragile membranes unable to bend the way flesh could, and they screamed. Suddenly, far from ruling the skies, as their species had once done, they plunged from them.

They hit the ground at horrific speeds. Their fragile bodies burst: arms and legs, chitin and eyes, ichor and assholes flying in all directions.

I didn't care. The second sentinel I threw at a pillar; its arms grabbed on, swinging, then locked itself in tight and close, as it started to pick out targets from this new, and considerably out of reach, vantage point.

No, I didn't care about that either; it'd been a single opportunity and I'd taken it on instinct.

No, what I cared about?

The queen.

She was huge and old, ten meters or so tall, hunched around a withered egg sac.

It looked as though it'd been fuller, once, and the sight of it triggered a new notification, one I cut from bothering me as soon as I recognized what it probably meant.

The queen was here, and she was ready for a fight. That was all that mattered right now.

She screamed at me in rage, and I felt the force of that scream in more than just sound.

Advanced Pheromonic Compound Identified: Nanites Assessing...

Countering...

The notification slid off me, as I snorted my disgust. It was pathetic. Compared to the greater dryads? It was amateurish level. It whimpered that I was tired, that I was small and afraid, and that I should lie down, that I should hope the queen forgets about me. I should curl up into a ball.

You know what?

Fuck that shit.

I twisted around, lining up on her as she tore herself free of the egg sac. Its massive bulk seemed to be cemented into the wall, corpses of hundreds, if not thousands of creatures bound to it, and used as incubators over the years.

She was segmented into three sections: one her upper body, with much longer, blade-like arms, one a smaller body, like a human or humanoid one, with a narrow waist and small three-fingered hands atrophied and held close in, the arms weak and palsied.

The last section was four long legs, each attached to the main abdomen, and they ended in grasping, claw-tipped feet.

It screeched and warbled at me again, and I threw myself at her, slamming a gravity bubble into the center of her humanoid section.

She twisted, crying out in pain as her stomach was crushed, like a wasp folding around a pin driven through it. She raised her head, then sprayed a viscous liquid at me, spitting it out.

I twisted, barely avoiding the majority. Gravity bubbles ripped it downward as I hit her again. Her blade-like arms frantically twisted and cut, carving through the air as she tried to fight whatever she could feel but not see on her skull.

It was all a distraction, though. No matter how painful the attacks were, there was one guaranteed way to end this—and fuck it, was I not the Devourer?

It was time to let my armor out to play.

The Stelek were an early attempt at creating living weapons for the wars the creators were fighting, that much was clear, but the rest? It was fucking obvious why they'd changed and abandoned that line of experimentation in favor of humanity and its variants.

I flew through the air. My skin shifted as more and more nanites pooled on the surface; my arms lifted to the heavens, my blades extending, shining.

It dragged its arms back, throwing its head back and screaming. Its head was narrow; lines of eyes roved back from the central point and the tip of the snout, which had split up and down, to show a standard jaw—if one lined with rows upon rows of teeth—now split further, rolling apart like a six-segmented flower petal opening.

Each segment had eyes on the exterior in a row leading back, and rows of flexing teeth that ran down the inside. A single mass in the center of the head glared out at me. Blood-red eyes gleamed, and it lunged forward, the jaws snapping shut around me.

I was intercepted, literal seconds before I'd have hit its chest, and as the petals closed, the teeth reached for me. Liquids spurted from the mess at the back of its throat, the red eyes staring malevolently in victory.

It washed across me, covering me. Acid warnings flashed as my nanites fought it. Steam and smoke burst from me, and the head angled upward, shaking itself, flicking like a dog would, desperate to drag me down its gullet.

I'd started to flex my tentacles, sinking them into the jaws around me, holding them at bay, when I grinned in the confines of my armor.

"Fuckin' amateur," I muttered, retracting the tentacles, as pseudopods lashed out from the back of the throat, wrapping around my arms, my legs, my torso.

It began to drag me deeper, presumably pleased at how easy it was, that its prey had "given up."

Then it screamed, and this time it was in agony.

The pseudopods tore and broke, snapping as the nanites ate through them. Tentacles punched out; their tips ended in sharp blades that dug deep into the flesh, before extending barbs, tearing and locking on, using the now stable and deeply rooted barbs to drag me farther into its throat.

It whipped its head about, frantically trying to dislodge me as I grabbed handfuls of flesh and pulled, fingers digging in as my new armor lived up to its name.

Webs of nanites lashed out, sticking to the mass all around and starting to feed.

I felt nanites in their tens of thousands being dragged inward, meat, genetics, cells, and more breaking down; the best of them were used to heal the punctures and tears that the teeth were making.

The acid filled its mouth with smoke, and I could no longer see. But I didn't need to, not really.

For every nanite that died, collapsing in the wash of acid, three more were ripped free and absorbed. And best of all? I hadn't even begun to play with my new toys yet. I triggered Emergency Synthesis, spending nanites at a rate of five to one. For every milliliter of the substance created, five nanite clusters collapsed.

The Tsunami nanite surprise—God, I needed a better name for that—wasn't ready yet; it was still coding, a tiny fragment of my nanites having been converted and stored, or that were in the process of it as I fought.

But the acid and the various biological weapons this fucker had used on me so far, either directly or through its minions? They were giving me so many new toys to play with it was unbelievable.

My Biological Warfare package was shifting, growing, learning more and more, and the synthesis of Death's Kiss that was now entirely unique to me?

That was ready.

The first small dose was, anyway.

Normally, a small dose and a giant fucking insect queen? Not a good combination.

Normally, however, I'd not be at the base of its mouth, braced, while my armor devoured its head, and my tentacles, spikes, and blades carved it a new fucking arsehole either.

Spoiler alert: it didn't end well for the fucker.

The mixture was small—literally, maybe enough to fill a test tube, that was it—and yeah, again, to a creature this size, not generally a serious risk.

However, an injection of a horrifically potent anesthetic and acid into the stem of its nervous system still sent it reeling. And by the time it'd felt it? It was too late.

That was the wonder of an anesthetic-based weapon. You didn't feel the fucker. It made the flesh numb; everything it touched went numb, and then? *Well,* nothing felt the acid, did it?

The liquid ate through the nerve stem. The head sagged limply; the brain, presumably somewhere deeper, went into spasms as more and more of the liquid was dragged down its connective tissues, watered down by the fluid it was carried in, but still potent as fuck.

By the time it reached the brain, and it shut down? I was halfway down the neck, surrounded by flesh and chitin that blackened and collapsed at my touch.

I literally burrowed deeper, grabbing handfuls of flesh, yanking, dragging myself inside. The web of interconnected nanites I dragged behind me fed on the queen, who in turn collapsed inward, practically dissolving.

More and more of my nanites came online, and the process picked up speed, a rolling wave of cellular degeneration.

Three minutes after the fucker had snapped its jaws shut around me, I stepped from its stomach. Then, meters of giant, abominable insect queen, the scourge of the underground, the nightmare that had fed upon Oracan parents and children, as well as who knew what the fuck else?

Eaten in its turn.

I stepped down. My armor shifted; fresh plates slid into place and new wings shivered as the cooler outside air touched them for the first time.

I was reborn, thanks to the masses of nanites that fucker had absorbed over the centuries. And although it might have been a medium-grade dinner, barely a decent steak compared to feeding on the Erlking and his kind would be?

It was a damn good start.

I flexed my wings, the surface of my armor wet and smoking, organic-looking in a way it'd never been before, as I faced the others.

"I'm back," I whispered, and I saw the satisfied smile on Ingrid's face in response.

CHAPTER THIRTY-NINE

Seven hours.

That's how long it took for both Belle and I to drain the corpses around us—the hundreds of Stelek that led the way back up to where we'd been, and the hundreds more that had been streaming in from the far reaches of the hive to defend the queen.

The vast majority had dropped dead when the queen died, some kind of psychic link, and that made our jobs considerably easier, thank you very much.

One passageway we found, though, had nothing in it. No bodies, anyway.

No, there was a lovely smear of recent passage, though. A shitload of still drying ichor, presumably left behind by the new queen, as she fled.

Evolving Quest Completed!

Evolving Quest complete: Cull the Interlopers: Level 2

The Stelek primary and secondary hives in the local area have been culled. Their relentless expansion has been stopped, and the ancient fortress city of Bashanti-Ulm has been freed. Cull their numbers to receive the following reward:

- ~~Eliminate Upper Stelek Hive~~
- ~~Eliminate Lower Stelek Hive~~
- ~~Eliminate Stelek Queen~~

Reward:

- **+5 Support Points**
- **+5 War Points**
- **+Access to Level 3 of the Evolving Quest**

*

Evolving Quest unlocked: Cull the Interlopers: Level 3

Before her death, and yet sensing the threat that drew near, the Stelek Queen and matriarch awoke and unleashed her daughter, the new queen. As the Stelek cannot have more than one local queen due to their nature, the infant queen was immediately forced out, slinking deeper into the depths of the caverns.

After killing the original Stelek queen, now, to gain additional points and a valuable source of resources, you must hunt down and eliminate the infant queen to receive the following reward:

- **Eliminate the Infant Queen and her nascent hive**

Reward:
- **+2 Support Points**
- **+2 War Points**

*

Quest Completed: Rescue the Oracan war party: Level 2

The Oracan war party was defeated and captured by the Stelek defenders. While the upper hive contained some survivors, the lower contained only corpses. For discovering this grisly truth, you receive the following reward:

- **+1 War Point**

I couldn't help but grin at it. The quest was done, and all that was left? A single Stelek queen, freshly birthed and leaving behind a trail a blind man could follow. Kill her, and I got two more War and two more Support points.

The others were getting three of their primary points as rewards for this. They'd missed the original points I'd gotten for the lycan stages, but that they were getting any rewards at all was awesome.

I was back up to seven damn War points available now, and five Support! Add in the single Espionage, and the three Weapon Skills? Fuck, yes.

"What do we do now?" Ingrid asked, and I hesitated, before speaking quickly.

Things had been a bit strained since I'd rejoined them, not least because they all thought I'd been an idiot to activate abilities when I knew there was a risk of frying my brain, and I felt like they'd abandoned me to grab the nanites for themselves.

It was a stupid thought, I damn well knew that, but still, the hunger and need for the nanites, the draw to replace my armor and be "me" again was a bit of an ongoing headfuck right now.

"We hunt the queen," I said, at the same time that Belle and Jonas spoke up.

"We need to share out the nanites first," Belle declared.

"I think we need to spend some of these points," Jonas answered. "Remember, something forced the Stelek up to the higher levels and they, in turn, forced the Oracan out. That queen might be five minutes away, and an easy kill, or she might be ten miles, or have flown off. It might take a month to find her, and we might get trapped down below."

"Really?" I growled. "We already gave her hours to escape!"

"You're the boss," Jonas acknowledged, wincing at the glare Ingrid gave him. "Both of you," he added. "I'm the hired muscle, but seriously? You need to consider this. At the very least, Belle is right...we need to split our nanites, right?"

"We do," Ingrid agreed, looking at me.

I hesitated, and nodded, reluctantly. "I agree."

"So, Belle, how many did we get?" she asked.

"Nearly three million," Belle replied, smiling. "We were lucky in that the Stelek had been harvesting the dead for a long time, and the hive was full. Split that five ways and—"

I held up my hand to stop her before she could finish.

"Four," I said firmly. "Split it four ways. Most of them came from the kills you did while I was wiped out, and I'm sorry for doing that. I did what I thought was right at the time, and I need to do it again. There's a shitload of nanites and points I need to assign. Either way, though? You killed these ones, and that's only fair."

"Thank you." Jonas nodded, and I saw the relieved look on the faces of those around me.

"What?" I asked, and Ingrid, looking at the others, spoke first.

"We were worried about you," she admitted. "You seemed to lose yourself before, desperate to get more nanites, and we were worried that they were addictive or something, that's all. Until recently, there was nobody else who could have used them, so you didn't have to share, and…"

I saw the worry in her eyes, the fear and the beginning of tears, making me curse as I stepped forward, wrapping her in my arms and pulling her close.

"I'm sorry," I said to them all, but mainly to her. "I've been a bit focused, haven't I?"

"Obsessed," Jonas agreed, before grinning. "Don't get me wrong…I understand it—I want the nanites too, and I know Scylla does."

"I want to be what I was," she whispered, nodding to me. "I want my body back, my abilities. I understand what it feels like to lose it, and how desperately you want it back."

"You've been feeling it too?" I asked, and she snorted.

"Steve, you've been without your armor and abilities for days? And you had them for what, a few years?"

"Months, really," I admitted.

Ingrid stepped back, looking up at me and smiling, before looking over at Scylla. "It was years, but most of that was spent drugged up or dead."

"I had my abilities for centuries, before I was locked away," Scylla whispered, and I winced as I realized the difference that would make. "I feel like I might collapse at any second, that I cannot lift my spear, that old age has robbed me of my life, when as an Arisen? I should never grow old."

"And now that you have your nanites?" I asked.

"I must use them. I must—" She straightened, looking around. "It is as an addiction. Like the tears of amethyst, should you use them regularly. For an addict, all else pales— your needs, your desires…nothing is important beyond that. So I have not pushed, I have not asked, for I cannot be sure it is my will that decides I need to use them, or if it be the nanites."

"We need to spend them now," Ingrid said. "Steve, how many did you get? I know we agreed that you keep what you kill, so the queen is yours, but the other corpses?"

"One and a half million," I admitted. "The queen had another million, which is nearly enough, with what I had, to reform my armor. The one and a half I harvested from the rest of the bodies is yours, not mine. But what do you want to do?"

"What do you mean?" Scylla frowned.

"I mean, do you want me to give you them as corrupt ones? Your systems are reset and active now, so you'll cleanse them eventually, but it'll take awhile…days, at least. Belle, can you clean them faster?"

"In hours," she said.

"Then you share out the ones you've got cleansed so far, and keep working on the rest?" I suggested, and she nodded.

The group settled down. The rest of us moved back from the mounds of corpses, while I sat, considering my armor.

I was actively feeling hunger, and not the "I could kill for a burrito" style either. All the corpses around us? Belle had stripped them of nanites, sure, but the corpses themselves were still there, and damn if I didn't want to feed on them.

I was starting to get the idea that a Devourer wasn't a good thing to have accidentally unlocked, when Ingrid finally got my attention.

"What's up?" I asked distractedly, getting a look from her. "What?"

"Belle asked you twice for the nanites," she said, and I blinked, having totally missed it.

"Shit," I grunted, then I hesitated, reaching out a hand to Belle. "How do we do this?"

"Well, there's a proven method for a male to share something with a female, but…" She laughed at the look on both Ingrid's and my faces as she went on. "But I think we can make do with the harvest tools!"

"You better," Ingrid grumbled, unsubtly, as she sat down next to me, making it clear that she was going nowhere until I'd finished this.

I extended my right arm and Belle did hers; our palms touched as the ports in both our wrists and knuckles opened at will.

I focused on wanting to transfer the one and a half million corrupted nanites to her. My tubules extended, her own growing up to match, and they sealed to each other, connecting us up.

For a second, it was all I could do to force out a breath as the world exploded in sensations.

I could feel the hard rock of the ground under my ass, *and under hers!* I felt her heartbeat, faster than my own, and the way her body shivered, the need for sunlight that made me wince as I recognized that yeah, she'd said it before, and I'd totally blanked on it.

She was a *plant*-based lifeform. She appeared "meaty" like a human was, but she wasn't. She didn't eat. She drank, sure, but primarily? She needed *sunlight*.

We'd been underground for ages, and she was starving.

She could enter into a hibernation mode, and she'd be fine, but all the while she was using the nanites and her new abilities? She was draining herself badly.

It was suddenly obvious in the skin around her eyes, the way she slumped slightly, the exhaustion. I couldn't believe I'd not seen it before. And now that I had? I couldn't not see it.

I felt the hunger in her as well, the desire, genetically programmed in her to hunt for men, the need for us, buried beneath the thin layer of self-control that she forced on herself, making her appear "respectable" in the eyes of the group.

For a split second, we stared into each other's eyes, and we knew each other in a million new ways, as our bodies were shared at the level of our nervous systems.

I knew then, that regardless of her appearance, we weren't as similar as she pretended. She was still my friend, but fuck me, the raging level of need that rushed through her all the time? Add in that now she was feeling my body, in a way that she'd never felt another? She felt the nerves and stimulus responses that rode through me, and I felt…the same in her.

We both stared, wide-eyed, as the nanites flowed, the million and a half corrupted flowing from me into her. I swallowed hard. Her need, feeding my desire, and her sensing it, and the unwitting flexing of my anatomy?

I felt the responding sensations growing in her, the hormonal response…

As soon as the transfer was done, I broke the connection, silently vowing that we really, *really* needed to find a better way to do this than that!

She straightened up, forcing a smile, and staggered off, muttering something about needing a minute to herself.

"What just happened?" Ingrid scowled, and I forced a smile.

"It was just…um…weird?" I offered lamely. "Sorry, I didn't expect that. The tubes? They connect to our nerves, so as long as we were connected, all I could feel was her body. All of it."

"You were feeling…"

"Not like that," I said quickly, shaking my head. "I mean, not in a horny way, but like doubling the sensations and so on, feeling the way she breathed and more. It was just weird." I was glad that, for once, the way I was sitting concealed the raging hard-on.

"Okay…" Ingrid frowned, then she kissed me. "Well, if you want to talk about it, I'm here, all right?"

"I'm fine," I lied, desperately trying to think of anything to calm my raging hunger.

It didn't help that the other side of it was that I was sure the hunger from my damn armor was growing more and more unmanageable.

It felt like I was next to a massive all-you-can-eat buffet after a week of dieting and living on fucking celery and all that pointless shit. Now I was basically just lying and saying no, I'd much prefer the bowl of celery, rather than the mass of steak and chips and so on.

It took control, and focus, to not just reach out to it. And the more I did that? The faster the horny side relaxed.

Ingrid stayed with me for a few more minutes, talking about little things, but I could see she was distracted too, and eventually I just said fuck it.

"You want to examine this place?" I asked her, and she nodded emphatically. "Go for it. I can't concentrate with the bodies here, so…"

"So you're going to destroy them?" she asked, and I nodded as I clambered to my feet.

The relief as I started was immense. The more I did that—harvesting the bodies—the less bothered I was by the others getting the nanites from Belle as she finished cleansing them.

I didn't understand it. I'd never been a greedy person. I mean, sure, I wanted more, in a general "keeping score" kind of a way, and I'd been poor as shit enough in my life to know that I hated that part of it, so I was determined to never be again. But, seriously?

I loved Ingrid. Nothing had changed there, despite the last few days being a bit weird between us as she adjusted to new situations, no longer me protecting her, but fighting as part of a team instead of being the lone weapon.

Now, though? I forced myself to look at my actions, and emotions, squarely in the face. I'd been the only one, the "special" one for so long that I wasn't liking sharing that status.

Basically, I was being a child, and I needed to grow the fuck up.

The armor? The hunger?

The more I examined that, the more I realized that it wasn't coming from the armor, not entirely. Sure, some of it was, but it was a yearning, a need. One that, as I pulled up the details, and checked them over? I understood.

The armor, and the active nanites that I was blending in with it, were responding to my subconscious will.

When I drained a body, when I "ate" them, like I had been? I had a small chance to harvest a percentage point and to add it to my own stats.

Without my armor and the nanites, I'd been desperately focused on needing to be stronger, and this was the result. When I'd fed on these fuckers, I'd been harvesting them, and I'd gained fifteen fucking points to my stats. Fifteen!

I pulled the stats up and stared at them hungrily, loving the changes, and wanting more!

Identifier: Biological Weapon Variant #Steve				
Species: Human		**Nanites available**: 19,576		
Threat Level: Iota		**Corrupted Nanites**: 1,247,142		
		Weaponized Nanites: 11,400		
Stat	**Current points**	**Description**	**Effect**	**Cost to Upgrade**
Body	6.0	Physical strength and capacity to absorb damage	+50 resistance to damage	600k
Reactions	4.5	Mental and physical reactions	Time Dilation= 4.5*4.2*10= 189+50%= 283.5 seconds	450k
IQ	4.9	Intelligence and the capability to utilize it in the real world	+39 to Assimilation of new technologies and capabilities	490k
Nimbleness	4.2	The capacity to utilize tools, weapons, and small devices	+32 to success with devices	420k
Dexterity	4.6	The ability to dodge and utilize larger items/devices	+36 chance to dodge	430k
Karmic Luck	5.1	The likelihood of an action to spawn an adverse/positive reaction	+41 chance to gain a favorable outcome in games of chance	5.1m

Perception	4.2	The ability to differentiate between details and spot threats at a distance	+32 likelihood to spot concealed items, details, or traps — see Reactions	420k
Control	3	The ability to control external systems		300k
Cybernetics	4	Integration of Cybernetic and Biogenetic augmentations and how likely they are to work		400k
Resonance	5	The capacity to use and integrate devices that require elemental resonances		500k

That was why my armor was driving my desperate need to feed on the bodies. If I was lucky, I'd gain more points. I'd gain the points mainly from the nanite-infused corpses, so I was unlikely to acquire any more from the corpses that Belle had left behind, but damn.

It was also a fucking relief as I'd been getting worried I'd end up a damn cannibal the way I was feeling.

It also meant that I could both learn to tamp this instinct down, and it was only likely to be an issue around masses of bodies, not generally. There was no risk of me wandering the local villages and feeding on people in my damn sleep, for example.

Fifteen points.

Fifteen points I'd gained in the end: twelve from the nanite-infused corpses I'd drained—and then given the nanites to Belle, as they were the others' kills—and three more from the drained corpses. It showed the massive difference between the two, and the huge room was now knee-deep in places with broken organic materials.

I'd explained what I was doing, and why, to Belle and the others as I worked, and with some guidance, Belle had taken some of the similar choices. With her understanding that the System Replenishment option was a good thing, and with a little tweaking and searching, an alternative option unlocked for her as well. In her case, it converted the majority of the corpses to a different kind of matter, one that was more compatible with her system, but the overall effect was the same.

Ingrid invested her points mainly in the Command tree, unlocking more bonuses for us all, better examination abilities and boosts. She could now augment one of us at a time, feeding additional energy into that one to enable them to, in turn, boost an ability of theirs.

Jonas and Scylla went down the path of War, of course, but with their additional points, I talked them through the layout, and what I'd gotten at each level.

Their options, again, were slightly different. Scylla, for example, had a sub-tree called Spartan, which was based around control of the body, absolute dedication to a physical ideal, to pushing herself to attain it, and to become the greatest warrior of the age once again.

Jonas gained one that was named Paladin, which was built around his fighting style—namely, that once he dedicated himself to an ideal, he'd fuckin' achieve it.

I took the piss out of him a bit for that, asking if he'd picked a god to follow or what, and he just smiled and offered to demonstrate his Smite.

It was a skill that allowed him to alter the effect of a bullet—before it was fired, obviously, coating it in nanites and making it happen through tech, not magic—and it ranged from armor-piercing, incendiary and high-explosive, to poison and more.

I'd recommended they look for their version of the tree that matched them, like I'd gone for Assassin primarily. It was the skill tree that matched me best, after all, and that was how they'd found those.

They both managed—just—to reach the most basic levels of armor crafting, and I was talking them through the designs I'd come up with when Ingrid shouted for us.

"Up!" she screamed, racing over, gesturing to the entrance on the far side. "We need to get up!"

"What's wrong?" I asked.

All of us drew our weapons, getting ready as she raced past, before falling and sprinting along behind her.

"The ship!" she called to us. "It's under attack!"

CHAPTER FORTY

The rest of the trip to the surface was a blur, and a hell of a one at that. The passages and caverns flashed past as we ran. My new internal changes made me curse and sweat, racing to keep up.

The ship was under attack, all right, and because of its value? Zac and the others were totally unwilling to relinquish it to the enemy.

I was both glad about that—I'd fought and literally fucking died for that ship—and I was snarling out my fury as well.

I'd died, but I'd fucking come back. Zac and the others? They had the *potential* to now, but I was betting they'd never get the chance.

The structure had been broken into in two areas. The first?

Close to the shore, probably the entrance I'd first used. It'd been found, and an absolute shitload of lycans, werecats, and vamps had poured in. How they'd managed that without flooding the ship I had no clue, but they'd done it.

Zac had shared images of them in a running battle with dozens of the smaller sentinels, and a handful of his much bigger personal designs.

They were holding their own currently. And the gamma lasers meant that, when they went down? They were weaker when they got back up.

That was great.

What wasn't, though, was the other force.

Xi-Ma—the massive creatures that I'd seen acting as guardians for the underground area at the end of the cave system.

Two of them strode through the ship, and in their wake, the ship reverted to the control of the security AI.

That fucker had to have been involved in this, and I grimly swore I'd hunt the little bastard out and grind it to silica under my boot for this.

There were custodians and a small handful of security sentinels traveling in their wake. And the only reason the ship hadn't already been lost? The Xi-Ma didn't seem to know where they were going.

I knew that the AI was trapped, locked away in its own emergency fallback bunker, so this plan had to have been put in place a while ago, or at the very least it'd set up contingencies "just in case."

Now I was paying for it, as I lumbered along, the others huffing and puffing as they did the same as me.

I'd managed to describe my armor to the others—the chest portion of it, at least—enough that they could mimic it.

They didn't have access to the power core tech, but that was fine. I did, and I also had a working Support sub-mind now. That sub-mind had enabled me to unlock two more levels of the power core tech, and a single level of RI.

Then, I'd demanded—and got—a quarter of a million nanites from each of them. None of them were happy about it, but it was the only way.

Now five power cores were growing on my back, even as my armor solidified and shifted, developing as we ran.

The trip to the surface should have taken at least two hours, probably more. And considering we were all more than capable of an under five-minute mile? That showed just how deep we were.

Groans rose as we dashed up the final set of stairs and into the throne room of the fortress, not even slowing slightly as we crossed it, and sprinted into the connecting passages.

"Fuck you, stairs!" Jonas groaned. "How the hell do women do that in the gym for so long?"

"They don't sprint up them for over an hour!" I huffed. My internal reserves drained at a horrific speed that made me insanely glad I'd not spent any of my nanites on improving my body.

The first of the cores clicked over from draining me, to activating, to powering up on its own. I let out a groan of relief, one that was echoed a minute later when the next repeated the process.

More and more clicked off, until the last—my own—changed over to internal power and I started to disconnect them.

"Here!" I called, slapping the first into the small of Ingrid's back, staggering her, as the power core locked into place. Her armor, a Command variant that was much, *much* smaller than ours, was basically closer to a modern infantry system, where ours looked more like we should be battling dragons, or monsters from thirty centuries plus into the future.

Regardless, as soon as the power core locked into place, her armor flowed up around it, sealing it in and coating the exterior with solid armor to protect it, as the smaller, secondary device attached to the power core shifted.

I'd talked the others through it as we'd run, seeing it was the only way that we could make this work, especially considering Dimi had been at the recycling plant when the shit had hit the fan.

He'd been in the middle of shipping Oracan back there, which had meant he'd been able to load up on an assault and rescue team. Mainly, they were Oracan, with a few humans from Anders's past to add modern tech to it. Anders was leading it, with Dave—Amanda had been forced to stay behind—and Dimi had dropped them off first, leaving them to assault the lycans, etc. from behind.

Then he'd set off for us, and as we reached the final stretch, the valley and the exit a matter of minutes ahead of us, he was still more than two hours away.

We could rest—sit about and wait for him—or we could go to him.

That was why we had the power cores, and the others were shifting their armor at my direction now.

The result was that we all now had chest and back pieces, helmets, and best of all? Wings and power cores.

The new design for the power cores were smaller and more powerful than ever before, as well as having an inbuilt RI to regulate them, making damn sure they weren't a risk to us, nor the world around, by developing into runaway fusion reactors and essentially blowing up.

The advantage? Beyond the obvious one of all of us living and so on, was that the secondary device that I'd created for each of them was also under the control of the RI.

It was a gravity inverter, and although I'd had to learn to use it myself, and I'd actually designed it, theirs was a lot simpler and needed no input from them.

It existed to streamline their flight, to reduce the effect of gravity on them, and to protect them a little from the effects of high-speed maneuvers.

Mine? No such protection, nor help, but I'd learned to do all of that and more on my own. They didn't have the time they needed to figure that shit out. Not right now.

I passed out the others, slapping them onto the back of their armor. They started to integrate them, desperately listening to me as I, moving back into the lead of the group, shouted out explanations of what they were going to feel, and how to deal with it.

The helmets would keep them safer, and when they crashed—not if, *when*— they were more likely to survive the impact, and be able to fly still, rather than the rest of us having to leave them behind to make their way along later.

There wasn't time to create a full-on atmospheric control for them, nor the rebreathers, the chemical and biological weapon facility, none of the majority of the systems that were regrowing in my armor now. They'd need to unlock those themselves, so I'd warned them the flight was going to be cold as a witch's tit. And breathing? It would be painful.

They'd be sucking down air as hard as they could to keep themselves going. If they blacked out? The best they could do was try to rest, when they'd recovered and woke, then follow along behind.

Again, I warned them, flying was dangerous and fucking hard. If they crashed? We had people in danger to a level that they simply wouldn't be. The rest of us would leave those who fell behind, well, behind.

They all agreed it was the best way, and despite the sheer number of times I said it? I still didn't know whether I could do it. Scylla and Jonas? Sure. Belle? She was a lot more of a friend, and yeah, I'd really struggle with that—not least because, you know, if for whatever reason she didn't survive?

That dick the Erlking would come for me, and as much as I ran my mouth off, I wasn't ready for that fight yet.

Ingrid, though? I genuinely didn't see that I could do that, as much as I intended to. I loved her, and unlike Jonas or Scylla, she wasn't built for this.

She was, however, I realized as we started to sprint up and down the rolling flights of stairs, able to augment us!

"Ingrid!" I called over the huffing of our breaths. "If I create a bubble of gravity around us, can you help me with it?"

"Prob...ably...?" She gasped, and I grunted, shifting in closer and scooping her up.

Rather than complain, she sagged against my chest, frantically trying to catch her breath as the sentinel that had been clinging to my shoulders moved. Scylla saw it and moved in closer to take it as it leapt from my back to her.

She caught it, swinging it around and resting it on her shoulders, where it wrapped its arms and legs around her, making sure it didn't bounce and throw off her rhythm.

Jonas had the other. I was still the strongest by a fair measure, and so I'd carried one on my own this far, while the other had leapt from Scylla to Jonas every five minutes or so.

Now, as the light of day bathed the end of the chamber ahead, I couldn't help but feel relieved.

We burst out into a gentle rainfall, steady and refreshing.

The river that ran down the side of the entrance was already swollen and rushing, but thankfully not deep. We splashed through the shallows and leapt to the far side, slipping and sliding on the wet grass as we forced our way up the hillside.

Ingrid struggled, and I set her down, taking her hand when she offered it. The pair of us managed a dozen steps before letting go by unspoken agreement.

Holding hands might be fucking romantic and all, but it was also making climbing the damn hill a lot harder.

A handful of minutes later, we burst from the brush, scrabbling up the last few meters to the top of the low hill.

We were all panting again, fucking exhausted, and I insisted we needed to take a few minutes to catch our breath, pointing out that if they used their wings? They needed to focus on it, just like they did regular muscles.

This seemed wrong to them—they were nanite constructions, after all—as Jonas commented, but I shook my head.

"I don't give two shits about right and wrong," I told them. "I can always feel the beat of my wings and the way I fly. Might be you designed your wings differently. Might be you don't need this shit. That's nice for you, but I know this is how *my* wings work, all right?"

The first flying lesson was a mess.

They all needed to learn, first of all, to split their attention: to tell the RI what they wanted, and also to move their wings.

Jonas complained that it'd be easier to fly the way I did sometimes—no wings, just fist out and alter gravity—and I laughed my ass off at how fucking stupid that was.

Should it be easier? Sure.

Was it easier? Fuck no.

To do that, I constantly made a thousand tiny adjustments in a complex pattern in the space around myself. I adjusted the gravity well against that generated by the fucking planet, making a million infinitesimal alterations unconsciously a fucking second, and now, when I considered how I did it? I had no clue how I managed it.

It was done in much the same way that I breathed.

I didn't focus on a single set of muscles or an individual one and order that to release while its opposite contracted. I didn't order my mouth to open, nor my throat to close off the "food" tube, and open whatever it was called that led to the lungs instead.

I didn't do any one of a billion possible things that were needed to breathe *consciously*—I just did them.

That was the same for the gravity manipulation. I'd done it so much, for so long, that I did it without thought now. When I'd first done it? I'd been lumbering through the sky, my wings doing most of the work as I used the gravity manipulation to help me.

That was a learned skill, and one that I'd managed thanks to the data I'd been able to download and internalize.

They had none of that, so for them? A simple RI to do the work while they gave it orders, and wings that they could learn to flex and fly with.

Jonas was determined that what worked for me was great and all, but he was sure he knew best, and Scylla agreed.

The pair of them did it their way, with my blessing, and drove themselves first into the air with whoops and cheers, and then into the river at the bottom of the hill at a hell of a speed, almost drowning themselves, and breaking multiple bones in the process.

After that, and they'd struggled back up the hill?

They listened.

Ingrid took to it well, beating her wings and lifting off, nudging the RI to help her to do things. And having flown with me plenty before, it helped there as well.

Belle? Well, she was annoyingly gifted at it.

She was the best of the group—after me—and although her landings were crap, she stayed aloft easily enough.

Thirty minutes after we'd reached the top of the hill, five minutes after Jonas and Scylla had made it back up, I cut the lesson short.

"We can't waste any more time," I said. "Every mile we manage to get closer to the others is a mile that Dimi doesn't have to travel over twice. We need to go."

The takeoff for the group was a mess, as each of them lumbered into the air behind me. I hovered there, beating my wings in a steady, rhythmical pattern.

I used them more as scoops to flick me around, then guide me, as anything these days, and the others picked up on that as we set off, at first flying low enough, and following the river as long as we could to make sure that if they crashed, they weren't too injured.

Ten minutes in, I took off the training wheels, and we started to climb. Each of us used the gravity inverters to send us along faster and faster.

Ingrid steadied out and focused, reaching out through the command link and pushing at me, helping to guide me, to make my energy usage more efficient, as I in turn used my much more powerful power core and my skilled and conscious usage of the gravity inverter to create a tunnel around us.

We picked up speed, doubling and more as we hit terminal velocity, then continued to accelerate.

We couldn't get up to "real" speeds, not like I'd done in escaping from the various air forces as I left Copenhagen. It just wasn't an option when we had to keep slowing for everyone to catch their breath and recover. But by the time Dimi appeared on the horizon?

We'd shaved a few hundred miles off the distance he needed to travel.

He rocketed wide around us, coming up from behind, slowing steadily, as he pulled alongside. The ramp at the back slowly lowered; lights inside came to life as they illuminated the interior, the sun already setting where we were, and I guided my little flock into place.

Ingrid led us, her command link making it easier for the others, projecting a line to follow. And although it wasn't easy? We all made it, furling our wings at the last second as I reached out—from my position as last in line—to boost the others in.

There were a lot of bruises, admittedly, and we were all tired, but as the rear ramp whirred steadily back up, the scream of the air being battered by the plane's intrusion dying, we knew we'd done all that we could.

I helped the others to seats, seeing a touch more respect in the eyes of Jonas and Scylla than I was used to as they thanked me, and I smiled, before heading up to the cabin to join Dimi.

He looked like shit.

Apparently, he'd had about an hour of sleep in the last twenty, and he was literally running on fumes now. But he was also well aware that the difference between us holding onto the ship, and Zac, Casey, Lars, Oxus, Paul and Courtney, of course, was him getting us there as fast as possible.

Currently, Zac was leading the massive Xi-Ma around the deepest parts of the ship with sacrificial creations, frantically trying to build more sentinels to take them out.

He'd been caught in the old "infrastructure vs. defenses" issue.

The basic thing was, he could have made a fuckload of sentinels and had them roaming the ship constantly, and he had made some, but that would mean that the amount that could be produced was always finite.

There'd only be, for example, a single large factory unit, or a limited number of units that could produce the parts needed. Instead, he'd made what he thought was a reasonable number, then he'd swapped to building and developing tech that would enable him to make more, and faster, in the future.

That wasn't to say that there weren't defenses in place—he wasn't an idiot— and he liked playing with guns enough that he was practically an honorary *American*, for fuck's sake.

There were turrets on the lead-up points to the main construction areas, and he'd made a hundred or more sentinels, which should have been more than enough to deal with pretty much anything.

The issue?

The Xi-Ma.

Lycans and more were going down fairly steadily, no real match to the defenses that were in place, but the Xi-Ma shredded the sentinels with ease. The only consolation was that they were at opposite ends of the ship currently.

The images we'd managed to get from Zac showed the massive figures striding through the long-dead ship, towering over everything.

They stood easily forty feet high—twelve or thirteen meters, I quickly worked it out —and with their glossy black skin, the golden jewelry they wore, and the dead white eyes?

They were a fucking horror.

Their eyes…it was always their eyes that drew me in, when I saw them. They were bulbous, white, and glowed. They were also insanely inhuman, making me think of the gleaming pearly white ones of deep-sea angler fish, rather than anything used for "real" vision.

Their mouths were similar as well, almost humanoid, but full of needle-like teeth that were longer than my hand. And when they opened their mouths?

They had what I could only call a fucking breath attack or a laser combined into one.

Literally, they screamed at something and a bright light streaked out, hitting it, causing the target to detonate, while their teeth, outlined by the light streaming out? Totally fine.

It made no fucking *sense* to me. It didn't seem possible, but there they were—large as life and twice as ugly.

Their bodies were humanoid, massively muscled, black as pitch and wearing Egyptian-style waist wraps, gold bracelets on their wrists and ankles, and a sheet of beaten gold across their chests like a damn big necklace or whatever.

Ingrid had identified it, and the waist wraps, when we'd seen them, saying something that sounded like a fuckin' sneeze to me, and I'd forgotten it as fast.

I didn't care what they *wore*—what I cared about was that their bodies, supposedly simple flesh by the way they walked, healed almost instantly.

Their bodies were those of a highly muscled man and woman, the kind who would have stood out as professional models and weightlifters—aside from the bumps and protrusions that ran here and there under the skin.

It looked more like they were wearing their armor under there, which was freaky as all fuck, as they moved so sinuously and gracefully.

Their heads, though?

They looked as though they'd been vacuum sealed, all the flesh and blood boiled away until there was only a skull, with skin as thin as parchment stretched across it.

The Xi-Ma were horrific creatures, and the first time I'd seen one? The system had basically told me to run like fuck.

I'd done it as well—hell, I'd ran like my dick was on fire…not beating it, but like there was a barrel at the other end and it was my only chance to save my sex life.

I stared at the video that Zac had sent, watching it repeatedly as the sentinels opened fire on them, carving thin lines into their chests that bubbled up with blood, before sealing over and healing in seconds.

I watched as the Xi-Ma responded, screaming out their own beams of white fire, carving the deck and scrap into gases. I saw sentinels explode, and walls falling.

In the distance, water roared, shimmering force fields flickering and holding back the ocean.

That made sense, I guessed. There had to be an emergency response to this kinda shit. And as powerful as the tech was? That did make sense.

Thank fuck we'd made the power plants and plugged them into the grid, all things considered, as otherwise the ship would be steadily flooding again.

"Are you all right?" I asked Dimi, who was hunched over the flight-stick, hanging onto it with one hand and a glowing green can of energy drink in the other.

He nodded, blinking owlishly, as he tried to focus, then sighed and shook his head, glancing at me and then back out at the mountains we were streaking past.

"Boss, I'm fucked," he admitted, grinning a little unsteadily. "A modern plane? Autopilot. You can use things like that and lock in altitude controls and….and…like a million other things, all right? You can make sure it all works and you can rest, right? This thing? I love her, but she's a constant fight to fly."

"Right?" I agreed, not really seeing it. We'd had people installing tech after all, and…

"You know that?" He nodded to the bank of instruments on the right-hand side of the plane.

"Yeah?"

"Fucking useless," he said cheerfully. "The only way we can use civilian air traffic systems, or military, is if we're plugged in, right?"

"Yeah, and we hacked that."

"Yeah, turns out that causes a fuckload of issues," he admitted grimly. "To be able to work out where we are, it needs to identify us, and when it does that? The system freaks, keeps identifying us as a missile, since besides that and top-secret prototypes? Nothing else flies like we do.

"So, you ignore the system, tell it not to report, and it can't identify the area properly—that means we get a rough map and some identifiers for what should be there, but that's it. You know how fucking scary it is when you pass a fully laden passenger jet that you didn't see coming, in three seconds? I do."

"Did they see you?"

"Oh, they saw me," he assured me dispiritedly, staring straight ahead out of the front windscreen. "They thought I was a missile at first, screaming out that they were a civilian flight under attack. I had to outrun fucking fighter jets, and all the while, the Oracan were screaming and threatening each other, fighting and throwing up. Why the hell do you think all the soft furnishings are gone? Our new call sign is the Vomit Comet."

"Are you all right?" I asked him again.

"Not even fucking close," he replied, forcing cheer into his voice. "But there's nobody shooting at me, not right now anyway, so that's nice. So, so far, you know there's no autopilot, there's no reliable navigation and plotting, and you know what else? It's fucking difficult to keep the entire goddamn route in your head at once."

"Right?"

"Not the general route, that's easy. No, I mean literally the full fucking route. And traveling at these speeds? I overshoot, and we are *gone*, man! Add in other planes, birds, smoke—hell, I saw a spy device once…*for about half a second.* Some weather balloon-looking motherfucker. Zip, boom! The drag tore it out of the sky. Whoever was using that must have had a hell of a surprise. I know I needed to change my damn shorts. I still do, actually."

He'd rattled all of that off, seemingly without stopping for a breath, clearly on the edge of a breakdown, and I cursed.

"Dimi, how long until we get there?" I asked. "Can you make it?"

"Oh yeah, I'll get us there," he assured me. "Land afterward? Maybe, maybe not, but I'll get us *there*."

"We need you still, Dimi, so if you need to? We can bail out and head for the ship under our own power. If you can hold on until then? If need be, we can point the plane at the sky, hit the engines to full and jump out."

"Fuck you, man, this is my plane!" He whimpered, clinging to the stick like his first born, as he blinked myopically at me. "And I told you, no autopilot! The program needs to be written from scratch to account for the things this beauty can do, and there's nobody in the world who could do that!"

"How long?" I asked him again, doing my best not to let him know how fucking worried I was. "How long 'til we get there?"

"An hour?" he guessed. "Maybe? We're all right now. We're heading for the Black Sea...maybe half an hour till we get there. I can relax for now. But once we get there? That's some of the busiest airspace on the planet, and I'll need to make quick changes of direction, so make sure you're all strapped in."

"Okay, man, do you need me here?" I asked, not wanting to leave him, but needing to check on the others.

"Nah, I'm okay. You go! Go have fun. And hey, gotta say, boss, we need bigger toilets on here, all right? And maybe a bed? I mean, for these flights, if I could get a bed, that'd be great..."

"If the autopilot worked?" I suggested, and he sighed and nodded.

"Shit, yeah, need one of those, or, you know, another pilot maybe?"

"Jonas," I muttered, eyes widening. "Fuck, hang on."

I ran back, finding Jonas half asleep, sitting in a seat talking quietly to Scylla as Belle and Ingrid talked about the nanites and their nature.

"Jonas, can you fly?" I asked him, cutting into his conversation. "A plane, I mean?"

"Well, I've had some lessons," he drawled. "I'm not that good, though, not really...too few hours in the seat, you know, and..."

"And get your arse up to the cockpit." I sighed, relief flooding me. "Dimi needs help, and you've got a clue, which is more than the rest of us have."

"Are you insane? This plane's nothing like what I've trained on and—"

"And Dimi is gonna fly us into a fucking mountain at this rate. Get up there and see what you can do. Even if it's just take the controls for long enough for him to have a piss, it's something," I ordered him.

"Fuck," he grumbled, grabbing the back of the seat and hauling himself up, then staggering as we hit a patch of turbulence, swearing as he staggered forward.

I turned to the others and explained the situation, finishing with: "And if the shit hits the fan? Get out. Get out of the plane. Remember—you can fly. And even if you're hurt when you land? A little time and you can walk it off."

"You've got such a way of looking on the bright side." Ingrid beamed at me, and I laughed, shrugging.

"Sorry, I just wanted to be clear."

"Steve, it's okay," she said softly, gripping my hand in hers as I leaned against the seats she and Belle were in. "We'll get to them. You know that, right?"

"We will," I agreed, knowing that she was asking for reassurance as much as she was offering it. "Have you heard from your father?"

"He's in the ship." She nodded. "He and the team have cut off the lycan reinforcements. They killed them fairly easily, as there weren't many left there, and the literal silver plating that one of Zac's people came up with for the bullets helped a lot."

"I bet." I snorted. "Are they staying down?"

"They are, but mainly because Far insisted that they cut the heads from the lycans before they move on. The Oracan like him, apparently, as he gives no mercy. Mor is furious with him. He told her he was going to 'arrange' things, not lead the charge himself, and she had no clue he was on the flight until it'd left. She's swearing he'll be dead by dawn, one way or another."

"Well, we'll make sure it's by her hand." I snorted. "We've got maybe an hour until we get there...are you all right?" I checked with all three of them, getting nods and various responses.

"Belle, do you know anything about the Xi-Ma?" I asked, getting a firm shake of the head from her.

"The Erlking spoke about some of their creations, but many were simply ignored or it chose not to discuss. It decided what we learned, and why, but it never mentioned them."

"Dammit," I grumbled. "I should have known, I guess."

"Nothing worthwhile is ever easy," Ingrid replied, smiling as she gripped my hand tighter. "We can do this, though, and once it's done? We've got points to spend, nanites, and we'll have the ship fully claimed. So don't worry, we can do this!"

"Reclaimed," I muttered.

"What?"

"I was given command rights over it by the Erlking," I pointed out. "Anyone else there now is trespassing, right?"

"I suppose so. I don't know what court we'd take them to, though?" She wrinkled her nose in thought, and I laughed.

"Fair point. Sorry, I was just thinking aloud."

"Steve?" Scylla said, and I looked at her. "The tentacles? Can you teach that?"

I hesitated, then shrugged. "You formed your armor, so probably?" I guessed, before getting comfy and focusing, causing a spike of nanites to lift from the palm of my hand, forming in the air. "So, the first thing here is…"

CHAPTER FORTY-ONE

The water, when I hit it, was dark, colder than I expected, and exploded in bubbles as I sank. My helmet kept water from rushing up my nose as I tombstoned into the depths.

I'd spoken to the others about the methods they'd need to alter their wings to the underwater version, and they were above me now, landing much more carefully as I sank.

I was to be the first wave, on my own. They were coming, and they'd be as fast as they could, but the Xi-Ma had gotten sick of chasing the sentinels that Zac had been leading them around with, and had apparently picked up Paul's scent.

He'd been scouting them, and they damn well knew it, it seemed. He'd fallen back, the sentinels sacrificing themselves to give him time, but the Xi-Ma were giving chase, and the turrets they'd hit a few minutes before had barely slowed them.

The original plan was that I was going for the rear entrance—heh—and Ingrid and the others were heading for another we'd found about halfway along the ship.

The hope was that we'd be able to pincer them between us, and Paul, being Paul, was heavily armed, so he'd be able to provide ammo and more guns.

That'd been the plan, and right up until about thirty seconds ago, it'd seemed a good one. That was when they'd turned and started chasing him and practically ignoring everything else.

They were fucking the ship up, carving walls and floors apart to get him, and he was running and gunning for all he was worth.

Courtney, his wife, had been setting up, ready for Paul to bring them to her, her high-powered rail gun sniper rifle hopefully enough to take them down.

Unfortunately, the lycans had sent a batch of their puppies, led by a pair of vamps, around the outside, successfully evading the sensors, and she'd been in a running fight for her life since then.

The way the day was going, I half expected Shamal and Athena to show up yet.

I dove, my wings rippling out around me like I'd once seen a squid on a natural history program do, sending me deep, and fast.

Fish blurred past me. A school that'd been too close exploded in all directions as I startled them, before I was twisting around and closing on a section of the ship I remembered.

It took me bare minutes to make it to the seabed, and a little longer to make it to the entrance. My wings flowed with a grace that was at odds with the way I struggled and swam.

Fuck it, though, because as soon as my fingers hit the air lock, I was sucked inside to the other side, empty and ready.

I crashed to the bottom, hammered by the weight of the ocean as it forced me down, until the pressure equalized. As soon as the upper entrance was sealed, the lower was opening. The seawater poured in, in a wild deluge as I refused to take the thirty seconds to purge it first.

The others might not have that time, and I had literal miles to cover here.

I was washed through, falling and twisting, planting my feet on the gangway and kicking off. I reformed my wings to their airborne configuration as I fell, catching the air even as I created a bubble of gravity.

I was practically fired from a cannon upward, arcing my wings, rolling and leveling out. The cold, long-dead halls of the ship were alive with the crash of water falling, the creak and boom of failing connectors as the gangway came apart, crumbling behind me, and I dove.

The passage that led from this cavernous section to the next lay just ahead. As I closed on it, the door opened. A mental ping from Zac made it clear he knew I was there, and was smoothing the way for me.

I accepted it, and a directional marker lit up before my eyes. I angled, tilting to the right slightly and picked up speed, snapping my wings in close as I passed through the doorway into the passage. The gravity bubble I had summoned kept me from slamming into the ground and buoyed me up.

The far door opened, and I readied myself, snapping my wings out as I burst from the narrow confines, and launched myself upward.

That was the pattern for the next several minutes: me creating tunnels of divergent gravity, dragging me this way and that, buoying me up and dragging me down, my wings booming like thunder as I heaved them hard, cupping the thin, old, and musty air in here, and using every trick at my disposal to get there as fast as I could.

There!

I heard the gunfire, the crack of rail gun fire, then the horrific hammering of what could only be the heavy machine gun version that mad bastard had taken to carrying.

A screech rang out and, in the distance, I saw a terrible bright-white light. A beam punched through the wall ahead and dragged sharply down; an entire section crashed free.

The beam lanced through the air, only to be caught by a ripple of red light. The damage it'd managed to do to the outer wall was caught by a similar field that stopped the water that was trying to cascade through...*for now.*

I saw scuttling shapes, and recognized the constructors that Zac had made, as they clearly worked to keep the ship together, flowing around the fight and keeping clear of the Xi-Ma as Paul attempted to take them down.

Howls and screams rang out as I got closer. I snarled my frustration, before snapping shut my wings, pulling my arms and legs in tight, and aiming for the section that the Xi-Ma had carved free.

I rocketed through, wings snapping back out as I saw one of the giant figures right before me. The bastard spun, apparently sensing me at the last second.

My wings snapped in again, and I switched them from wings to tentacles; my left rolled in and split far faster than my right.

I used the right, and longer, more formed wing, to snap one last time, flipping me into a roll. The trident this massive bastard stabbed out with passed literal inches to my side thanks to the roll.

My blades slid out. The vorpal blade reached out to carve the trident apart...only to fill the air with a horrific buzzing screech as the air was filled with sparks, and both the blade and the trident took damage.

I broke off. My vision filled with damage notifications, and a tentacle flashed out, latching onto the trident and tugging me in close.

Leading with the harvest blade, I dug it into the fucker's chest. The tentacle released as soon as I was in the right trajectory, and I flipped my feet up.

Landing, half standing on the chest of the "male" of the pair, my weapon digging in the top flesh, only to be stopped by something solid beneath, I pulled as hard as I could on the harvest blade.

The Xi-Ma screeched in outrage. Its eyes bugged wide and the glow appeared in its throat.

I dove sideways. A gravity bubble ripped to the left, and it followed. The blast carved more of the wall apart before it cut off abruptly. I reoriented, aiming, catching myself as I tumbled free...and then was smashed from behind by a kick or a punch—who knew what it'd been, besides damn hard—and I was sent flying. Pain screamed at me as I flipped end over end to crash into a pile of debris.

I lay there, blinking, trying to get my brain back in gear, before a hand grabbed me roughly, dragging—or *trying* to drag—me out of the way.

Blinking, I saw Paul standing over me, his machine gun braced; a belt feed from a box on his back started to rattle as he opened fire, before he released me, unable to keep the gun on target and try to drag my heavy ass at the same time.

The bullets hammered into the nearest giant, and this time, it was its turn to stagger. The bullets didn't seem to do a huge amount of damage, but they were unable to resist the force of physics, even as the flesh knit closed the wounds it was busy taking.

I shook myself, glaring up and forcing myself to my feet, before diving aside and taking both me and Paul down as another blast of the white beam tore through the air where we'd been a second before.

It cut off again, almost as soon as it started, and the creature staggered. One hand raised to its left eye, blood like tar fountaining free as it wailed its outrage.

Its partner spun and screeched in a direction deeper into the massive room, as Paul shoved me off him.

"That's Court! She just saved your stupid life, so fucking do something with it!" he roared at me, before pulling a grenade free, priming, and hurling it, all in one smooth, practiced motion.

"Motherfucker!" I growled, getting to my feet in time to see the one with his eye put out pulling its hand free, as bullet fragments oozed out and the eye slowly reformed. "What the fuck does it take to kill these things...?" I mumbled in shock.

"More than I had in this!" Paul snapped, dumping his gun and ripping free a long-bladed hunting knife and a tomahawk. "Time to fuck some shit up!" He grinned, manically.

"Get back, you fucking idiot," I snapped, shaking my head. "They're too strong for you!"

"Devil Dogs!" Paul roared. "Oorah!" He ran at the nearest one.

He barely managed to land a blow, as I ran after him, before the Xi-Ma kicked out. A shallow gaping wound carved into the flesh of the shin, spraying blood as Paul vanished into the darkness with a cry of pain and breaking bones.

I dodged it, time dilation triggering at a thought as I slashed at the leg. It raised its massive bare foot, the toes webbed together as it passed me, and I slid sideways, the harvest blade carving flesh easily.

Whatever was under the skin was here as well, but…but I realized for the first time, with time literally slowed, just how thick with nanites the fucker was.

Its blood was practically solid with them—no goddamn wonder it healed so fast and the damn time-dilation effect was barely enough to keep me in the fight still.

I dragged more and more free: tentacles lashed out to punch into the skin, anchors deployed and dragged me in close as I desperately drank the nanites free, my armor shifting on instinct.

I'd thickened it up before using most of the nanites I'd had to form the chest and back, as well as the helm, but this?

I tore nanites free in their thousands by the second, and as they entered me, they were converted by my will to weaponized at a terrific rate.

The tentacles dug in deeper, the ends blooming with the Devourer nanites.

I felt it—the armoring that was beneath the surface weakened—and the Xi-Ma screeched in outrage, twisting, trying to look down at me as I stabbed deeper, wrapping my arms and legs around it, dragging my way upward, like a spider monkey.

It staggered, trying to fix its gaze on me. Its leg gave way as it toppled sideways. One hand reached out for me, the other trying to break its fall; the trident clanged, forgotten, to the floor.

The other one spun, seemingly in slow motion. Its trident came up as it twisted and leapt toward me, seemingly not wanting to use its scream-beam on its partner or whatever it was.

Instead, it stabbed out, rushing forward, trying to pluck me free.

I grinned, shoving out with a gravity well, sending a burst of energy at its right foot just as it shifted its weight, the slow motion run as that foot came down, ready to take all the creature's weight.

Instead, the ankle twisted; the foot yanked sideways and it fell, smashing into a pile of debris. Twisted metal flew in all directions as it screeched out its rage.

I'd fucked up, though, drunk on the nanites I'd been feasting on, distracted by the other, as the one I'd been clambering up smashed a hand across my chest.

Its claws were out—strange how I'd missed them before, but now, as they flew at me, they were all I could see.

Each of them at least ten inches long, glistening and sharp as fuck, they smashed into me, carving lengthy lines down my armor and sending me onto the floor…bouncing, I hit that hard.

I groaned. My right arm was whipped into an unnatural angle; my right leg, the one I'd landed on along with the arm, was *definitely* broken.

A boom rang out. The hand that had been reaching for me jerked back as a fresh hole appeared in it, and my tentacle rippled out, punching into the deck and lifting me.

I backed up, the tentacles carrying me as I lifted my left arm, coughing in pain and snarling as I used some of the nanites I'd stolen to form a gravity cannon.

It spun up. The first ring formed, then the second. But before I could form the third, a trident hurtled out of the darkness.

I dove to the side, my aim and concentration broken. The cannon disintegrated. Compressed waves of gravity expanded out in all directions as it exploded, hurling me through the air to crash into a pile of nearby debris.

I laid there, stunned, my left arm stripped down to the bone and blood splattered everywhere. The vorpal blade was fucked up *again*. That was my first fuzzy thought. I was going to have to remake that bastard all over again!

Then I blinked, realizing that getting *that* distracted in a fight? Not a good thing.

Fortunately, that was when a new arrival made her presence known.

Scylla landed hard on the back of the farthest Xi-Ma—the female, maybe— as it struggled to get back to its feet, shoving debris aside.

I didn't give a damn about its sexuality, and they wore waist wraps, so I cared even less, but Scylla drove her spear down hard enough that it clearly sank deeper than anything else had to date.

It screamed, twisting and reaching back, flailing at Scylla, trying to get her off, as its partner, the one whose leg I'd been shredding, screeched in outrage.

That one rolled, coming to its feet as I shoved free of the debris.

My right arm was broken, although snapping back into place with terrifying speed now, and my left? Well, from the middle of the forearm up? It looked pretty shredded.

From that point down?

There were twisted sections of metallic bones that were visible, the rest long gone.

I snarled in fury. A sudden barrage of coordinated fire ripped into the one closest to me as it tried to run to the other's aid. It staggered and fell, keening as a loud bark over the rest of the gunfire announced its eye being taken again.

My tentacles punched into the deck, clamping in and propelling me forward at a thought. Gravity hammers slammed into the pair from all angles, keeping them off-balance as I frantically covered the distance to the nearest.

It turned.

My time dilation was still active, giving me the precious milliseconds I needed to dodge as it unleashed the beam at me, but damn it was close.

I leapt, landing to the left, and jumped farther. It twisted, trying to follow me…

I could feel the battle all around me suddenly sliding into place as Ingrid arrived, knowing that the barrage of fire that now cut off was from Jonas, Ingrid, and Courtney, and that the last of the sentinels were battling the last of the lycans and vamps.

I grinned inside my helm, before throwing myself down, triggering two gravity bubbles at once: one above me, shoved me down; one below the other Xi-Ma, shoved it upward.

The scream-beam of the other Xi-Ma punched into its chest as it rose, the one I'd goaded into firing shutting off with a hiss of horror, but it was too late.

They might be armored to fuck against our more normal weapons, but they sure as shit didn't like each other's.

A hole was burned halfway through the other's chest and it collapsed backward, stunned, as Scylla leapt free, dragging her spear out of its back.

It crashed down hard, stunned, and somehow, that crazy bastard Paul was there again, limping out of the darkness to leap onto its arm.

He swung the tomahawk down, again and again. The blade was stopped by the armoring under the flesh, but with every chop, black blood fountained free. That arm, the right, as he leaned half across it, shuddered. The damage he was doing combined with the damage to its chest was enough to stop it reacting for a vital few seconds. A fresh bark echoed out; the head snapped sideways as a new round flashed across the outer surface of both eyes from the side.

It screamed in pain, blinded, and shoved off, twisting and sending Paul flying. Its one good arm rose to cover its eyes, as Scylla lunged from the side.

The tip of her spear sank into the now exposed armpit. And rather than being stopped by the subdermal armoring? It sank deep.

I flexed my tentacles, flinging myself into the air, pulling all but two of my tentacles in, covering my body in the nanite film and grabbing onto the fucker that had just attacked me with the beam weapon. It was frozen, stunned, half blind, and with one side of the world now dark to it, it missed my move until the last second.

I landed atop it, on its chest, and I stabbed out. The harvest blade cut a shallow wound. It dragged more and more of its nanites free. My two tentacles lashed around it, gripping its arms and flexing to hold them back from me. A third tentacle formed from the top of my head and punched upward, sinking into the joint where the jaw met the throat—this time not taking anything, but instead delivering.

The other's scream cut off with a gurgle as Scylla shoved the spear over a meter into its chest via the armpit, carving through lungs, into who knew what organs were in there, and it collapsed.

It was clearly what Belle had been waiting for, as she leapt from the darkness, ramming her harvest tool forward and into its head.

The tendrils flashed out and struck hard. A solid dozen of them wove around fingers and flailing arms to punch deep, entering through eyes, ears, mouth, and nose.

Belle shredded its brain, and as its arms fell loose, she started to rip great quantities of nanites free.

The one I was atop had stiffened as my tentacle punched deep, then ignored it, the wound small compared with the pain my Devourer armor was causing it, literally eating its flesh and feeding on it, repairing and regrowing my body as its withered.

There was a lot of the fucker, though, and it was never going to go down easy.

It broke free of the tentacles I'd used to pin it, and slammed its arms around me, crushing me to its chest. Then it howled in pain and dug its claws in, ripping me free and flinging me at the others.

I hit the ground hard, bouncing and sliding before my tentacles could gain traction and stop me. Then I shoved myself back up, feeling *much* fucking better, despite the battering I'd just taken, for the meal my armor was still processing.

The nanites in their thousands poured across me, and I couldn't help but smile as I looked at the figure that tried to force its way back to its feet, reaching out with one hand to grab its trident, then turning its head to face us.

It opened its mouth, the light starting to glow…

"Oh, I don't fucking think so, pal," I snapped, closing my right fist.

Its jaw snapped shut. The glow of the beam illuminated its head briefly from within as it burst to life, right up until the skull detonated.

There was a second of silence as the Xi-Ma's corpse, braced on one arm, still fought to deny its death. Then reality caught up with it, and it crashed backward. Great gouts of blood erupted from the severed neck.

The one that Belle was feeding from twitched and quivered, jerking as random neurons fired, triggered by the mass that rolled over them, and she cried out in pleasure, gasping with the sheer number of nanites she was recovering.

I turned with the others, battered, bruised, and bloody, but unbroken as a new figure landed nearby. Its pretentious smart suit made it stand out all the more as it hissed and grabbed onto Paul's throat.

"Stop! All of you, stop what you're doing, or I'll kill this...argh!" It'd barely got the words out when Paul, unrisen as he might be, stabbed the fucker in its stomach with the long dagger, before slashing it across the muscles of its upper arms.

He wrapped his arm around the vampire's own and flexed, ripping its now weakened grip from his throat and locking it into an arm bar, before lifting it and slamming it into the pile of debris behind it.

It had a second of shocked, stunned pain, as it looked up from what it'd assumed quite rightly was the weakest of us, before he punched it in the face.

Its skull was nanite reinforced, so it took the blow. Although the ex-marine was still human and had the lowest number of nanites of all of us, even those relative few, when combined with the years of training, the skill, the unbridled aggression, and adding in finally the tomahawk and dagger, augmented with otherworldly tech?

The vamp didn't stand a fucking chance.

EPIL⊙GUE

T he physical reality of the chicken-shit box, as Paul called it, and the Faraday cage that Zac named it, was a bit underwhelming, all things considered.

We'd ripped our way through the box we'd created to hold it, finding the gleaming structure had long since powered down. And when we did?

Utterly unimpressive.

It was about a meter long on all sides, square and gleaming. A powerful current flowed across it, and it now sat suspended in a vat of gleaming nanites that helped to form the electromagnetic shield.

Reaching out with a tentacle of nanites, I sank it into the bed of glistening "blank" ones, and they rippled in welcome, before flowing joyously up the tentacle and back to me.

I plucked the box from the hollow it now rested in, ignoring the charge as my nanites filtered it, and stabbed a connection into it.

The remaining time dilation I'd cut off earlier was more than enough for this. I held the box in one hand and accessed the Espionage tree, flicking down it, and spending the extra point in the Cyber-Espionage section.

The sub-mind processed the data flawlessly, and I barely noticed the change, save that instead of a single point of entry, the nanite spike grew nine more.

Ten spikes stabbed into the box, burrowing deep and overwhelming the remnant of the security AI in a matter of seconds.

I fancied I heard a tiny squawk of protest, before Tsunami was unleashed into it, rewriting the little fucker, and making sure it knew who its new master was.

I grunted, eyes flickering as the sub-mind parsed the data the security AI had access to; the remnants of the ship lit in my mind as more and more sections unlocked. The areas that had been reclaimed by its automated systems during the Xi-Ma incursion flickered, then rejoined the rest of the ship happily.

Deep space transmitters were being marked, relay points, security caches that were designed to survive even the most horrific of impacts flashing that they existed, even if they were far from our reach, scattered and buried miles away under eons of silt and ocean floor.

I sensed other ships out there. Their security AIs flashed complicated pattern recognition requests, before realizing what I was and severing the connection.

More and more points failed, cutting off, dropping free, leaving the ship as isolated as I'd wrongly believed it to be before, and now I saw why.

When I'd attacked it, when it'd truly assessed the likelihood of it losing control of the site as high, it'd apparently accessed a secure cache.

Not only had it activated long buried and lost protocols that allowed it to start to strip its precious ruined equipment apart, rebuilding and kick-starting a recovery process, but the primary reason it'd had to do that?

It was required to report the breach.

It'd done that, accessing and activating a transmitter that had been damaged, rebuilding it and linking to the long-dormant planetary network.

And five signals had responded.

Of those five, three were repeaters that fed into other security AIs in similarly poor positions. They'd accepted a data dump of the events and would essentially be on the lookout for me, while activating increased security measures of their own.

The remaining two?

One had flashed to life, startling a small group of ancient creatures. They'd attempted to respond to it, and had been identified as trespassing local life-forms. That connection had been severed.

The last, though? That was different.

One of the creators had responded, accepting the contact, and ordering the security AI to strip the entire system, to rebuild its primary production center, and how to do that.

It'd been the reason that the AI didn't just keep throwing minor escalations at me, and at the end had instead gone all out, stripping and rebuilding the center of the ship.

It'd been ordered to repair the heart of the ship, to reform it, and to create a production center, to build an *army*.

Had it been this bastard that had sent the Xi-Ma then? They were massively stronger than the arisen after all, so maybe? The creator had been pissed after all.

No...

No, it'd been *furious* that one of the descendants of its malfunctioning early creations had dared to set foot aboard one of its possessions, and it had ordered that the ship's security AI produce an army, as well as the parts and facilities it needed to erase this stain upon its honor.

It'd not been wasting its time like the Erlking, I saw.

Oh no, it'd been sleeping away the ages, confident in its knowledge that sooner or later, the conclave that had banished it to this mudball of a world would realize the mistake they had made, and return it to power.

For it, unlike the millennia that had passed for the Erlking, making it calmer and reflective, the war was *yesterday*. The pogrom was still ongoing across the stars, and the rage it felt that its playthings had disobeyed their betters was palpable.

I saw all of this, even as I felt that connection, and I realized that the fucker was still active and right there!

It was there, staring at me across the gulf between us, raging, and...and I felt fear! It hated me, hated what I was, everything that I'd become, and it was afraid as well!

It was weak, still entombed, desiccated and ruined by the sleep of the ages. And now, while its body was revived? It was vulnerable. Vulnerable to the unthinkable: the true death.

I blinked. The connection severed in the same second that I wondered where it could be, the creature having enough power to do that, to read my mind. And as the contact faded?

One last point became clear.

It had to have been *that* fucker who'd named me Devourer. It'd tagged me with a death mark, more than happy to kill me, just because I existed without its permission.

Well, fuck *that!*

I growled, even as the security AI's last redoubts failed, and the last lockouts gave way.

The ship was claimed, now I saw, as every system that still functioned accepted us.

I reached out and closed my mental fingers around the ship's core, a single message from the remains of the AI printing in my mind.

Welcome, Reclaimer.

THE END OF

BOOK THREE

ARISE 4: DEVOURER

By Jez Cajiao

There's a new player in the great game,
and the Elders edicts hold no sway over them...

Steve and the team hold the ship but only for now. Yet the world is swiftly waking to the new reality, the vultures are circling, and keeping the ship looks to be at least as hard as taking it ever was.

Time is never on Steve's side, but the knowledge that he agreed to present himself before the only faction he's not at war with, and the Elders have no patience for delays, only add to his stress.

He's out of time, out of tricks, and patience? That's a luxury long gone. But while Steve might be running low on many things, his reservoir of brutality is far from dry. Good thing too, because one of the god-like creators has cast her ominous gaze on him now, and as far as she's concerned, he and all his kind are vermin.

What will the vermin do, when the exterminators are called?

Buy on Amazon

QUEST ACADEMY

By Brian J. Nordon

A world infested by demons.
An Academy designed to train Heroes to save humanity from annihilation.
A new student's power could make all the difference.

Humans have been pushed to the brink of extinction by an ever-evolving demonic threat. Portals are opening faster than ever, Towers bursting into the skies and Dungeons being mined below the last safe havens of society. The demons are winning.

Quest Academy stands defiantly against them, as a place to train the next generation of Heroes. The Guild Association is holding the line, but are in dire need of new blood and the powerful abilities they could bring to the battlefront. To be the saviors that humanity needs, they need to surpass the limits of those that came before them.

In a war with everything on the line, every power matters. With an adaptive enemy, comes the need for a constant shift in tactics. A new age of strategy is emerging, with even the unlikeliest of Heroes making an impact.

Salvatore Argento has never seen a demon.
He has never aspired to become a Hero.
Yet his power might be the one to tip the odds in humanity's favor.

Buy on Amazon

WANDERING WARRIOR

By Michael Head

A divine quest to deliver justice.
One year to accomplish his mission.
After nineteen planets, there's something different about this one.

James Holden has reached the maximum level there is for a human. That's perfect, since he's the only one of his kind. A wandering warrior, without control of his destination, tossed between universes by gods who've failed to tell him why. James is the lone Judge on a new world in need of someone to balance the scales. He isn't afraid to do so with extreme prejudice. As the Chief Justice, he has to right the wrongs the innocent can't fix themselves.

As James quickly discovers, the roots of corruption run deep. Guilds choose to protect themselves rather than the people. Monsters roam the wilderness unchecked. Judgment is usually a decision between right and wrong, but nothing is ever that simple. This time, being the strongest human won't be enough to punish the guilty. James might have to recruit some new blood, even if he prefers to work alone.

On his twentieth world, he is going to win, no matter the cost. James will have to find a way to break past the limits of the system if he's going to have a chance at making a difference.

Buy on Amazon

KNIGHTS OF ETERNITY

By Rachel Ní Chuirc

When Zara awoke in chains she thought she'd gone mad.

She was Zara the Fury - mistress of flame and fear. Her name was whispered across the land, from ramshackle taverns to the royal court. Even the heroic Gilded Knights thought twice before crossing her path.

She was feared—*respected*

Now she was curled up on a dirt floor on her fiancé's orders. Valerius, leader of the Gilded, mocks her cries for help. And the kingdom is on the brink of war over the missing Lady Eternity…

But that wasn't why Zara thought she had gone mad.

The reason why is that the last thing she remembered was blood, an arcade screen, and the gun that changed everything.

But no chains can hold the Fury, and when she gets out?
The world is going to *burn*.

Coming Soon!

www.legionpublishers.com

REVIEWS

Hey! Well, I hope you enjoyed the book! If so, please, please remember to leave a review. It's massively important, as not only does it let others know about the book, but it also tells Amazon that the book is worth promoting, and makes it more likely that more people will see it.

That, in turn, will hopefully keep me able to keep writing full-time, while listening to crazy German bands screaming in my ears, and frankly, I kinda really like that!

If you want to spread the good word, that'd be amazing. And if you know of anyone who might be interested in stocking my books, I'm happy to reach out and send them samples, but honestly, if you enjoy my madness, that's massive for me.

Thank you.

FACEBOOK AND SOCIAL MEDIA

If you want to reach out, chat or shoot the shit, you can always find me on either my author page here:

www.facebook.com/JezCajiaoAuthor

OR

We've recently set up a new Facebook group to spread the word about cool LitRPG books. It's dedicated to two very simple rules;

1; Lets spread the word about new and old brilliant LitRPG books.
2: Don't be a Dick!

They sound like really simple rules, but you'd be amazed…

Come join us!

www.facebook.com/groups/litrpglegion

I'm also on Discord here: **https://discord.gg/u5JYHscCEH**

Or I'm reaching out on other forms of social media atm, I'm just spread a little thin that's all!

You're most likely to find me on Discord, but please, don't be offended when I don't approve friend requests on my personal Facebook pages. I did originally, and several people abused that, sending messages to my family and being generally unpleasant, hence, the author page:

www.facebook.com/JezCajiaoAuthor

I hope you understand.

PATREON!

Okay then, now for those of you that don't know about Patreon, its essentially a way to support your favorite nutcases, you can sign up for a day or a month or a year, and you get various benefits for it, ranging from my heartfelt thanks, to advance access to the books, to me sending them books, naming characters and more.

At the time of me writing this, the advanced Patreon readers are halfway through Arise 4: Devourer. By the time this launches? I *think* they'll be around the end of the book, and getting ready to start on Arise 5 as well, so yeah, you get plenty for the support!

There's two of my wonderful supporters out there that I have to thank personally as well; ASeaInStorm and Steve Messina, thank you both!

www.patreon.com/Jezcajiao

LEGION

Okay everybody, if you've not yet seen or heard, well, the secret is out! My wife Chrissy, and our friend Geneva and I have launched the Legion Publishers! We're taking on new authors, as well as experienced ones, focusing primarily on the LitRPG side of things, but we're open to anything really, with one very clear rule that guides our company:

Don't be a dick.

That's it. Our contracts aren't hidden behind layers of legalese, you can find them here:

www.legionpublishers.com/legioncontract

If you want to reach out an ask any questions, get an idea of the support we offer, and possibly become part of the family? We'd love to hear from you, just tap the link and fill in the form:

www.legionpublishers.com/contact-and-submissions

Hope you're having a good one!

-Jez, Chrissy and Geneva

RECOMMENDATIONS

I'm often asked for personal recommendations, so if this book has whetted your appetite for more LitRPG, please have a look at the following, these are brilliant series by brilliant authors!

The Ten Realms by Michael Chatfield

The Land by Aleron Kong

Challengers Call by Nathan A. Thompson

Quest Academy by Brian J. Nordon

Wandering Warrior by Michael Head

Endless Online by M H Johnson

The Good Guys/Bad Guys by Eric Ugland

God of the Feast by Kevin Sinclair

The Wayward Bard by Lars Machmüller

LITRPG!

To learn more about LitRPG, talk to other authors including myself, and to just have an awesome time, please join the LitRPG Group

www.facebook.com/groups/LitRPGGroup

FACEBOOK

There's also a few really active Facebook groups I'd recommend you join, as you'll get to hear about great new books, new releases and interact with all your (new) favorite authors! (I may also be there, skulking at the back and enjoying the memes…)

www.facebook.com/groups/LitRPGsociety/

www.facebook.com/groups/LitRPG.books/

www.facebook.com/groups/LitRPGforum/

www.facebook.com/groups/gamelitsociety/

Printed in Great Britain
by Amazon

29144479R00238